Faceless

Faceless

Bruce Sutherland

Published by Zebra Press
an imprint of Random House Struik (Pty) Ltd
Company Reg. No. 1966/003153/07
80 McKenzie Street, Cape Town, 8001
PO Box 1144, Cape Town, 8000, South Africa

www.zebrapress.co.za

First published 2011

1 3 5 7 9 10 8 6 4 2

Publication © Zebra Press 2011
Text and illustrations © Bruce Sutherland

Cover images © Bruce Sutherland

PUBLISHER: Marlene Fryer
MANAGING EDITOR: Ronel Richter-Herbert
COVER DESIGNER: Monique Oberholzer
PRODUCTION MANAGER: Valerie Kömmer

Printed and bound by Paarl Media, Jan van Riebeeck Drive, Paarl, South Africa

978 1 77022 283 0 (print)
978 1 77022 284 7 (ePub)
978 1 77022 285 4 (PDF)

IMAGES OF AFRICA
PHOTO LIBRARY

Over 50 000 unique African images available to purchase
from our image bank at www.imagesofafrica.co.za

To my loyal friends, family and readers, this book is dedicated to you.
Without your encouragement, support and input,
Faceless would not exist, on the interwebs or in this format.

Thank you,
Bruce Sutherland

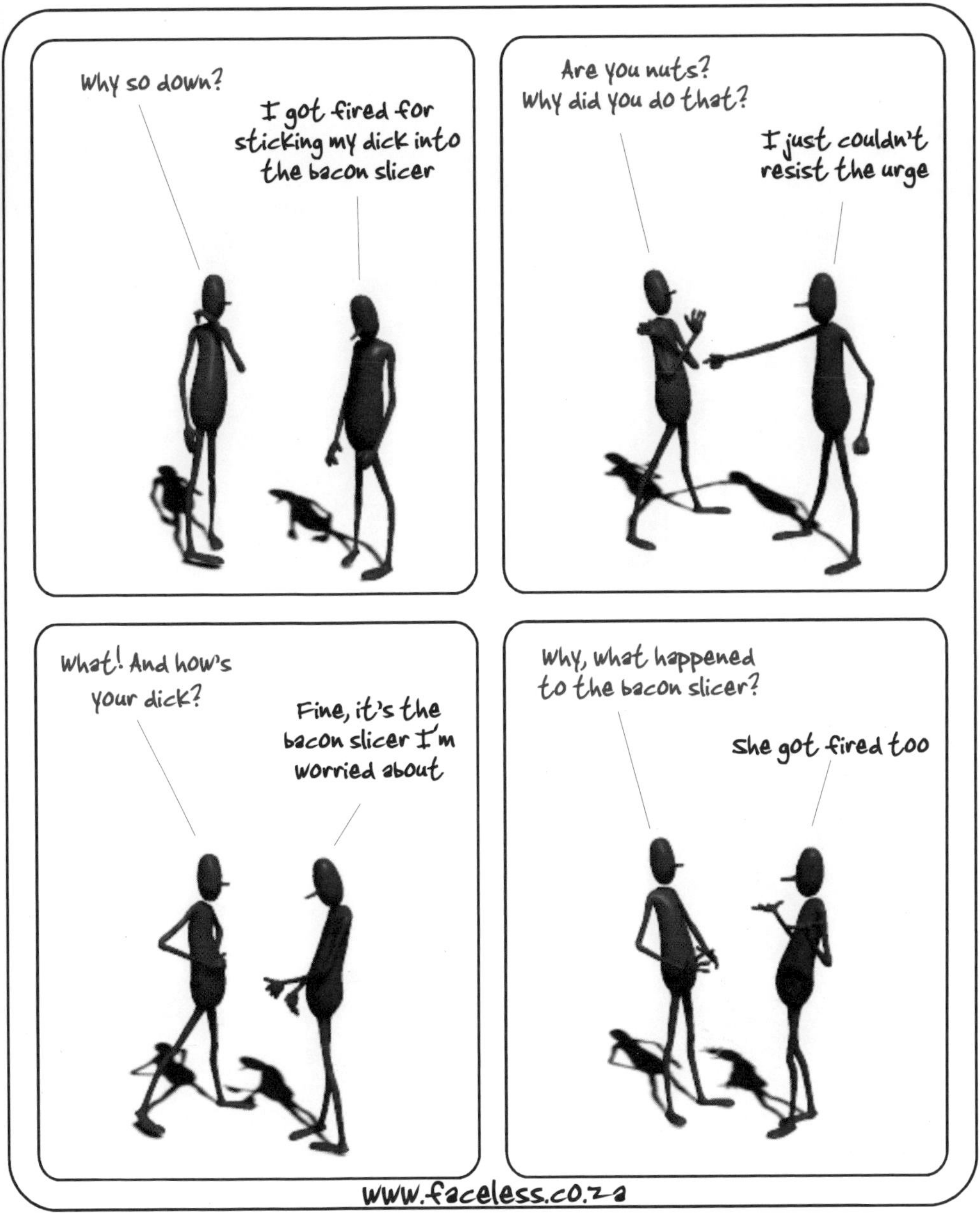
Why so down?
I got fired for sticking my dick into the bacon slicer
Are you nuts? Why did you do that?
I just couldn't resist the urge
What! And how's your dick?
Fine, it's the bacon slicer I'm worried about
Why, what happened to the bacon slicer?
She got fired too
www.faceless.co.za

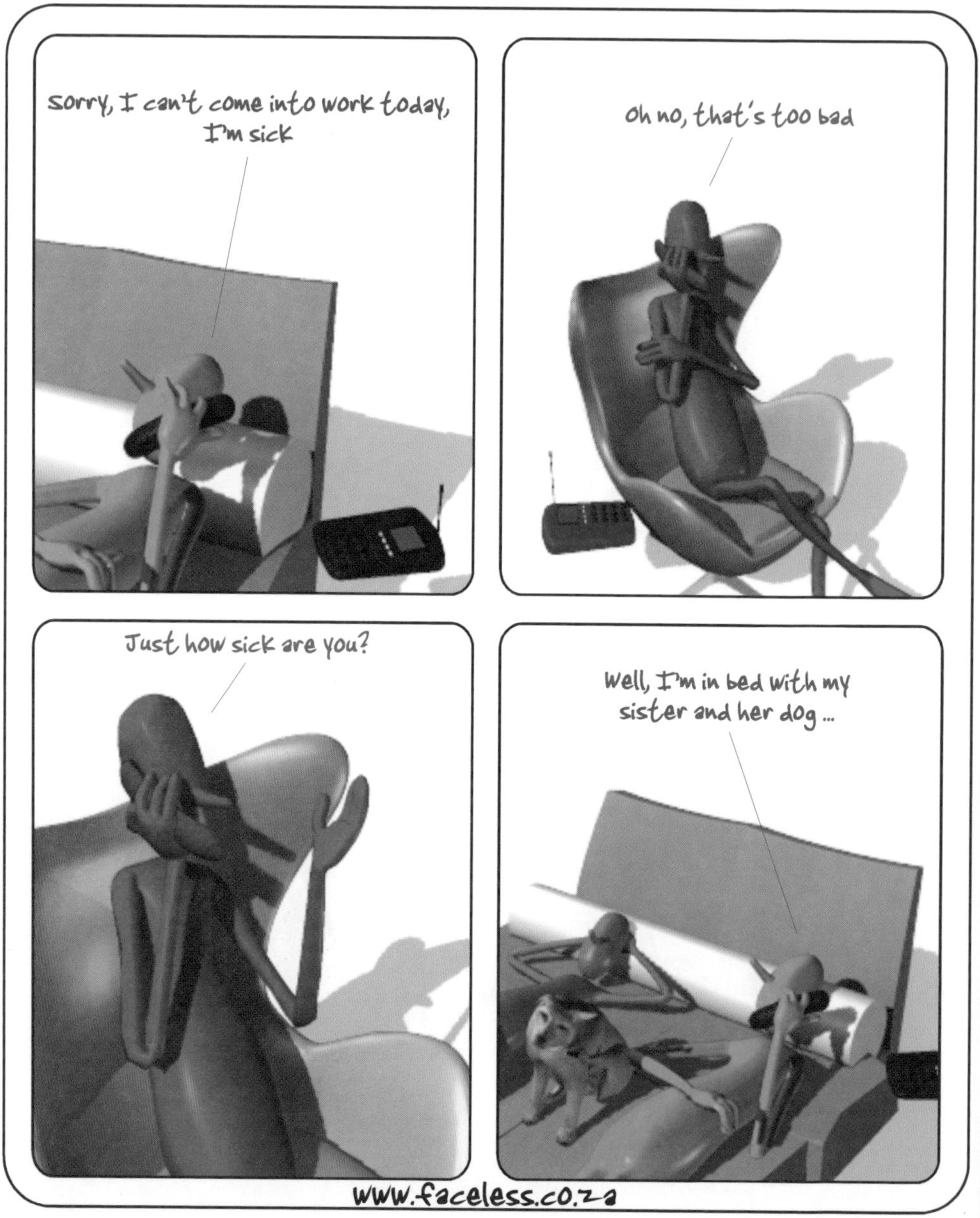
sorry, I can't come into work today, I'm sick
Oh no, that's too bad
Just how sick are you?
Well, I'm in bed with my sister and her dog ...
www.faceless.co.za

Doctor, I'm really concerned. I found my daughter and the boy next door together
They were naked, examining each other's bodies and giggling
That's nothing to worry about, it's pretty normal
Well, I don't know, it worries me AND it worries her husband, too!
www.faceless.co.za

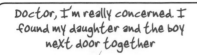

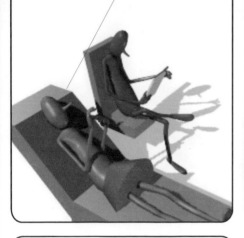

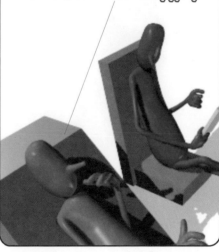

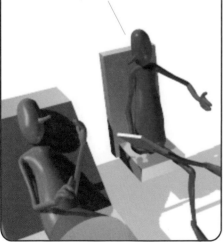

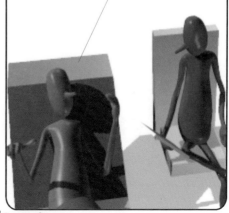

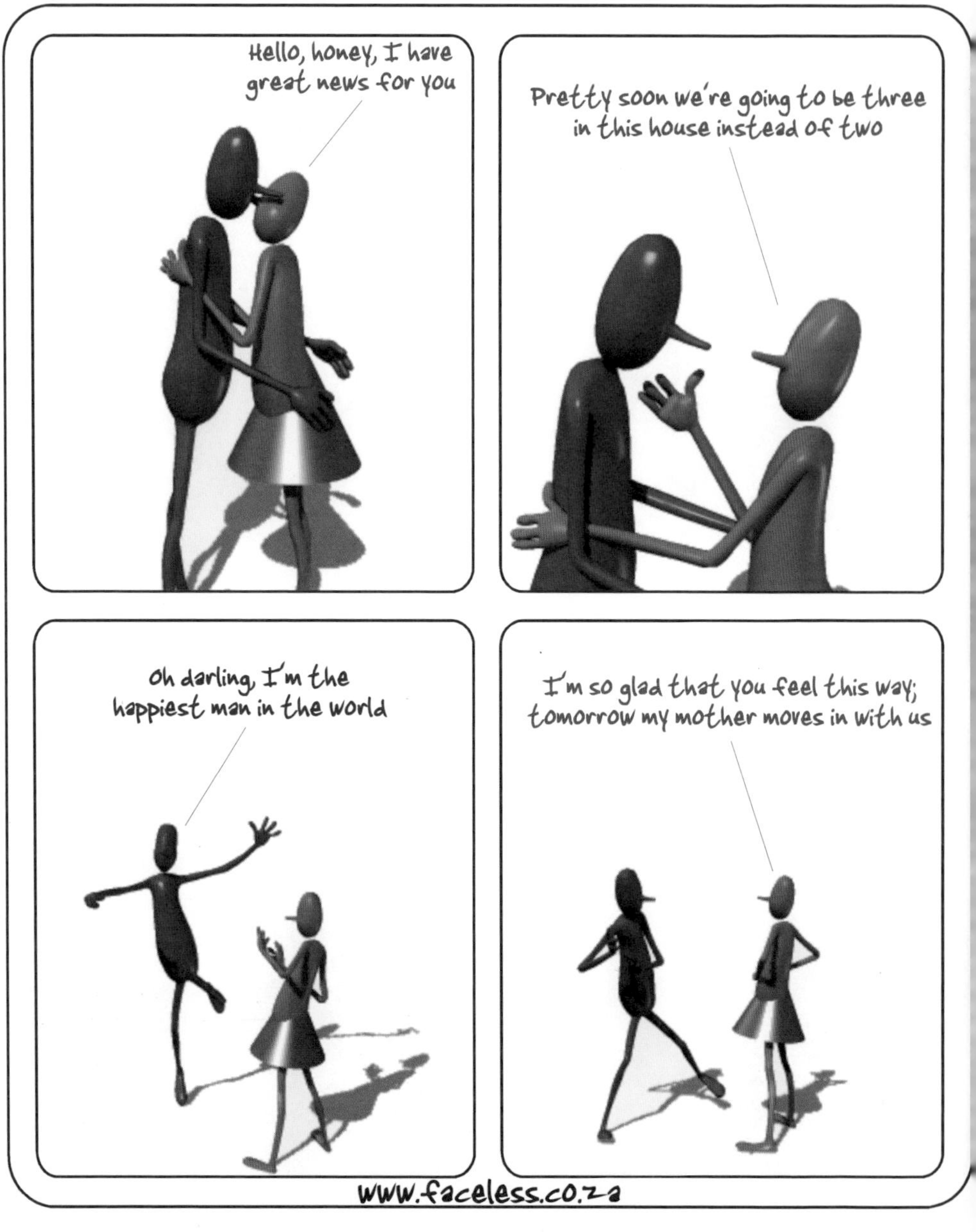
Hello, honey, I have great news for you
Pretty soon we're going to be three in this house instead of two
Oh darling, I'm the happiest man in the world
I'm so glad that you feel this way; tomorrow my mother moves in with us
www.faceless.co.za

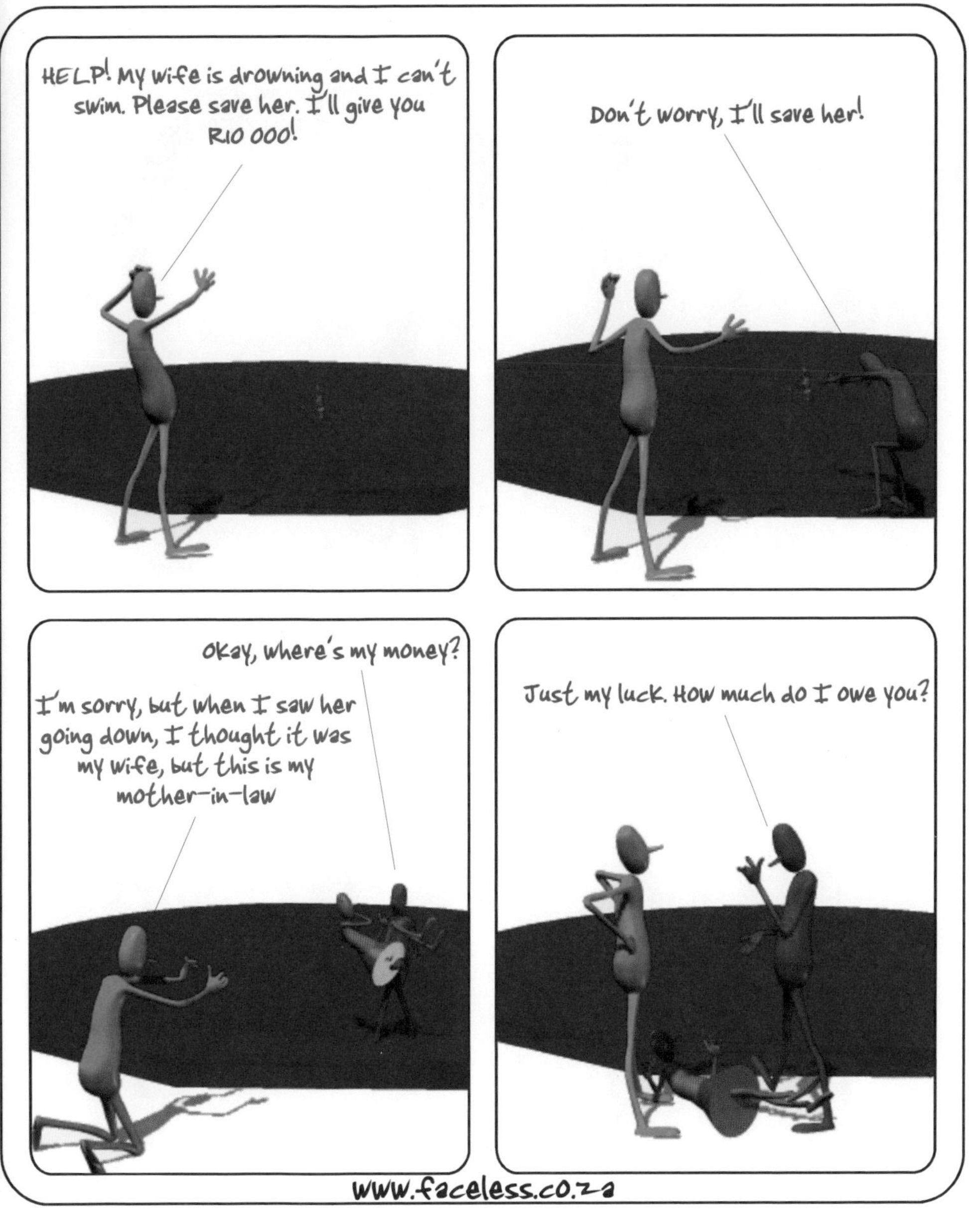
HELP! My wife is drowning and I can't swim. Please save her. I'll give you R10 000!
Don't worry, I'll save her!
Okay, where's my money?
I'm sorry, but when I saw her going down, I thought it was my wife, but this is my mother-in-law
Just my luck. How much do I owe you?
www.faceless.co.za

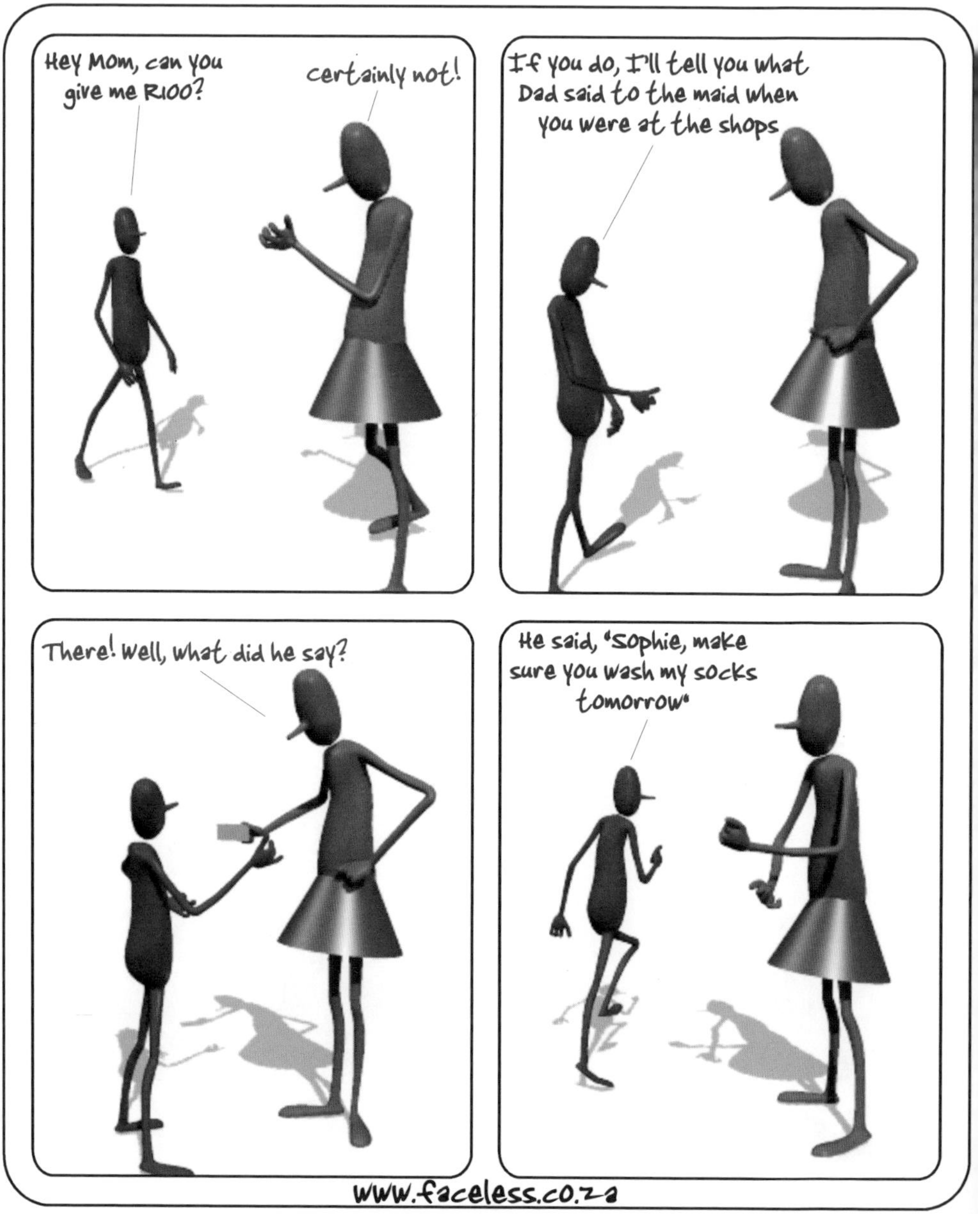
Hey Mom, can you give me R100?
certainly not!
If you do, I'll tell you what Dad said to the maid when you were at the shops
There! Well, what did he say?
He said, "Sophie, make sure you wash my socks tomorrow"

www.faceless.co.za

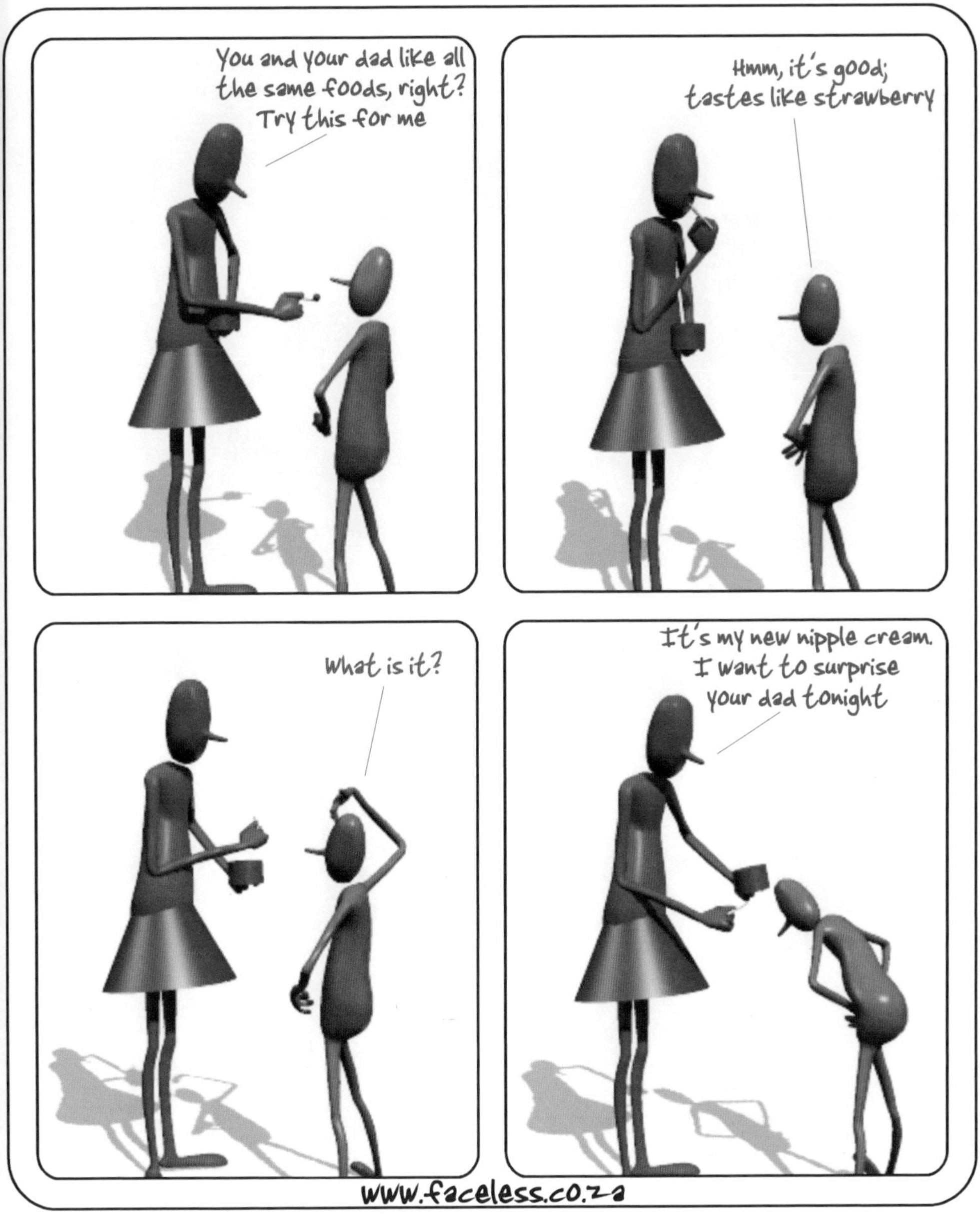
You and your dad like all the same foods, right? Try this for me
Hmm, it's good; tastes like strawberry
What is it?
It's my new nipple cream. I want to surprise your dad tonight
www.faceless.co.za

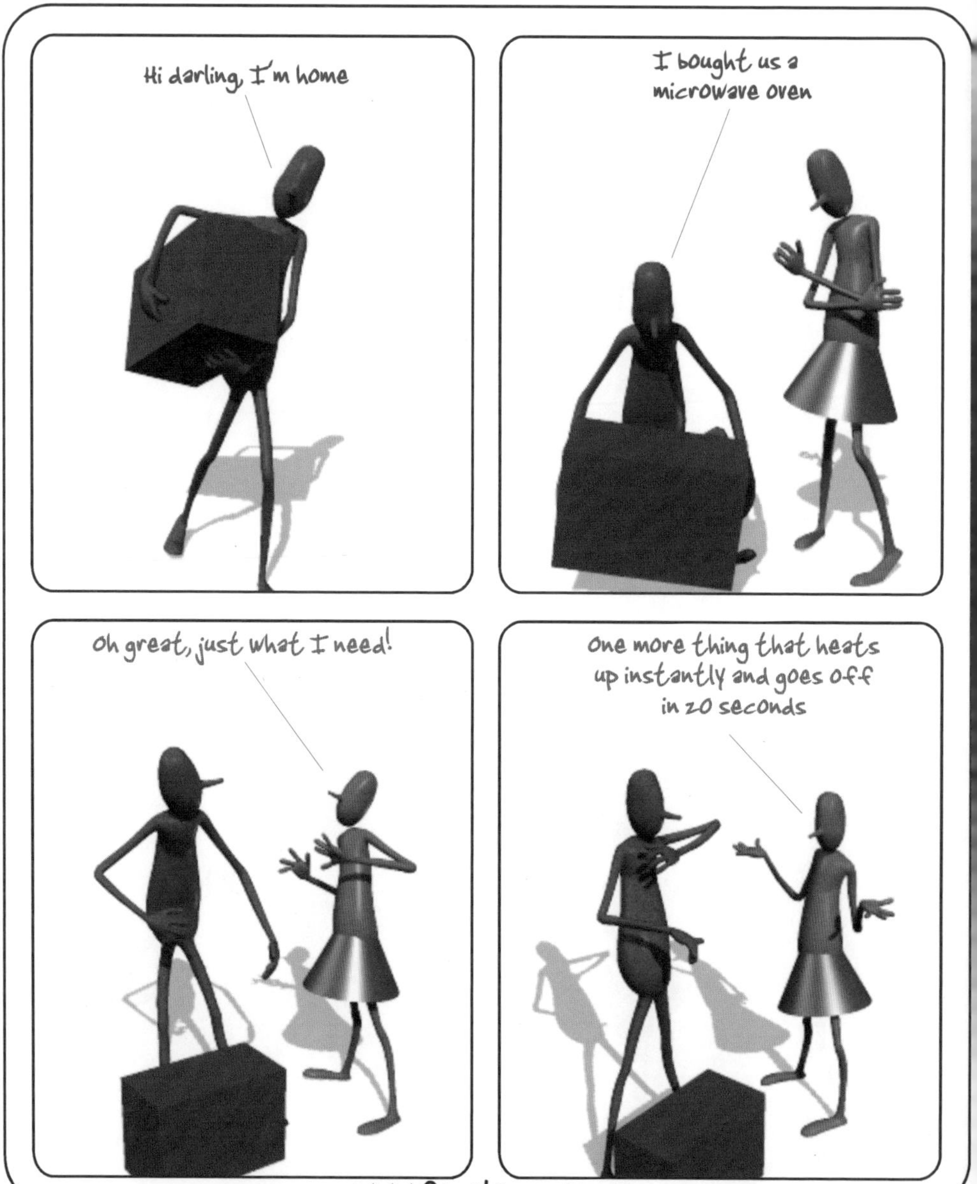
Hi darling, I'm home
I bought us a microwave oven
Oh great, just what I need!
One more thing that heats up instantly and goes off in 20 seconds
www.faceless.co.za

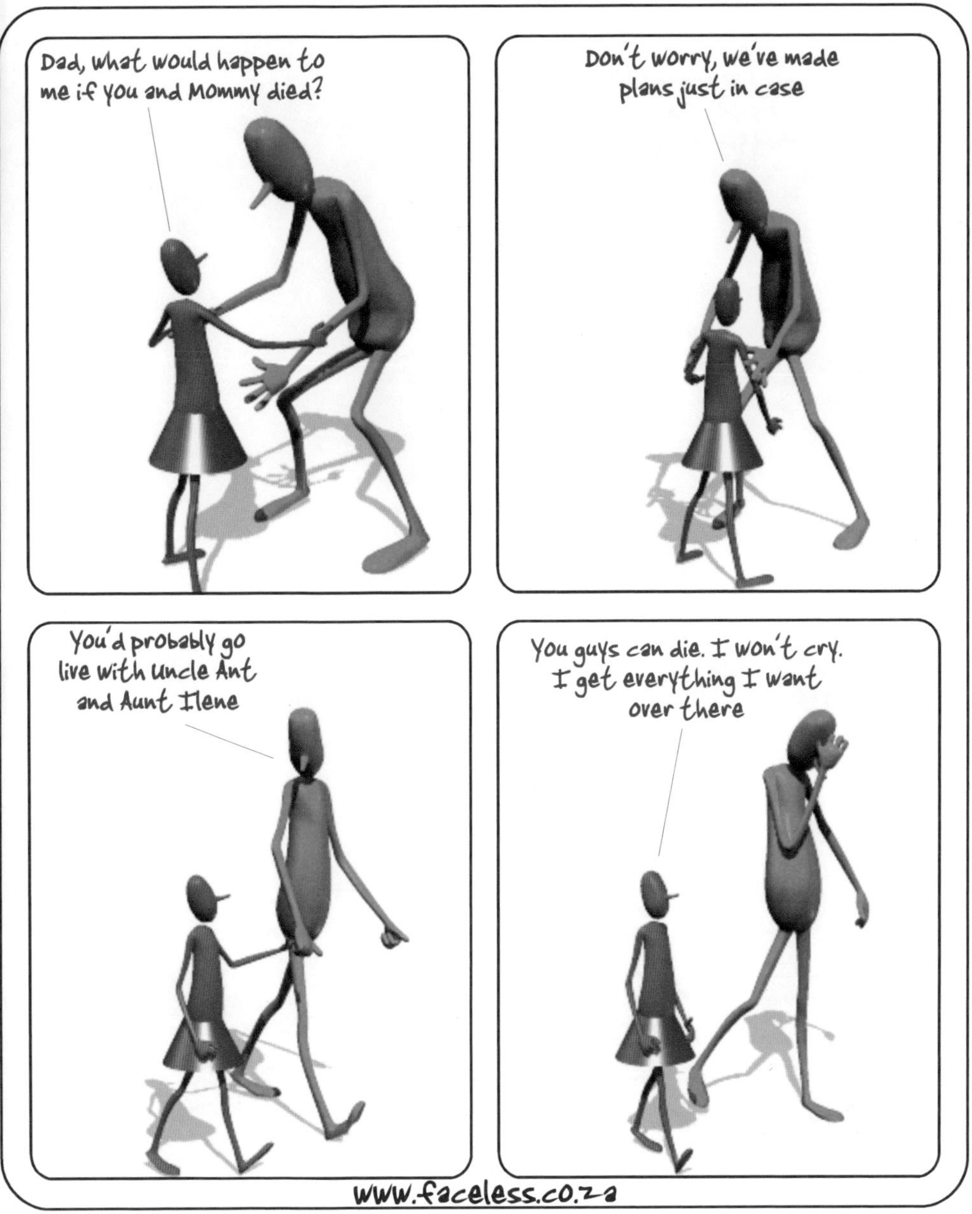
Dad, what would happen to me if you and Mommy died?
Don't worry, we've made plans just in case
You'd probably go live with Uncle Ant and Aunt Ilene
You guys can die. I won't cry. I get everything I want over there
www.faceless.co.za

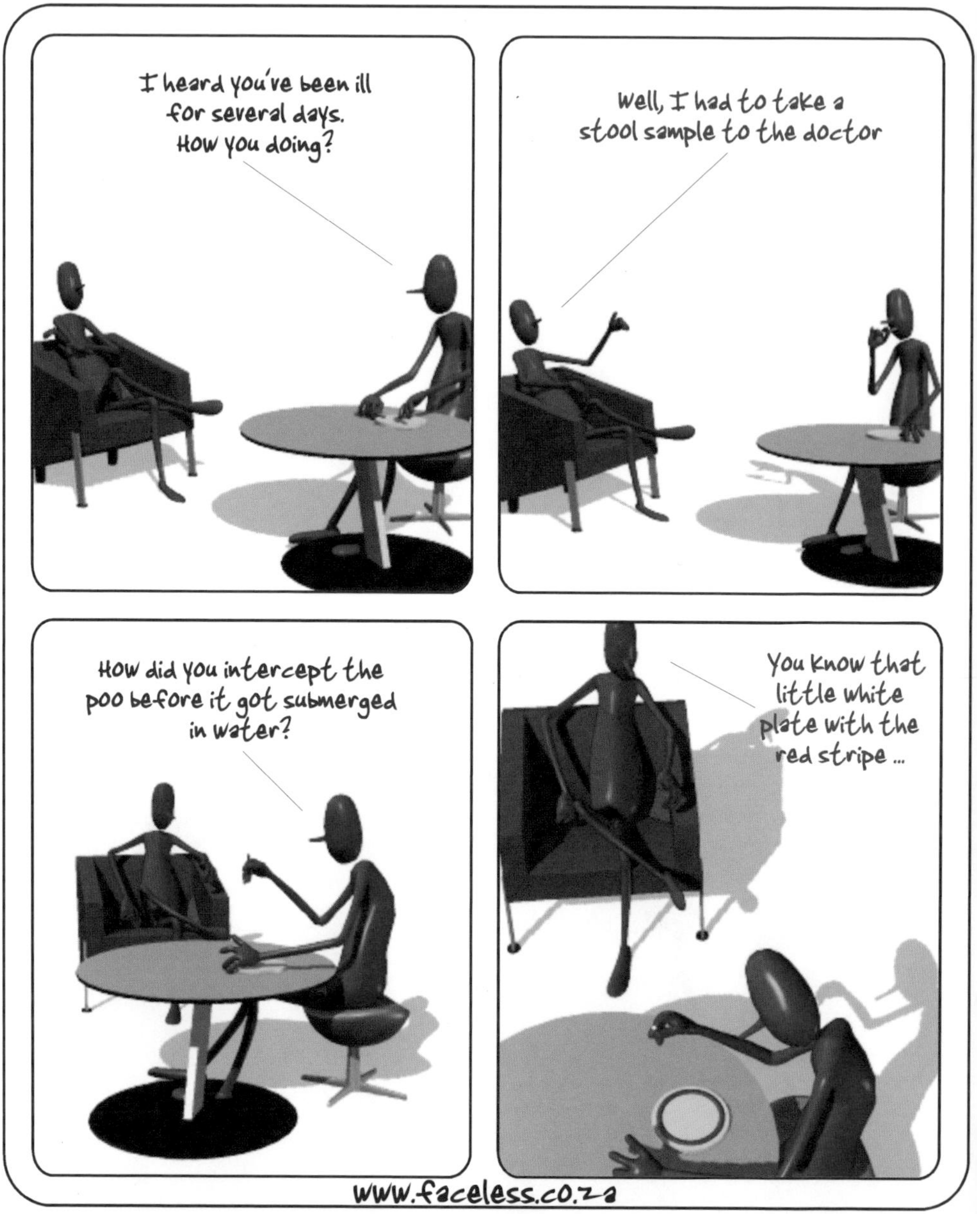
I heard you've been ill
for several days.
How you doing?
Well, I had to take a
stool sample to the doctor
How did you intercept the
poo before it got submerged
in water?
You know that
little white
plate with the
red stripe ...
www.faceless.co.za

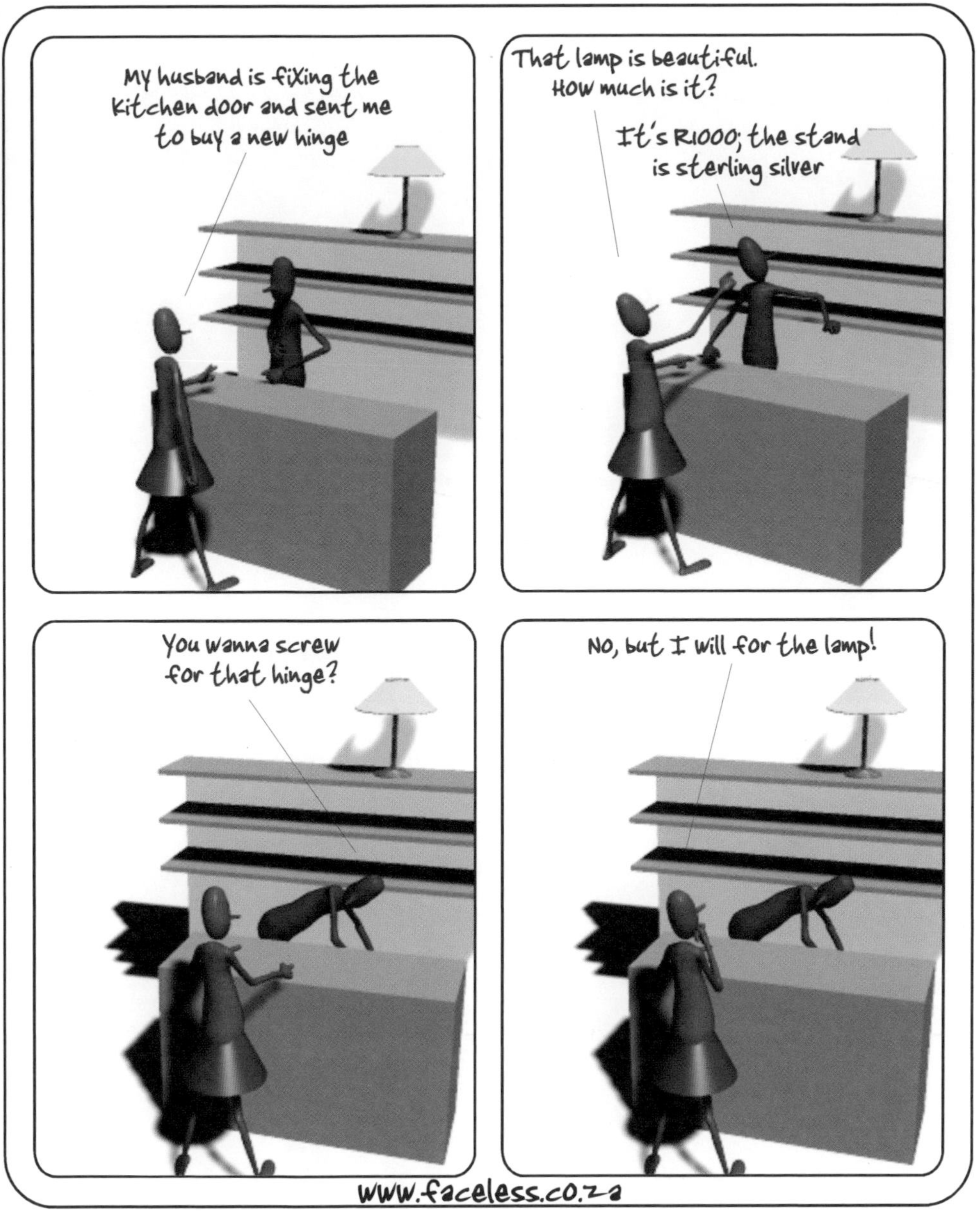
My husband is fixing the kitchen door and sent me to buy a new hinge
That lamp is beautiful. How much is it?
It's R1000; the stand is sterling silver
You wanna screw for that hinge?
No, but I will for the lamp!
www.faceless.co.za

Now that we're engaged, I think we should have pet names for each other
I'm going to call you "Tiger" because you remind me of a tiger being so muscular
You remind me of a zebra
Why?
Because of your stretch marks

www.faceless.co.za

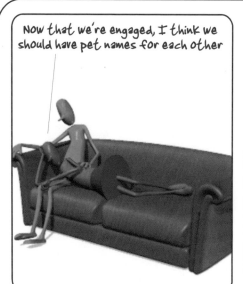

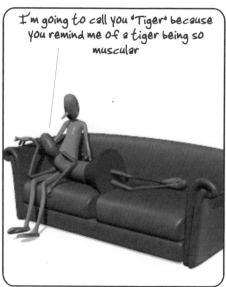

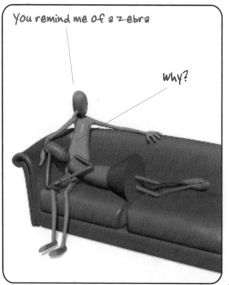

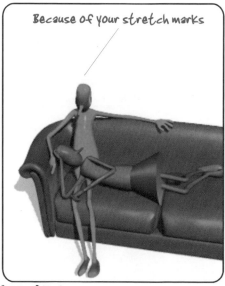

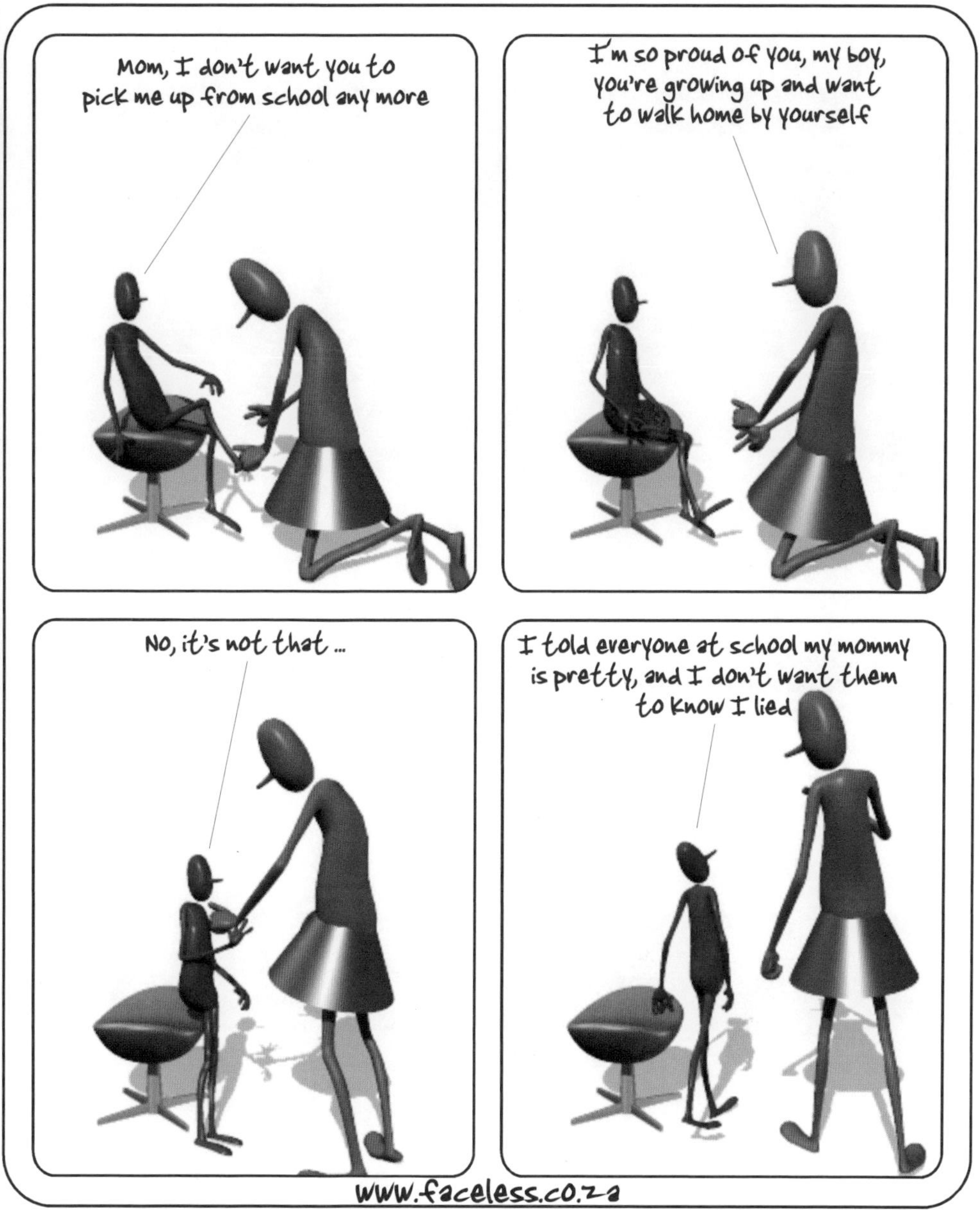
Mom, I don't want you to pick me up from school any more
I'm so proud of you, my boy, you're growing up and want to walk home by yourself
No, it's not that ...
I told everyone at school my mommy is pretty, and I don't want them to know I lied
www.faceless.co.za

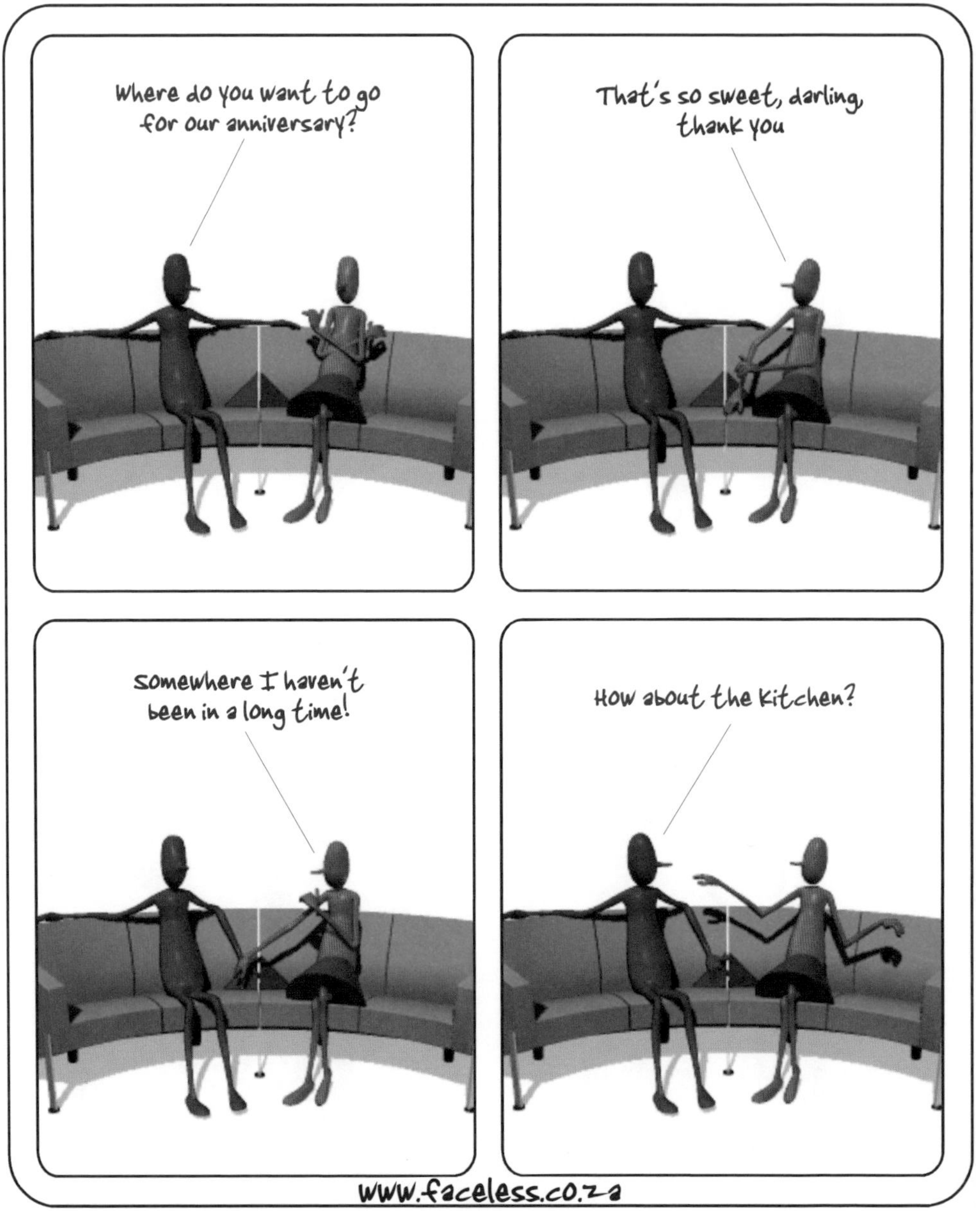
Where do you want to go for our anniversary?
That's so sweet, darling, thank you
Somewhere I haven't been in a long time!
How about the kitchen?
www.faceless.co.za

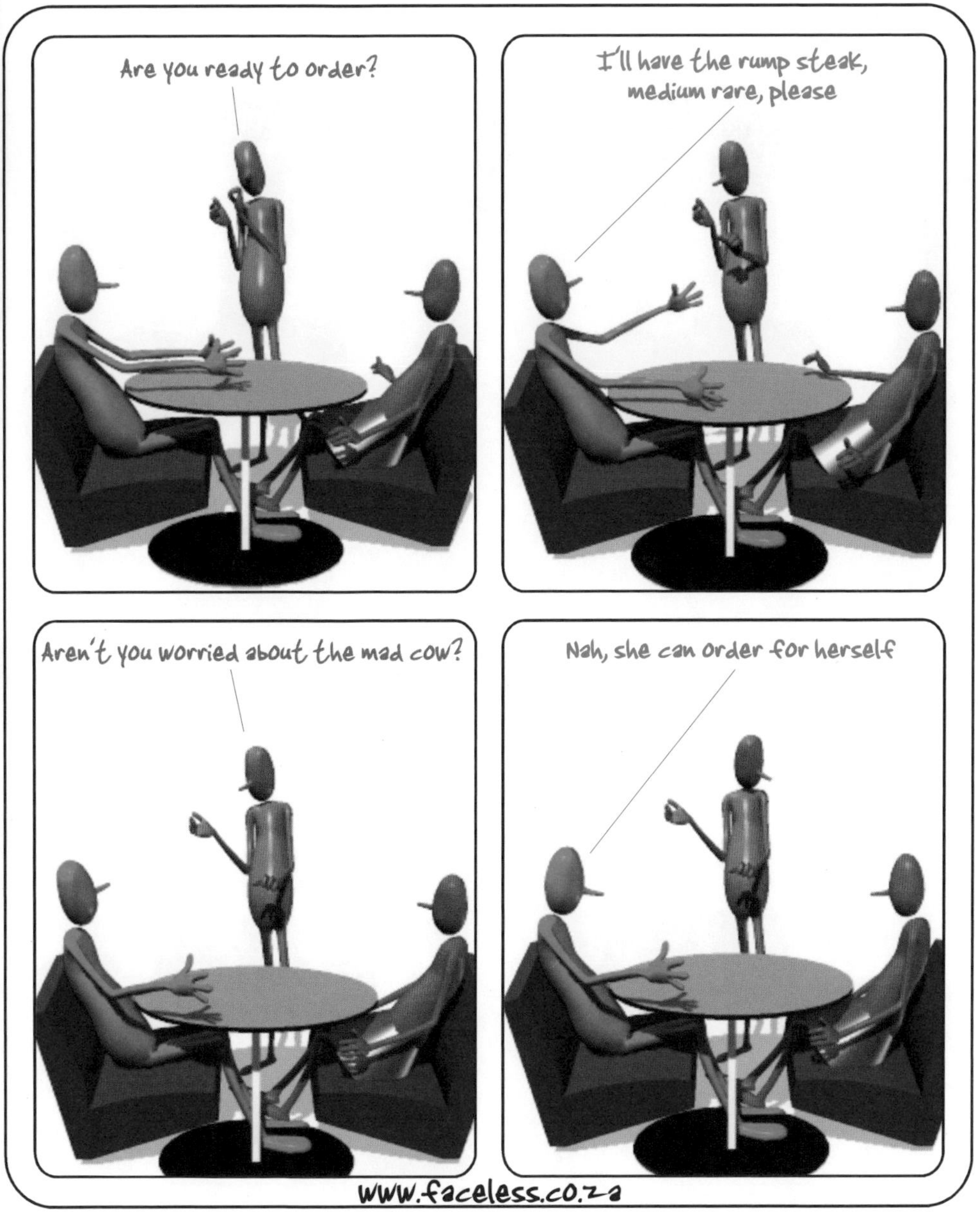
Are you ready to order?
I'll have the rump steak, medium rare, please
Aren't you worried about the mad cow?
Nah, she can order for herself
www.faceless.co.za

I know money is tight, but we've done this month's shopping and there's a little left over. I want to buy some beer
Yes, but I want to buy some new cold cream for my face
And beer costs R120 for a case, while the cold cream only costs R85
Maybe so, but the beer will make you look better at night than the cold cream
www.faceless.co.za

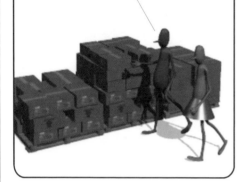

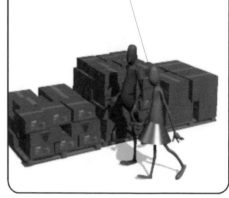

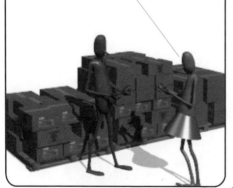

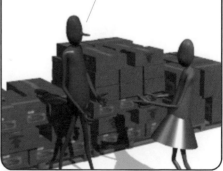

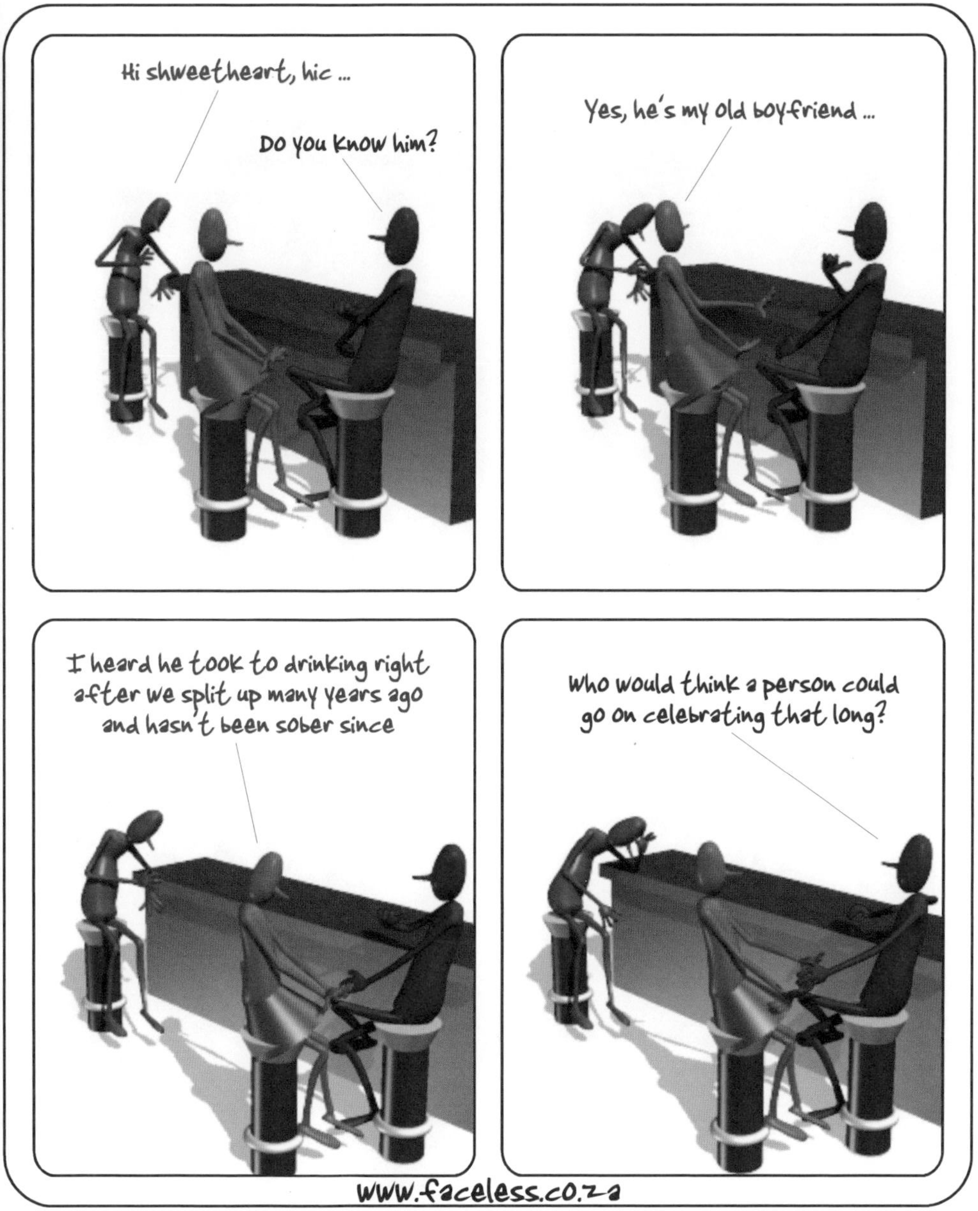
Hi shweetheart, hic ...
Do you know him?
Yes, he's my old boy-friend ...
I heard he took to drinking right after we split up many years ago and hasn't been sober since
Who would think a person could go on celebrating that long?
www.faceless.co.za

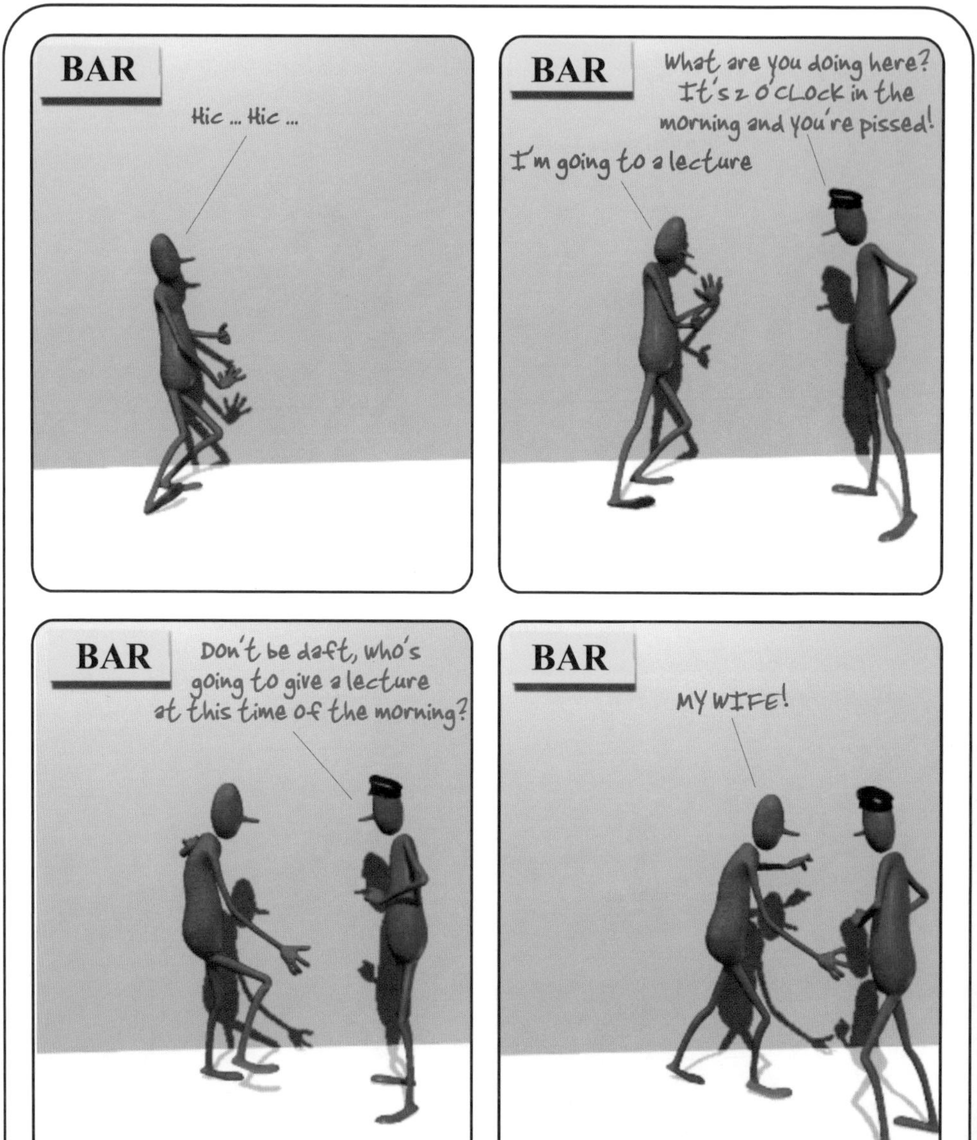
BAR
Hic ... Hic ...
BAR
What are you doing here? It's 2 O'CLOCK in the morning and you're pissed!
I'm going to a lecture
BAR
Don't be daft, who's going to give a lecture at this time of the morning?
BAR
MY WIFE!

www.faceless.co.za

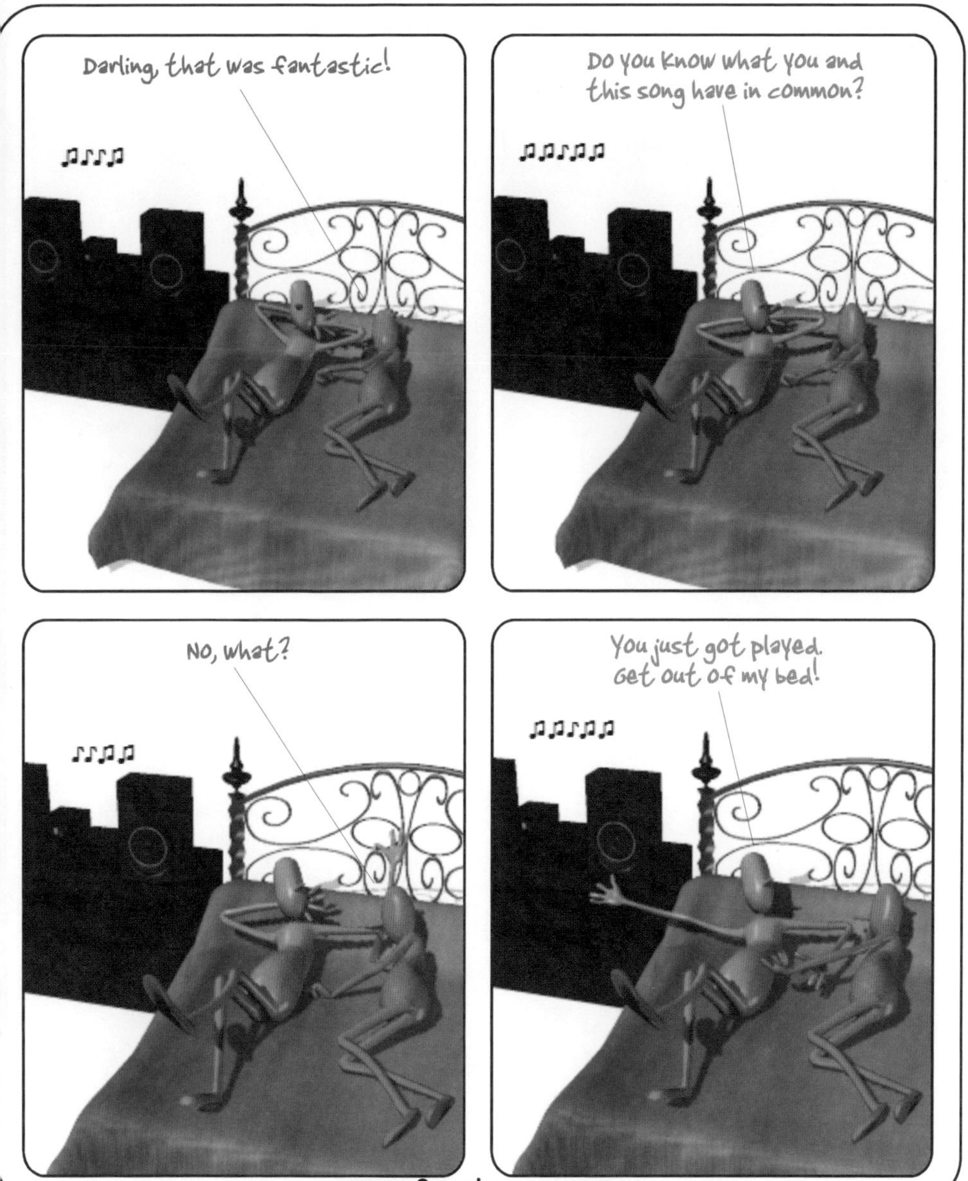
Darling, that was fantastic!
Do you know what you and this song have in common?
No, what?
You just got played. Get out of my bed!

www.faceless.co.za

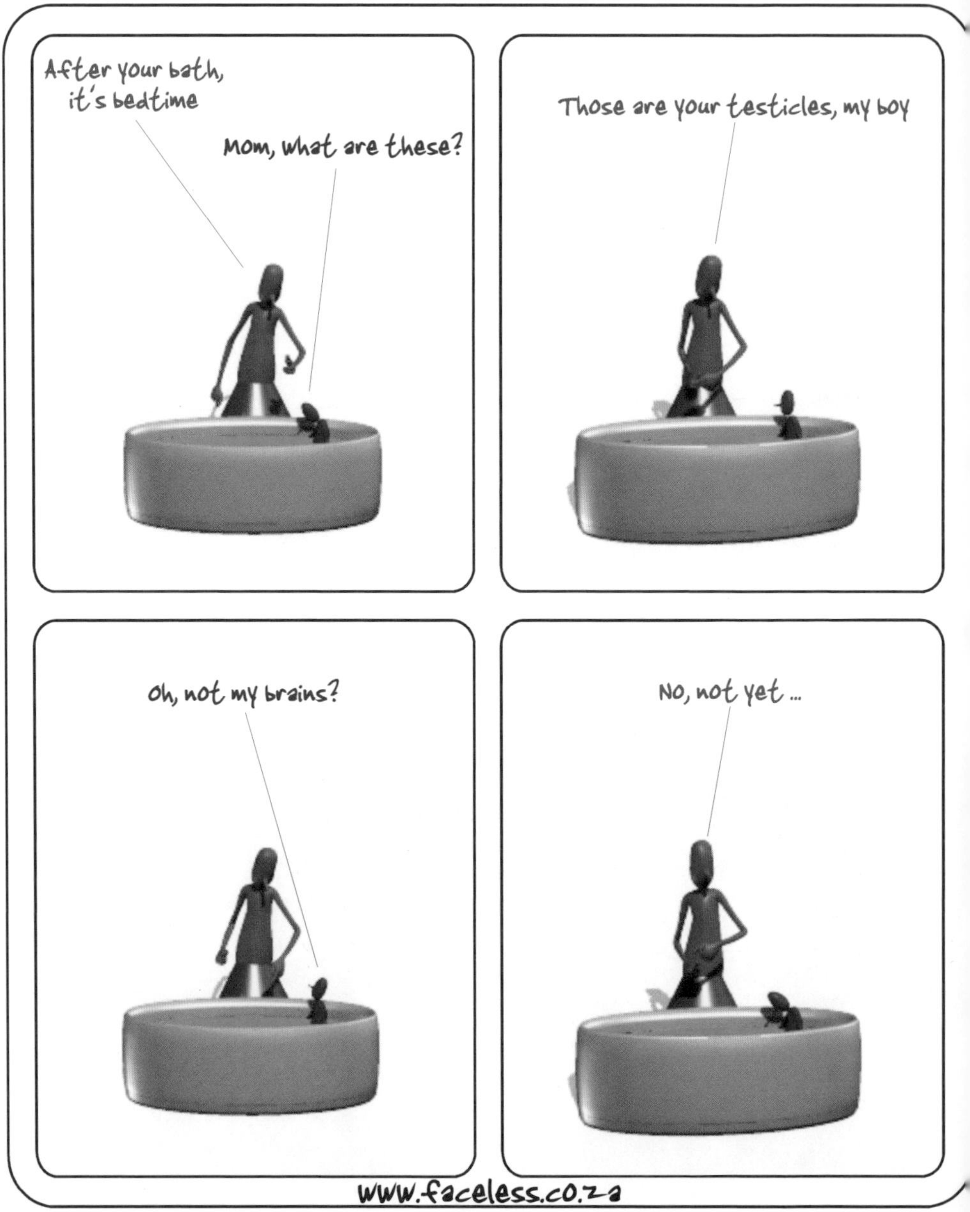
After your bath, it's bedtime
Mom, what are these?
Those are your testicles, my boy
Oh, not my brains?
No, not yet ...
www.faceless.co.za

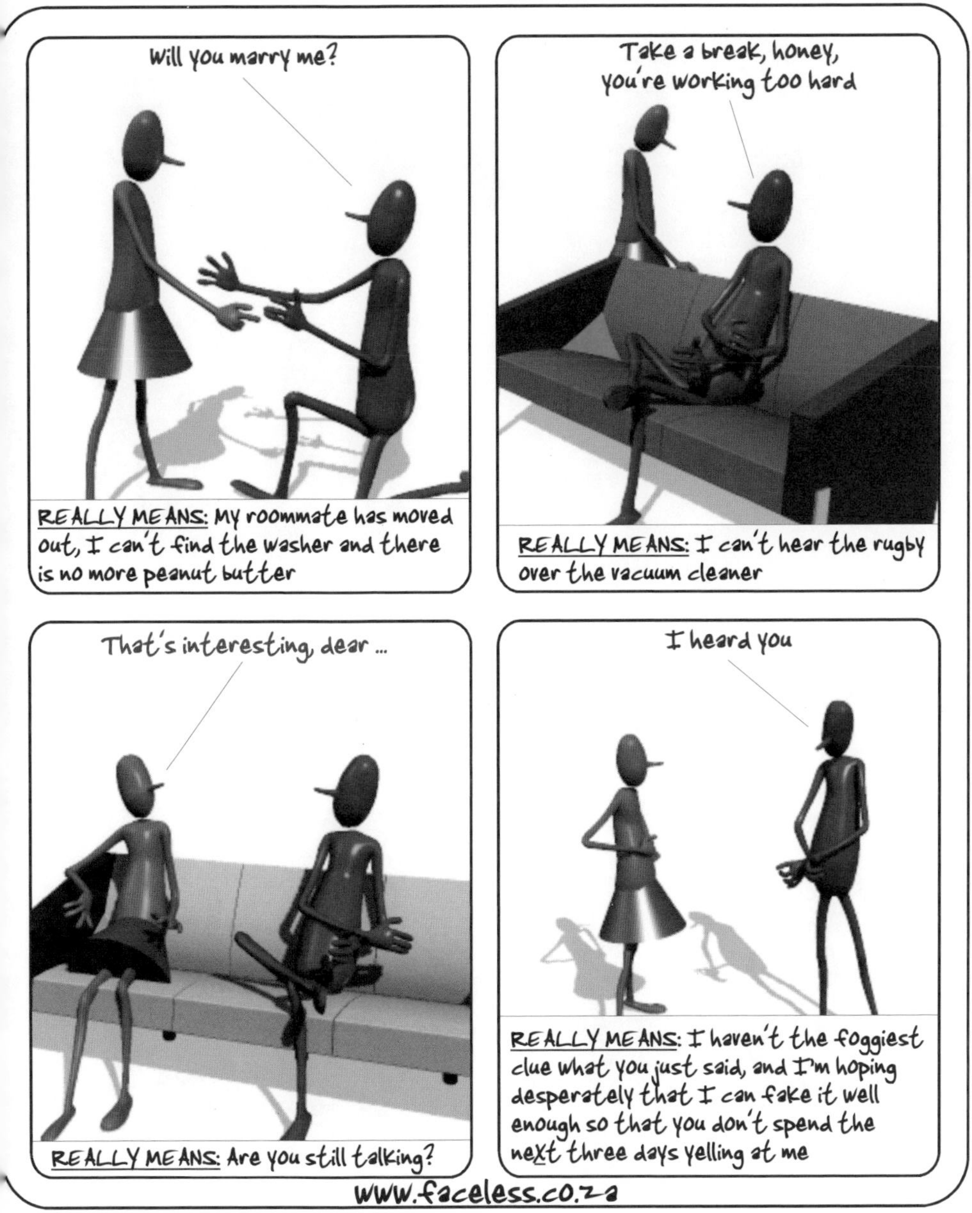

Will you marry me?
REALLY MEANS: My roommate has moved out, I can't find the washer and there is no more peanut butter
Take a break, honey, you're working too hard
REALLY MEANS: I can't hear the rugby over the vacuum cleaner
That's interesting, dear ...
REALLY MEANS: Are you still talking?
I heard you
REALLY MEANS: I haven't the foggiest clue what you just said, and I'm hoping desperately that I can fake it well enough so that you don't spend the next three days yelling at me
www.faceless.co.za

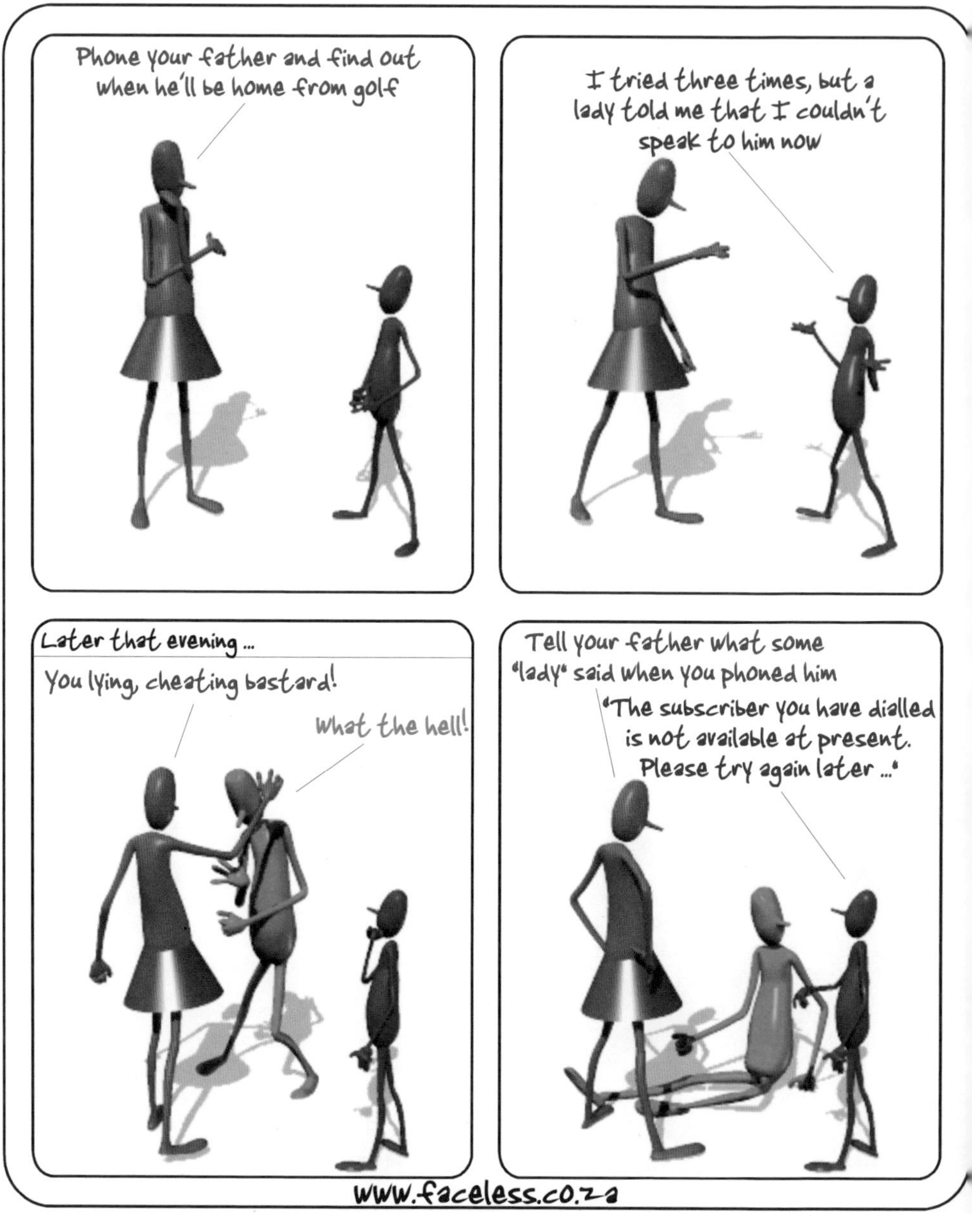
Phone your father and find out when he'll be home from golf
I tried three times, but a lady told me that I couldn't speak to him now
Later that evening ...
You lying, cheating bastard!
What the hell!
Tell your father what some "lady" said when you phoned him
"The subscriber you have dialled is not available at present. Please try again later ..."
www.faceless.co.za

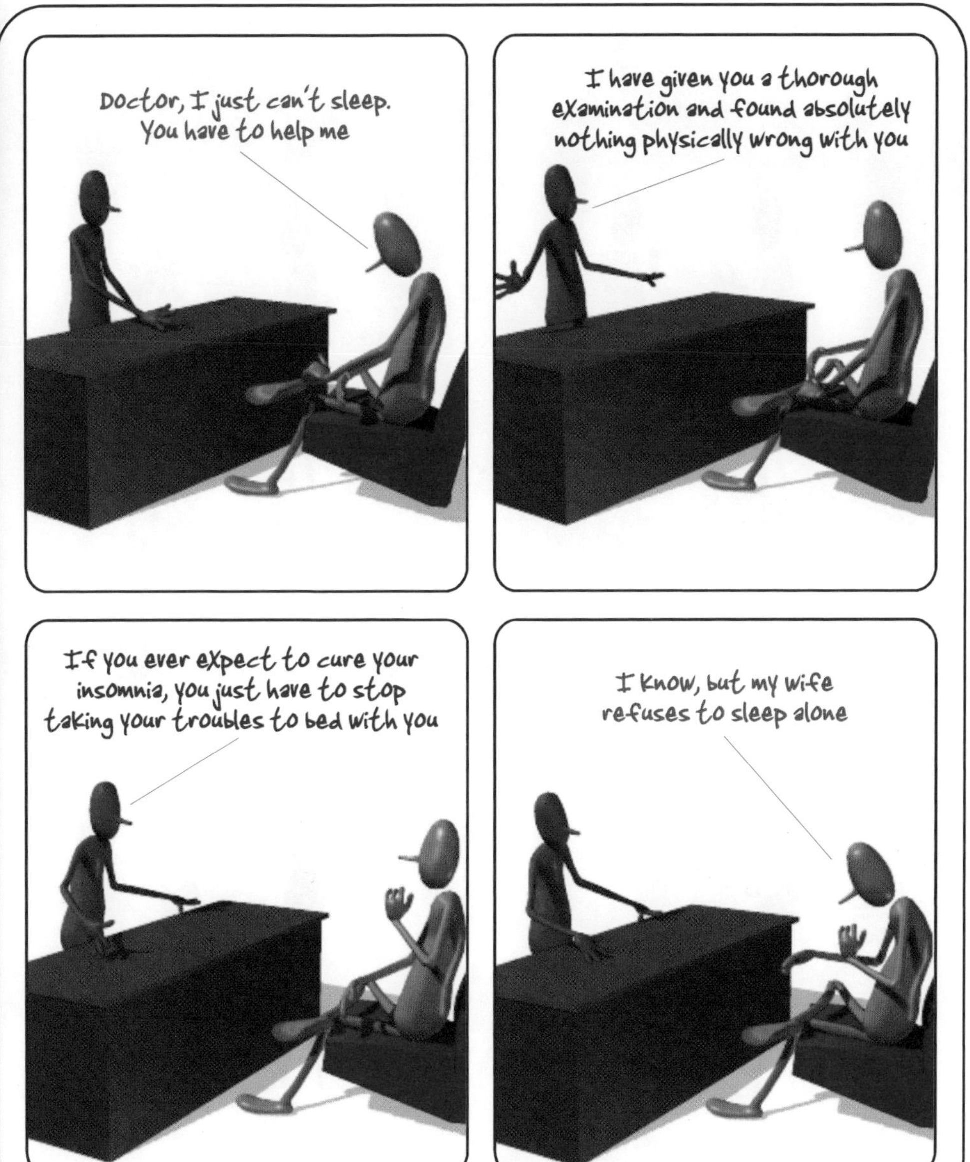
Doctor, I just can't sleep. You have to help me
I have given you a thorough examination and found absolutely nothing physically wrong with you
If you ever expect to cure your insomnia, you just have to stop taking your troubles to bed with you
I know, but my wife refuses to sleep alone
www.faceless.co.za

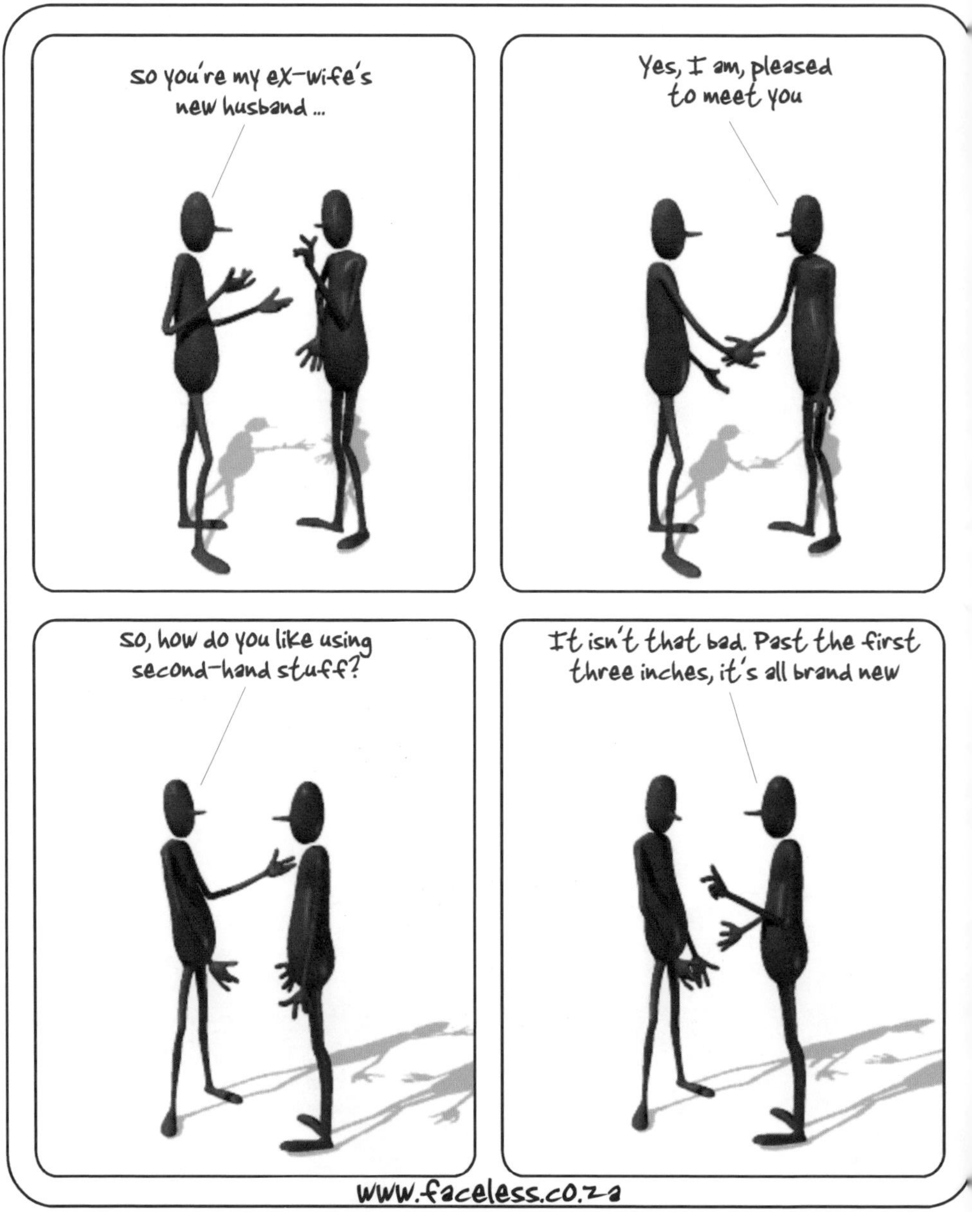
so you're my ex-wife's new husband ...
Yes, I am, pleased to meet you
so, how do you like using second-hand stuff?
It isn't that bad. Past the first three inches, it's all brand new
www.faceless.co.za

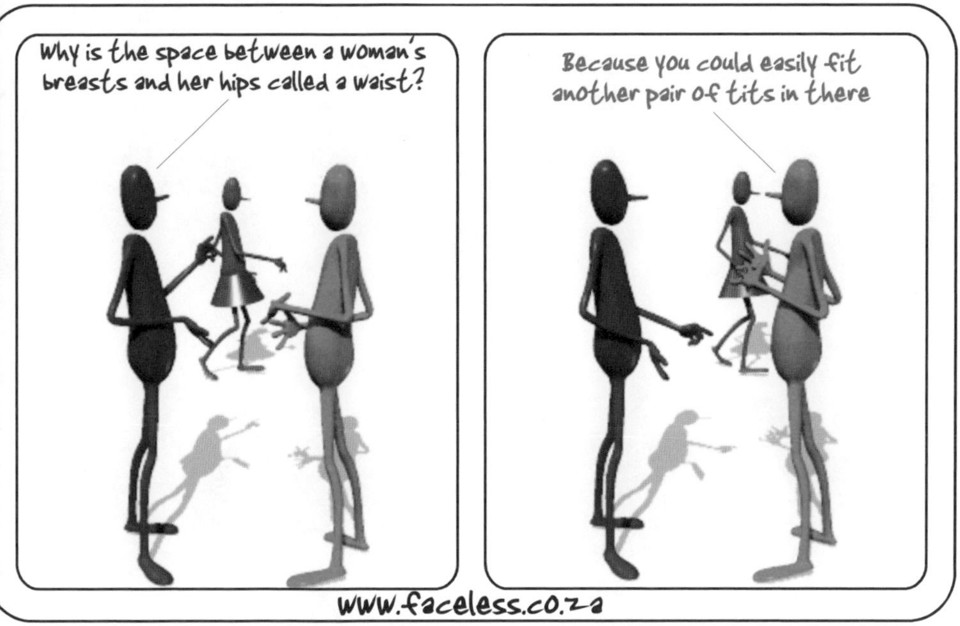
Why is the space between a woman's breasts and her hips called a waist?
Because you could easily fit another pair of tits in there
www.faceless.co.za

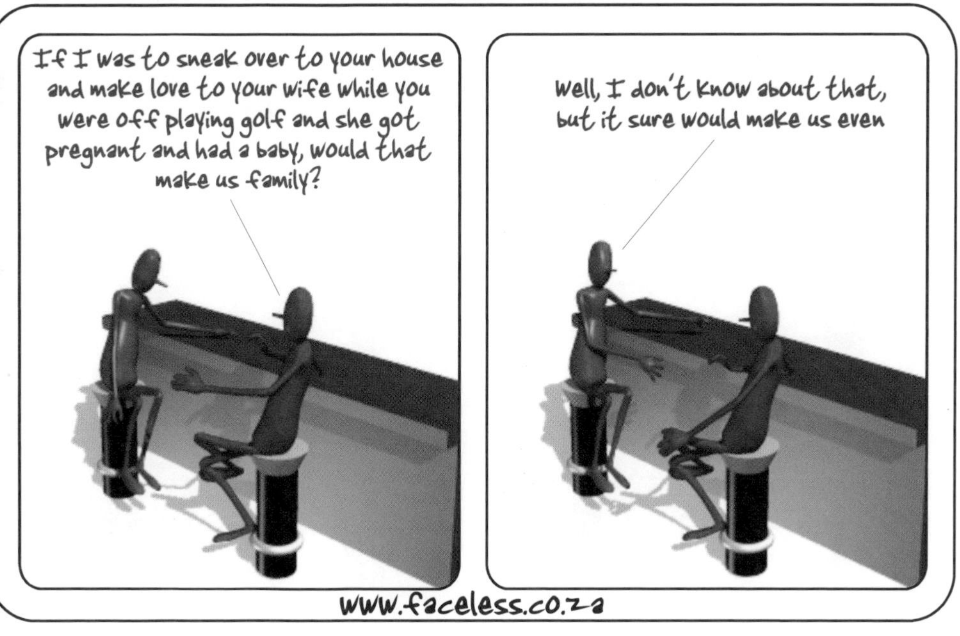
If I was to sneak over to your house and make love to your wife while you were off playing golf and she got pregnant and had a baby, would that make us family?
Well, I don't know about that, but it sure would make us even
www.faceless.co.za

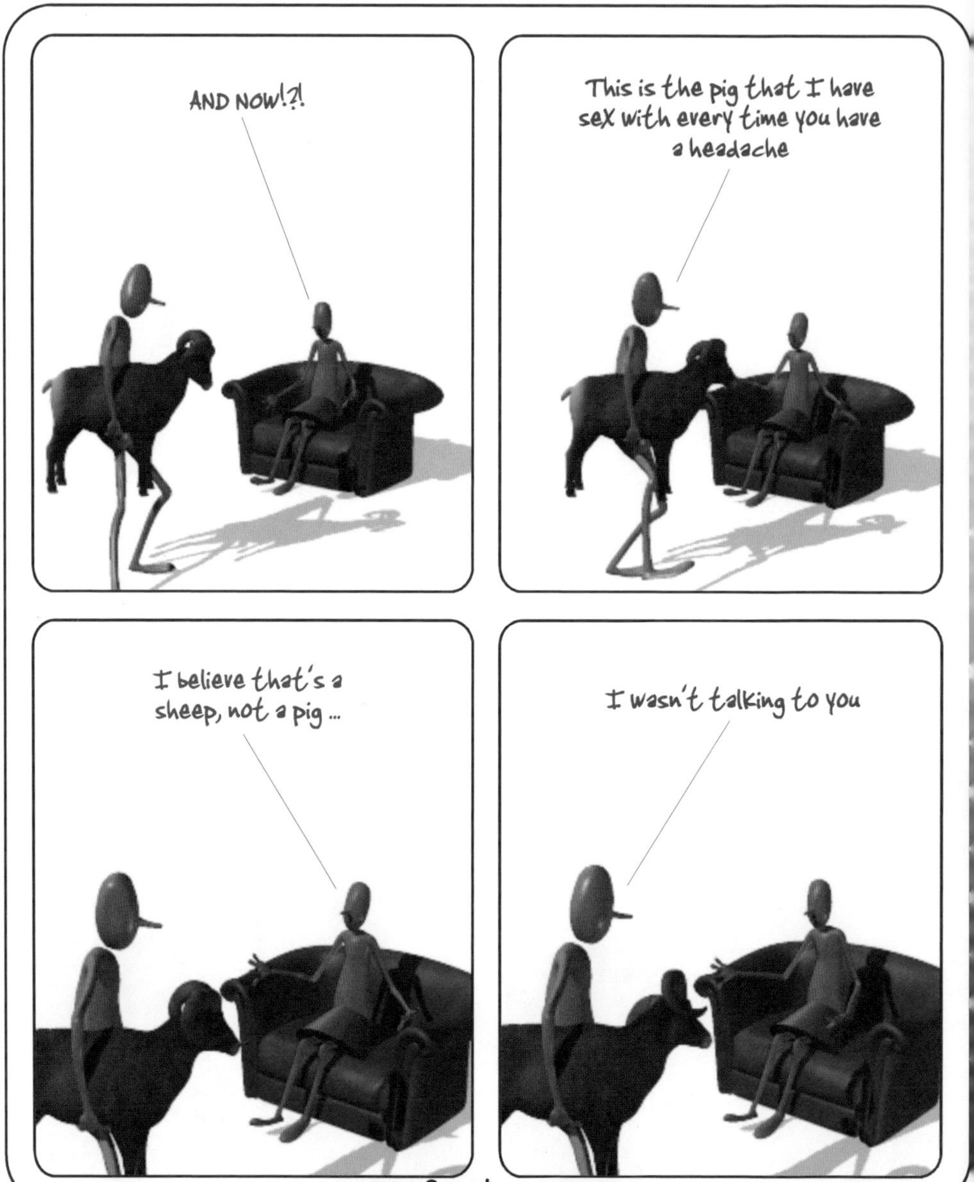
AND NOW!?!
This is the pig that I have sex with every time you have a headache
I believe that's a sheep, not a pig ...
I wasn't talking to you
www.faceless.co.za

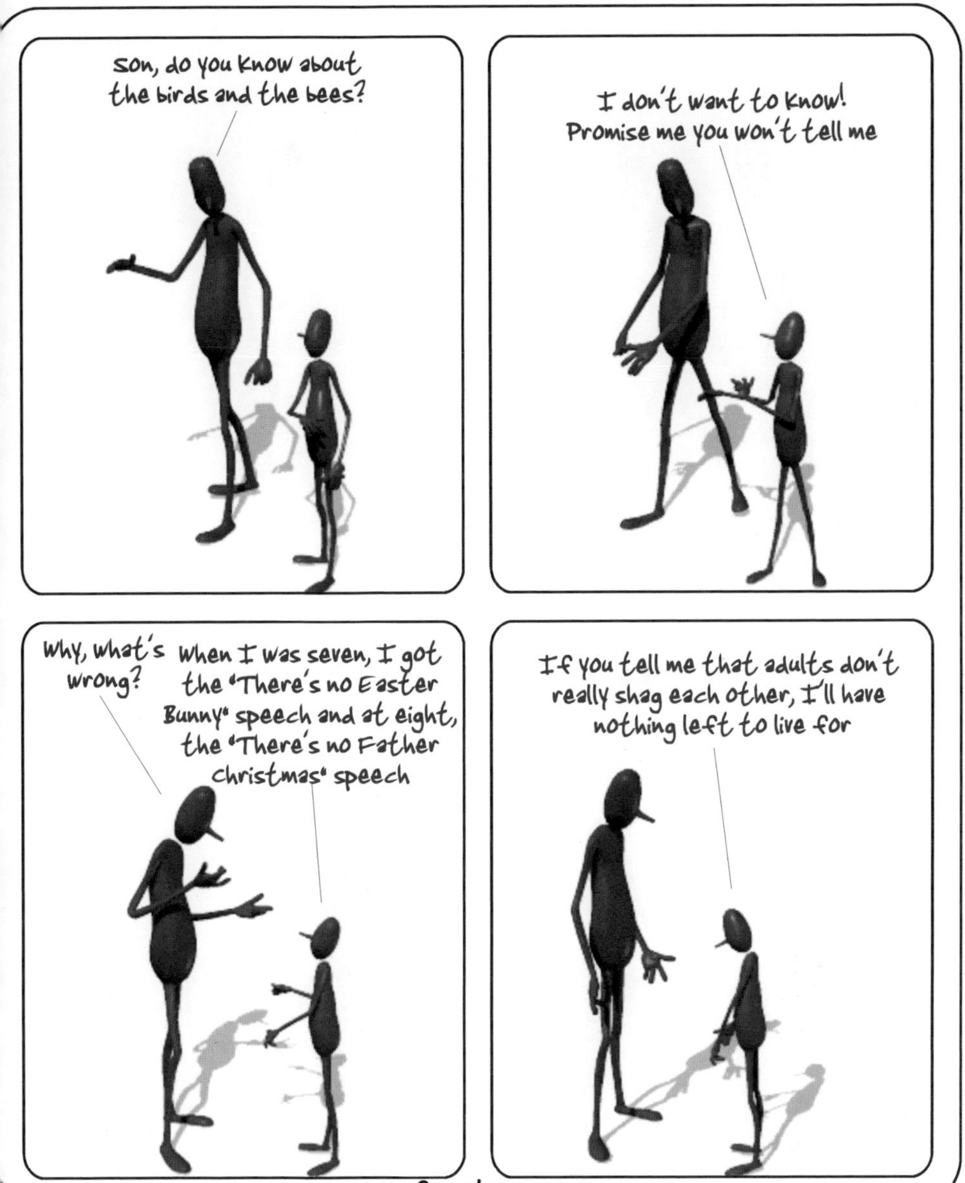
Son, do you know about the birds and the bees?
I don't want to know! Promise me you won't tell me
Why, what's wrong?
When I was seven, I got the "There's no Easter Bunny" speech and at eight, the "There's no Father Christmas" speech
If you tell me that adults don't really shag each other, I'll have nothing left to live for
www.faceless.co.za

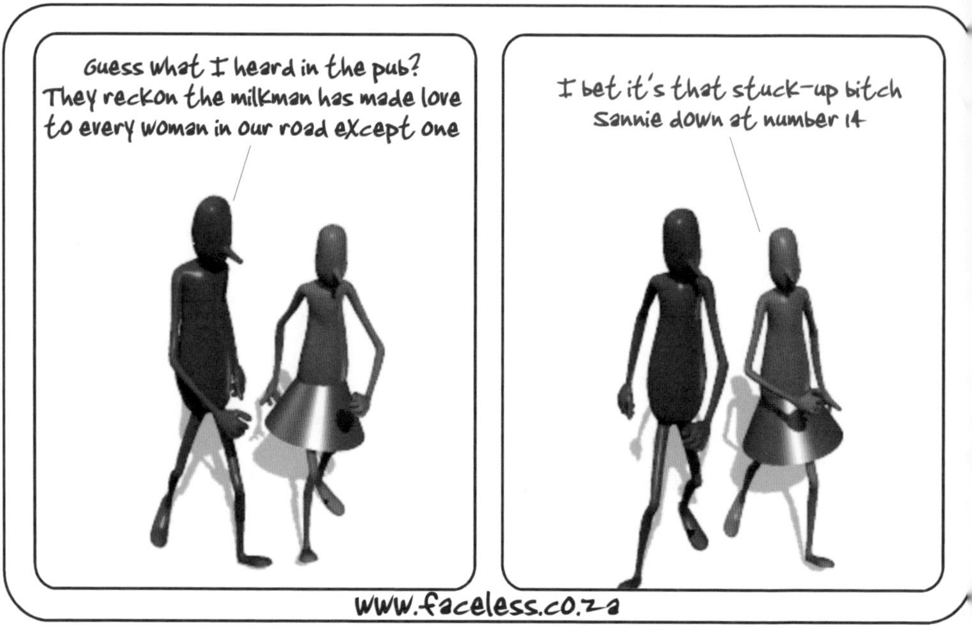
Guess what I heard in the pub? They reckon the milkman has made love to every woman in our road eXcept one
I bet it's that stuck-up bitch Sannie down at number 14
www.faceless.co.za

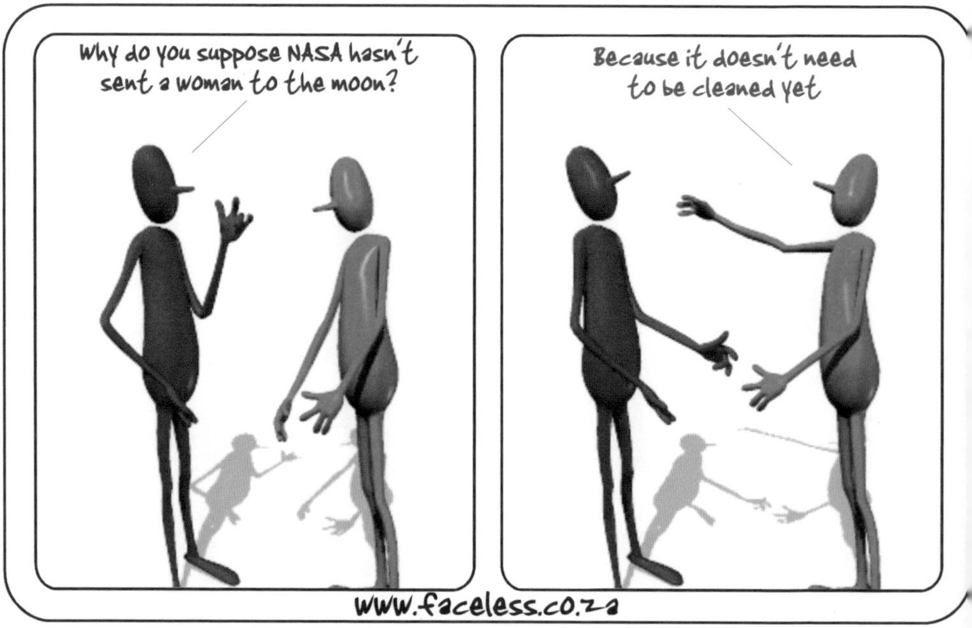
Why do you suppose NASA hasn't sent a woman to the moon?
Because it doesn't need to be cleaned yet
www.faceless.co.za

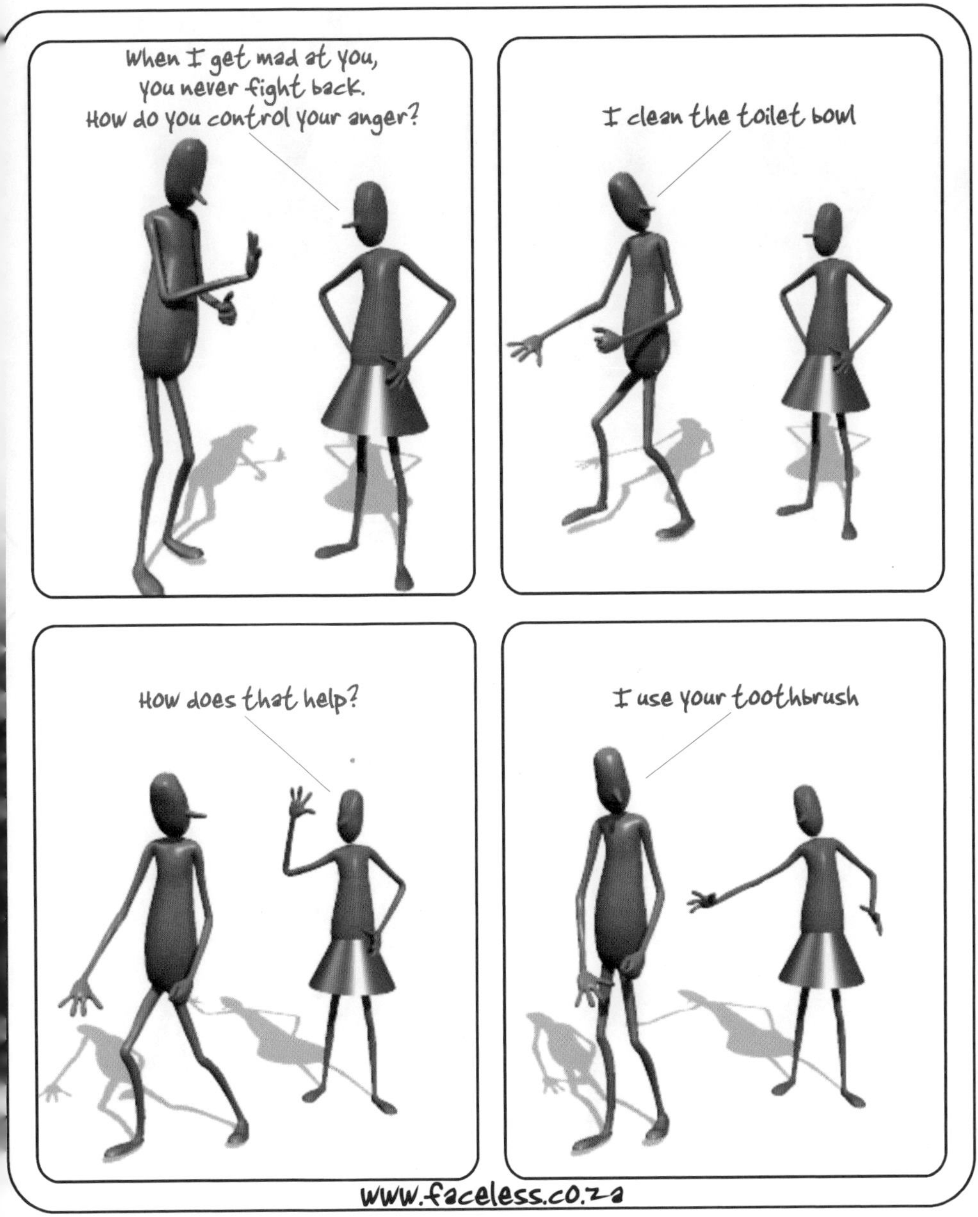
When I get mad at you,
you never fight back.
How do you control your anger?
I clean the toilet bowl
How does that help?
I use your toothbrush
www.faceless.co.za

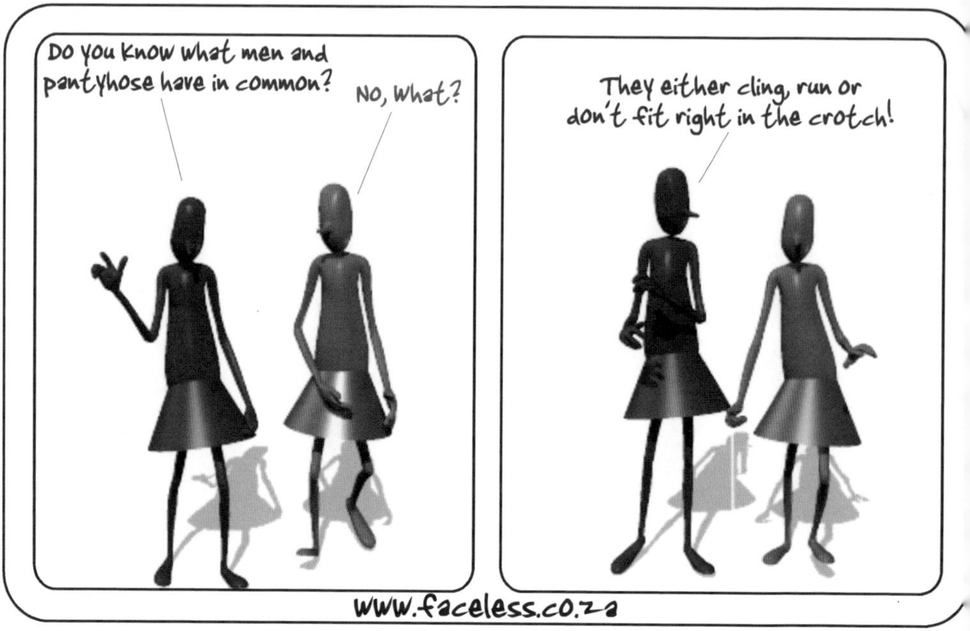
Do you know what men and pantyhose have in common?
No, what?
They either cling, run or don't fit right in the crotch!
www.faceless.co.za

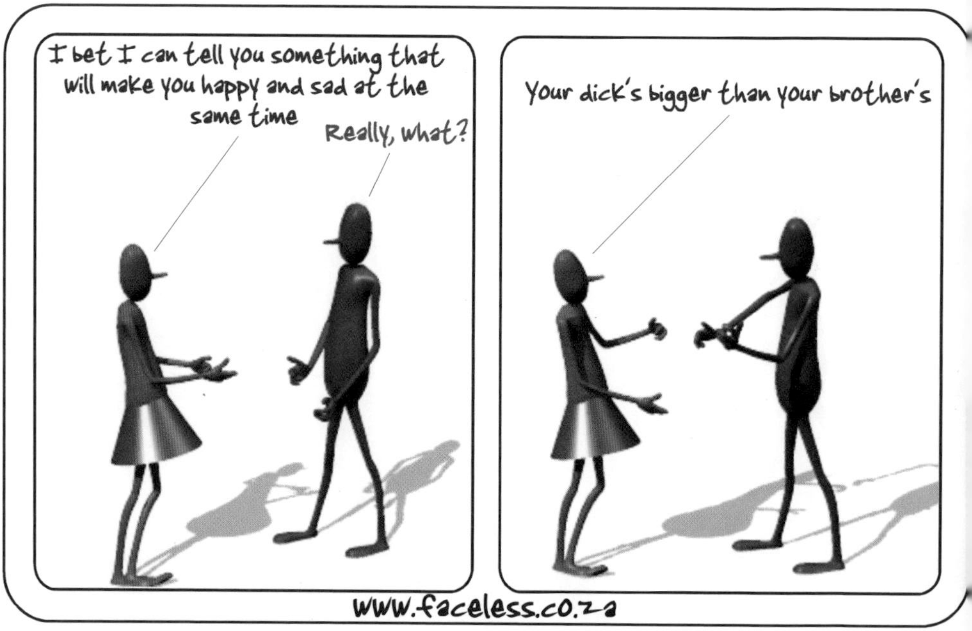
I bet I can tell you something that will make you happy and sad at the same time
Really, what?
Your dick's bigger than your brother's
www.faceless.co.za

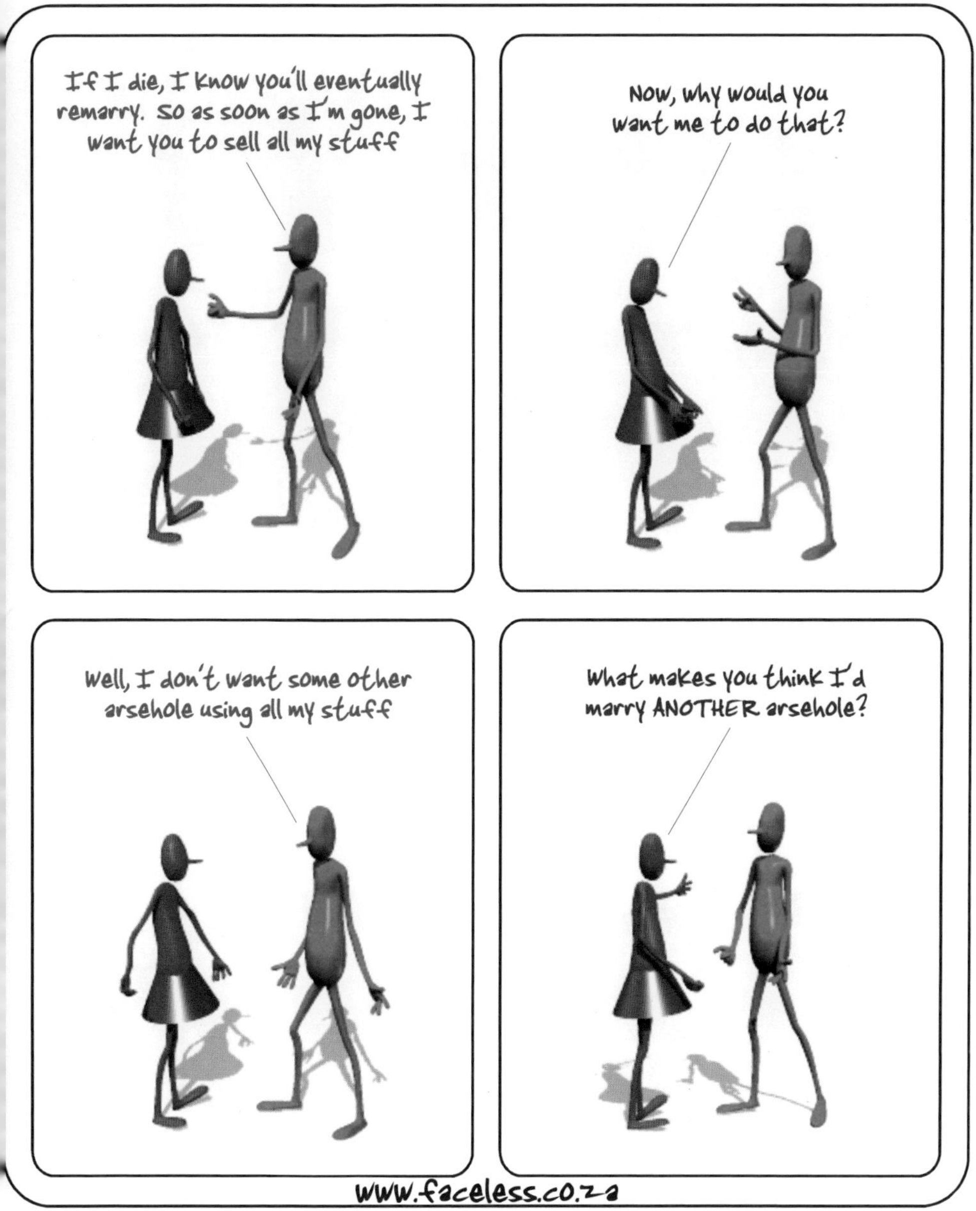
If I die, I know you'll eventually remarry. So as soon as I'm gone, I want you to sell all my stuff
Now, why would you want me to do that?
Well, I don't want some other arsehole using all my stuff
What makes you think I'd marry ANOTHER arsehole?
www.faceless.co.za

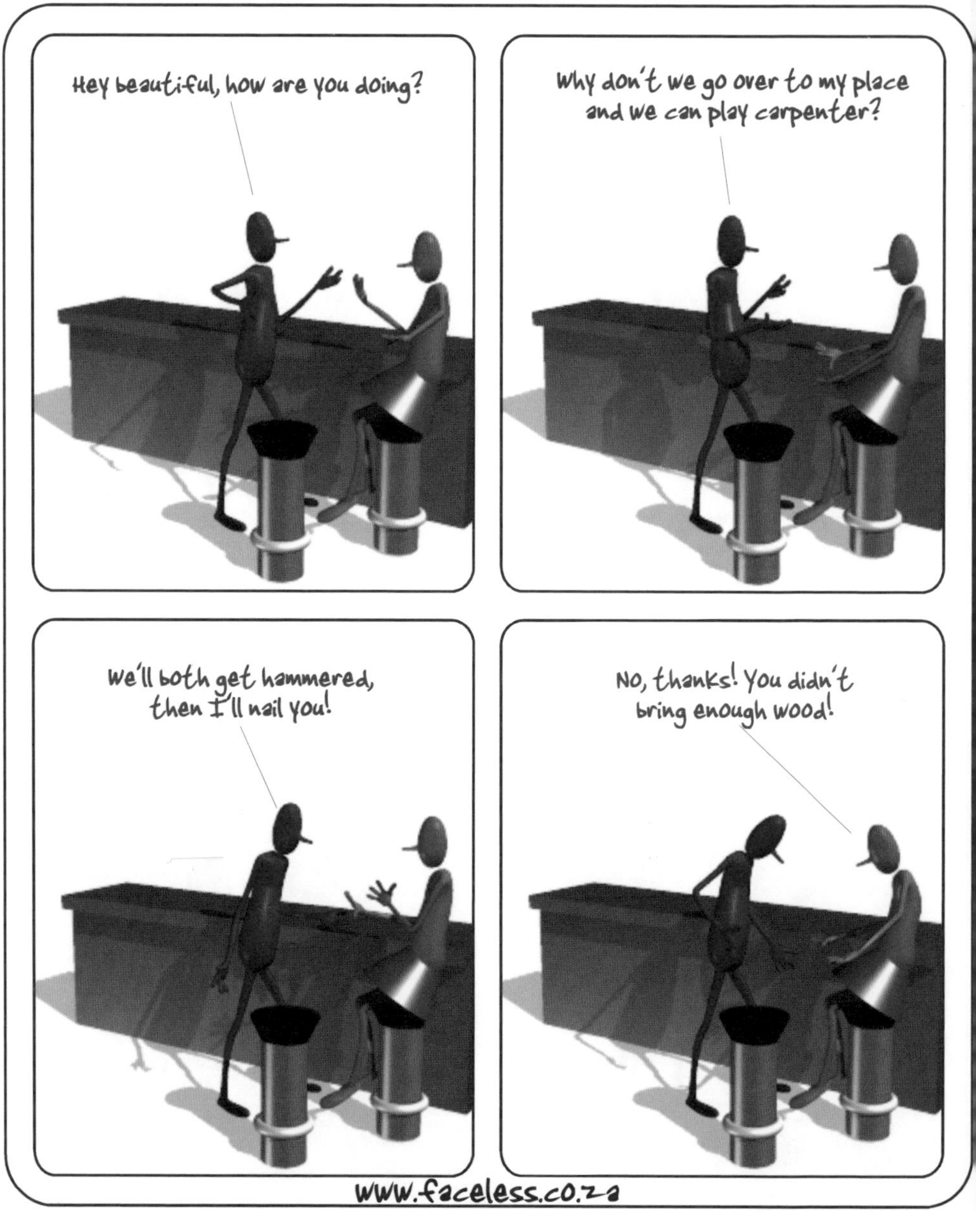
Hey beautiful, how are you doing?
Why don't we go over to my place and we can play carpenter?
We'll both get hammered, then I'll nail you!
No, thanks! You didn't bring enough wood!
www.faceless.co.za

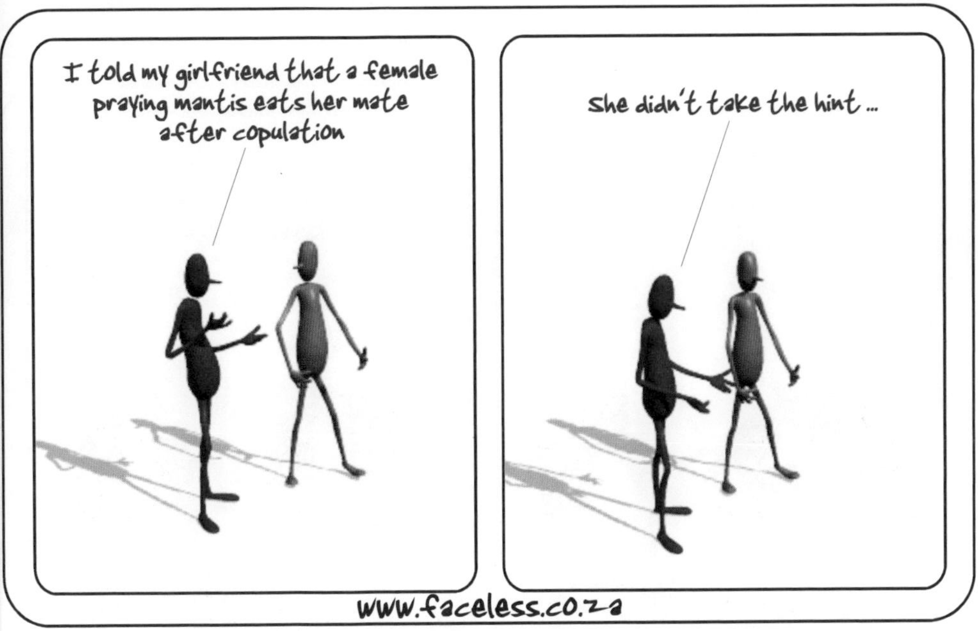
I told my girlfriend that a female praying mantis eats her mate after copulation
She didn't take the hint ...
www.faceless.co.za

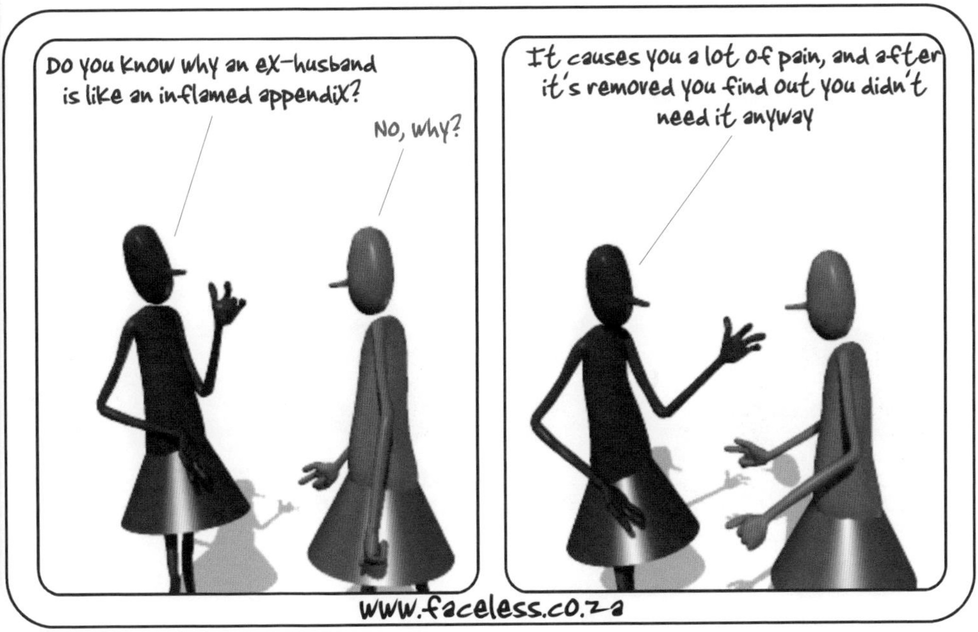
Do you know why an ex-husband is like an inflamed appendix?
No, why?
It causes you a lot of pain, and after it's removed you find out you didn't need it anyway
www.faceless.co.za

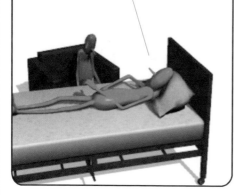

Dear, you have been with me all through the bad times. When I got fired, you were there to support me

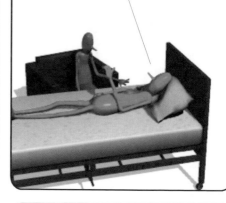

When my business failed, you were there. When I got shot, you were by my side. When we lost the house, you stayed right here

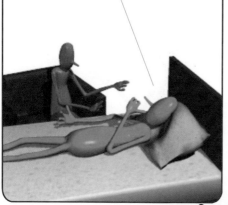

Now that I'm dying, you are still by my side ... Do you know what?

What, dear?

I think you're bad luck

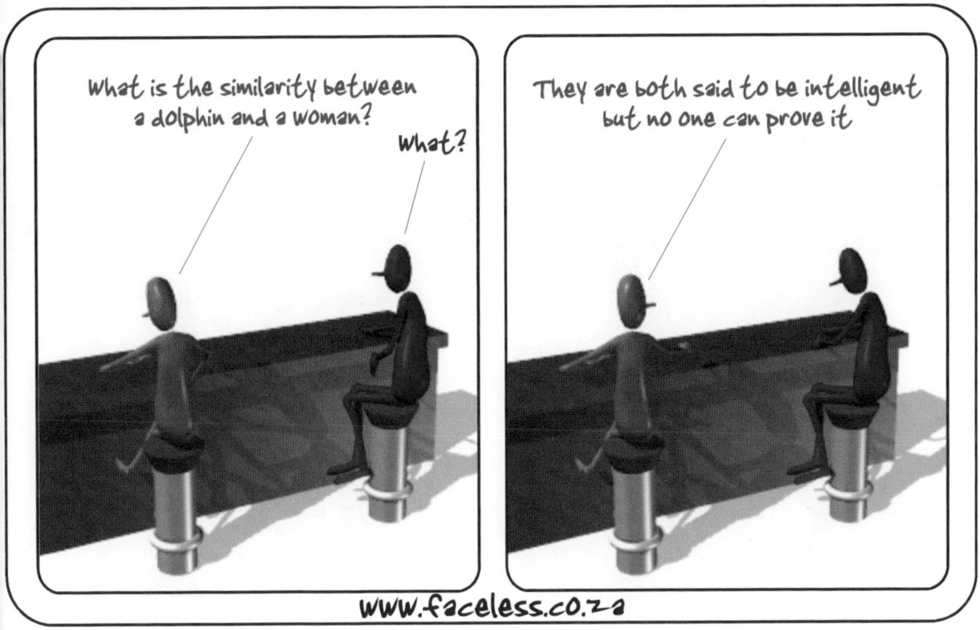
What is the similarity between a dolphin and a woman?
What?
They are both said to be intelligent but no one can prove it
www.faceless.co.za

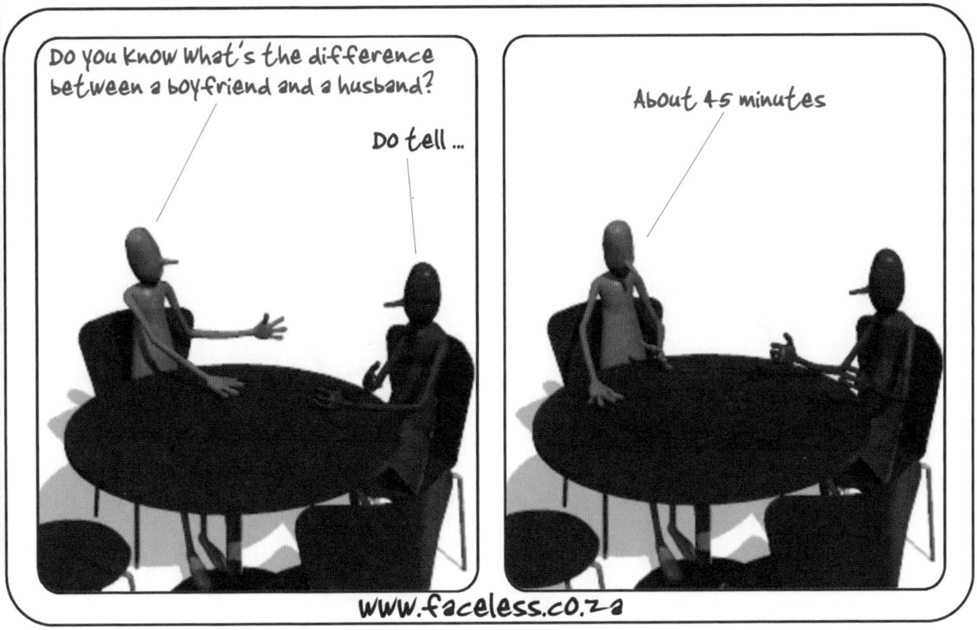
Do you know what's the difference between a boyfriend and a husband?
Do tell ...
About 45 minutes
www.faceless.co.za

Have you tried the new "rodeo" sex position yet?
I haven't even heard of that one; what is it?
Well, it's where you get your wife down on all fours and you mount her from behind
Then you reach around and cup each one of her breasts in your hands and whisper in her ear, "Boy, these feel just like your sister's"
Then you try and stay on for eight seconds
www.faceless.co.za

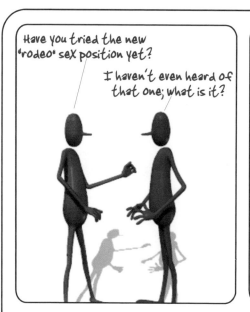

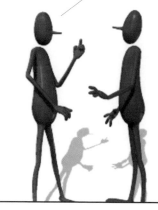

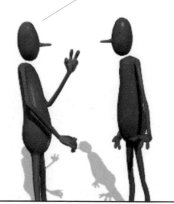

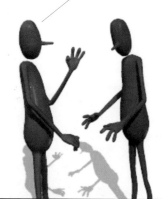

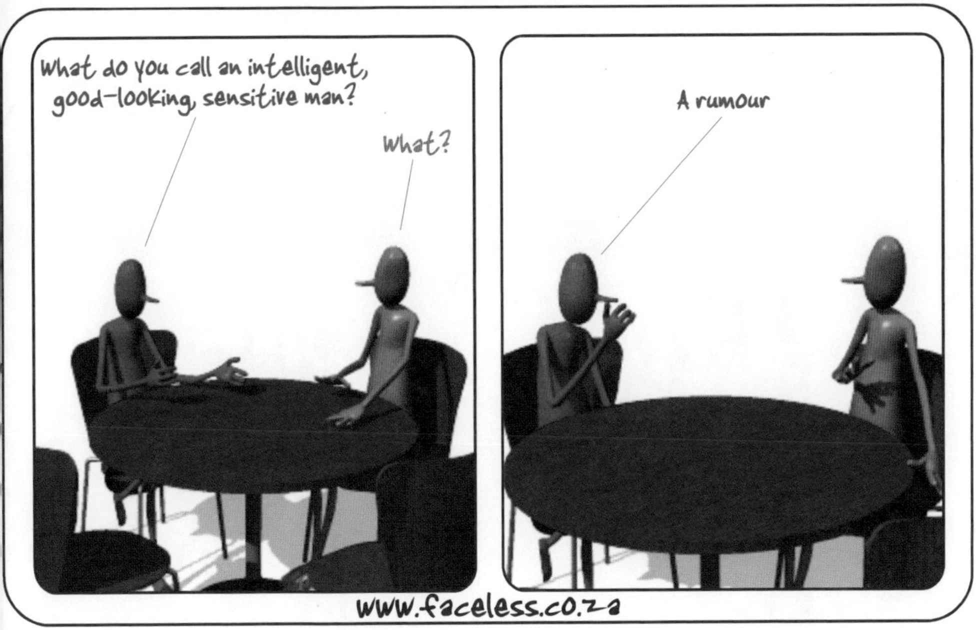
What do you call an intelligent, good-looking, sensitive man?
What?
A rumour
www.faceless.co.za

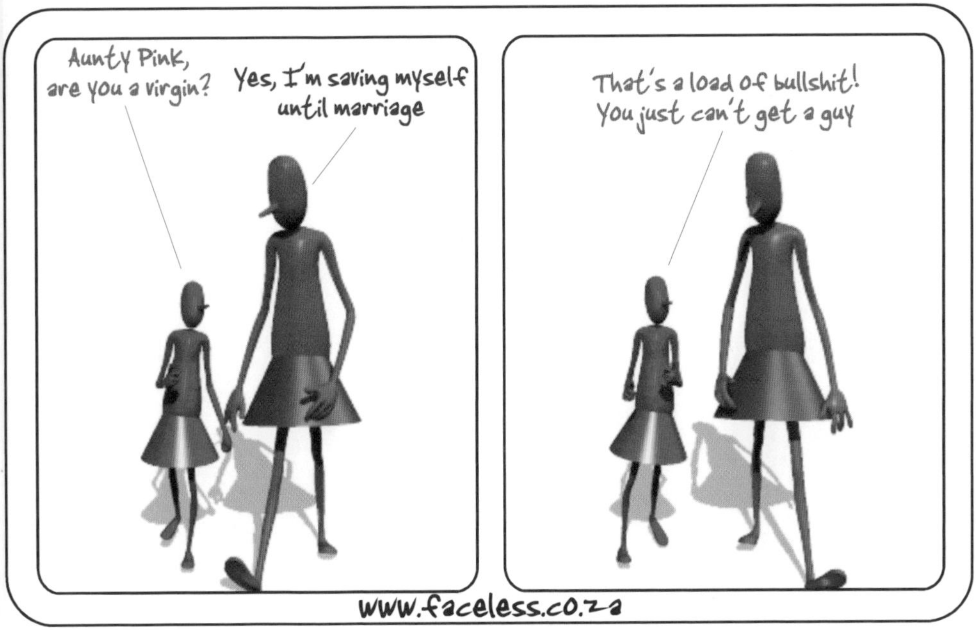
Aunty Pink, are you a virgin?
Yes, I'm saving myself until marriage
That's a load of bullshit! You just can't get a guy
www.faceless.co.za

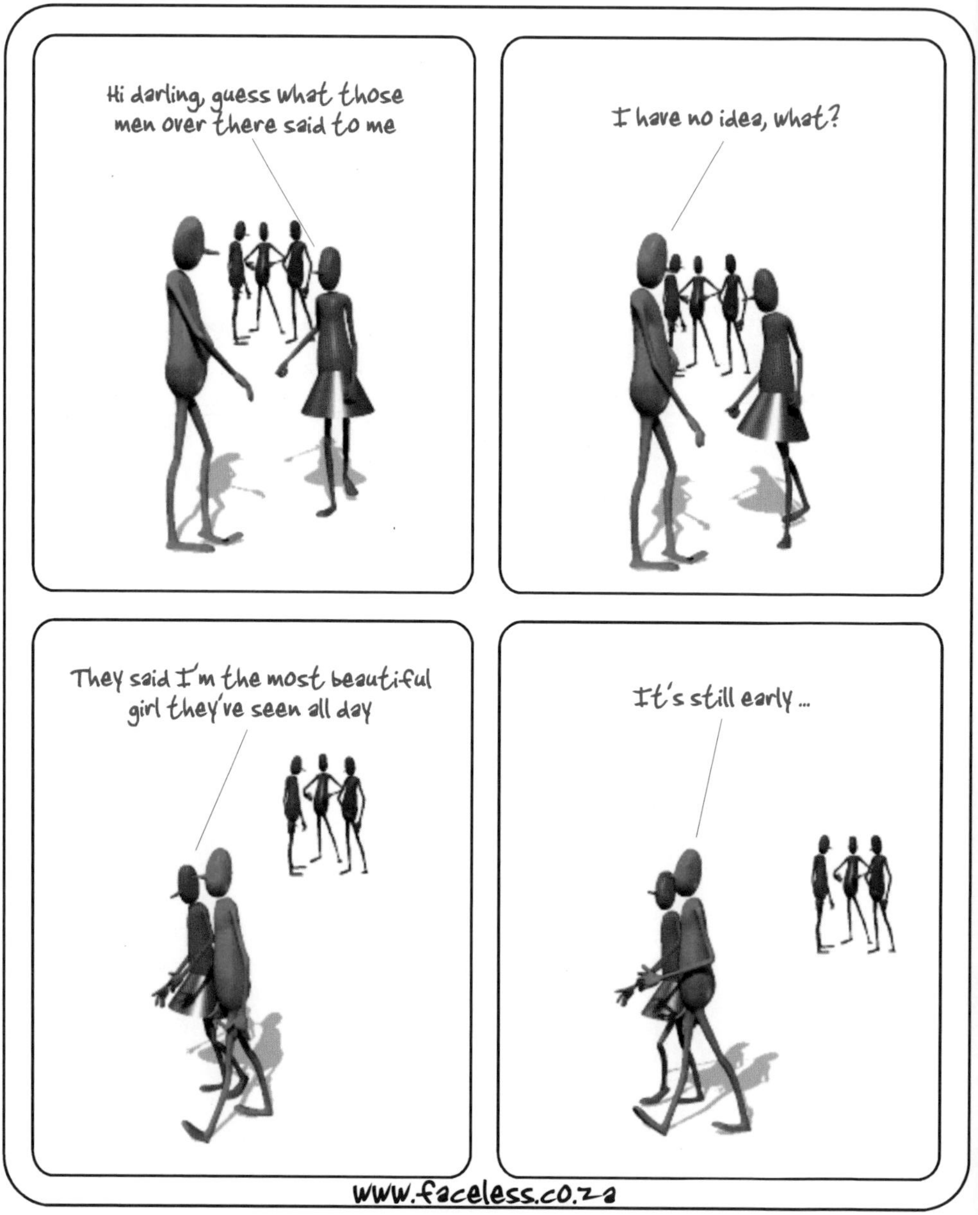
Hi darling, guess what those men over there said to me
I have no idea, what?
They said I'm the most beautiful girl they've seen all day
It's still early ...
www.faceless.co.za

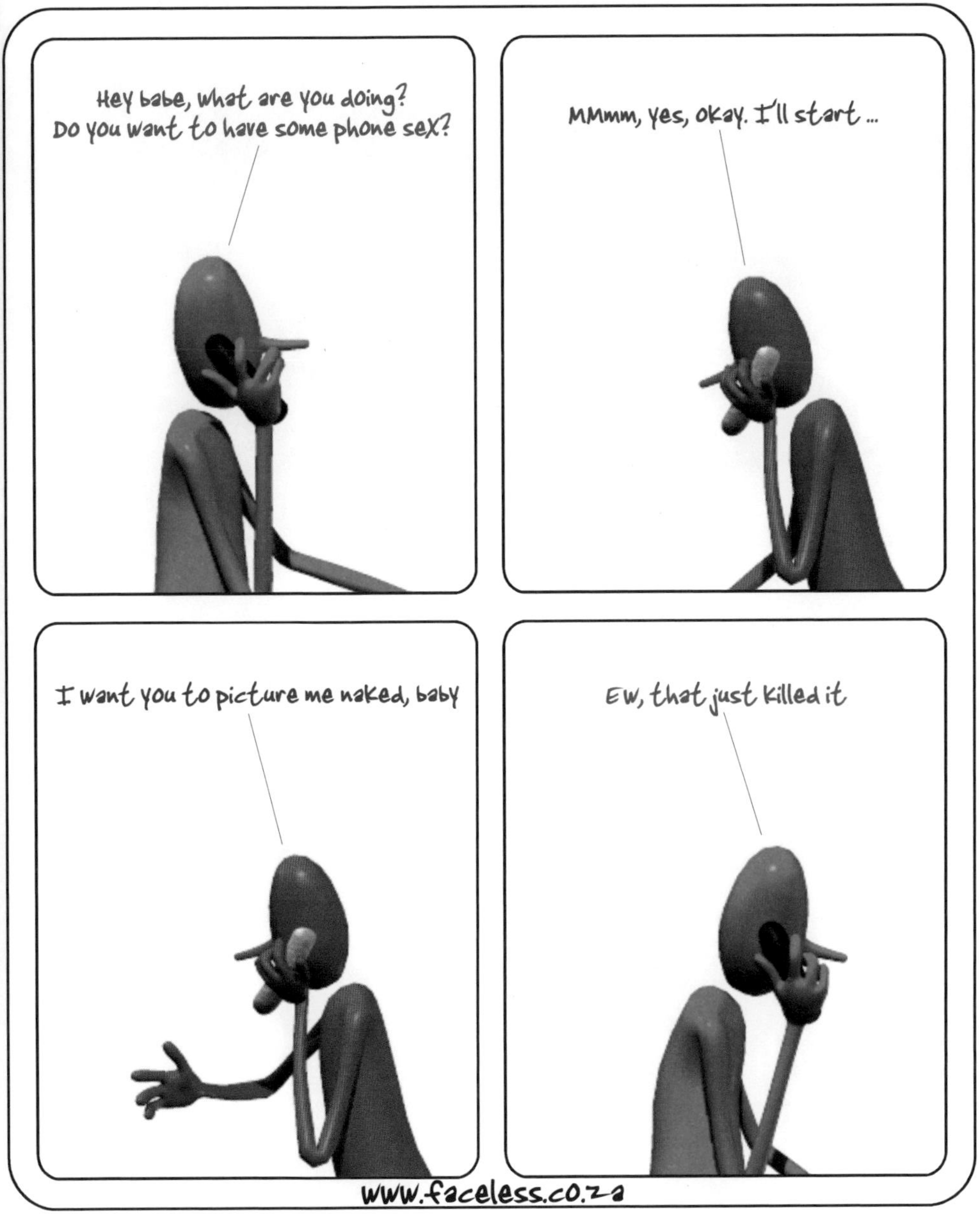
Hey babe, what are you doing?
Do you want to have some phone sex?
MMmm, yes, okay. I'll start ...
I want you to picture me naked, baby
Ew, that just killed it
www.faceless.co.za

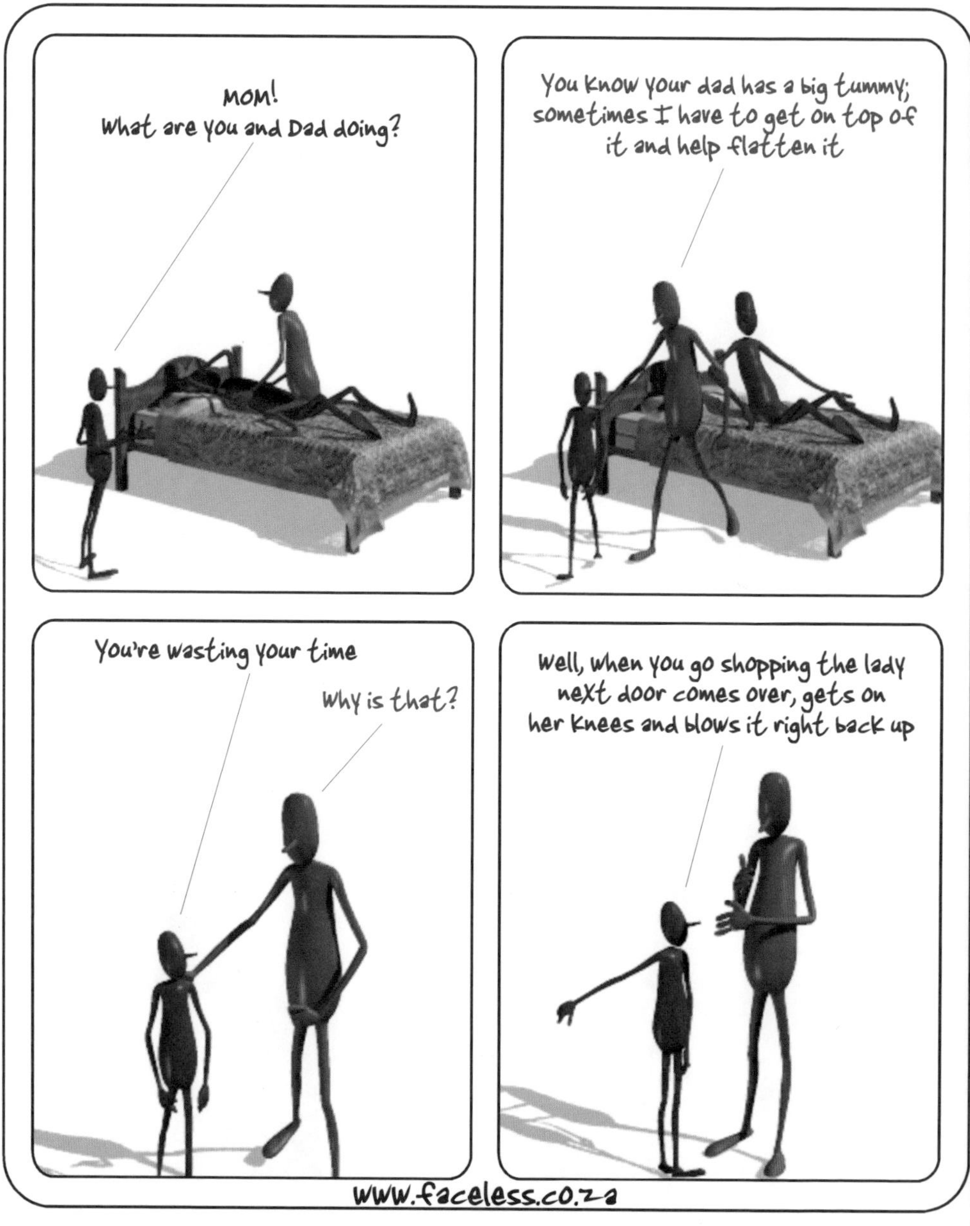
MOM!
What are you and Dad doing?
You know your dad has a big tummy; sometimes I have to get on top of it and help flatten it
You're wasting your time
Why is that?
Well, when you go shopping the lady next door comes over, gets on her knees and blows it right back up
www.faceless.co.za

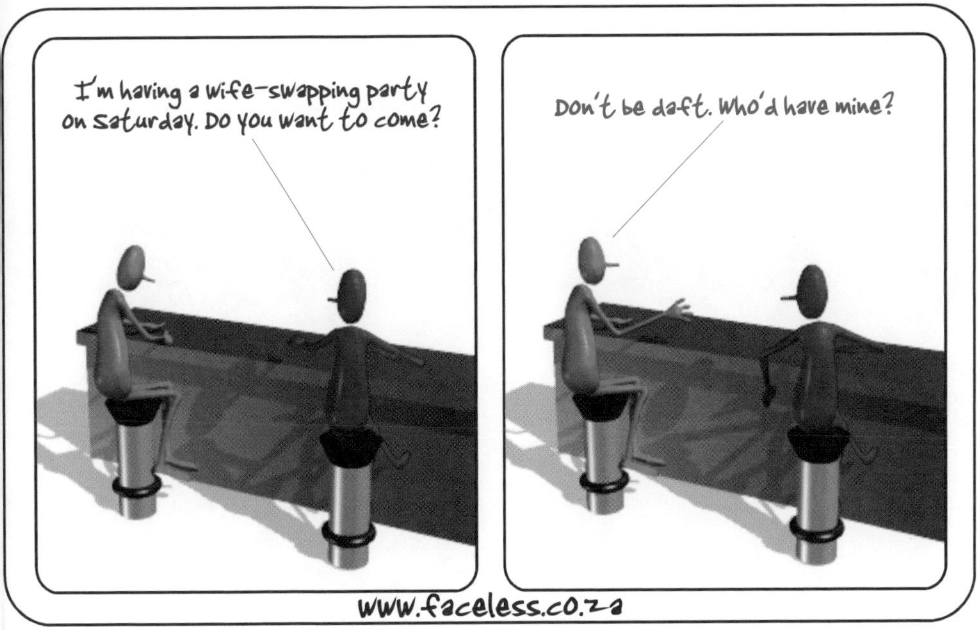
I'm having a wife-swapping party on saturday. Do you want to come?
Don't be daft. Who'd have mine?
www.faceless.co.za

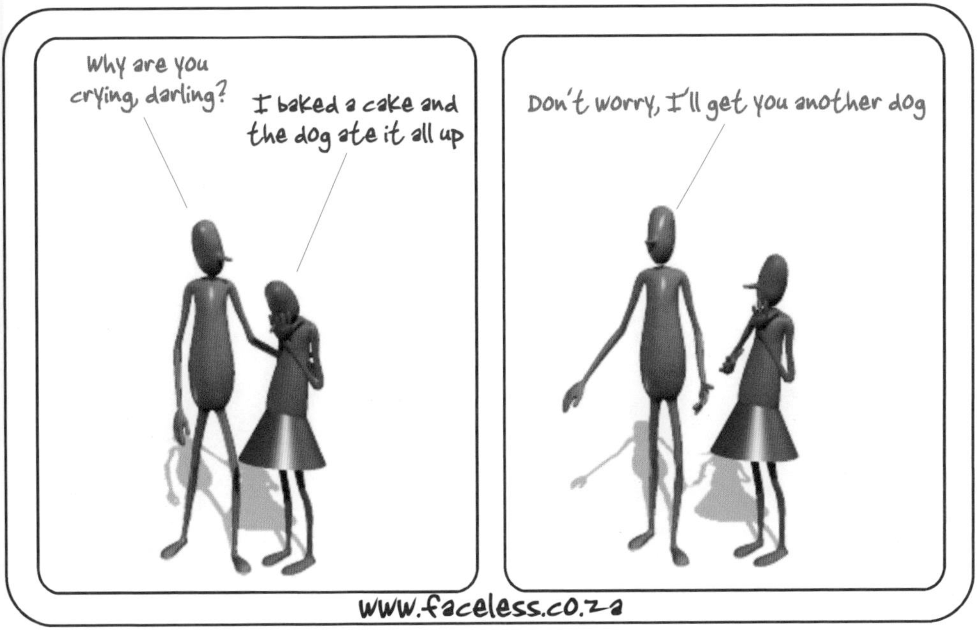
Why are you crying, darling?
I baked a cake and the dog ate it all up
Don't worry, I'll get you another dog
www.faceless.co.za

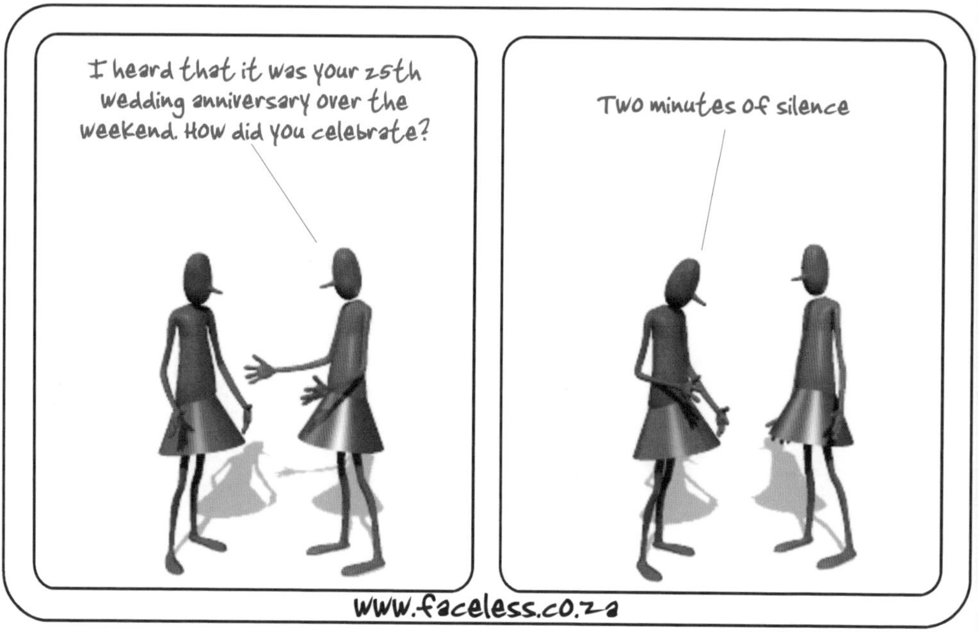
I heard that it was your 25th wedding anniversary over the weekend. How did you celebrate?
Two minutes of silence
www.faceless.co.za

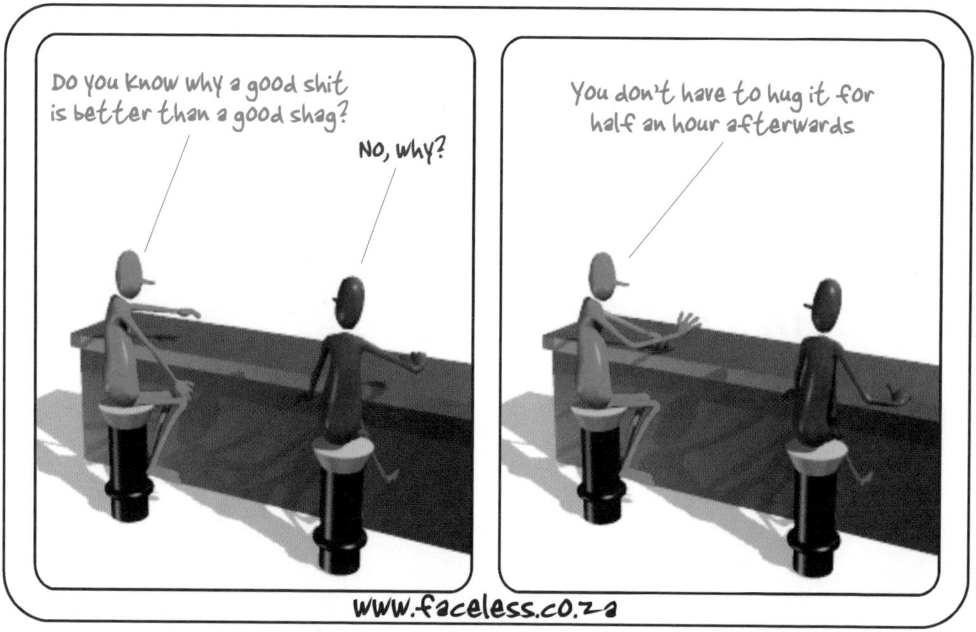
Do you know why a good shit is better than a good shag?
No, why?
You don't have to hug it for half an hour afterwards
www.faceless.co.za

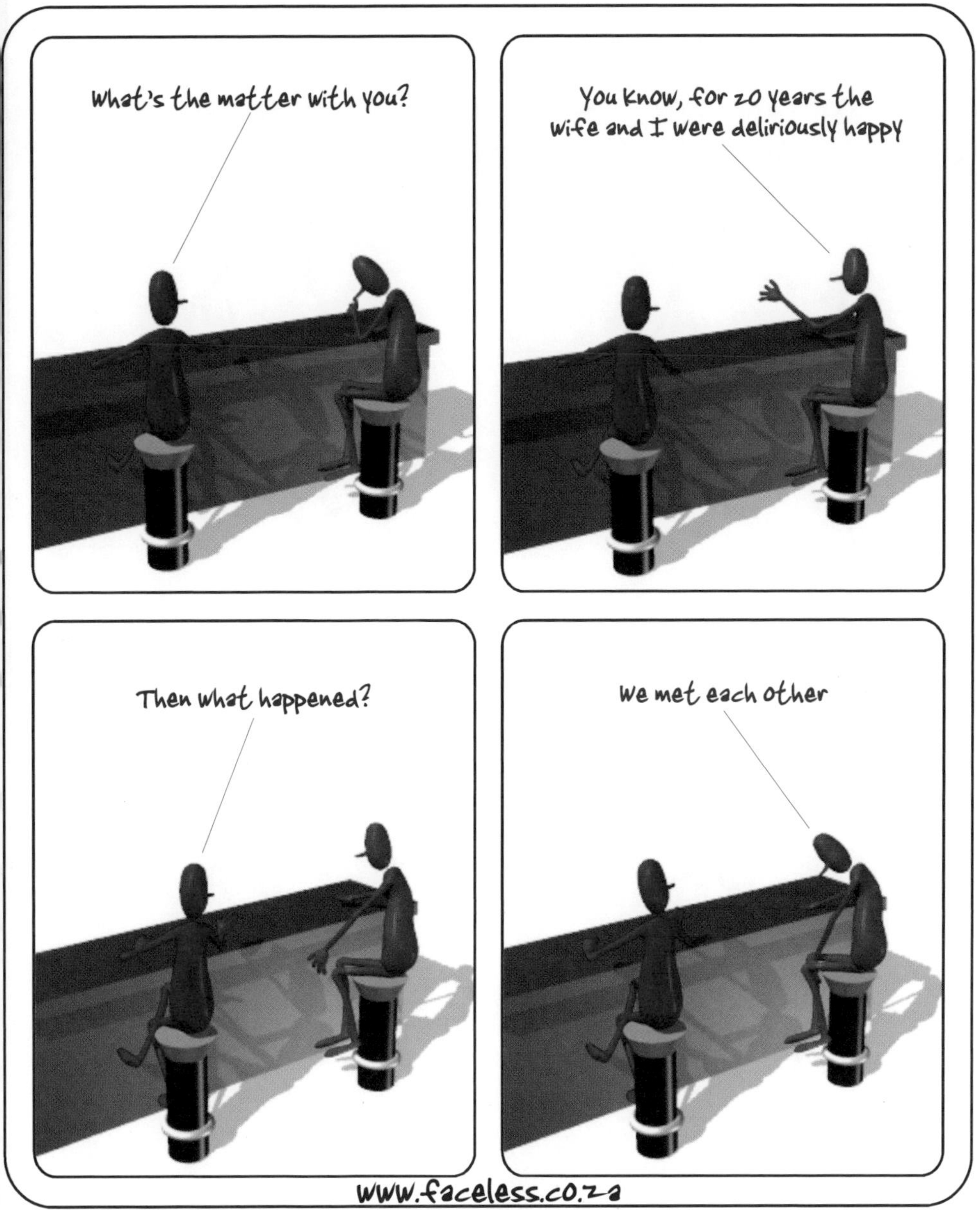
What's the matter with you?
You know, for 20 years the wife and I were deliriously happy
Then what happened?
We met each other
www.faceless.co.za

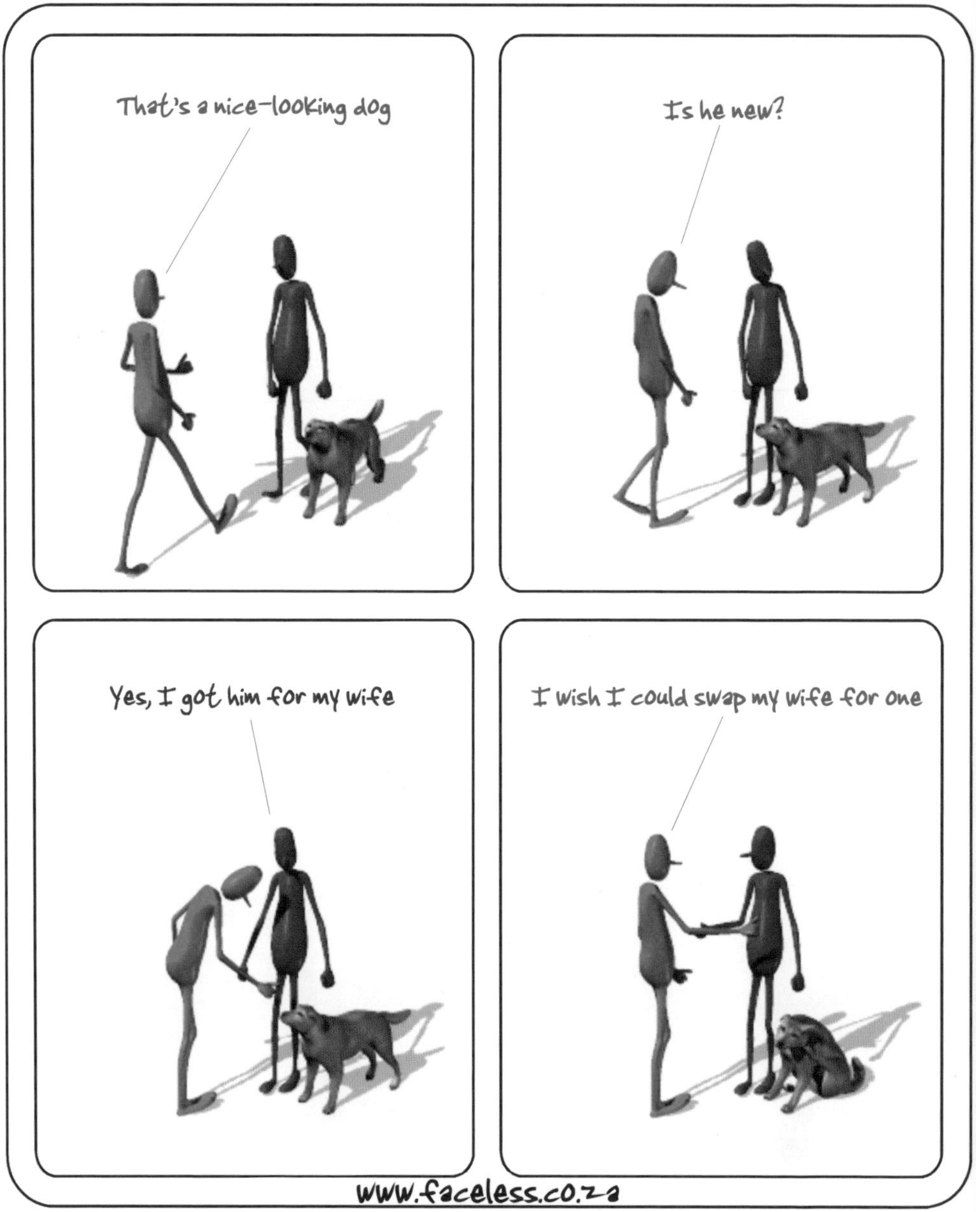
That's a nice-looking dog
Is he new?
Yes, I got him for my wife
I wish I could swap my wife for one
www.faceless.co.za

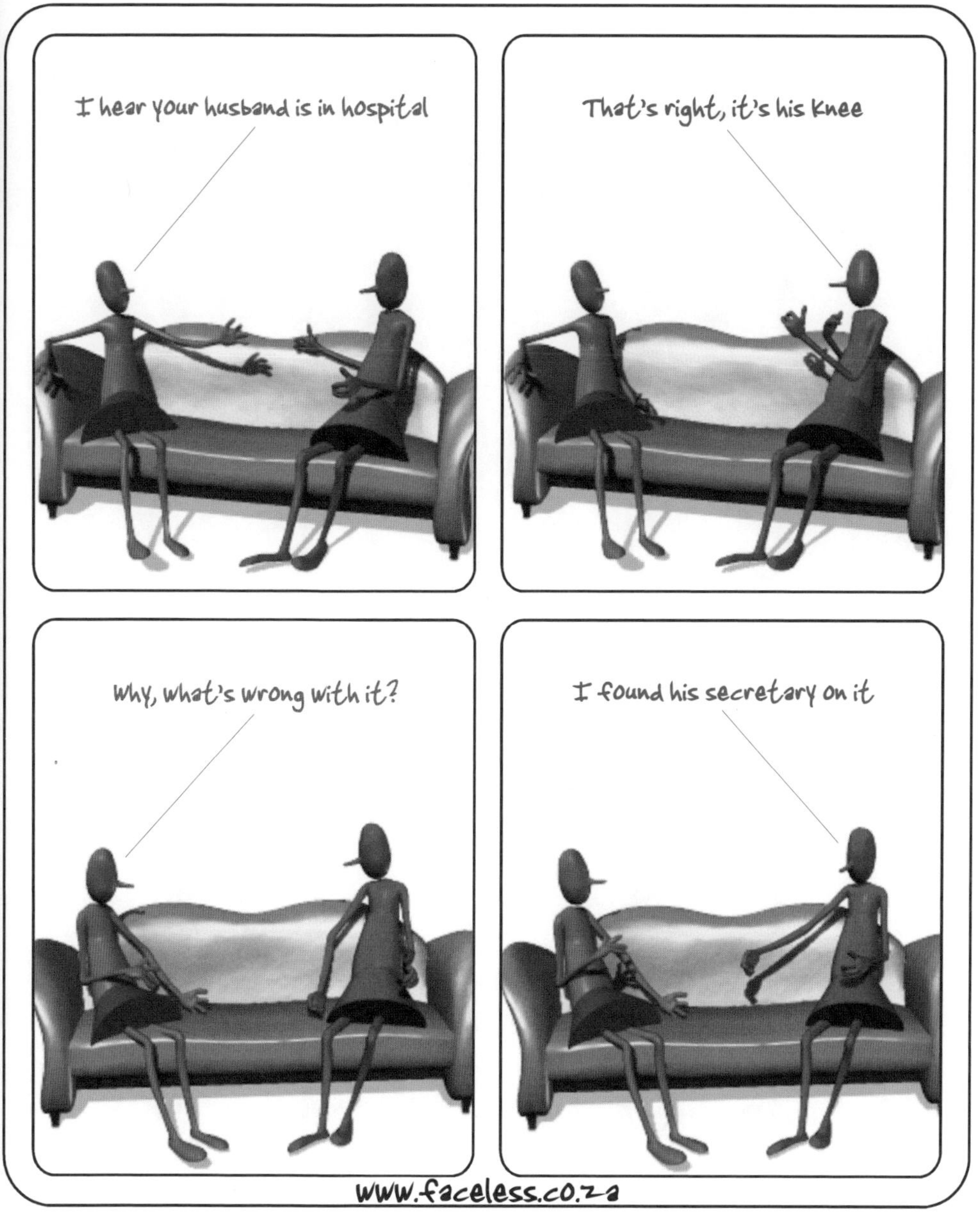
I hear your husband is in hospital
That's right, it's his knee
Why, what's wrong with it?
I found his secretary on it
www.faceless.co.za

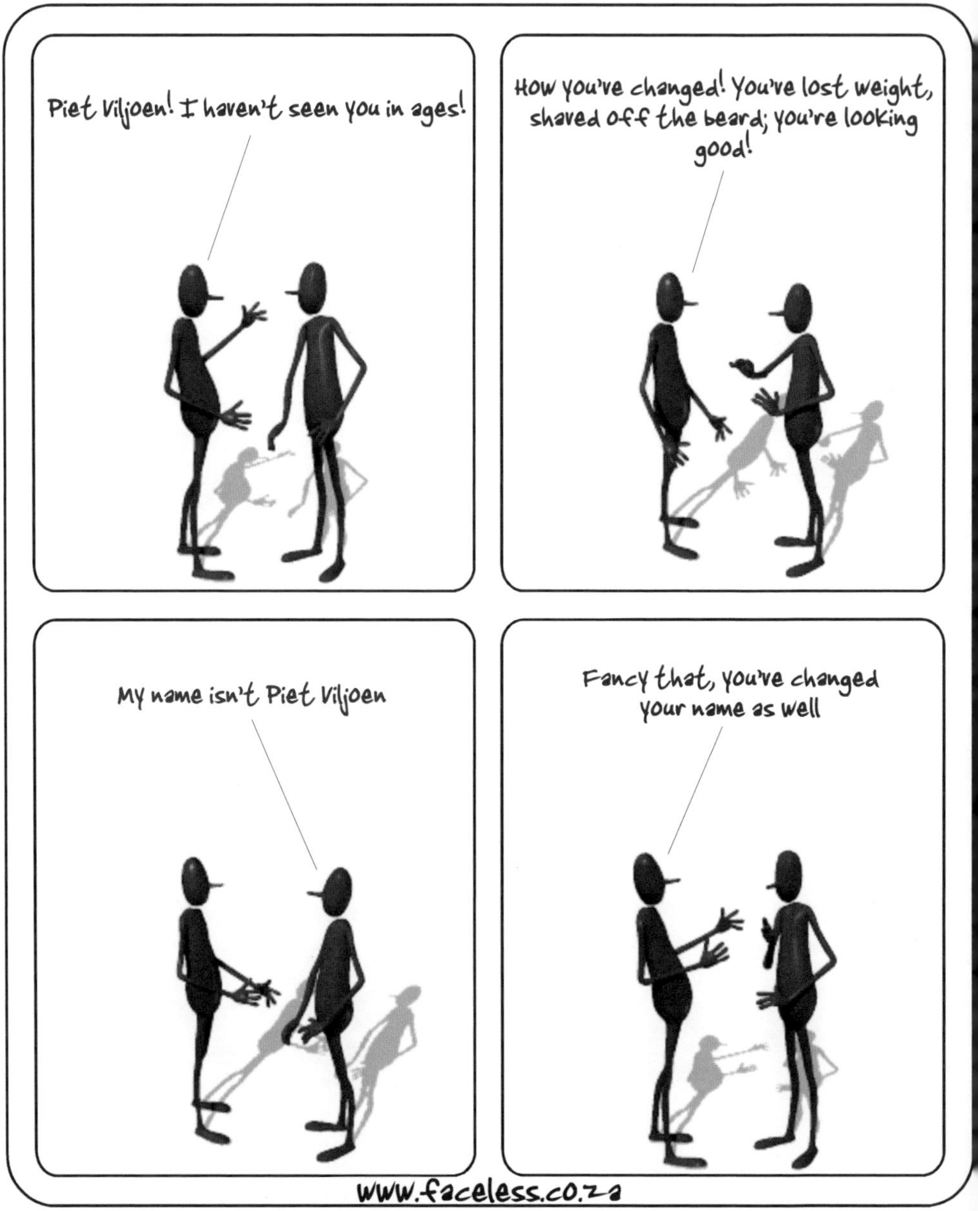
Piet Viljoen! I haven't seen you in ages!
How you've changed! You've lost weight, shaved off the beard; you're looking good!
My name isn't Piet Viljoen
Fancy that, you've changed your name as well
www.faceless.co.za

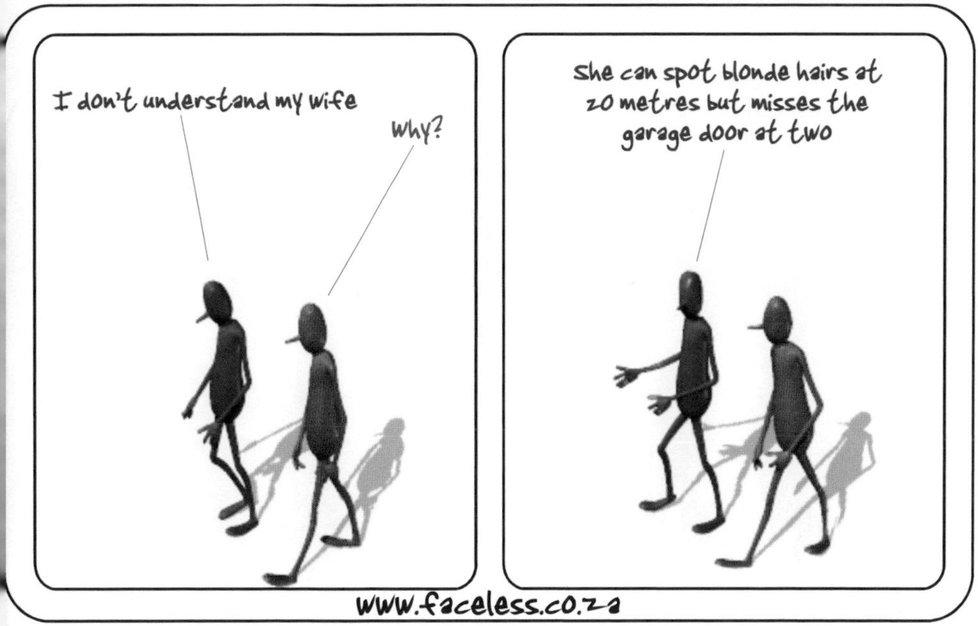
I don't understand my wife
Why?
She can spot blonde hairs at 20 metres but misses the garage door at two
www.faceless.co.za

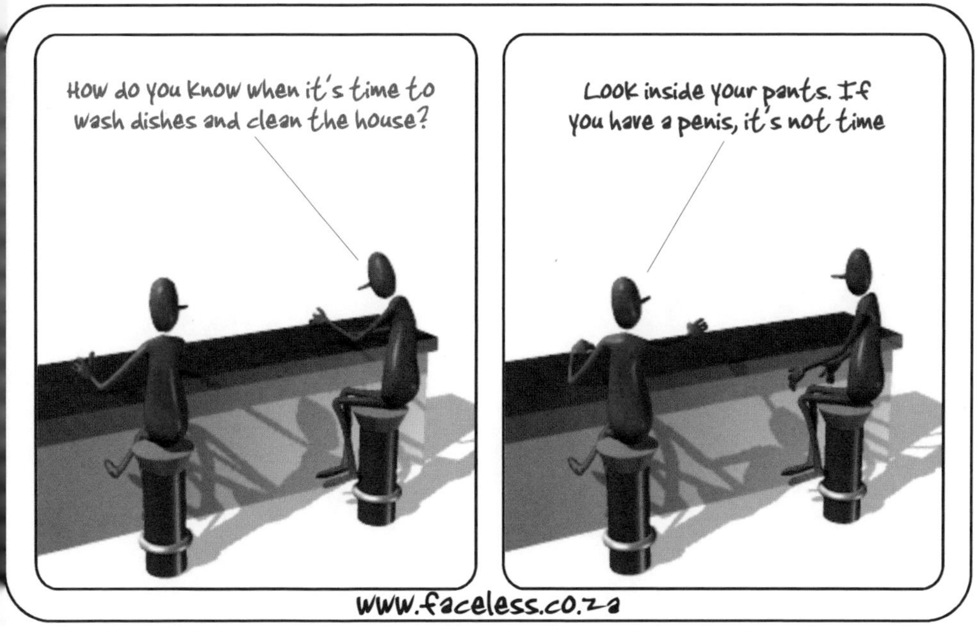
How do you know when it's time to wash dishes and clean the house?
Look inside your pants. If you have a penis, it's not time
www.faceless.co.za

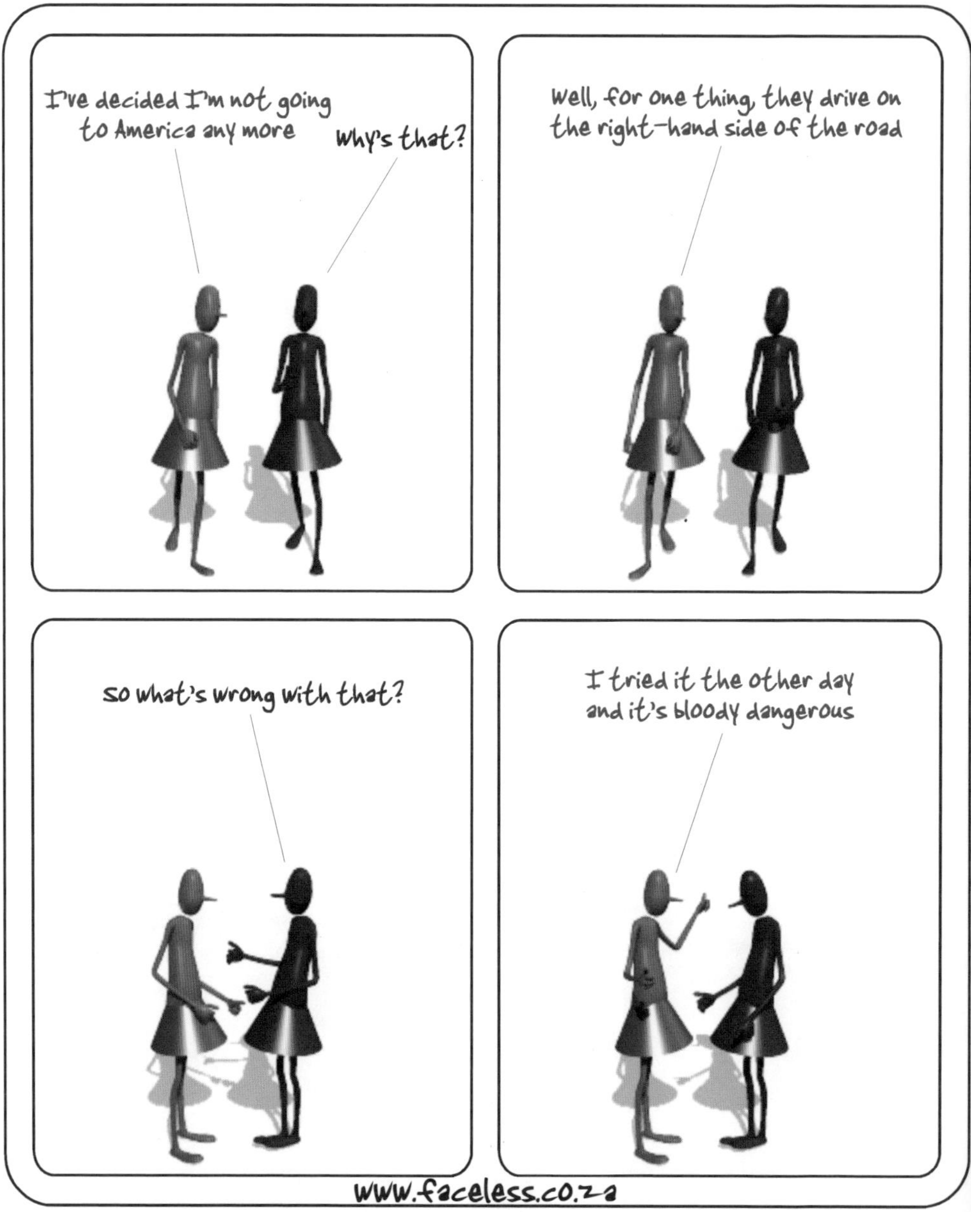
I've decided I'm not going to America any more
Why's that?
Well, for one thing, they drive on the right-hand side of the road
so what's wrong with that?
I tried it the other day and it's bloody dangerous
www.faceless.co.za

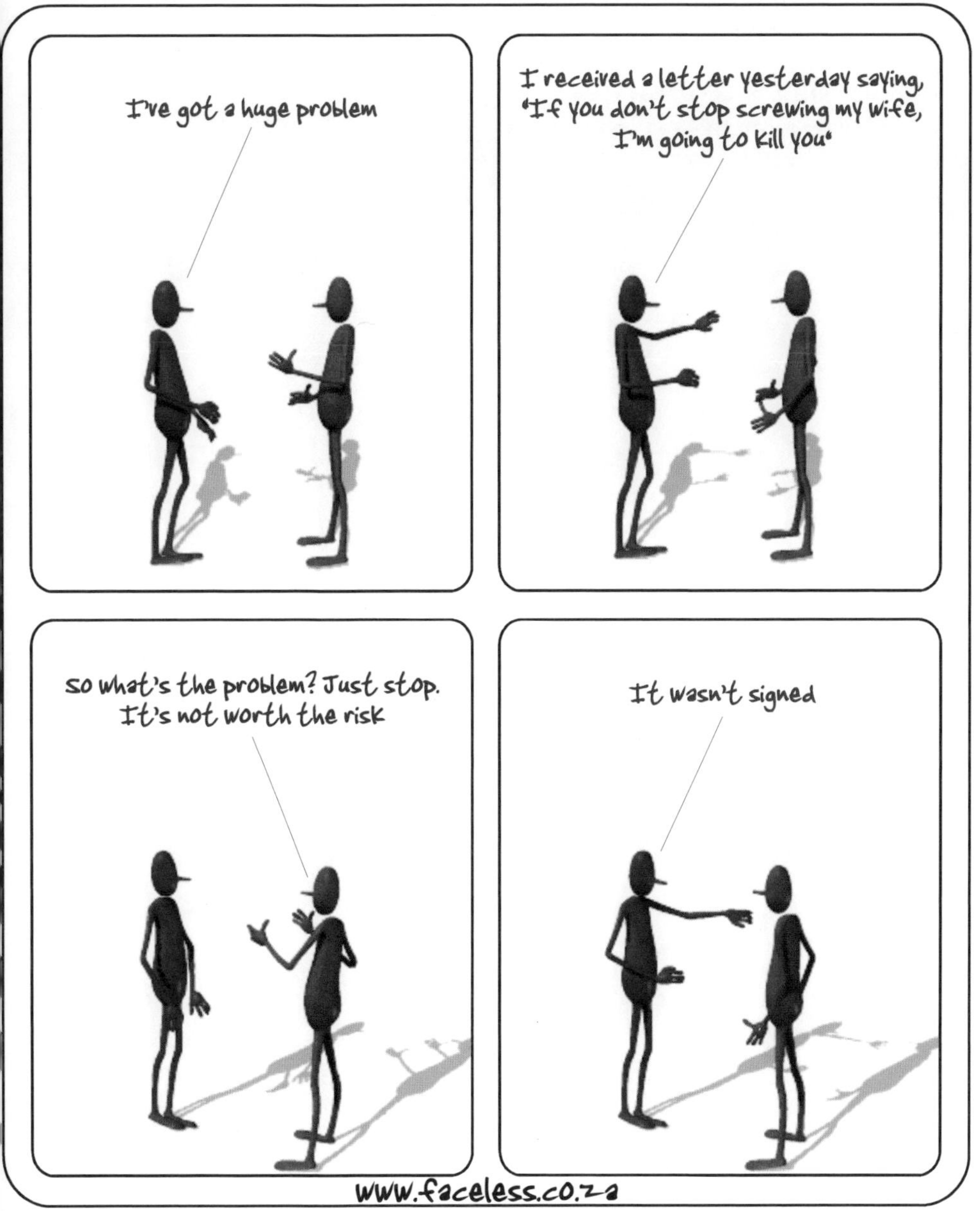
I've got a huge problem
I received a letter yesterday saying, "If you don't stop screwing my wife, I'm going to kill you"
so what's the problem? Just stop. It's not worth the risk
It wasn't signed
www.faceless.co.za

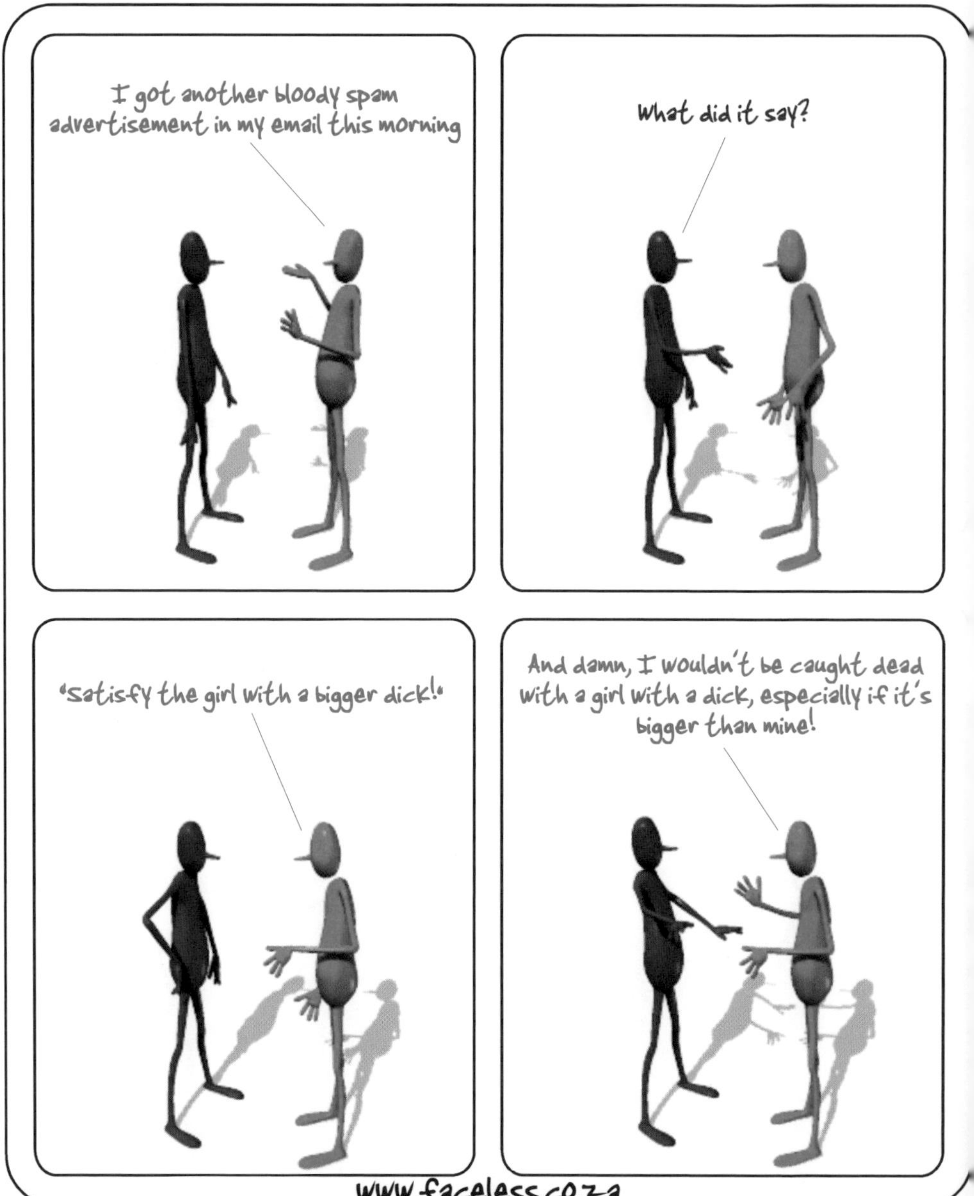
I got another bloody spam advertisement in my email this morning
What did it say?
"Satisfy the girl with a bigger dick!"
And damn, I wouldn't be caught dead with a girl with a dick, especially if it's bigger than mine!
www.faceless.co.za

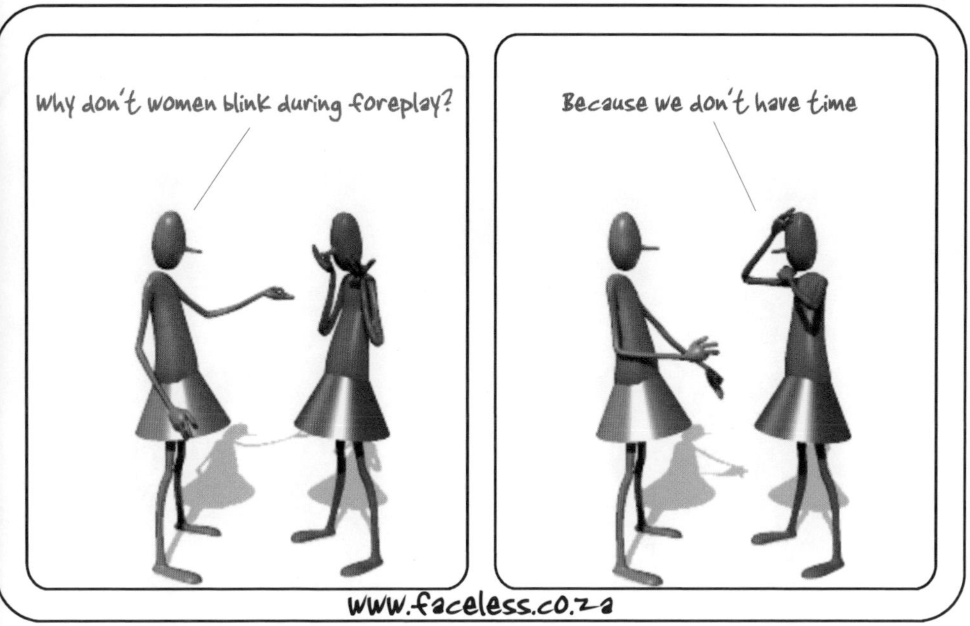
Why don't women blink during foreplay?
Because we don't have time
www.faceless.co.za

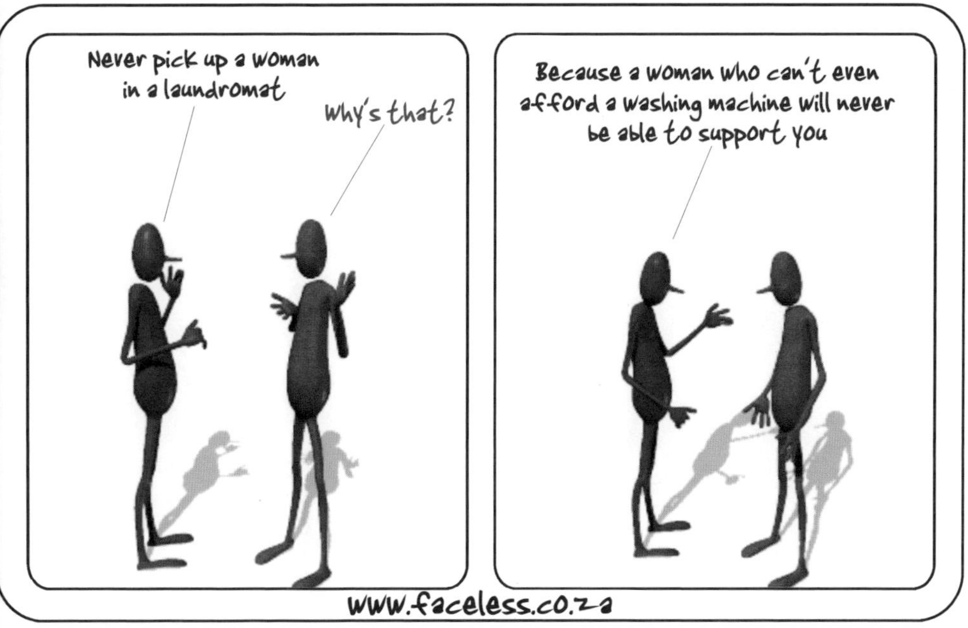
Never pick up a woman in a laundromat
Why's that?
Because a woman who can't even afford a washing machine will never be able to support you
www.faceless.co.za

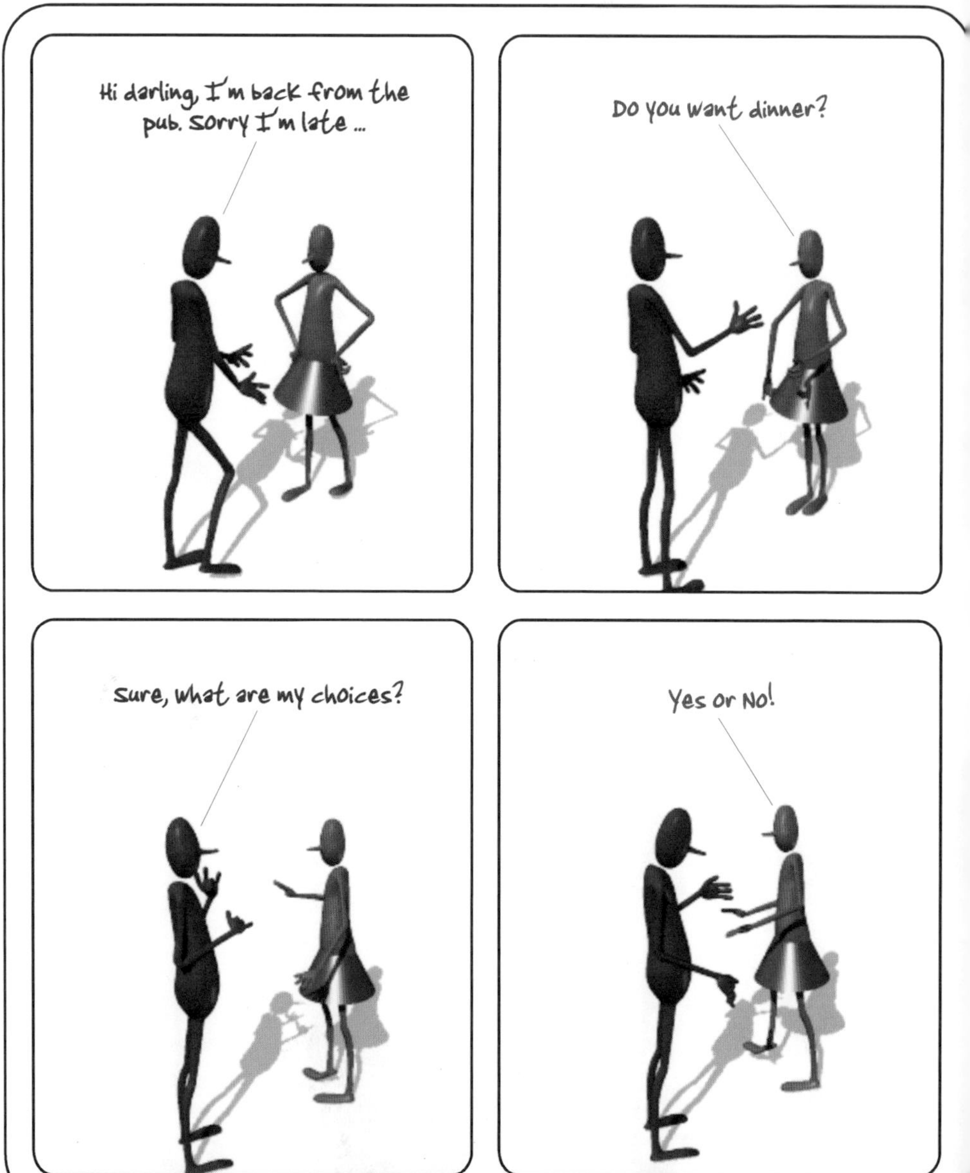
Hi darling, I'm back from the pub. Sorry I'm late ...
Do you want dinner?
Sure, what are my choices?
Yes or No!
www.faceless.co.za

I'm horny, want to have some fun?
Babe, we just had sex last night
so?
Why don't we wait a while so you've had some time to tighten back up
www.faceless.co.za

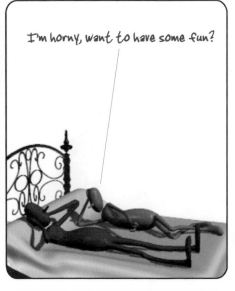

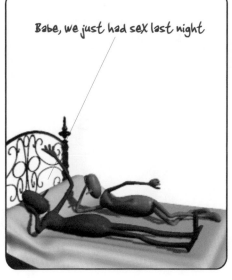

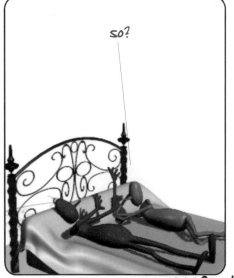

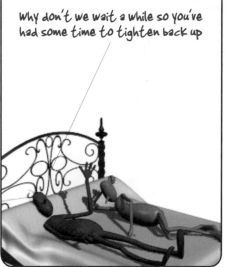

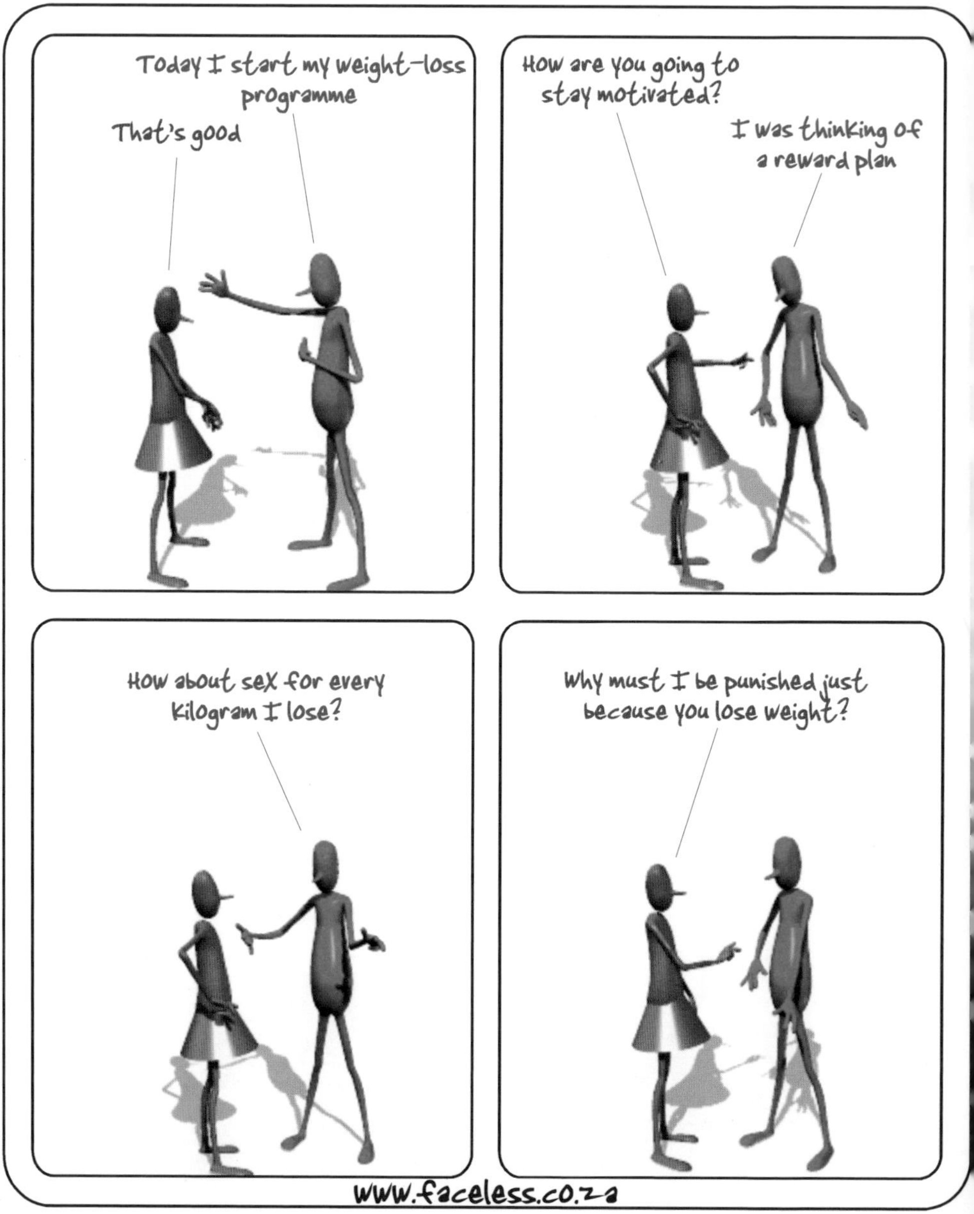
Today I start my weight-loss programme
That's good
How are you going to stay motivated?
I was thinking of a reward plan
How about sex for every kilogram I lose?
Why must I be punished just because you lose weight?
www.faceless.co.za

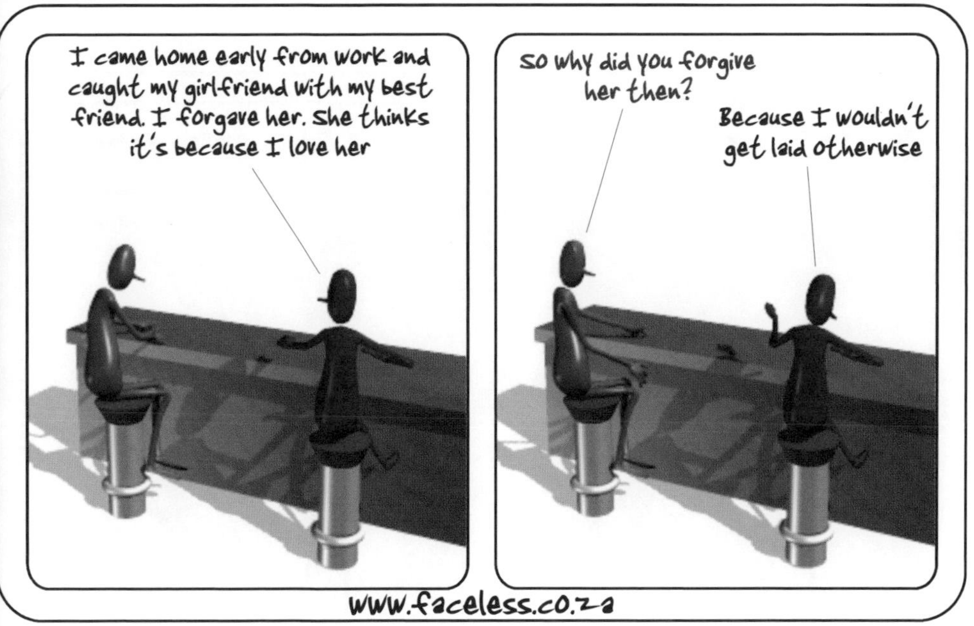
I came home early from work and caught my girlfriend with my best friend. I forgave her. She thinks it's because I love her
So why did you forgive her then?
Because I wouldn't get laid otherwise
www.faceless.co.za

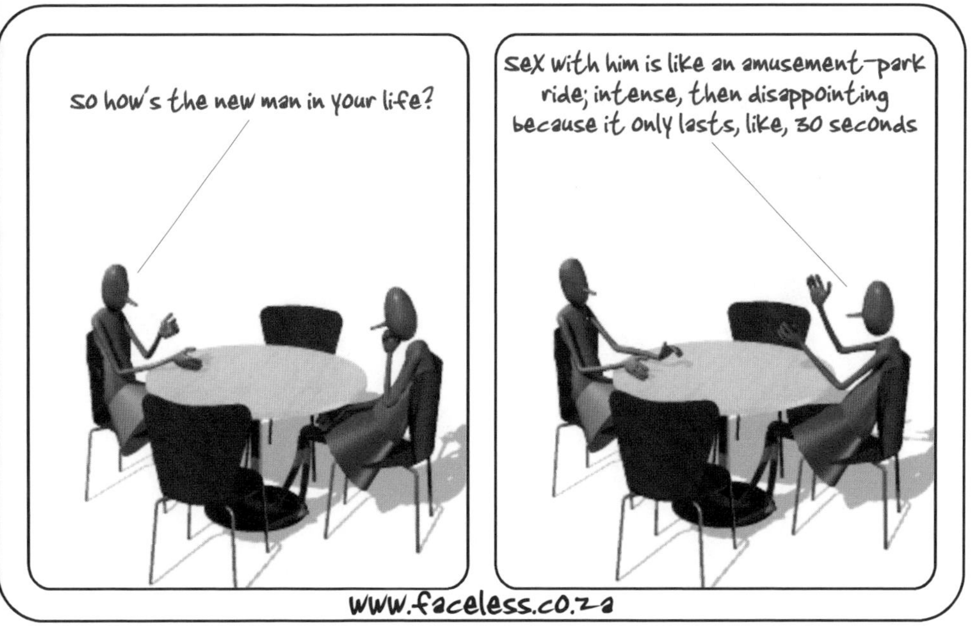
So how's the new man in your life?
Sex with him is like an amusement-park ride; intense, then disappointing because it only lasts, like, 30 seconds
www.faceless.co.za

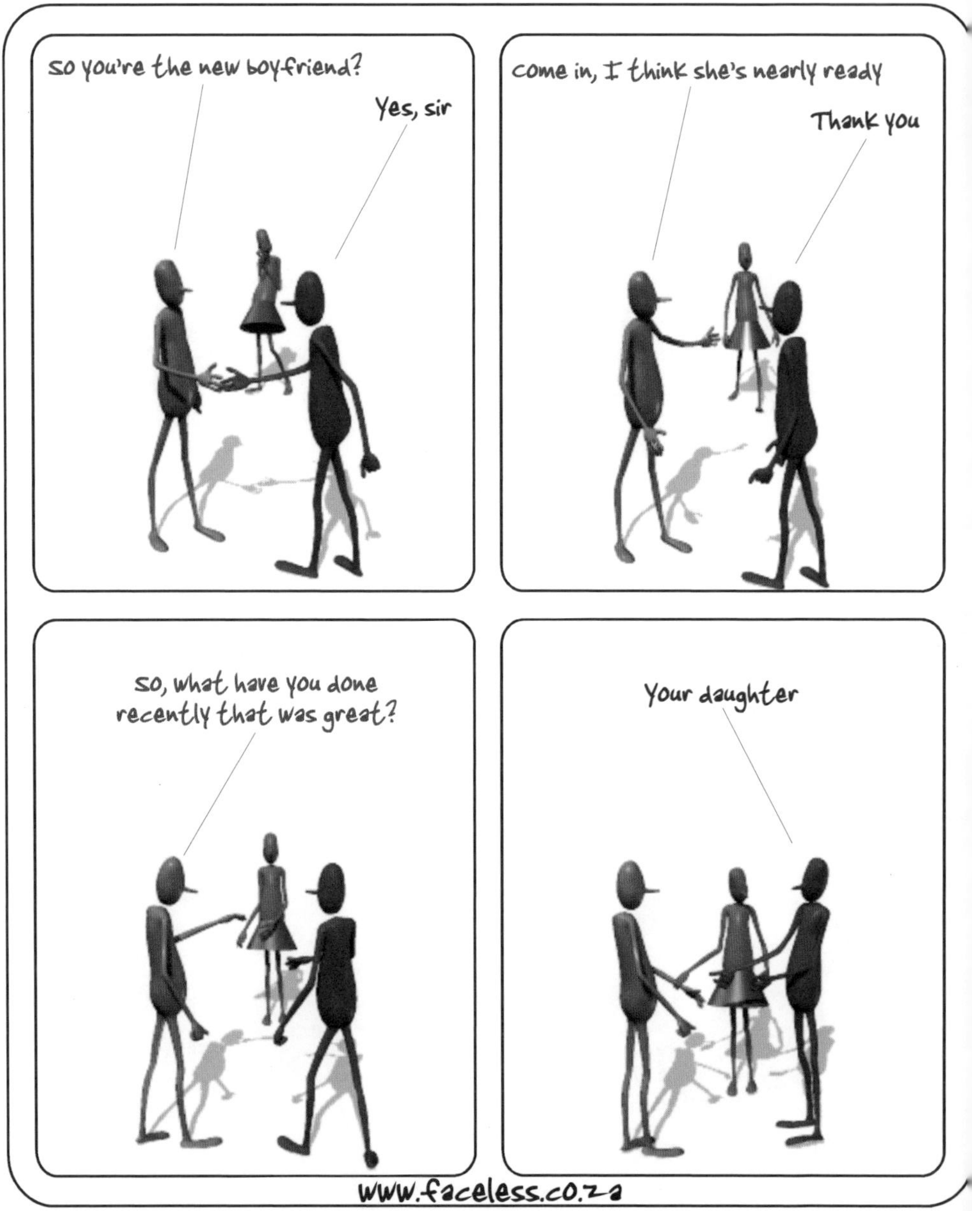

so you're the new boyfriend?
Yes, sir
come in, I think she's nearly ready
Thank you
so, what have you done recently that was great?
Your daughter
www.faceless.co.za

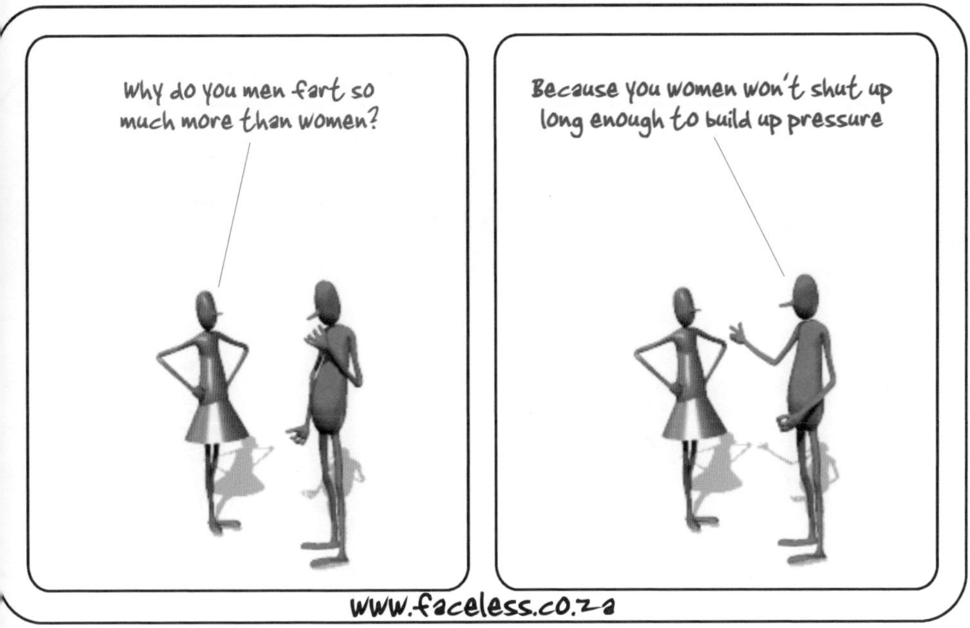
Why do you men fart so much more than women?
Because you women won't shut up long enough to build up pressure
www.faceless.co.za

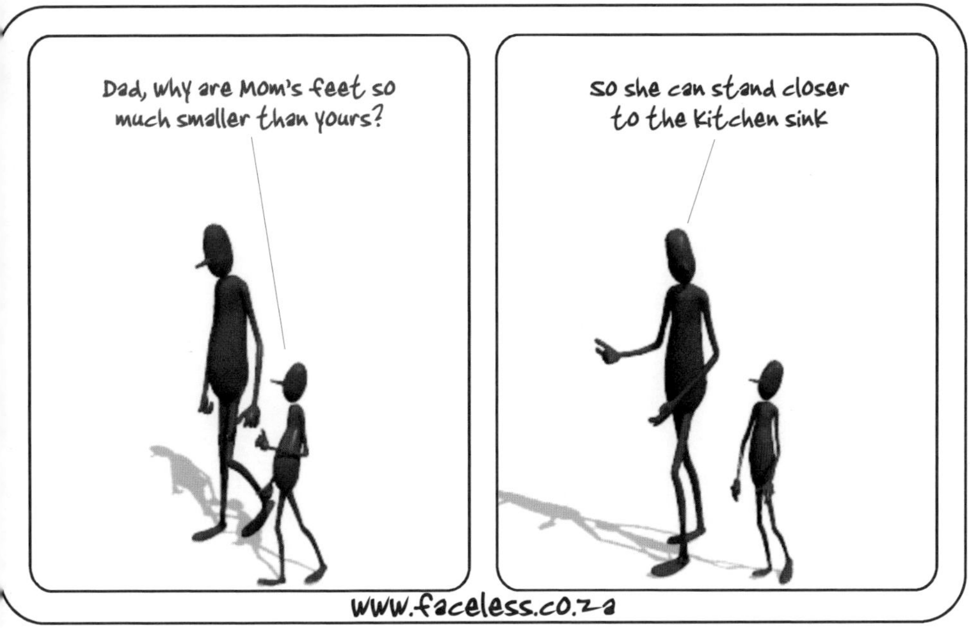
Dad, why are Mom's feet so much smaller than yours?
So she can stand closer to the kitchen sink
www.faceless.co.za

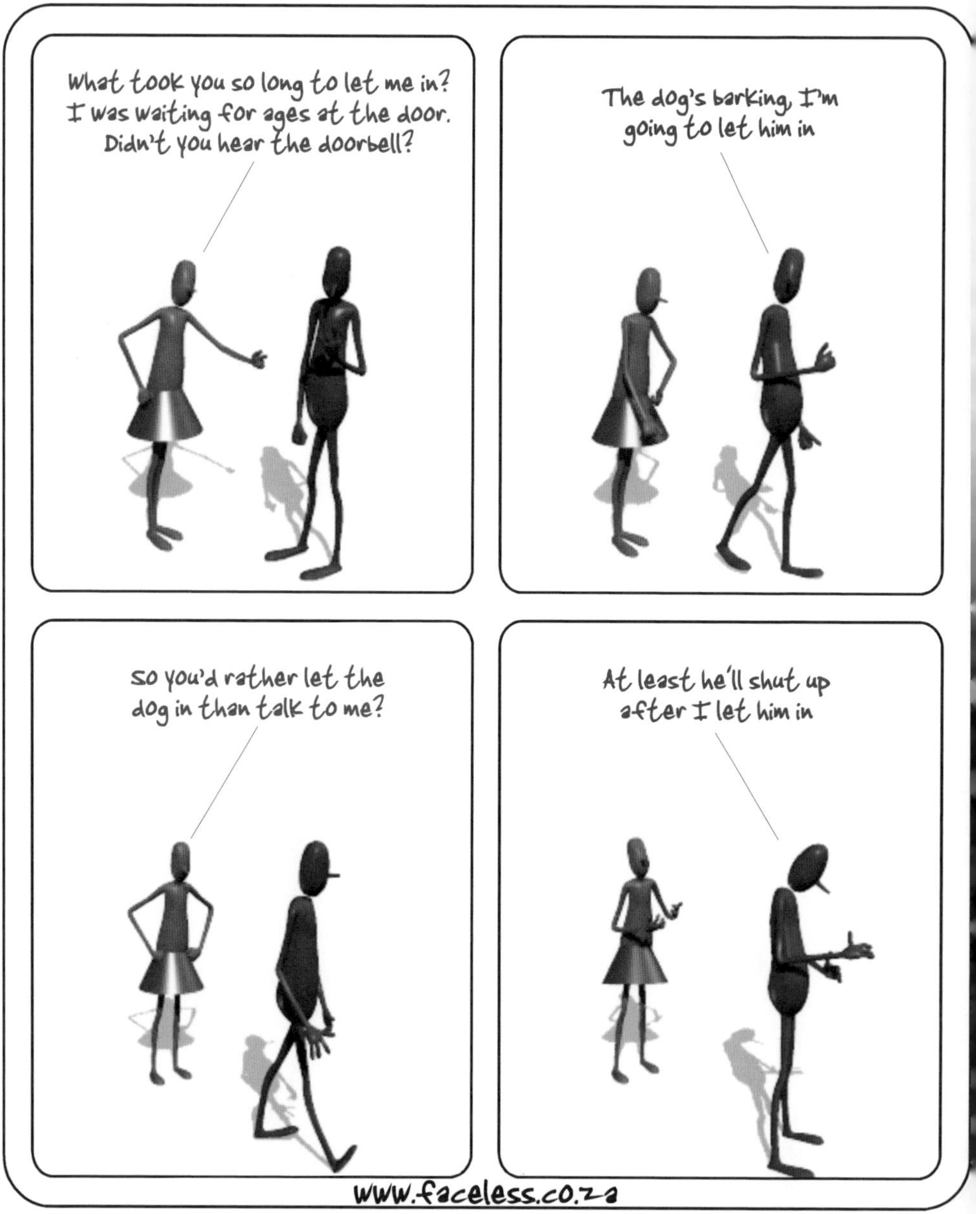
What took you so long to let me in? I was waiting for ages at the door. Didn't you hear the doorbell?
The dog's barking, I'm going to let him in
So you'd rather let the dog in than talk to me?
At least he'll shut up after I let him in
www.faceless.co.za

Hey babe, ready for some action?
No, I have a headache
Perfect, I was just in the bathroom powdering my dick with Grand-Pa ...
You can take it orally or as a suppository - it's up to you
www.faceless.co.za

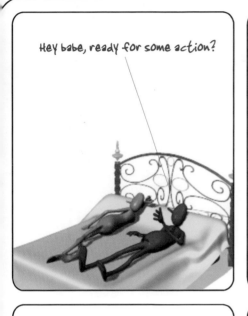

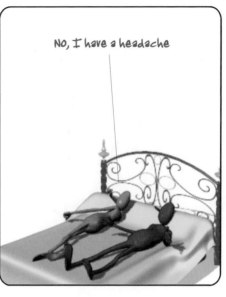

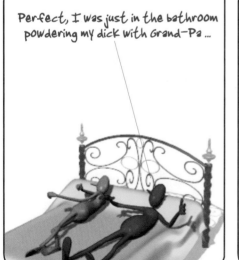

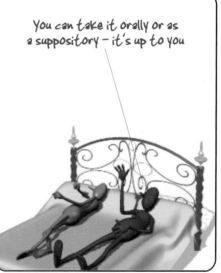

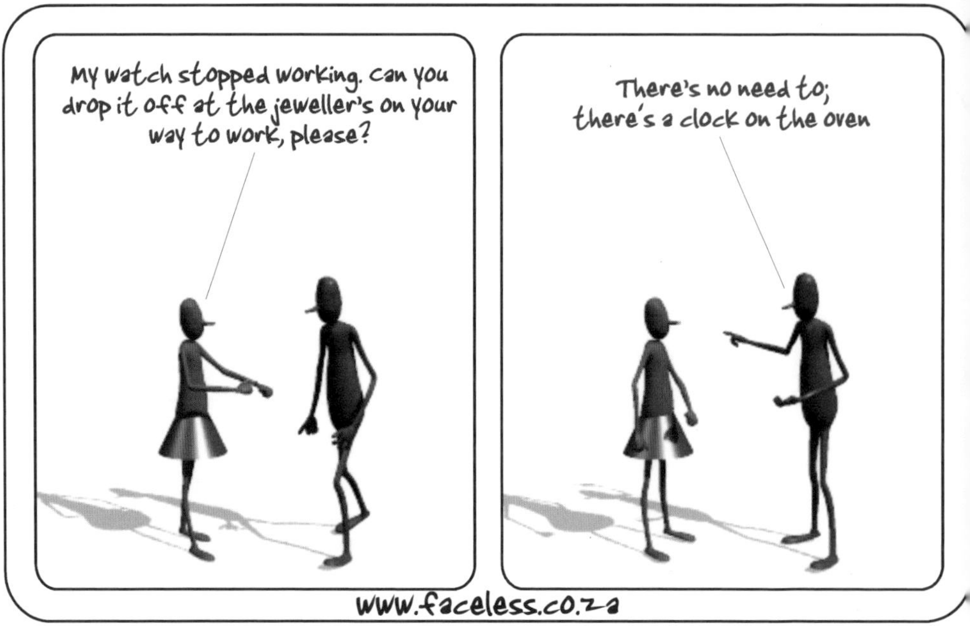
My watch stopped working. Can you drop it off at the jeweller's on your way to work, please?
There's no need to; there's a clock on the oven
www.faceless.co.za

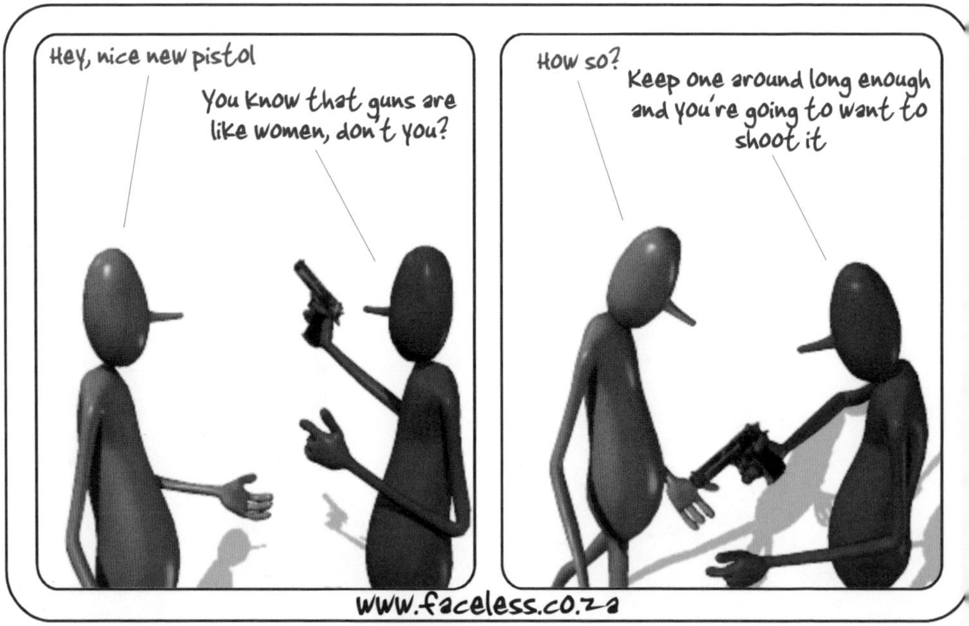
Hey, nice new pistol
You know that guns are like women, don't you?
How so?
Keep one around long enough and you're going to want to shoot it
www.faceless.co.za

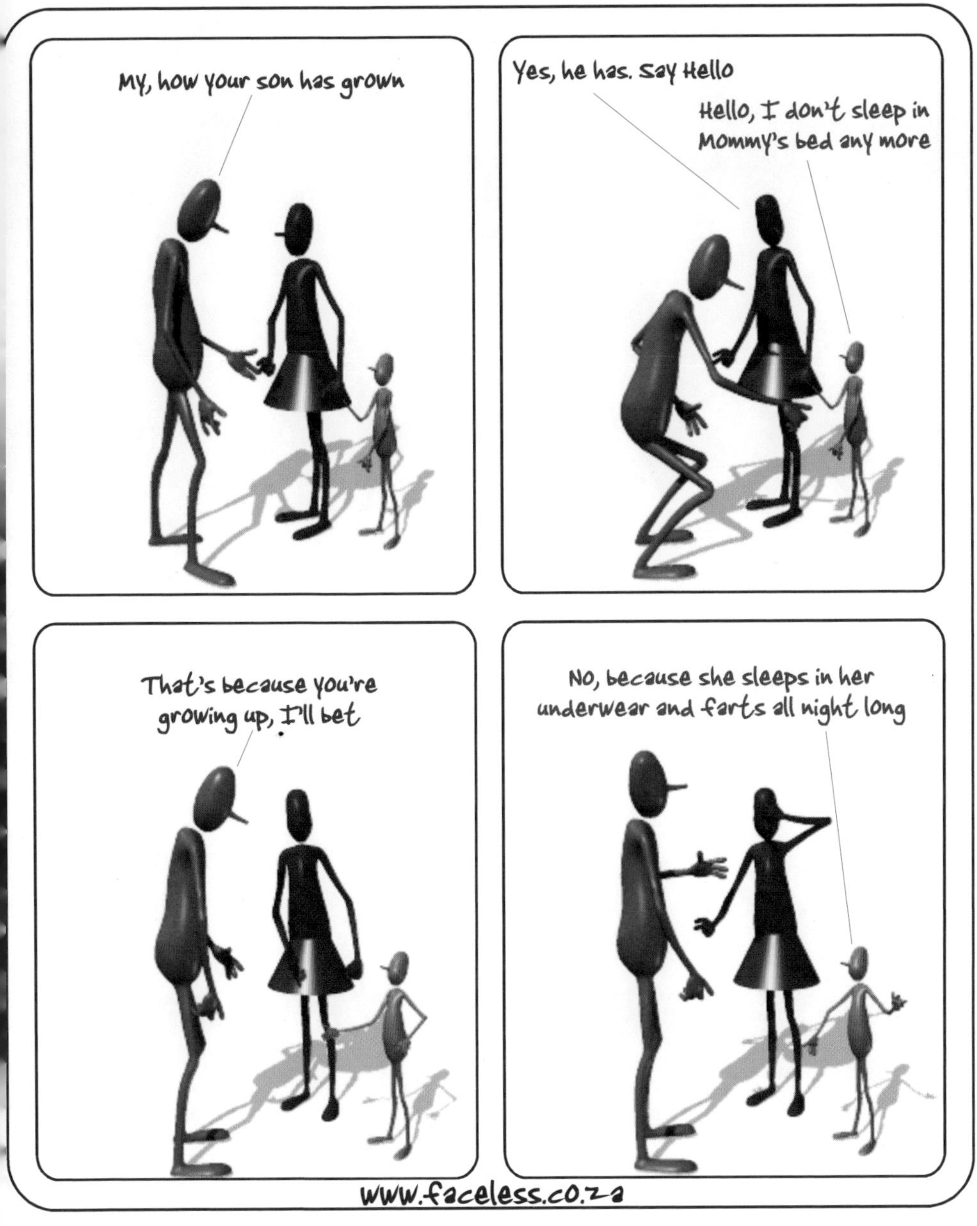
My, how your son has grown
Yes, he has. Say Hello
Hello, I don't sleep in Mommy's bed any more
That's because you're growing up, I'll bet
No, because she sleeps in her underwear and farts all night long
www.faceless.co.za

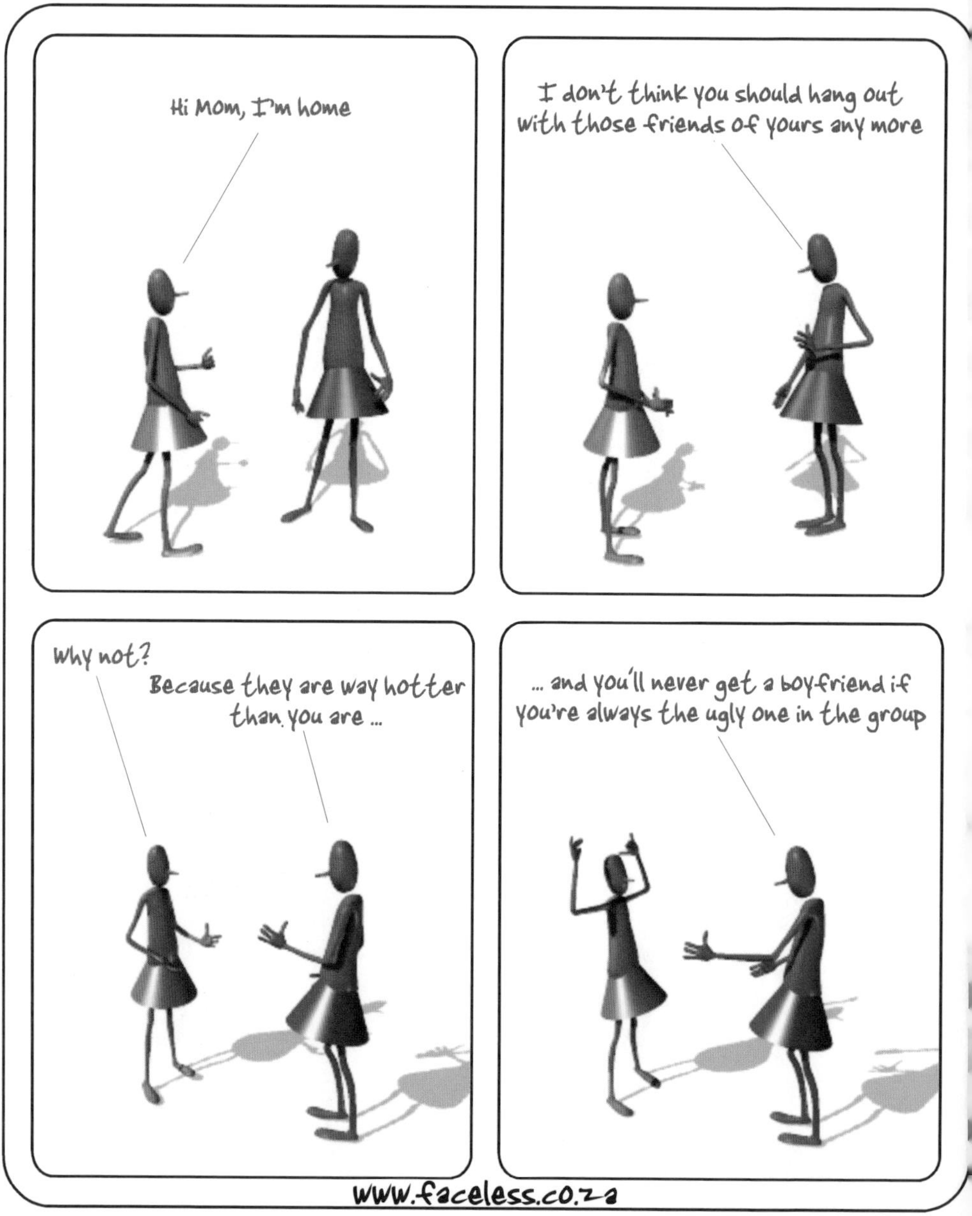
Hi Mom, I'm home
I don't think you should hang out with those friends of yours any more
Why not?
Because they are way hotter than you are ...
... and you'll never get a boyfriend if you're always the ugly one in the group
www.faceless.co.za

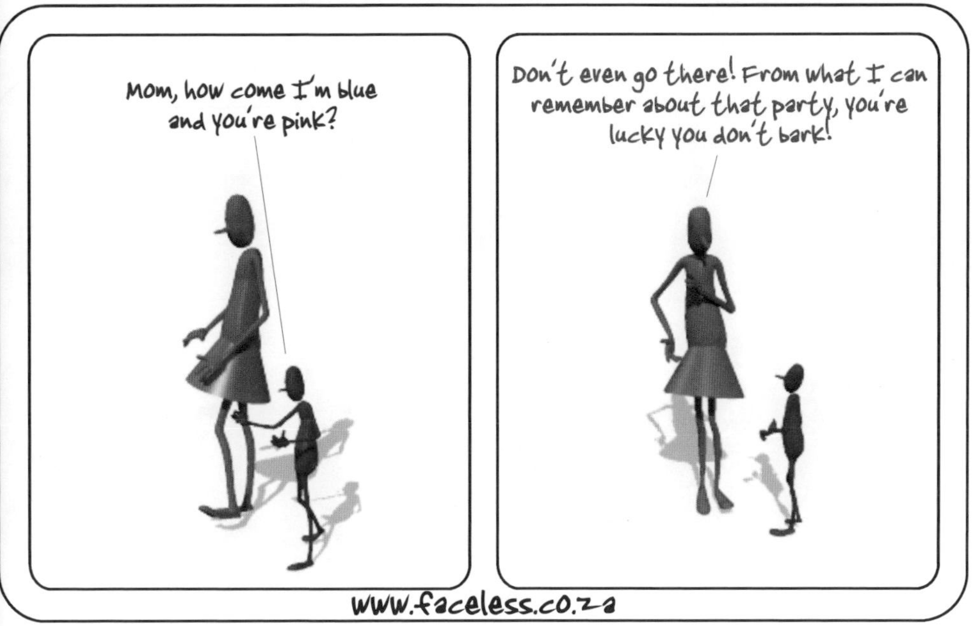
Mom, how come I'm blue and you're pink?
Don't even go there! From what I can remember about that party, you're lucky you don't bark!
www.faceless.co.za

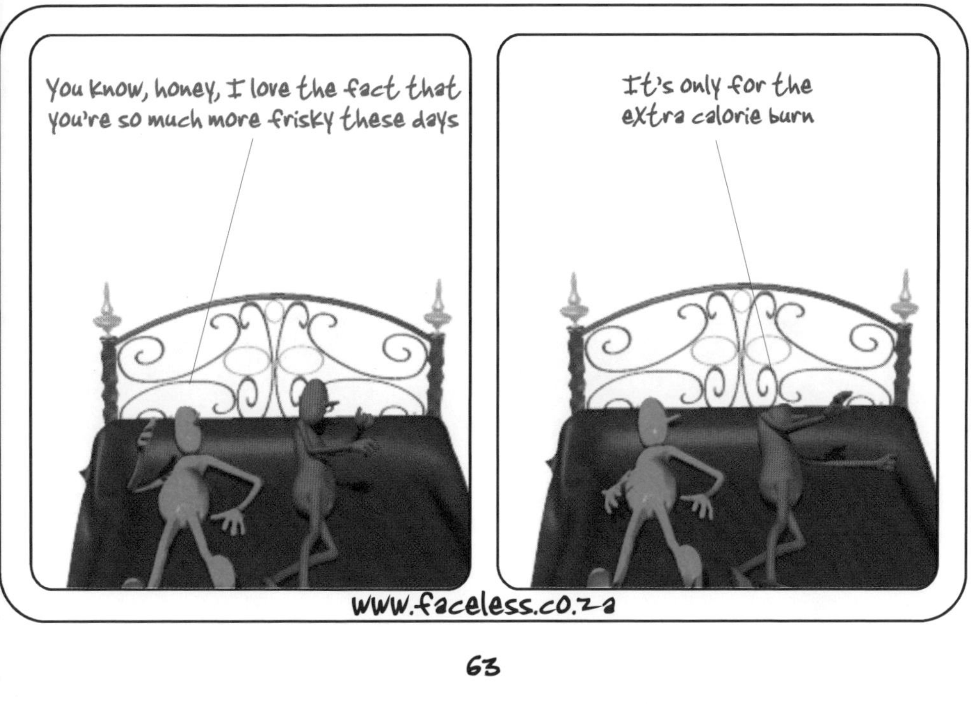
You know, honey, I love the fact that you're so much more frisky these days
It's only for the extra calorie burn
www.faceless.co.za

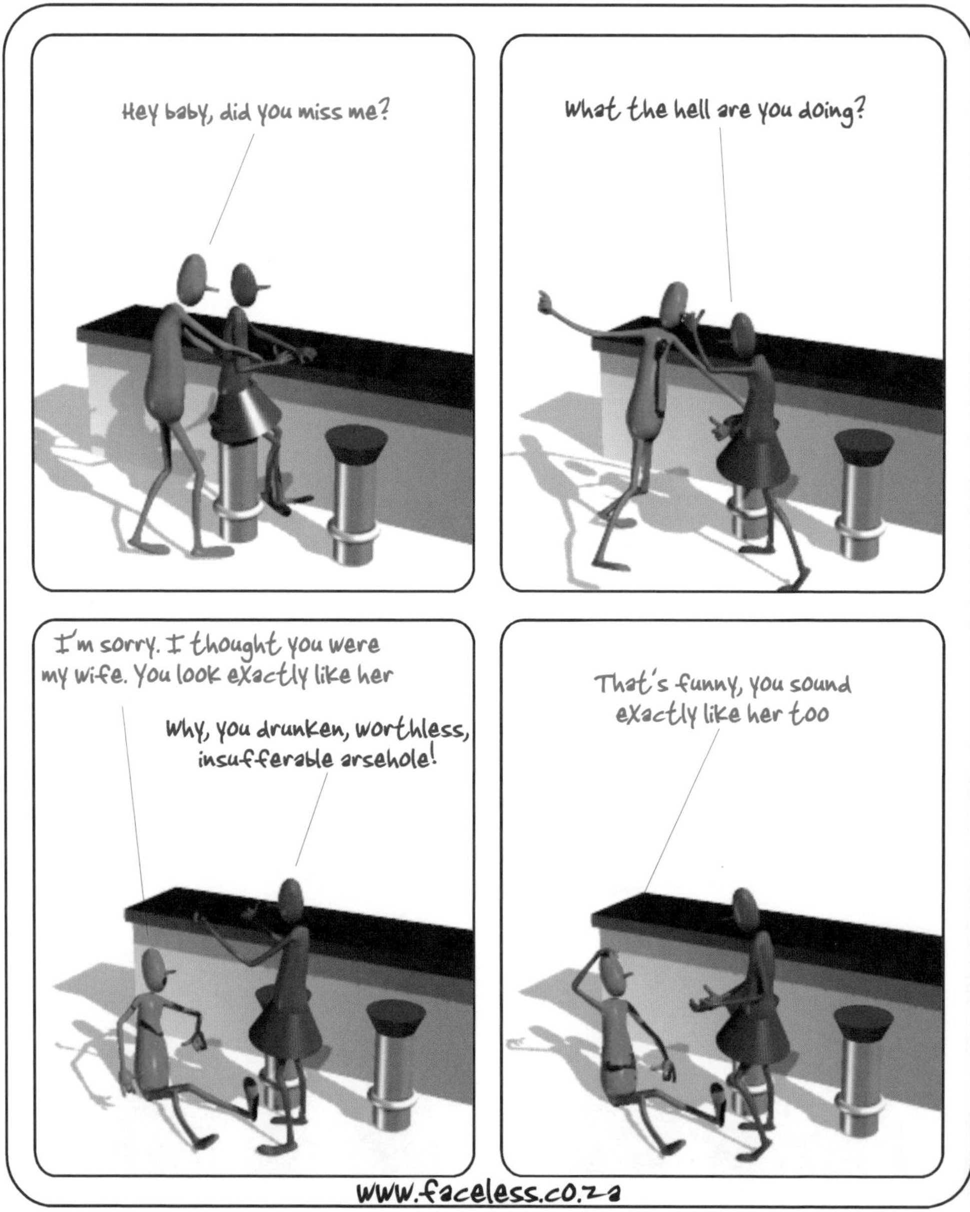
Hey baby, did you miss me?
What the hell are you doing?
I'm sorry. I thought you were my wife. You look exactly like her
Why, you drunken, worthless, insufferable arsehole!
That's funny, you sound exactly like her too
www.faceless.co.za

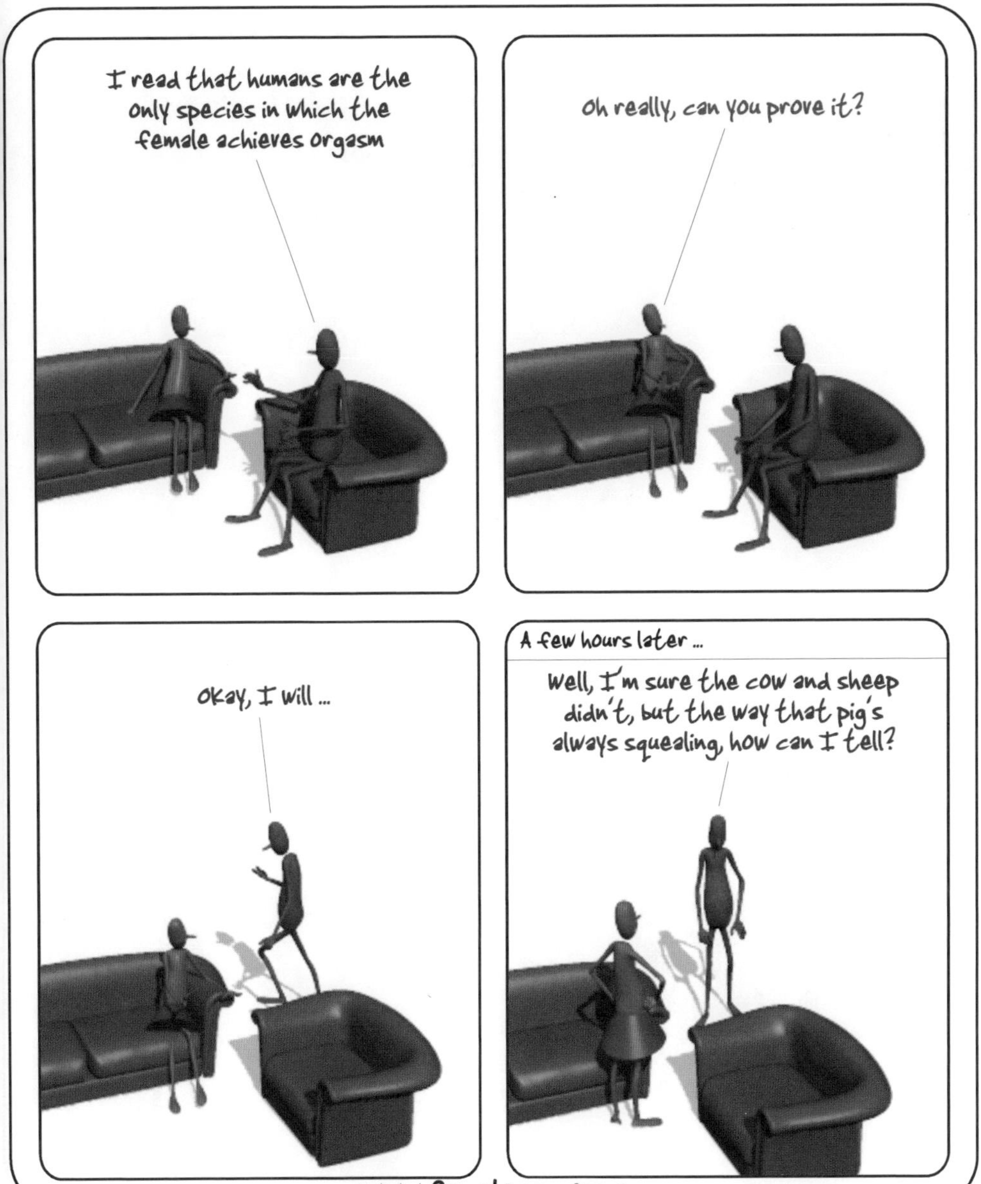
I read that humans are the only species in which the female achieves orgasm
Oh really, can you prove it?
Okay, I will ...
A few hours later ...
Well, I'm sure the cow and sheep didn't, but the way that pig's always squealing, how can I tell?
www.faceless.co.za

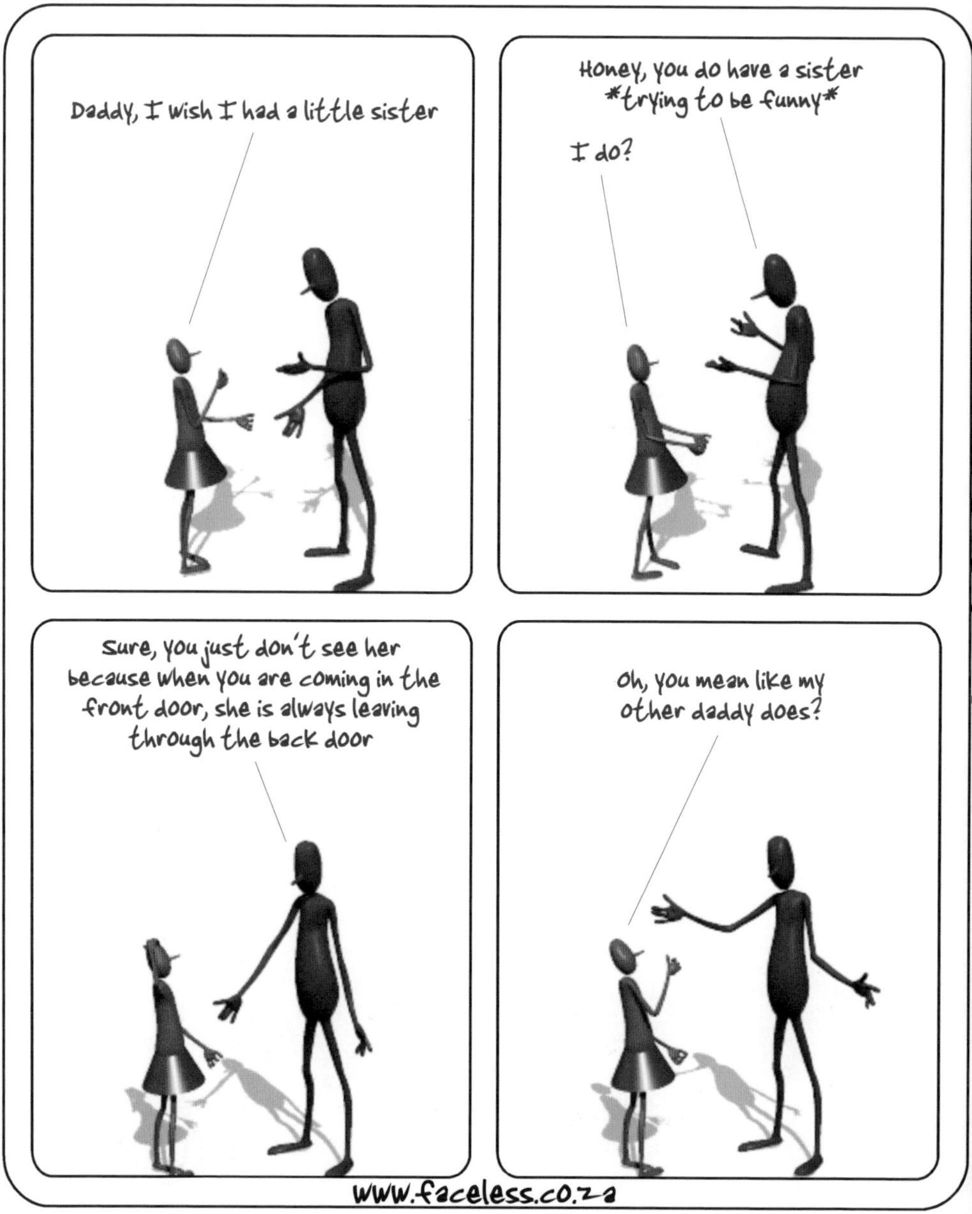
Daddy, I wish I had a little sister
Honey, you do have a sister *trying to be funny*
I do?
Sure, you just don't see her because when you are coming in the front door, she is always leaving through the back door
Oh, you mean like my other daddy does?
www.faceless.co.za

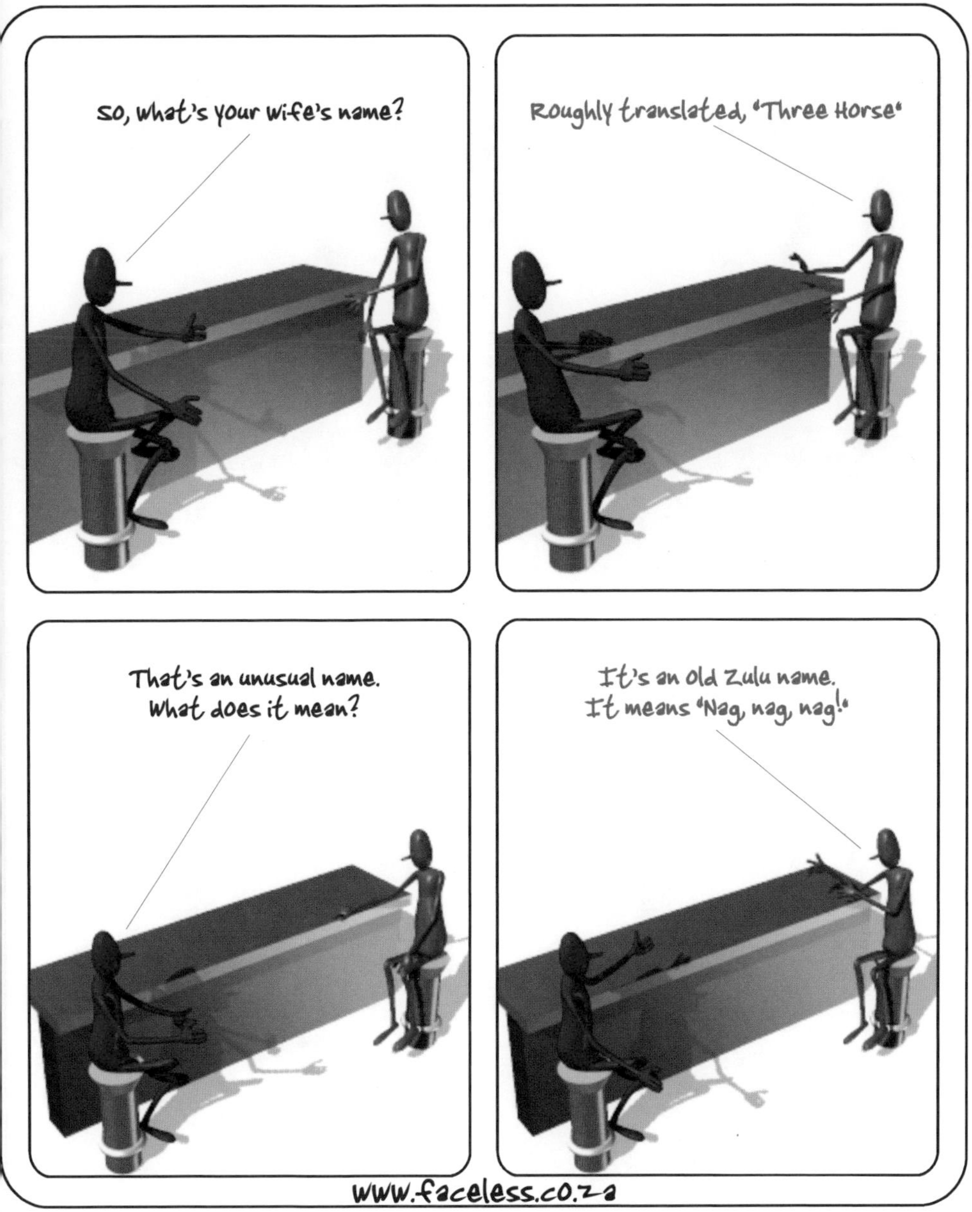
So, what's your wife's name?
Roughly translated, "Three Horse"
That's an unusual name. What does it mean?
It's an old Zulu name. It means "Nag, nag, nag!"
www.faceless.co.za

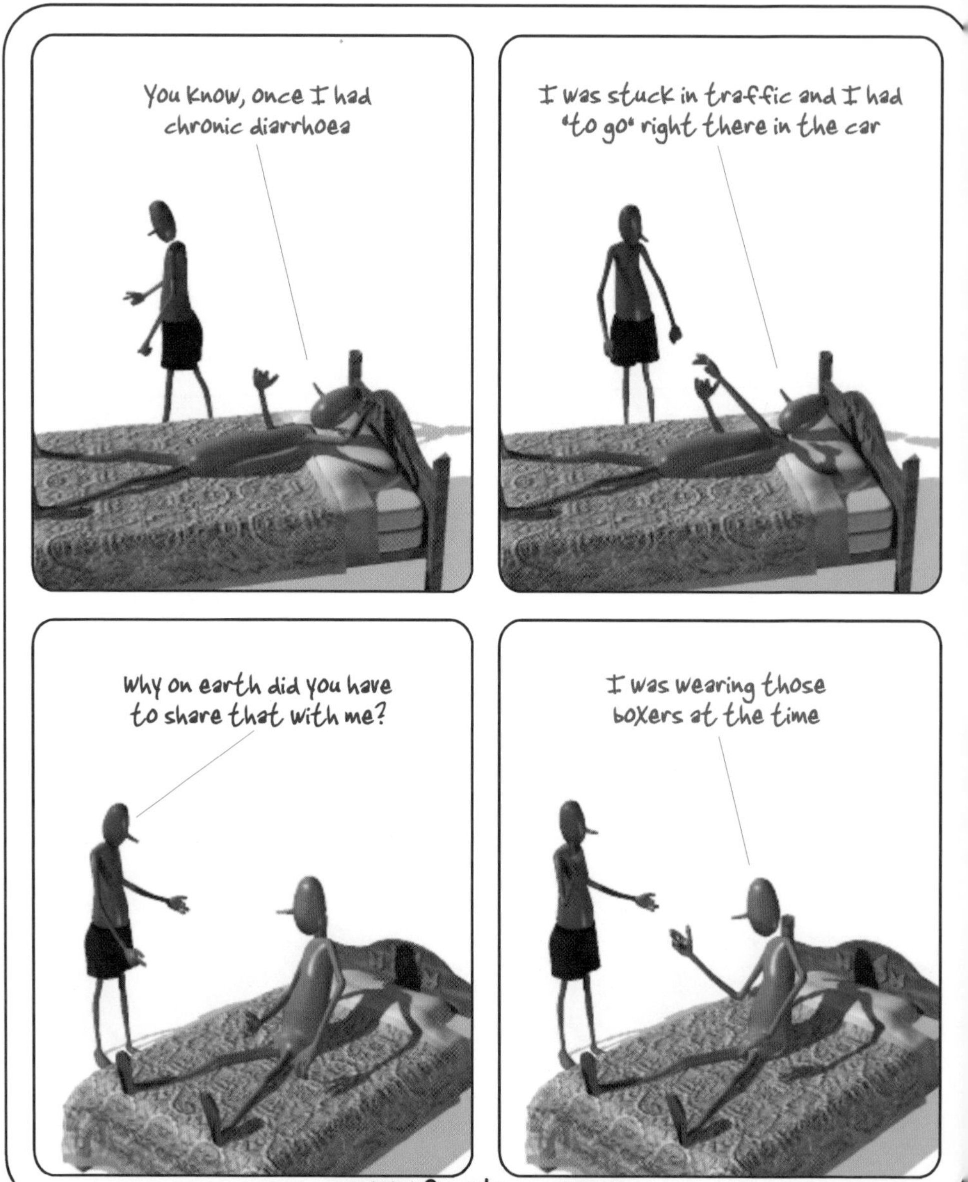
You know, once I had chronic diarrhoea
I was stuck in traffic and I had "to go" right there in the car
Why on earth did you have to share that with me?
I was wearing those boxers at the time
www.faceless.co.za

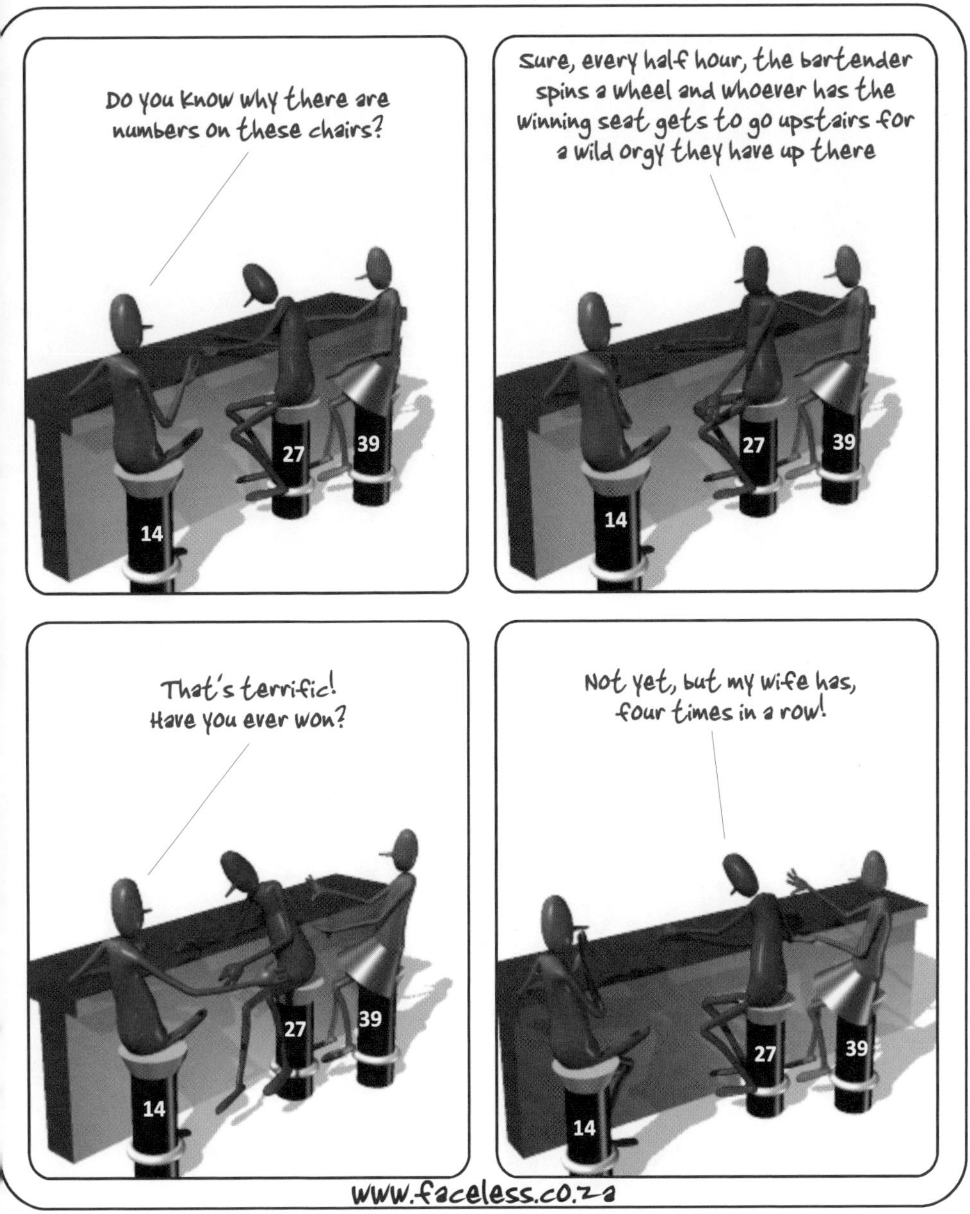
Do you know why there are numbers on these chairs?
Sure, every half hour, the bartender spins a wheel and whoever has the winning seat gets to go upstairs for a wild orgy they have up there
That's terrific! Have you ever won?
Not yet, but my wife has, four times in a row!
14
27
39
www.faceless.co.za

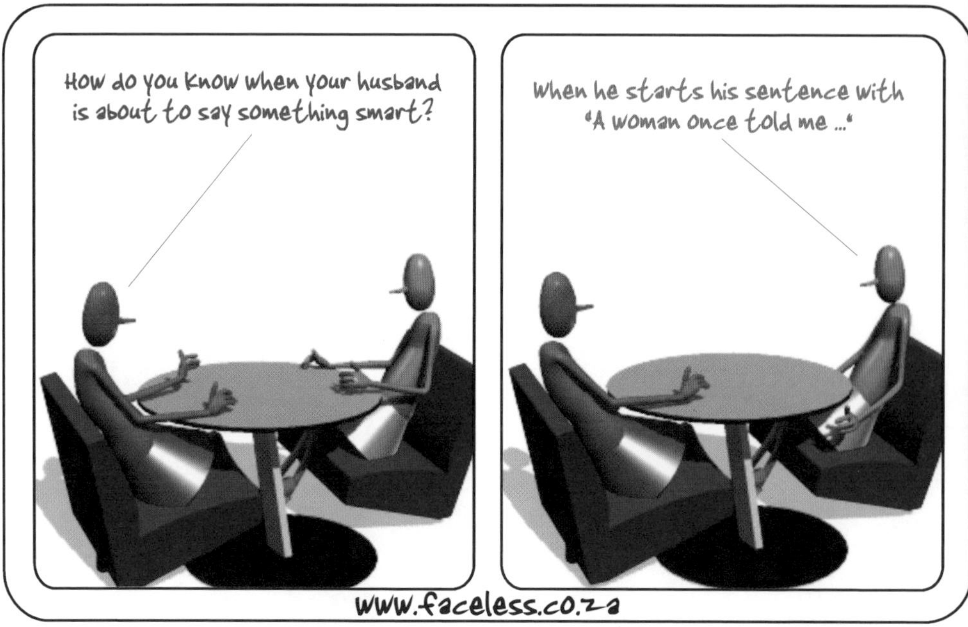
How do you know when your husband is about to say something smart?
When he starts his sentence with "A woman once told me ..."
www.faceless.co.za

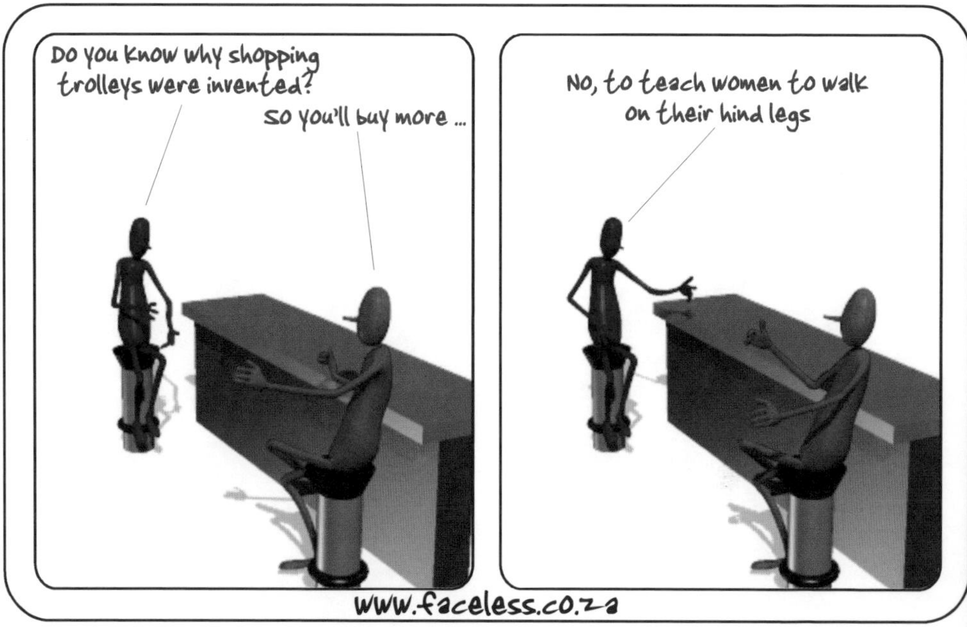
Do you know why shopping trolleys were invented?
So you'll buy more ...
No, to teach women to walk on their hind legs
www.faceless.co.za

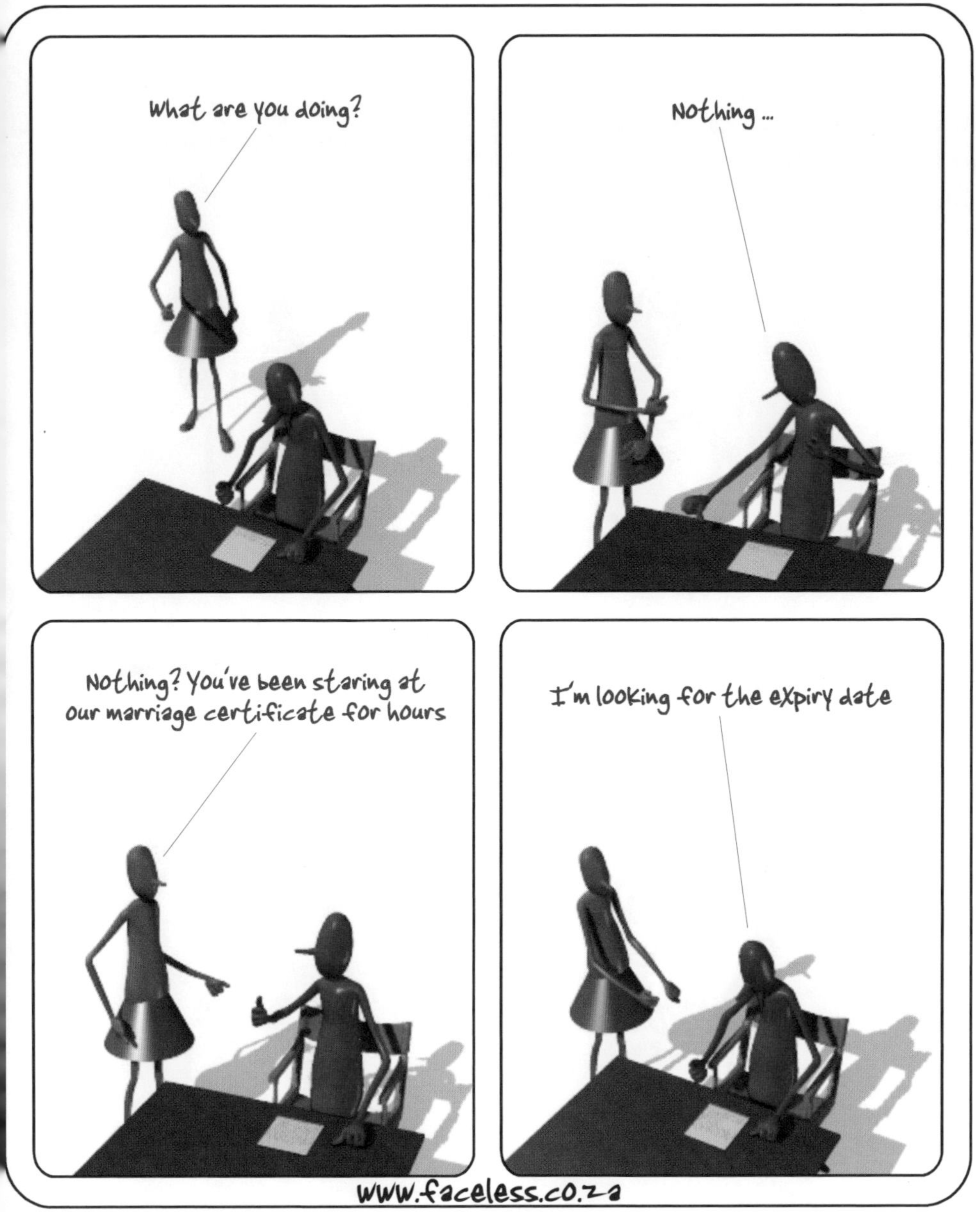
What are you doing?
Nothing ...
Nothing? You've been staring at our marriage certificate for hours
I'm looking for the expiry date
www.faceless.co.za

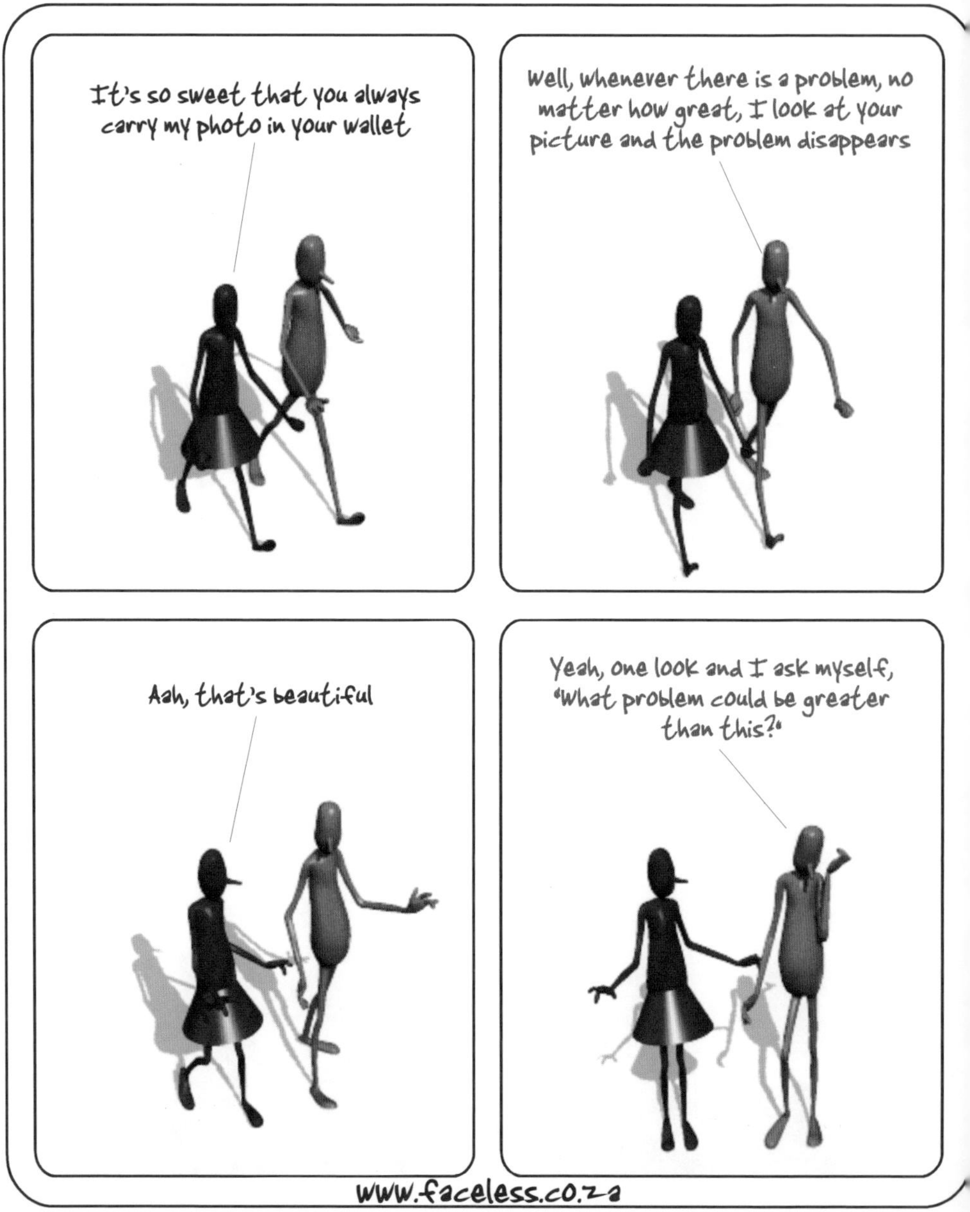
It's so sweet that you always carry my photo in your wallet
Well, whenever there is a problem, no matter how great, I look at your picture and the problem disappears
Aah, that's beautiful
Yeah, one look and I ask myself, "What problem could be greater than this?"
www.faceless.co.za

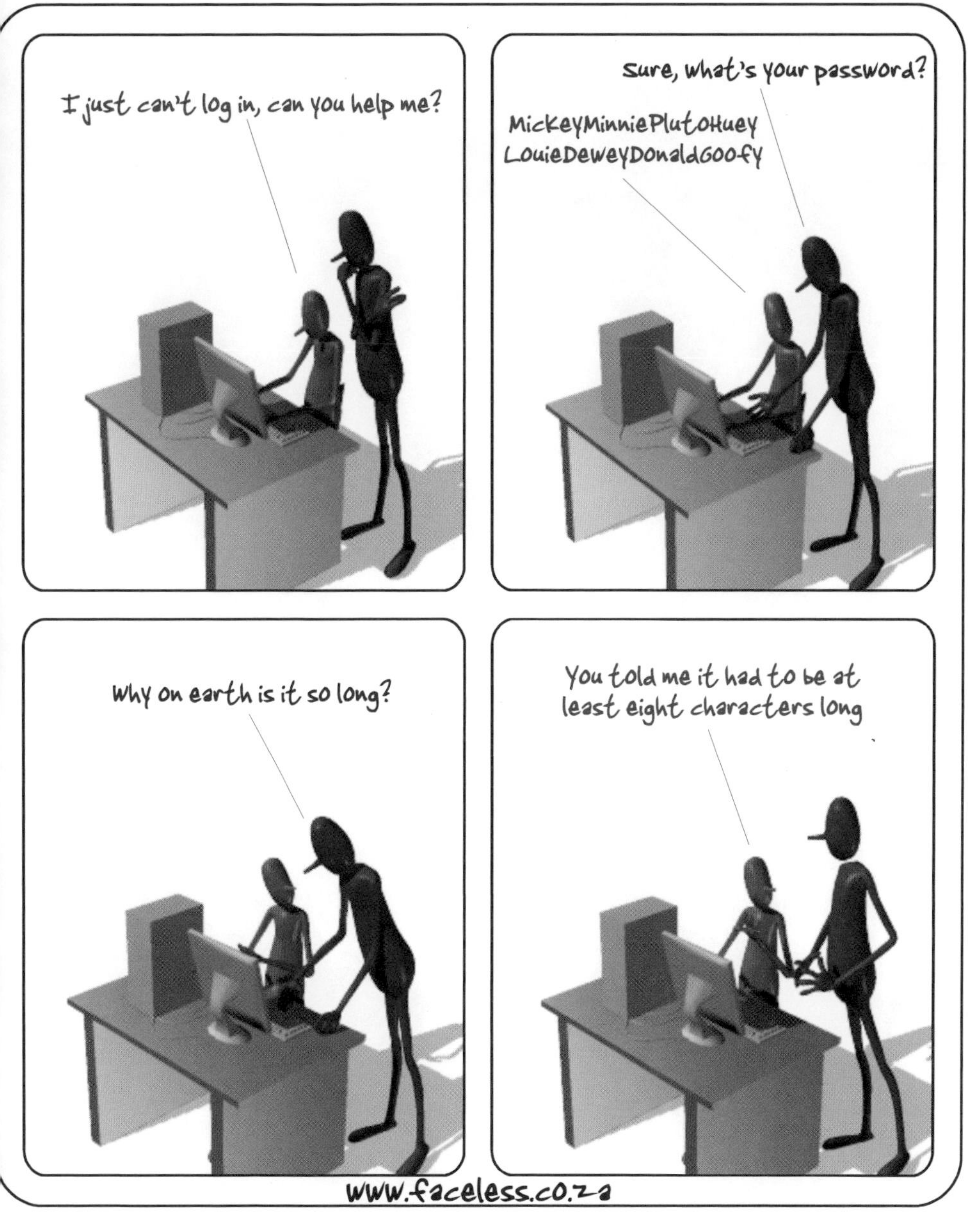
I just can't log in, can you help me?
Sure, what's your password?
MickeyMinniePlutoHuey
LouieDeweyDonaldGoofy
Why on earth is it so long?
You told me it had to be at
least eight characters long
www.faceless.co.za

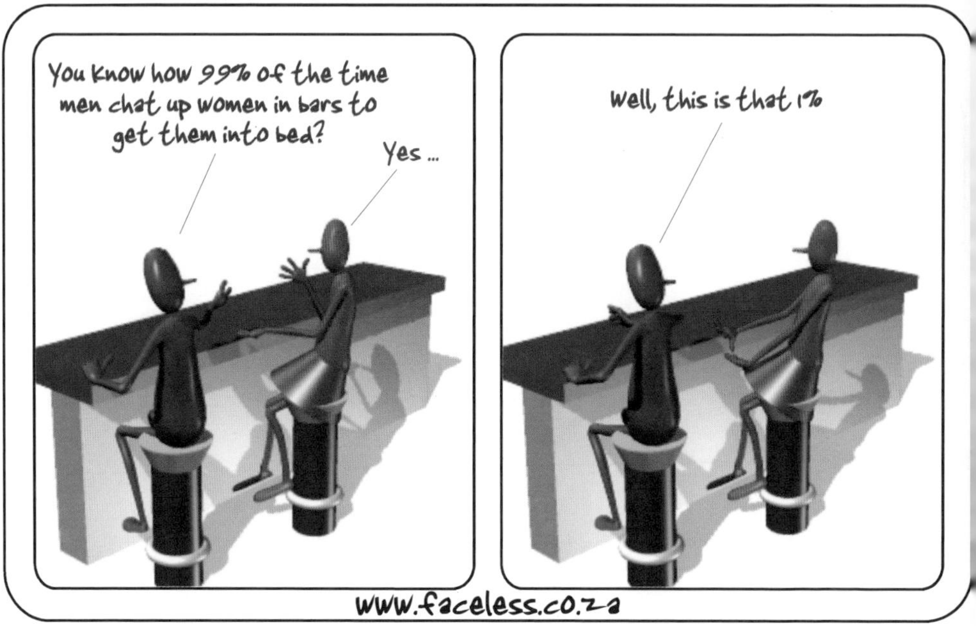
You know how 99% of the time men chat up women in bars to get them into bed?
Yes ...
Well, this is that 1%
www.faceless.co.za

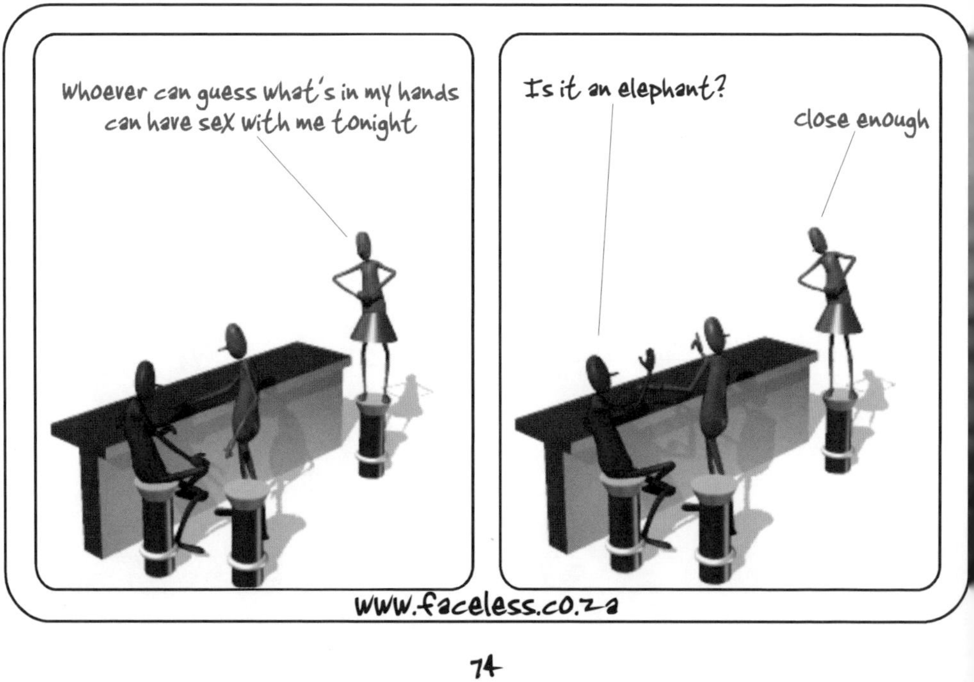
Whoever can guess what's in my hands can have sex with me tonight
Is it an elephant?
close enough
www.faceless.co.za

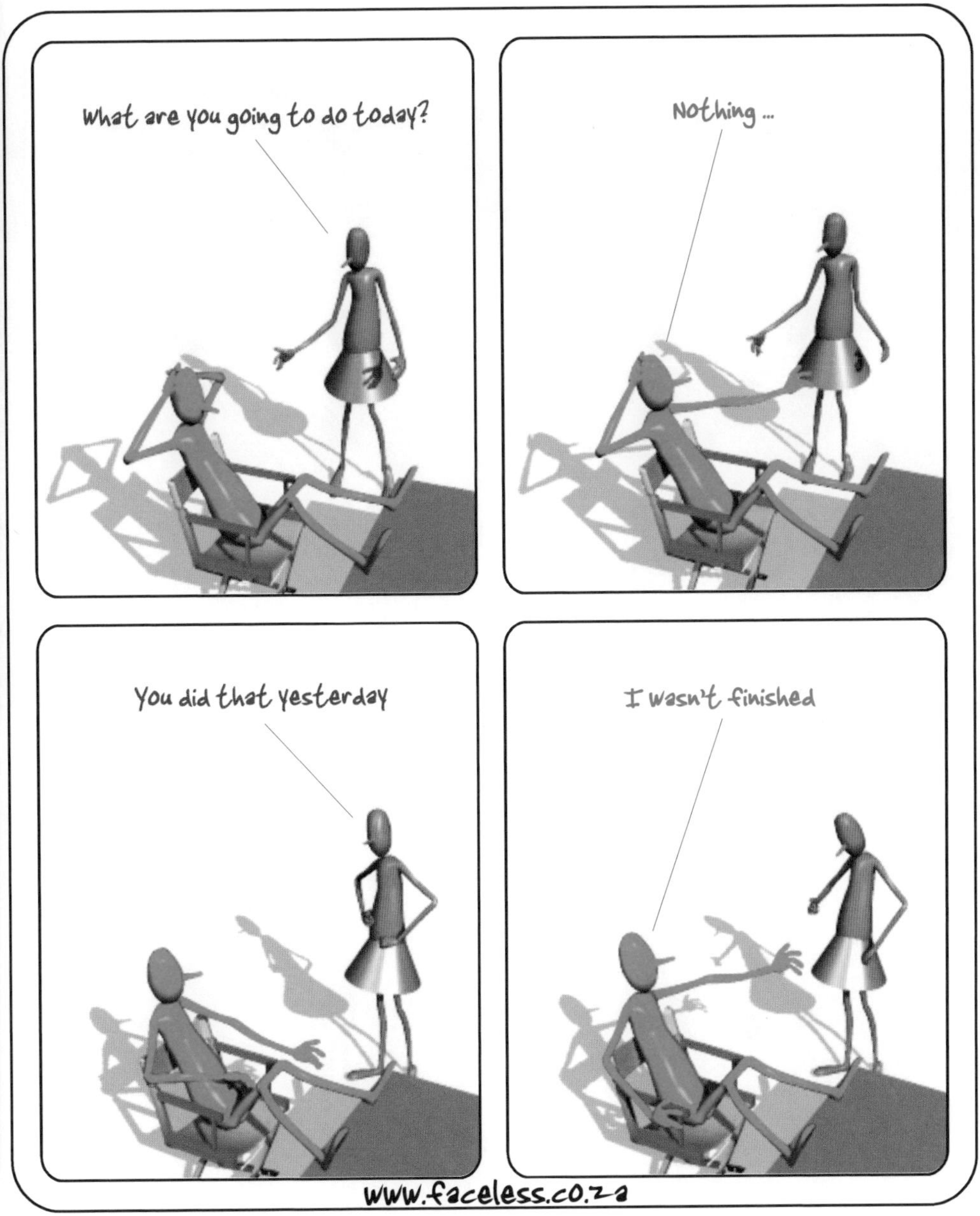
What are you going to do today?
Nothing ...
You did that yesterday
I wasn't finished
www.faceless.co.za

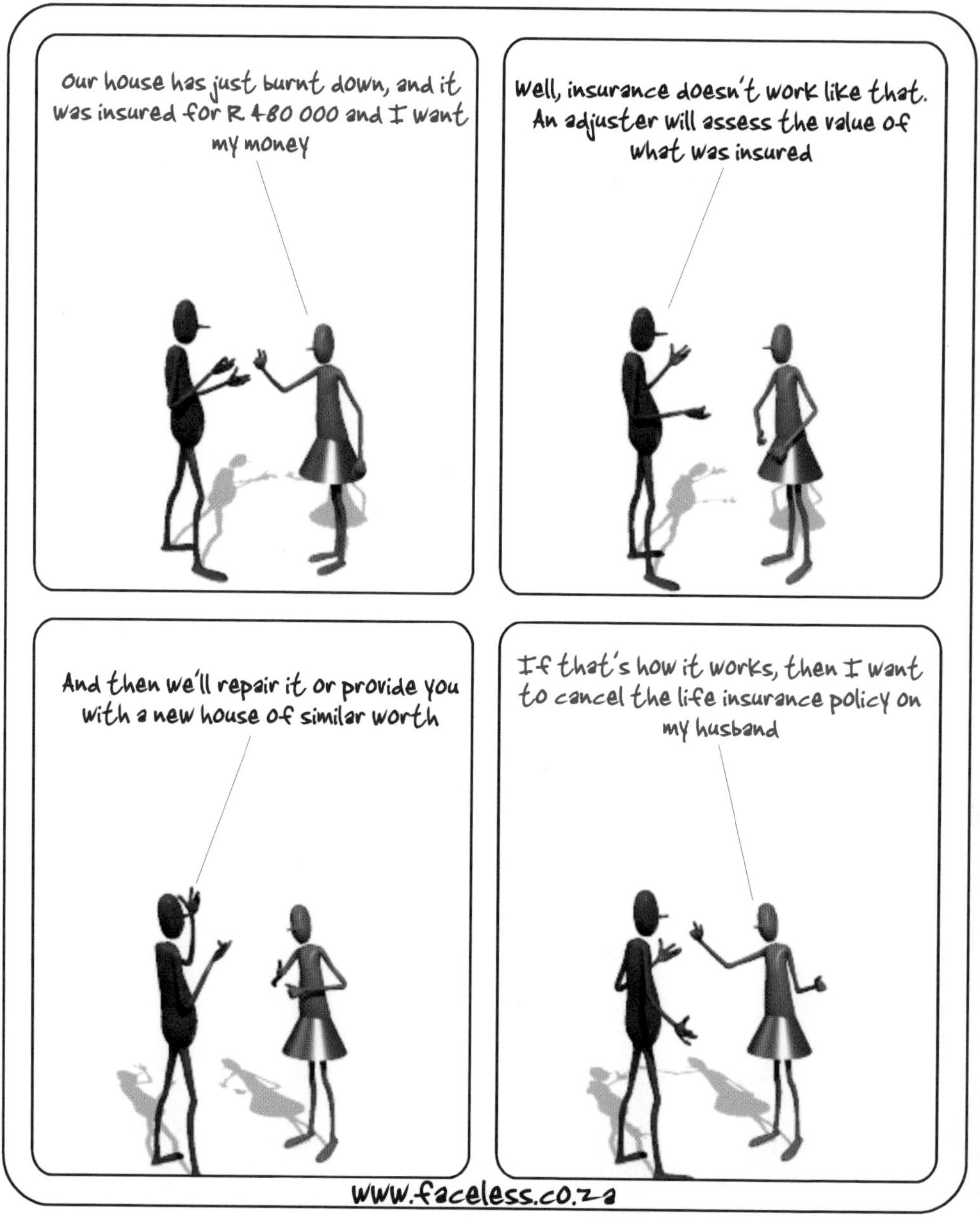

Our house has just burnt down, and it was insured for R 480 000 and I want my money
Well, insurance doesn't work like that. An adjuster will assess the value of what was insured
And then we'll repair it or provide you with a new house of similar worth
If that's how it works, then I want to cancel the life insurance policy on my husband
www.faceless.co.za

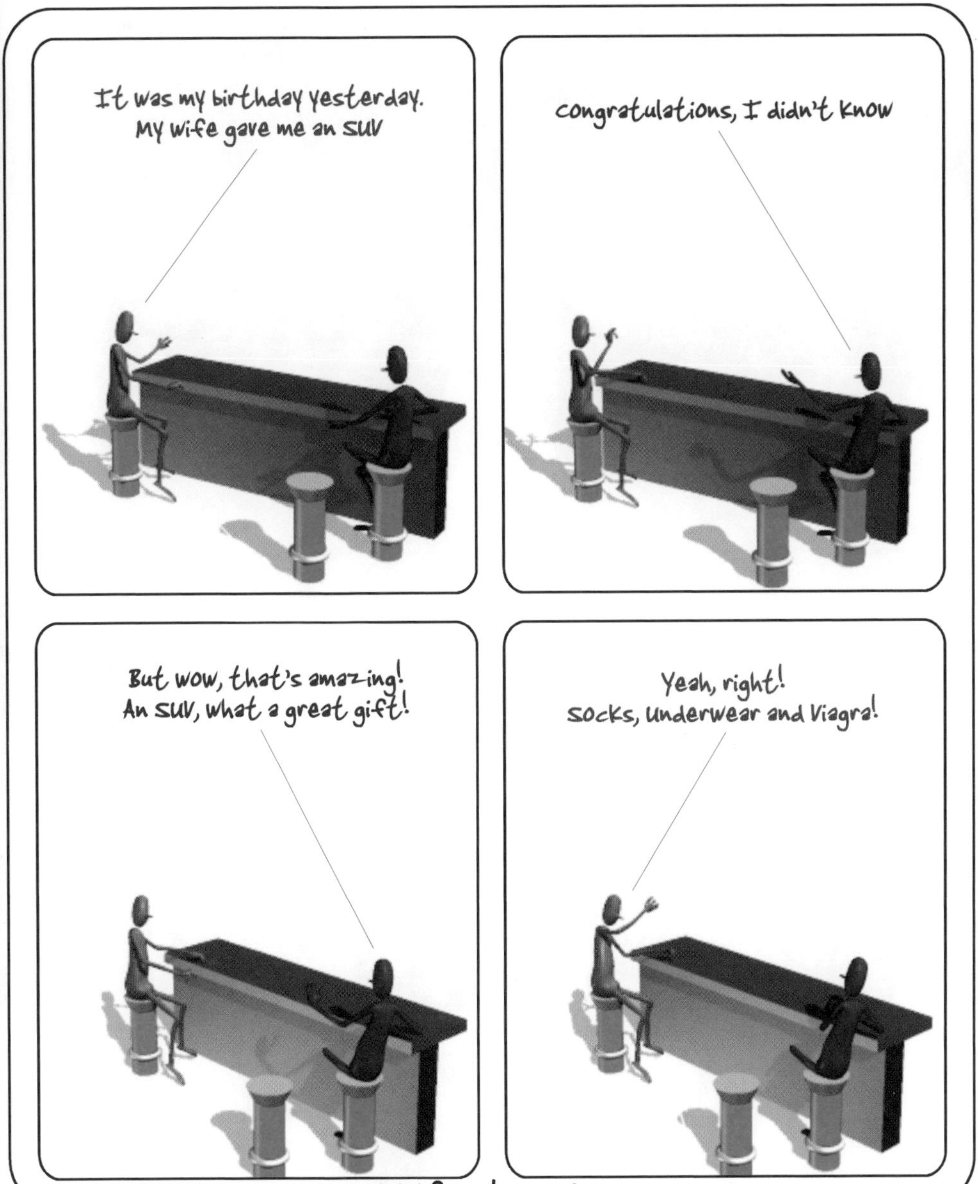
It was my birthday yesterday.
My wife gave me an SUV
congratulations, I didn't know
But wow, that's amazing!
An SUV, what a great gift!
Yeah, right!
Socks, Underwear and Viagra!
www.faceless.co.za

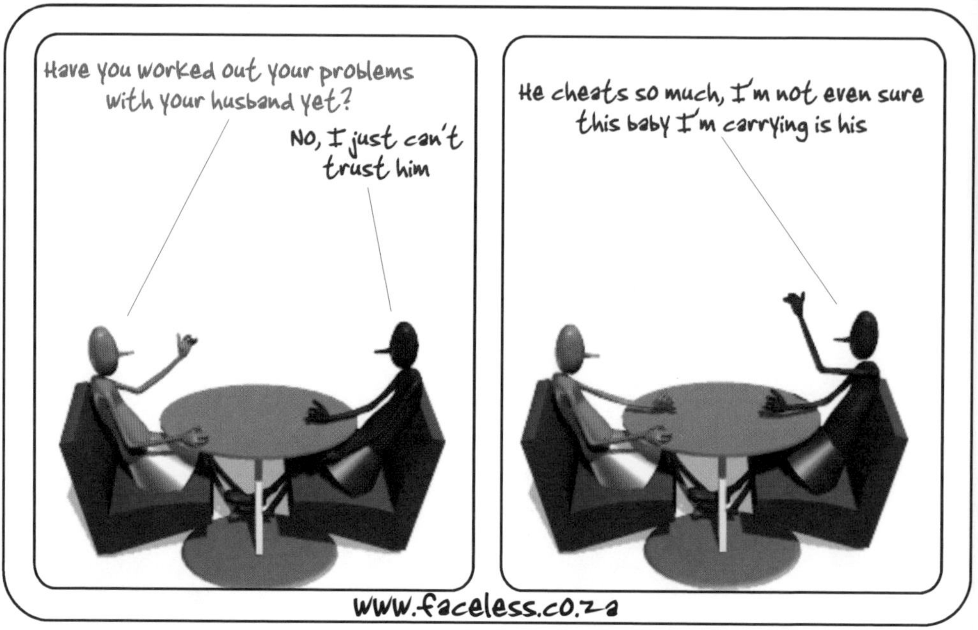
Have you worked out your problems with your husband yet?
No, I just can't trust him
He cheats so much, I'm not even sure this baby I'm carrying is his
www.faceless.co.za

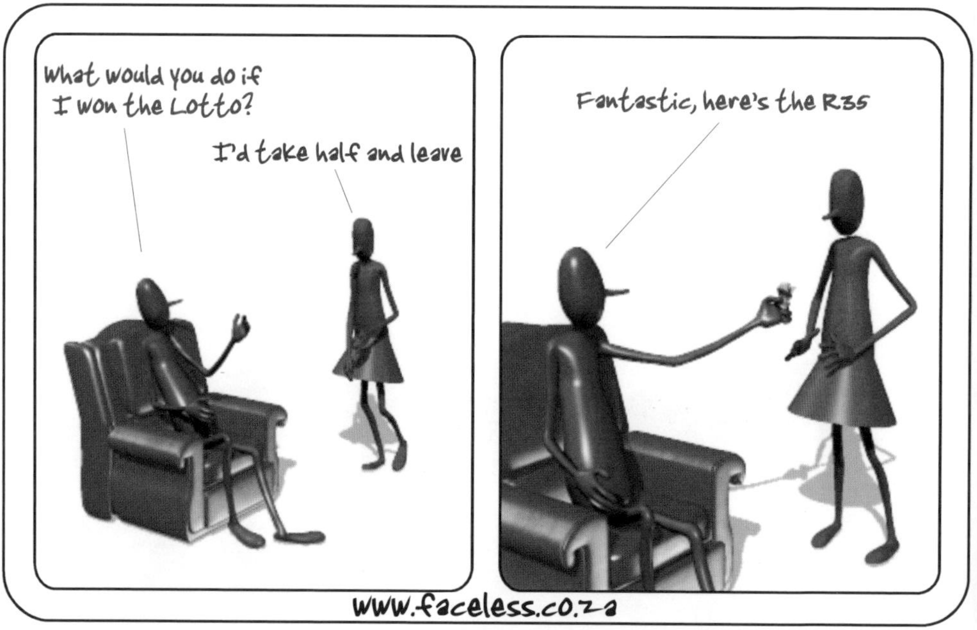
What would you do if I won the Lotto?
I'd take half and leave
Fantastic, here's the R35
www.faceless.co.za

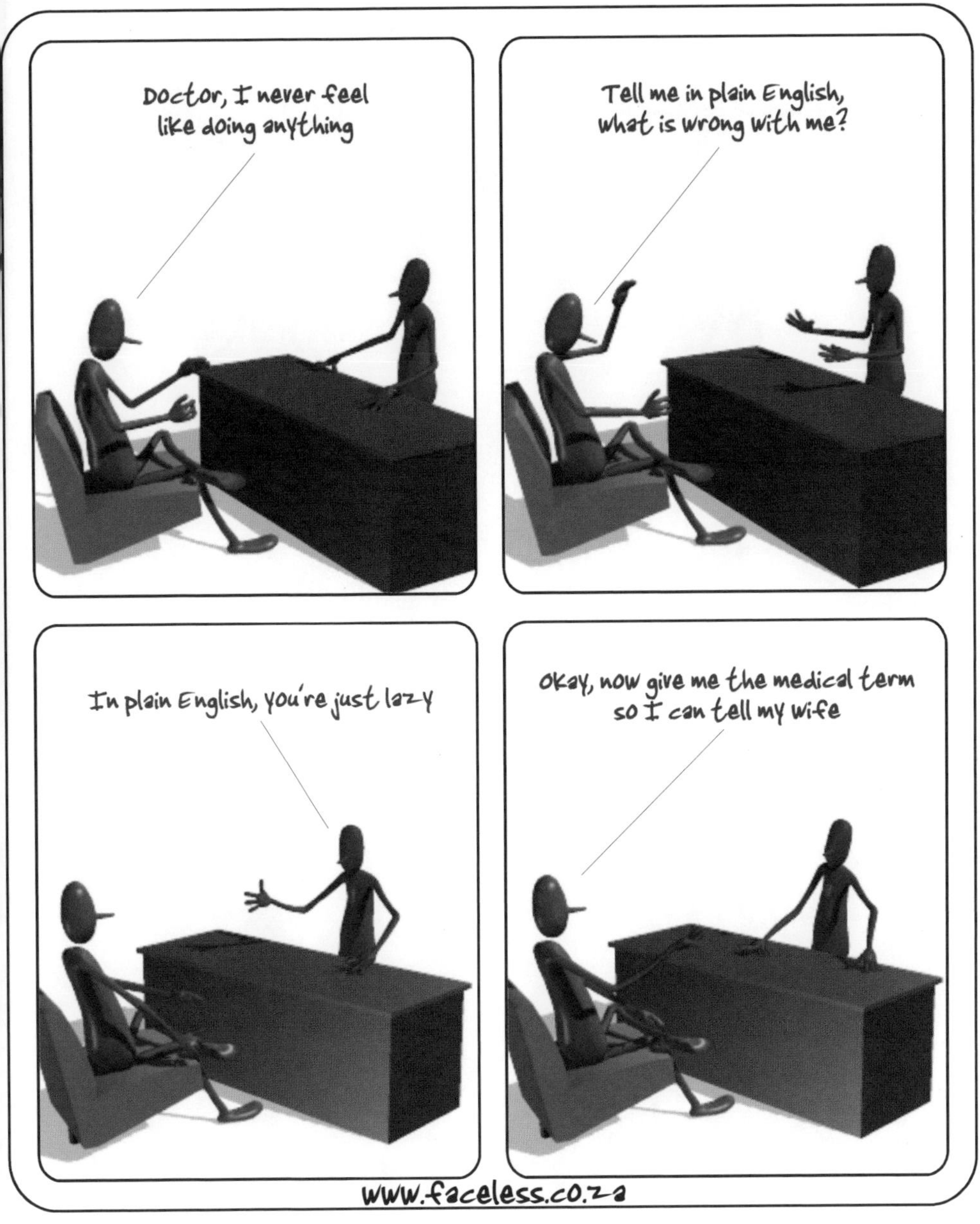
Doctor, I never feel like doing anything
Tell me in plain English, what is wrong with me?
In plain English, you're just lazy
Okay, now give me the medical term so I can tell my wife
www.faceless.co.za

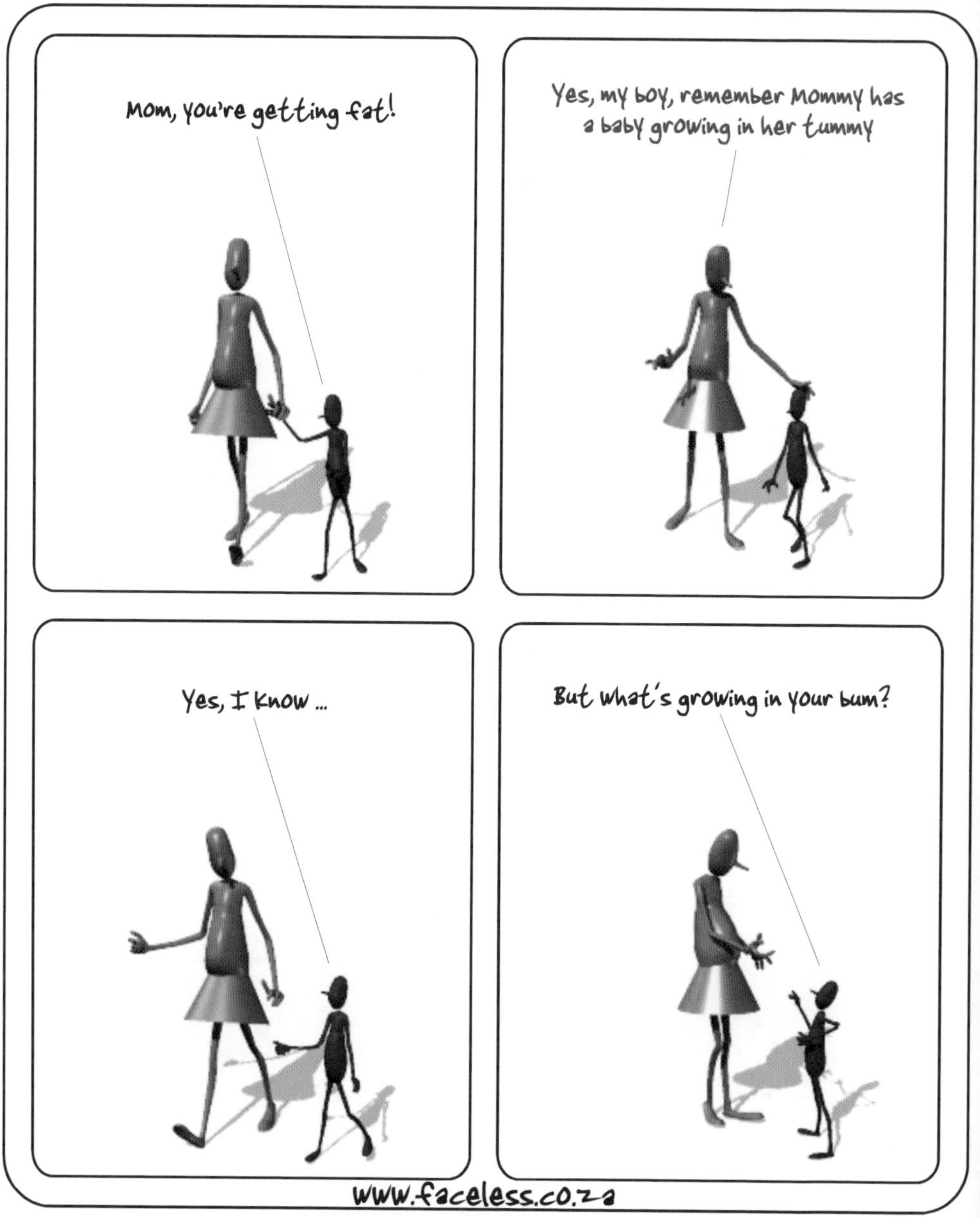
Mom, you're getting fat!
Yes, my boy, remember Mommy has a baby growing in her tummy
Yes, I know ...
But what's growing in your bum?
www.faceless.co.za

Hurry up and hit the damn ball already!
My wife is watching me from the clubhouse, so I want this to be a perfect shot
Impossible!
You'll never hit her from here!
www.faceless.co.za

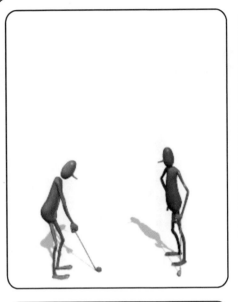

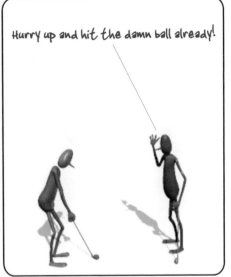

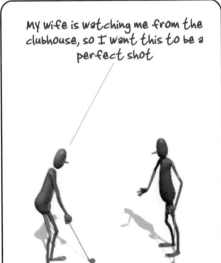

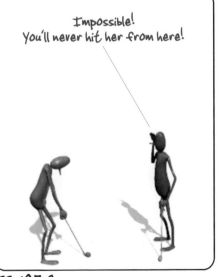

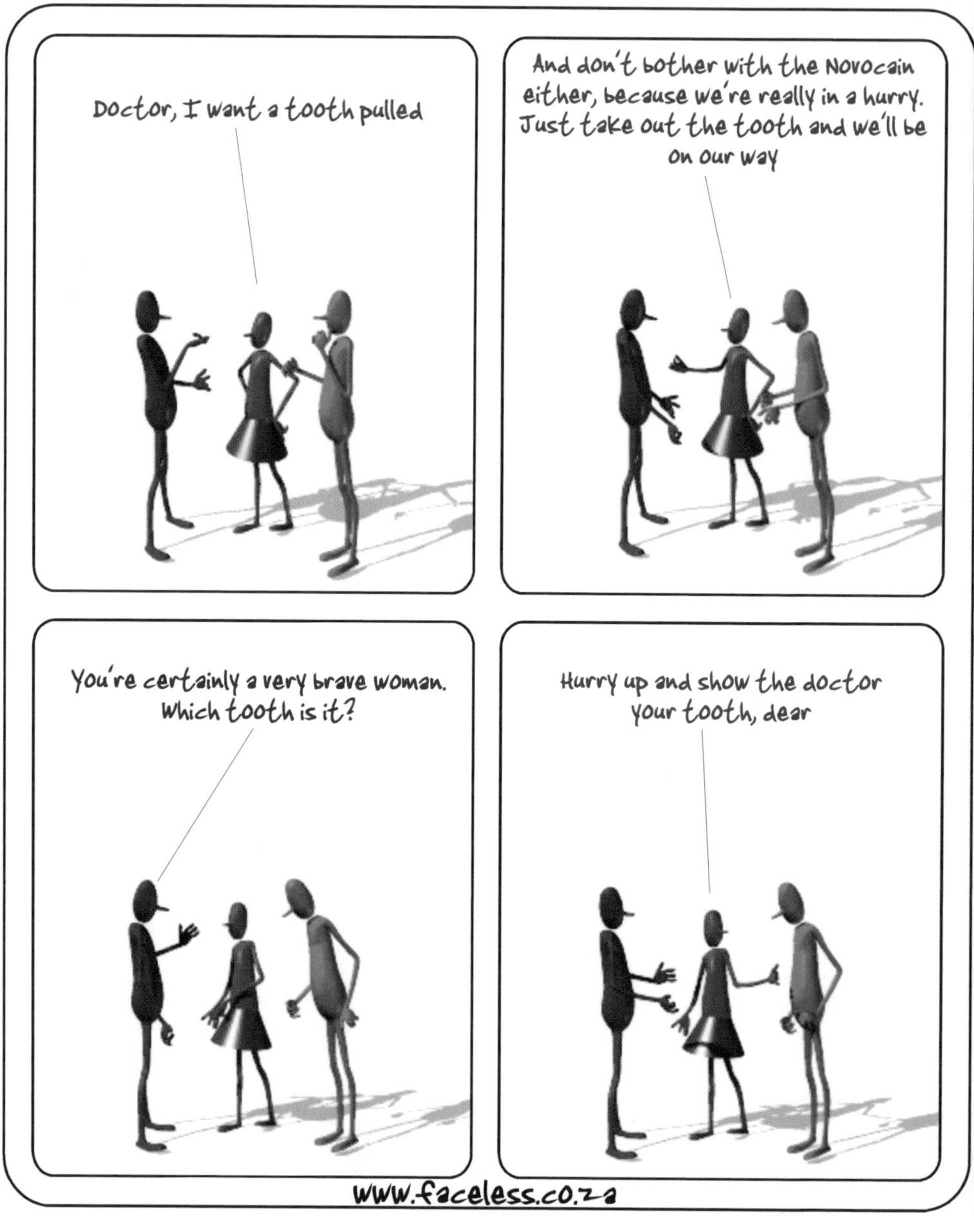
Doctor, I want a tooth pulled
And don't bother with the Novocain either, because we're really in a hurry. Just take out the tooth and we'll be on our way
You're certainly a very brave woman. Which tooth is it?
Hurry up and show the doctor your tooth, dear
www.faceless.co.za

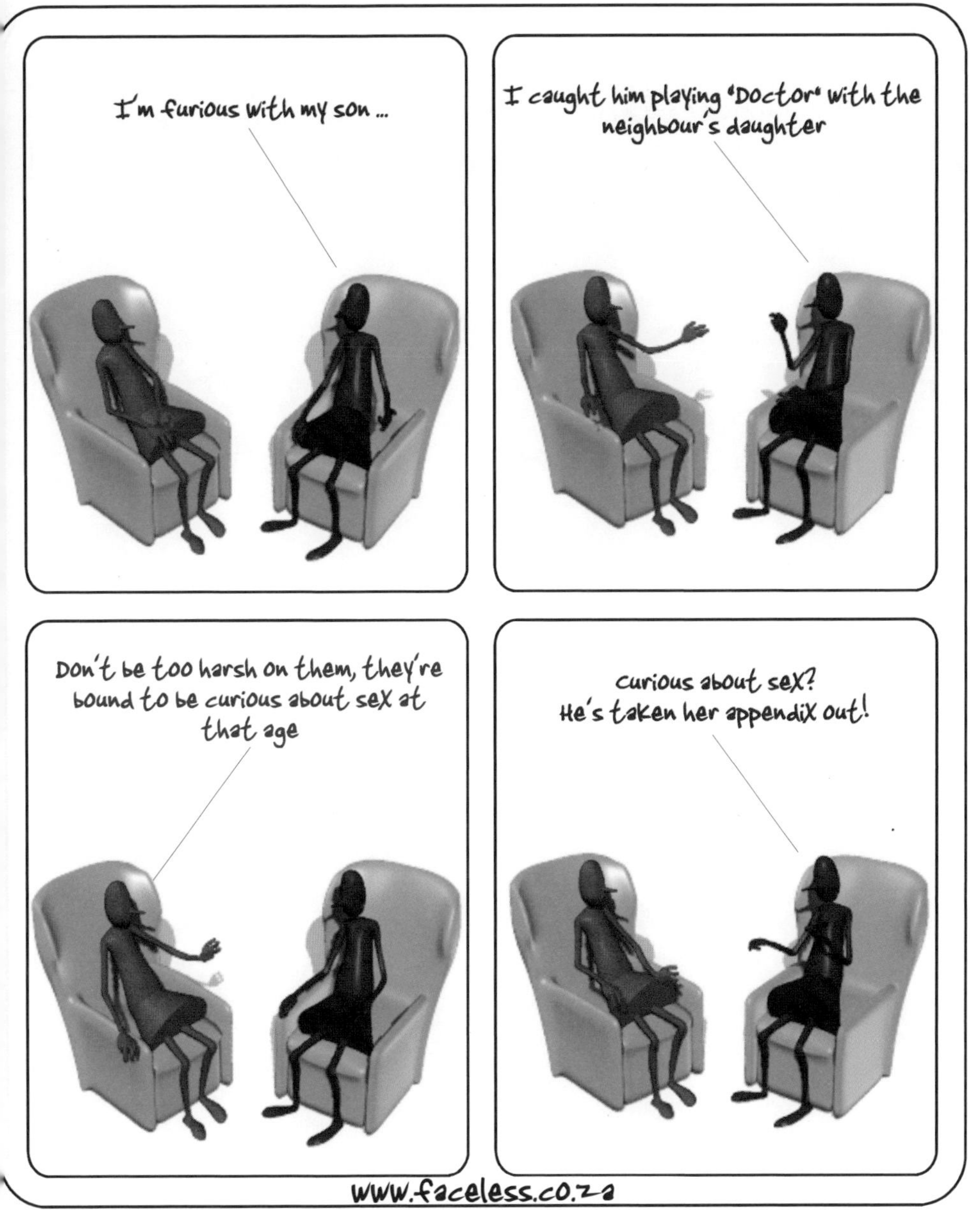
I'm furious with my son ...
I caught him playing "Doctor" with the neighbour's daughter
Don't be too harsh on them, they're bound to be curious about sex at that age
curious about sex? He's taken her appendiX out!
www.faceless.co.za

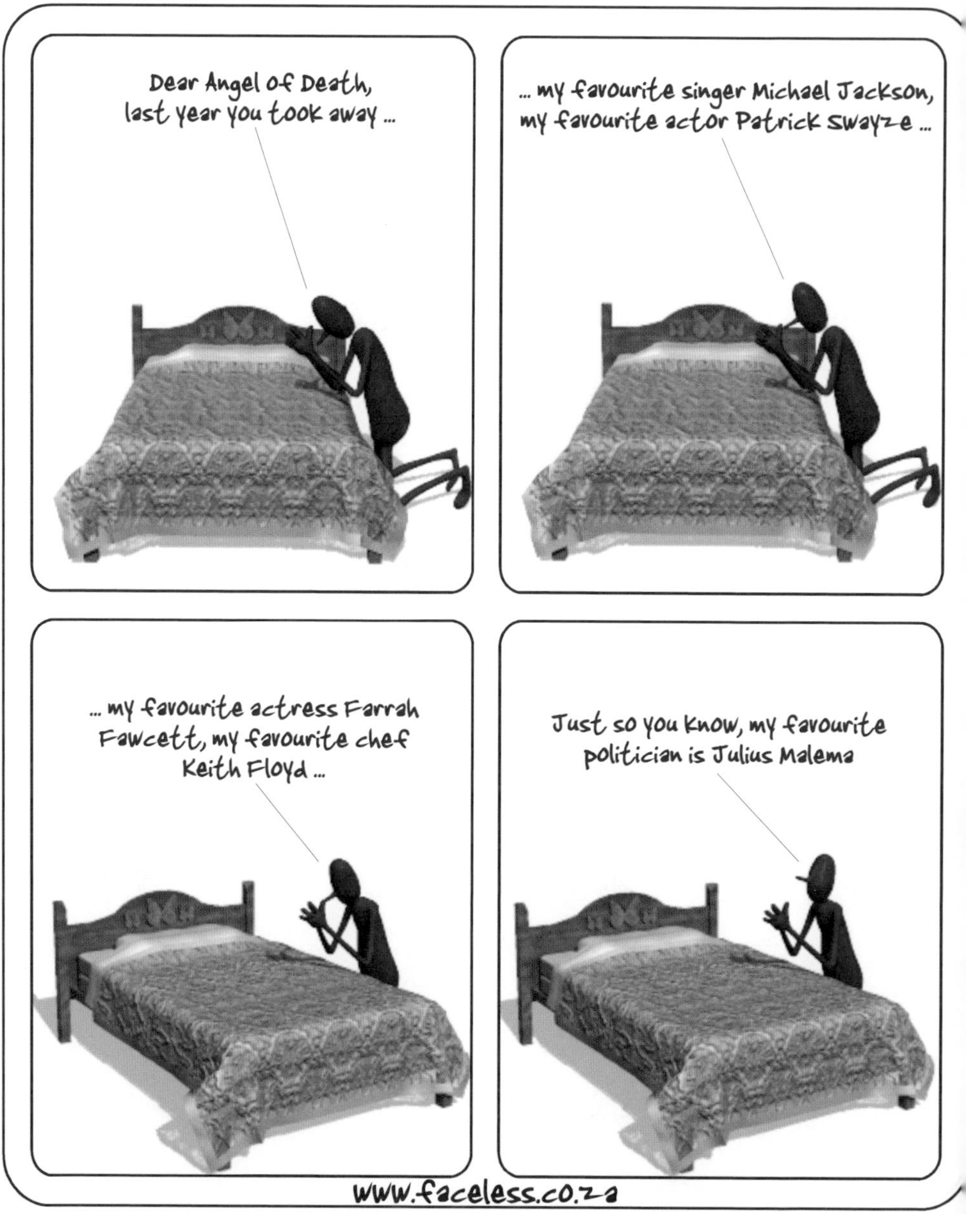

Dear Angel of Death, last year you took away ...
... my favourite singer Michael Jackson, my favourite actor Patrick Swayze ...
... my favourite actress Farrah Fawcett, my favourite chef Keith Floyd ...
Just so you know, my favourite politician is Julius Malema
www.faceless.co.za

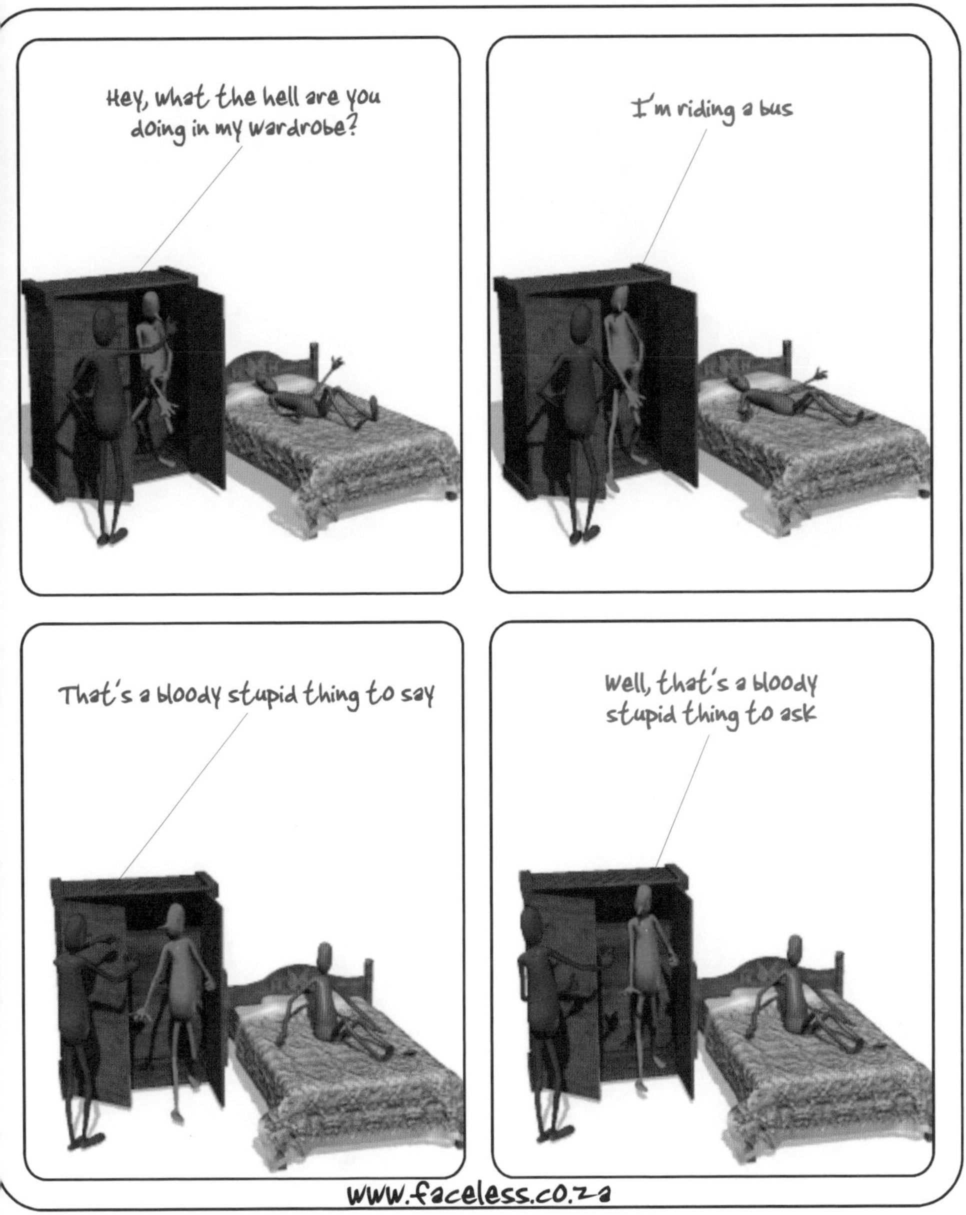
Hey, what the hell are you doing in my wardrobe?
I'm riding a bus
That's a bloody stupid thing to say
Well, that's a bloody stupid thing to ask
www.faceless.co.za

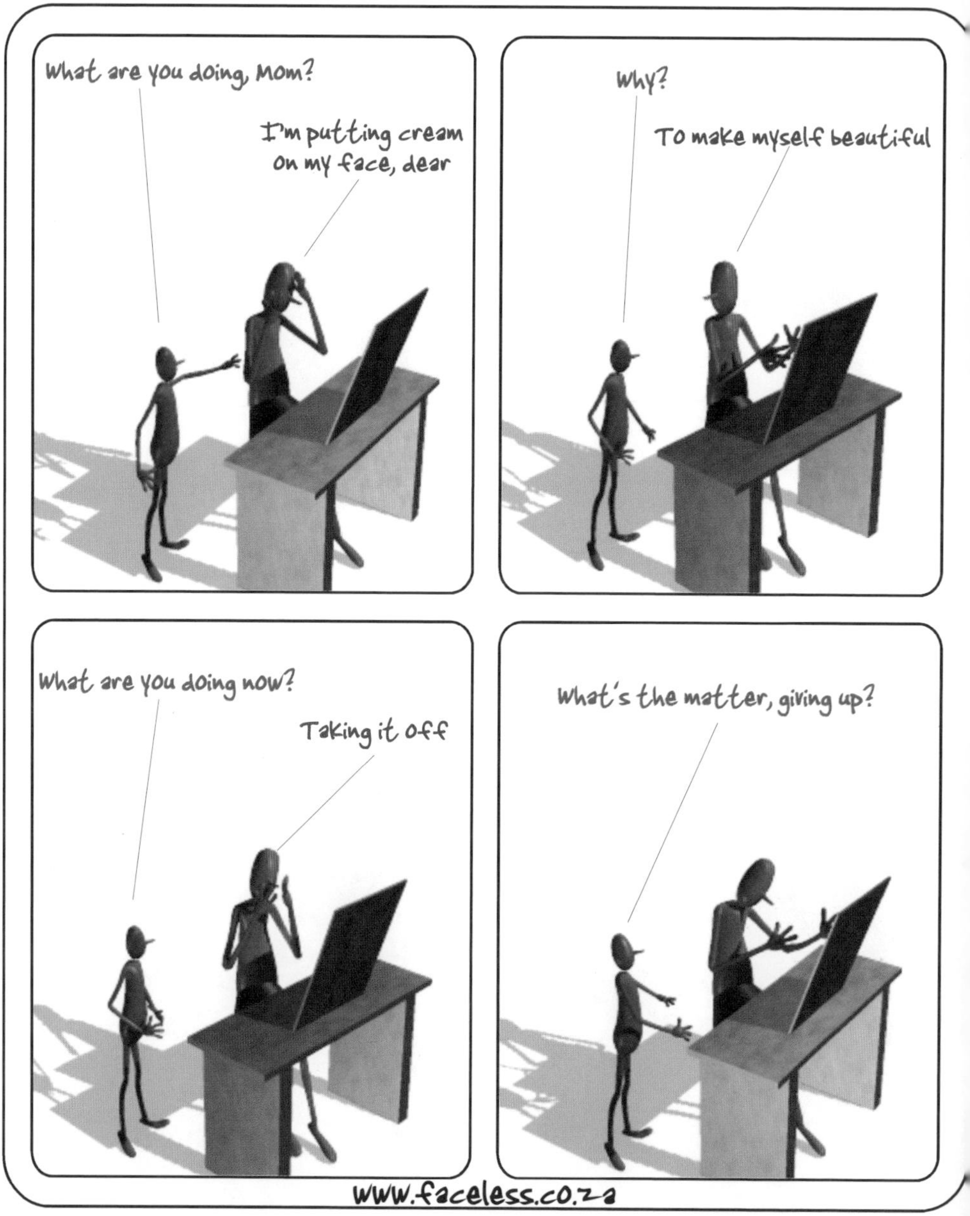
What are you doing, Mom?
I'm putting cream on my face, dear
Why?
To make myself beautiful
What are you doing now?
Taking it off
What's the matter, giving up?
www.faceless.co.za

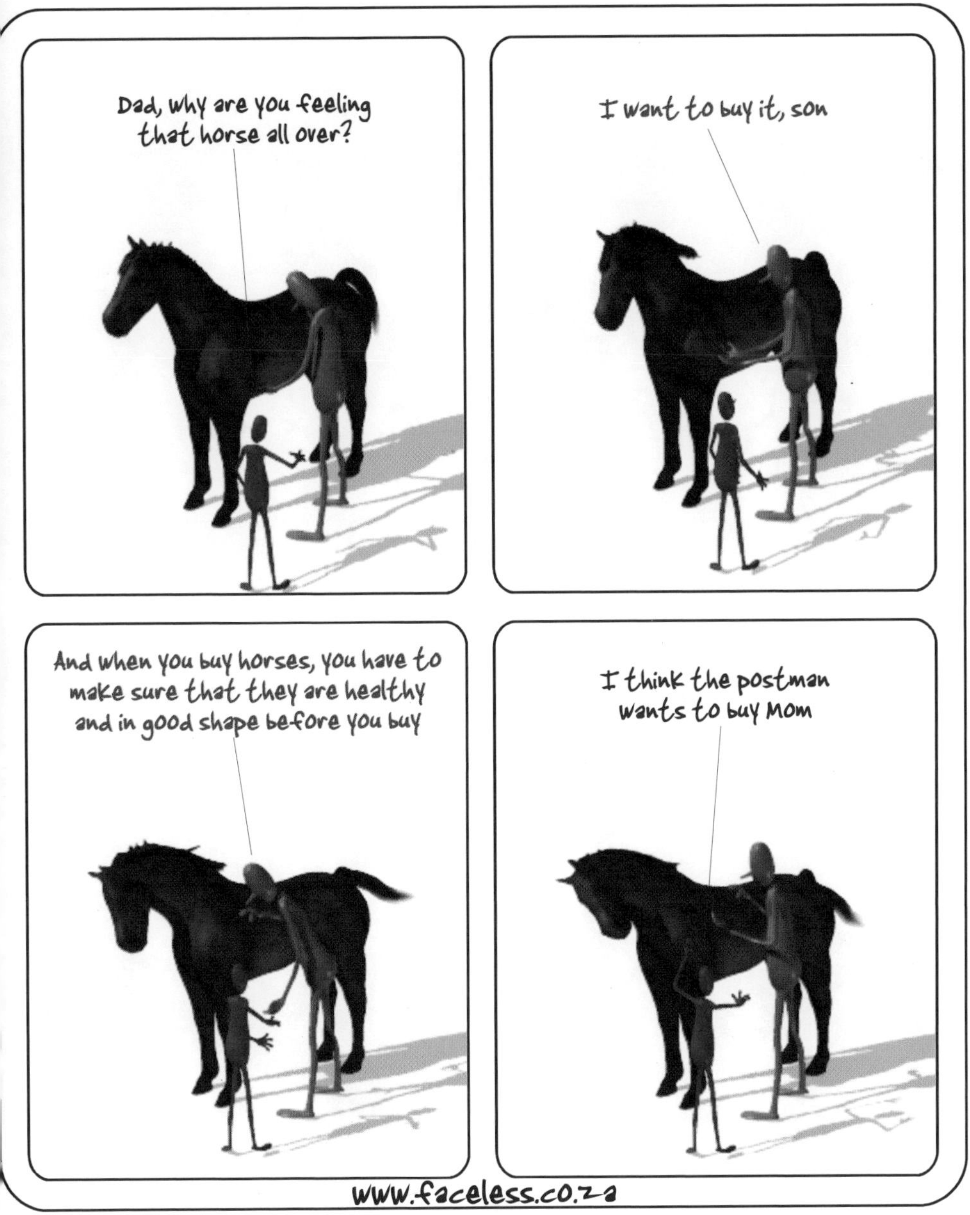

Dad, why are you feeling that horse all over?
I want to buy it, son
And when you buy horses, you have to make sure that they are healthy and in good shape before you buy
I think the postman wants to buy Mom
www.faceless.co.za

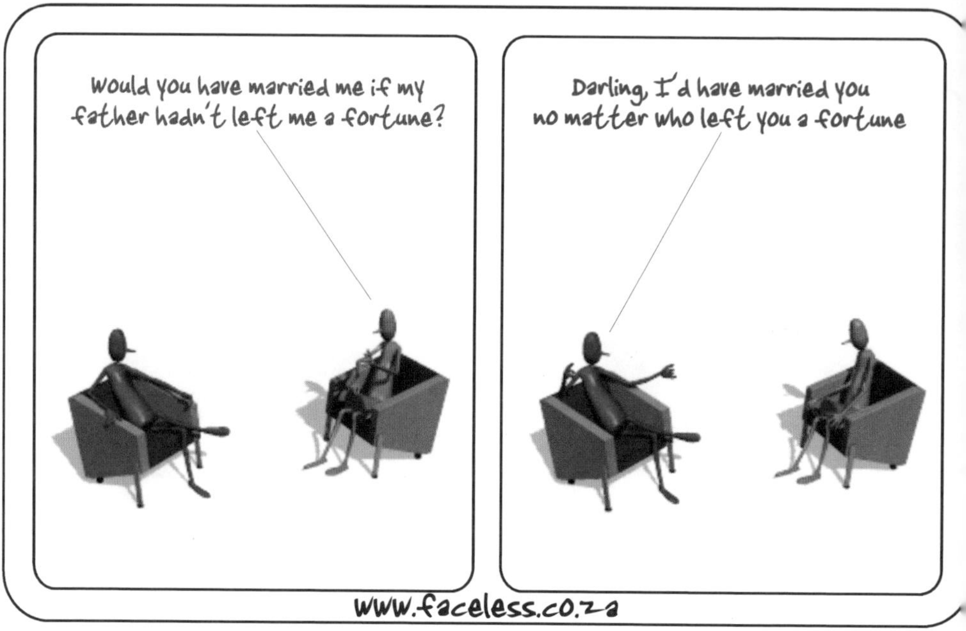
Would you have married me if my father hadn't left me a fortune?
Darling, I'd have married you no matter who left you a fortune
www.faceless.co.za

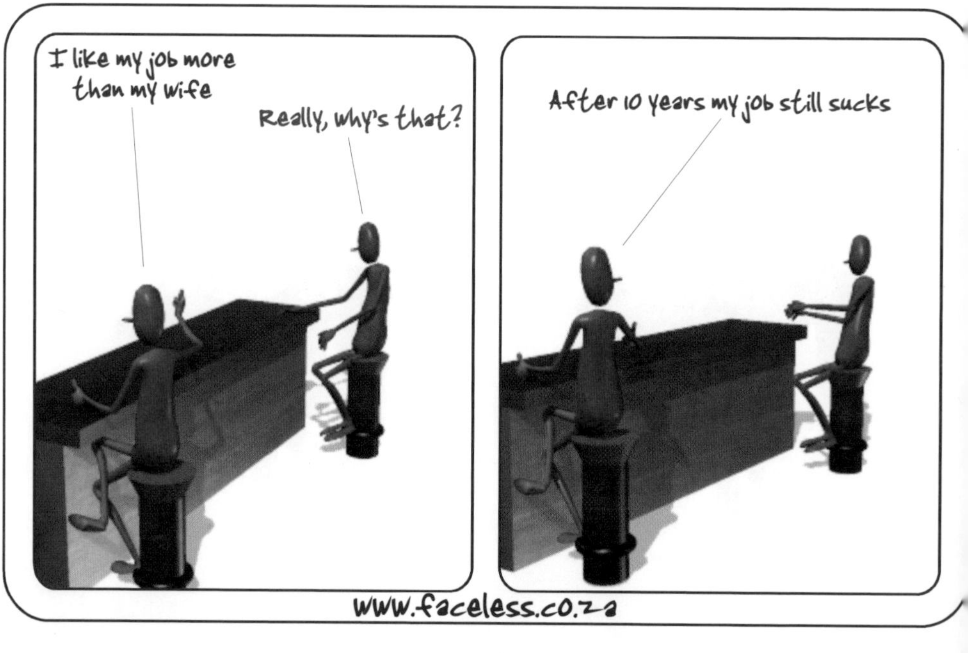
I like my job more than my wife
Really, why's that?
After 10 years my job still sucks
www.faceless.co.za

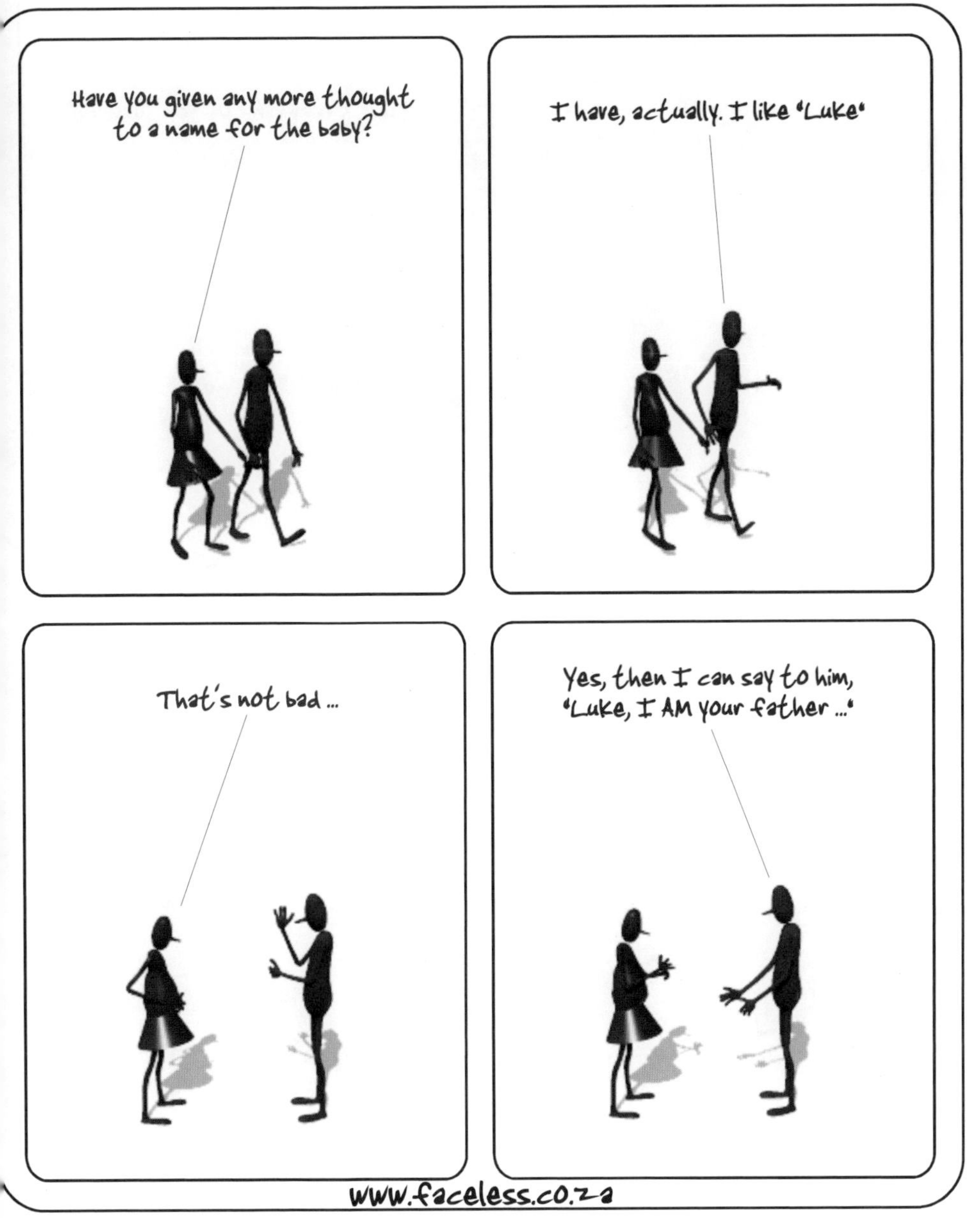
Have you given any more thought to a name for the baby?
I have, actually. I like "Luke"
That's not bad ...
Yes, then I can say to him, "Luke, I AM your father ..."
www.faceless.co.za

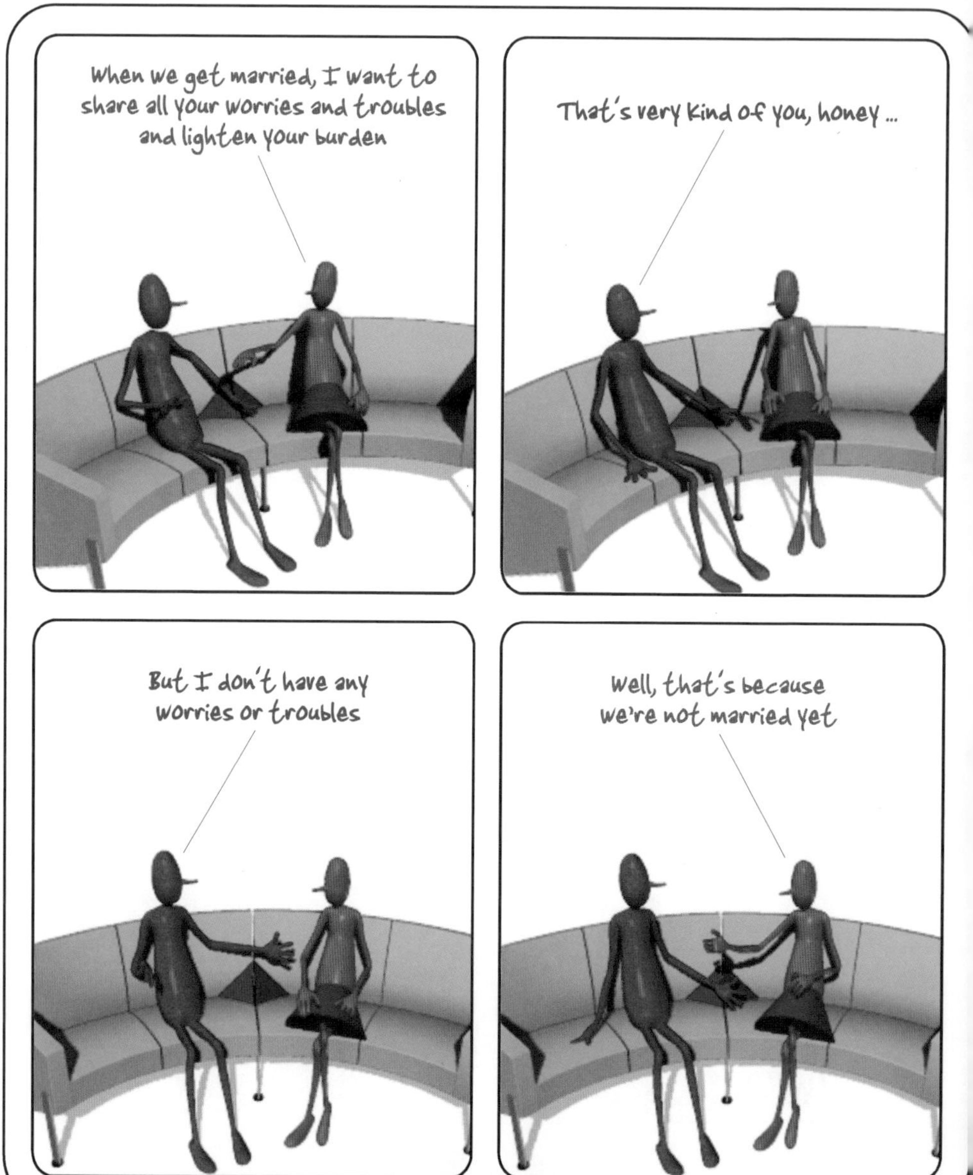
When we get married, I want to share all your worries and troubles and lighten your burden
That's very kind of you, honey ...
But I don't have any worries or troubles
Well, that's because we're not married yet
www.faceless.co.za

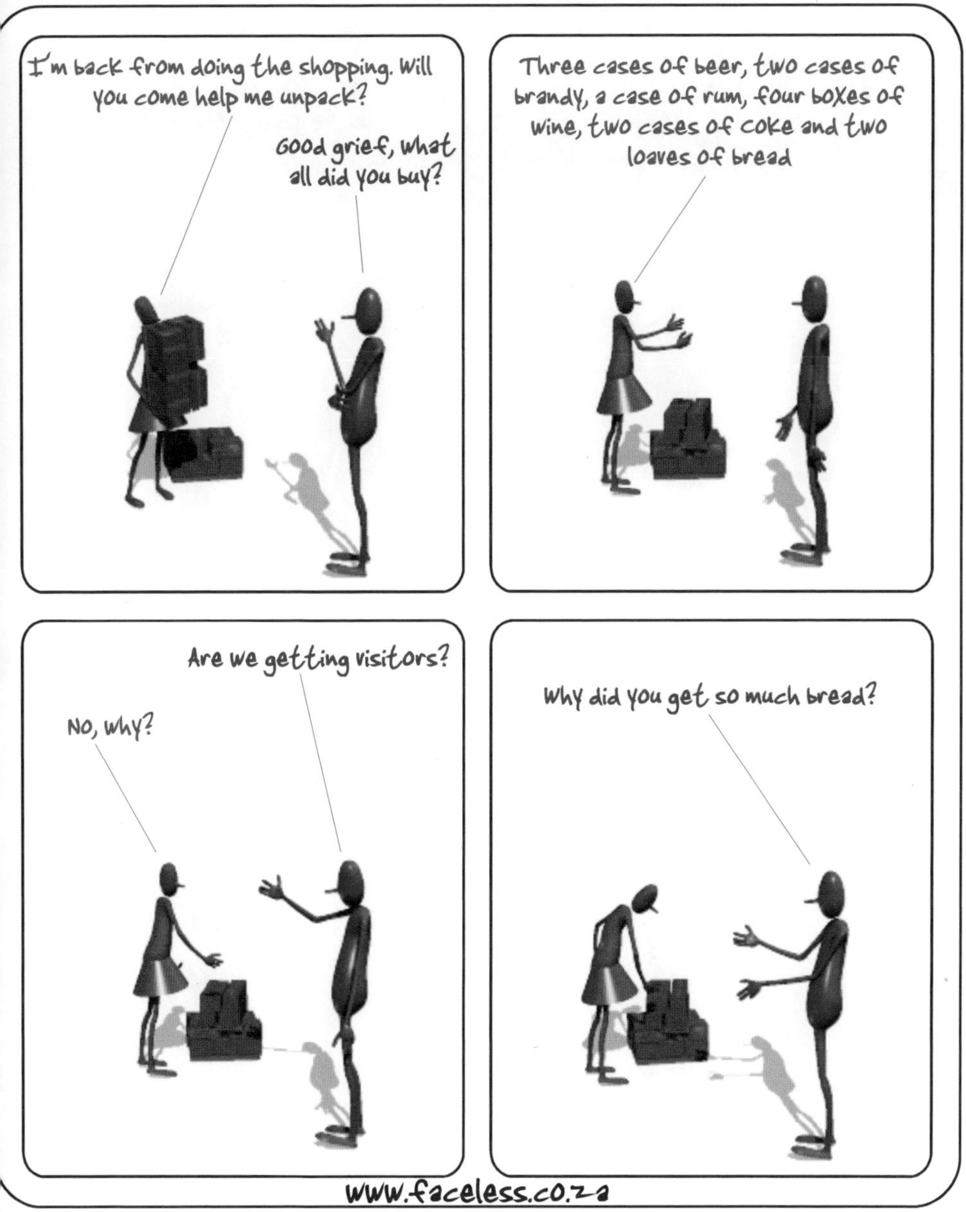
I'm back from doing the shopping. Will you come help me unpack?
Good grief, what all did you buy?
Three cases of beer, two cases of brandy, a case of rum, four boxes of wine, two cases of coke and two loaves of bread
Are we getting visitors?
No, why?
Why did you get so much bread?
www.faceless.co.za

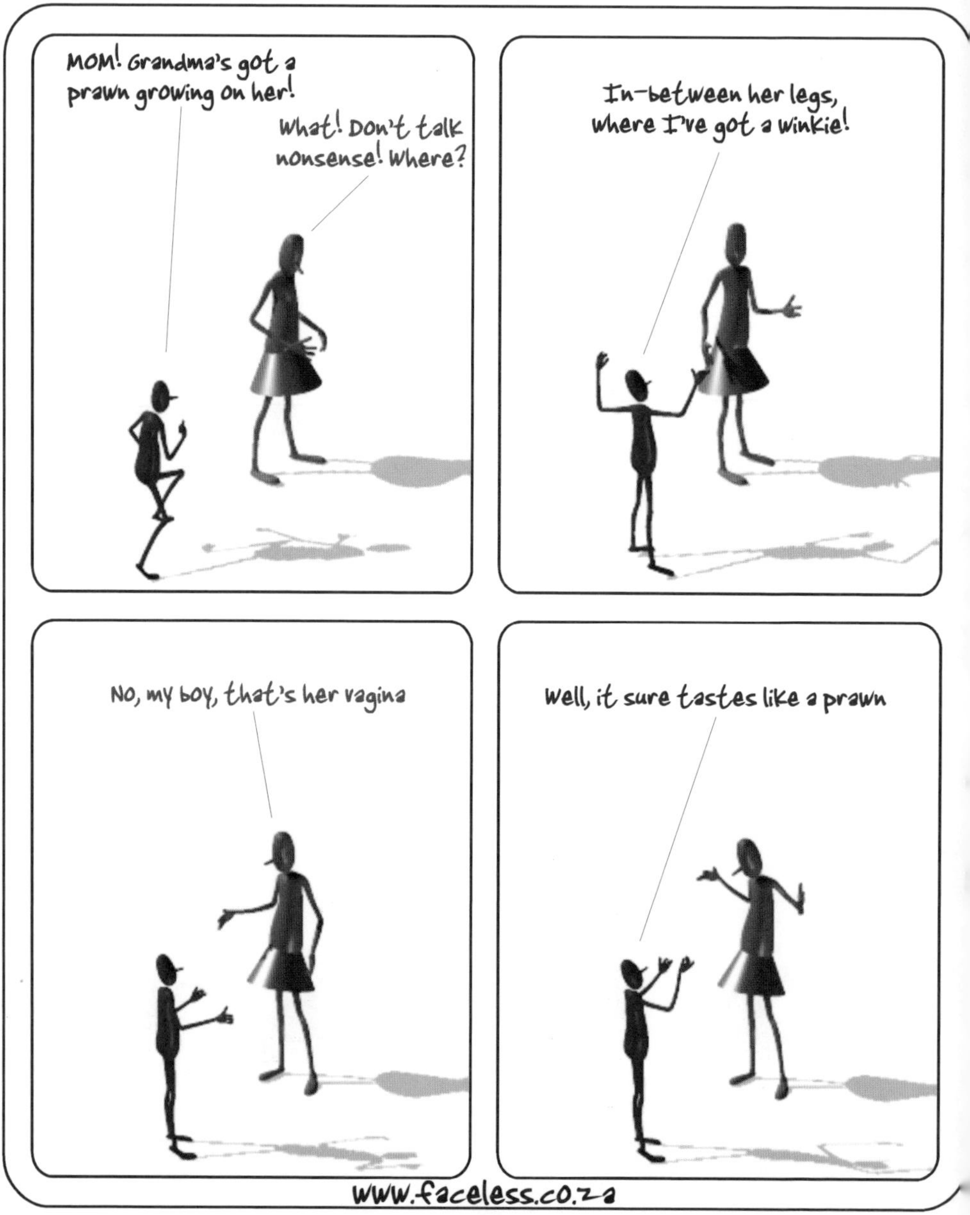
MOM! Grandma's got a prawn growing on her!
What! Don't talk nonsense! Where?
In-between her legs, where I've got a winkie!
No, my boy, that's her vagina
Well, it sure tastes like a prawn
www.faceless.co.za

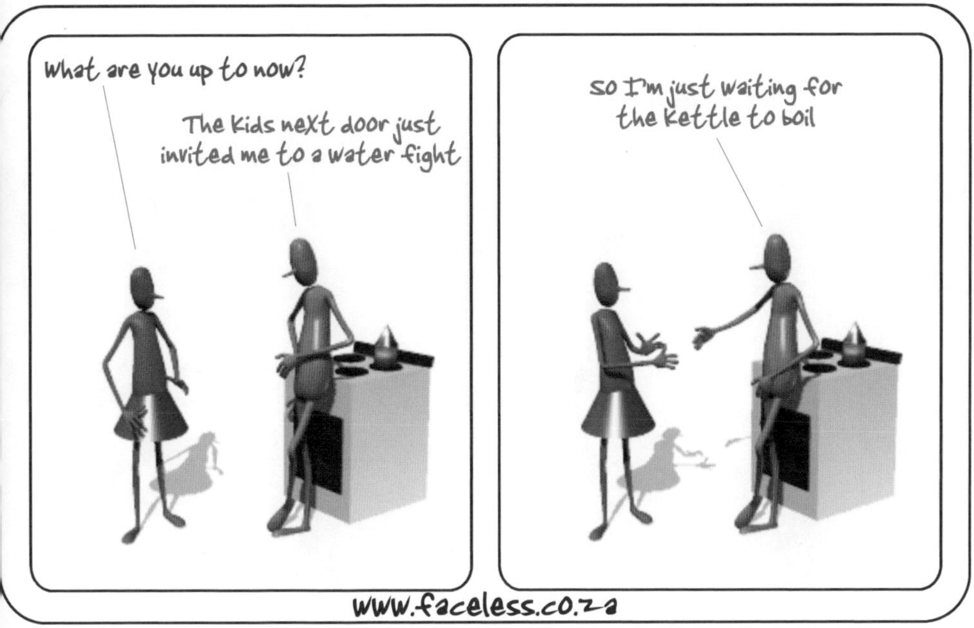
What are you up to now?
The kids next door just invited me to a water fight
so I'm just waiting for the kettle to boil
www.faceless.co.za

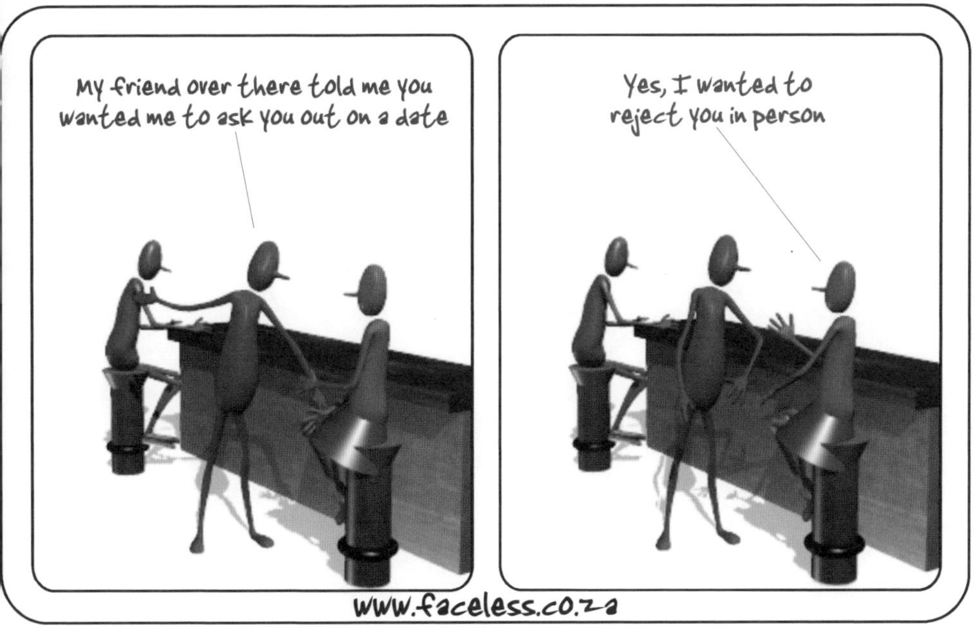
My friend over there told me you wanted me to ask you out on a date
Yes, I wanted to reject you in person
www.faceless.co.za

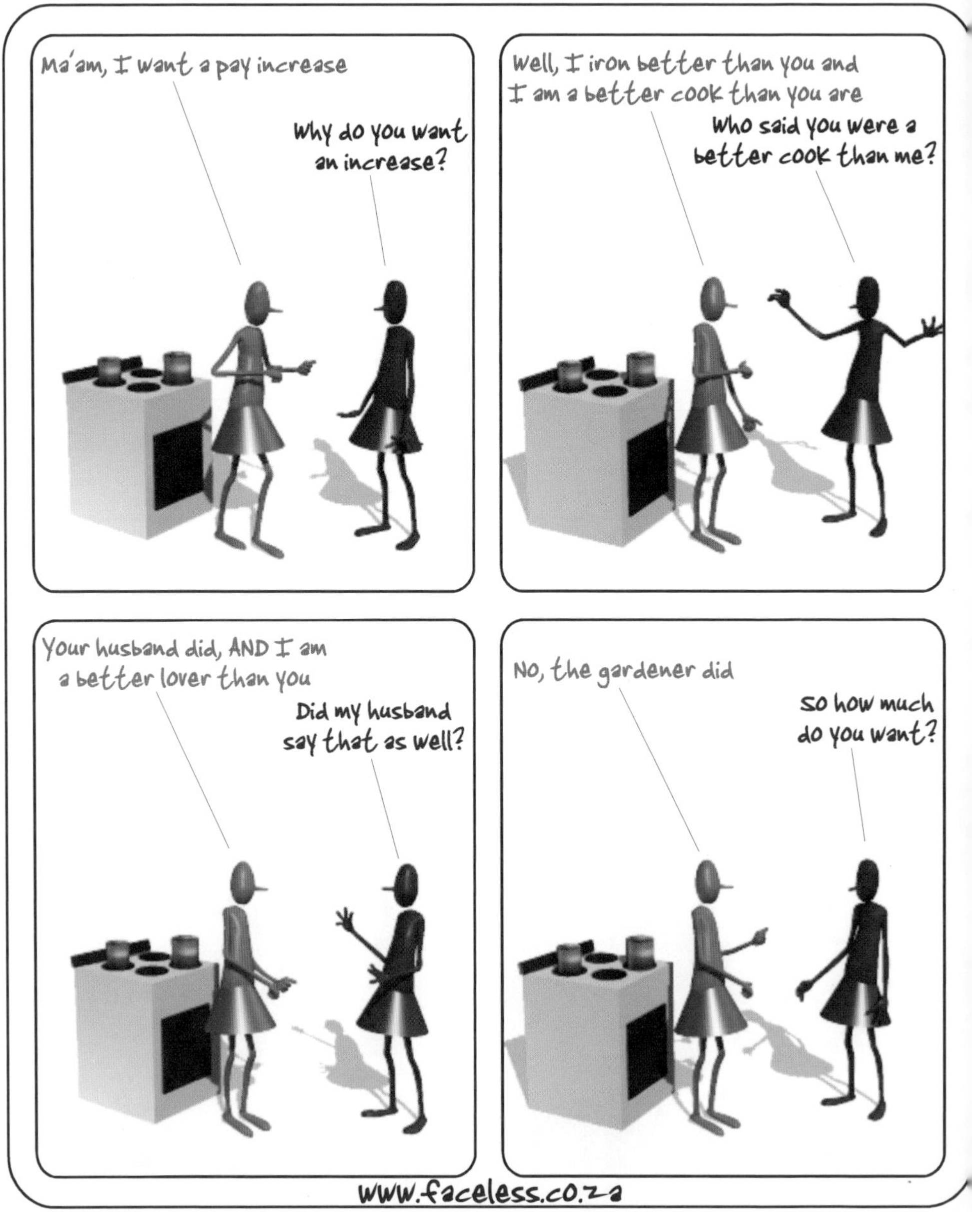
Ma'am, I want a pay increase
Why do you want an increase?
Well, I iron better than you and I am a better cook than you are
Who said you were a better cook than me?
Your husband did, AND I am a better lover than you
Did my husband say that as well?
No, the gardener did
So how much do you want?
www.faceless.co.za

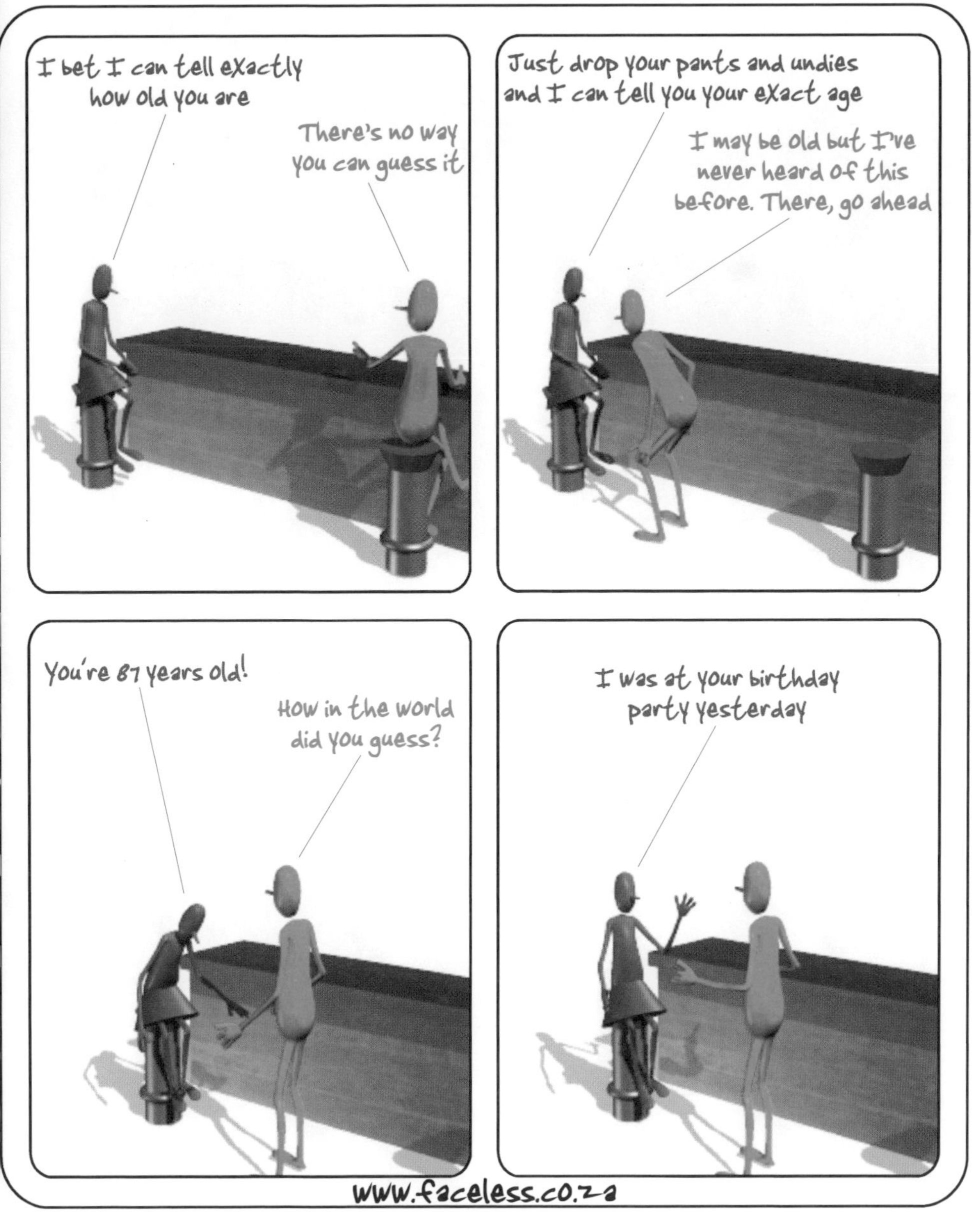
I bet I can tell exactly how old you are
There's no way you can guess it
Just drop your pants and undies and I can tell you your exact age
I may be old but I've never heard of this before. There, go ahead
You're 87 years old!
How in the world did you guess?
I was at your birthday party yesterday

www.faceless.co.za

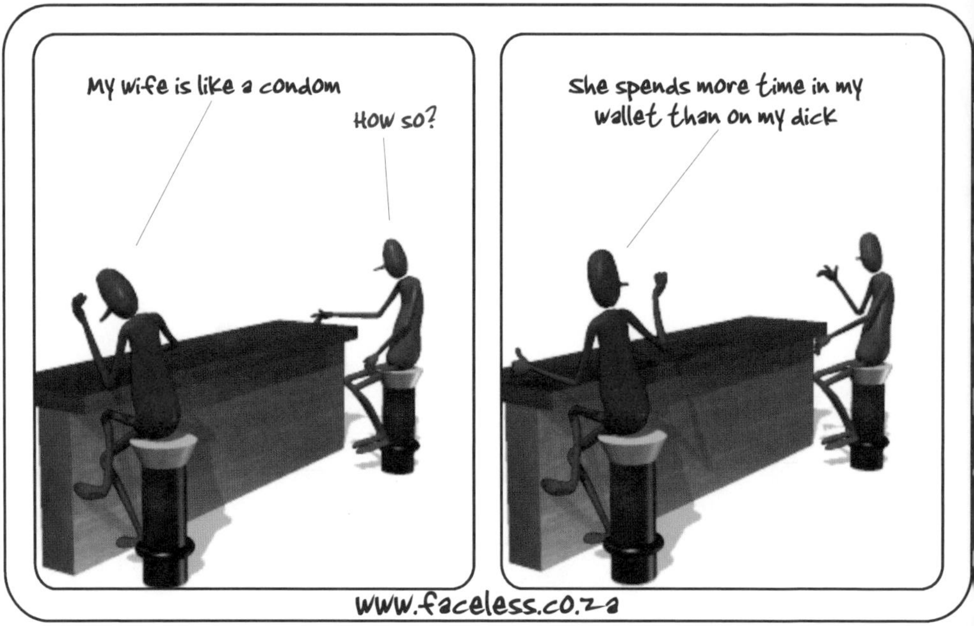
My wife is like a condom
How so?
She spends more time in my wallet than on my dick
www.faceless.co.za

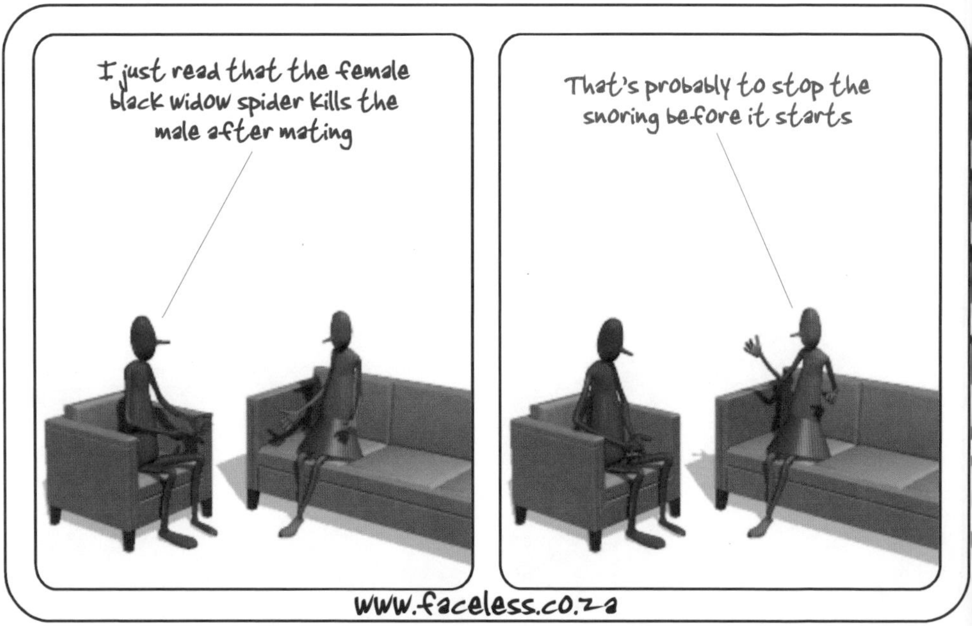
I just read that the female black widow spider kills the male after mating
That's probably to stop the snoring before it starts
www.faceless.co.za

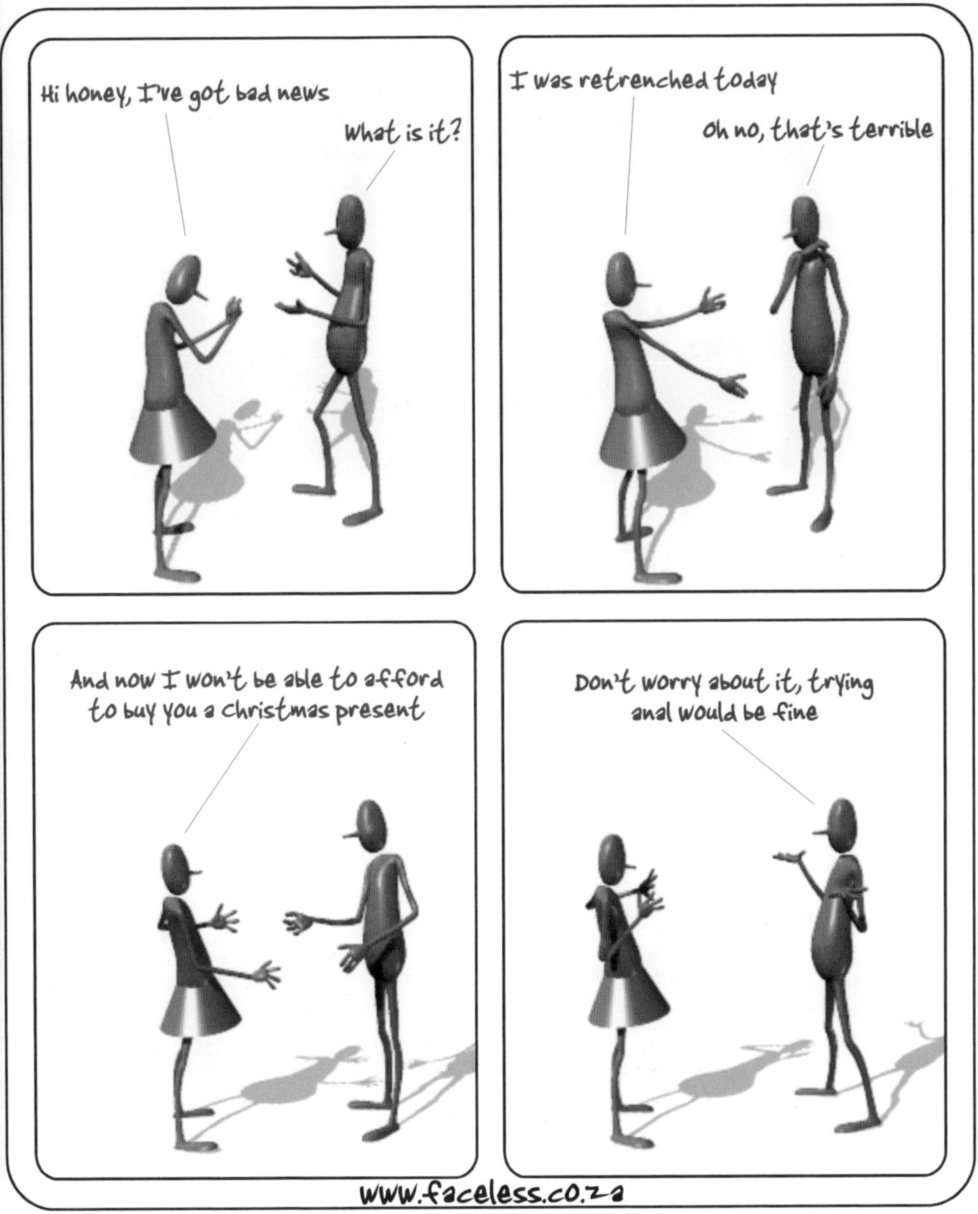
Hi honey, I've got bad news
What is it?
I was retrenched today
Oh no, that's terrible
And now I won't be able to afford to buy you a christmas present
Don't worry about it, trying anal would be fine
www.faceless.co.za

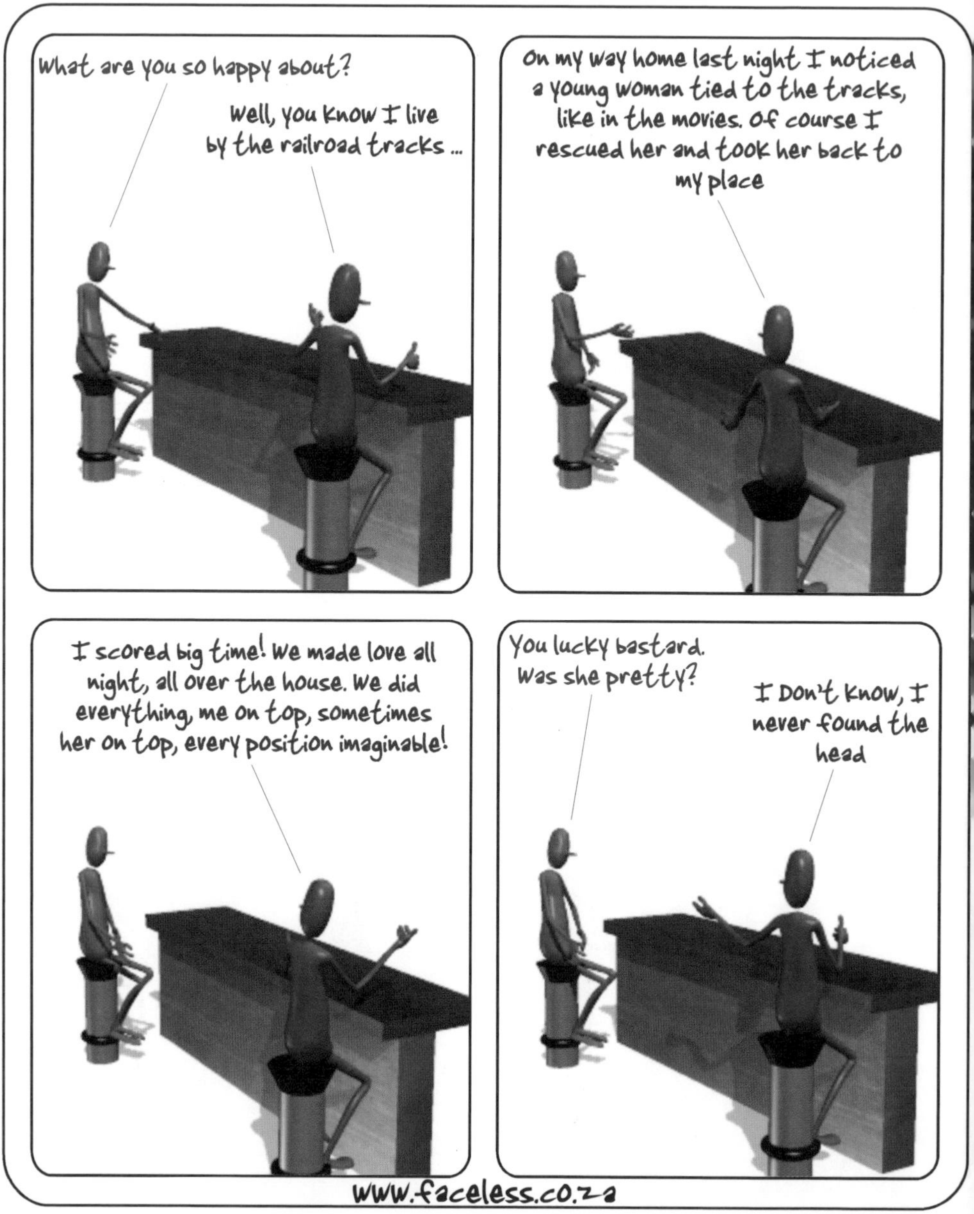
What are you so happy about?
Well, you know I live by the railroad tracks ...
On my way home last night I noticed a young woman tied to the tracks, like in the movies. Of course I rescued her and took her back to my place
I scored big time! We made love all night, all over the house. We did everything, me on top, sometimes her on top, every position imaginable!
You lucky bastard. Was she pretty?
I Don't know, I never found the head
www.faceless.co.za

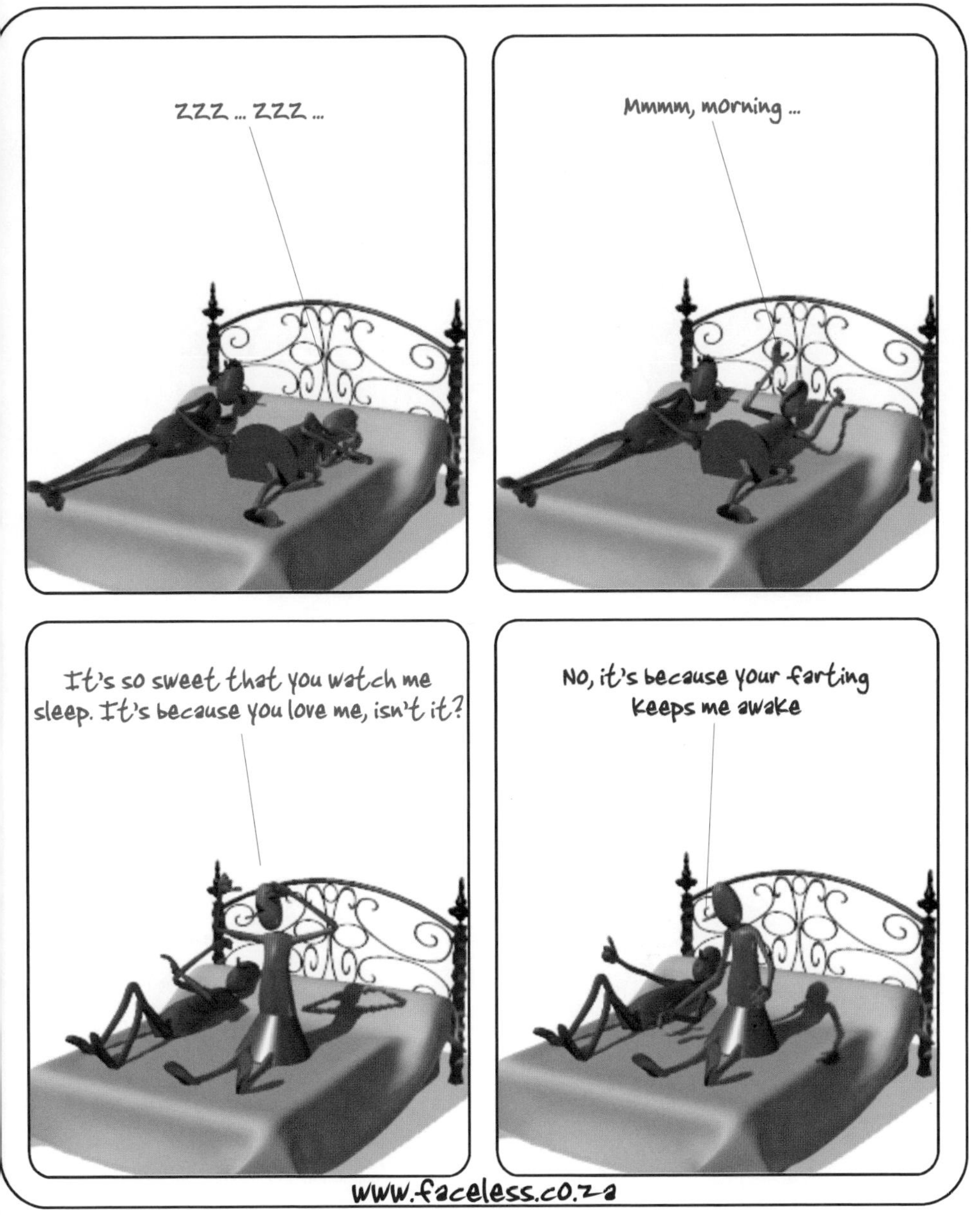
ZZZ ... ZZZ ...
Mmmm, morning ...
It's so sweet that you watch me sleep. It's because you love me, isn't it?
No, it's because your farting keeps me awake
www.faceless.co.za

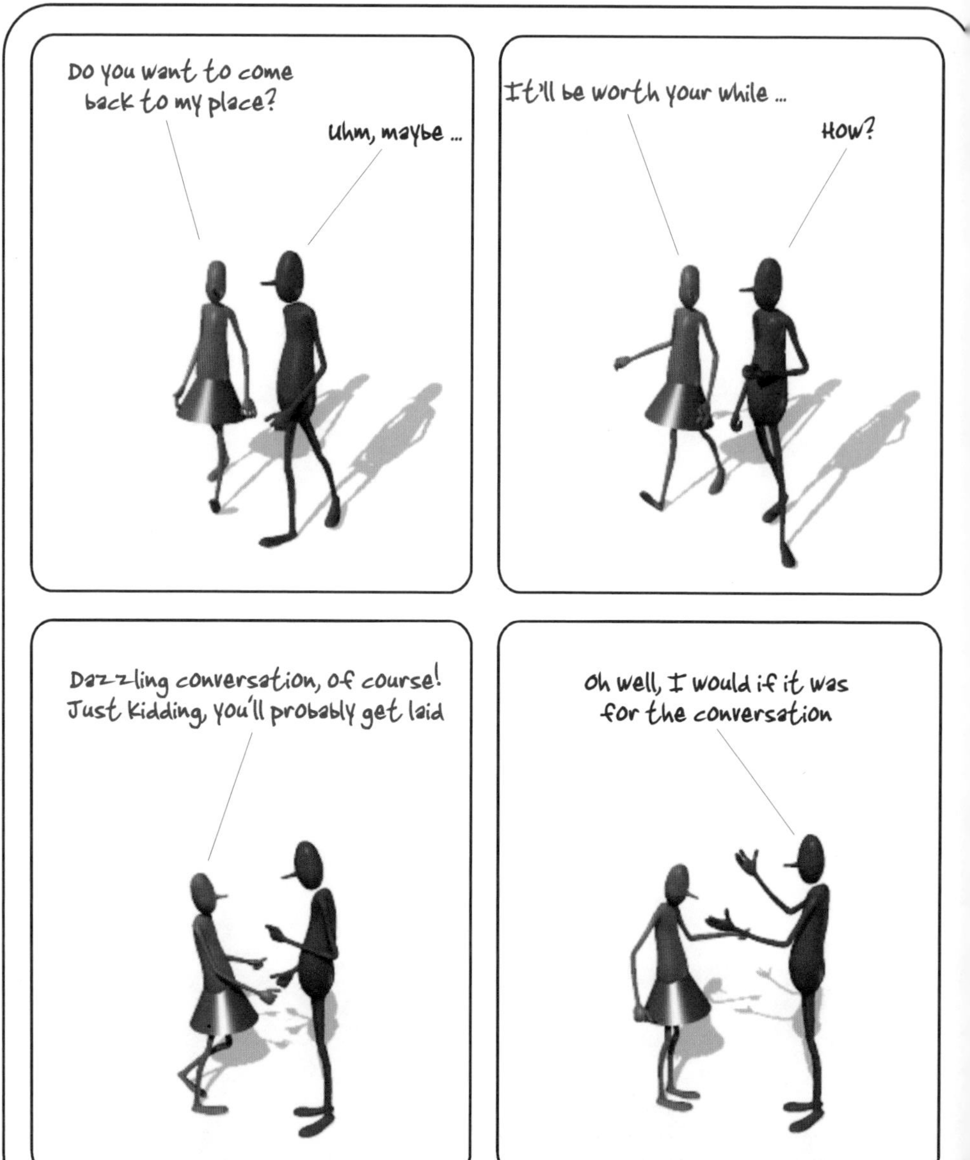
Do you want to come back to my place?
Uhm, maybe ...
It'll be worth your while ...
How?
Dazzling conversation, of course! Just kidding, you'll probably get laid
Oh well, I would if it was for the conversation
www.faceless.co.za

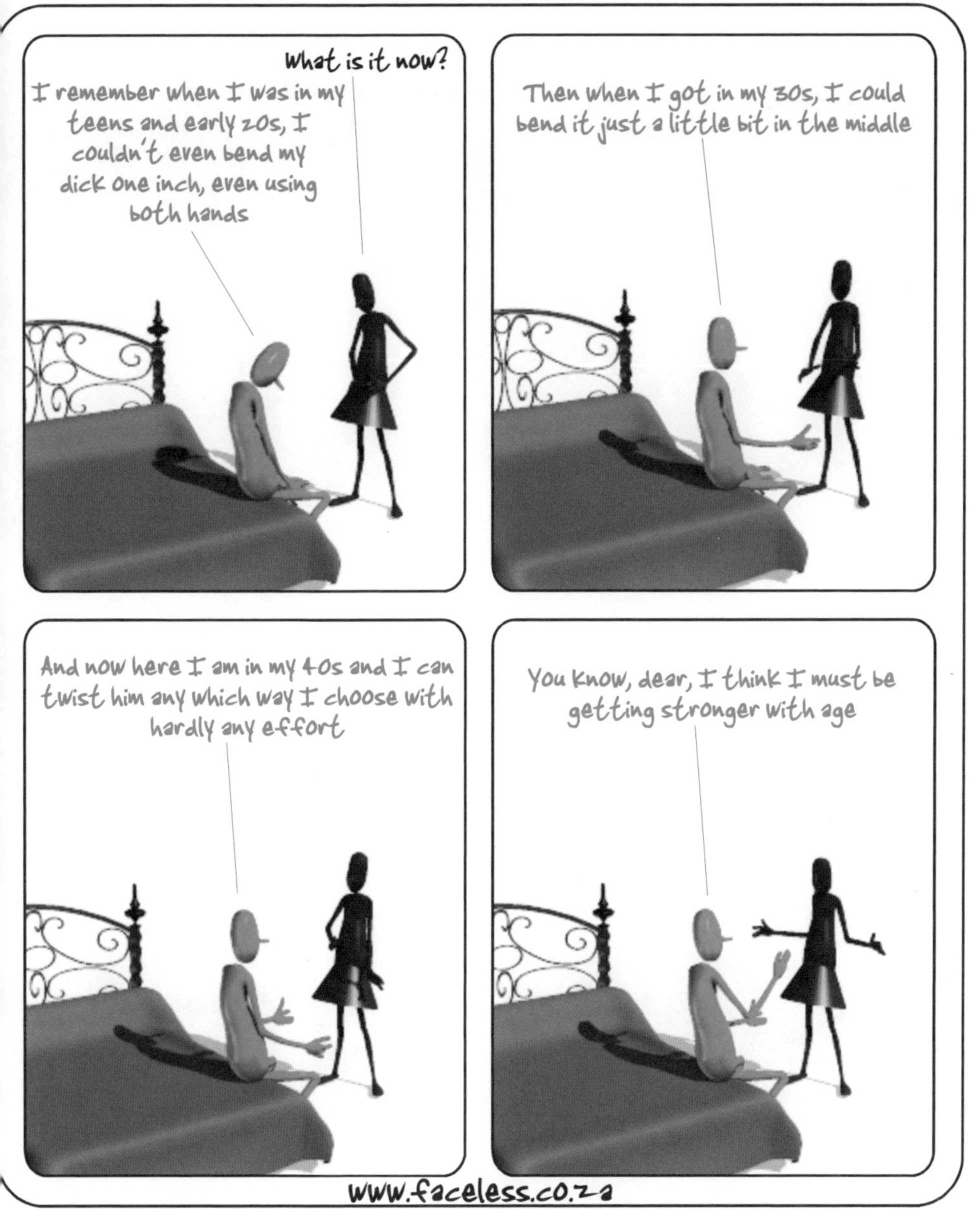
What is it now?
I remember when I was in my teens and early 20s, I couldn't even bend my dick one inch, even using both hands
Then when I got in my 30s, I could bend it just a little bit in the middle
And now here I am in my 40s and I can twist him any which way I choose with hardly any effort
You know, dear, I think I must be getting stronger with age
www.faceless.co.za

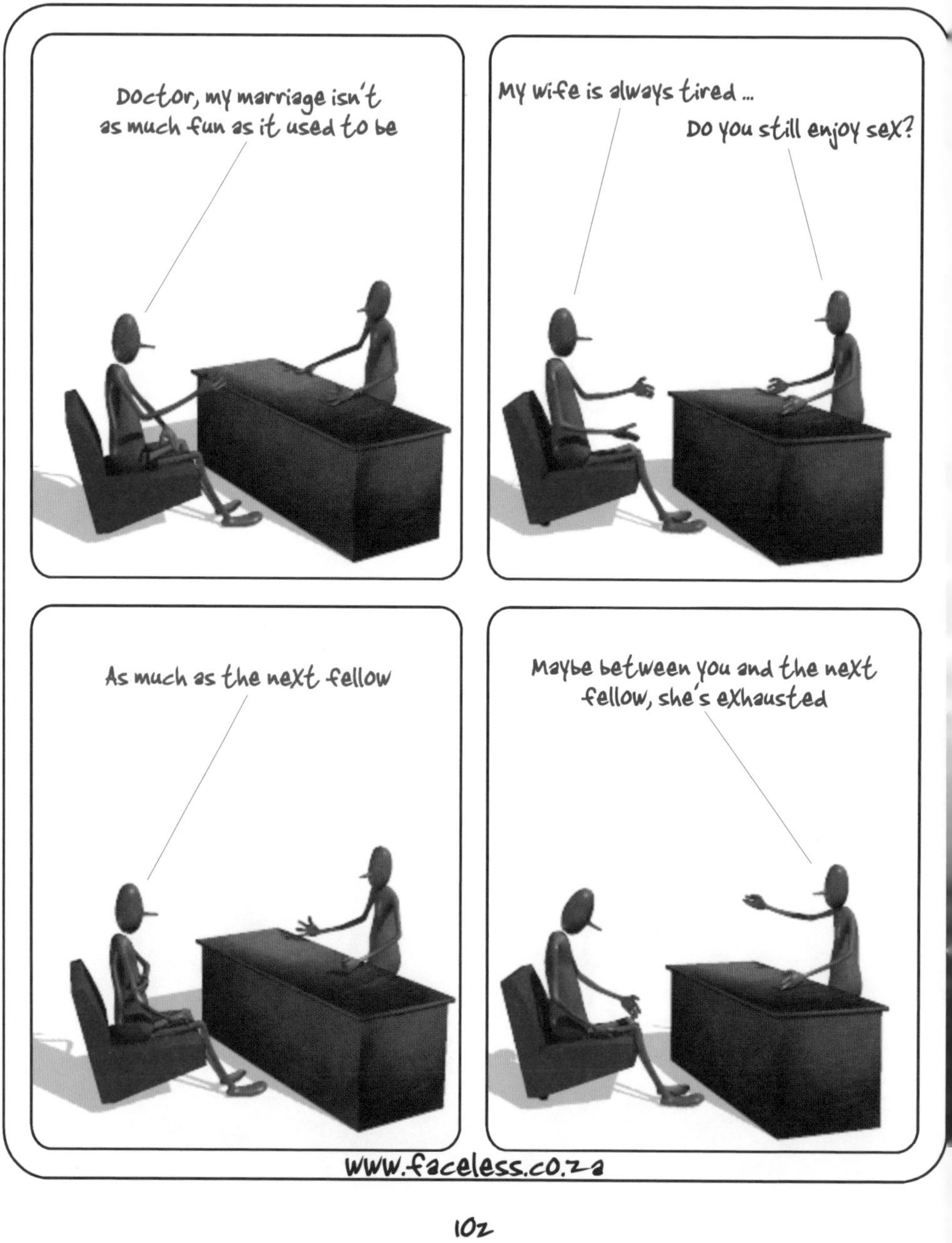
Doctor, my marriage isn't as much fun as it used to be
My wife is always tired ...
Do you still enjoy sex?
As much as the next fellow
Maybe between you and the next fellow, she's exhausted
www.faceless.co.za

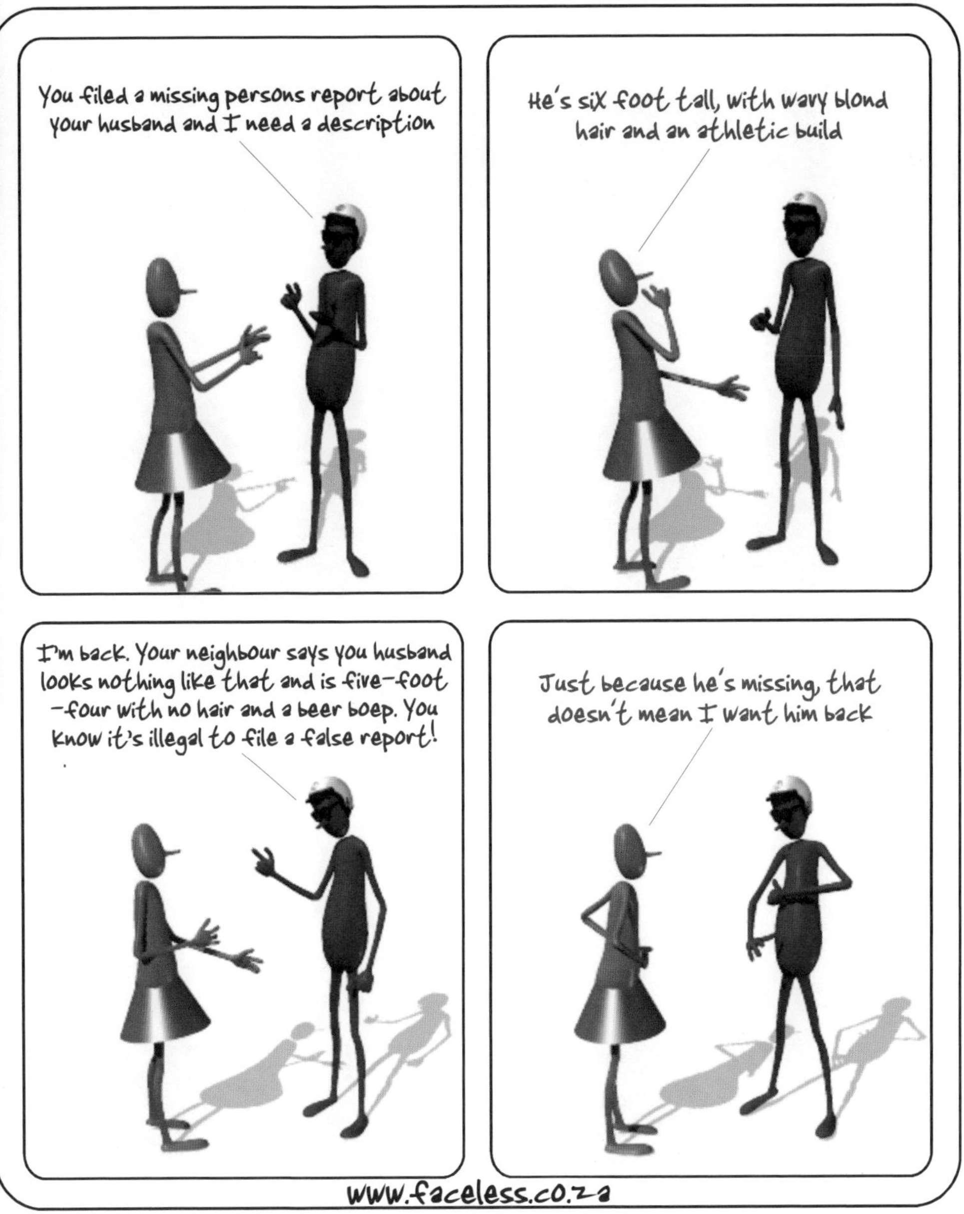
You filed a missing persons report about your husband and I need a description
He's six foot tall, with wavy blond hair and an athletic build
I'm back. Your neighbour says you husband looks nothing like that and is five-foot -four with no hair and a beer boep. You know it's illegal to file a false report!
Just because he's missing, that doesn't mean I want him back

www.faceless.co.za

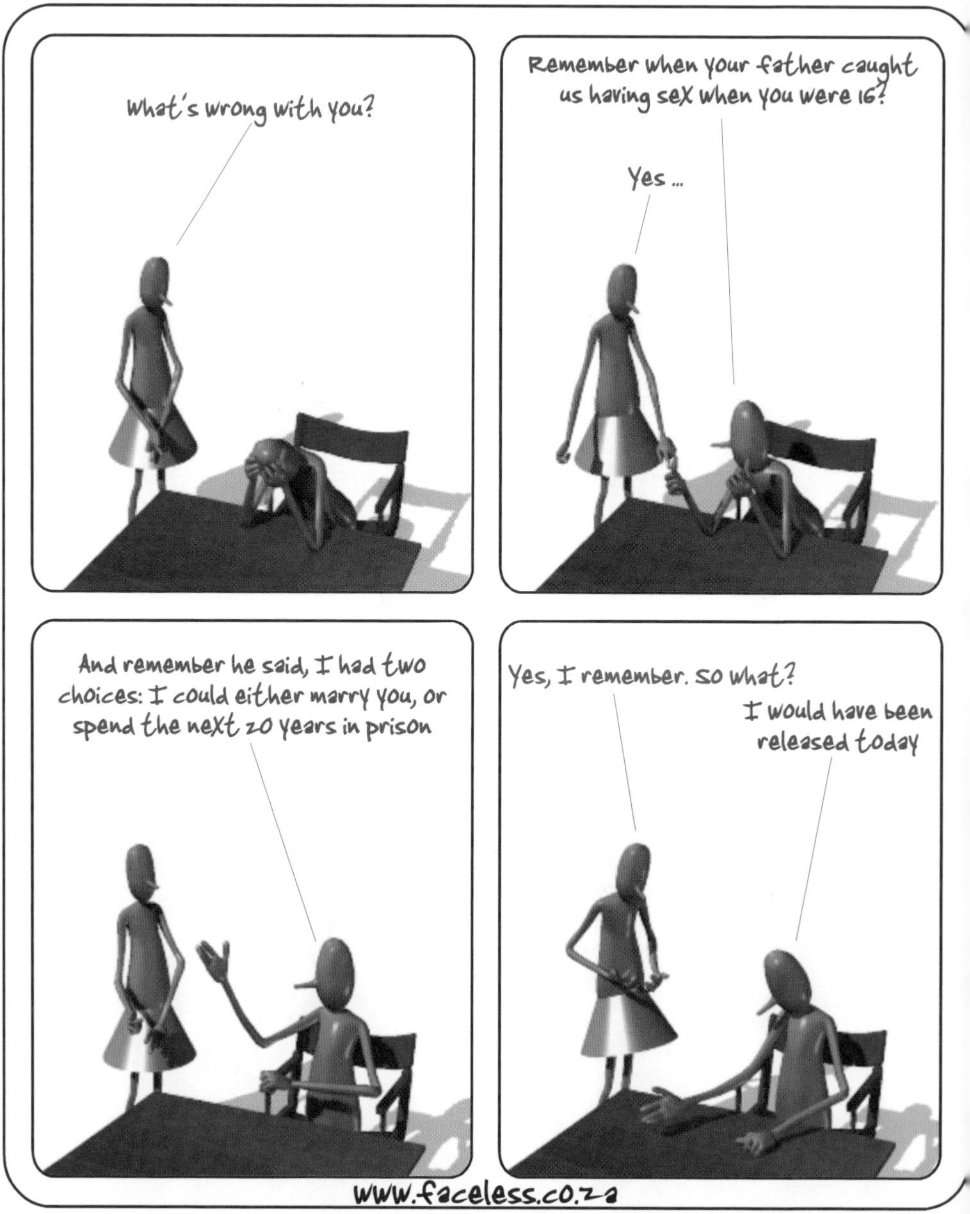
What's wrong with you?
Remember when your father caught us having sex when you were 16?
Yes ...
And remember he said, I had two choices: I could either marry you, or spend the next 20 years in prison
Yes, I remember. so what?
I would have been released today
www.faceless.co.za

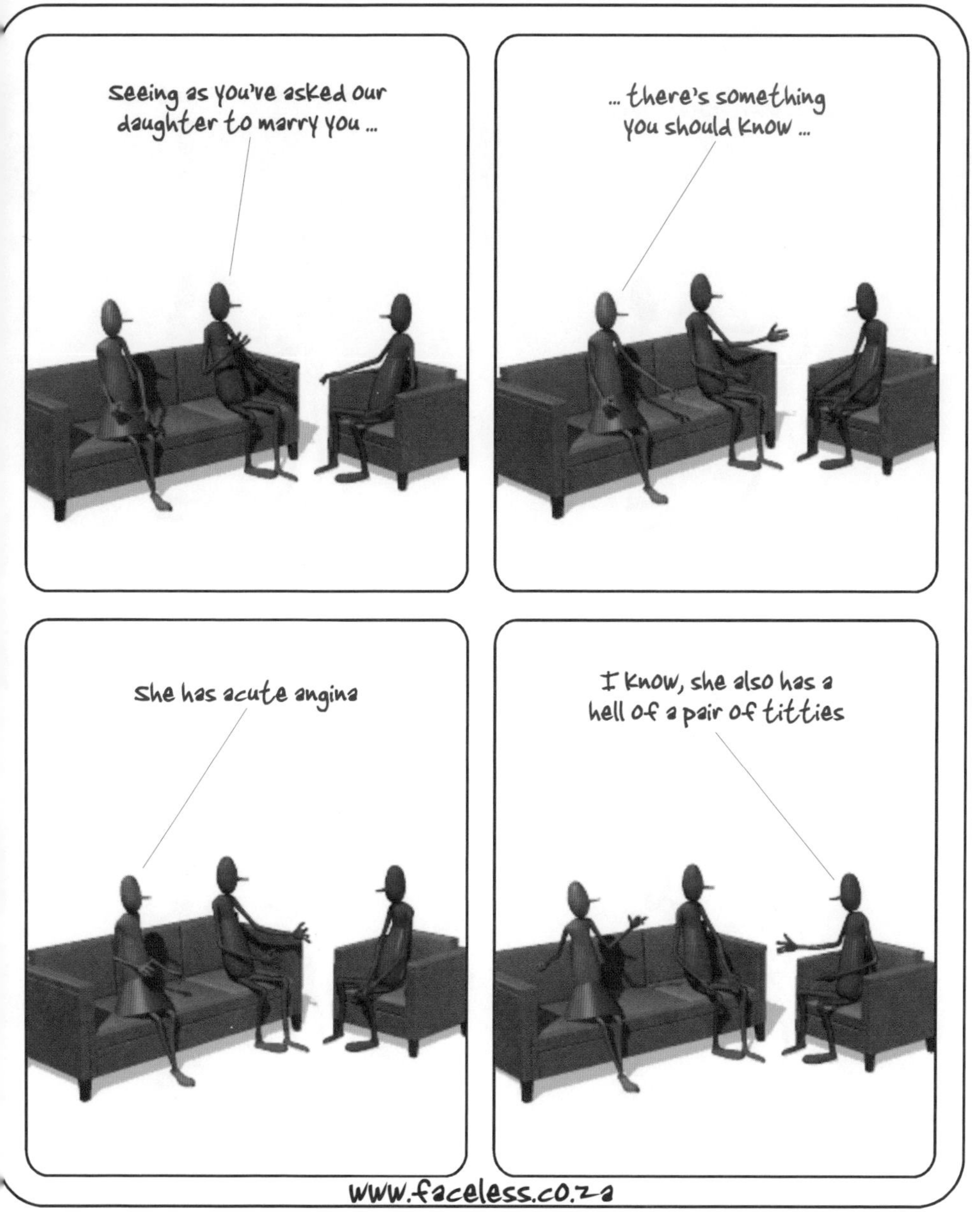
Seeing as you've asked our daughter to marry you ...
... there's something you should know ...
She has acute angina
I know, she also has a hell of a pair of titties
www.faceless.co.za

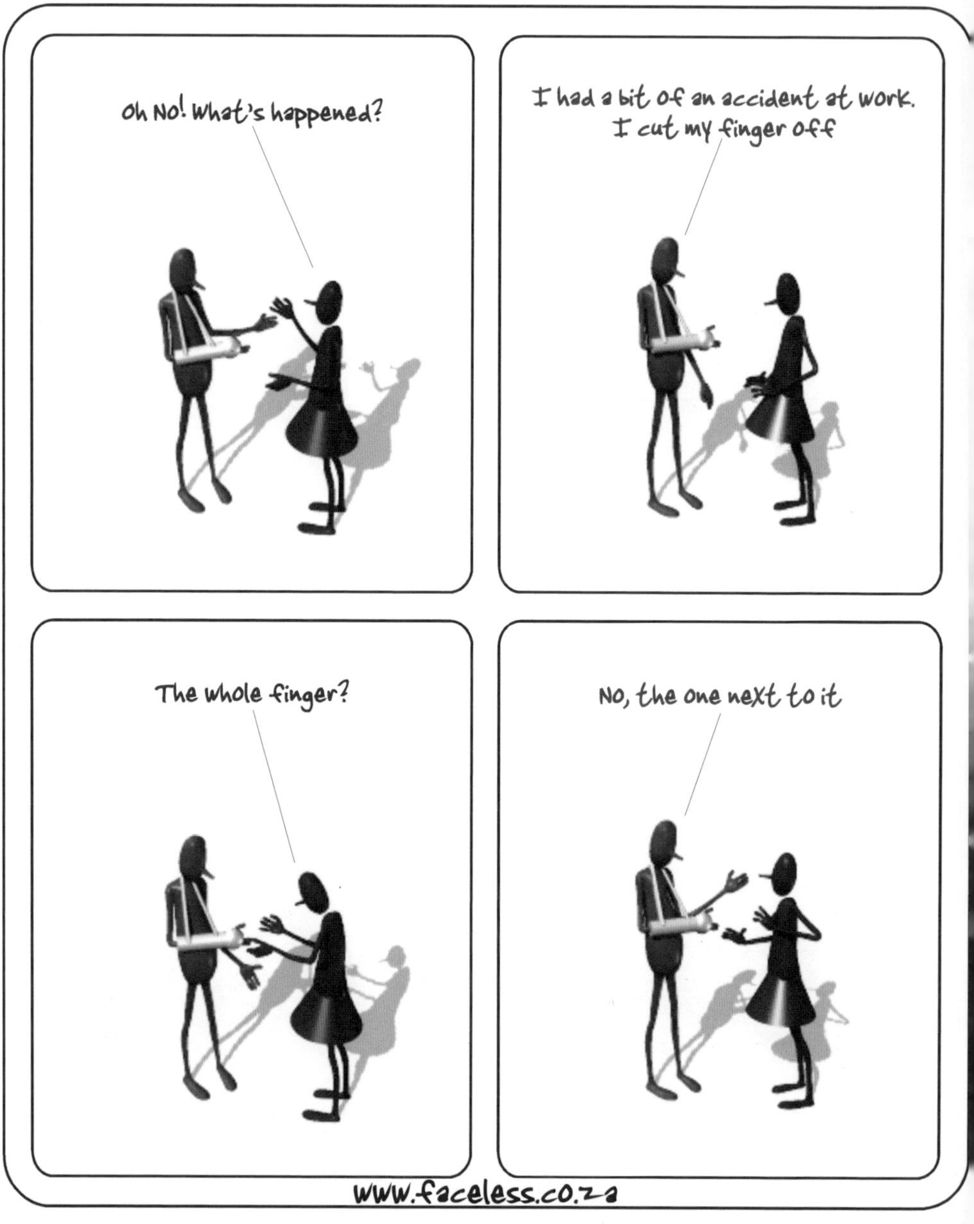
Oh No! What's happened?
I had a bit of an accident at work. I cut my finger off
The whole finger?
No, the one next to it

www.faceless.co.za

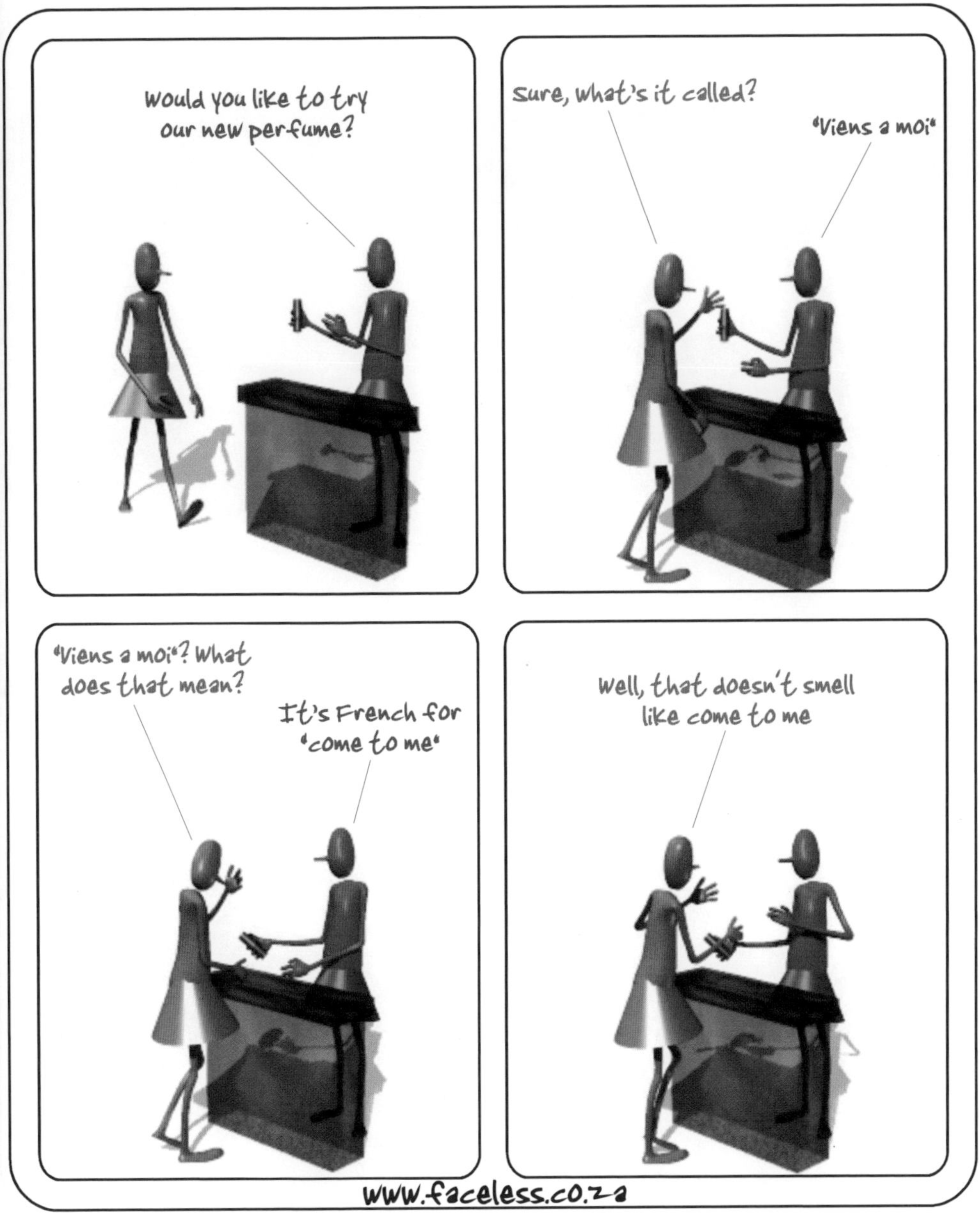
Would you like to try our new perfume?
Sure, what's it called?
"Viens a moi"
"Viens a moi"? What does that mean?
It's French for "come to me"
Well, that doesn't smell like come to me
www.faceless.co.za

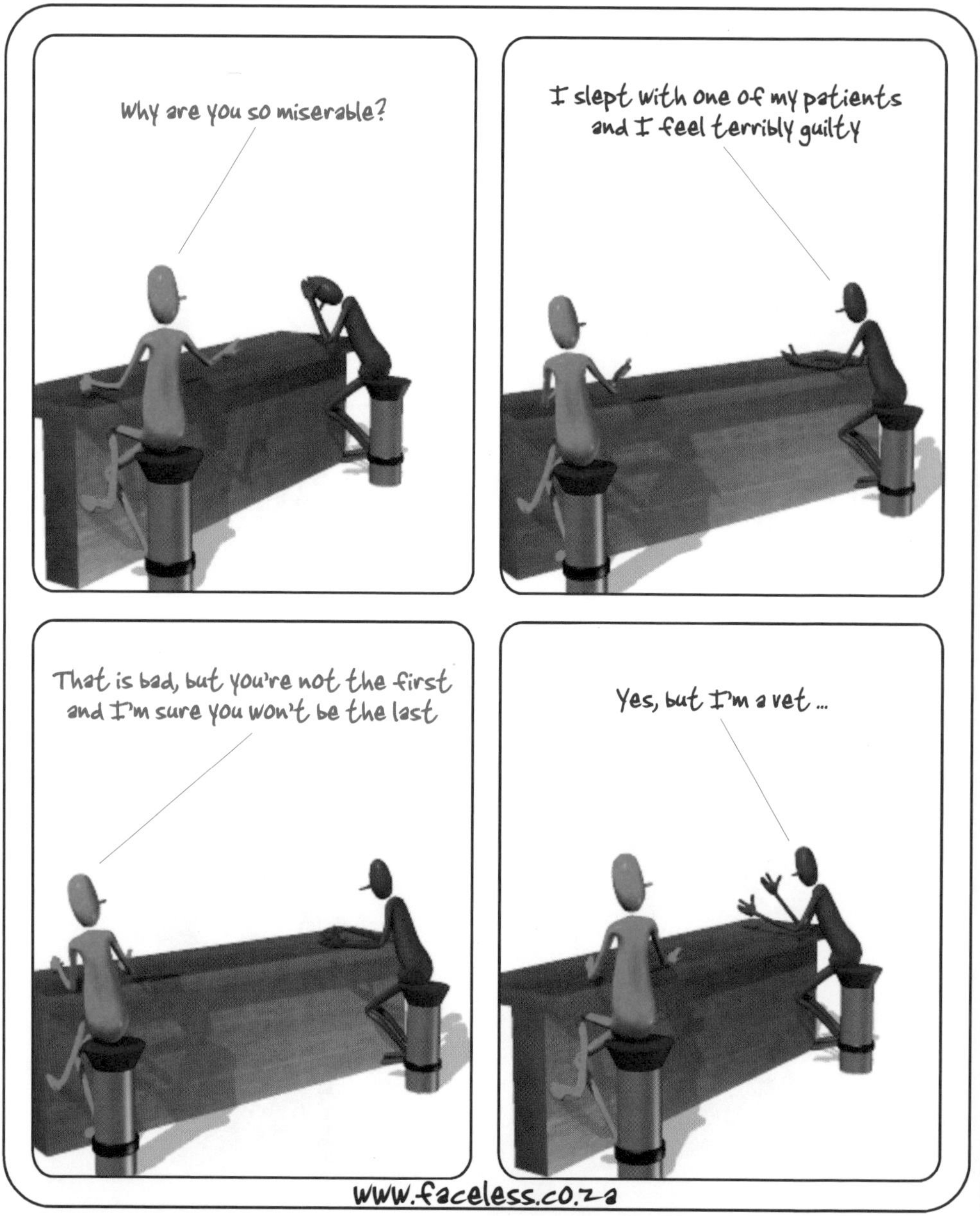
Why are you so miserable?
I slept with one of my patients and I feel terribly guilty
That is bad, but you're not the first and I'm sure you won't be the last
Yes, but I'm a vet ...
www.faceless.co.za

Just put a deposit down on a brand new Porsche and mentioned it on Facebook
What did you say?
I said, "I can't wait for the new 911 to arrive!"
Next thing I know, 4000 Muslims have added me as a friend
www.faceless.co.za

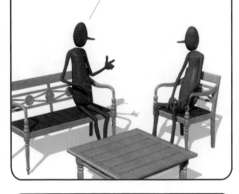

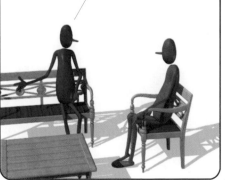

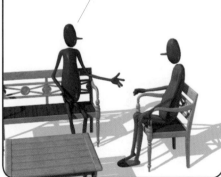

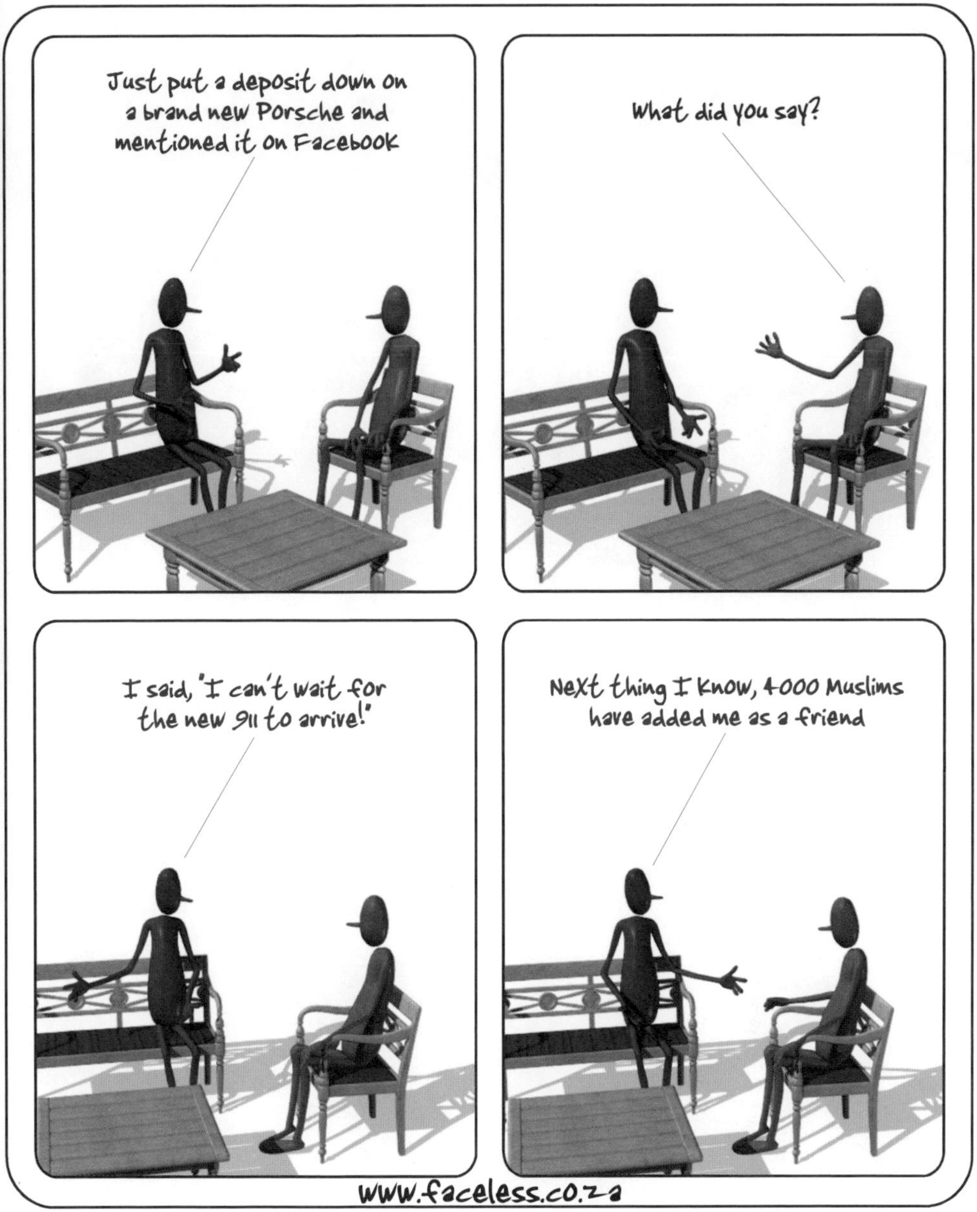

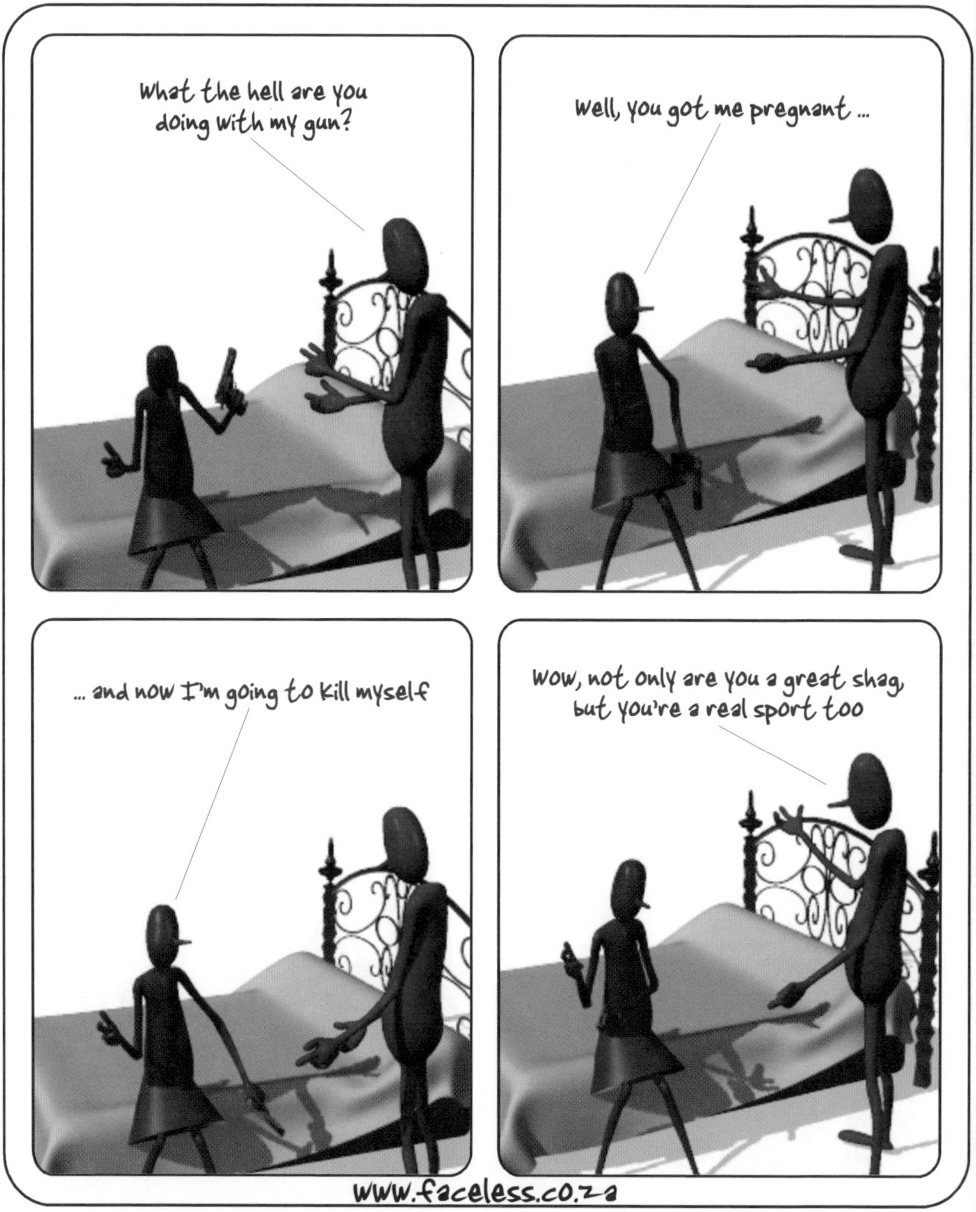
What the hell are you doing with my gun?
Well, you got me pregnant ...
... and now I'm going to kill myself
Wow, not only are you a great shag, but you're a real sport too
www.faceless.co.za

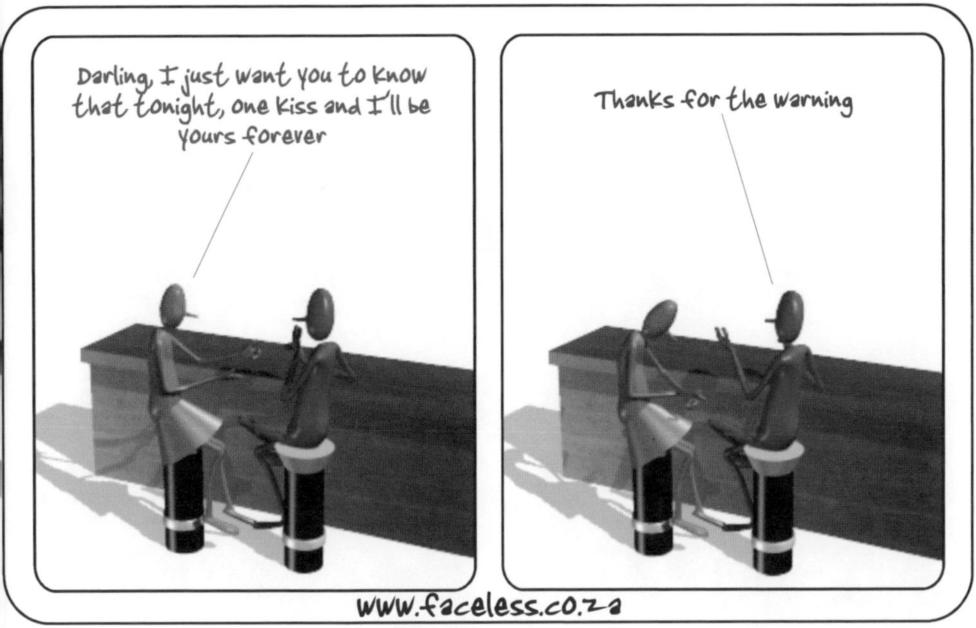
Darling, I just want you to know that tonight, one kiss and I'll be yours forever
Thanks for the warning
www.faceless.co.za

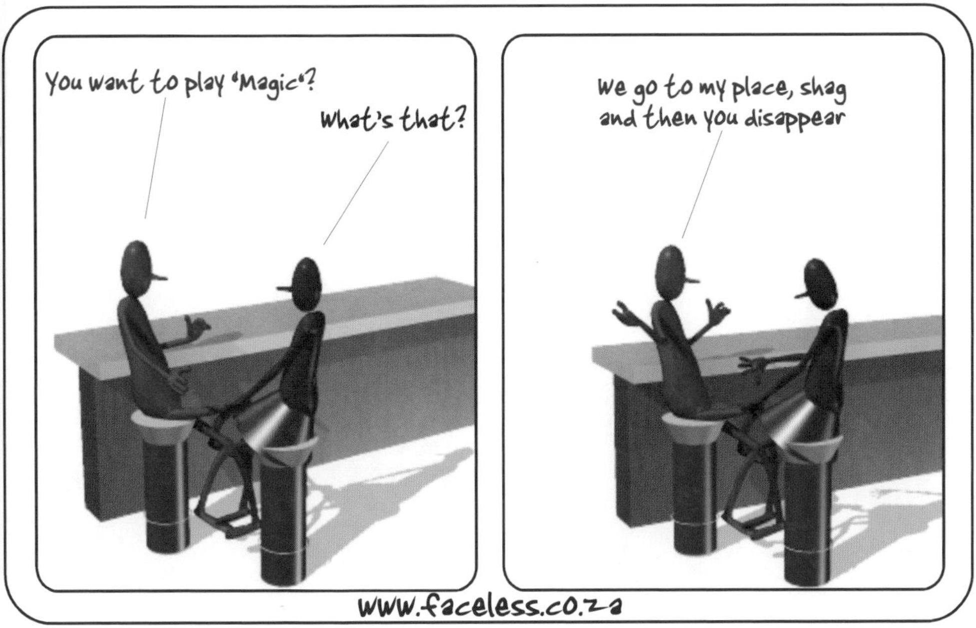
You want to play "Magic"?
What's that?
We go to my place, shag and then you disappear
www.faceless.co.za

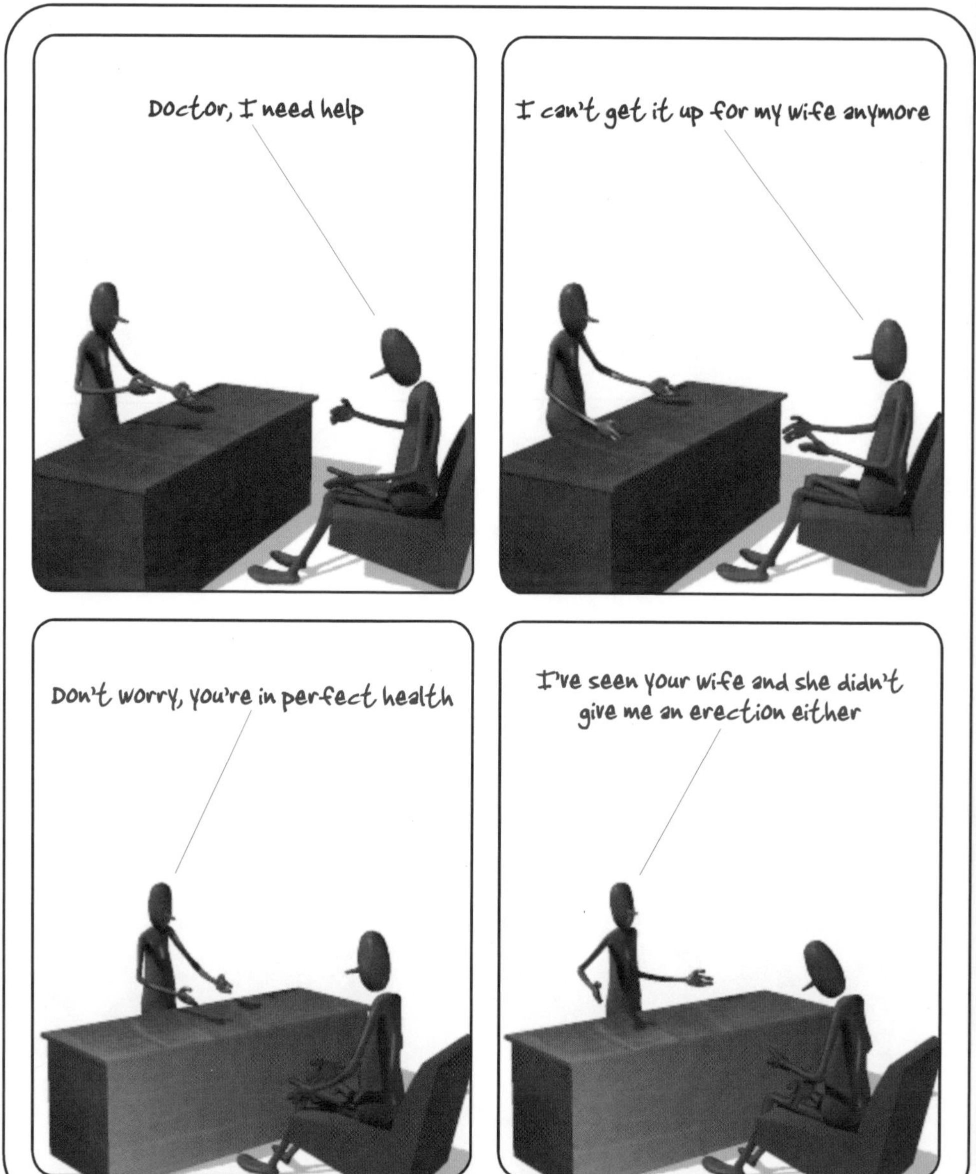
Doctor, I need help
I can't get it up for my wife anymore
Don't worry, you're in perfect health
I've seen your wife and she didn't give me an erection either
www.faceless.co.za

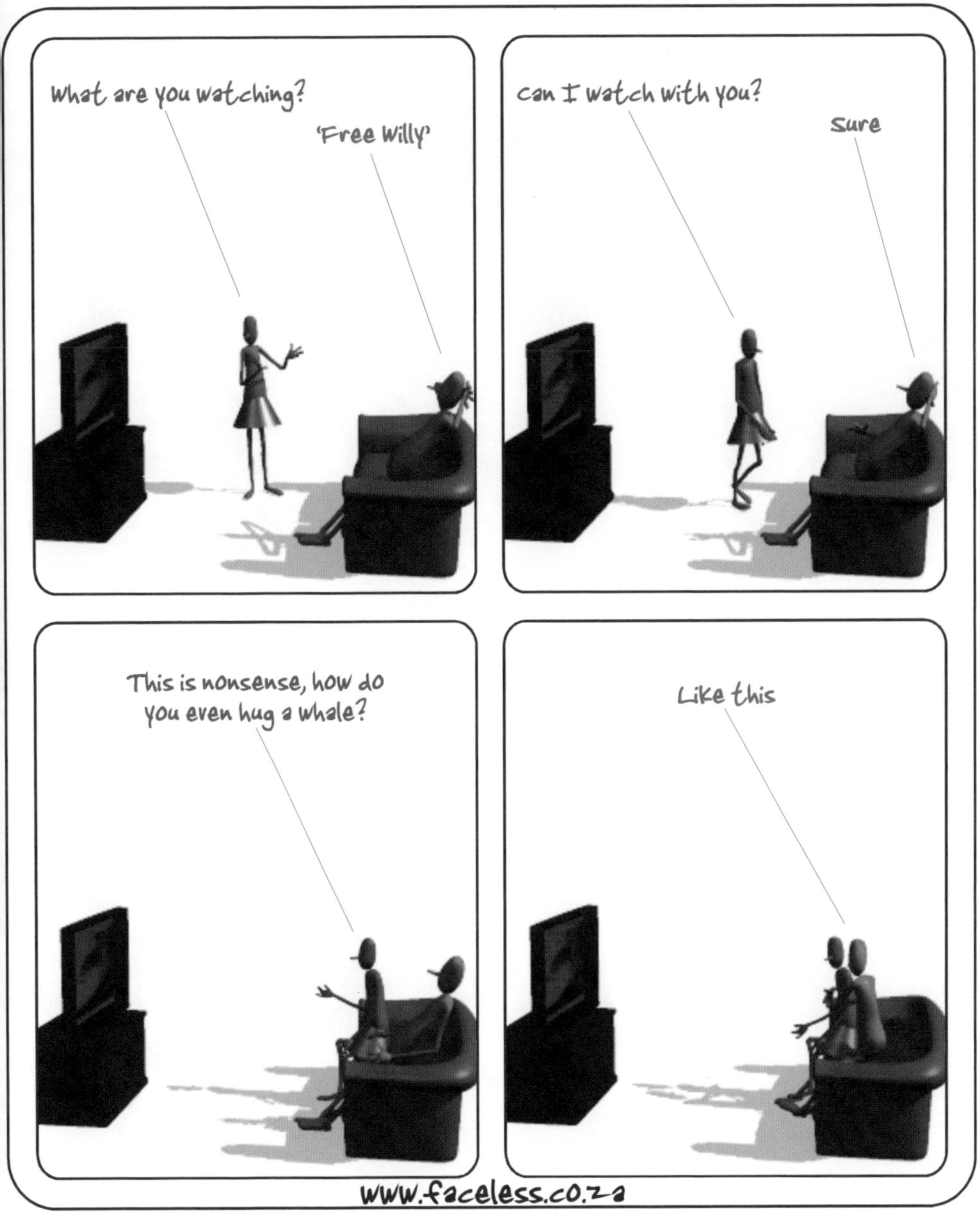
What are you watching?
'Free Willy'
Can I watch with you?
Sure
This is nonsense, how do you even hug a whale?
Like this
www.faceless.co.za

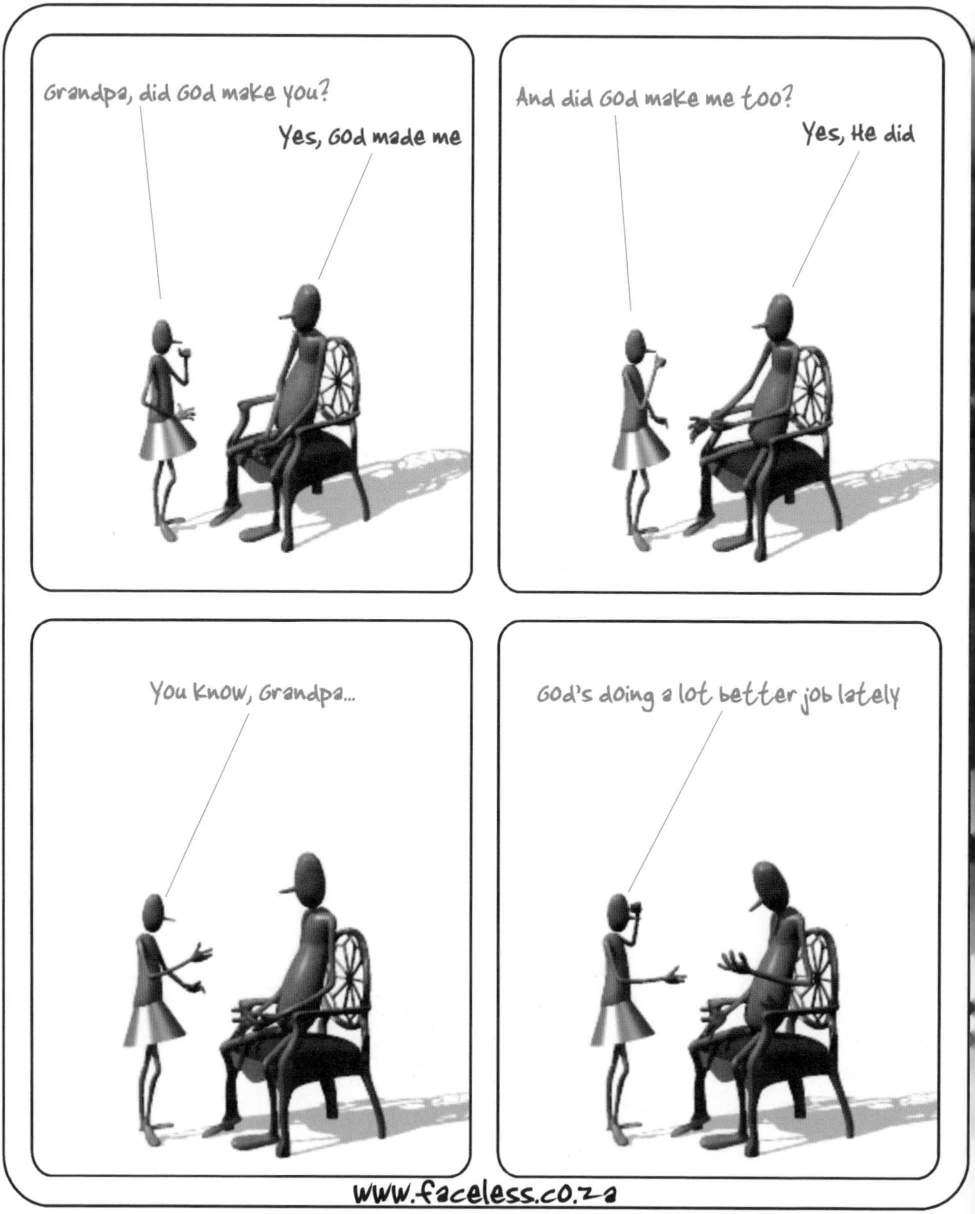
Grandpa, did God make you?
Yes, God made me
And did God make me too?
Yes, He did
You know, Grandpa...
God's doing a lot better job lately
www.faceless.co.za

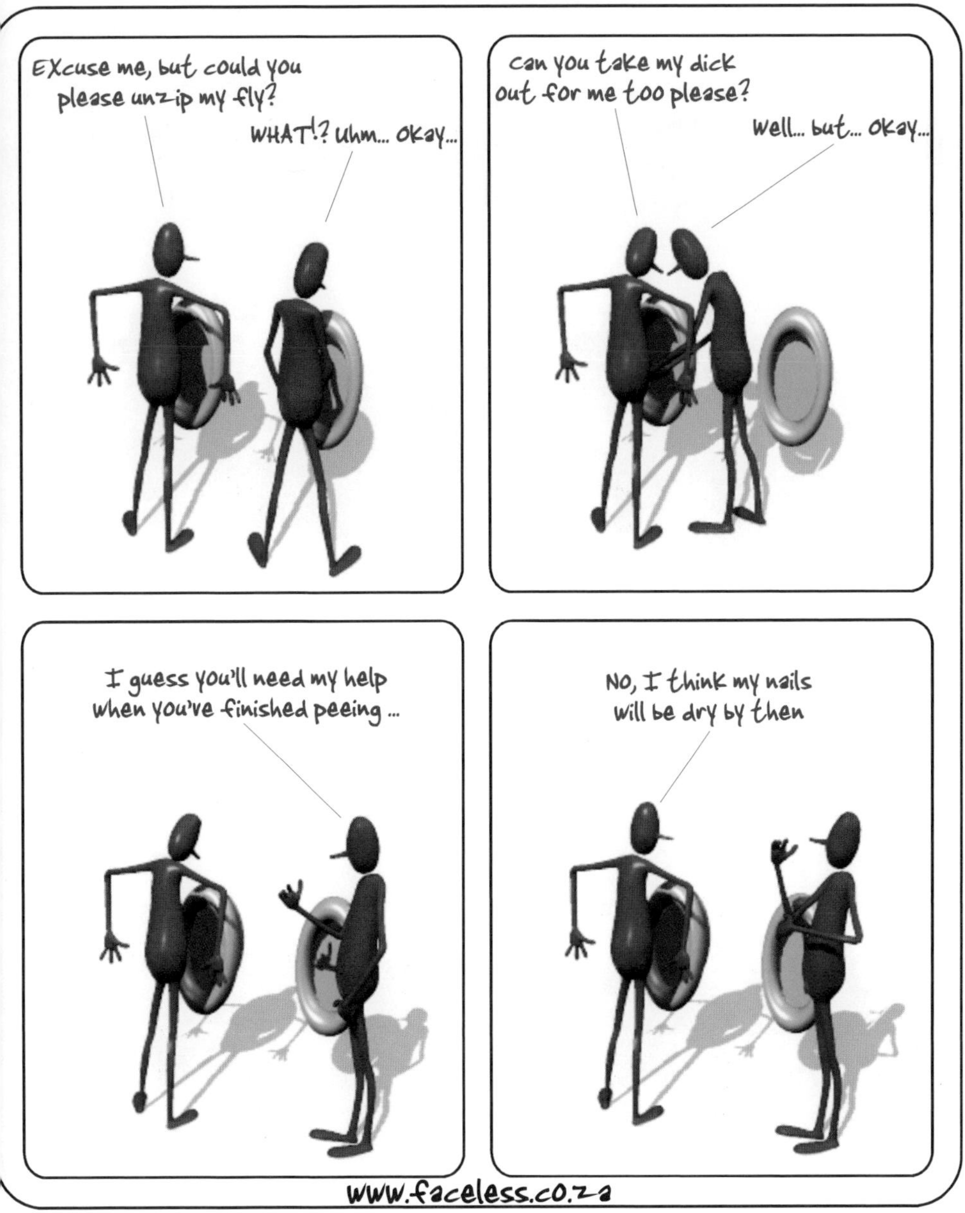
EXcuse me, but could you please unzip my fly?
WHAT!? uhm... okay...
can you take my dick out for me too please?
Well... but... okay...
I guess you'll need my help when you've finished peeing ...
No, I think my nails will be dry by then
www.faceless.co.za

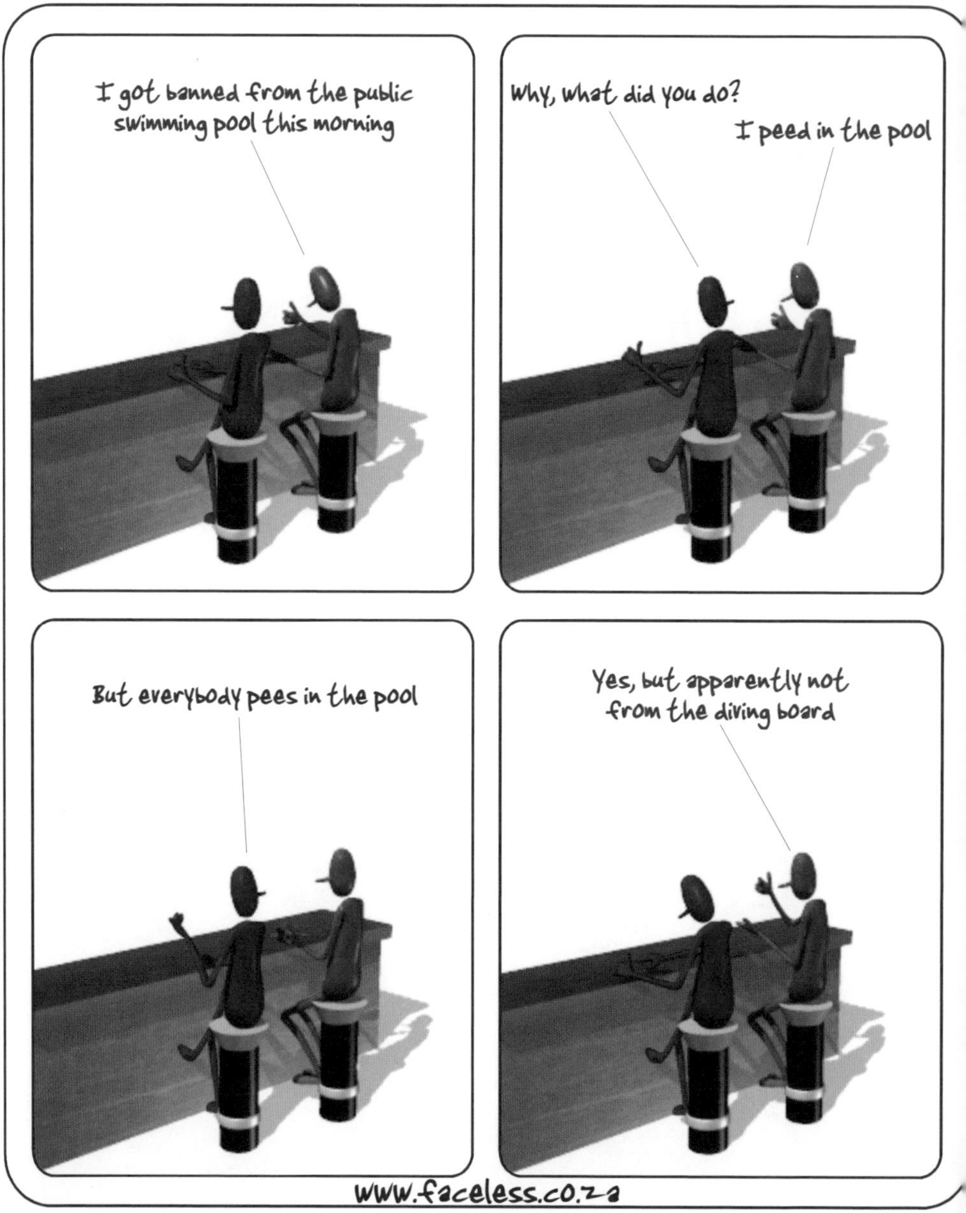
I got banned from the public swimming pool this morning
Why, what did you do?
I peed in the pool
But everybody pees in the pool
Yes, but apparently not from the diving board

www.faceless.co.za

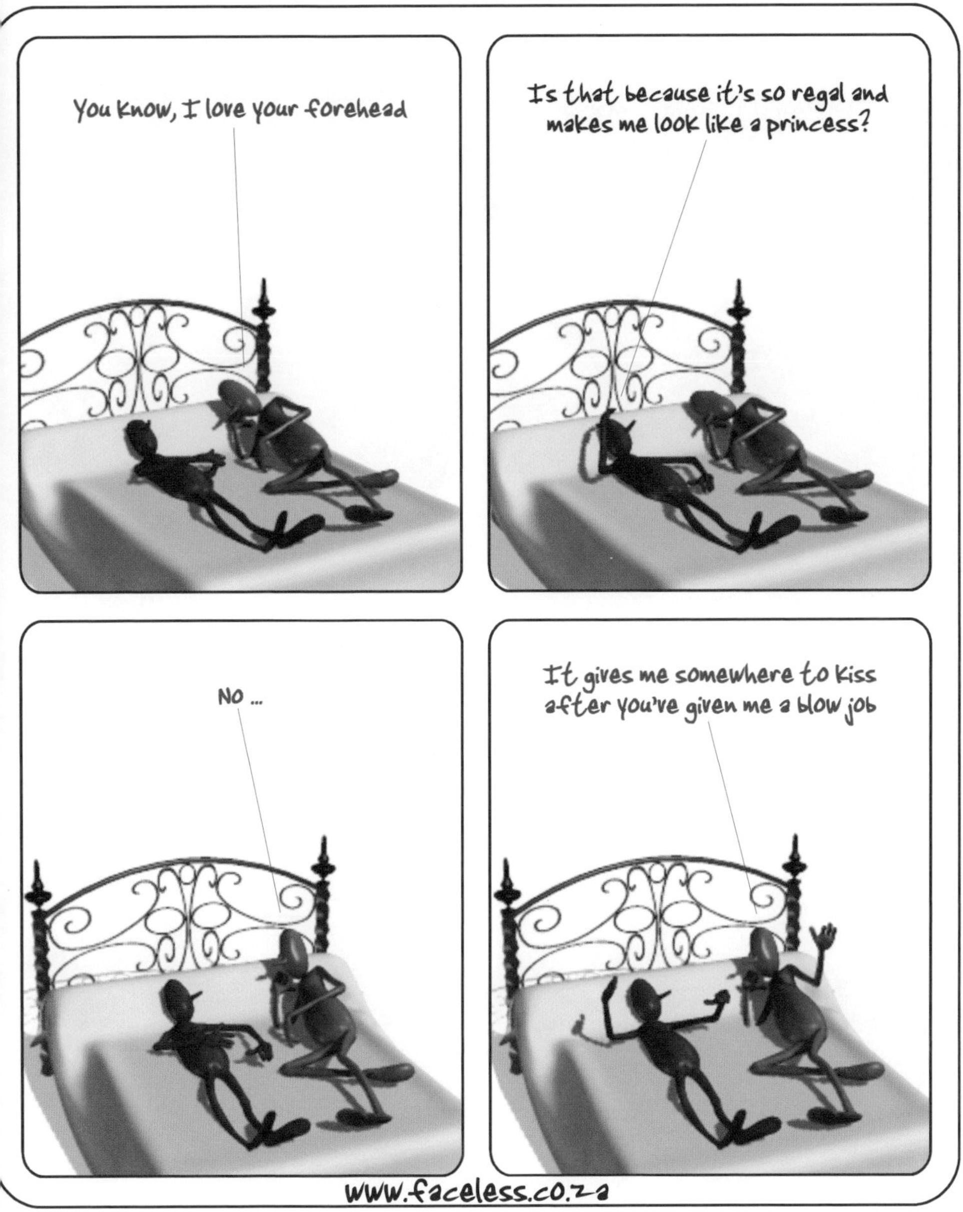
You know, I love your forehead
Is that because it's so regal and makes me look like a princess?
No ...
It gives me somewhere to kiss after you've given me a blow job
www.faceless.co.za

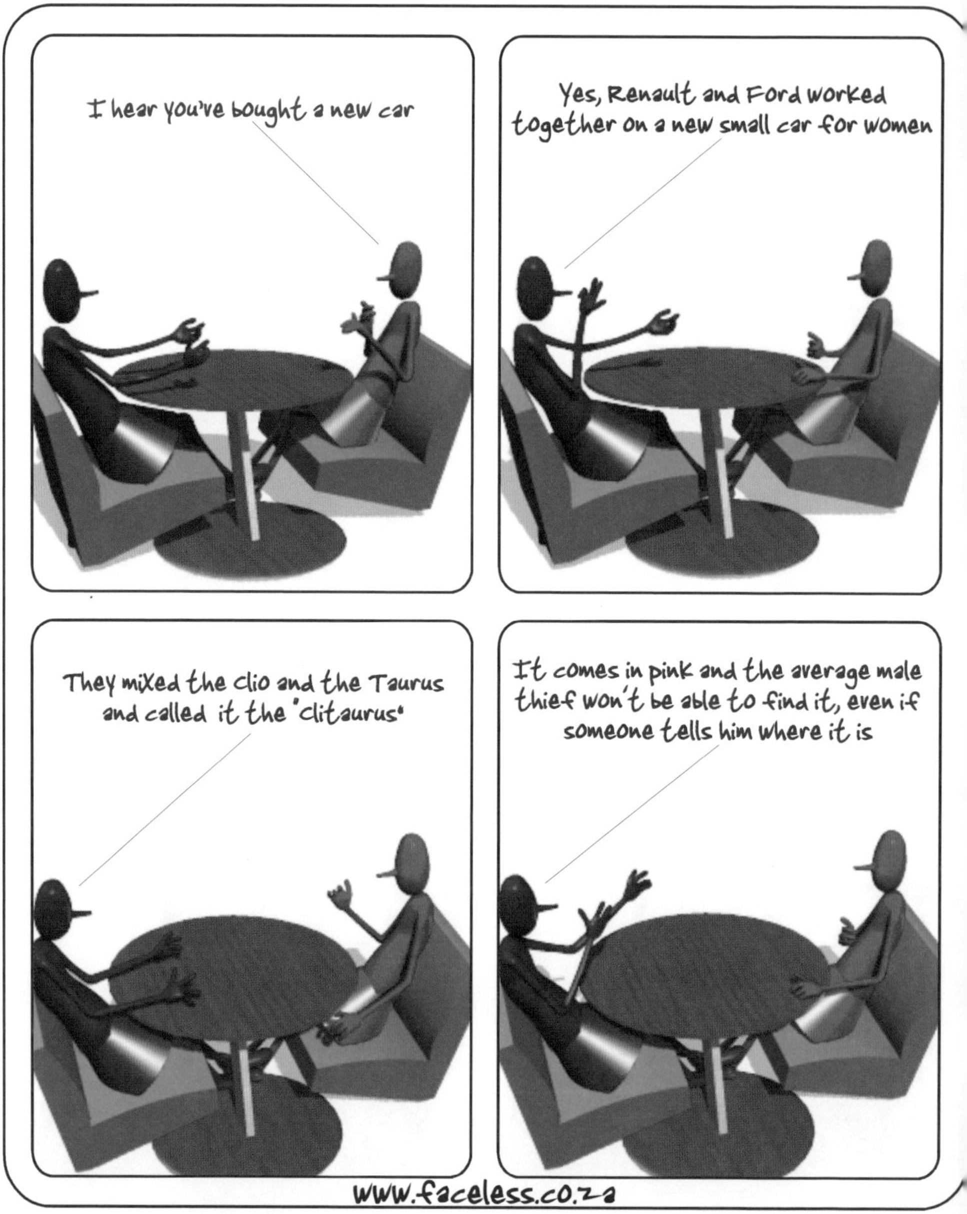
I hear you've bought a new car
Yes, Renault and Ford worked together on a new small car for women
They mixed the clio and the Taurus and called it the "clitaurus"
It comes in pink and the average male thief won't be able to find it, even if someone tells him where it is
www.faceless.co.za

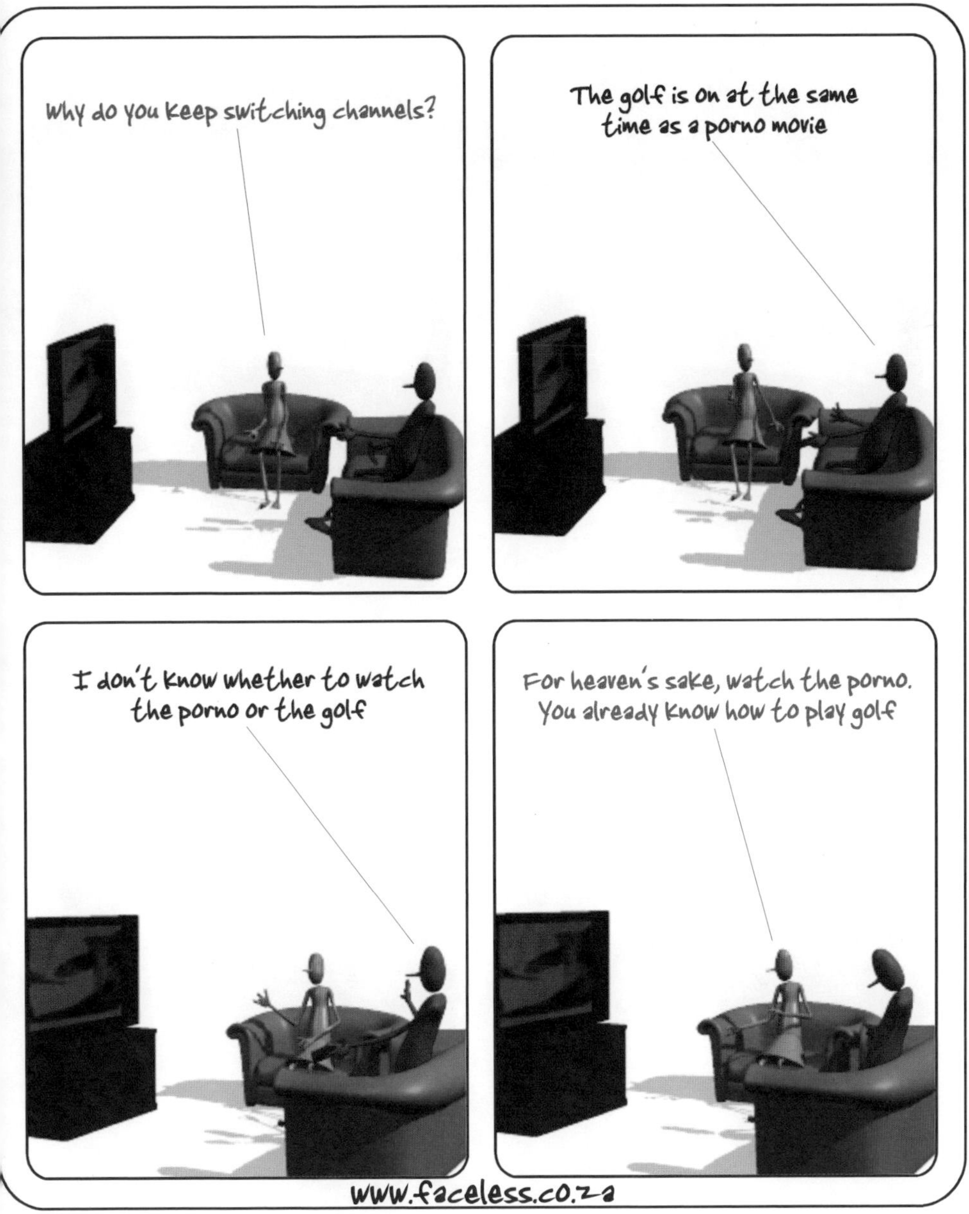
Why do you keep switching channels?
The golf is on at the same time as a porno movie
I don't know whether to watch the porno or the golf
For heaven's sake, watch the porno. You already know how to play golf
www.faceless.co.za

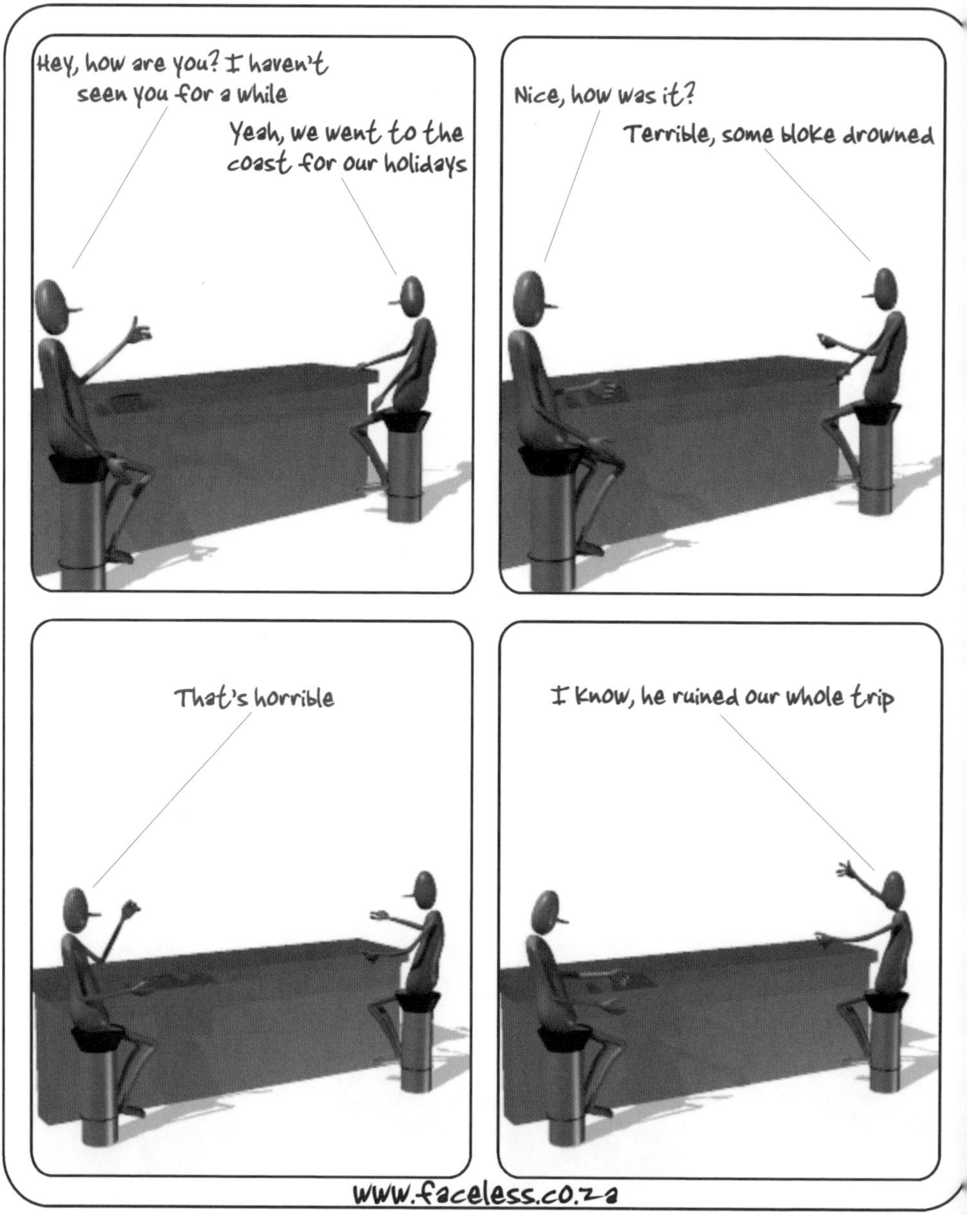
Hey, how are you? I haven't seen you for a while
Yeah, we went to the coast for our holidays
Nice, how was it?
Terrible, some bloke drowned
That's horrible
I know, he ruined our whole trip
www.faceless.co.za

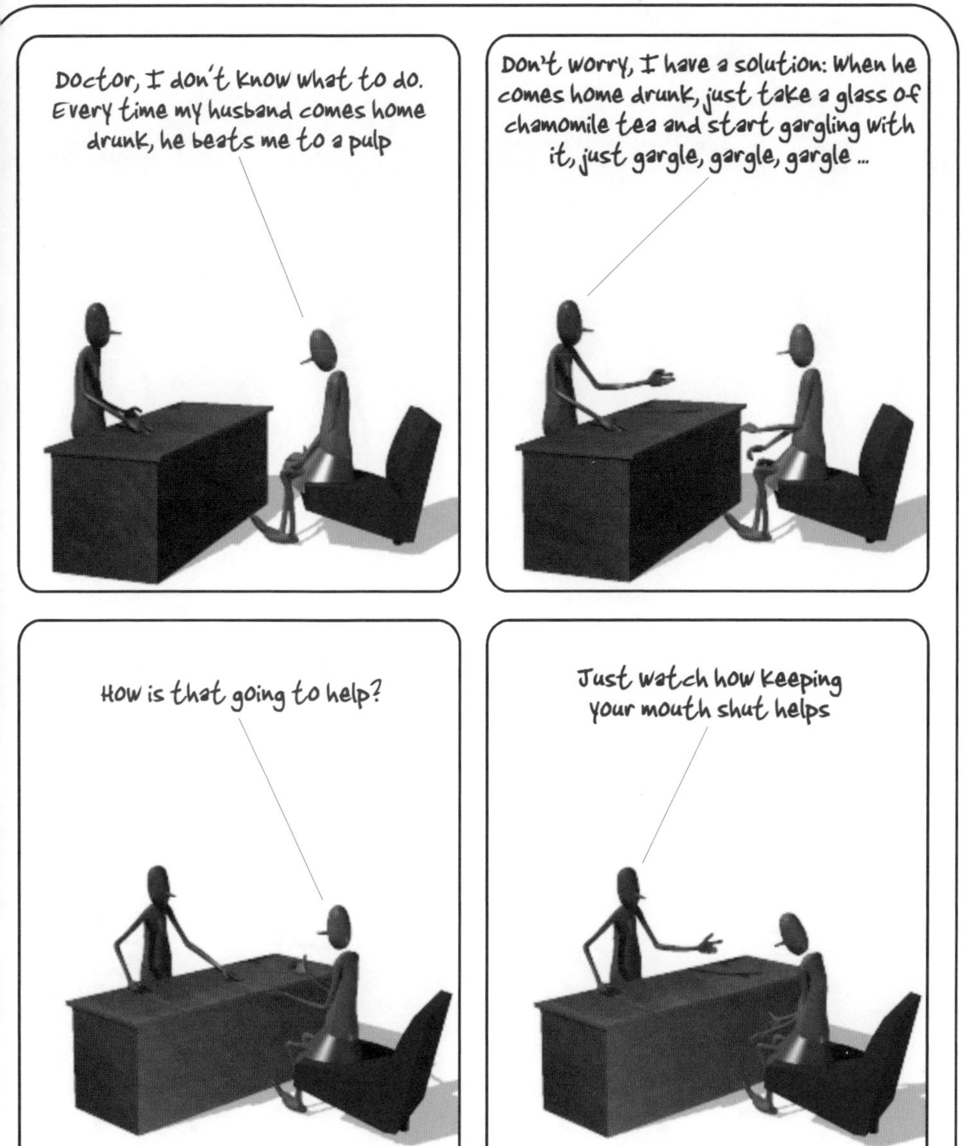
Doctor, I don't know what to do. Every time my husband comes home drunk, he beats me to a pulp
Don't worry, I have a solution: When he comes home drunk, just take a glass of chamomile tea and start gargling with it, just gargle, gargle, gargle ...
How is that going to help?
Just watch how keeping your mouth shut helps
www.faceless.co.za

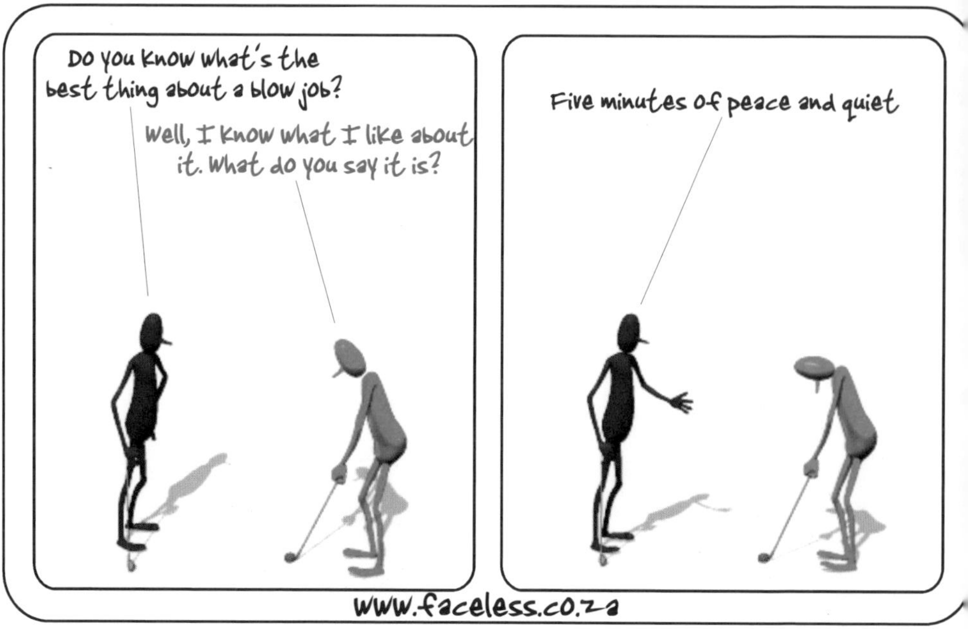
Do you know what's the best thing about a blow job?
Well, I know what I like about it. What do you say it is?
Five minutes of peace and quiet
www.faceless.co.za

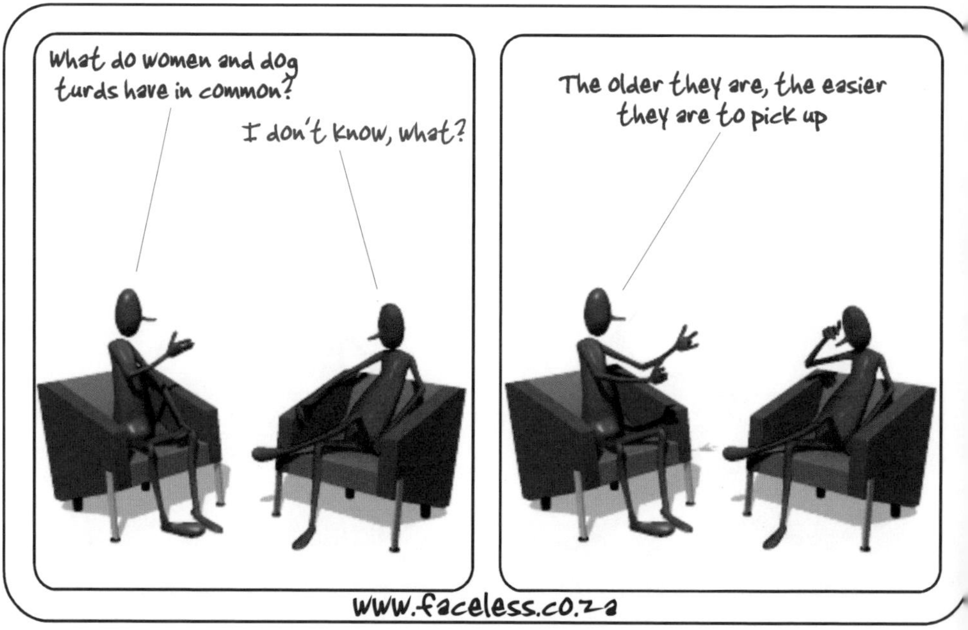
What do women and dog turds have in common?
I don't know, what?
The older they are, the easier they are to pick up
www.faceless.co.za

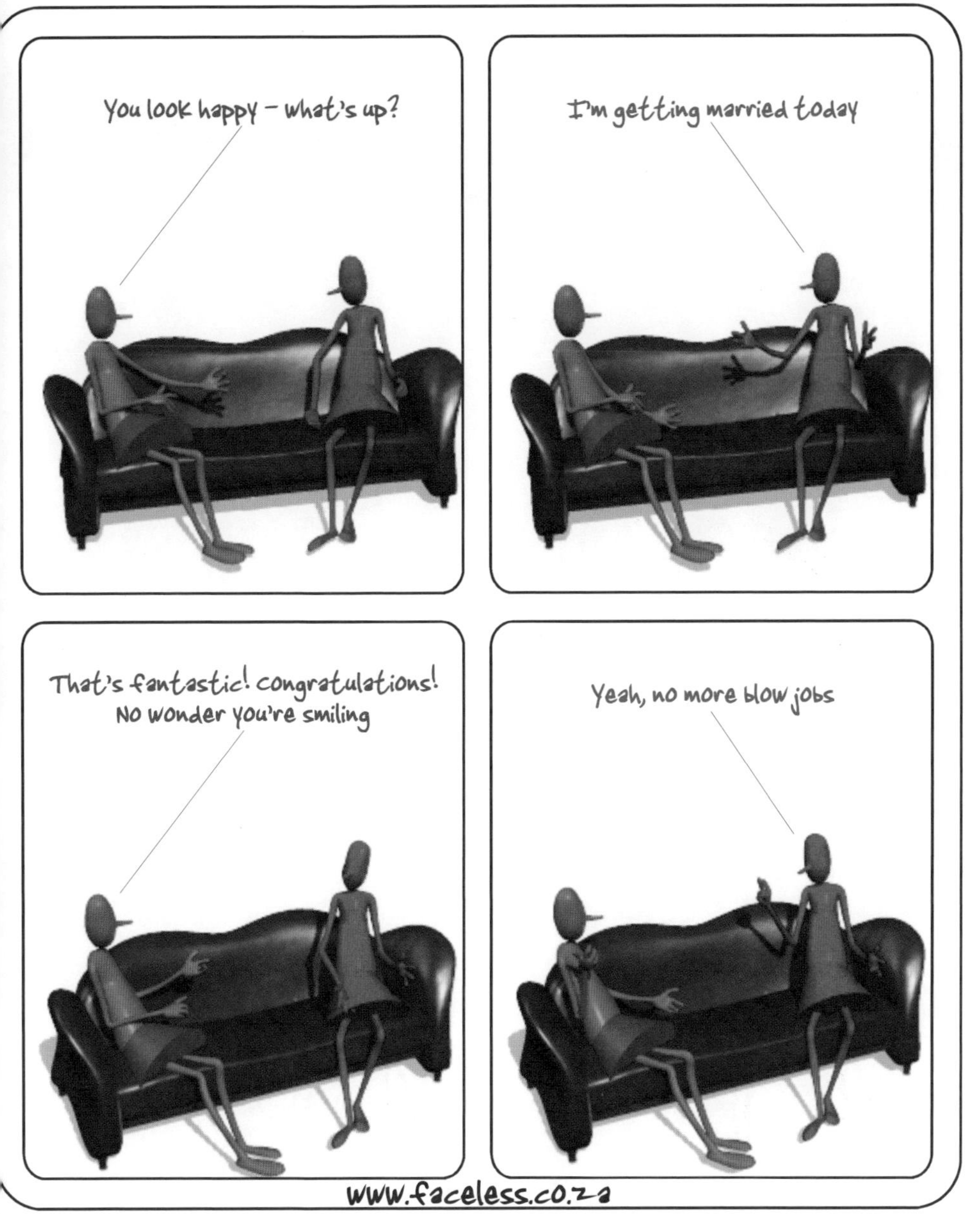
You look happy – what's up?
I'm getting married today
That's fantastic! congratulations!
No wonder you're smiling
Yeah, no more blow jobs
www.faceless.co.za

How was your Valentine's Day?

A disaster. He came home, scoffed down his food, got on top of me, shagged me for three minutes, rolled over and fell asleep. How about yours?

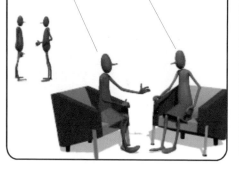

Fantastic, he got home, took me out to dinner, after we took a walk, back home he lit candles, had ages of foreplay. We made love and then we talked for an hour. It was like in a fairytale

How was your Valentine's Day?

Magic! Dinner was on the table, I ate, screwed my wife and fell asleep. What about you?

Horrible. I got home, no dinner because the power was off, I had to take her out to dinner which was so expensive that we couldn't afford a cab so we had to walk. I was so angry that I couldn't get it up, then I couldn't cum, and then I couldn't fall asleep for another hour

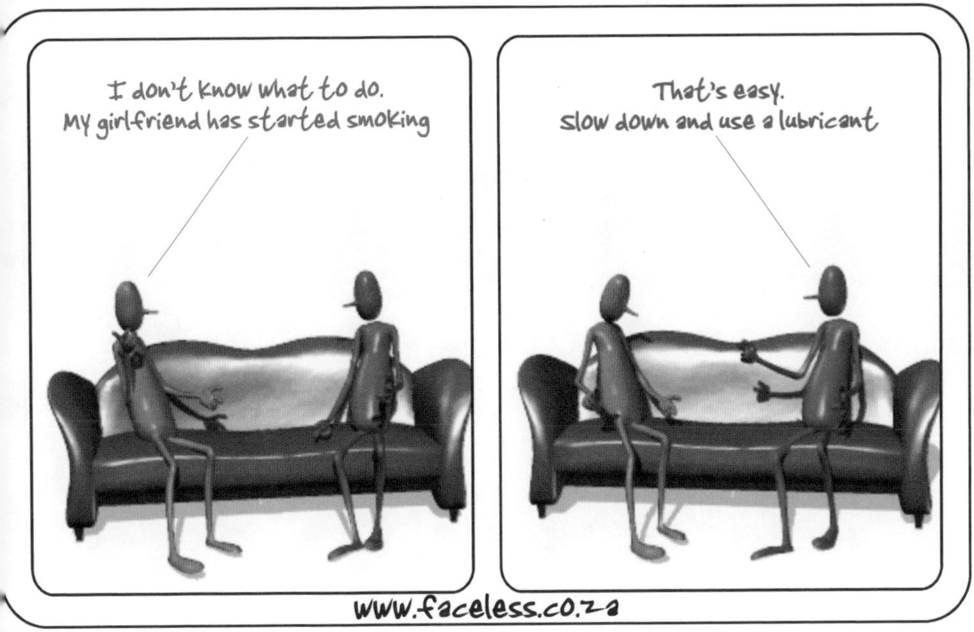
I don't know what to do.
My girlfriend has started smoking
That's easy.
Slow down and use a lubricant
www.faceless.co.za

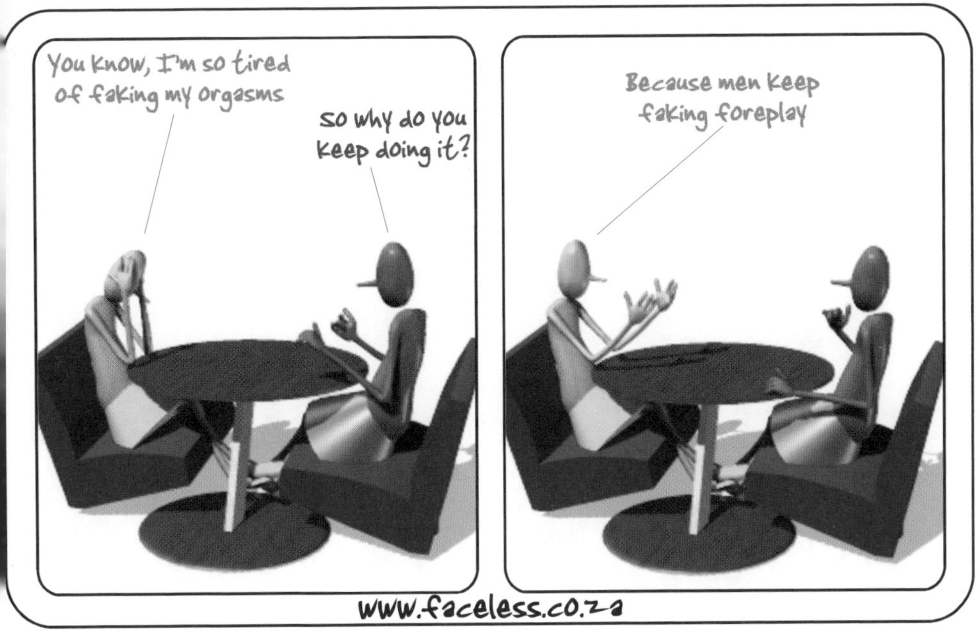
You know, I'm so tired
of faking my orgasms
So why do you
keep doing it?
Because men keep
faking foreplay
www.faceless.co.za

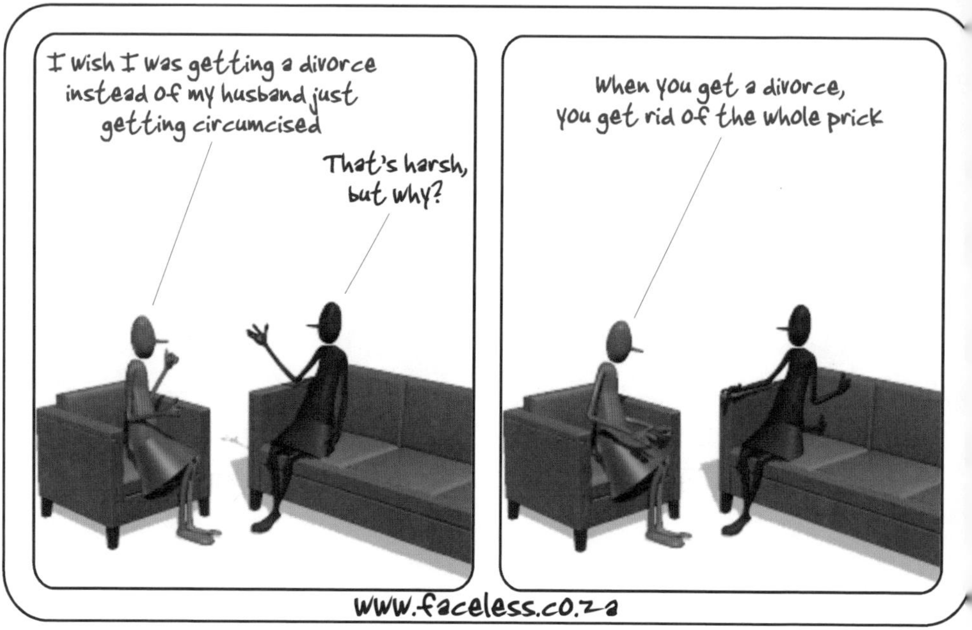
I wish I was getting a divorce instead of my husband just getting circumcised
That's harsh, but why?
When you get a divorce, you get rid of the whole prick
www.faceless.co.za

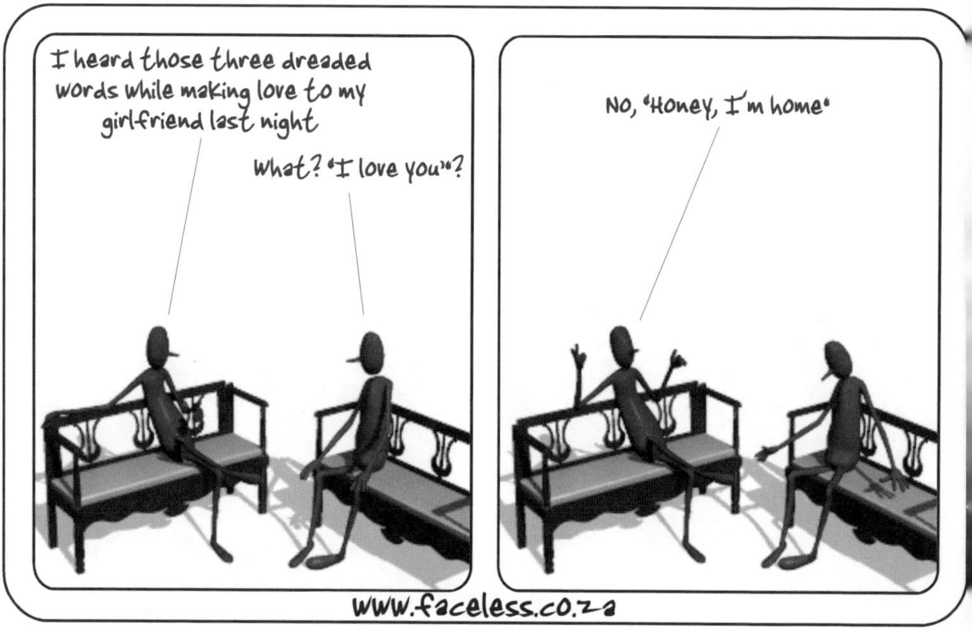
I heard those three dreaded words while making love to my girlfriend last night
What? "I love you"?
No, "Honey, I'm home"
www.faceless.co.za

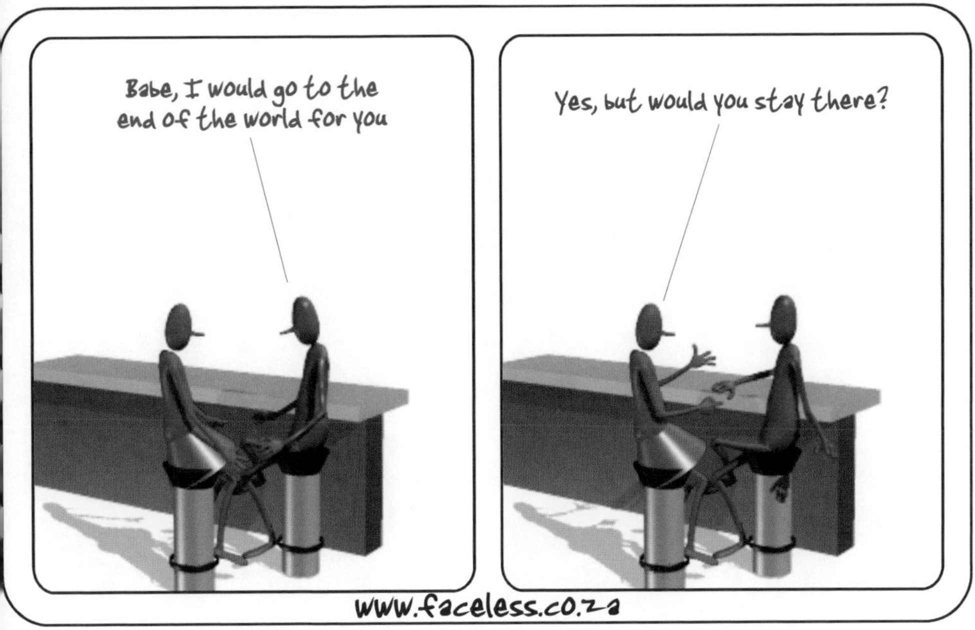
Babe, I would go to the end of the world for you
Yes, but would you stay there?
www.faceless.co.za

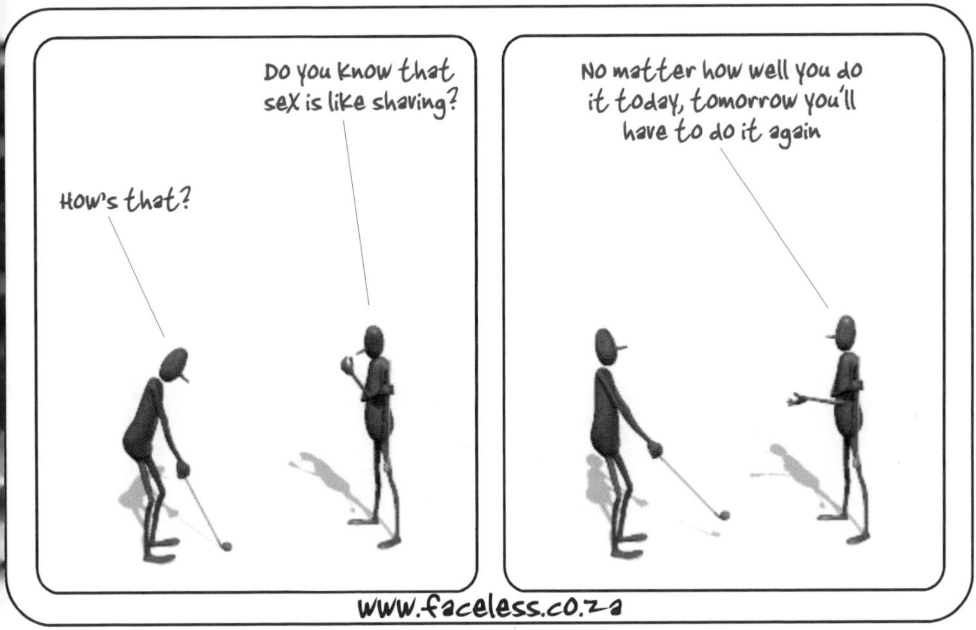
Do you know that sex is like shaving?
How's that?
No matter how well you do it today, tomorrow you'll have to do it again
www.faceless.co.za

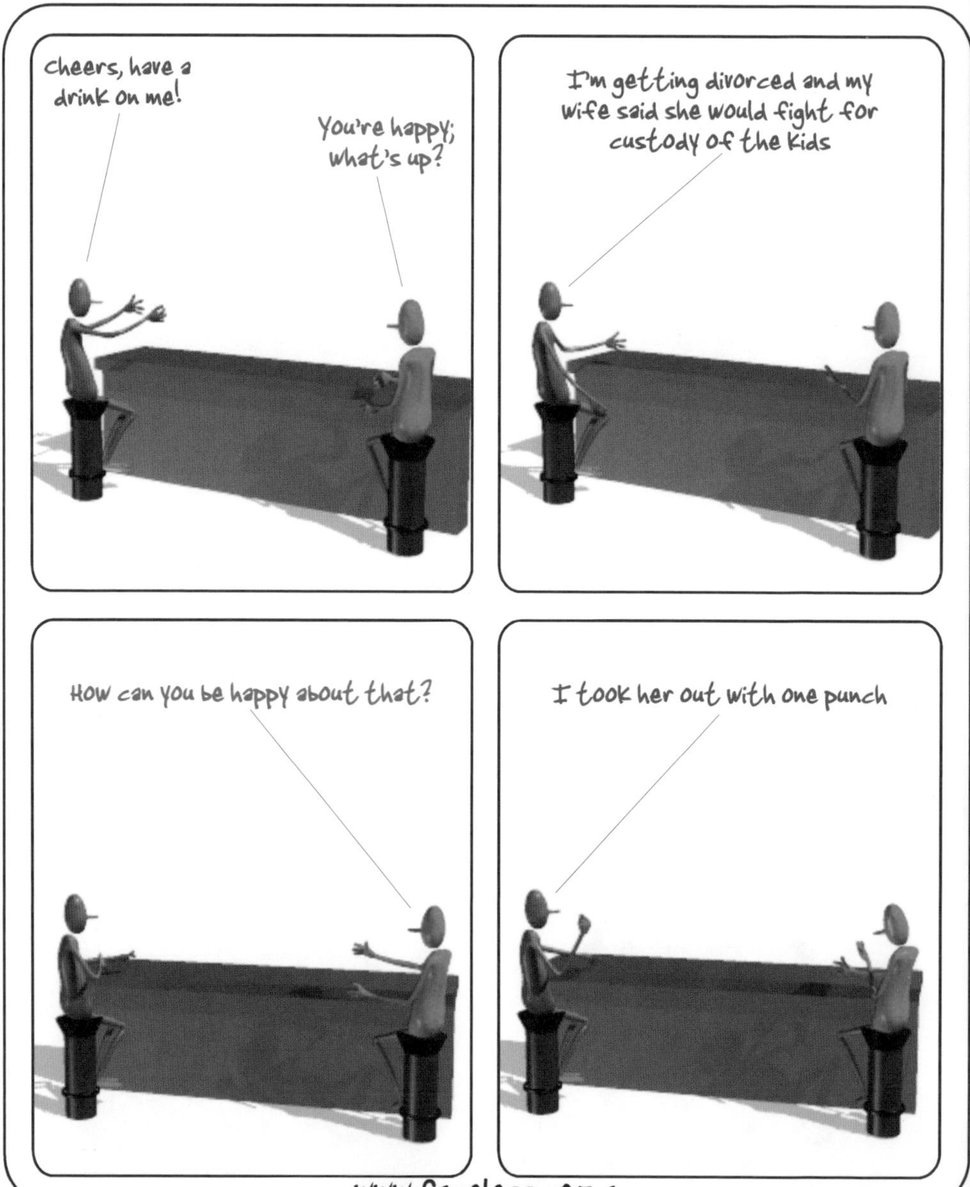

Cheers, have a drink on me!
You're happy; what's up?
I'm getting divorced and my wife said she would fight for custody of the kids
How can you be happy about that?
I took her out with one punch
www.faceless.co.za

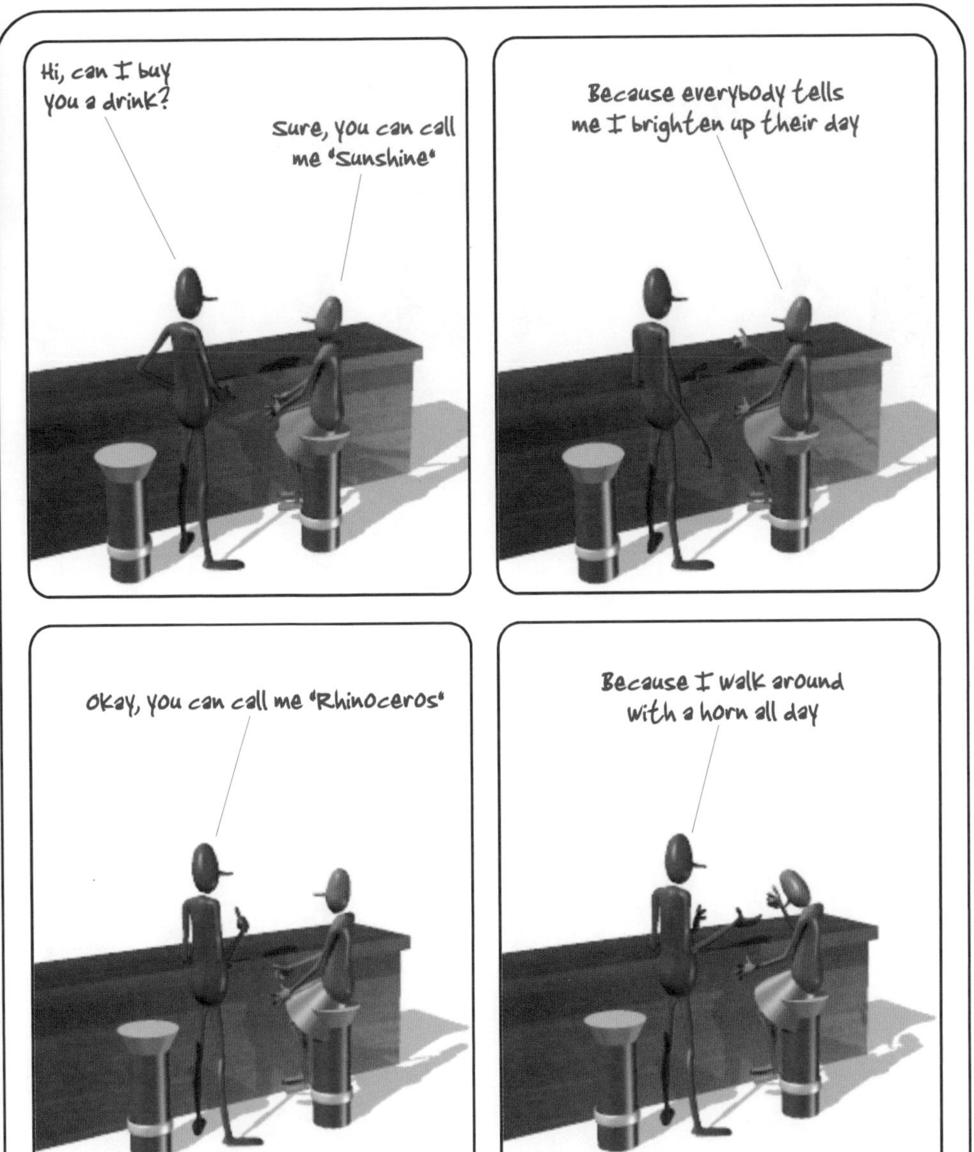
Hi, can I buy you a drink?
Sure, you can call me 'Sunshine'
Because everybody tells me I brighten up their day
Okay, you can call me 'Rhinoceros'
Because I walk around with a horn all day
www.faceless.co.za

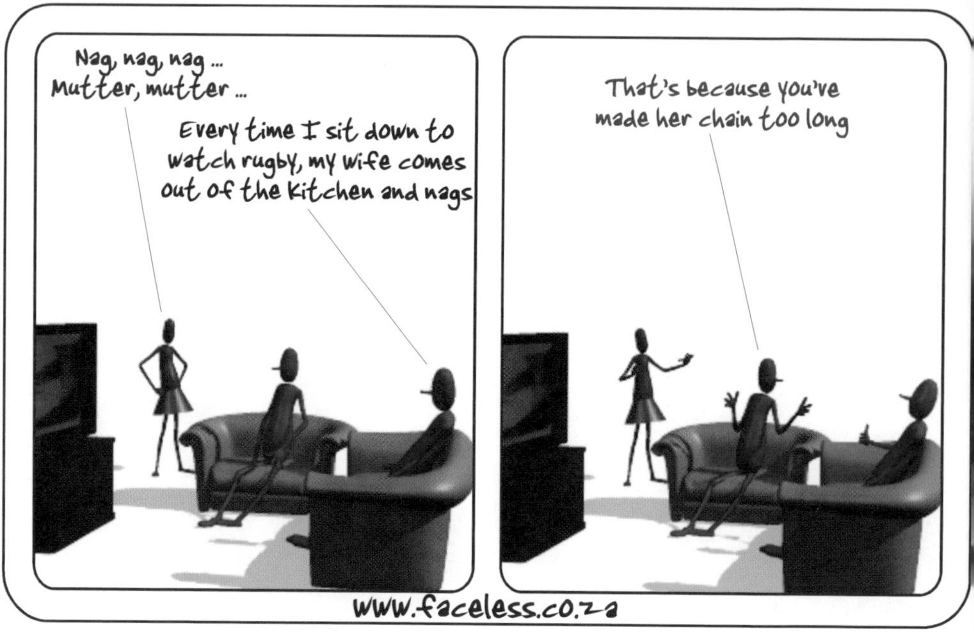
Nag, nag, nag ...
Mutter, mutter ...
Every time I sit down to watch rugby, my wife comes out of the kitchen and nags
That's because you've made her chain too long
www.faceless.co.za

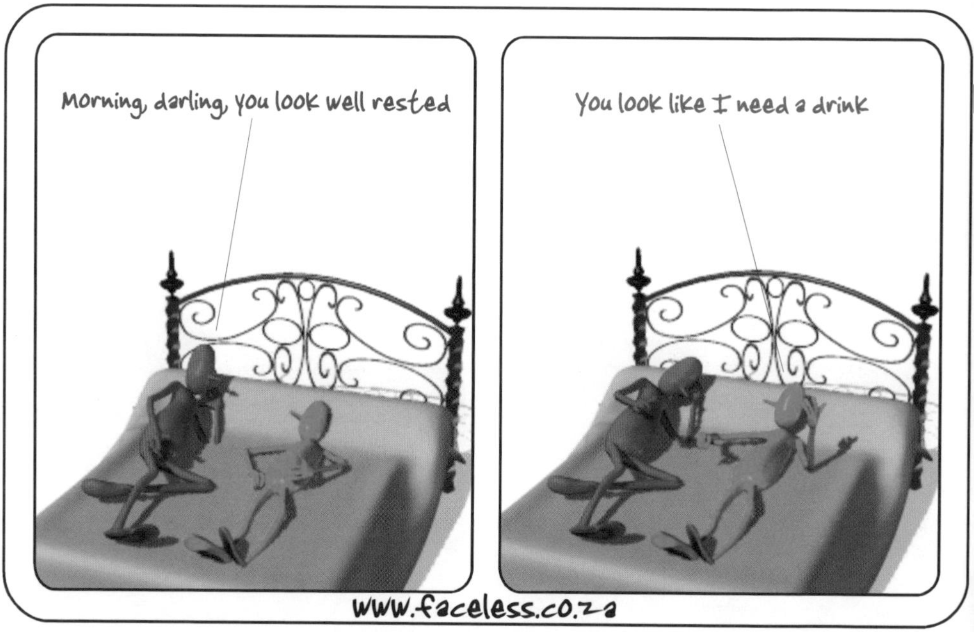
Morning, darling, you look well rested
You look like I need a drink
www.faceless.co.za

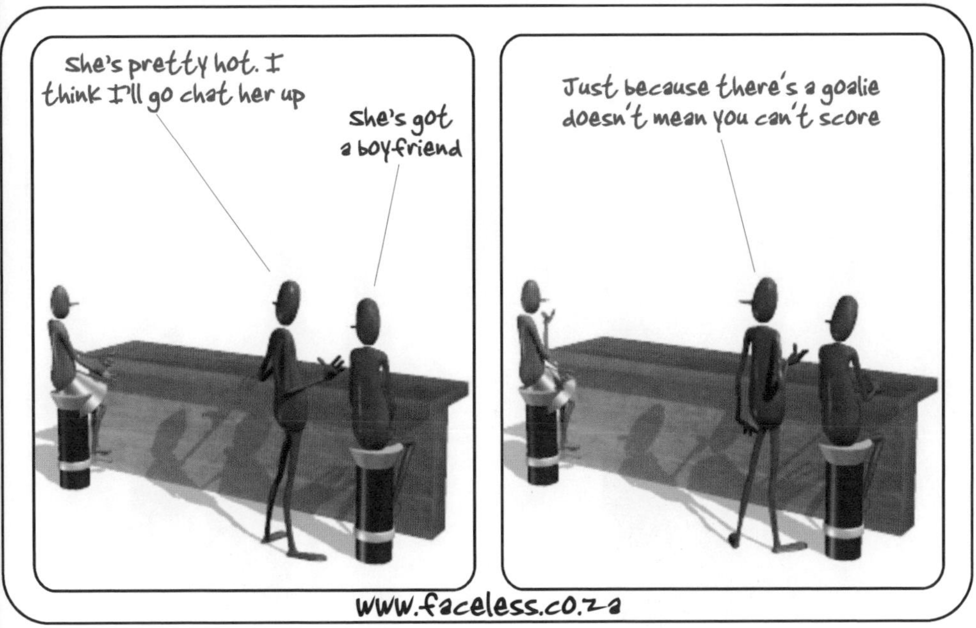
She's pretty hot. I think I'll go chat her up
She's got a boyfriend
Just because there's a goalie doesn't mean you can't score
www.faceless.co.za

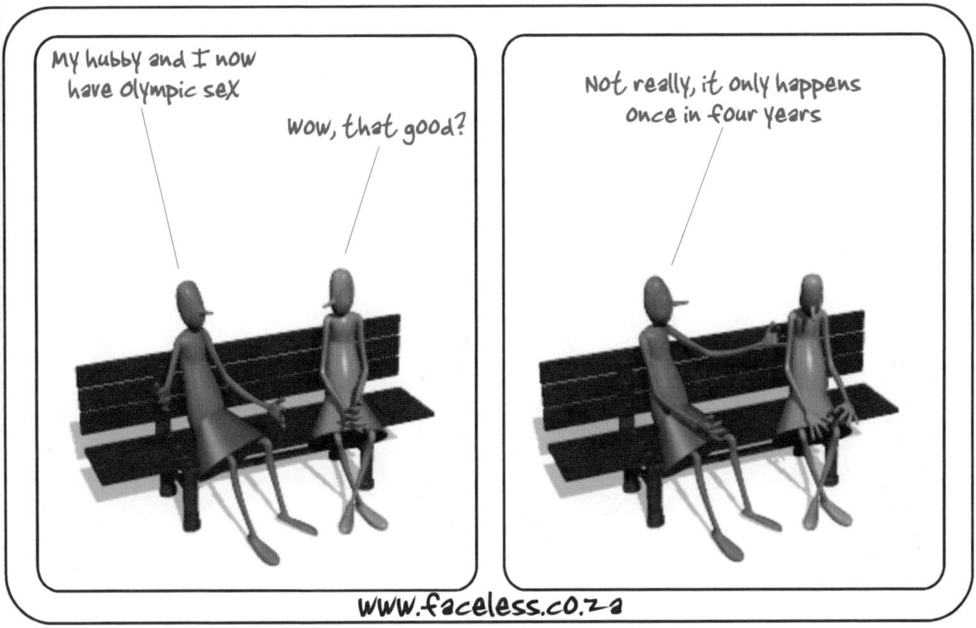
My hubby and I now have olympic sex
Wow, that good?
Not really, it only happens once in four years
www.faceless.co.za

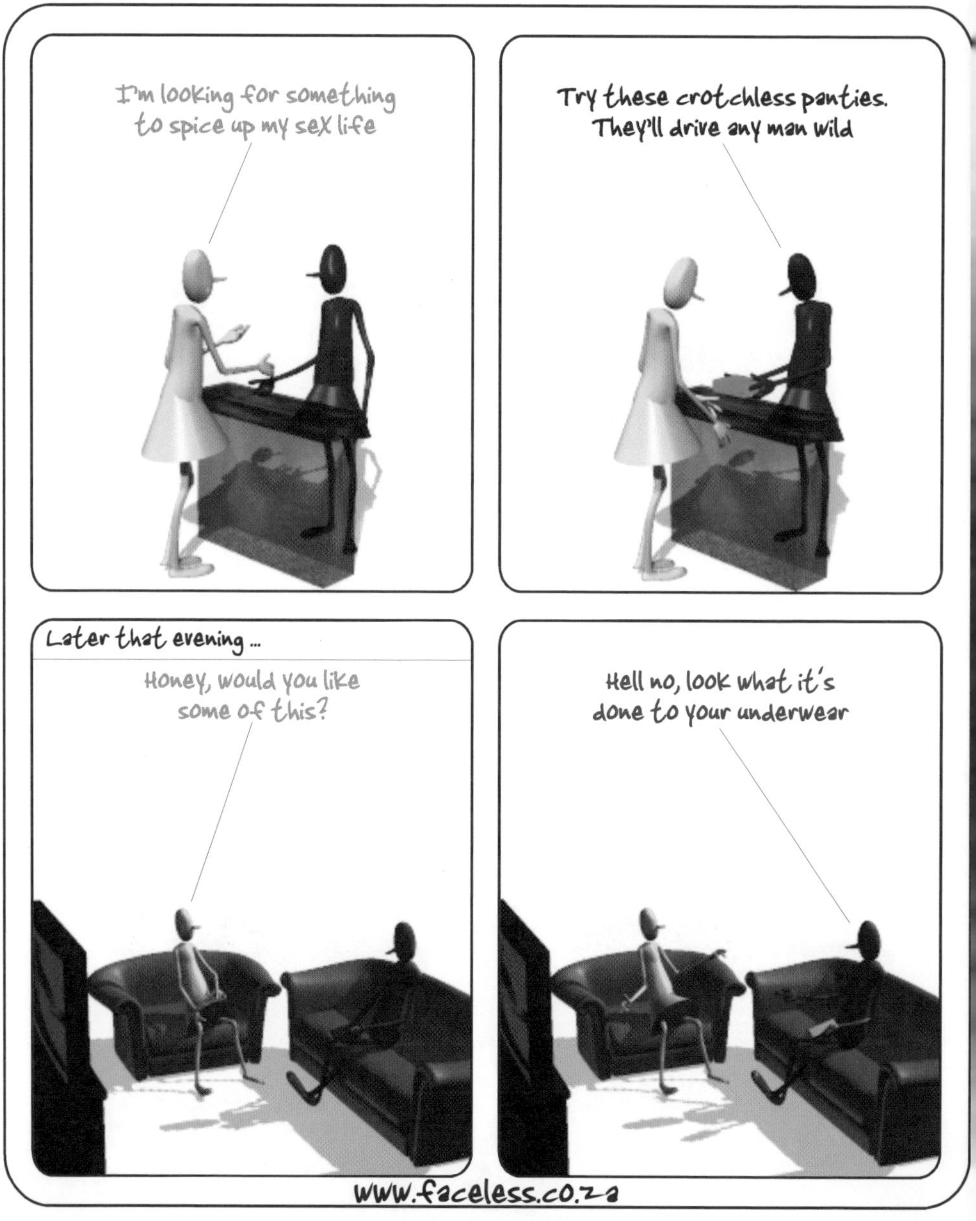
I'm looking for something to spice up my sex life
Try these crotchless panties. They'll drive any man wild
Later that evening ...
Honey, would you like some of this?
Hell no, look what it's done to your underwear
www.faceless.co.za

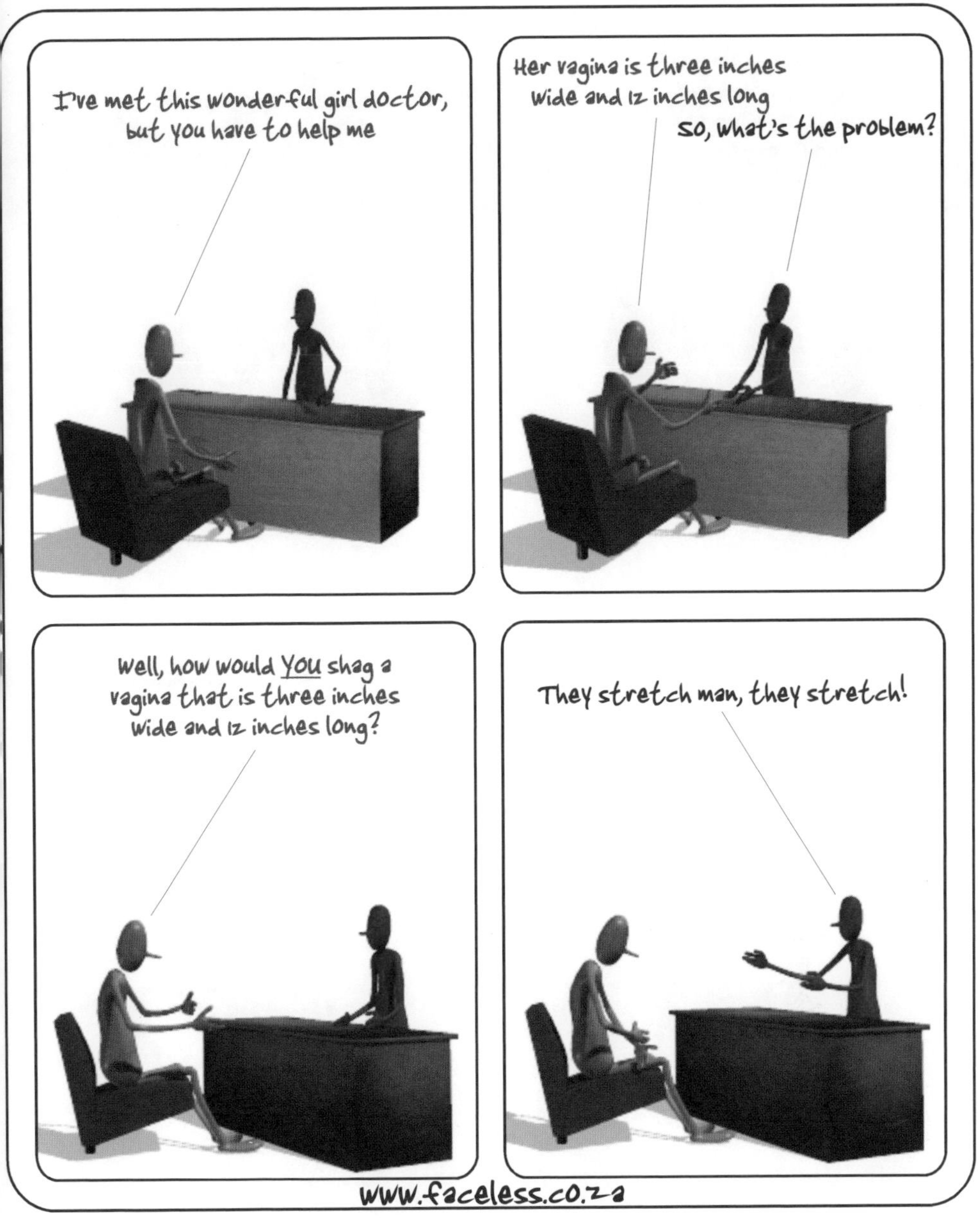
I've met this wonderful girl doctor, but you have to help me
Her vagina is three inches wide and 12 inches long
So, what's the problem?
Well, how would YOU shag a vagina that is three inches wide and 12 inches long?
They stretch man, they stretch!
www.faceless.co.za

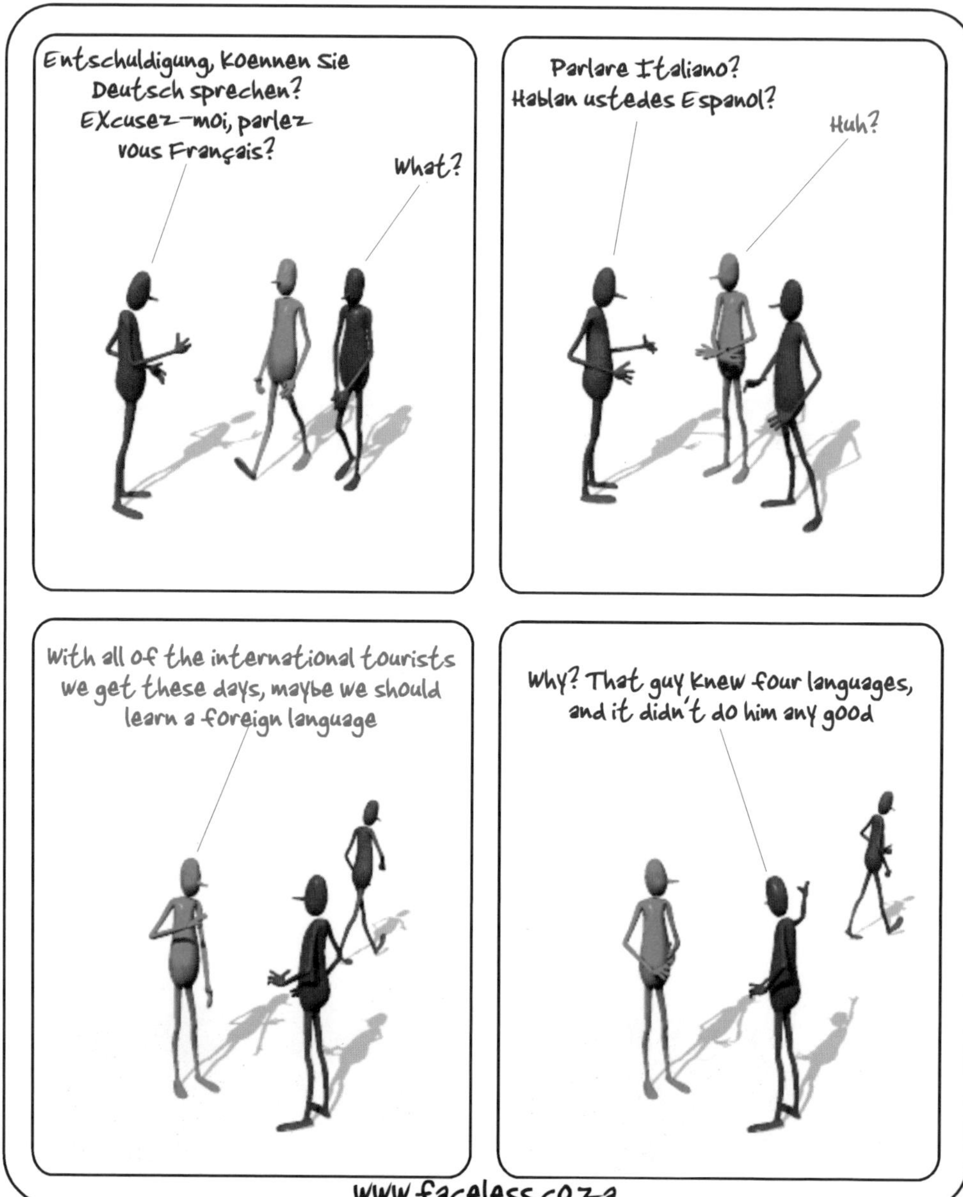

Entschuldigung, Koennen Sie Deutsch sprechen? EXcusez-moi, parlez vous Français?
What?
Parlare Italiano? Hablan ustedes Espanol?
Huh?
With all of the international tourists we get these days, maybe we should learn a foreign language
Why? That guy Knew four languages, and it didn't do him any good
www.faceless.co.za

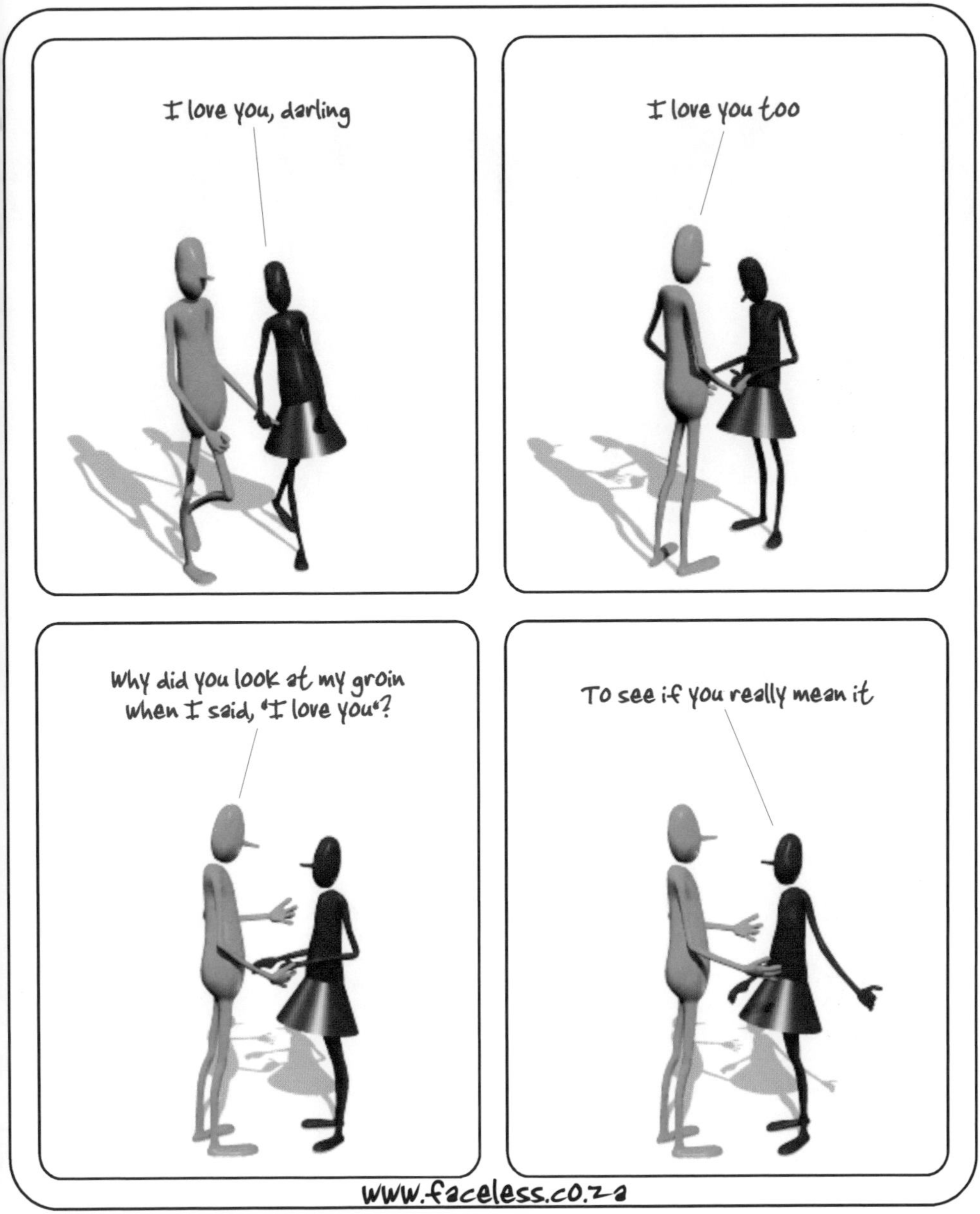
I love you, darling
I love you too
Why did you look at my groin when I said, "I love you"?
To see if you really mean it
www.faceless.co.za

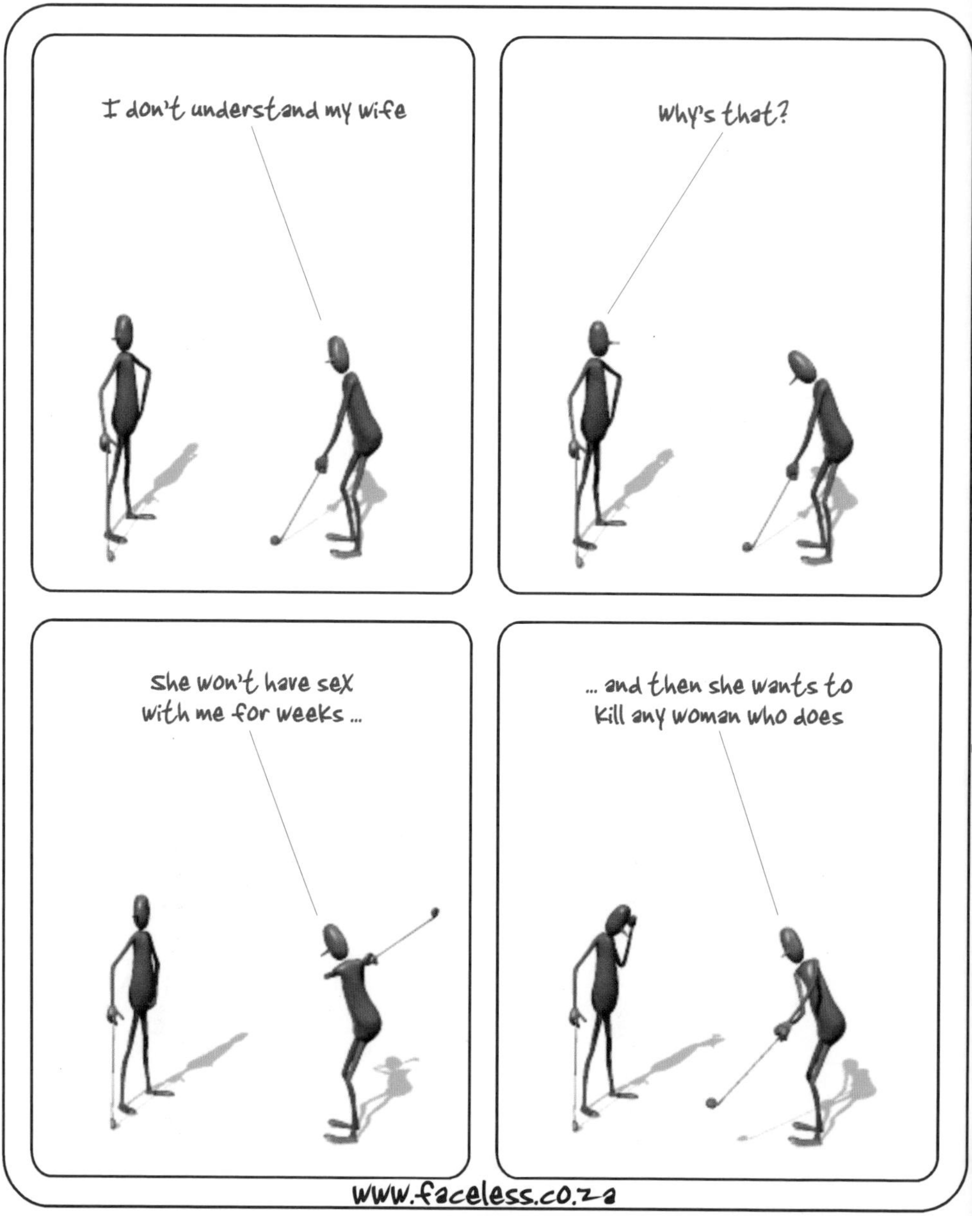
I don't understand my wife
Why's that?
she won't have sex with me for weeks ...
... and then she wants to kill any woman who does
www.faceless.co.za

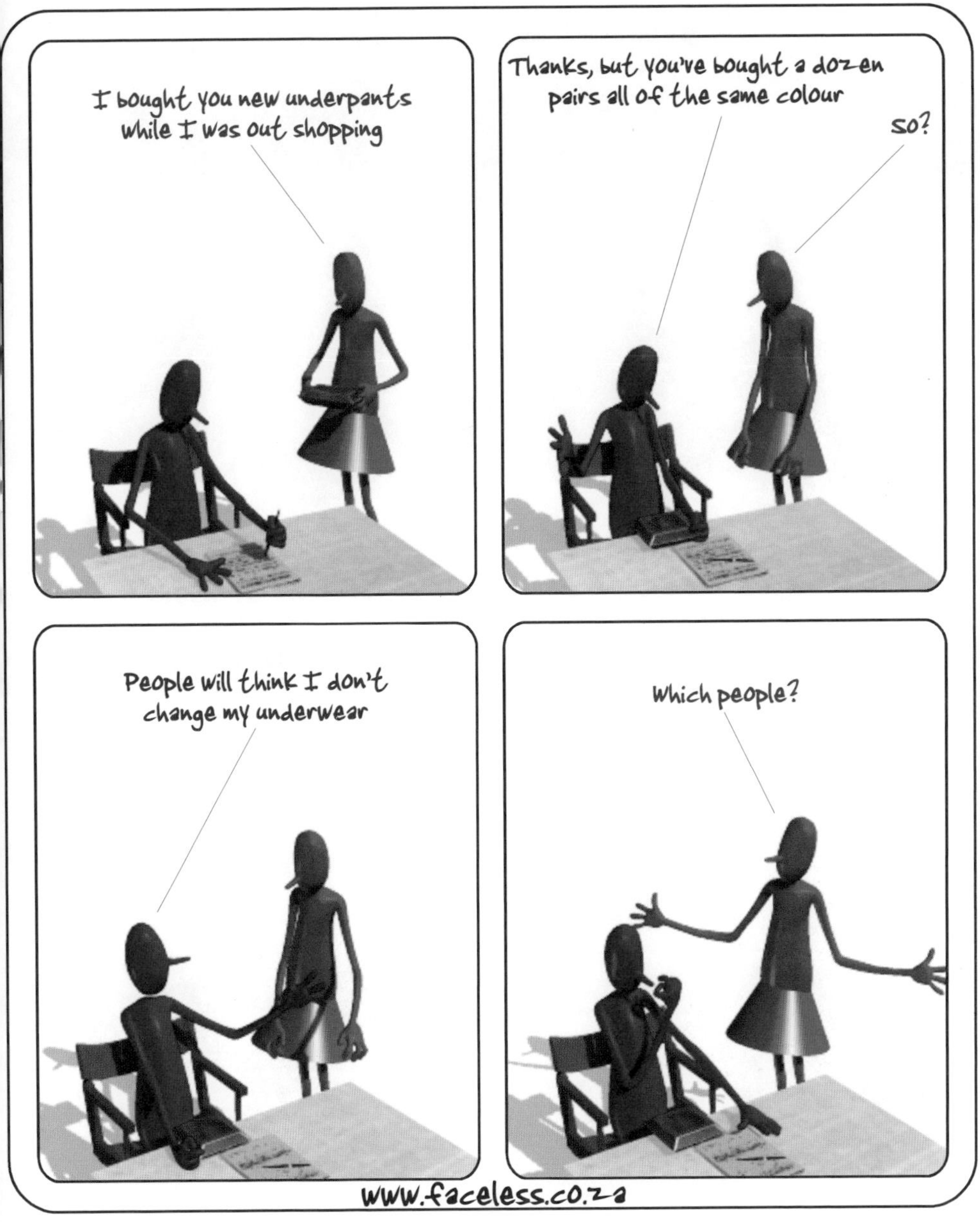
I bought you new underpants while I was out shopping
Thanks, but you've bought a dozen pairs all of the same colour
so?
People will think I don't change my underwear
Which people?
www.faceless.co.za

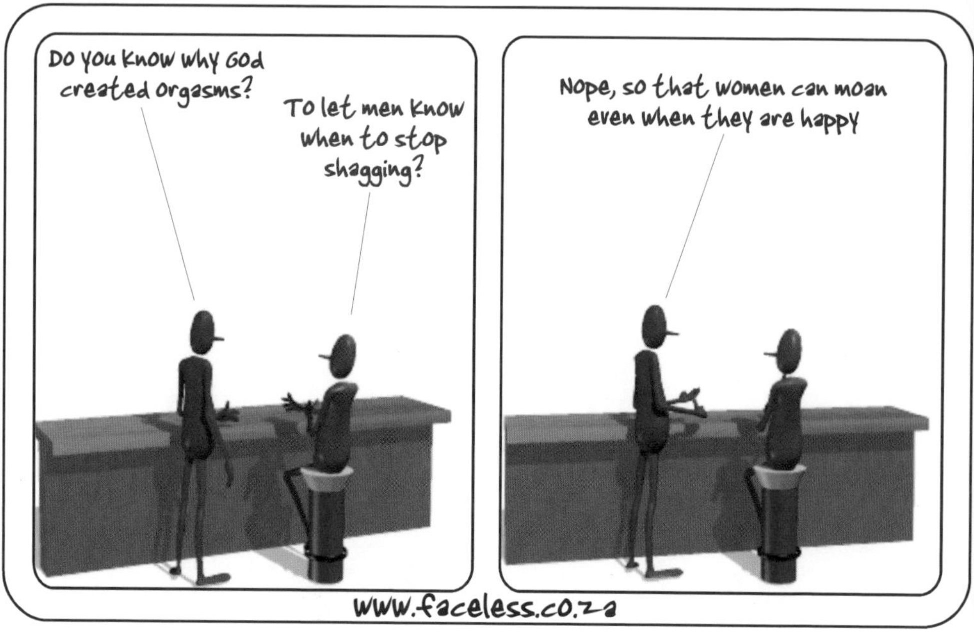
Do you know why God created orgasms?
To let men know when to stop shagging?
Nope, so that women can moan even when they are happy
www.faceless.co.za

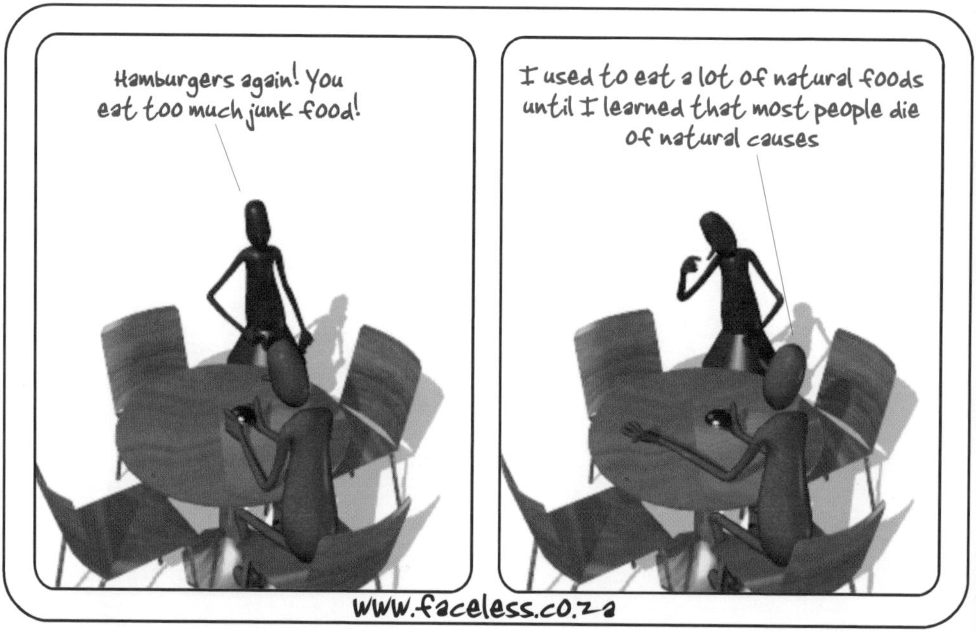
Hamburgers again! You eat too much junk food!
I used to eat a lot of natural foods until I learned that most people die of natural causes
www.faceless.co.za

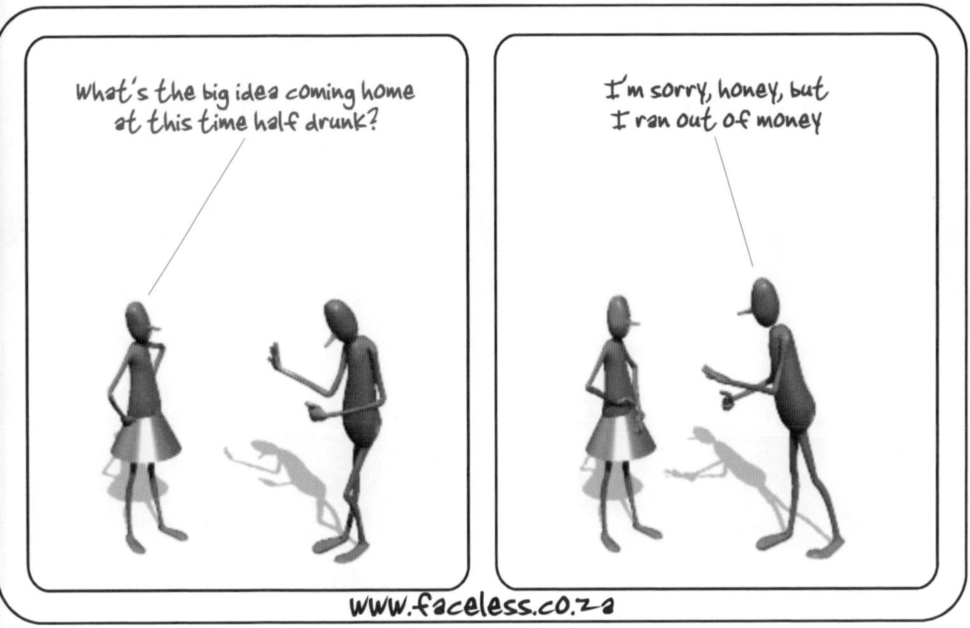
What's the big idea coming home at this time half drunk?
I'm sorry, honey, but I ran out of money
www.faceless.co.za

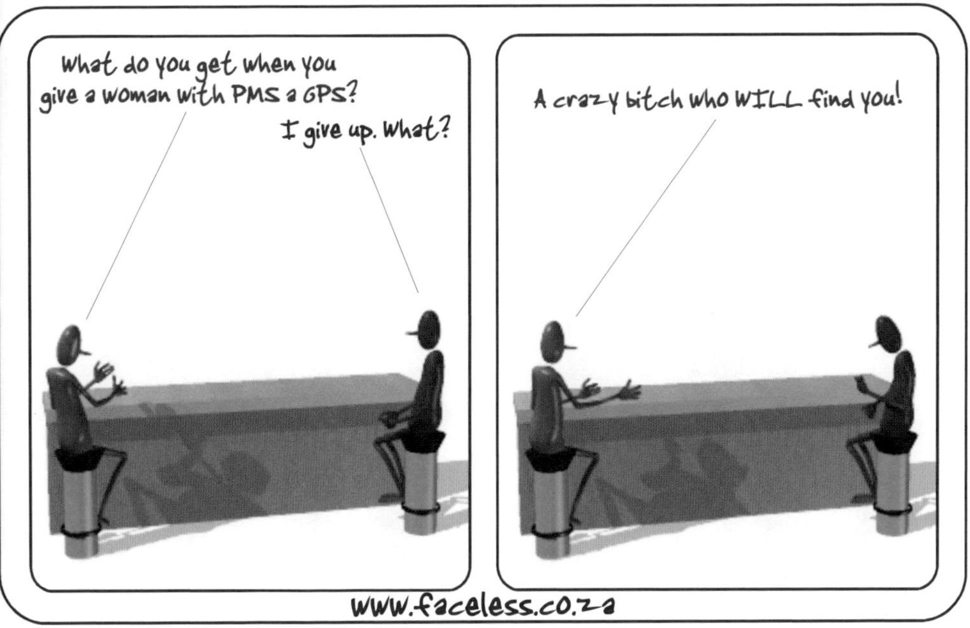
What do you get when you give a woman with PMS a GPS?
I give up. What?
A crazy bitch who WILL find you!
www.faceless.co.za

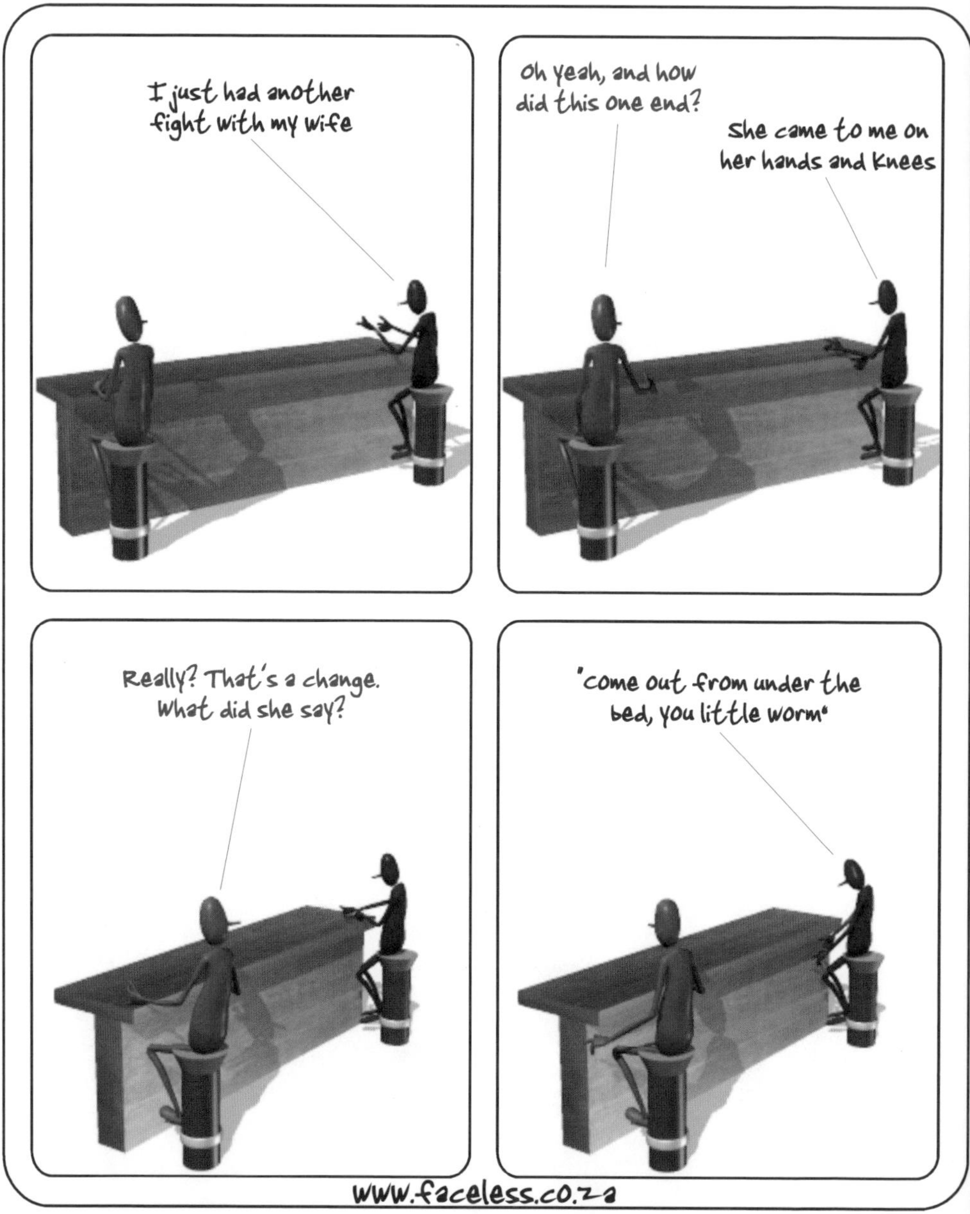
I just had another fight with my wife
Oh yeah, and how did this one end?
She came to me on her hands and knees
Really? That's a change. What did she say?
"come out from under the bed, you little worm"
www.faceless.co.za

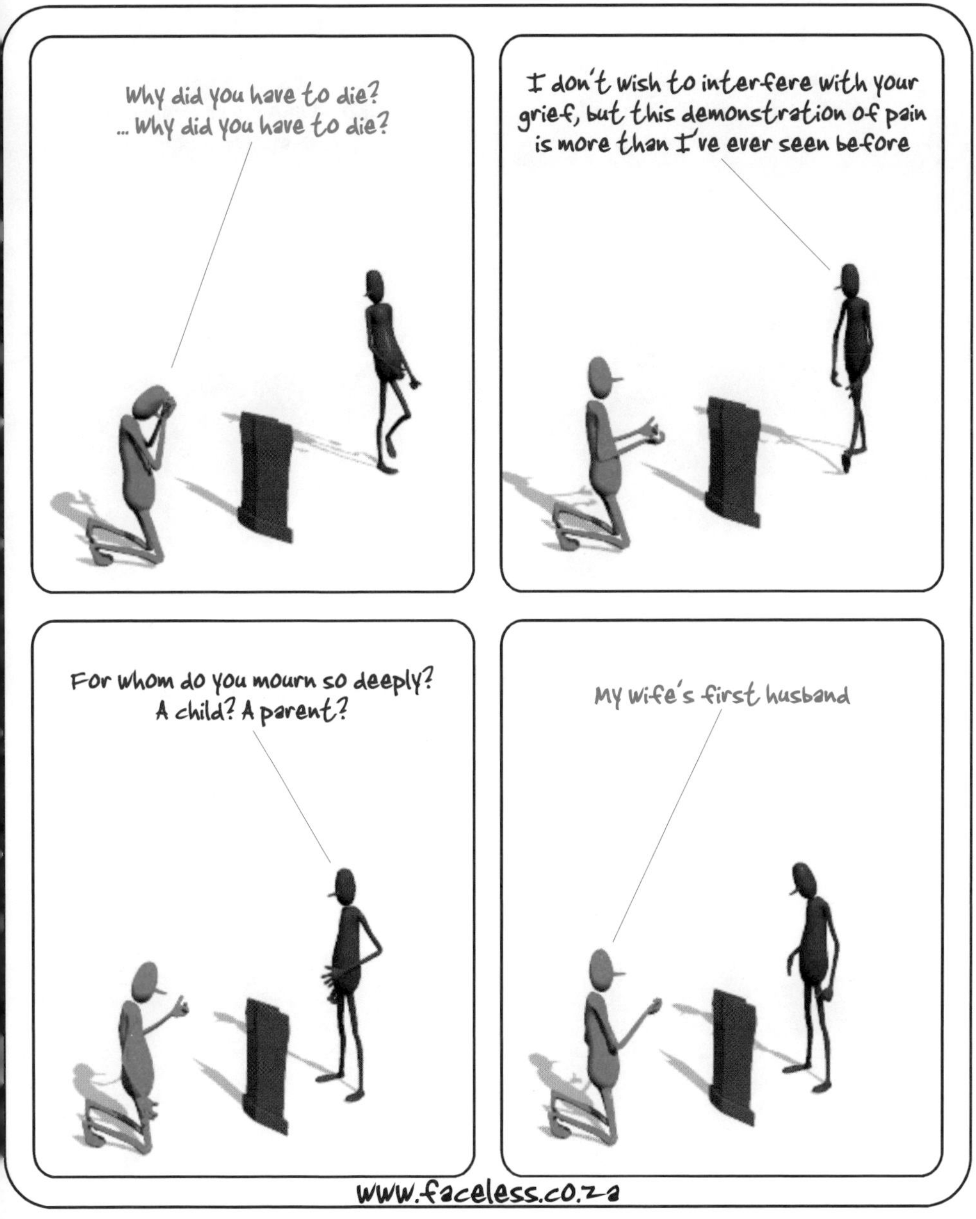
Why did you have to die?
... Why did you have to die?
I don't wish to interfere with your grief, but this demonstration of pain is more than I've ever seen before
For whom do you mourn so deeply? A child? A parent?
My wife's first husband
www.faceless.co.za

I just broke up with a girl because she had a seemingly incurable speech impediment
I'm shocked. I've never known you to be one to be prejudiced against handicaps
What was the girl's problem?
She couldn't say "yes"
www.faceless.co.za

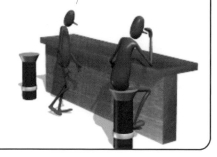

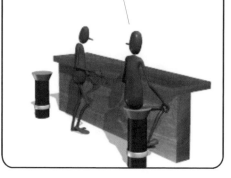

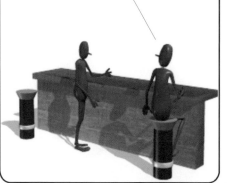

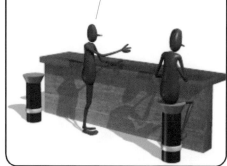

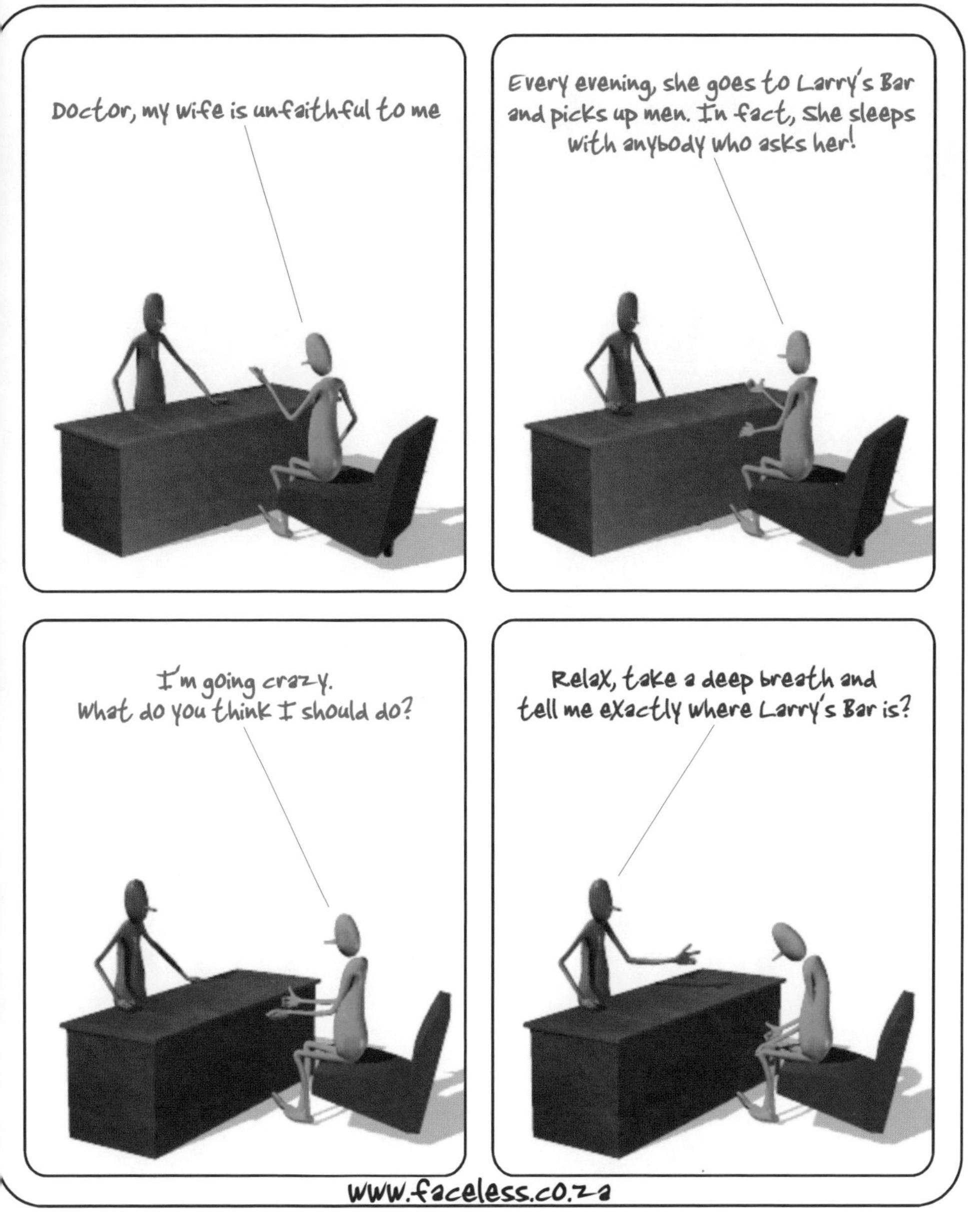
Doctor, my wife is unfaithful to me
Every evening, she goes to Larry's Bar and picks up men. In fact, she sleeps with anybody who asks her!
I'm going crazy. What do you think I should do?
Relax, take a deep breath and tell me exactly where Larry's Bar is?
www.faceless.co.za

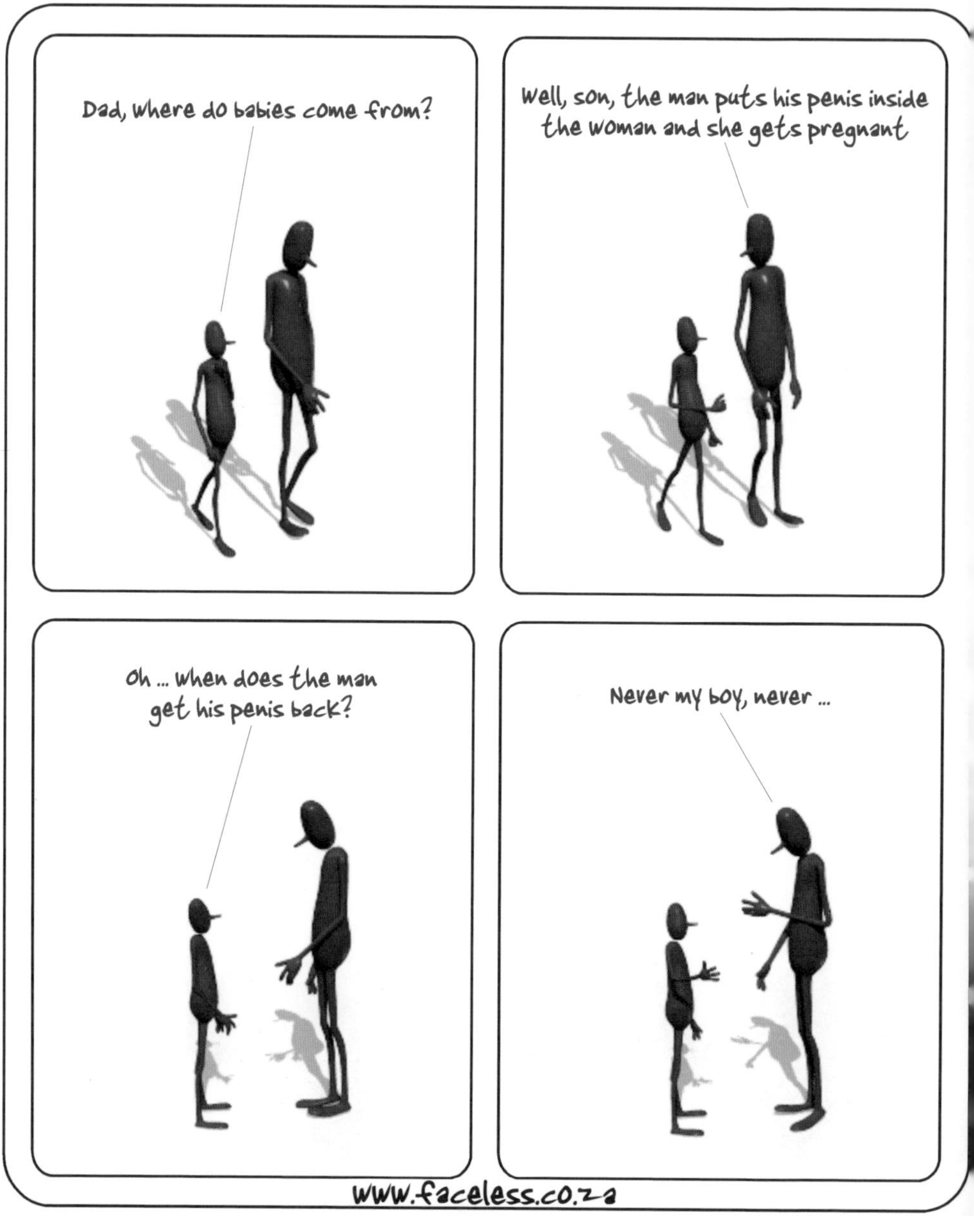
Dad, where do babies come from?
Well, son, the man puts his penis inside the woman and she gets pregnant
Oh ... when does the man get his penis back?
Never my boy, never ...
www.faceless.co.za

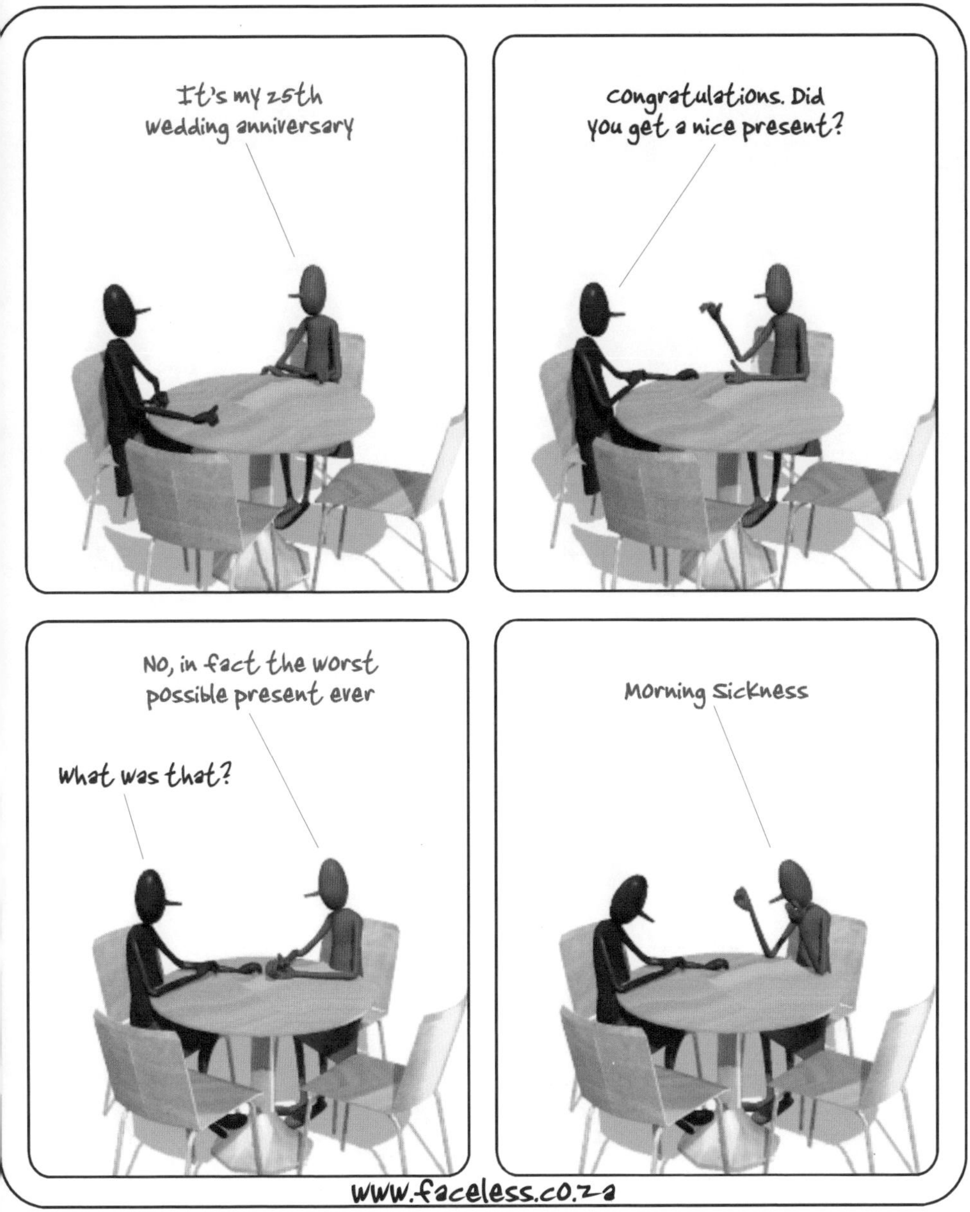
It's my 25th wedding anniversary
congratulations. Did you get a nice present?
No, in fact the worst possible present ever
What was that?
Morning Sickness
www.faceless.co.za

As my lawyer, I want you to put a few things in my will
sure, go ahead
First, I want to be cremated, and, second, I want my ashes scattered all over woolworths
uhm, okay, why woolworths?
Then I'll be sure my daughters visit me twice a week
www.faceless.co.za

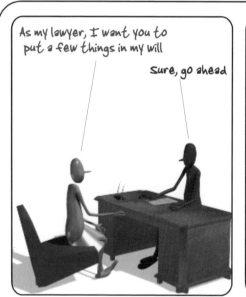

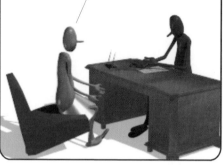

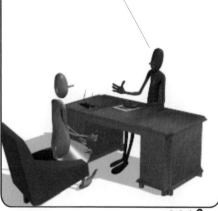

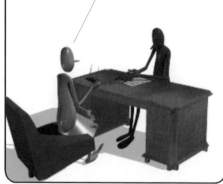

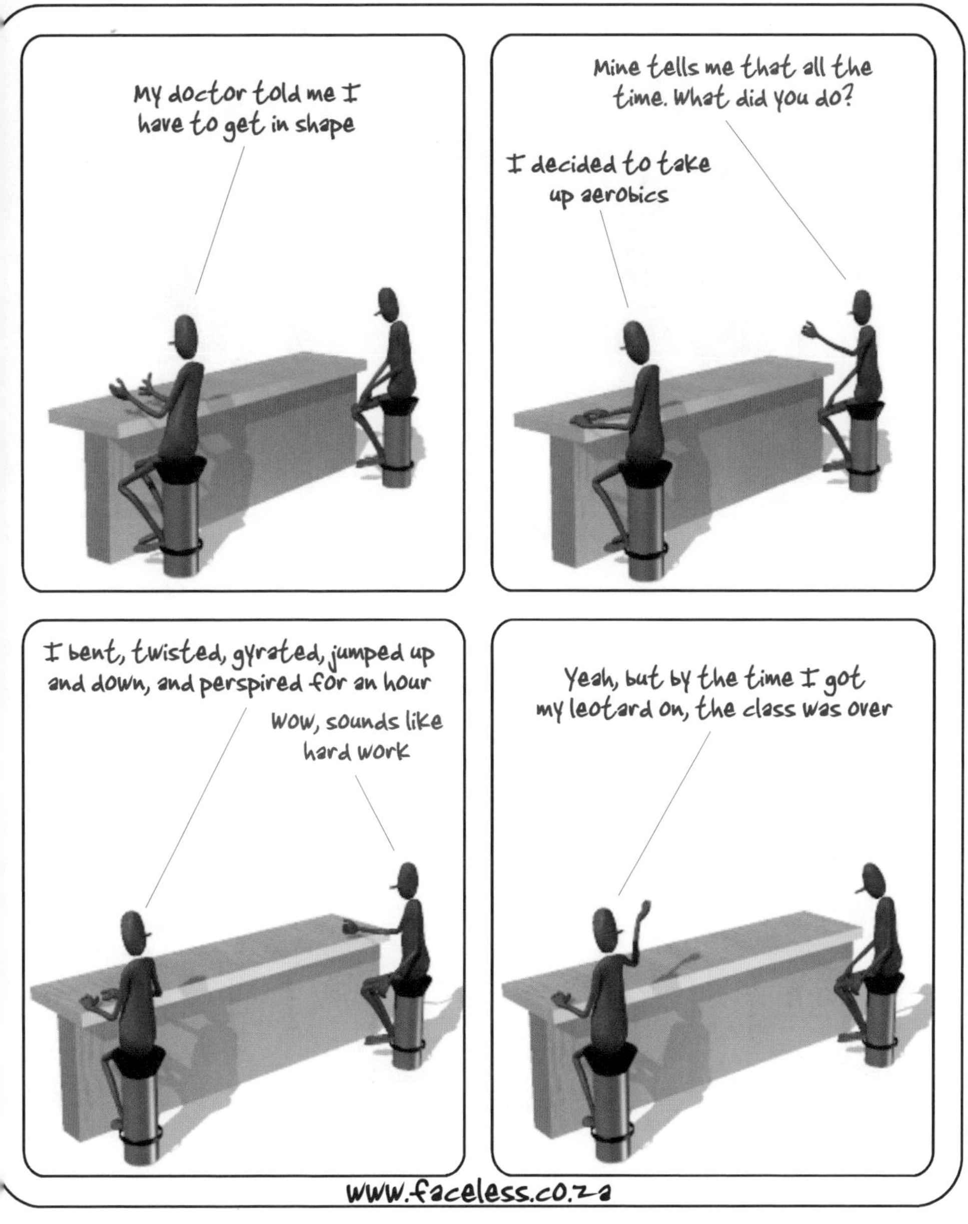
My doctor told me I have to get in shape
Mine tells me that all the time. What did you do?
I decided to take up aerobics
I bent, twisted, gyrated, jumped up and down, and perspired for an hour
Wow, sounds like hard work
Yeah, but by the time I got my leotard on, the class was over
www.faceless.co.za

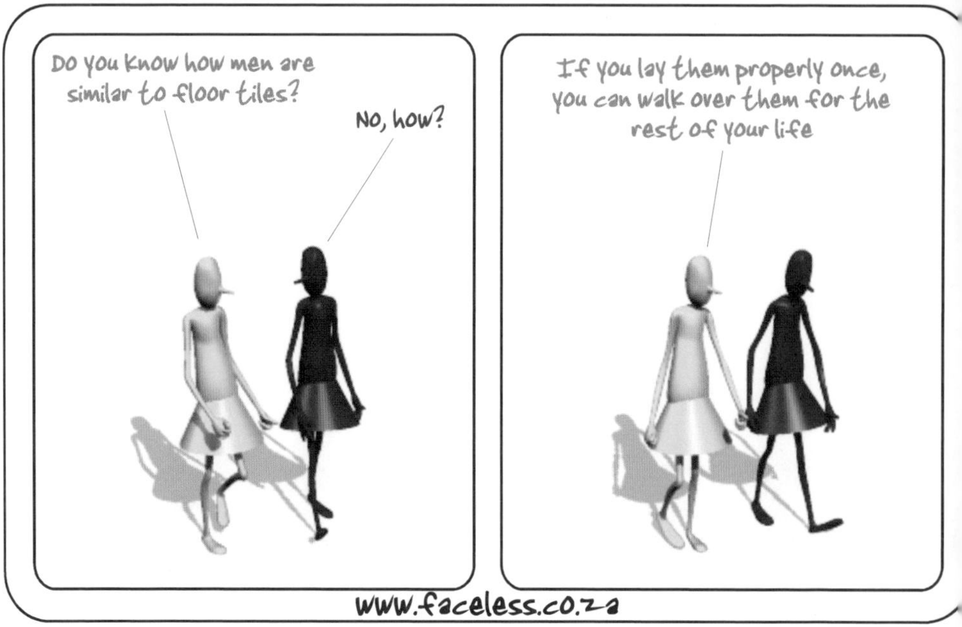
Do you know how men are similar to floor tiles?
No, how?
If you lay them properly once, you can walk over them for the rest of your life
www.faceless.co.za

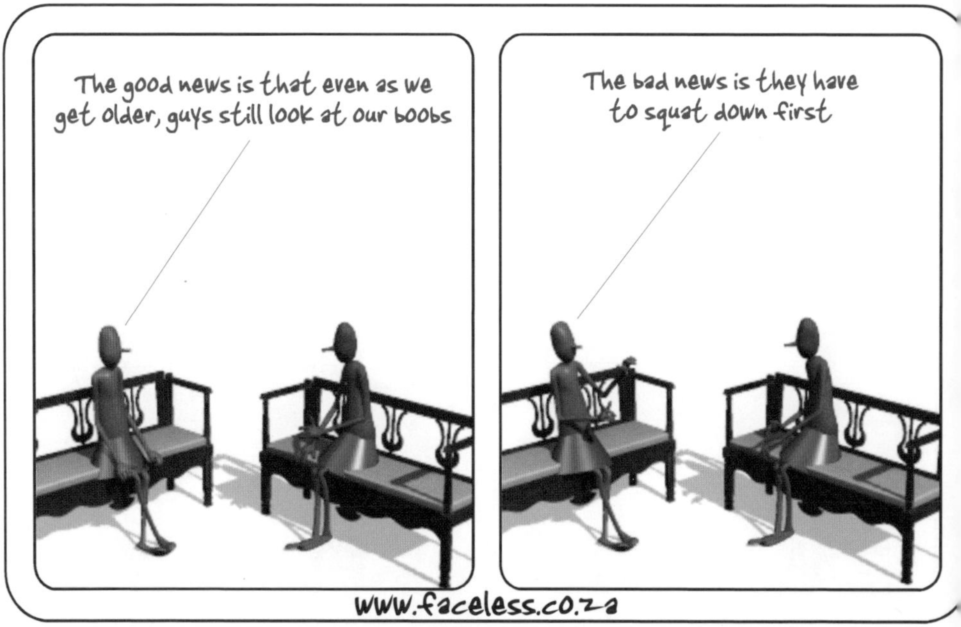
The good news is that even as we get older, guys still look at our boobs
The bad news is they have to squat down first
www.faceless.co.za

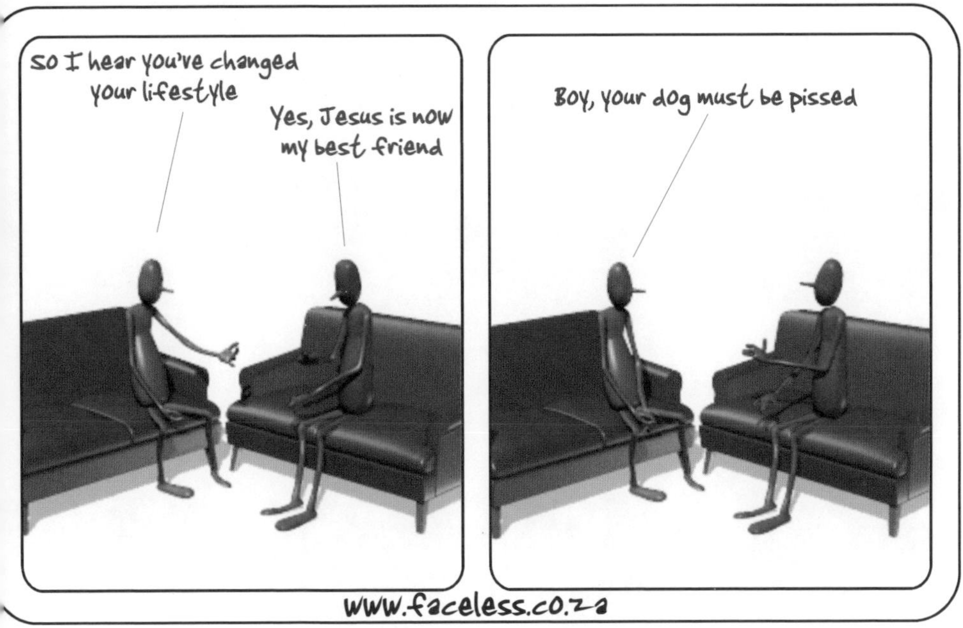
so I hear you've changed your lifestyle
Yes, Jesus is now my best friend
Boy, your dog must be pissed
www.faceless.co.za

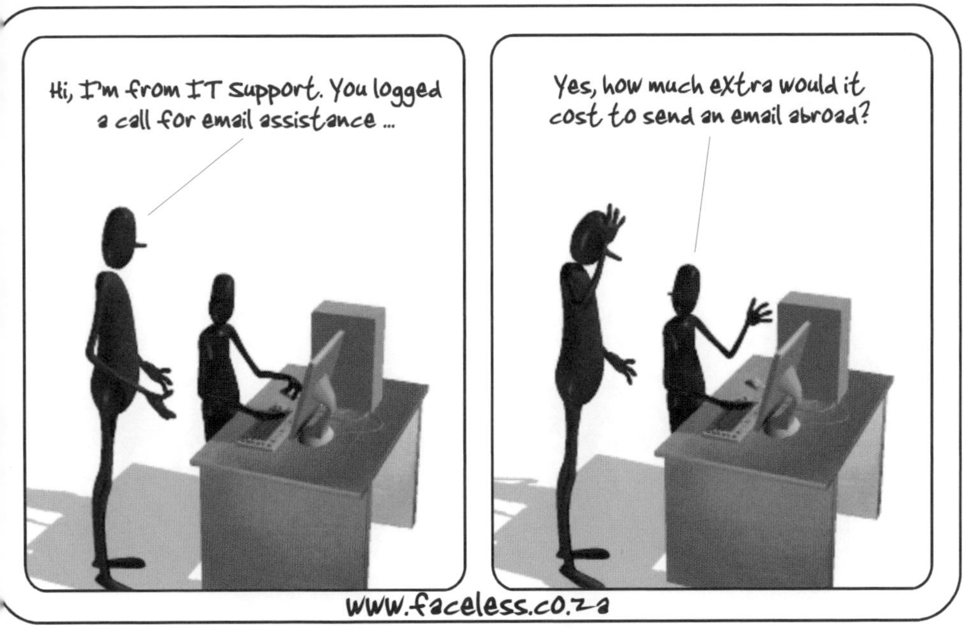
Hi, I'm from IT support. You logged a call for email assistance ...
Yes, how much extra would it cost to send an email abroad?
www.faceless.co.za

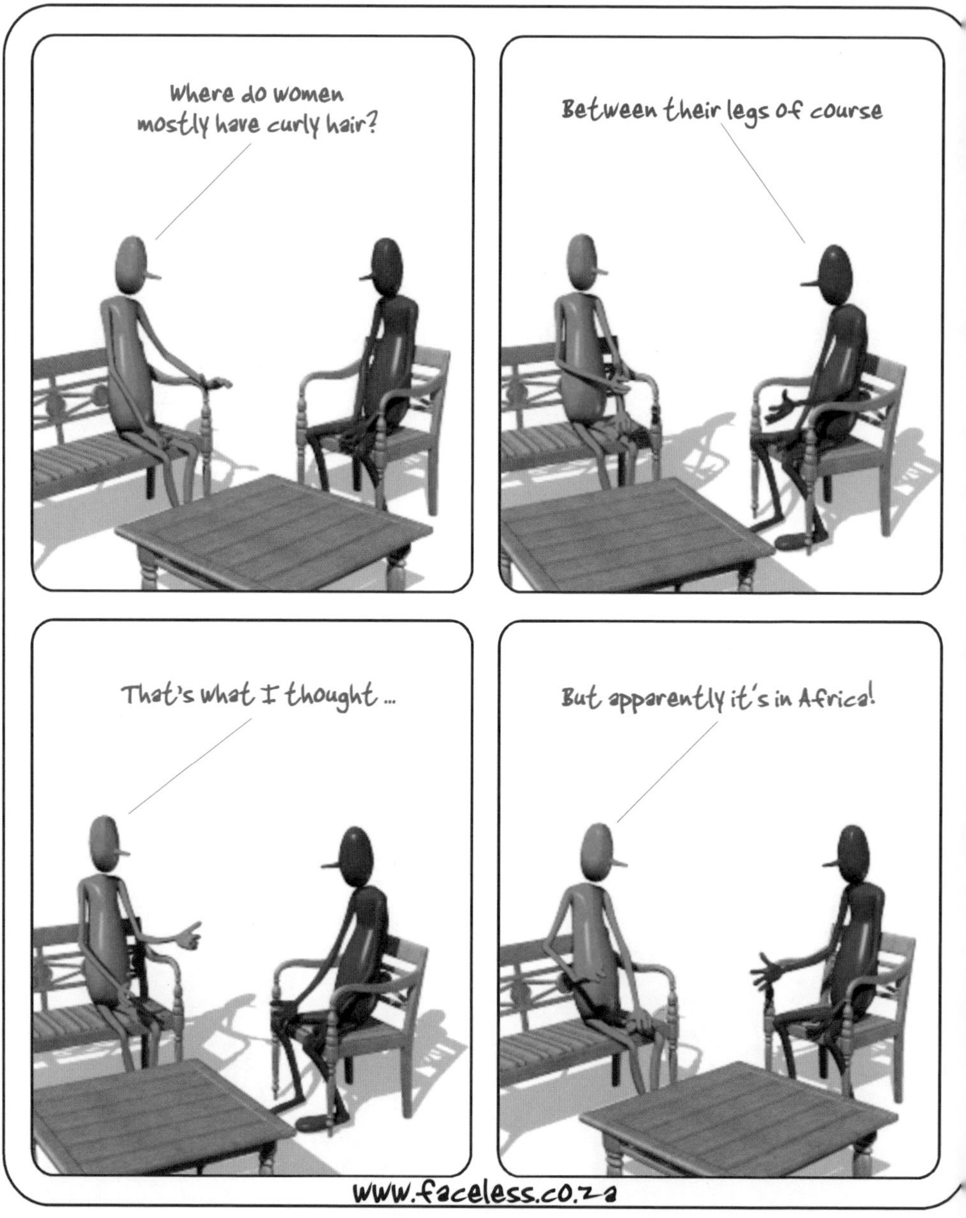
Where do women mostly have curly hair?
Between their legs of course
That's what I thought ...
But apparently it's in Africa!
www.faceless.co.za

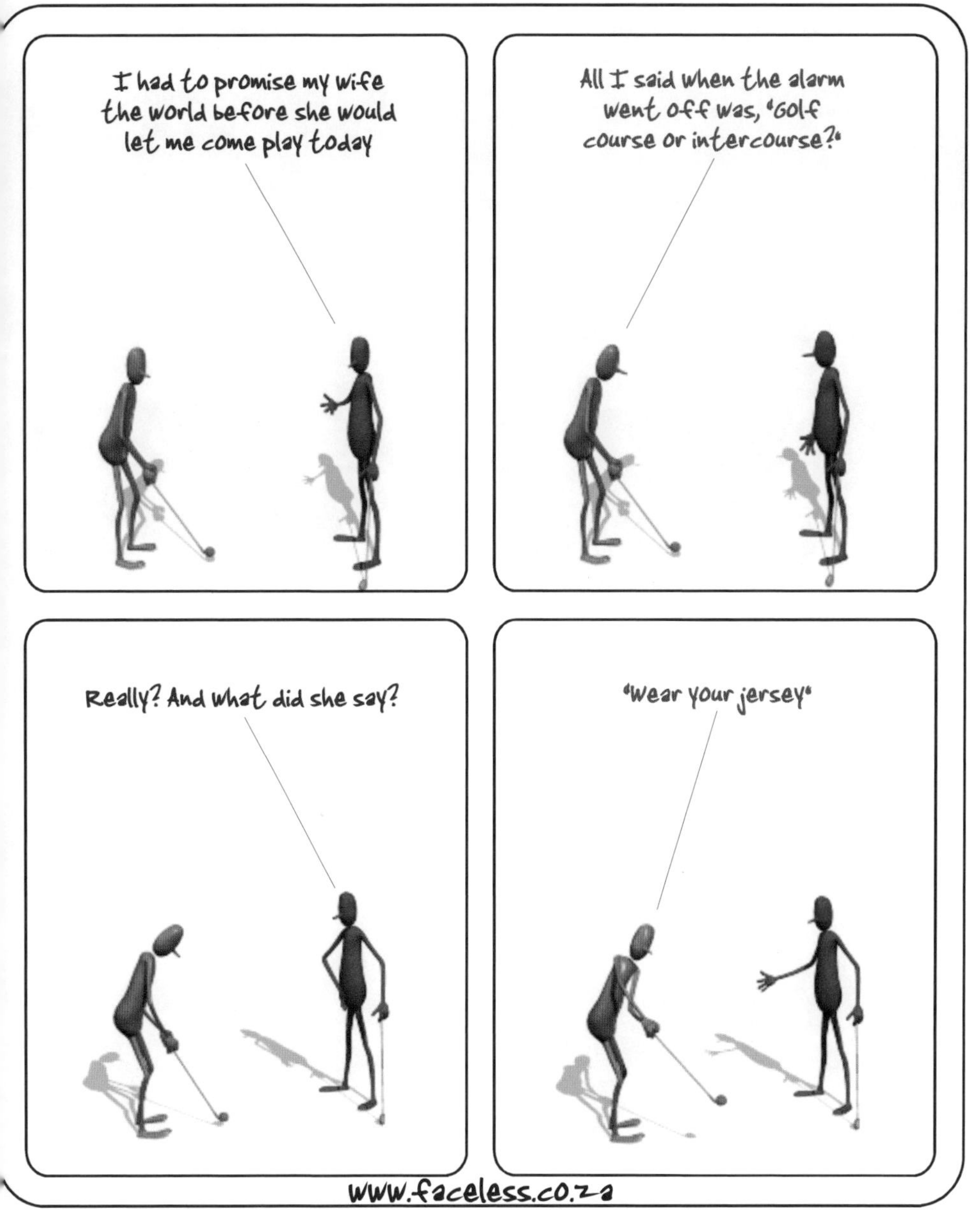
I had to promise my wife the world before she would let me come play today
All I said when the alarm went off was, "Golf course or intercourse?"
Really? And what did she say?
"Wear your jersey"
www.faceless.co.za

Your mom's the best sex in town!
I did your mom this morning, and it was sw-e-et!
And your mom liked it!
Go home, Dad, you're drunk!
www.faceless.co.za

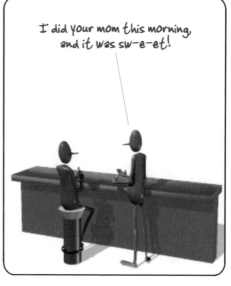

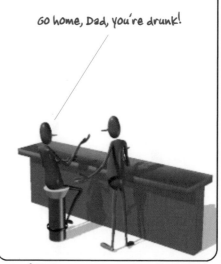

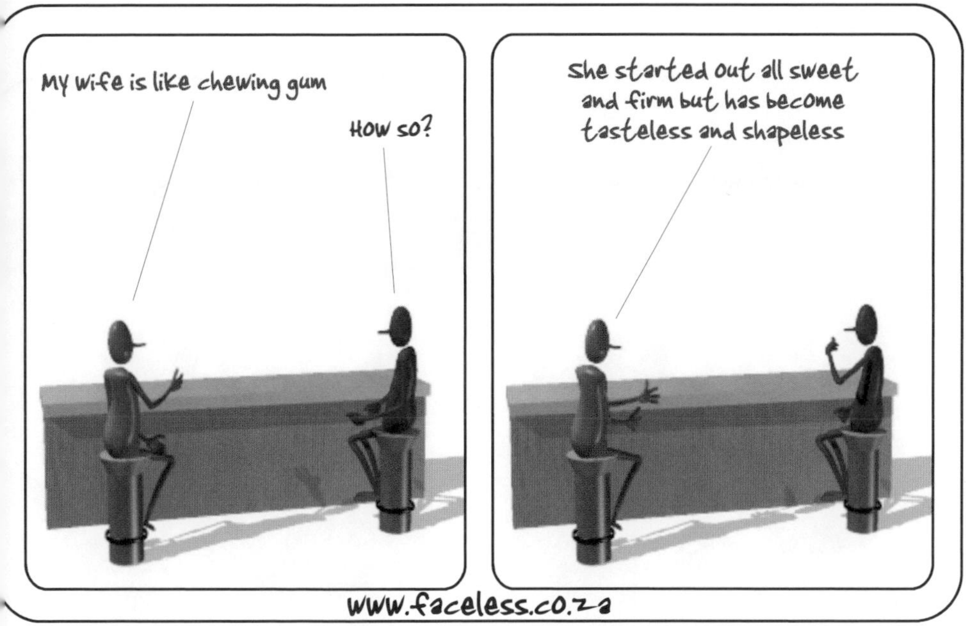
My wife is like chewing gum
How so?
She started out all sweet and firm but has become tasteless and shapeless
www.faceless.co.za

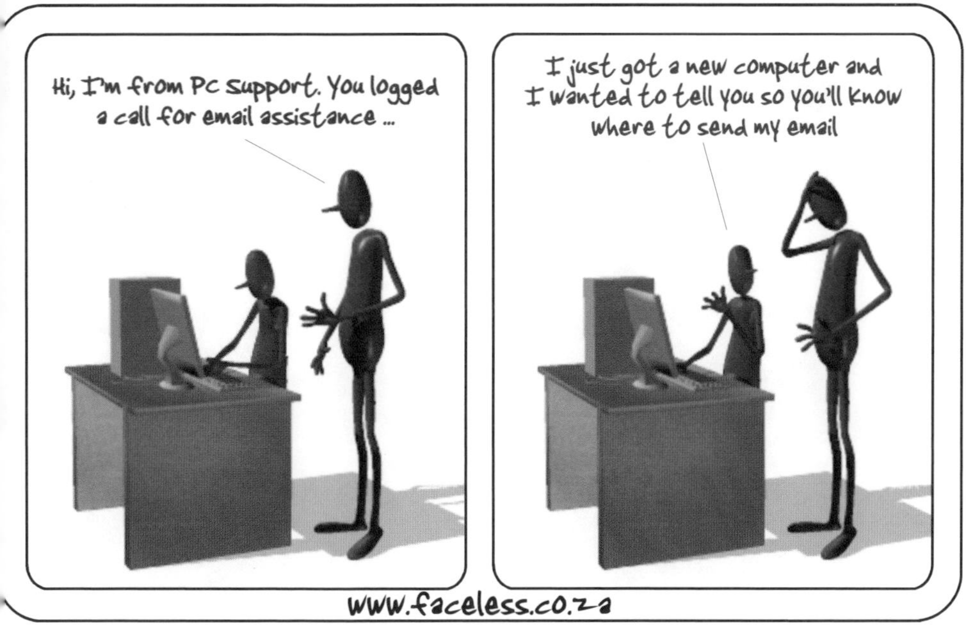
Hi, I'm from PC support. You logged a call for email assistance ...
I just got a new computer and I wanted to tell you so you'll know where to send my email
www.faceless.co.za

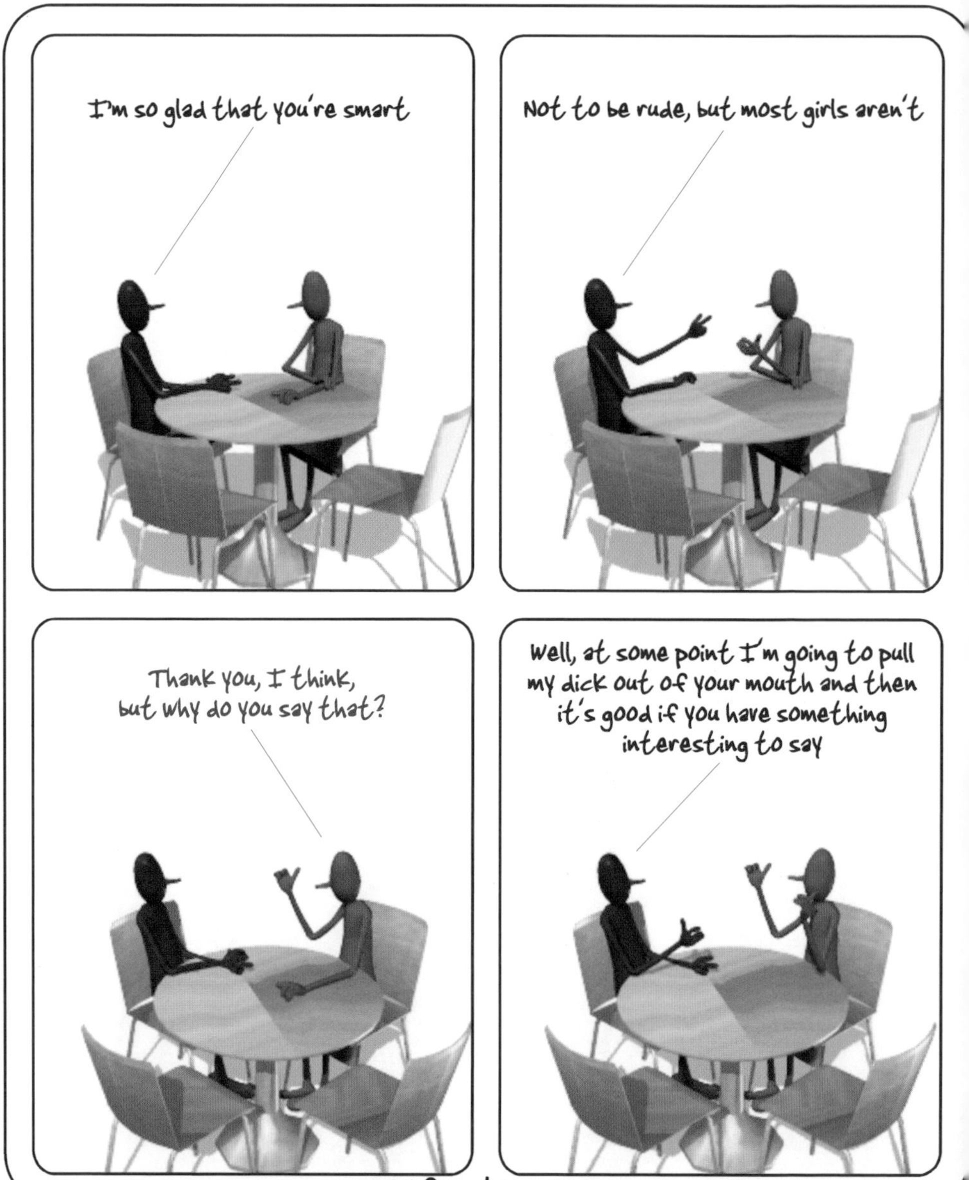

I'm so glad that you're smart
Not to be rude, but most girls aren't
Thank you, I think, but why do you say that?
Well, at some point I'm going to pull my dick out of your mouth and then it's good if you have something interesting to say
www.faceless.co.za

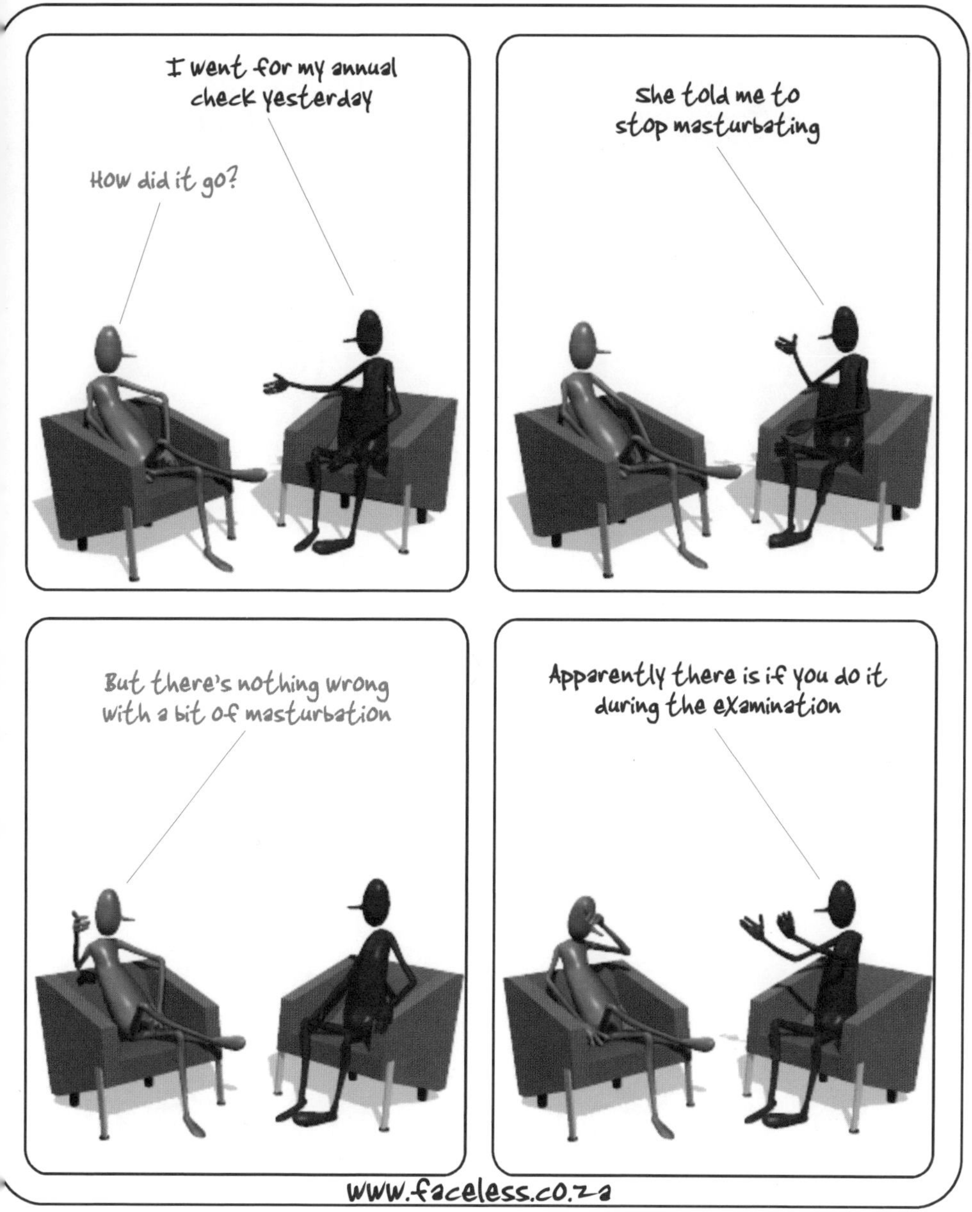
I went for my annual check yesterday
How did it go?
she told me to stop masturbating
But there's nothing wrong with a bit of masturbation
Apparently there is if you do it during the examination
www.faceless.co.za

Darling, I know this is our first baby, but you have to handle the pain
Get it out of me! Give me the drugs!
You did this to me, you bastard!
If you remember, I wanted to stick it up your butt and you said it would hurt too much
www.faceless.co.za

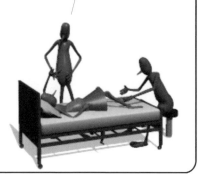

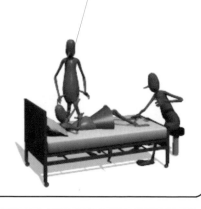

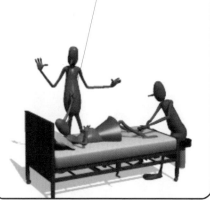

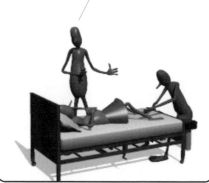

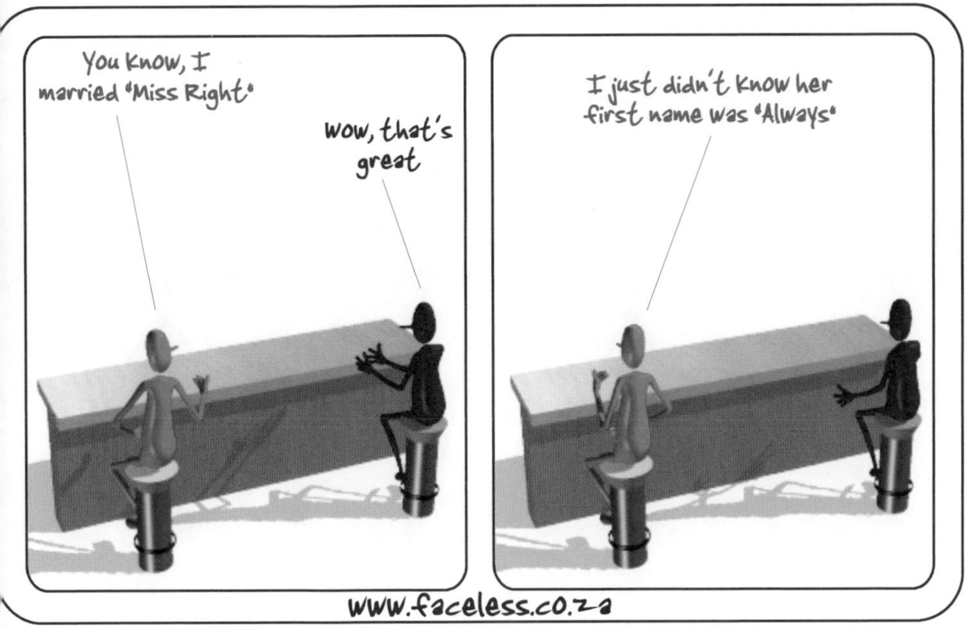
You know, I married "Miss Right"
wow, that's great
I just didn't know her first name was "Always"
www.faceless.co.za

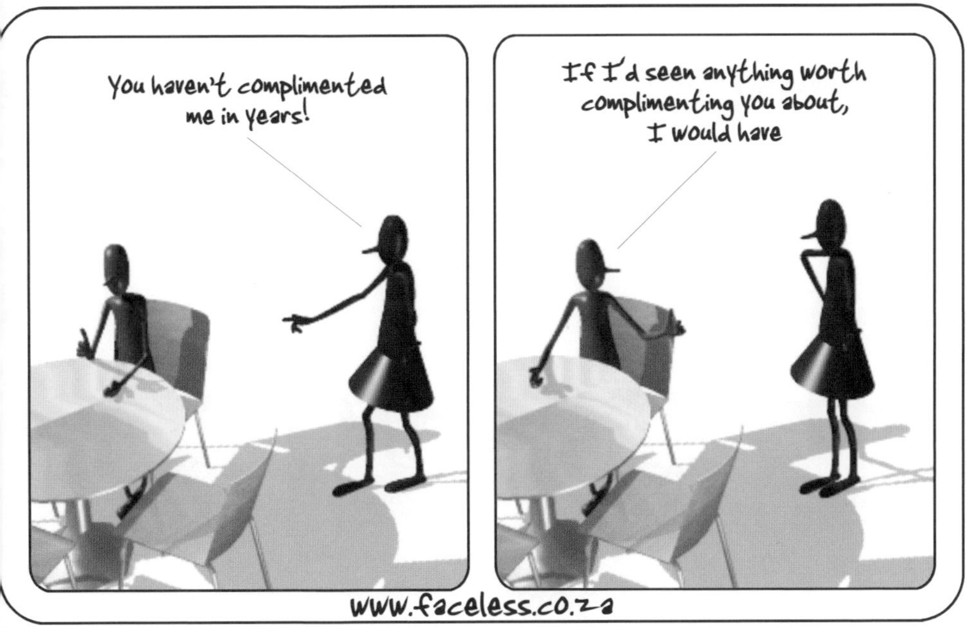
You haven't complimented me in years!
If I'd seen anything worth complimenting you about, I would have
www.faceless.co.za

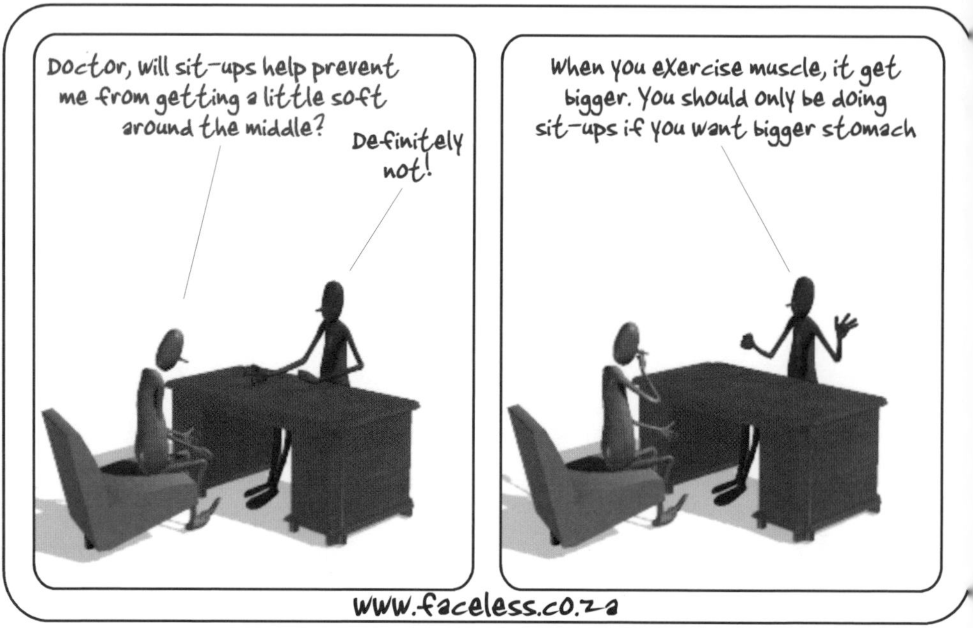
Doctor, will sit-ups help prevent me from getting a little soft around the middle?
Definitely not!
When you eXercise muscle, it get bigger. You should only be doing sit-ups if you want bigger stomach
www.faceless.co.za

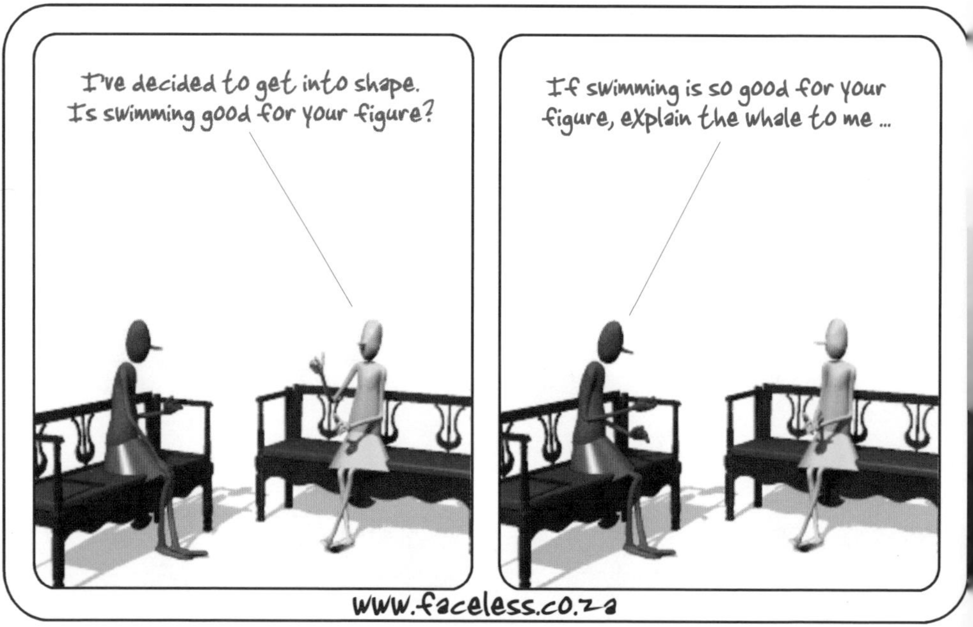
I've decided to get into shape. Is swimming good for your figure?
If swimming is so good for your figure, eXplain the whale to me ...
www.faceless.co.za

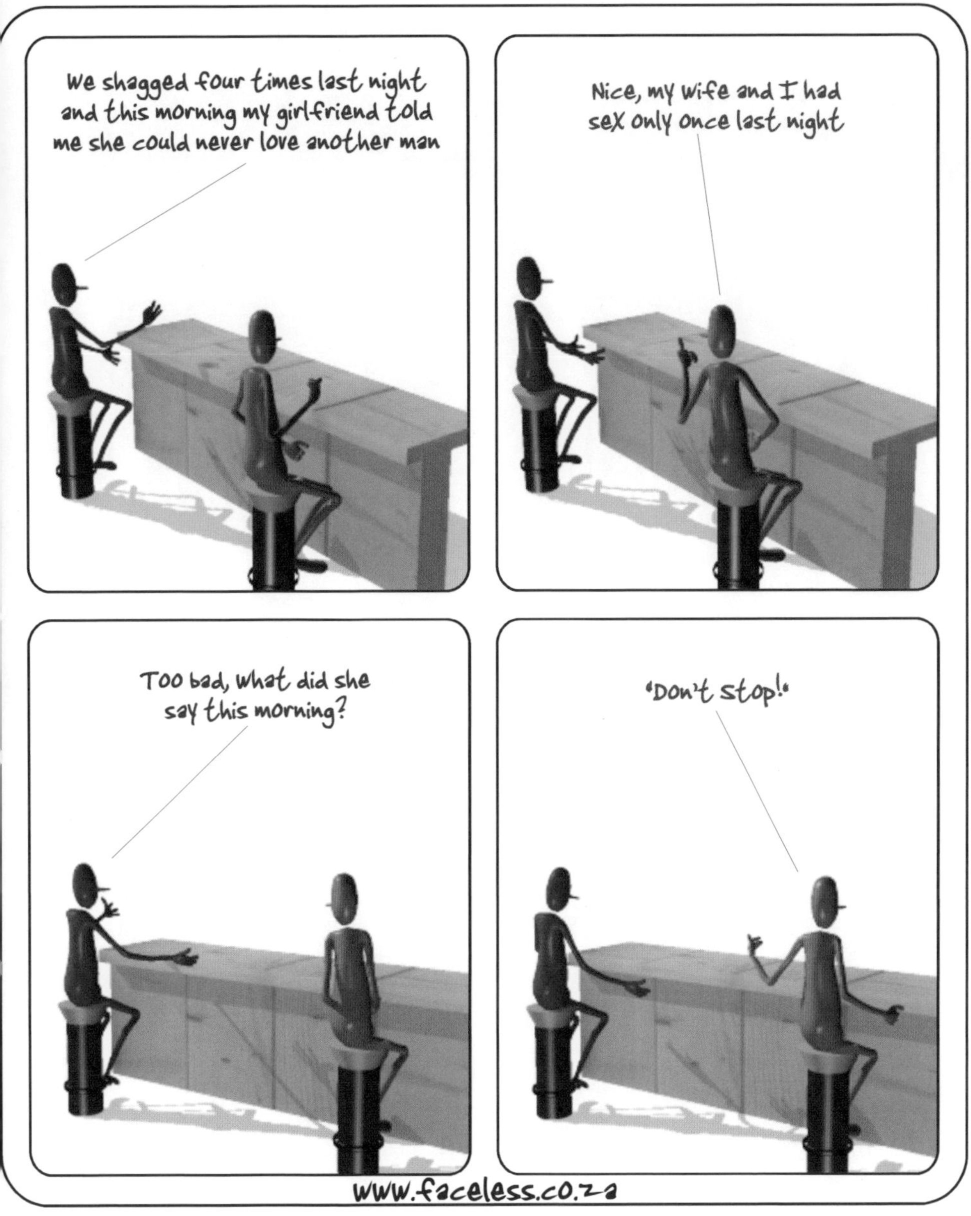
We shagged four times last night and this morning my girlfriend told me she could never love another man
Nice, my wife and I had sex only once last night
TOO bad, what did she say this morning?
"Don't stop!"
www.faceless.co.za

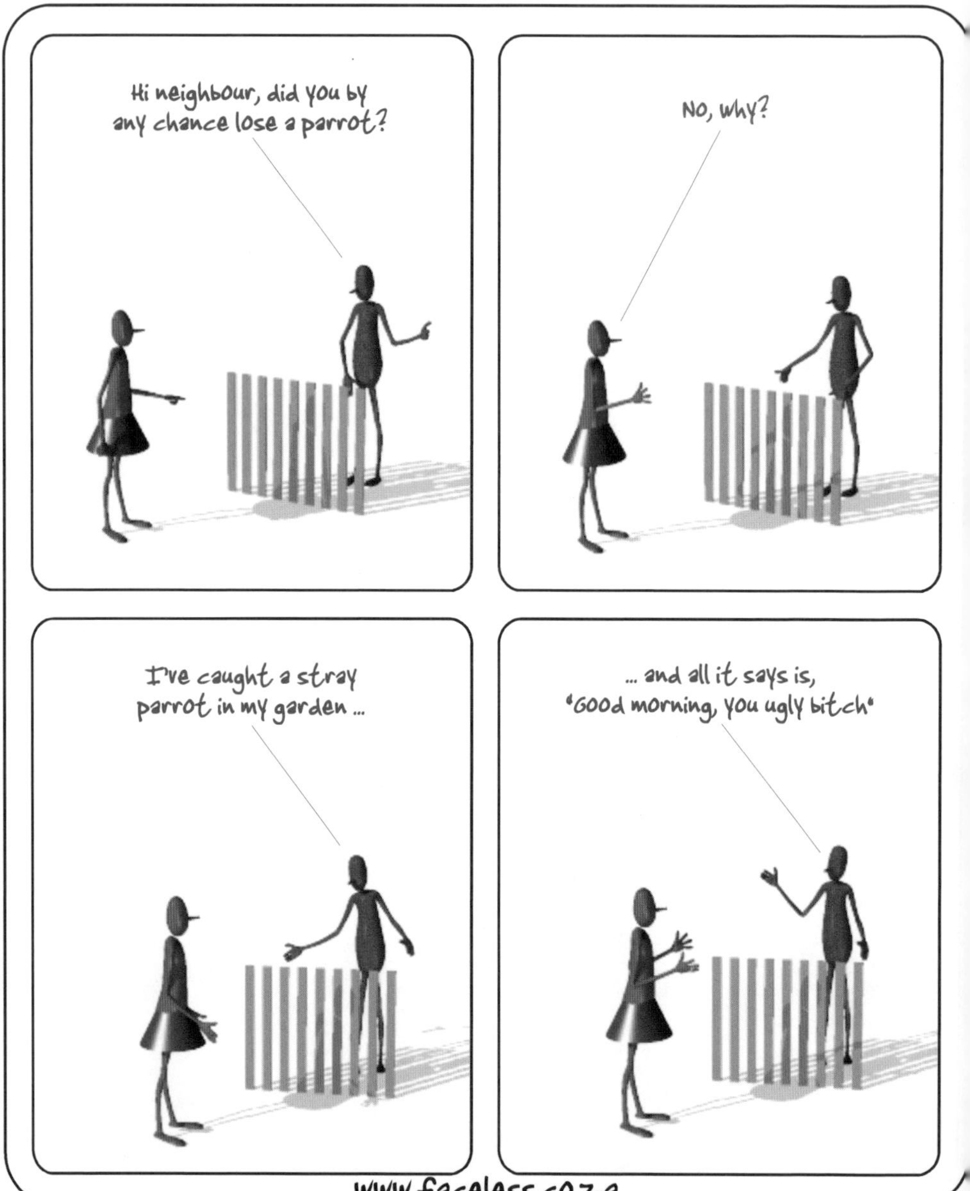

Hi neighbour, did you by any chance lose a parrot?
No, why?
I've caught a stray parrot in my garden ...
... and all it says is, "Good morning, you ugly bitch"
www.faceless.co.za

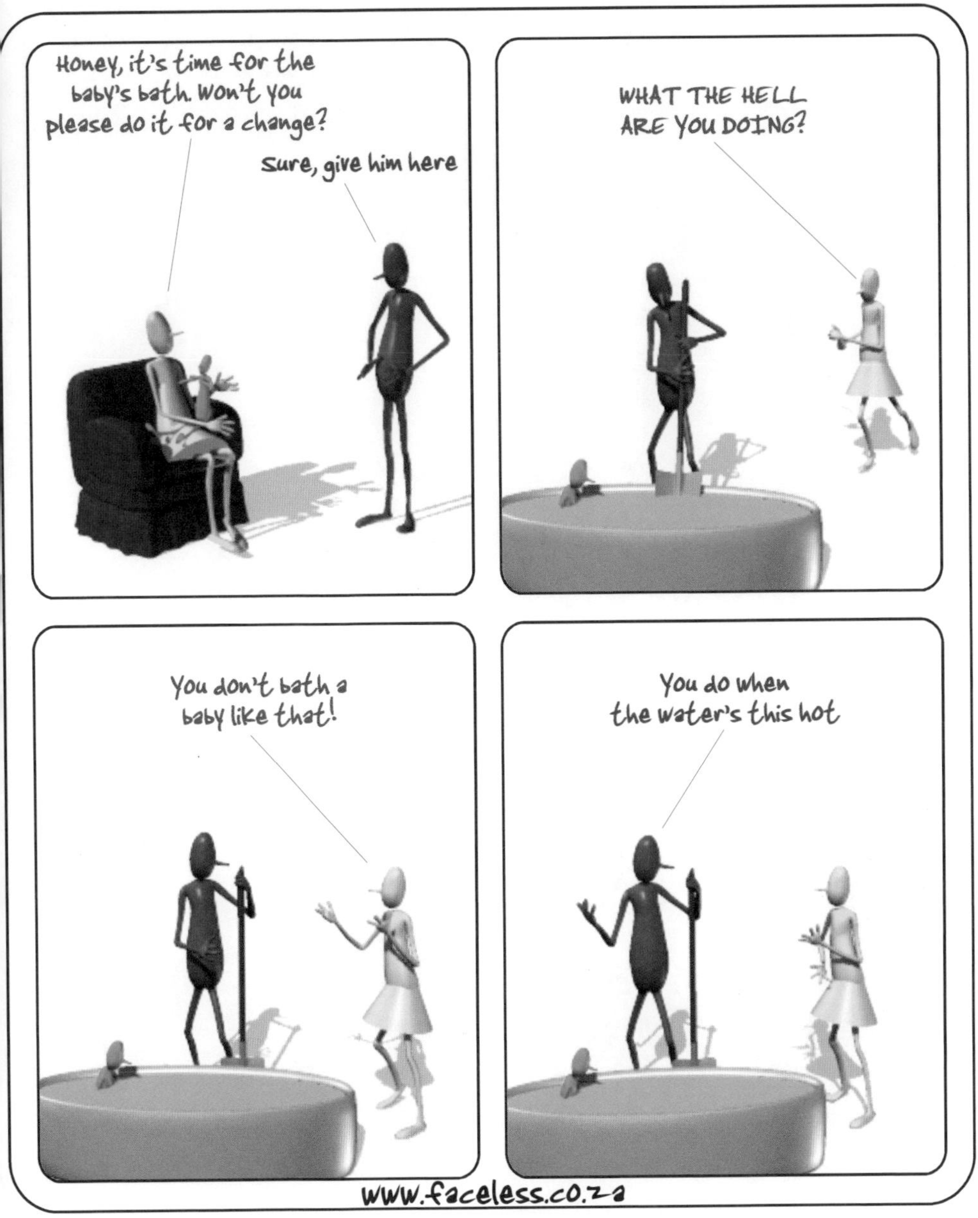
Honey, it's time for the baby's bath. Won't you please do it for a change?
Sure, give him here
WHAT THE HELL ARE YOU DOING?
You don't bath a baby like that!
You do when the water's this hot
www.faceless.co.za

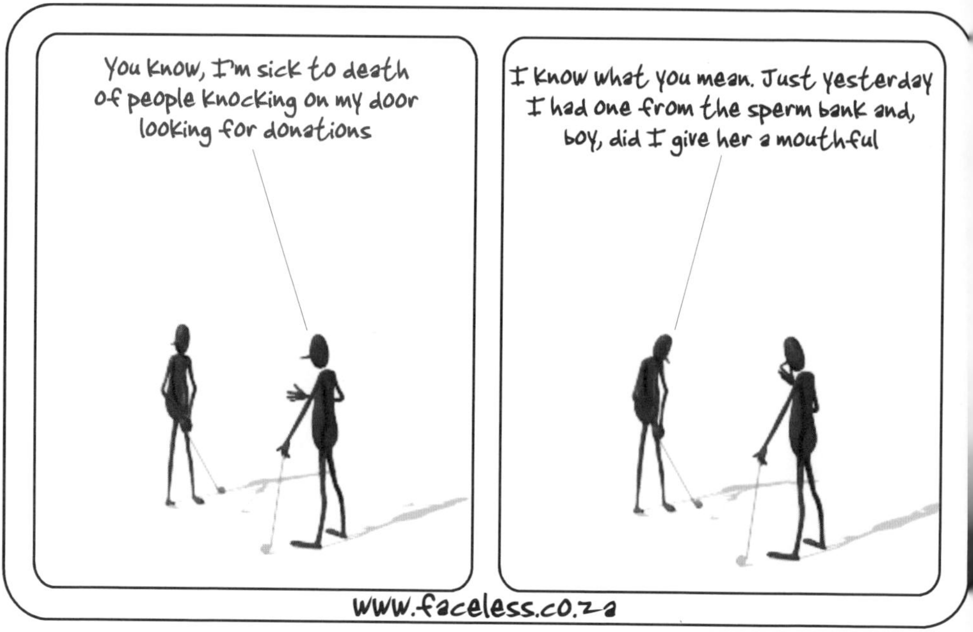
You know, I'm sick to death of people knocking on my door looking for donations
I know what you mean. Just yesterday I had one from the sperm bank and, boy, did I give her a mouthful
www.faceless.co.za

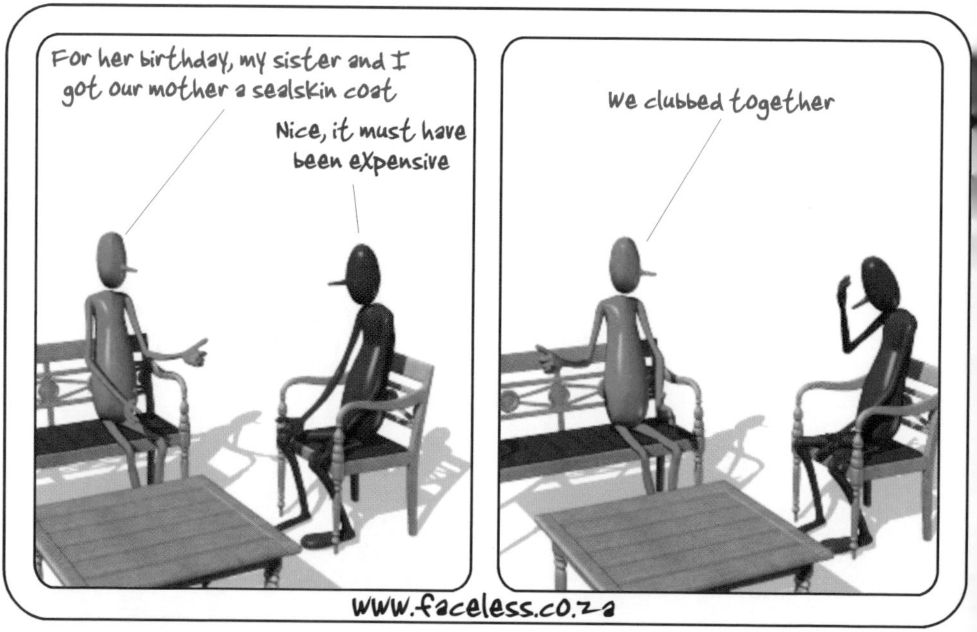
For her birthday, my sister and I got our mother a sealskin coat
Nice, it must have been expensive
We clubbed together
www.faceless.co.za

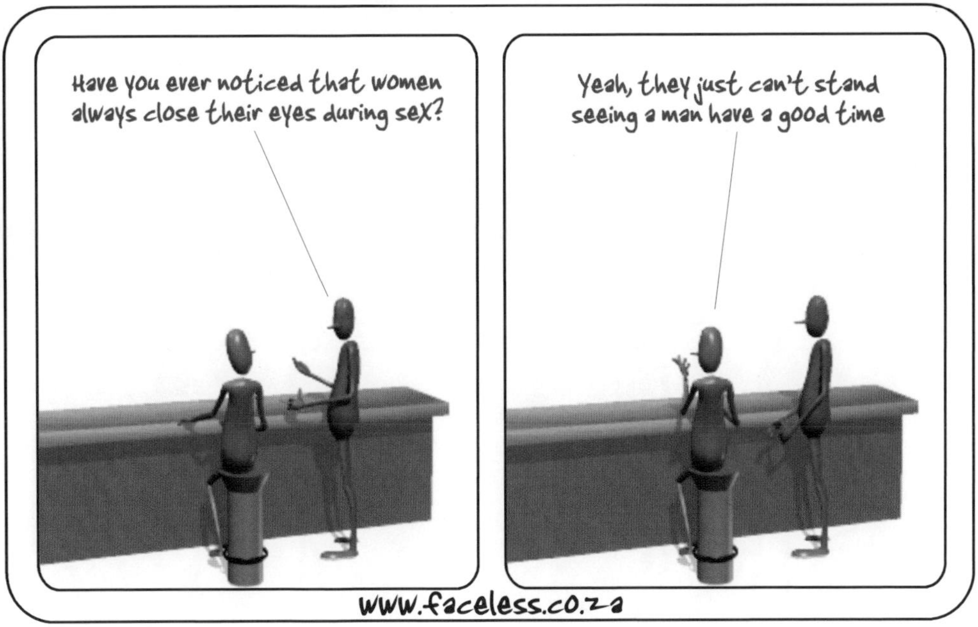
Have you ever noticed that women always close their eyes during sex?
Yeah, they just can't stand seeing a man have a good time
www.faceless.co.za

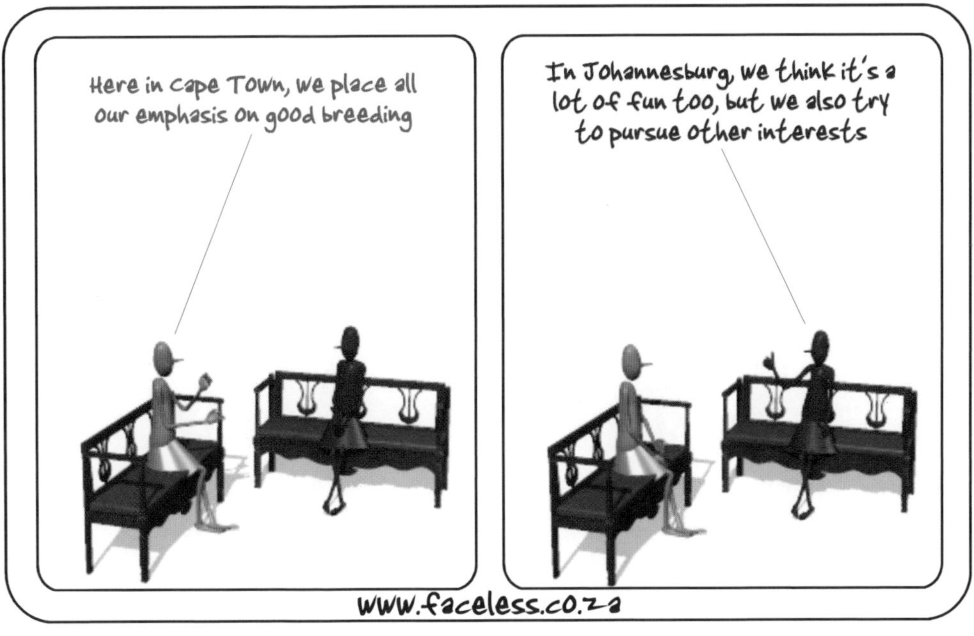
Here in Cape Town, we place all our emphasis on good breeding
In Johannesburg, we think it's a lot of fun too, but we also try to pursue other interests
www.faceless.co.za

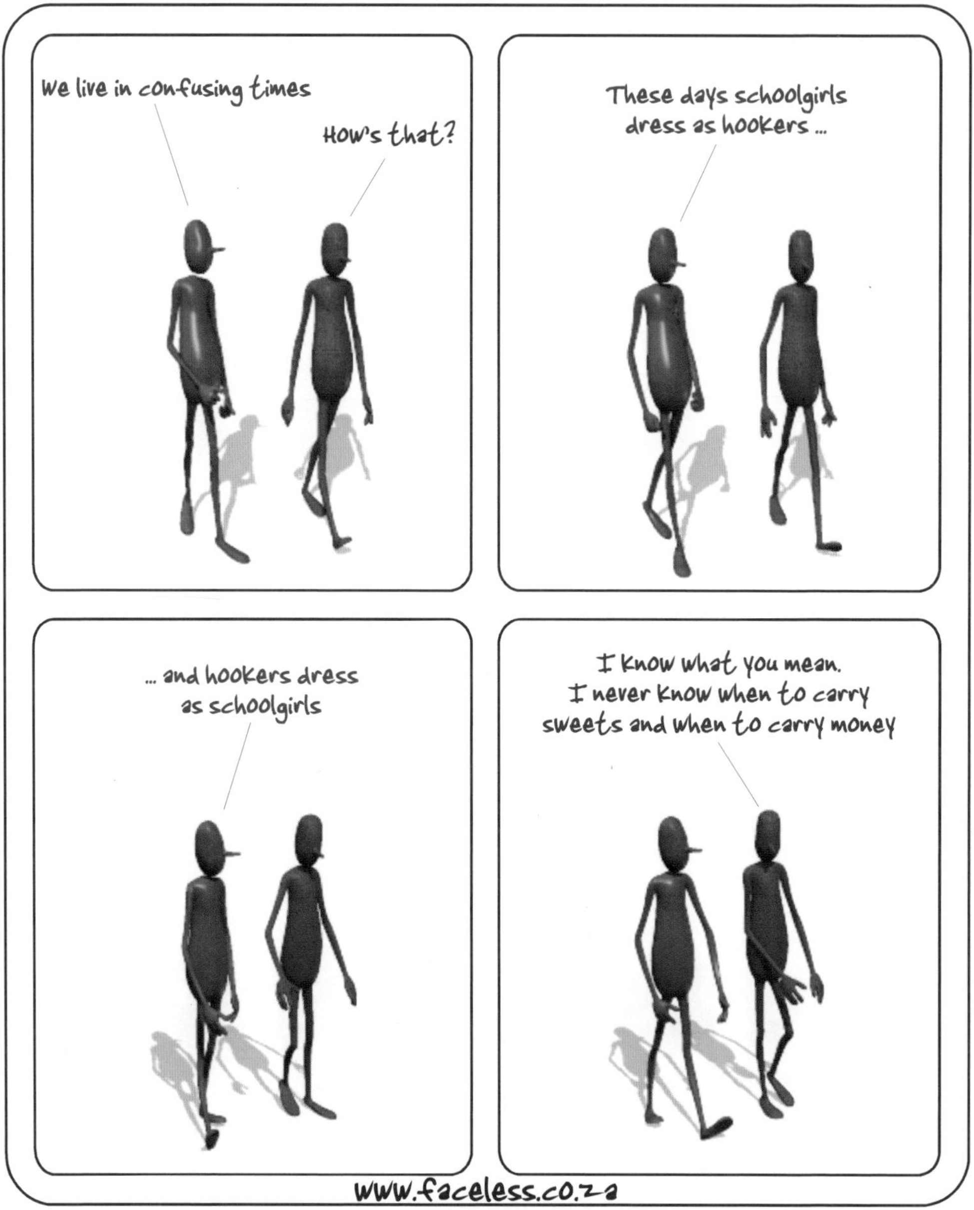
We live in confusing times
How's that?
These days schoolgirls dress as hookers ...
... and hookers dress as schoolgirls
I know what you mean. I never know when to carry sweets and when to carry money
www.faceless.co.za

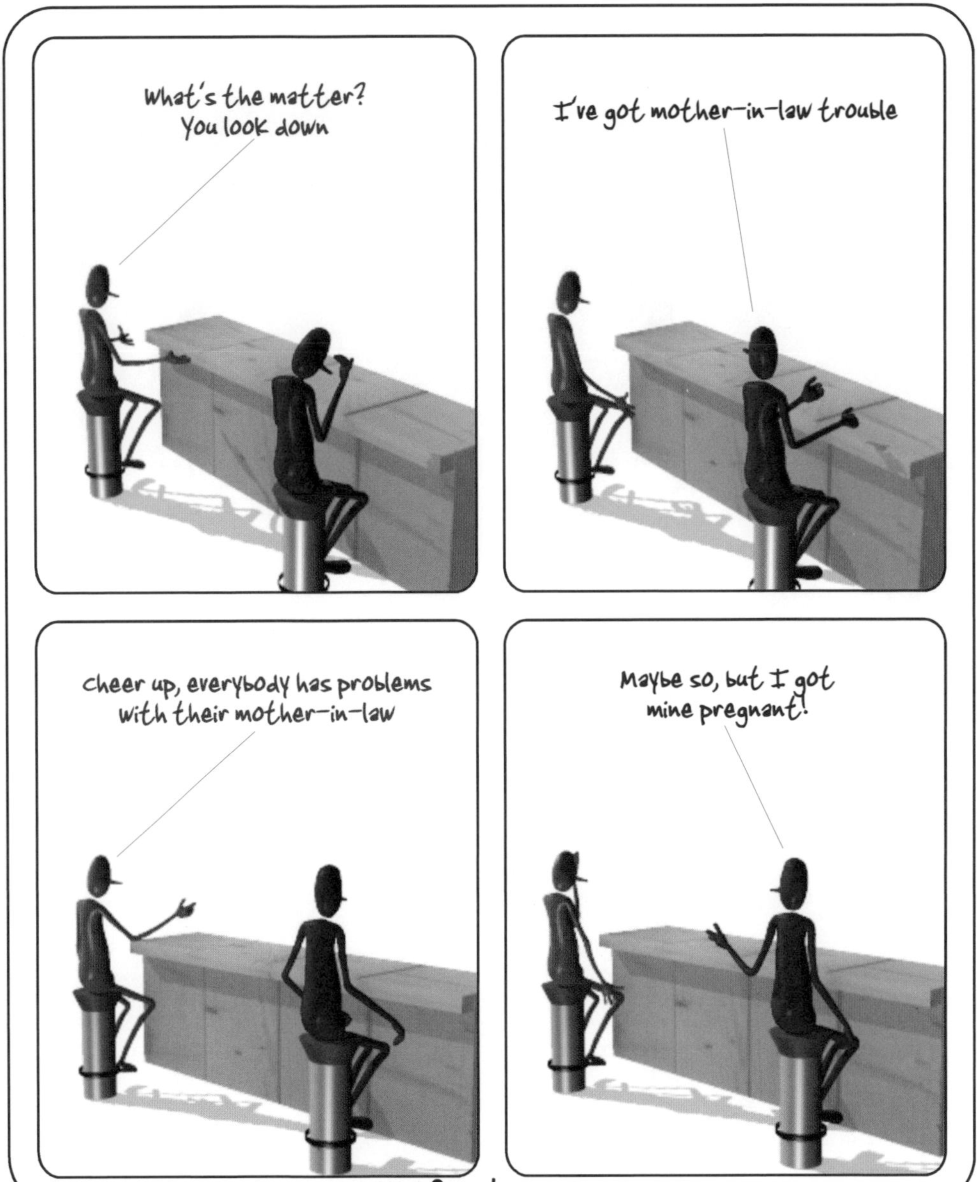
What's the matter? You look down
I've got mother-in-law trouble
Cheer up, everybody has problems with their mother-in-law
Maybe so, but I got mine pregnant!
www.faceless.co.za

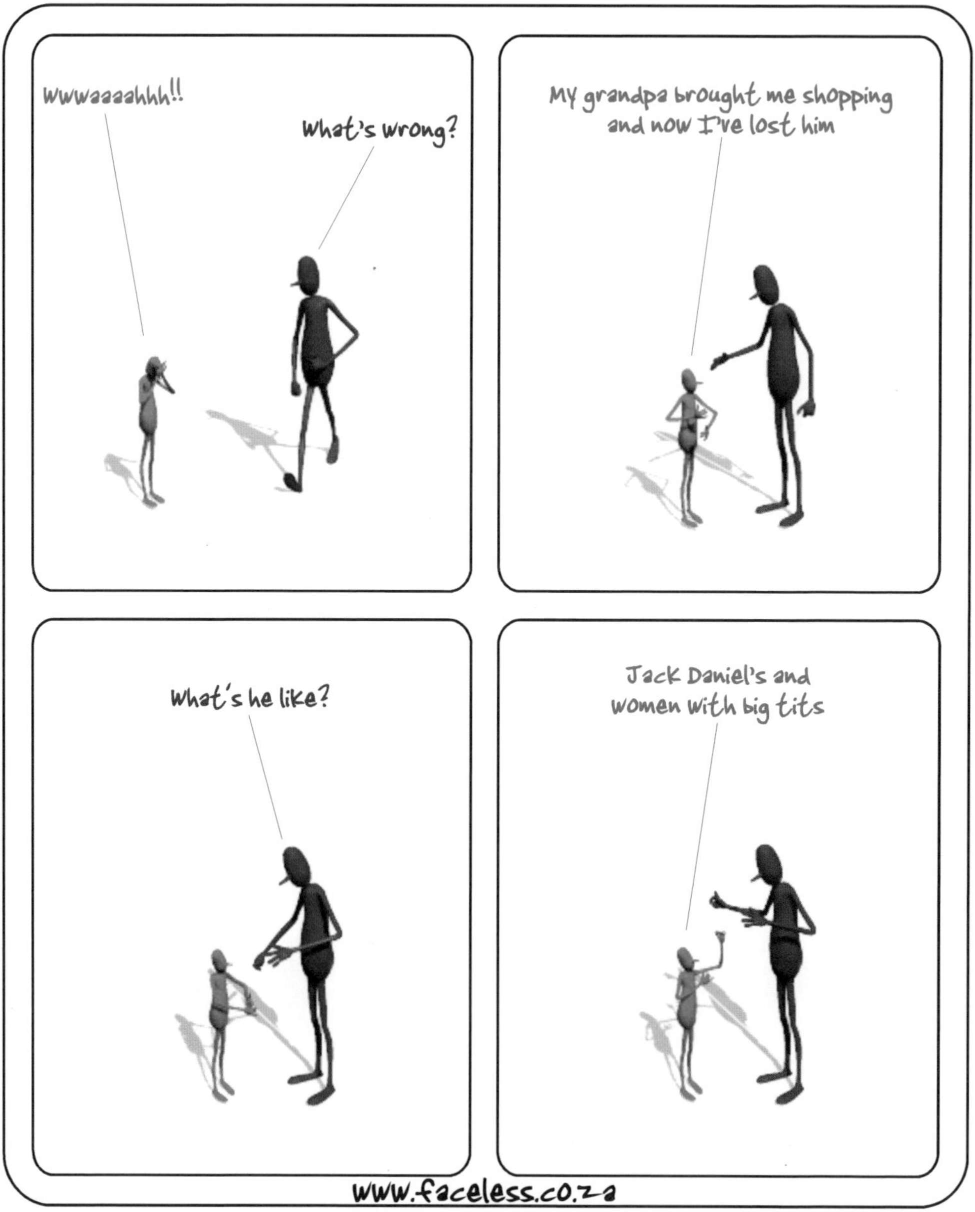
Wwwaaaahhh!!
What's wrong?
My grandpa brought me shopping and now I've lost him
What's he like?
Jack Daniel's and women with big tits
www.faceless.co.za

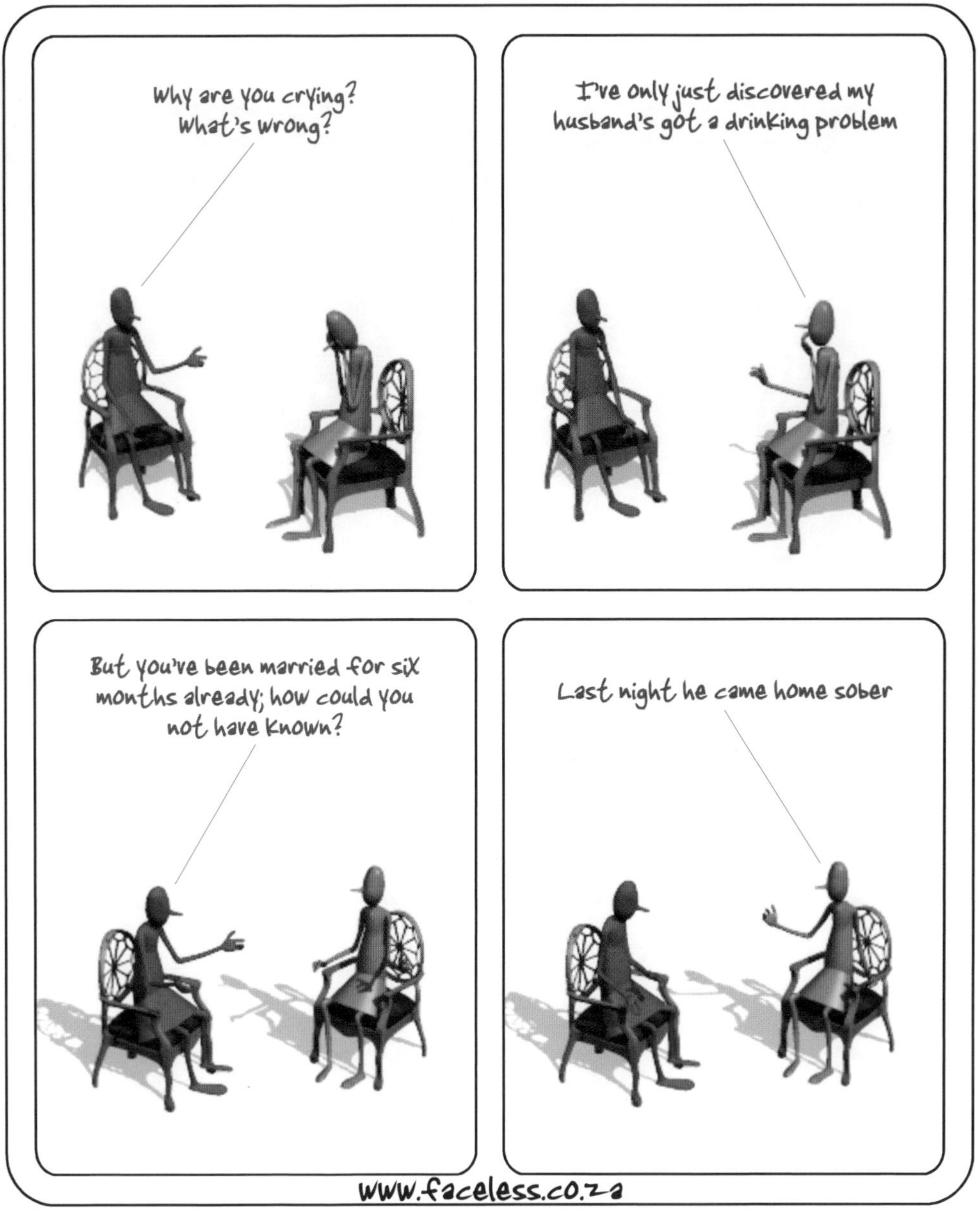
Why are you crying? What's wrong?
I've only just discovered my husband's got a drinking problem
But you've been married for six months already; how could you not have known?
Last night he came home sober
www.faceless.co.za

Since we got married, my wife has changed me - she stopped me drinking, smoking and partying all night
She taught me to dress well, enjoy fine arts, appreciate gourmet cooking and classical music
Sounds like you may be bitter because she changed you so drastically
I'm not bitter. Now that I'm so improved, she just isn't good enough for me
www.faceless.co.za

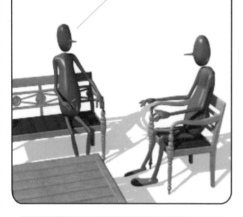

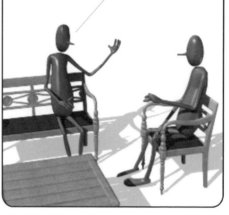

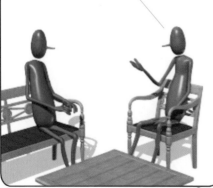

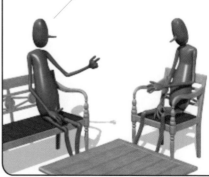

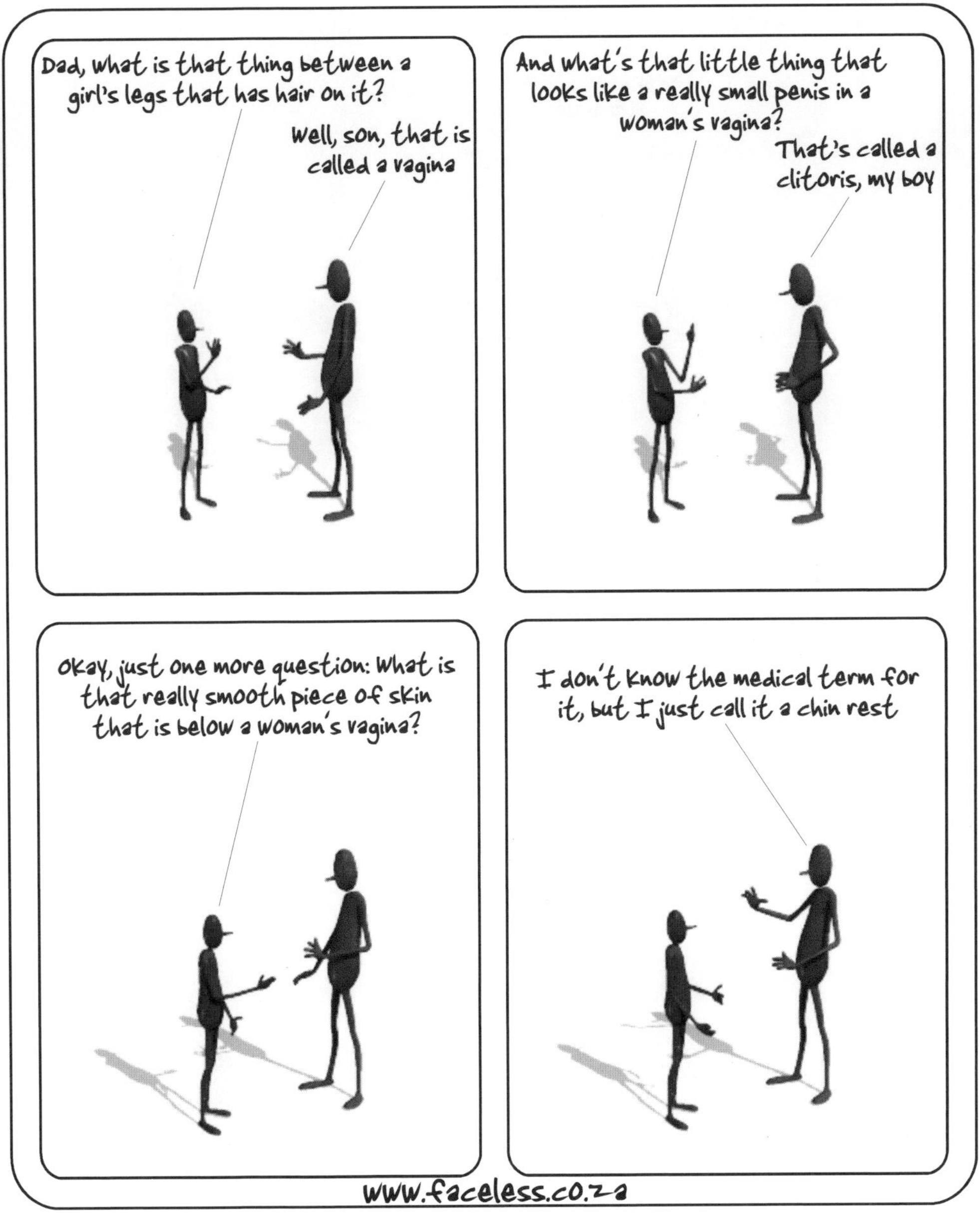
Dad, what is that thing between a girl's legs that has hair on it?
Well, son, that is called a vagina
And what's that little thing that looks like a really small penis in a woman's vagina?
That's called a clitoris, my boy
Okay, just one more question: What is that really smooth piece of skin that is below a woman's vagina?
I don't know the medical term for it, but I just call it a chin rest
www.faceless.co.za

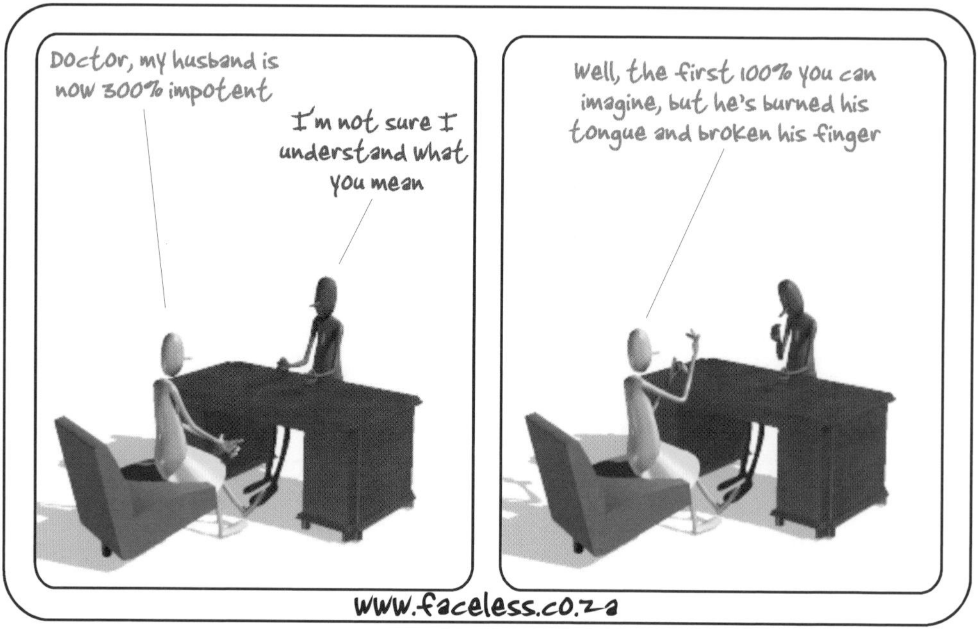
Doctor, my husband is now 300% impotent
I'm not sure I understand what you mean
Well, the first 100% you can imagine, but he's burned his tongue and broken his finger
www.faceless.co.za

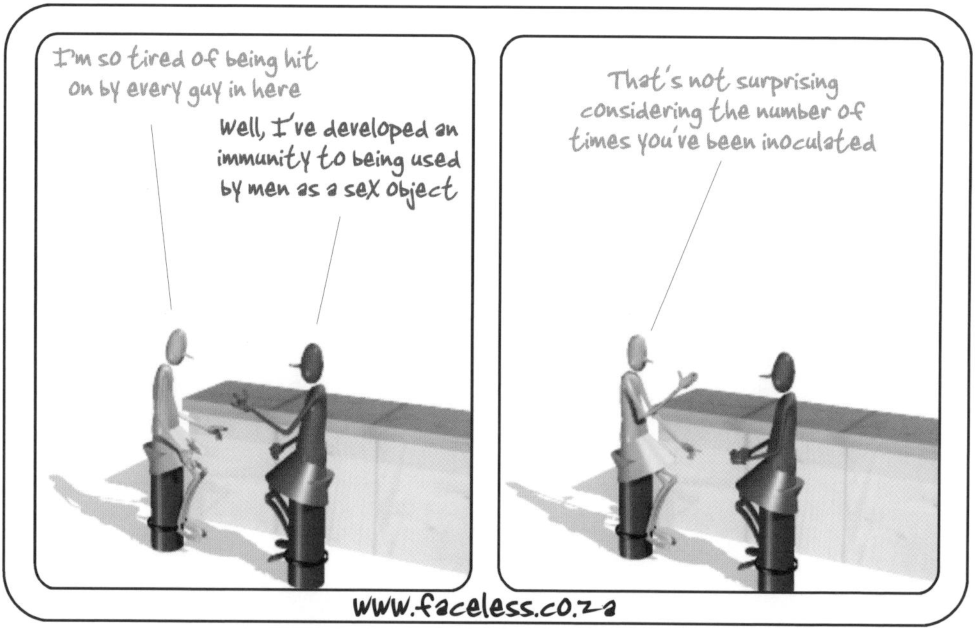
I'm so tired of being hit on by every guy in here
Well, I've developed an immunity to being used by men as a sex object
That's not surprising considering the number of times you've been inoculated
www.faceless.co.za

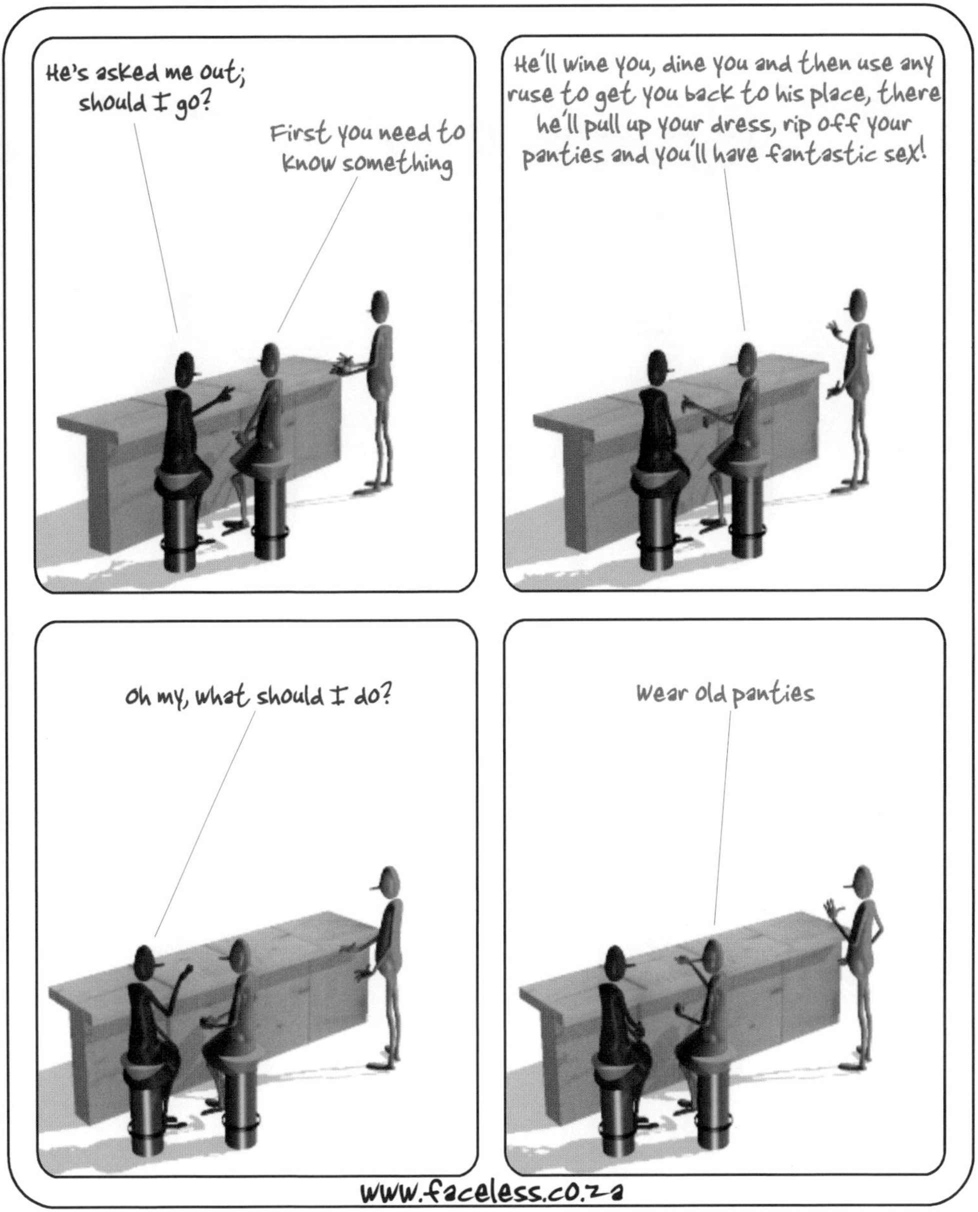
He's asked me out; should I go?
First you need to know something
He'll wine you, dine you and then use any ruse to get you back to his place, there he'll pull up your dress, rip off your panties and you'll have fantastic sex!
Oh my, what should I do?
Wear old panties
www.faceless.co.za

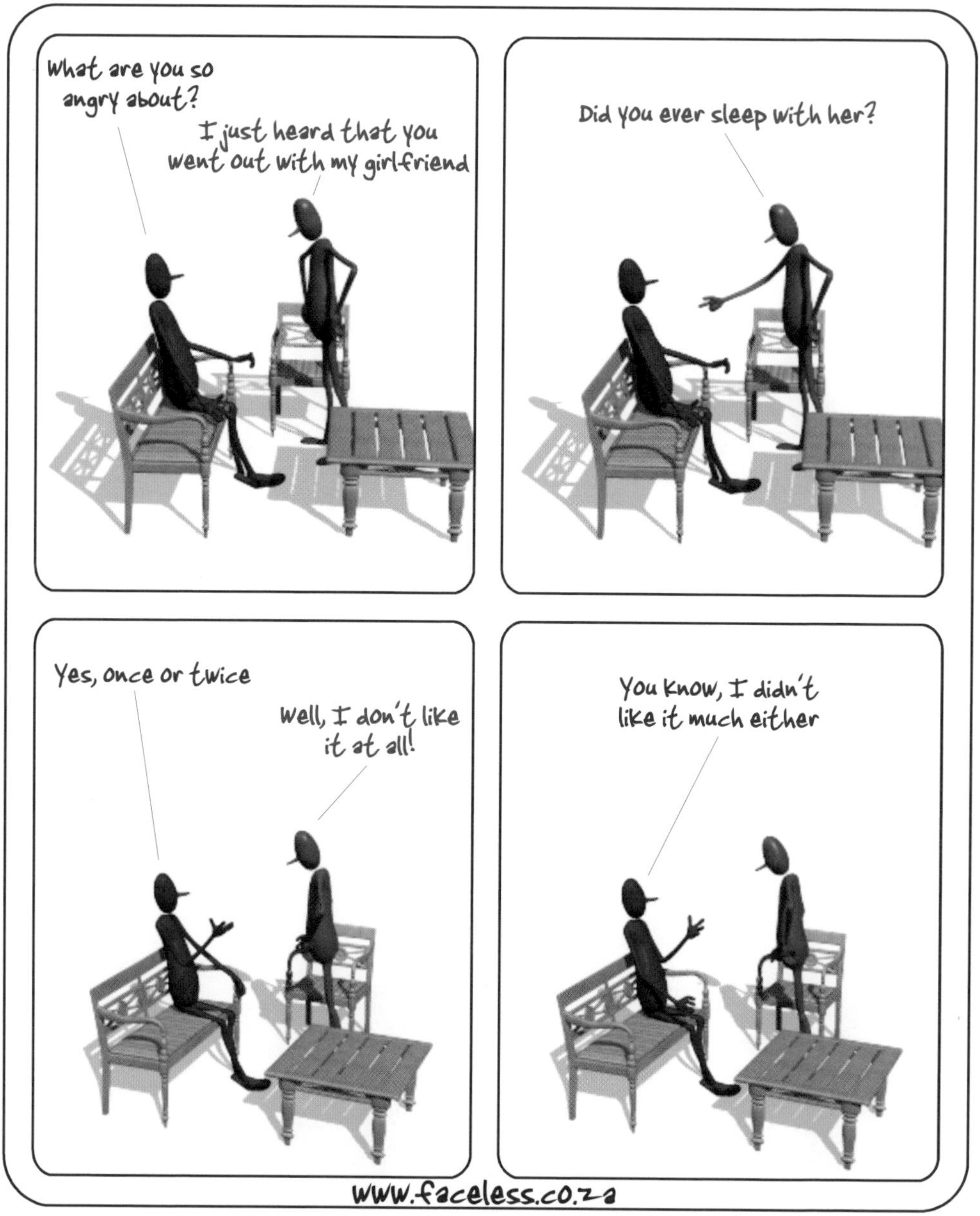
What are you so angry about?
I just heard that you went out with my girlfriend
Did you ever sleep with her?
Yes, once or twice
Well, I don't like it at all!
You know, I didn't like it much either
www.faceless.co.za

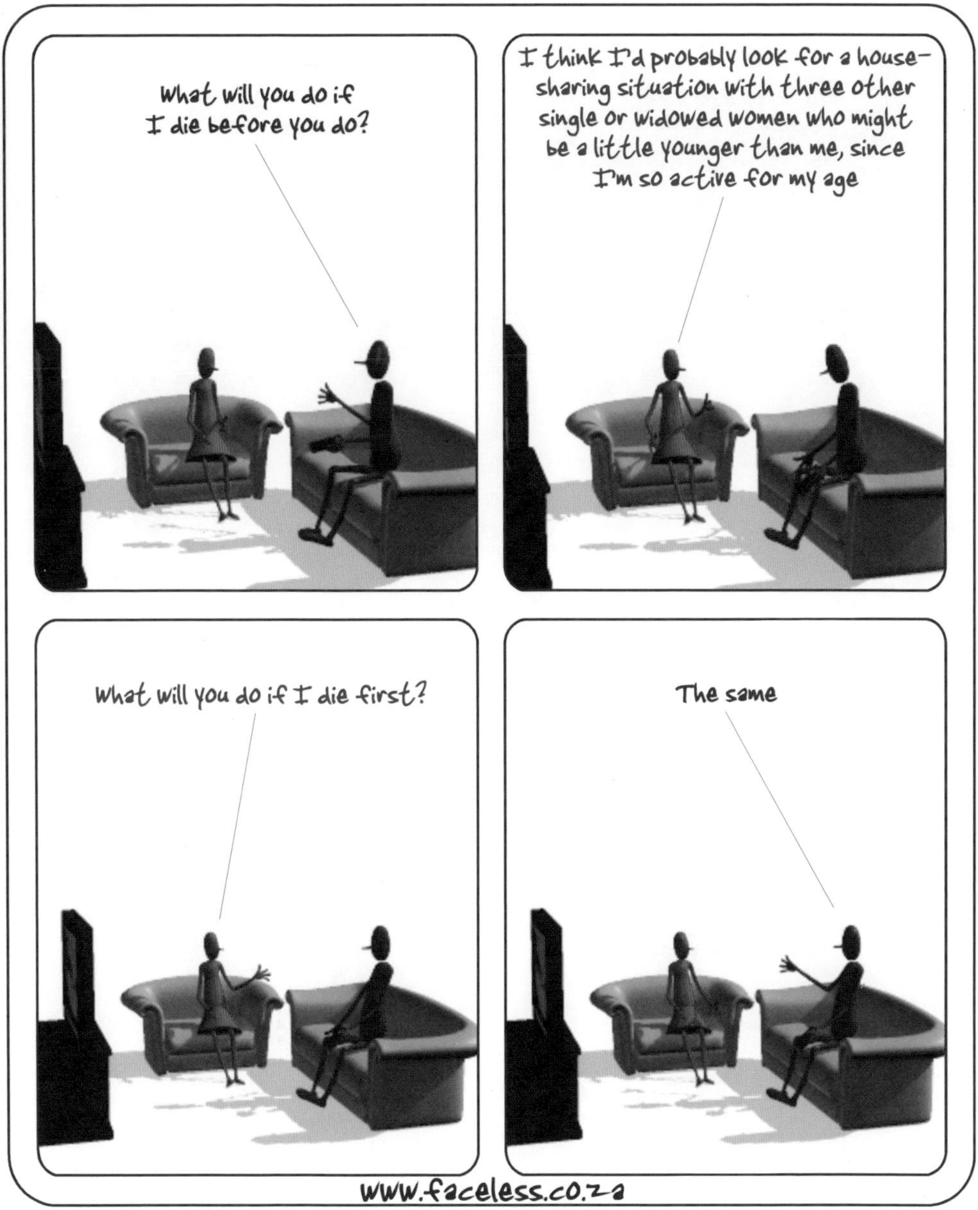
What will you do if
I die before you do?
I think I'd probably look for a house-sharing situation with three other single or widowed women who might be a little younger than me, since I'm so active for my age
What will you do if I die first?
The same
www.faceless.co.za

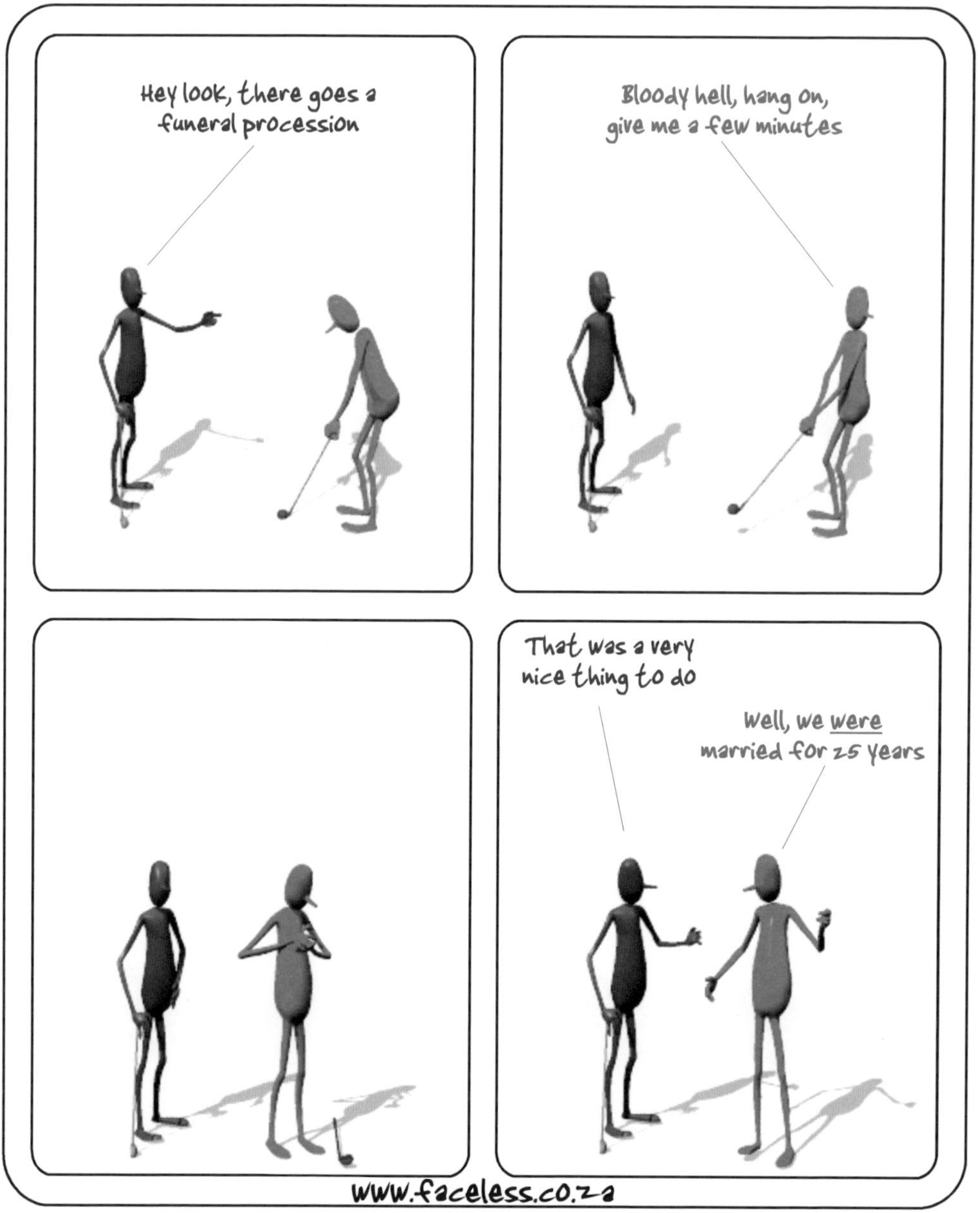
Hey look, there goes a funeral procession
Bloody hell, hang on, give me a few minutes
That was a very nice thing to do
Well, we were married for 25 years
www.faceless.co.za

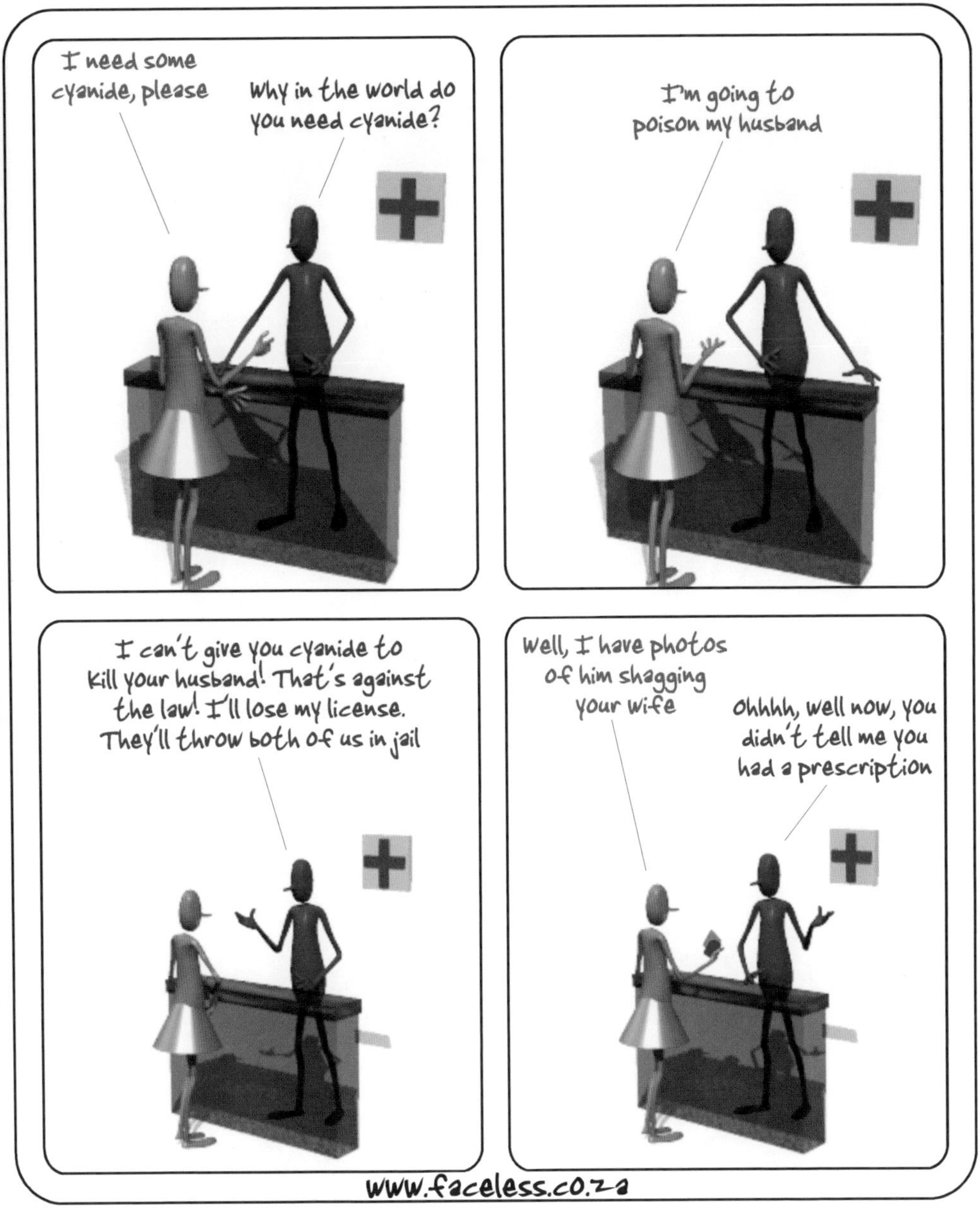
I need some cyanide, please
Why in the world do you need cyanide?
I'm going to poison my husband
I can't give you cyanide to kill your husband! That's against the law! I'll lose my license. They'll throw both of us in jail
Well, I have photos of him shagging your wife
Ohhhh, well now, you didn't tell me you had a prescription
www.faceless.co.za

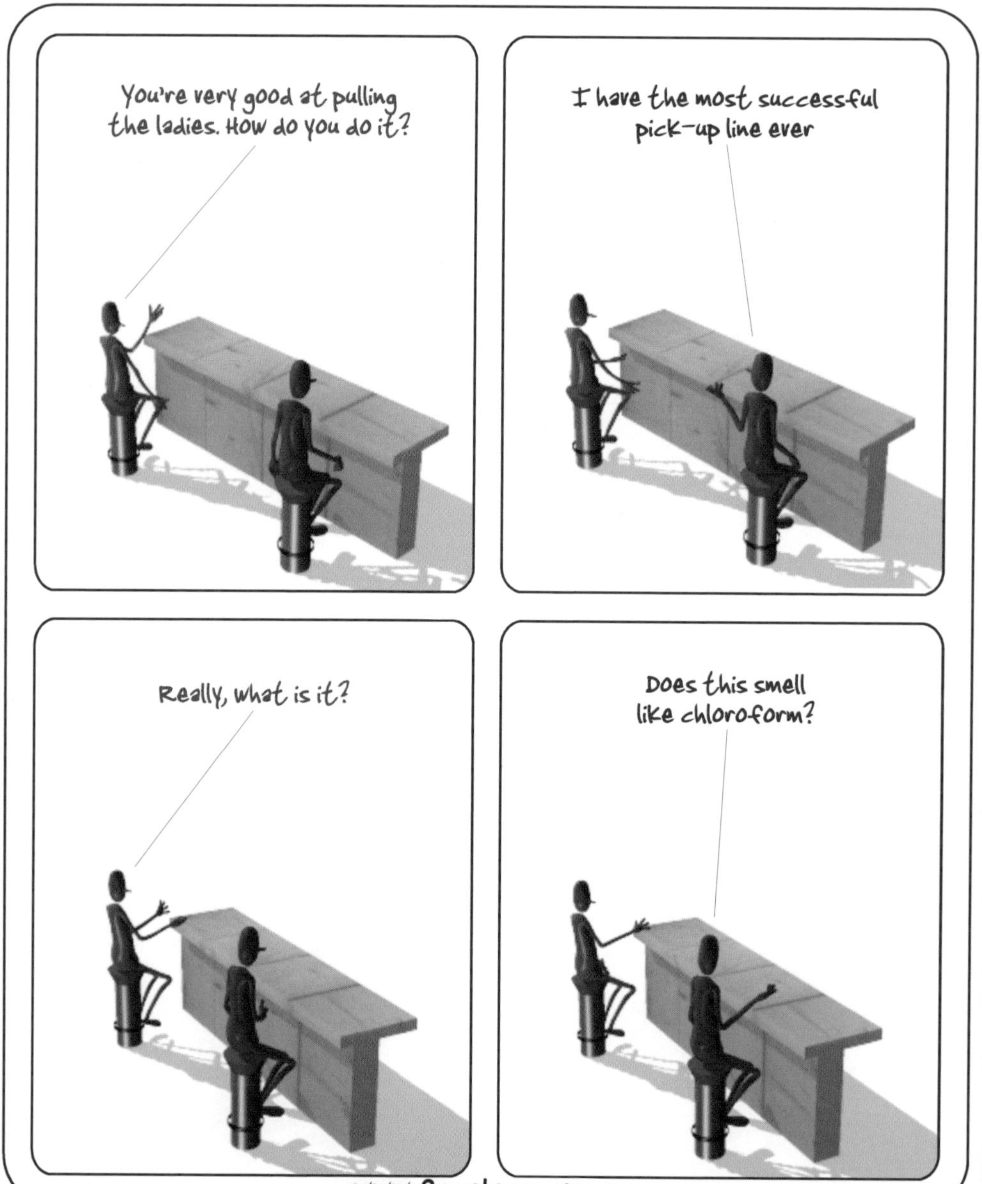
You're very good at pulling the ladies. How do you do it?
I have the most successful pick-up line ever
Really, what is it?
Does this smell like chloroform?
www.faceless.co.za

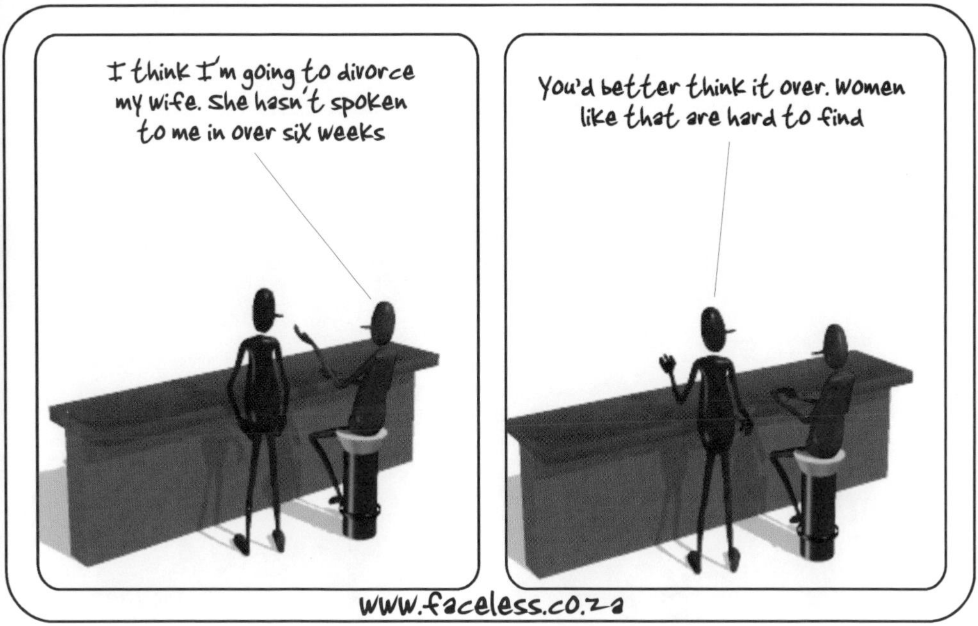
I think I'm going to divorce my wife. She hasn't spoken to me in over six weeks
You'd better think it over. Women like that are hard to find
www.faceless.co.za

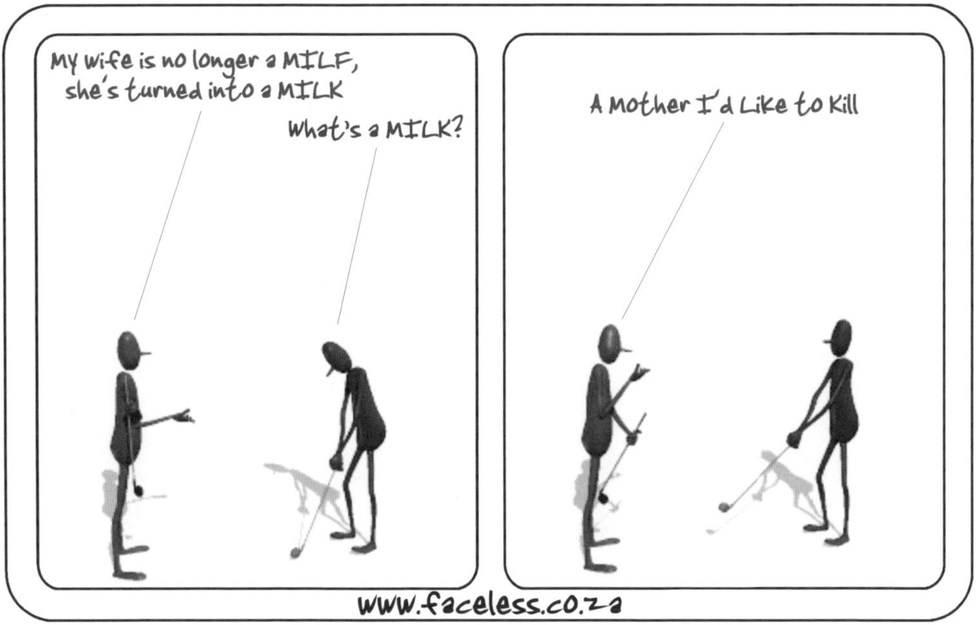
My wife is no longer a MILF, she's turned into a MILK
What's a MILK?
A Mother I'd Like to Kill
www.faceless.co.za

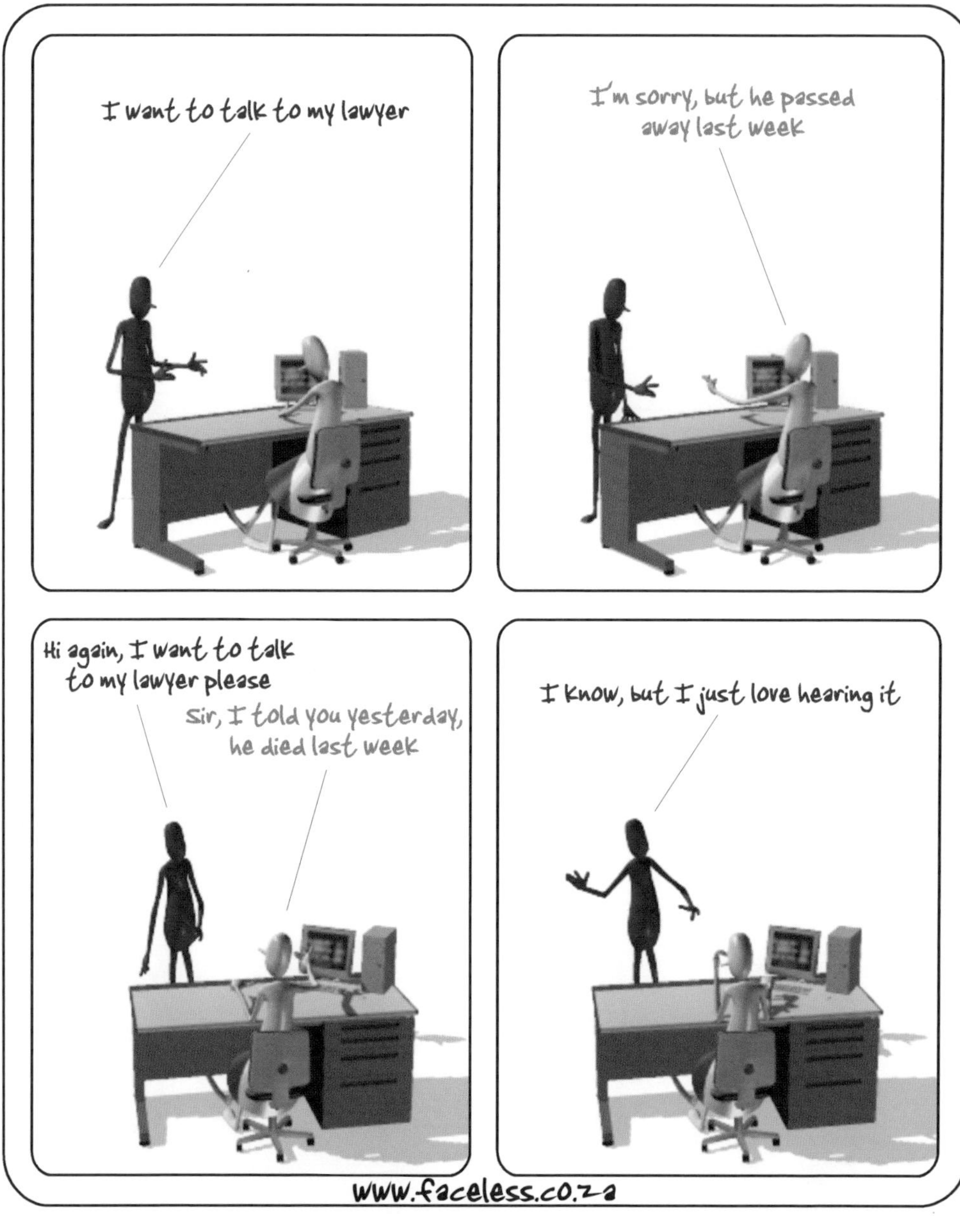
I want to talk to my lawyer
I'm sorry, but he passed away last week
Hi again, I want to talk to my lawyer please
Sir, I told you yesterday, he died last week
I know, but I just love hearing it
www.faceless.co.za

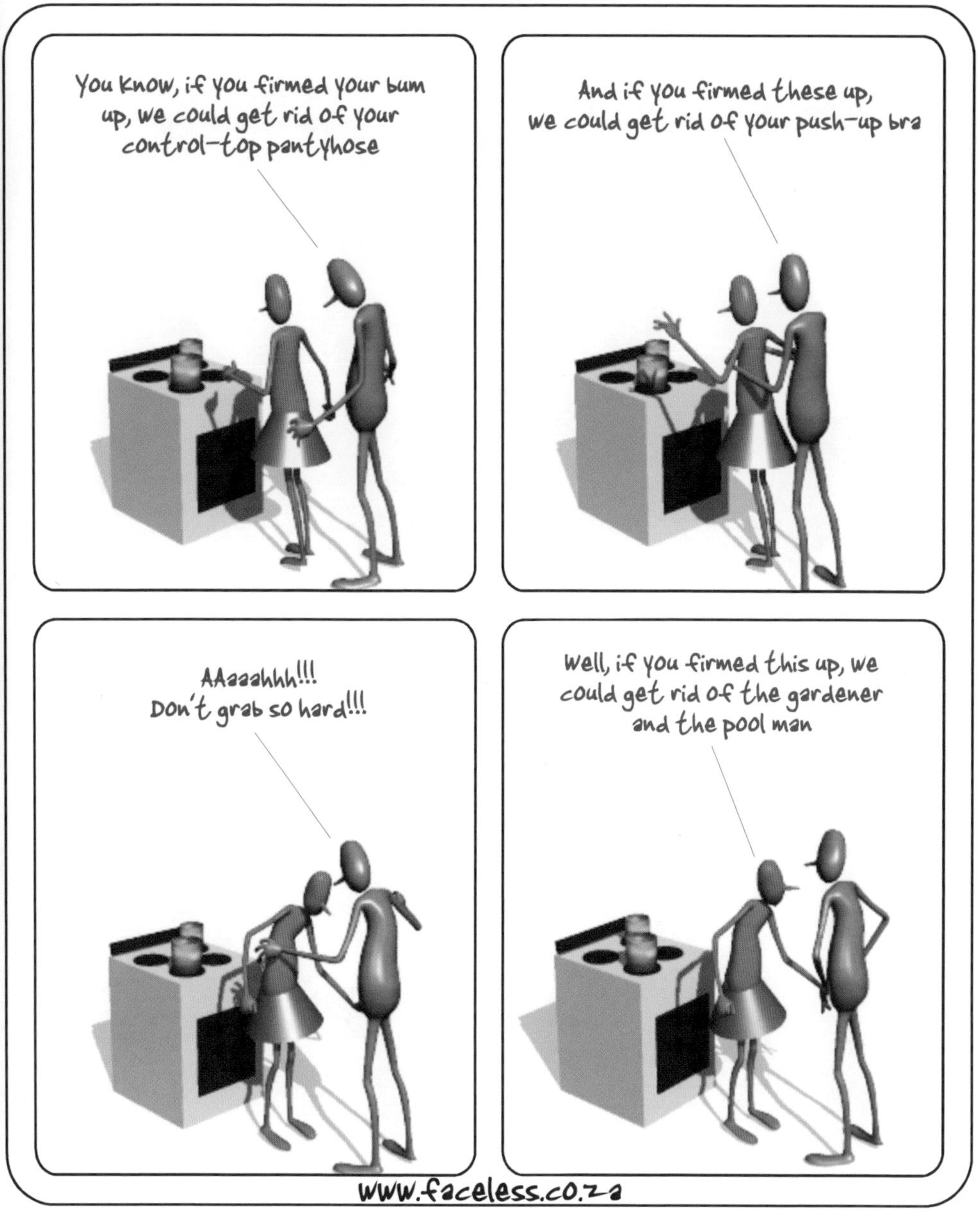
You know, if you firmed your bum up, we could get rid of your control-top pantyhose
And if you firmed these up, we could get rid of your push-up bra
AAaaahhh!!! Don't grab so hard!!!
Well, if you firmed this up, we could get rid of the gardener and the pool man
www.faceless.co.za

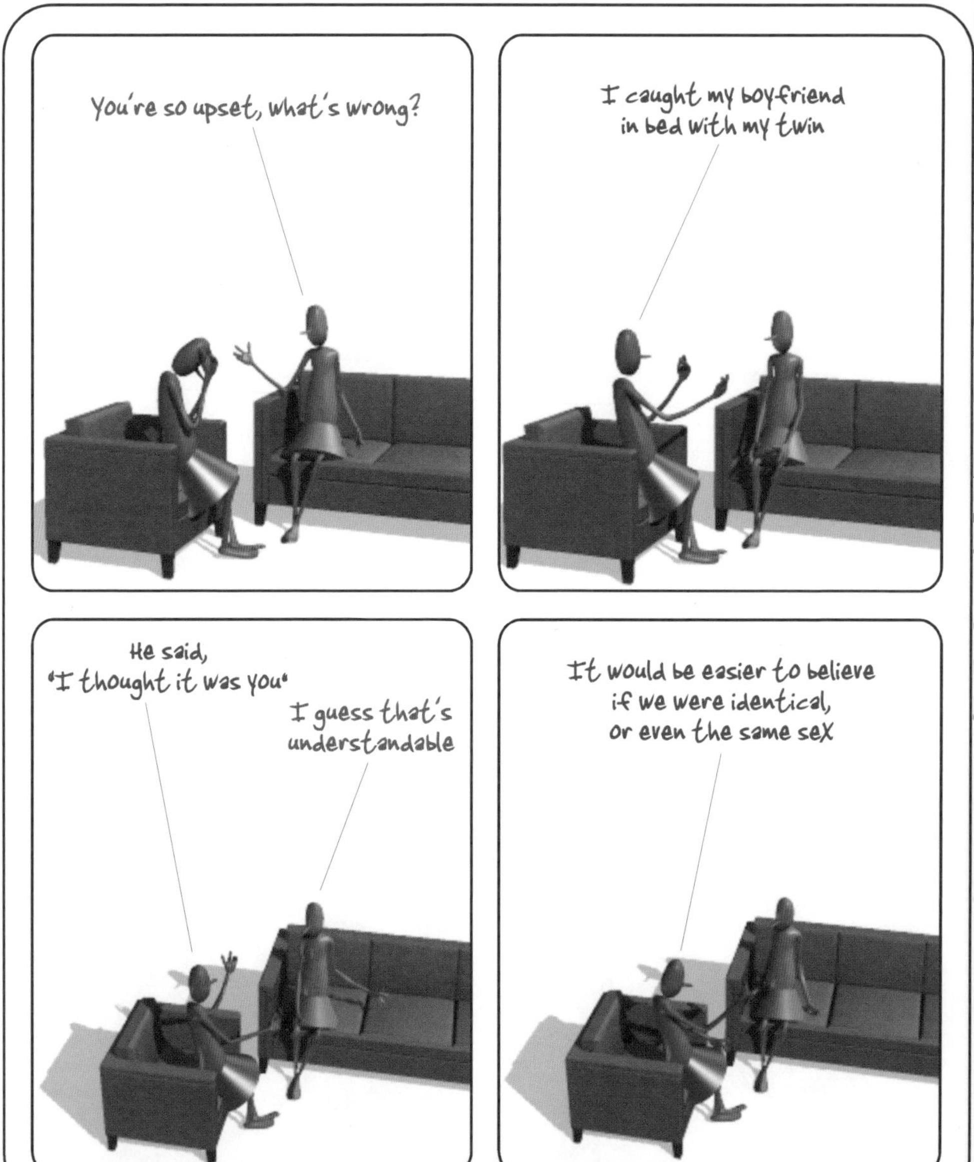
You're so upset, what's wrong?
I caught my boyfriend in bed with my twin
He said, "I thought it was you"
I guess that's understandable
It would be easier to believe if we were identical, or even the same sex
www.faceless.co.za

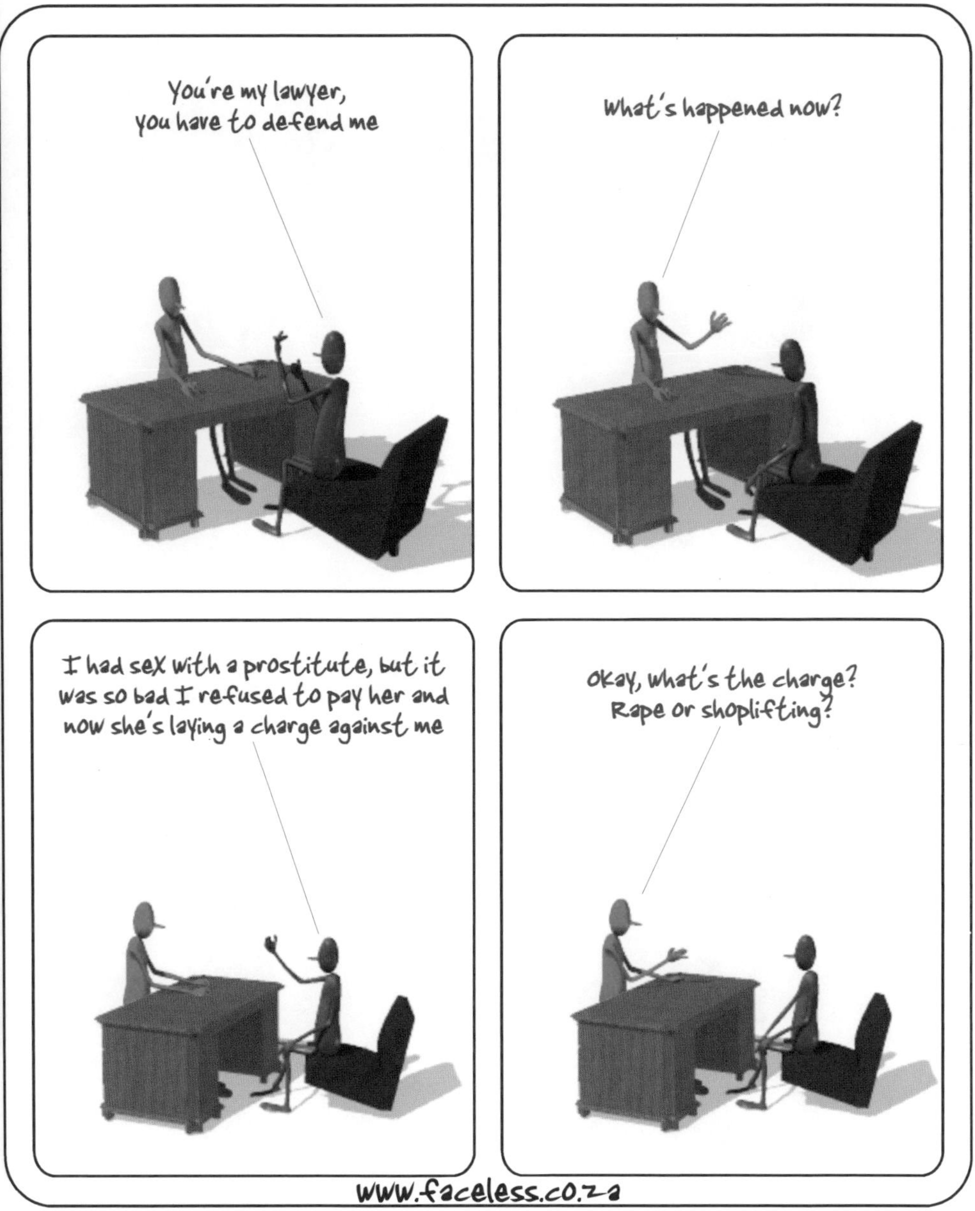
You're my lawyer, you have to defend me
What's happened now?
I had sex with a prostitute, but it was so bad I refused to pay her and now she's laying a charge against me
Okay, what's the charge? Rape or shoplifting?
www.faceless.co.za

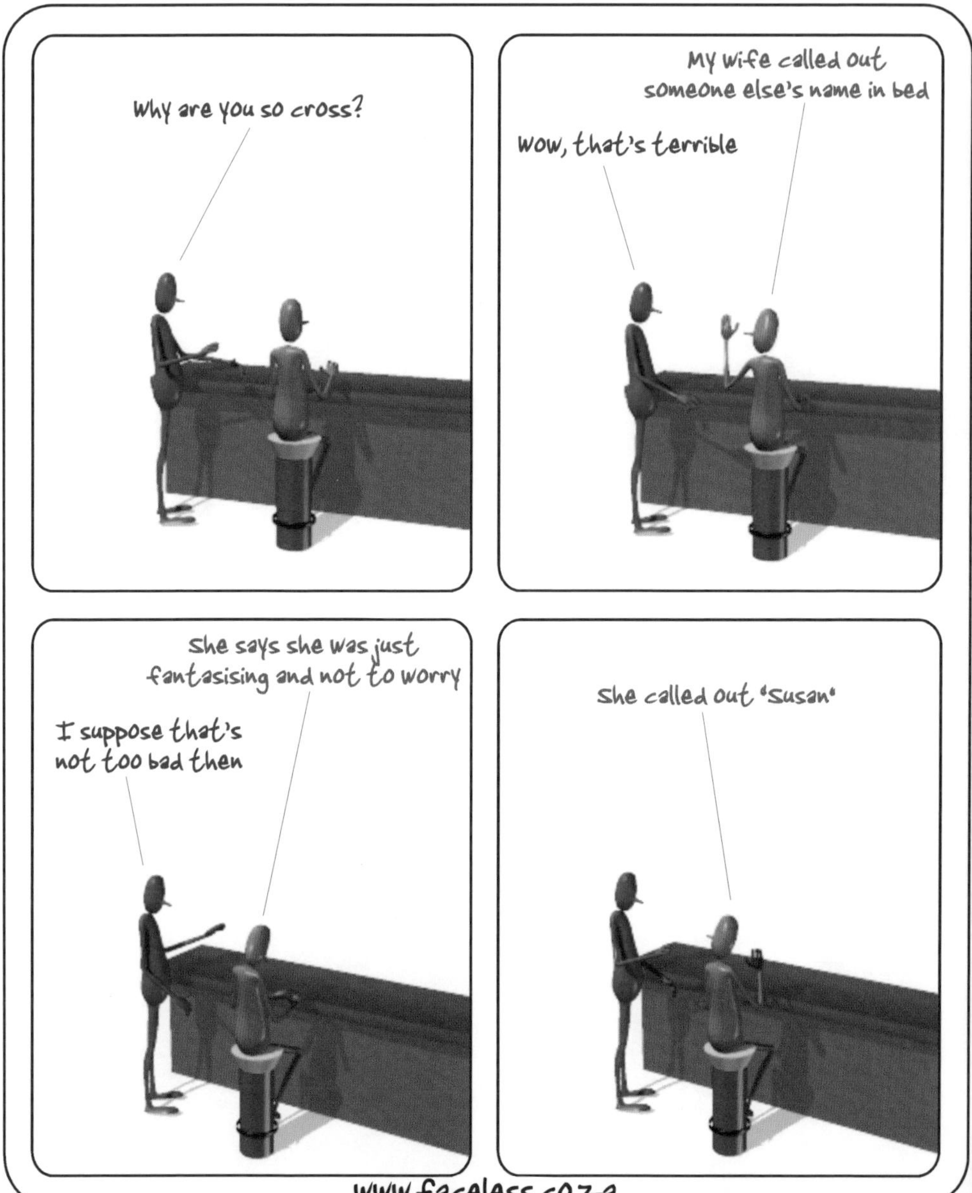
Why are you so cross?
My wife called out someone else's name in bed
Wow, that's terrible
She says she was just fantasising and not to worry
I suppose that's not too bad then
She called out "Susan"
www.faceless.co.za

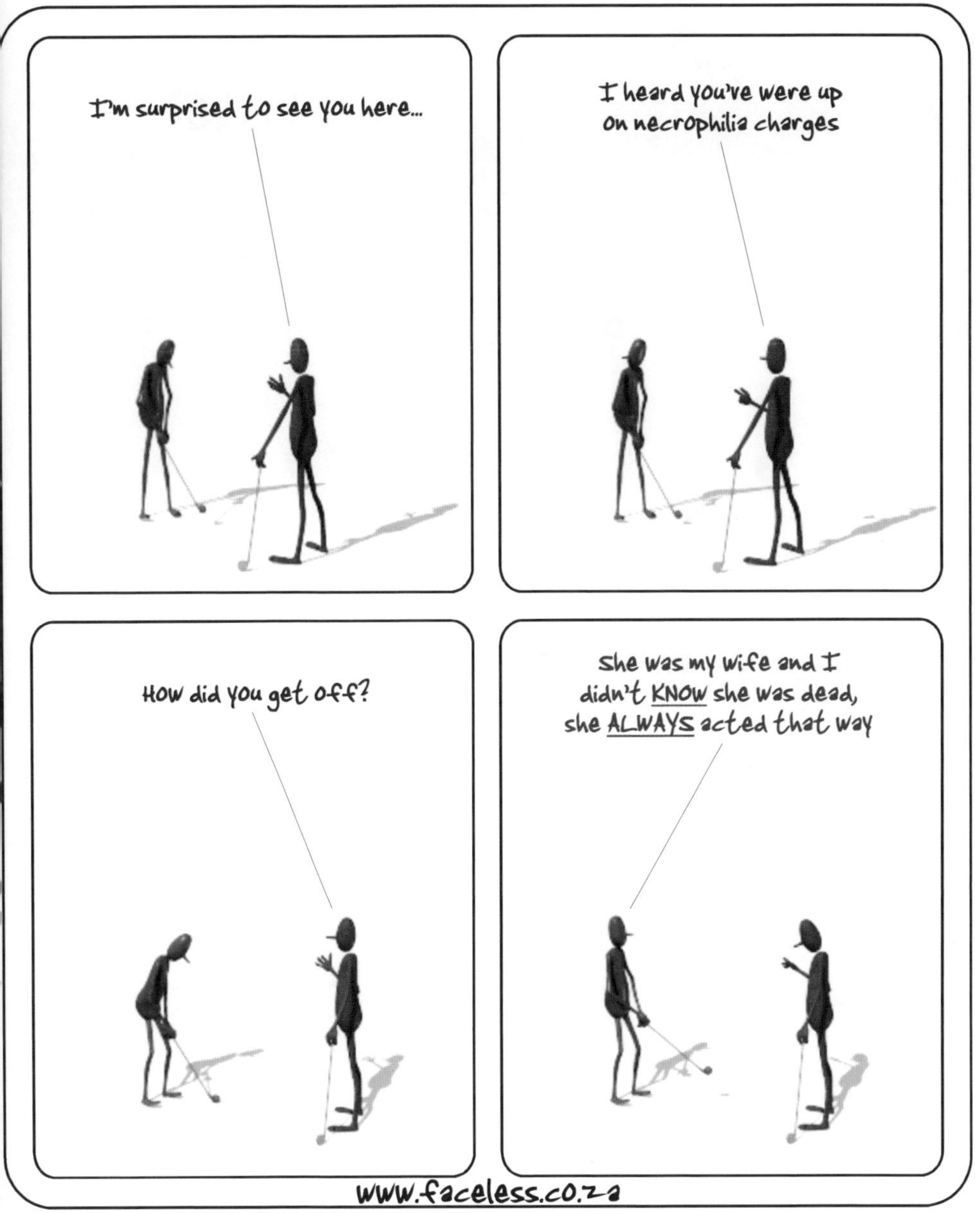
I'm surprised to see you here...
I heard you've were up on necrophilia charges
How did you get off?
She was my wife and I didn't KNOW she was dead, she ALWAYS acted that way
www.faceless.co.za

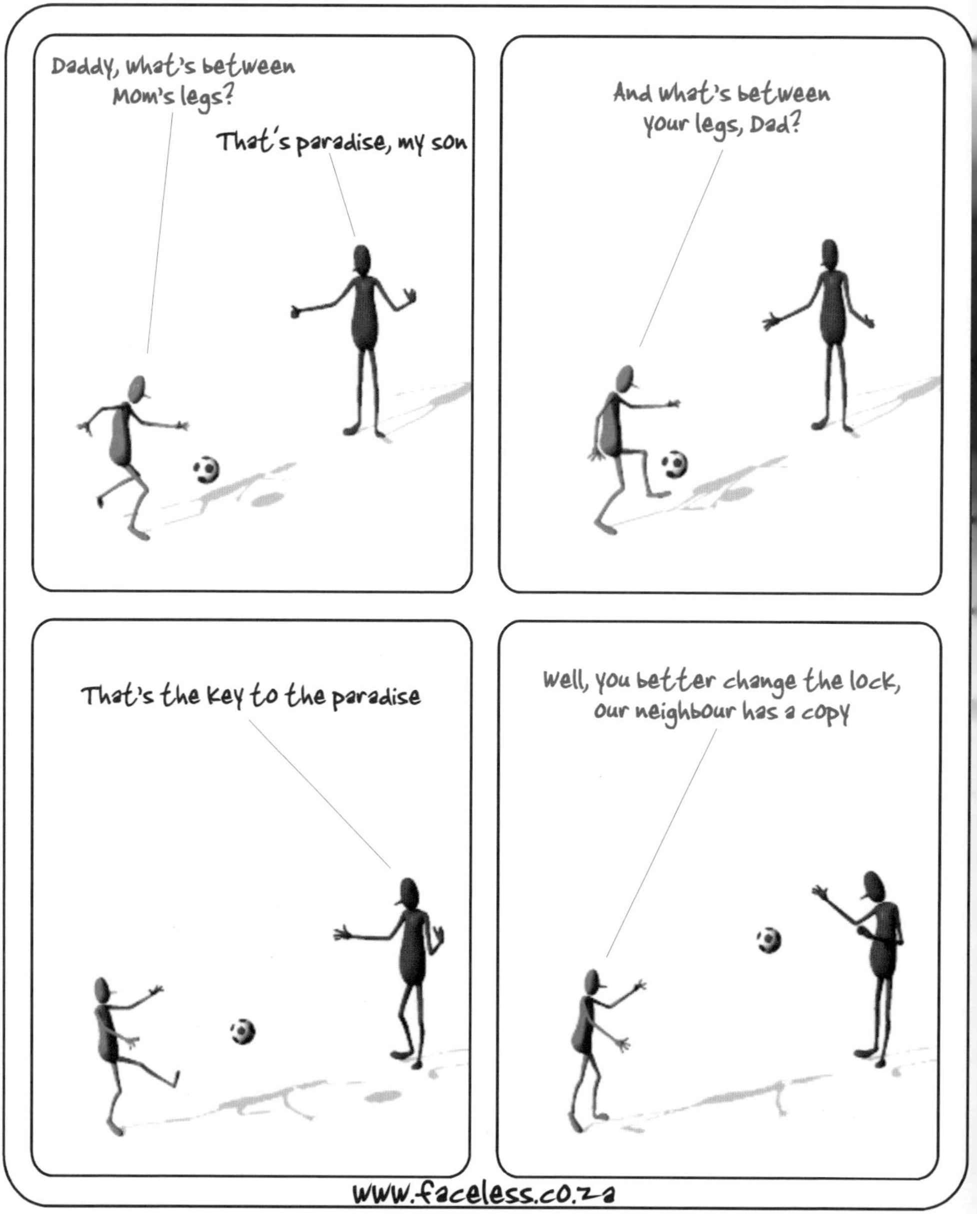
Daddy, what's between Mom's legs?
That's paradise, my son
And what's between your legs, Dad?
That's the key to the paradise
Well, you better change the lock, our neighbour has a copy
www.faceless.co.za

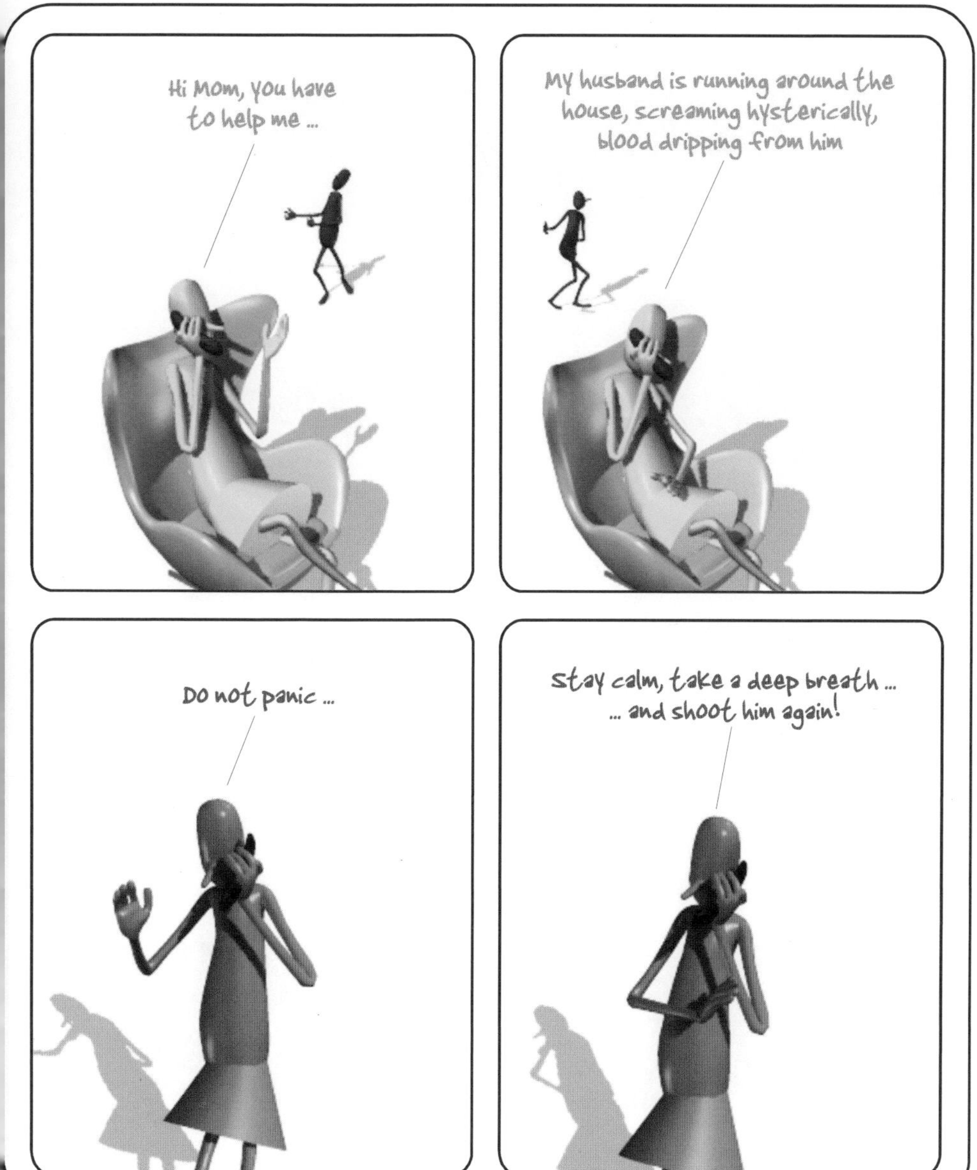
Hi Mom, you have to help me ...
My husband is running around the house, screaming hysterically, blood dripping from him
Do not panic ...
Stay calm, take a deep breath ...
... and shoot him again!
www.faceless.co.za

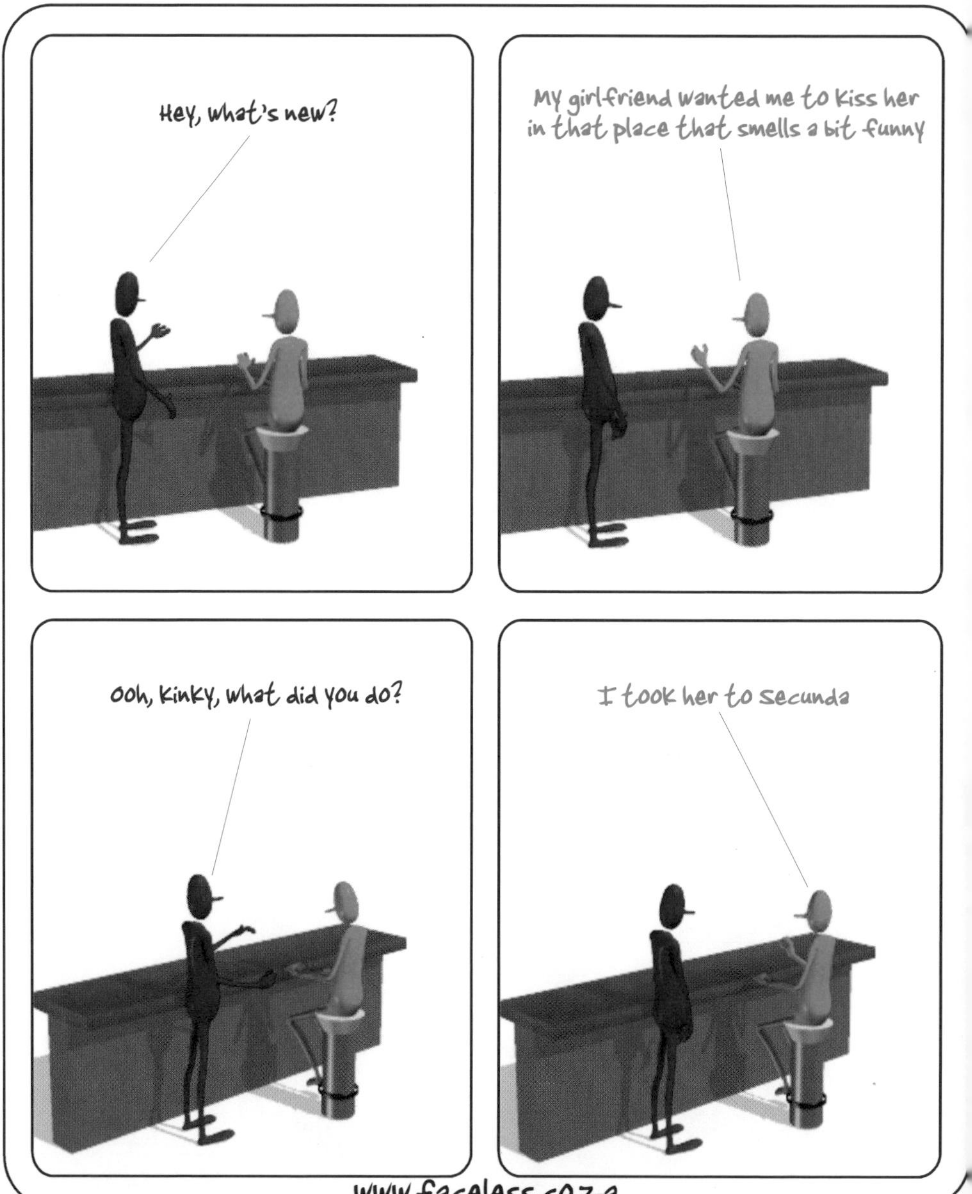
Hey, what's new?
My girlfriend wanted me to kiss her in that place that smells a bit funny
Ooh, kinky, what did you do?
I took her to secunda
www.faceless.co.za

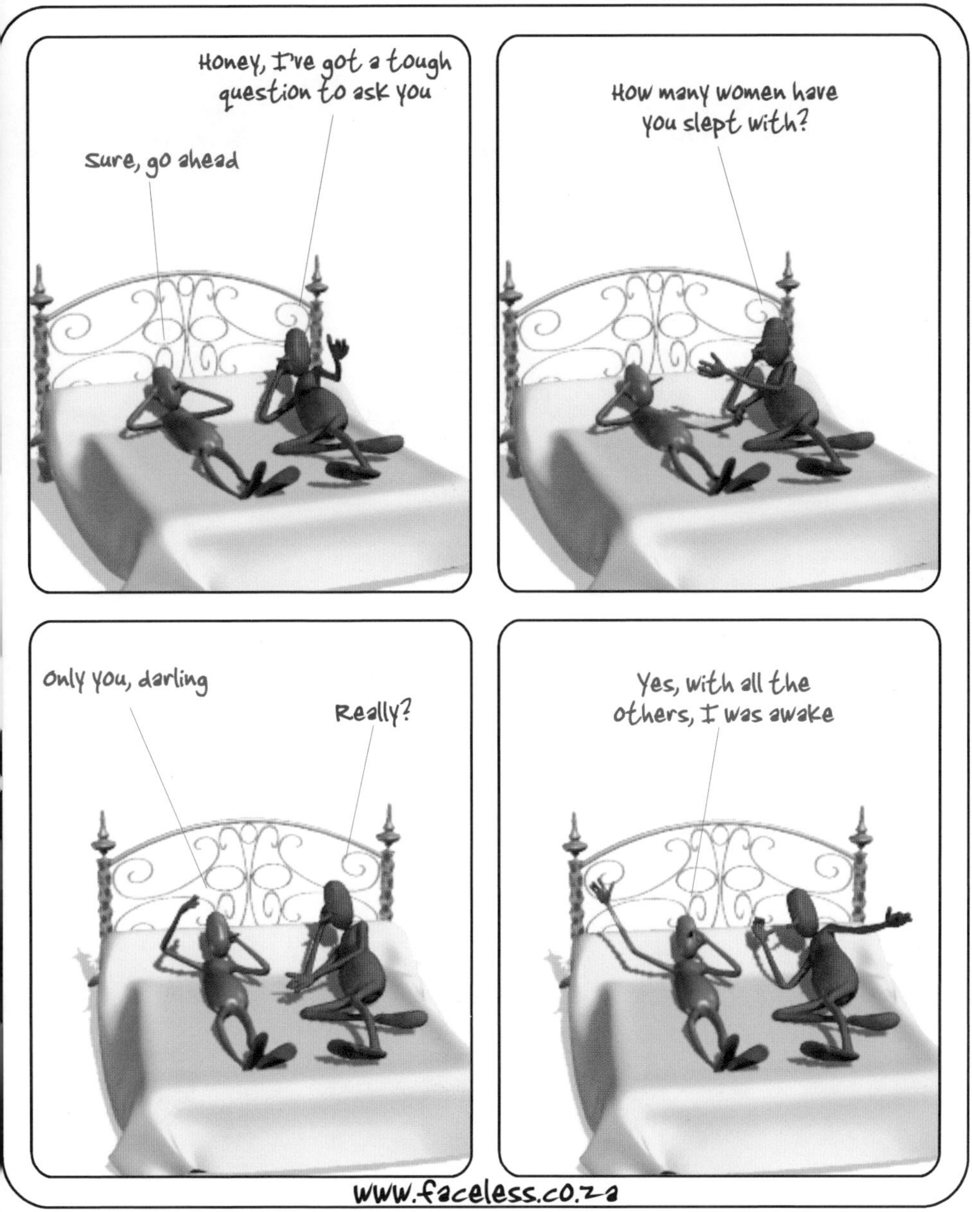
Honey, I've got a tough question to ask you
Sure, go ahead
How many women have you slept with?
Only you, darling
Really?
Yes, with all the others, I was awake
www.faceless.co.za

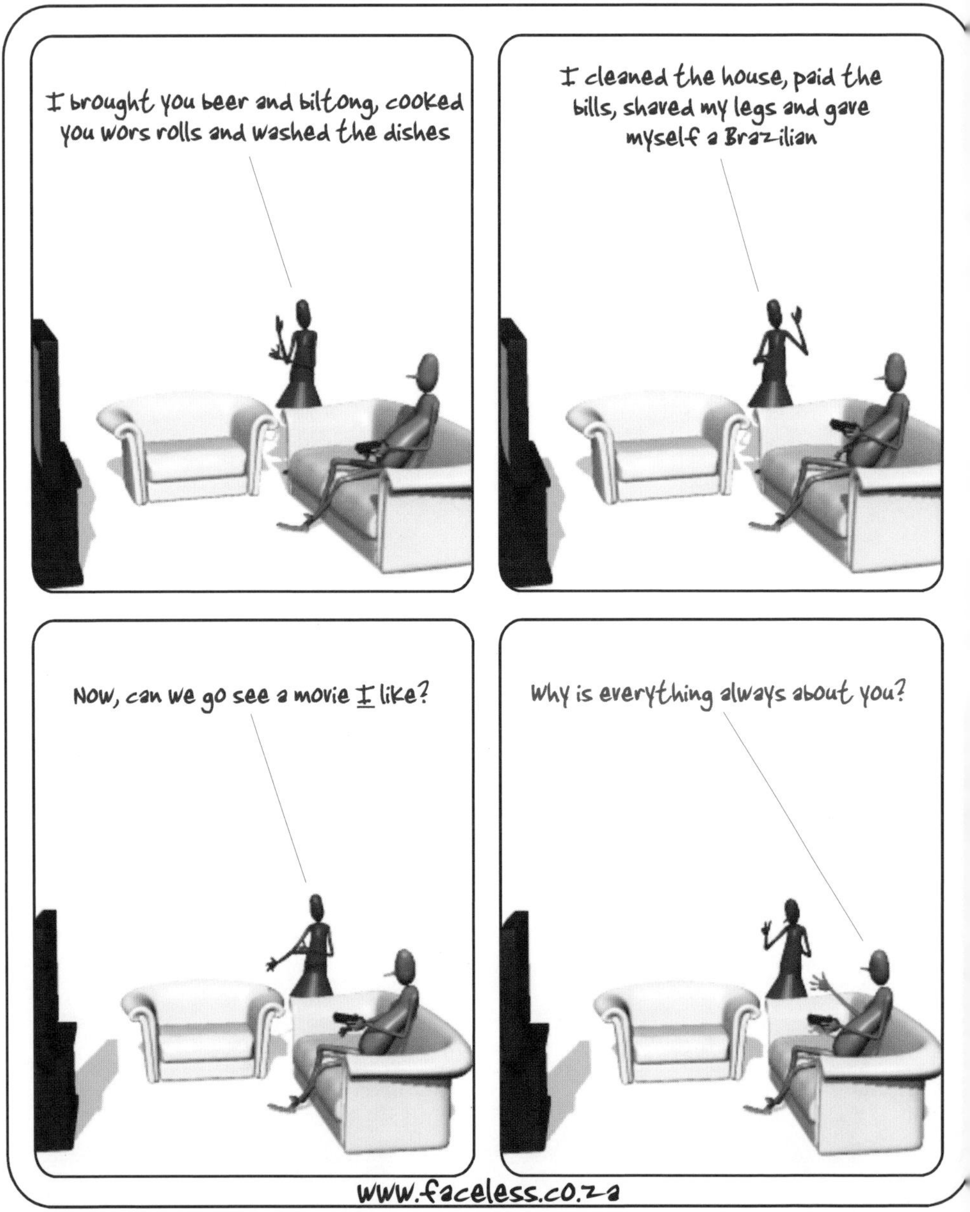
I brought you beer and biltong, cooked you wors rolls and washed the dishes
I cleaned the house, paid the bills, shaved my legs and gave myself a Brazilian
Now, can we go see a movie I like?
Why is everything always about you?
www.faceless.co.za

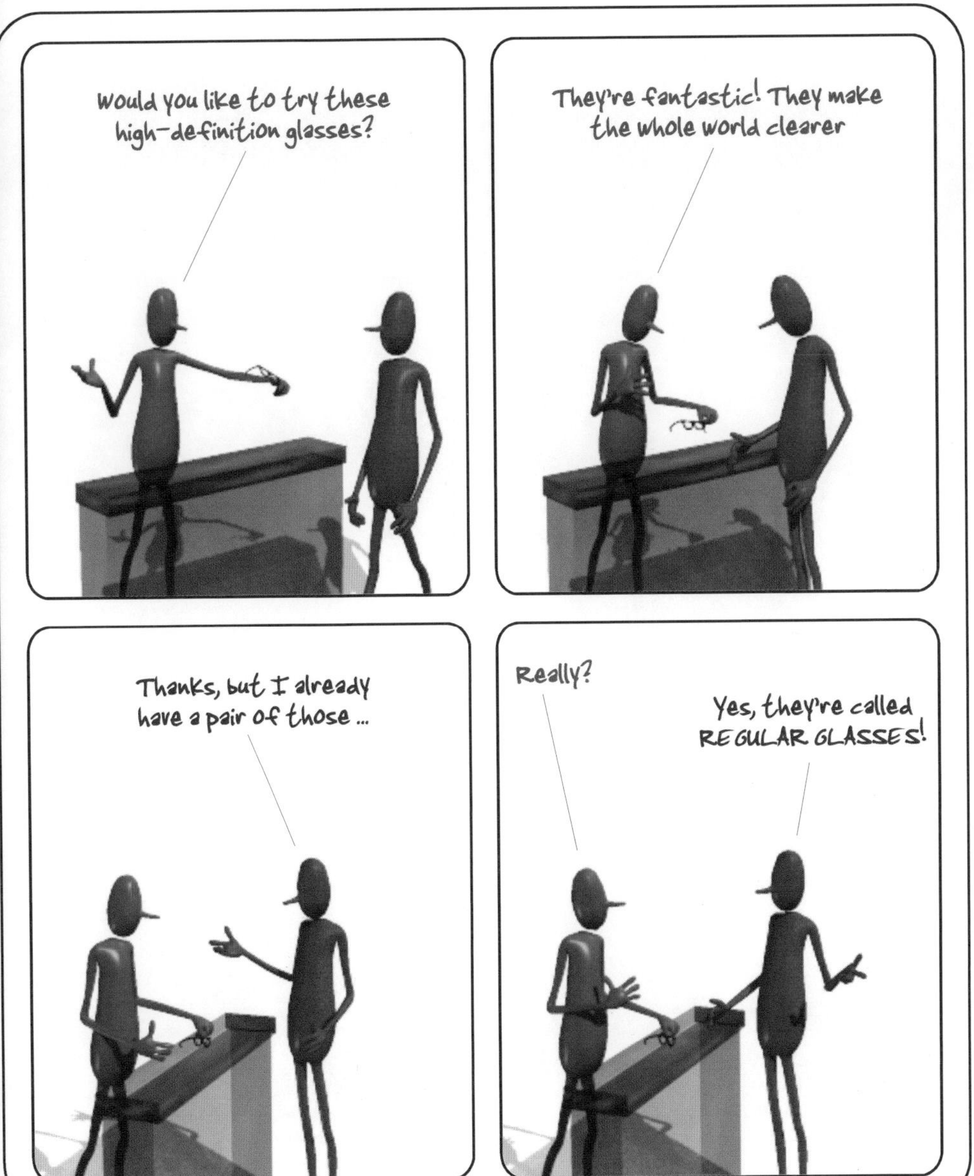
Would you like to try these high-definition glasses?
They're fantastic! They make the whole world clearer
Thanks, but I already have a pair of those ...
Really?
Yes, they're called REGULAR GLASSES!
www.faceless.co.za

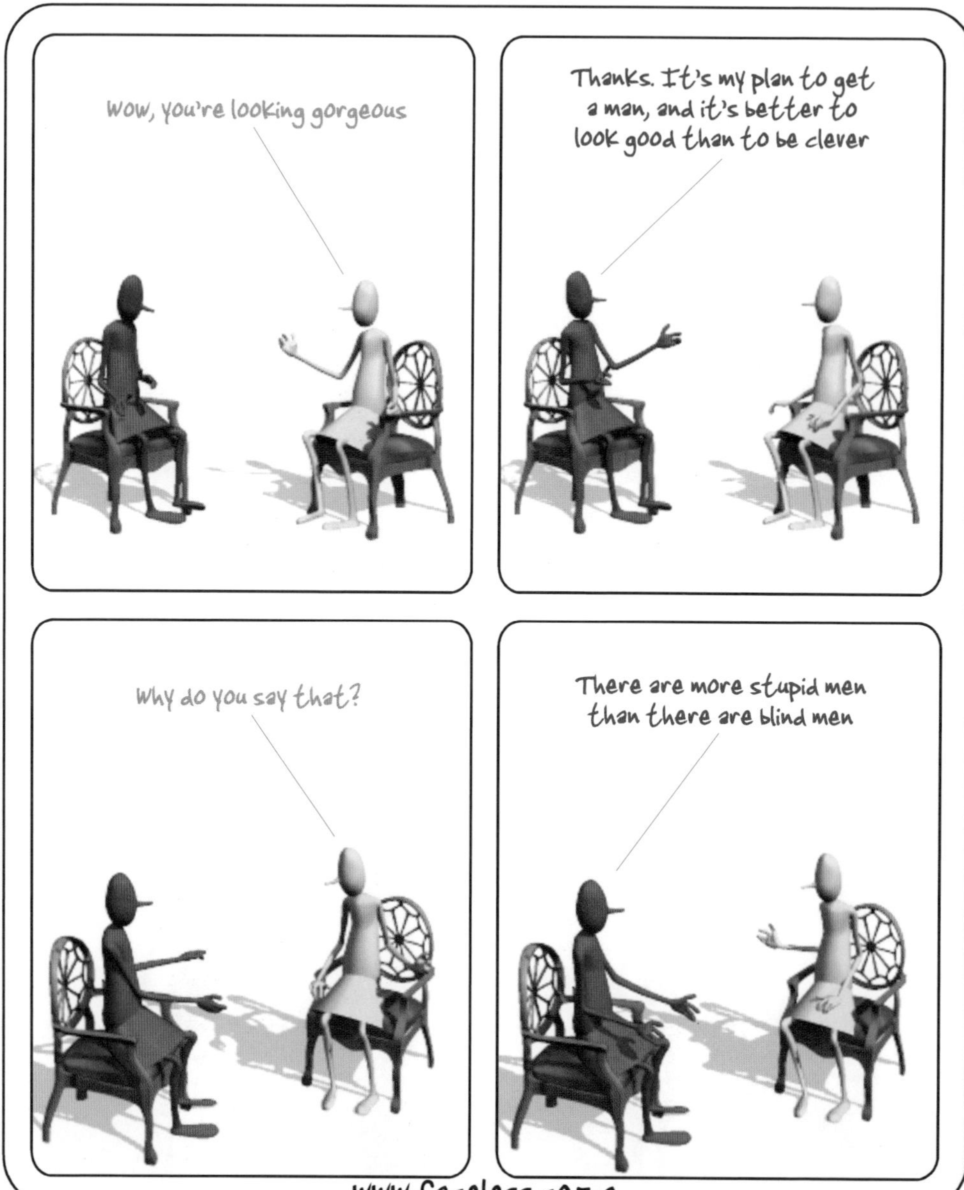
Wow, you're looking gorgeous
Thanks. It's my plan to get a man, and it's better to look good than to be clever
Why do you say that?
There are more stupid men than there are blind men
www.faceless.co.za

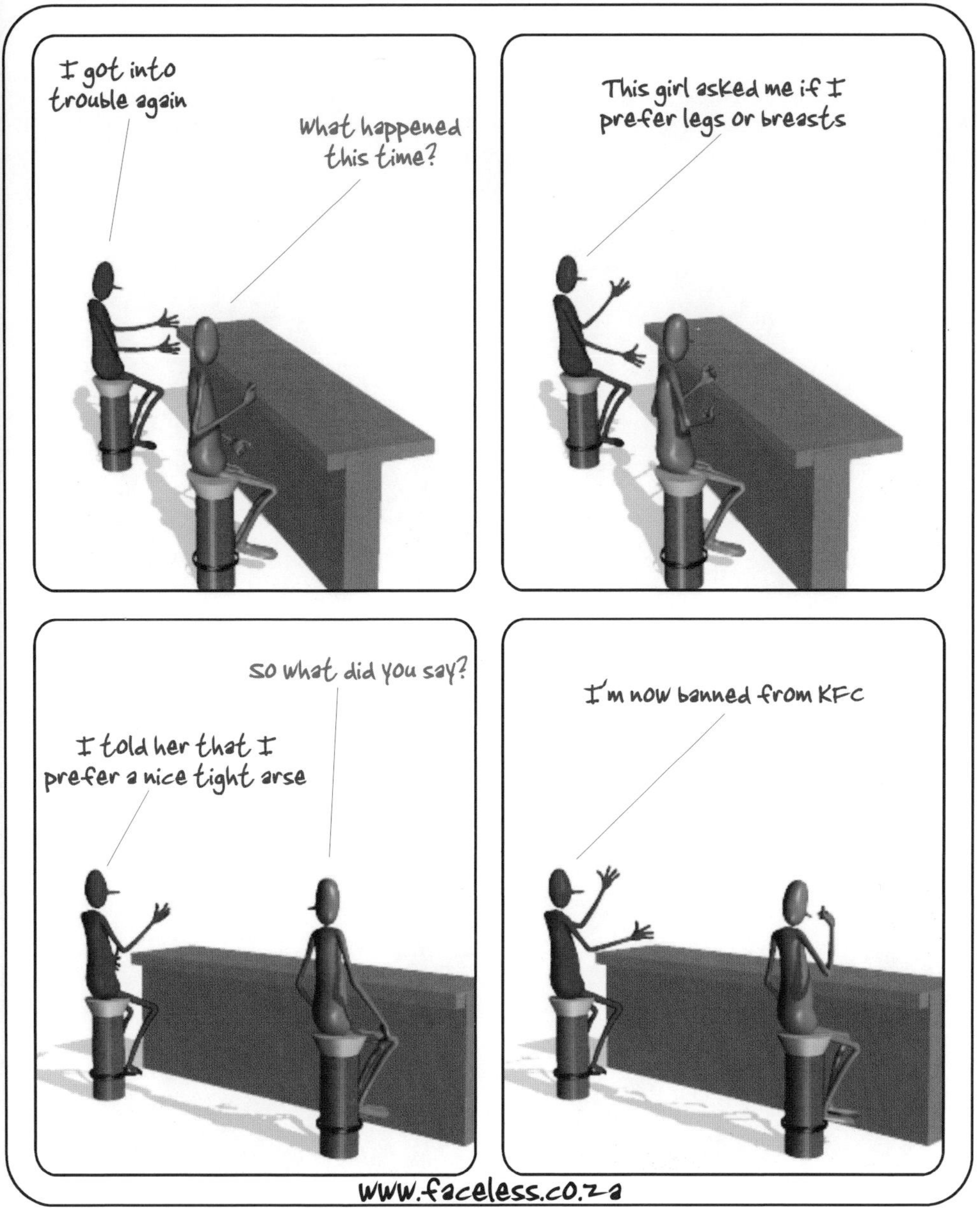
I got into trouble again
What happened this time?
This girl asked me if I prefer legs or breasts
so what did you say?
I told her that I prefer a nice tight arse
I'm now banned from KFC
www.faceless.co.za

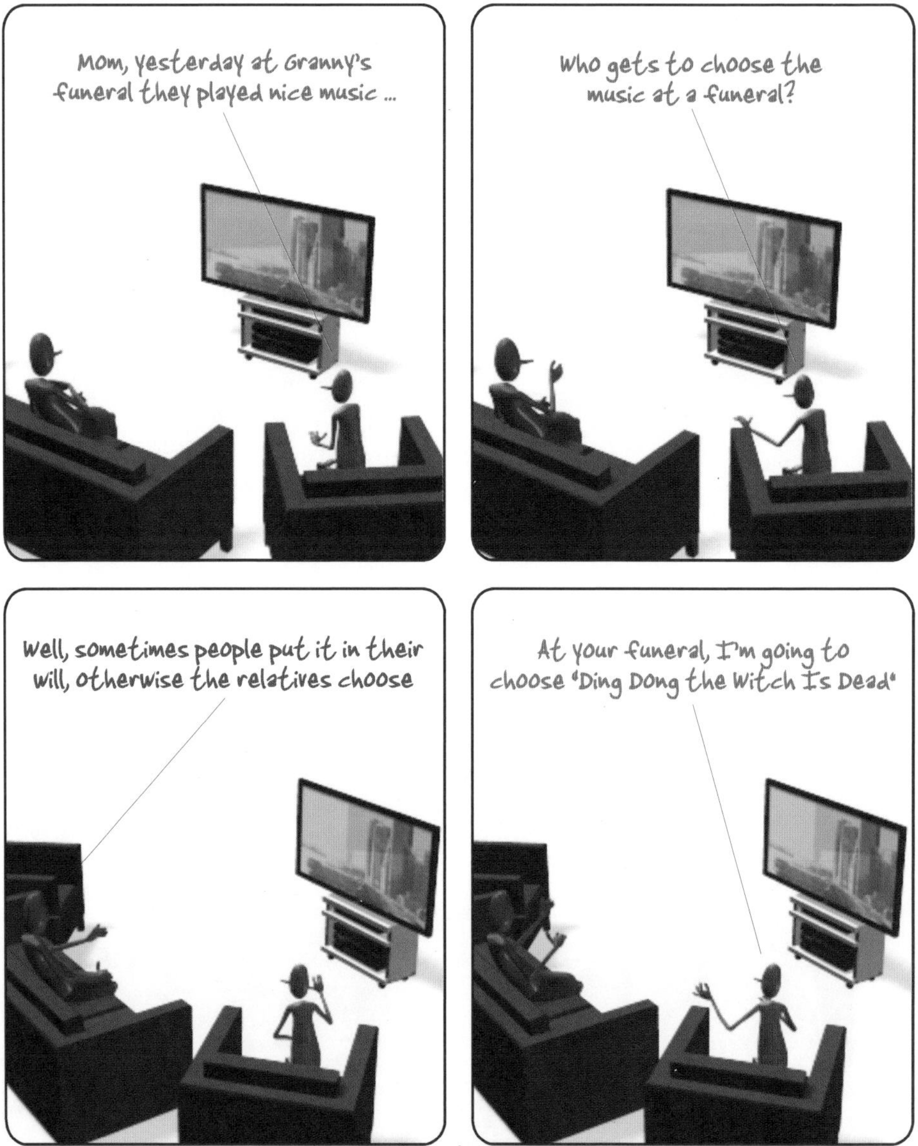
Mom, yesterday at Granny's funeral they played nice music ...
Who gets to choose the music at a funeral?
Well, sometimes people put it in their will, otherwise the relatives choose
At your funeral, I'm going to choose "Ding Dong the Witch Is Dead"

www.faceless.co.za

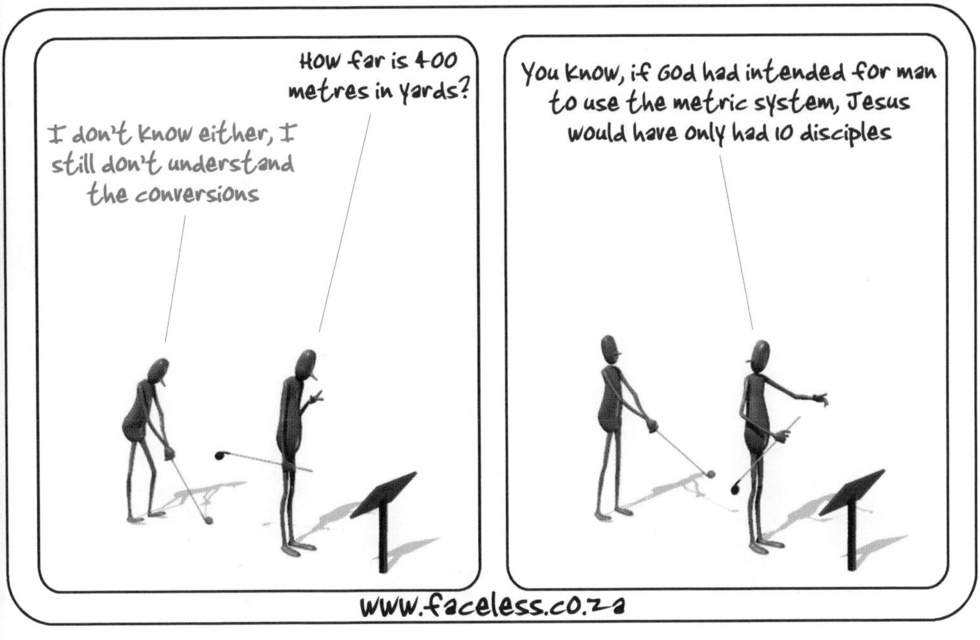
How far is 400 metres in yards?
I don't know either, I still don't understand the conversions
You know, if God had intended for man to use the metric system, Jesus would have only had 10 disciples
www.faceless.co.za

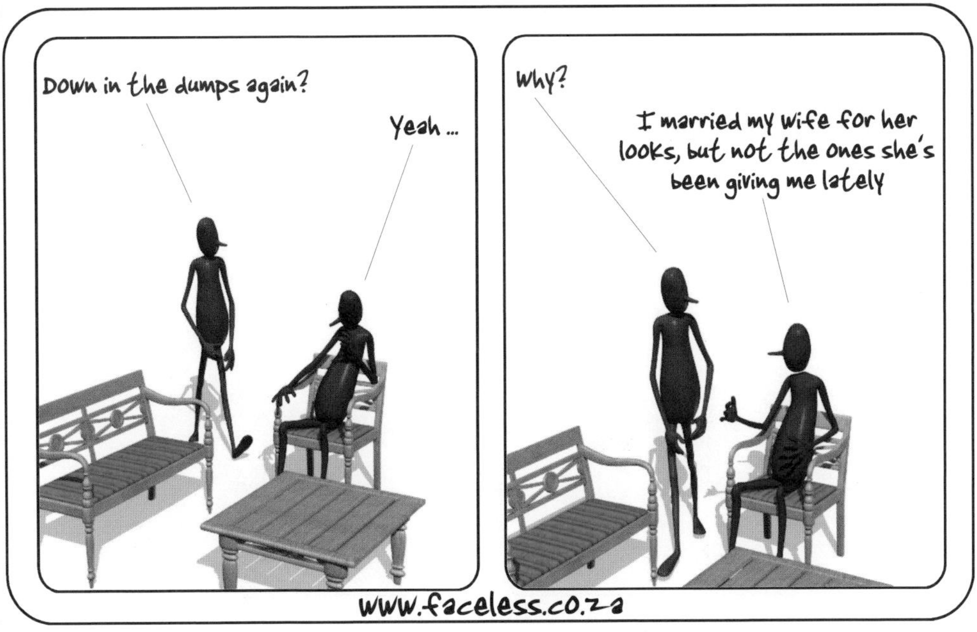
Down in the dumps again?
Yeah ...
Why?
I married my wife for her looks, but not the ones she's been giving me lately
www.faceless.co.za

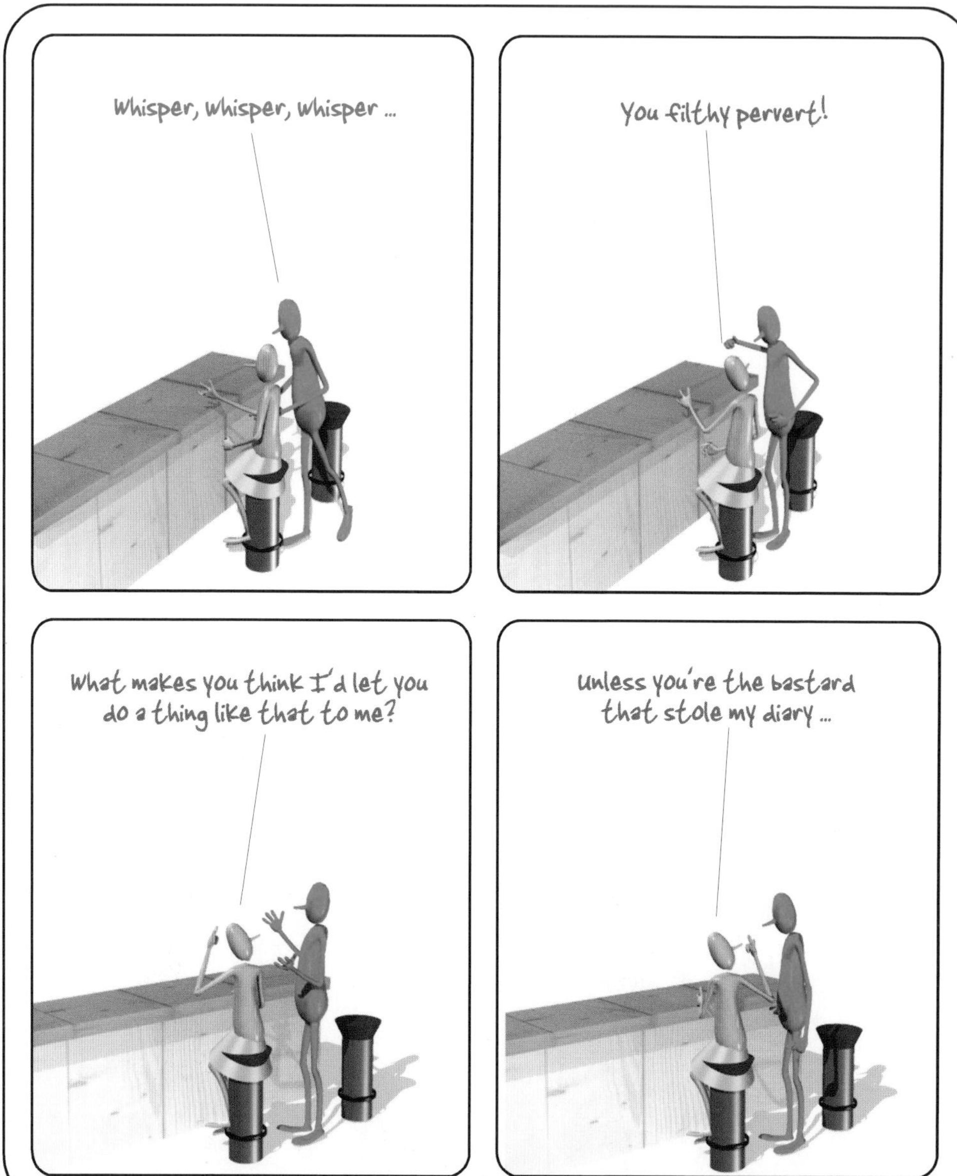
Whisper, whisper, whisper ...
You filthy pervert!
What makes you think I'd let you do a thing like that to me?
Unless you're the bastard that stole my diary ...
www.faceless.co.za

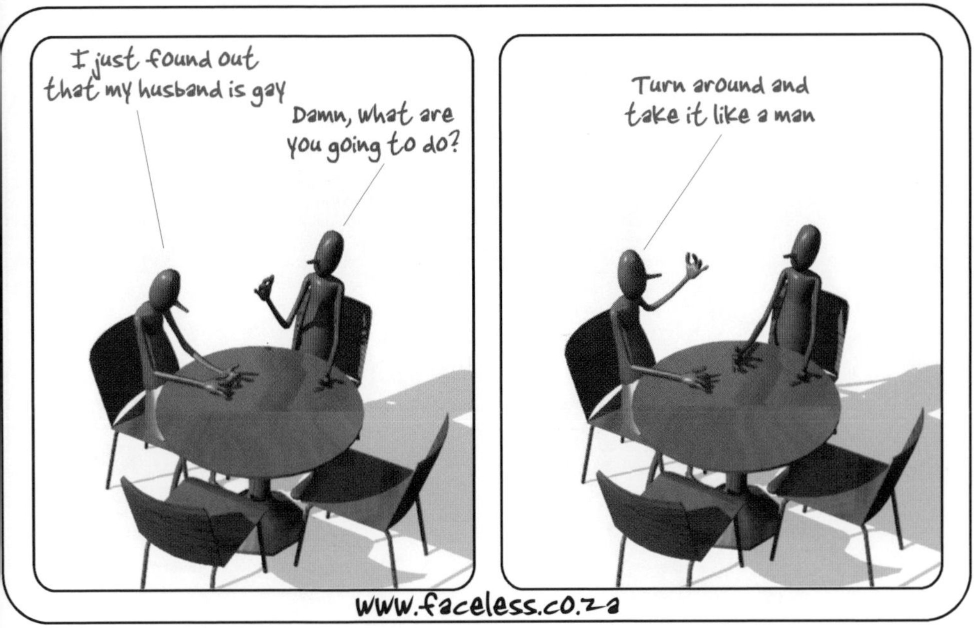
I just found out that my husband is gay
Damn, what are you going to do?
Turn around and take it like a man
www.faceless.co.za

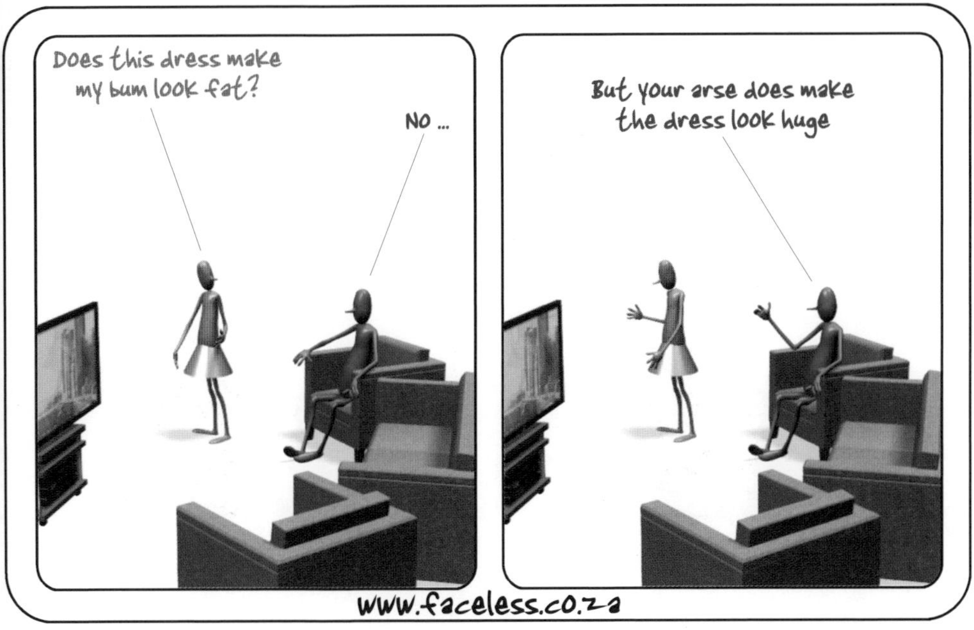
Does this dress make my bum look fat?
NO ...
But your arse does make the dress look huge
www.faceless.co.za

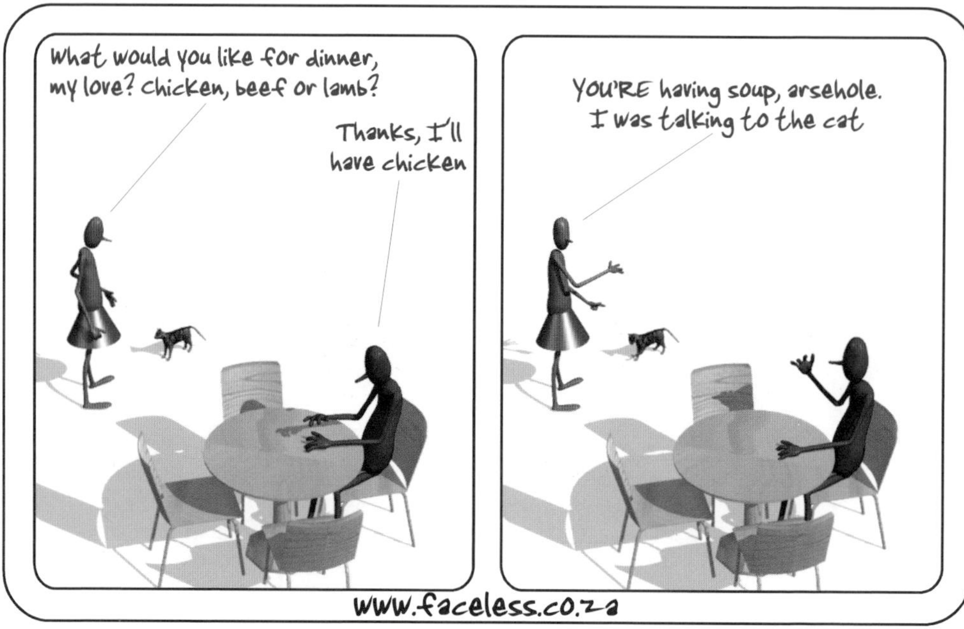
What would you like for dinner, my love? chicken, beef or lamb?
Thanks, I'll have chicken
YOU'RE having soup, arsehole. I was talking to the cat
www.faceless.co.za

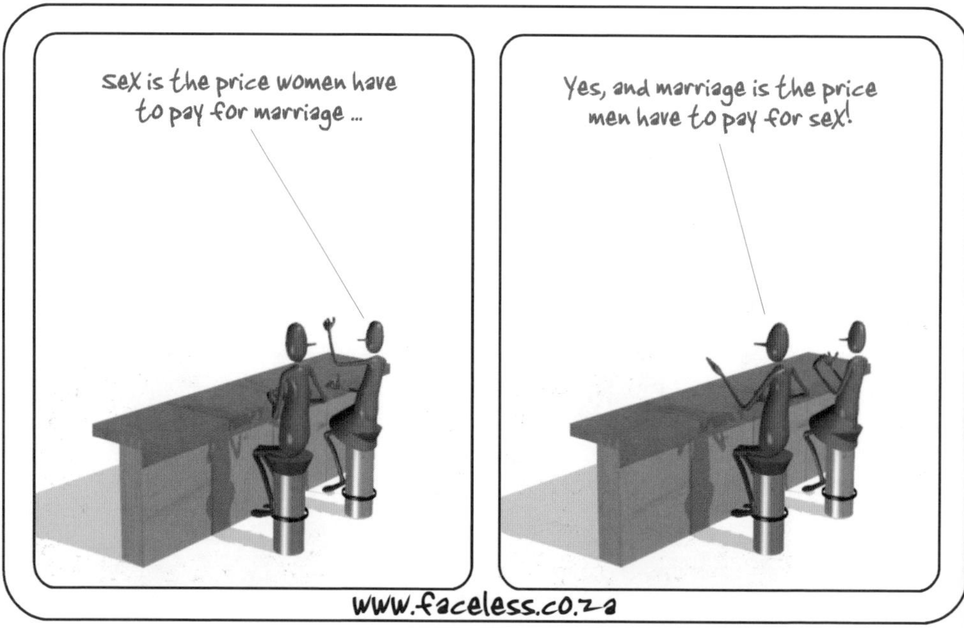
sex is the price women have to pay for marriage ...
Yes, and marriage is the price men have to pay for sex!
www.faceless.co.za

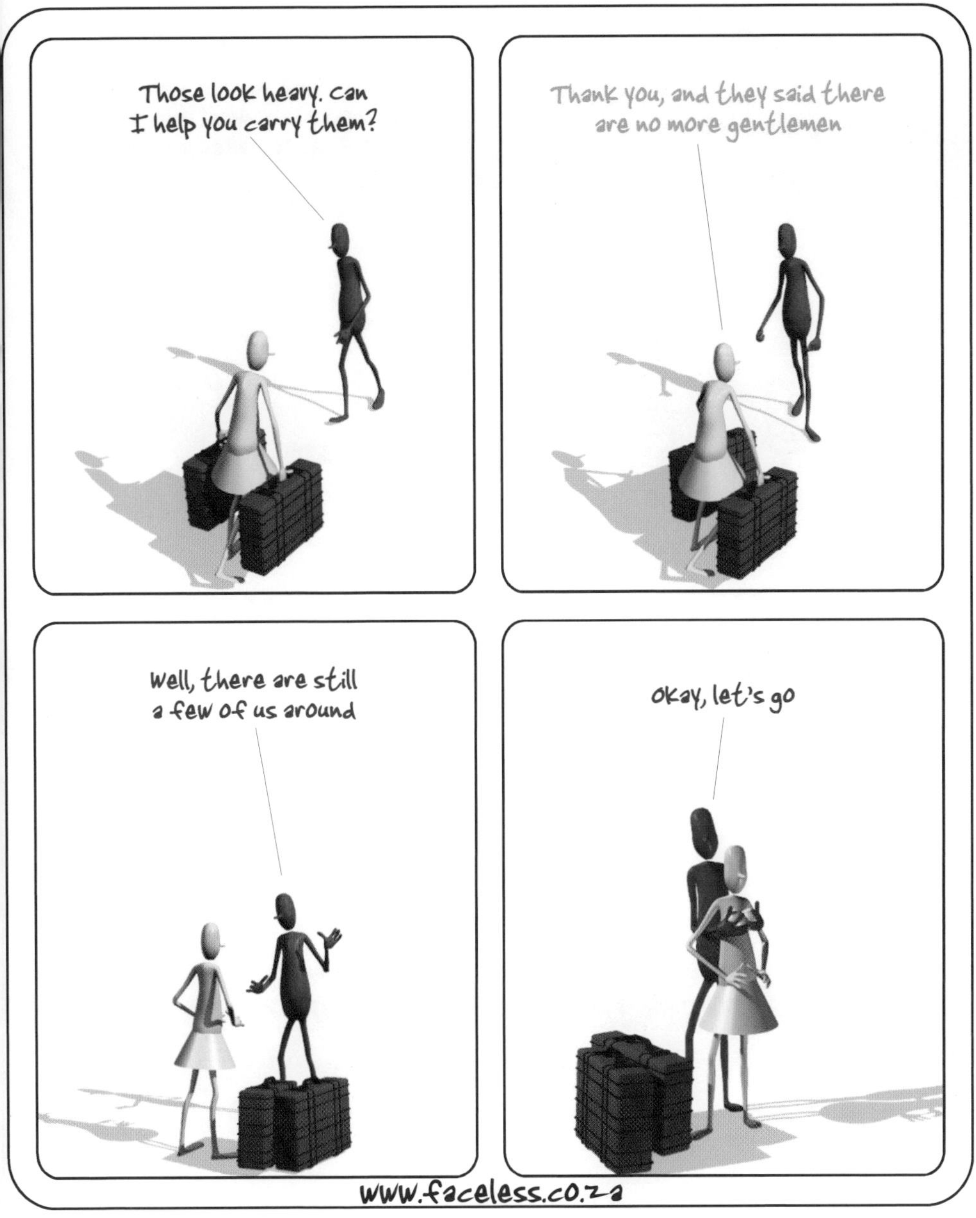
Those look heavy. can I help you carry them?
Thank you, and they said there are no more gentlemen
Well, there are still a few of us around
okay, let's go
www.faceless.co.za

I watched a documentary on TV last night about how bad our food is for us

They said, 'Red meat is awful; soft drinks corrode your stomach lining; chinese food is loaded with MSG ...'

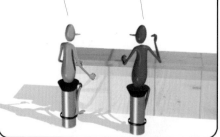

'High-fat diets can be disastrous and there are millions of germs in our drinking water'

Damn, and what food causes the most grief and suffering?

Wedding cake

I know you're growing up, and as you're almost 18, you know about sex and being responsible
I still worry and hope you'll be sensible ...
But just in case, I've bought you some condoms for your date tonight
Oh Mom! You don't have to worry about that! I'm dating Susan!
www.faceless.co.za

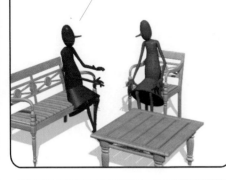

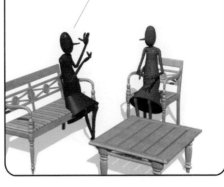

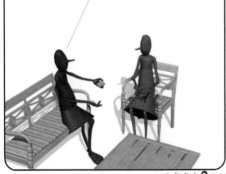

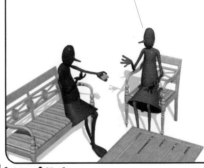

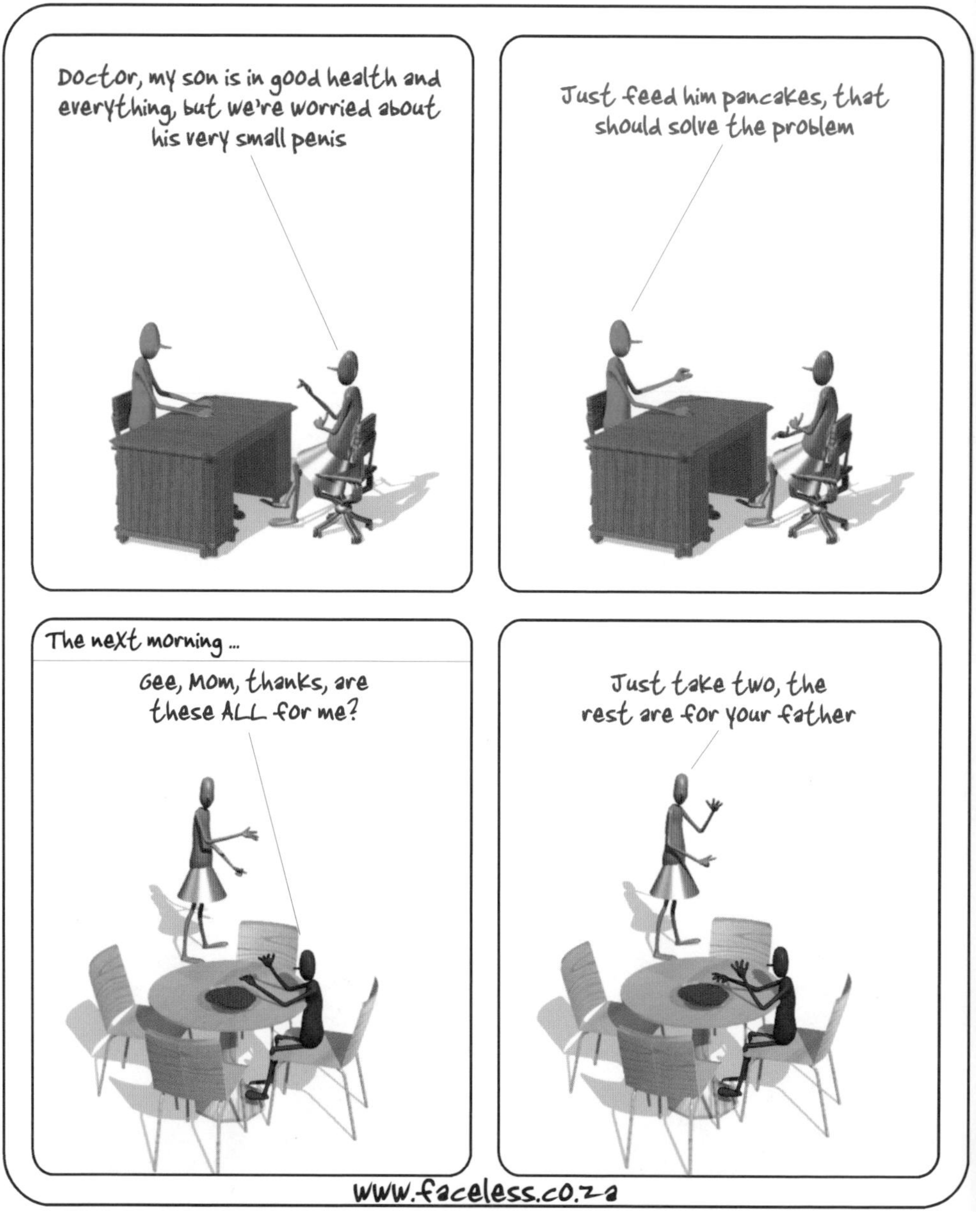
Doctor, my son is in good health and everything, but we're worried about his very small penis
Just feed him pancakes, that should solve the problem
The next morning ...
Gee, Mom, thanks, are these ALL for me?
Just take two, the rest are for your father
www.faceless.co.za

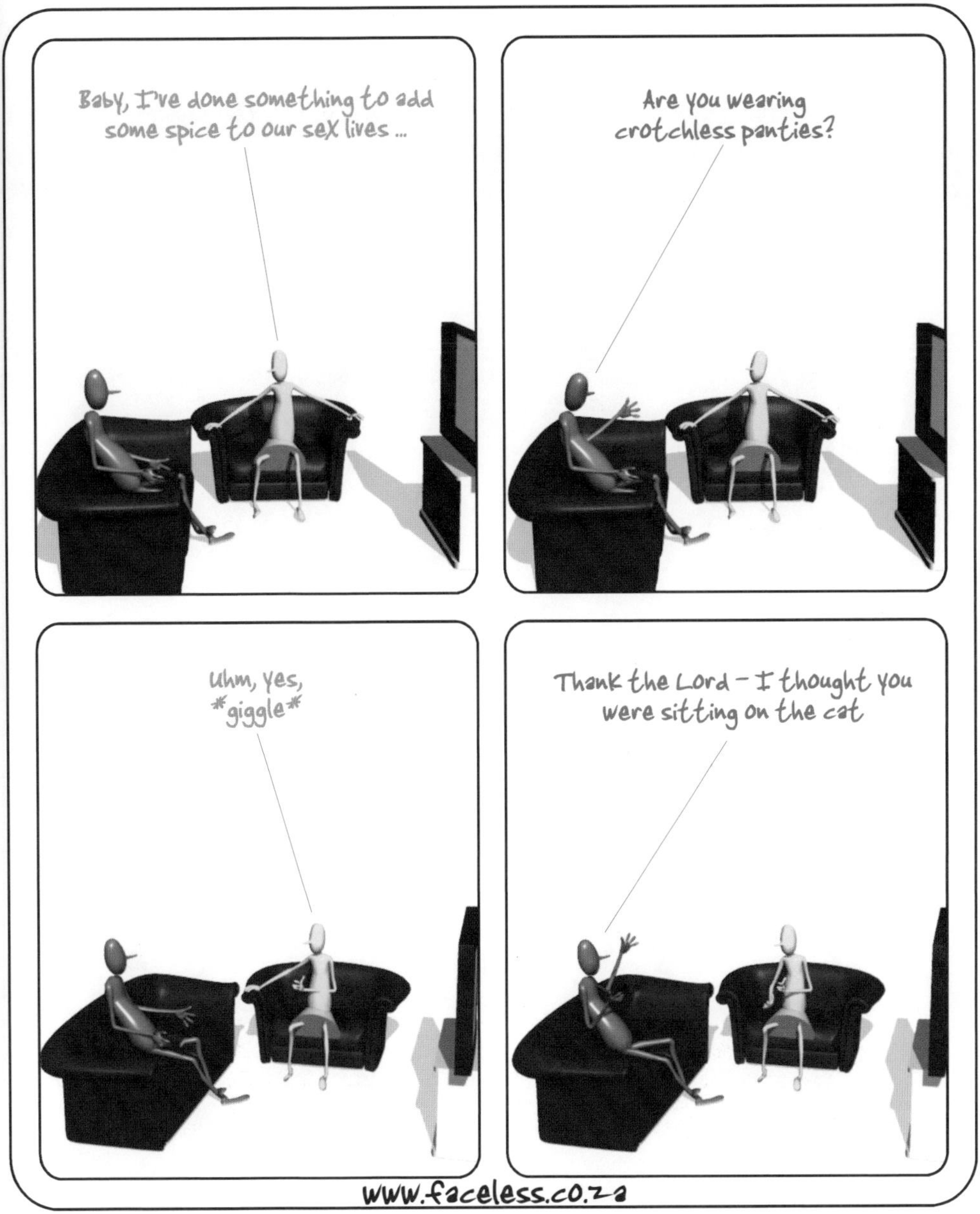
Baby, I've done something to add some spice to our sex lives ...
Are you wearing crotchless panties?
Uhm, yes, *giggle*
Thank the Lord - I thought you were sitting on the cat
www.faceless.co.za

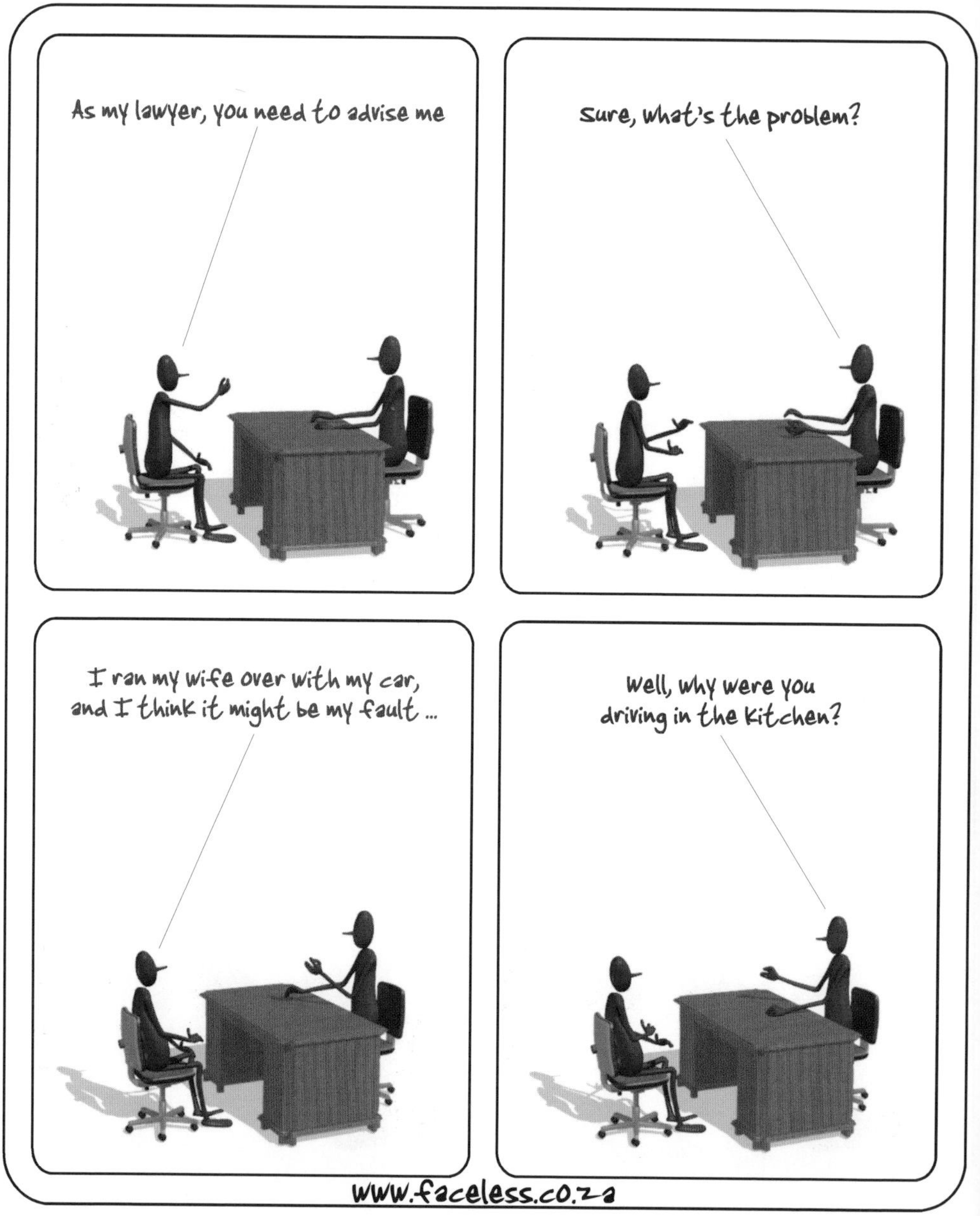
As my lawyer, you need to advise me
Sure, what's the problem?
I ran my wife over with my car, and I think it might be my fault ...
Well, why were you driving in the kitchen?
www.faceless.co.za

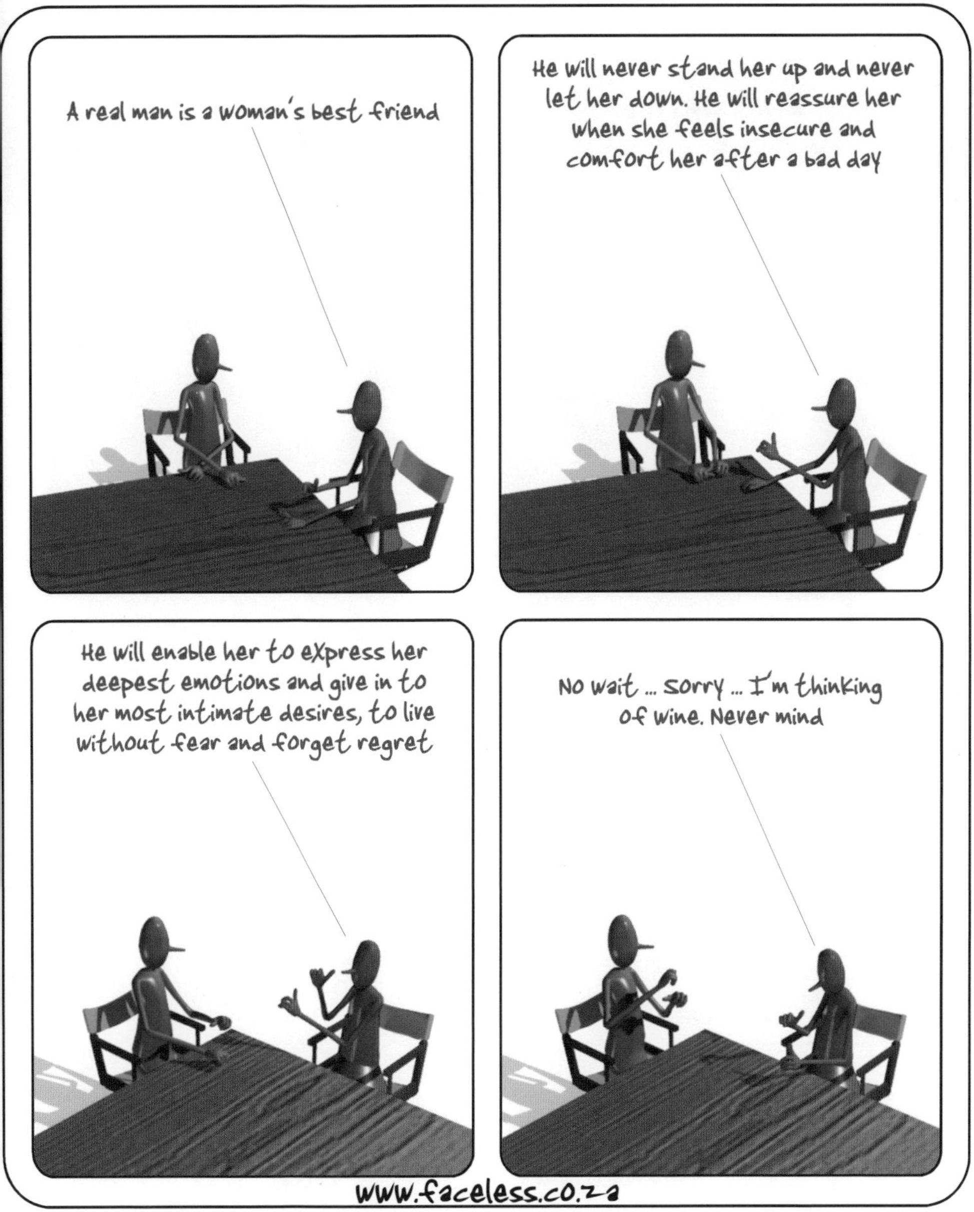
A real man is a woman's best friend
He will never stand her up and never let her down. He will reassure her when she feels insecure and comfort her after a bad day
He will enable her to express her deepest emotions and give in to her most intimate desires, to live without fear and forget regret
No wait ... sorry ... I'm thinking of wine. Never mind
www.faceless.co.za

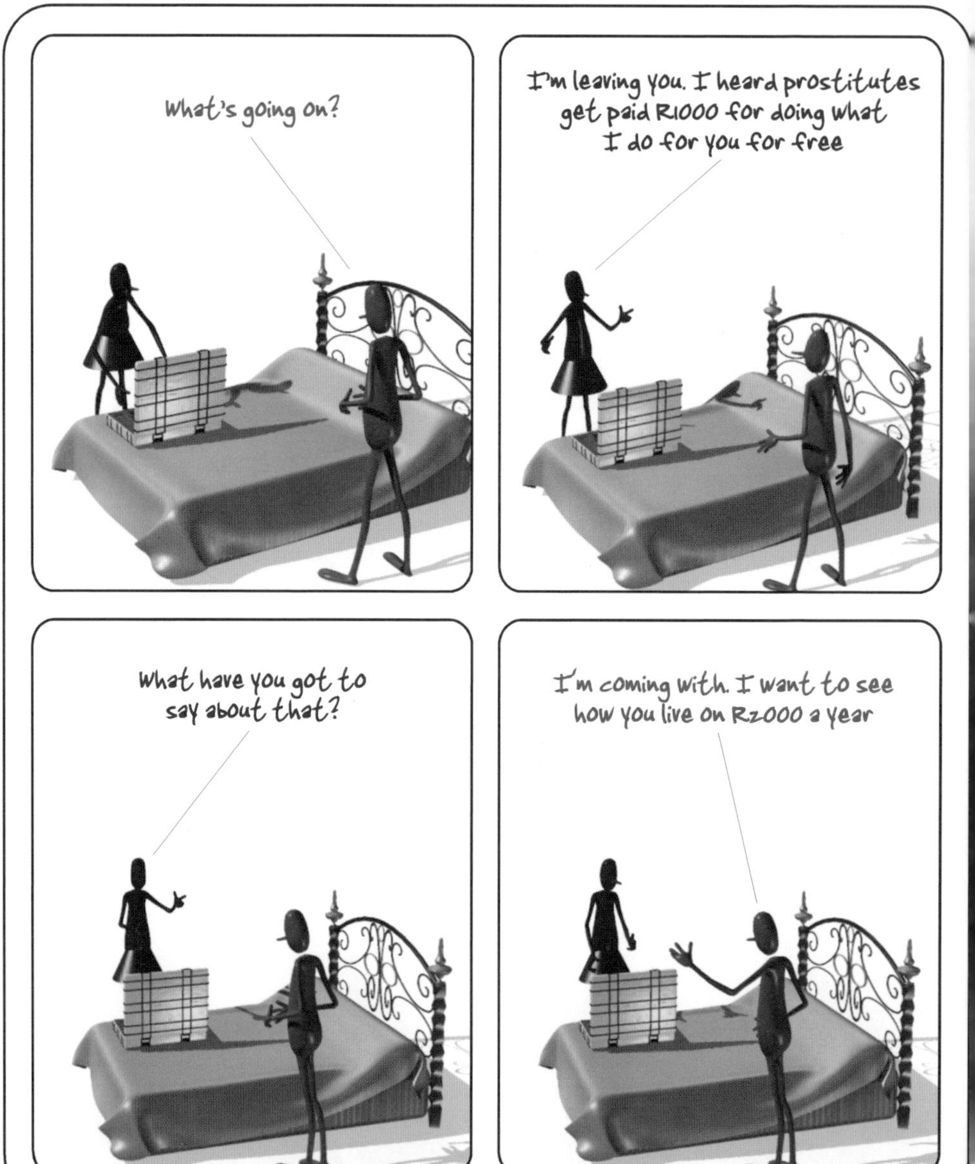
What's going on?
I'm leaving you. I heard prostitutes get paid R1000 for doing what I do for you for free
What have you got to say about that?
I'm coming with. I want to see how you live on R2000 a year
www.faceless.co.za

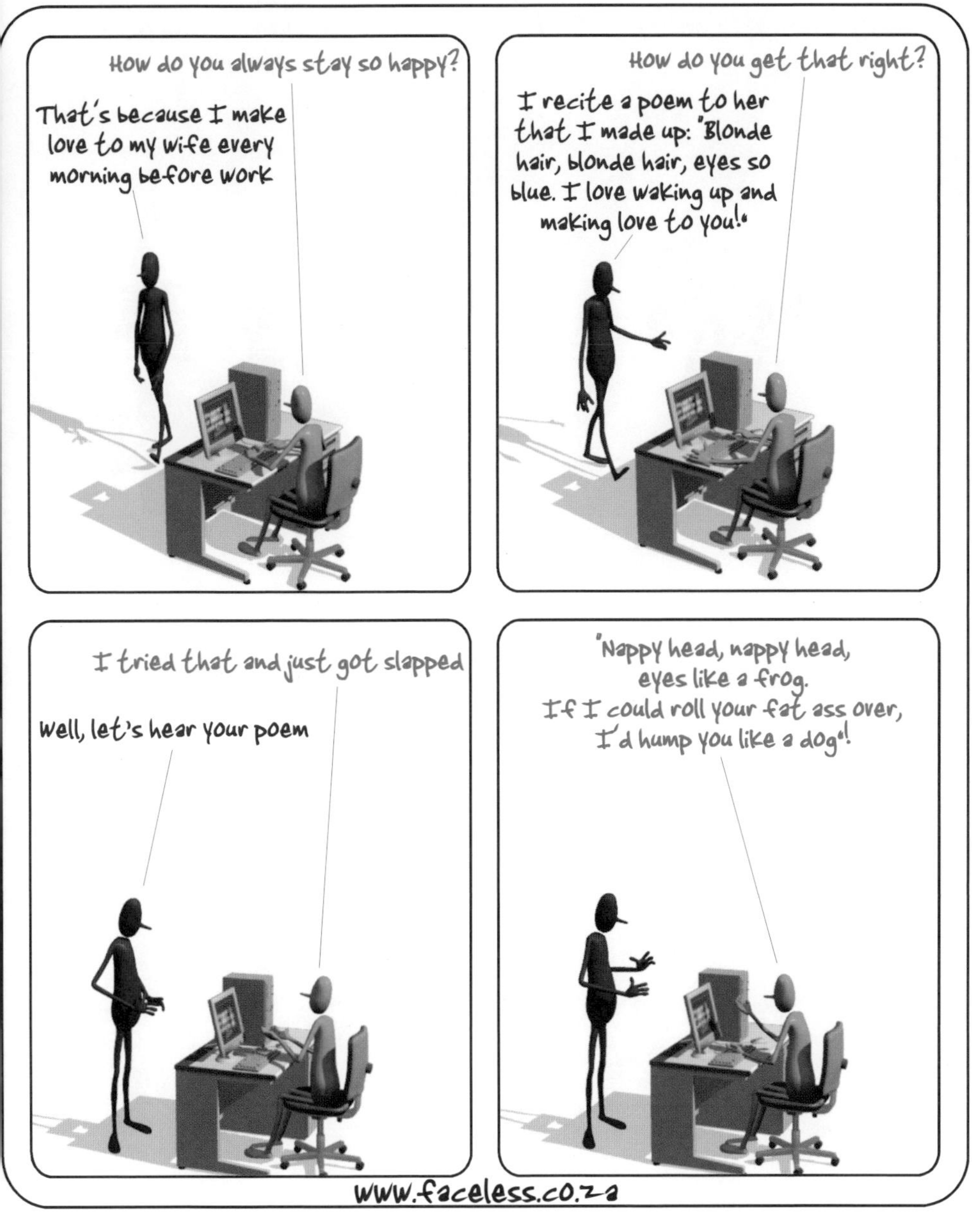
How do you always stay so happy?
That's because I make love to my wife every morning before work
How do you get that right?
I recite a poem to her that I made up: "Blonde hair, blonde hair, eyes so blue. I love waking up and making love to you!"
I tried that and just got slapped
Well, let's hear your poem
"Nappy head, nappy head, eyes like a frog. If I could roll your fat ass over, I'd hump you like a dog"!
www.faceless.co.za

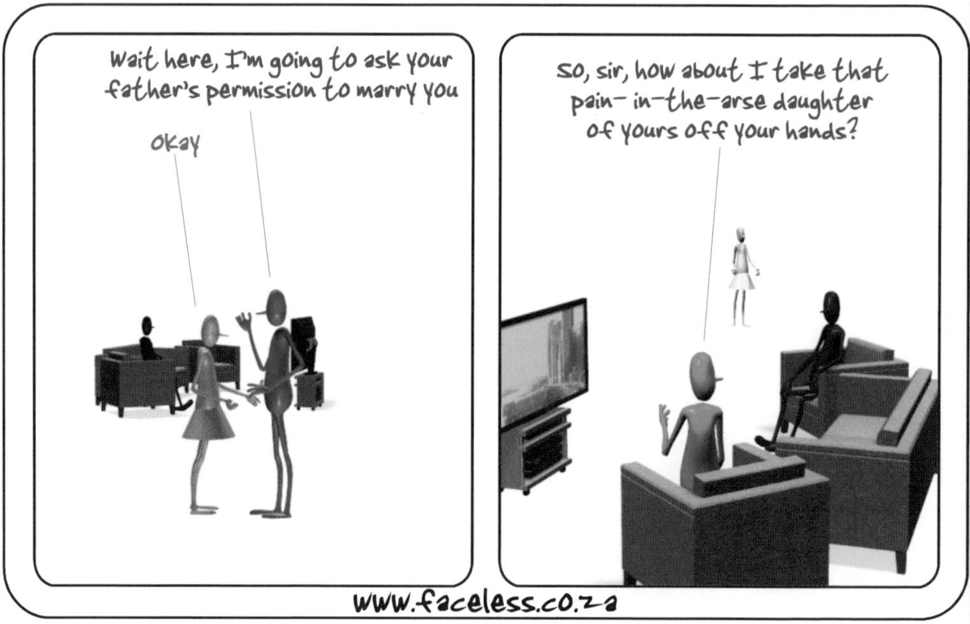
Wait here, I'm going to ask your father's permission to marry you
Okay
So, sir, how about I take that pain- in-the-arse daughter of yours off your hands?
www.faceless.co.za

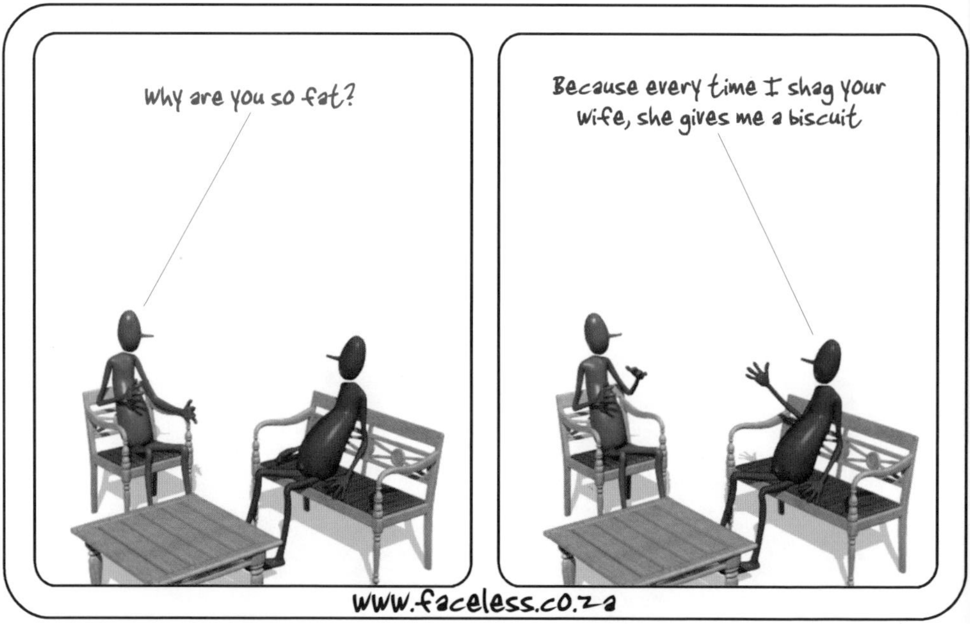
Why are you so fat?
Because every time I shag your wife, she gives me a biscuit
www.faceless.co.za

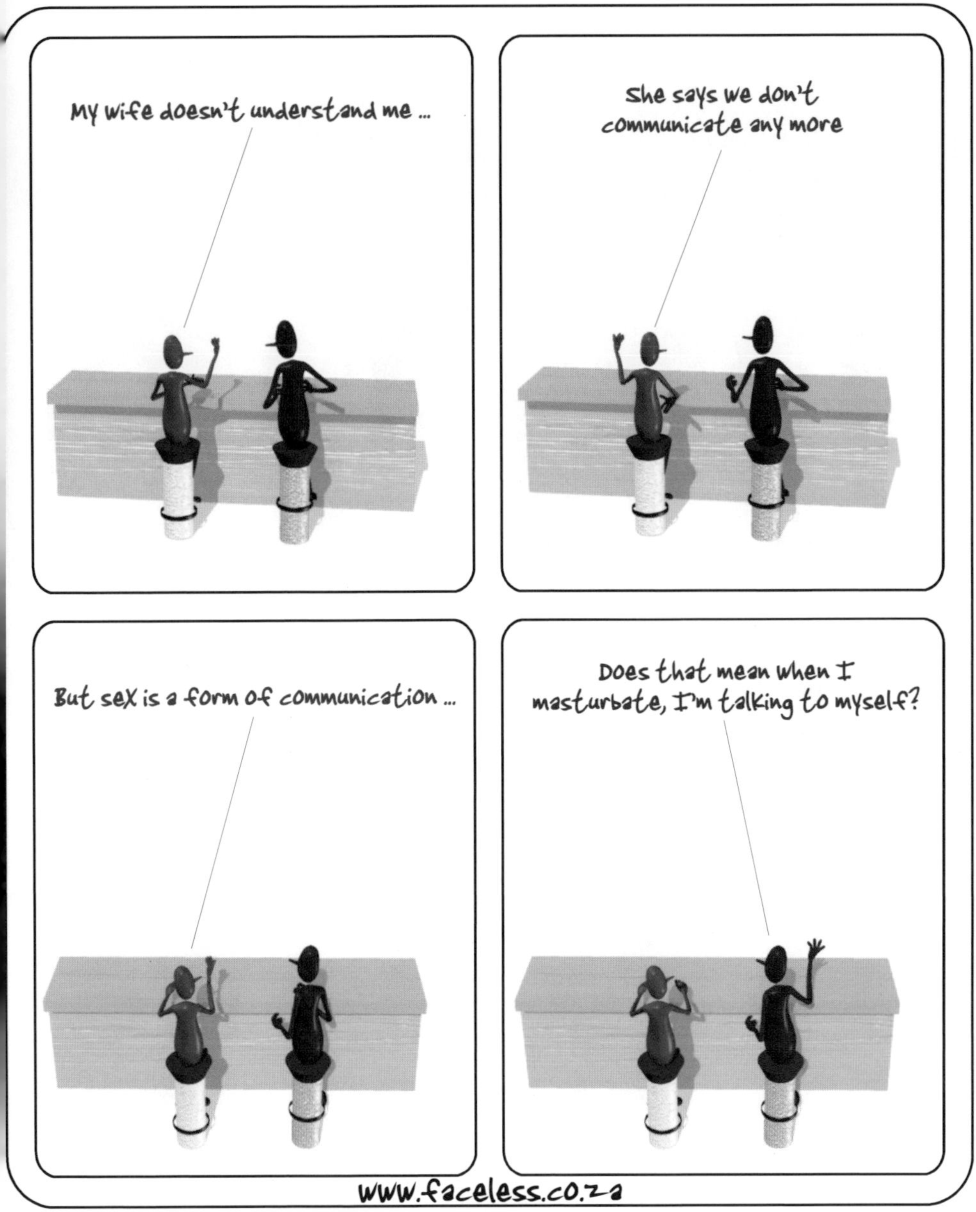

My wife doesn't understand me ...
She says we don't communicate any more
But sex is a form of communication ...
Does that mean when I masturbate, I'm talking to myself?
www.faceless.co.za

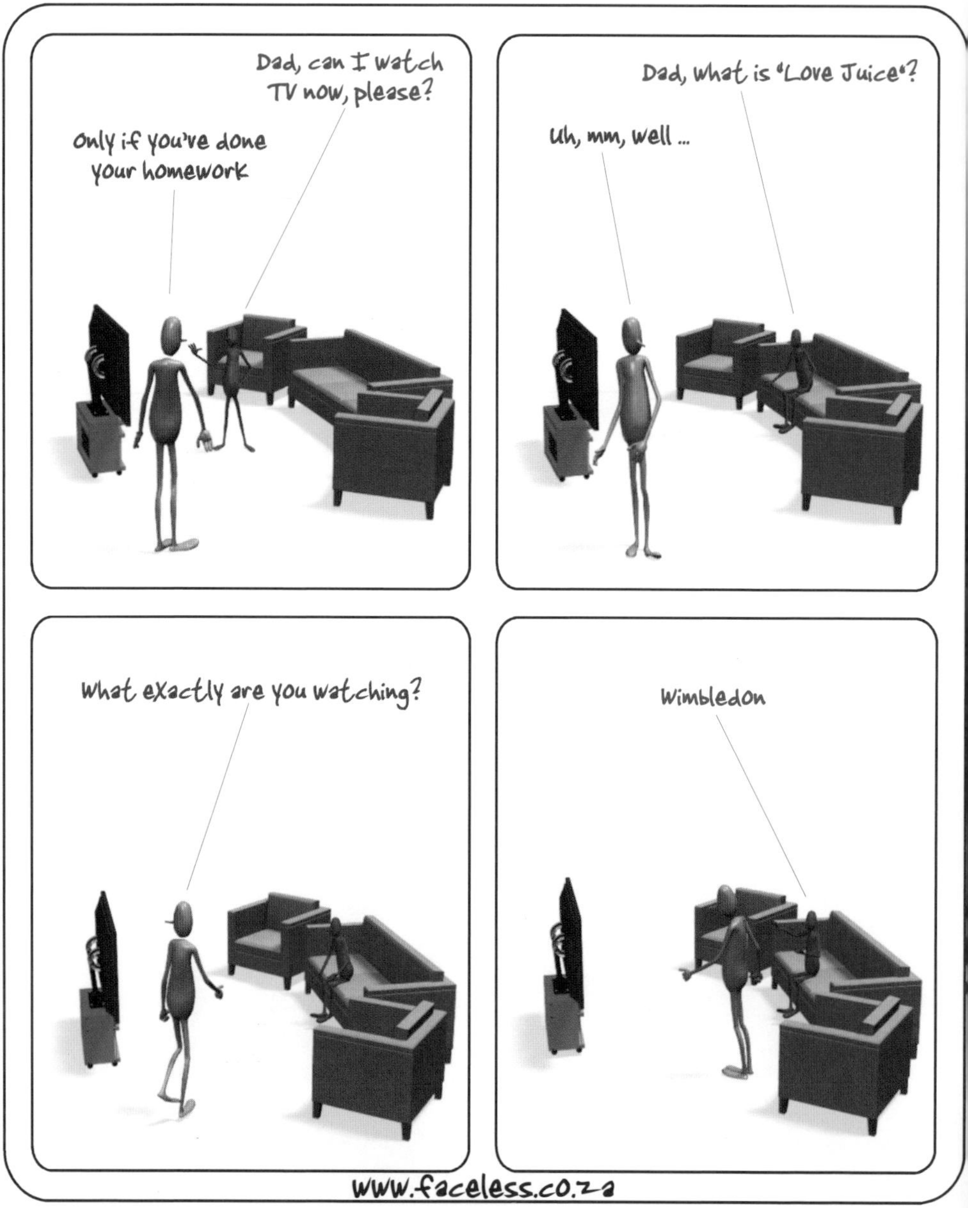
Dad, can I watch TV now, please?
Only if you've done your homework
Dad, what is "Love Juice"?
Uh, mm, well ...
What exactly are you watching?
Wimbledon
www.faceless.co.za

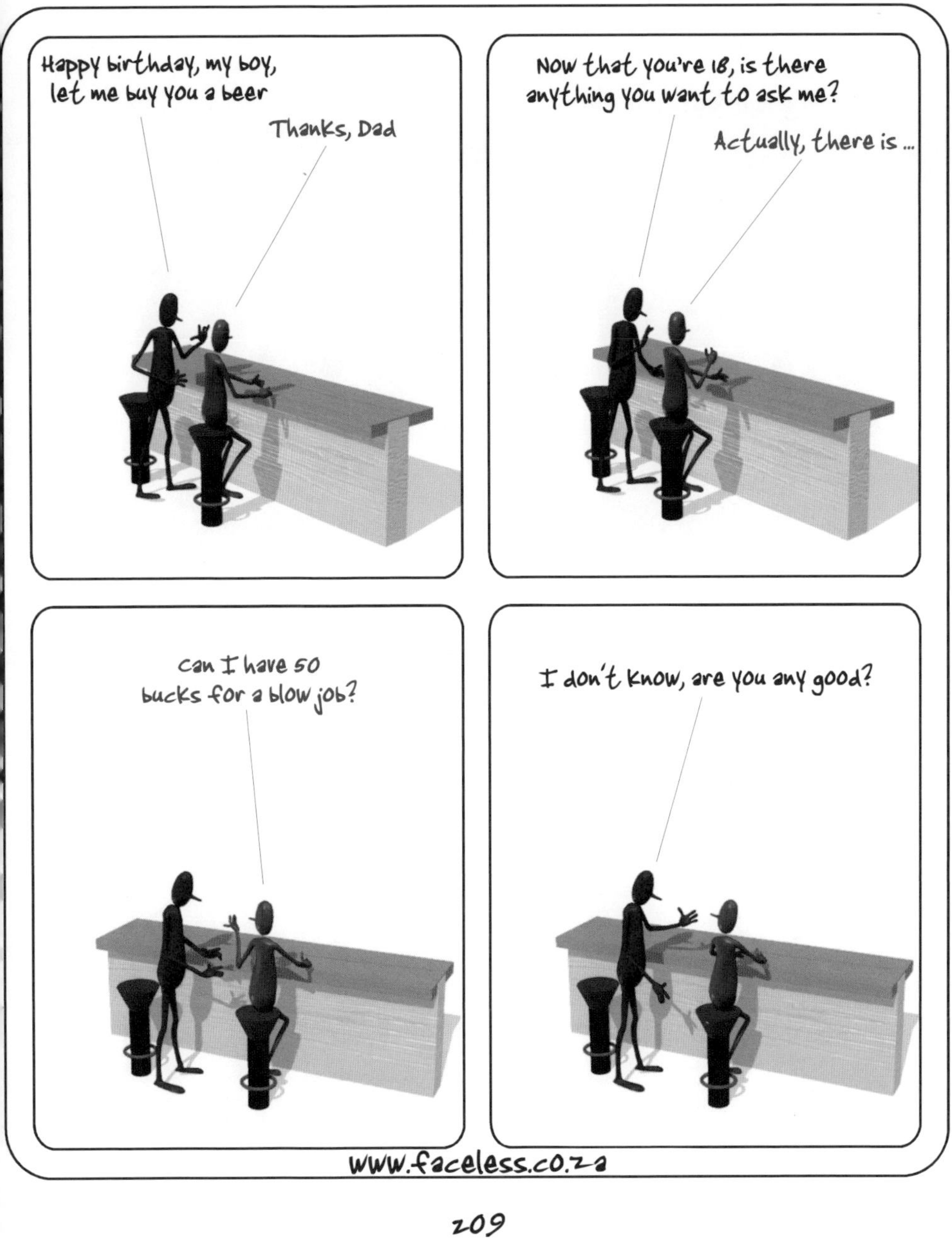
Happy birthday, my boy, let me buy you a beer
Thanks, Dad
Now that you're 18, is there anything you want to ask me?
Actually, there is ...
can I have 50 bucks for a blow job?
I don't know, are you any good?
www.faceless.co.za

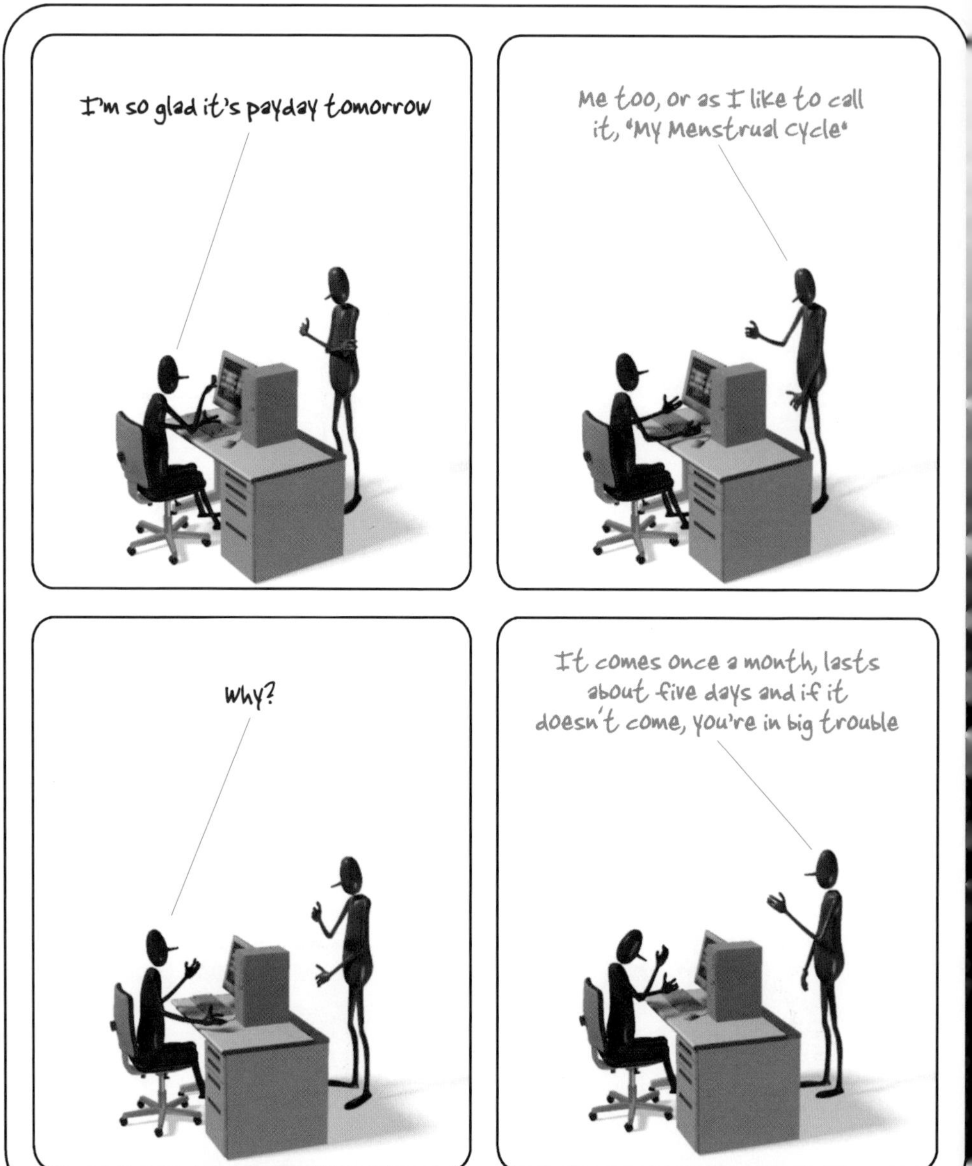
I'm so glad it's payday tomorrow
Me too, or as I like to call it, "My Menstrual cycle"
Why?
It comes once a month, lasts about five days and if it doesn't come, you're in big trouble
www.faceless.co.za

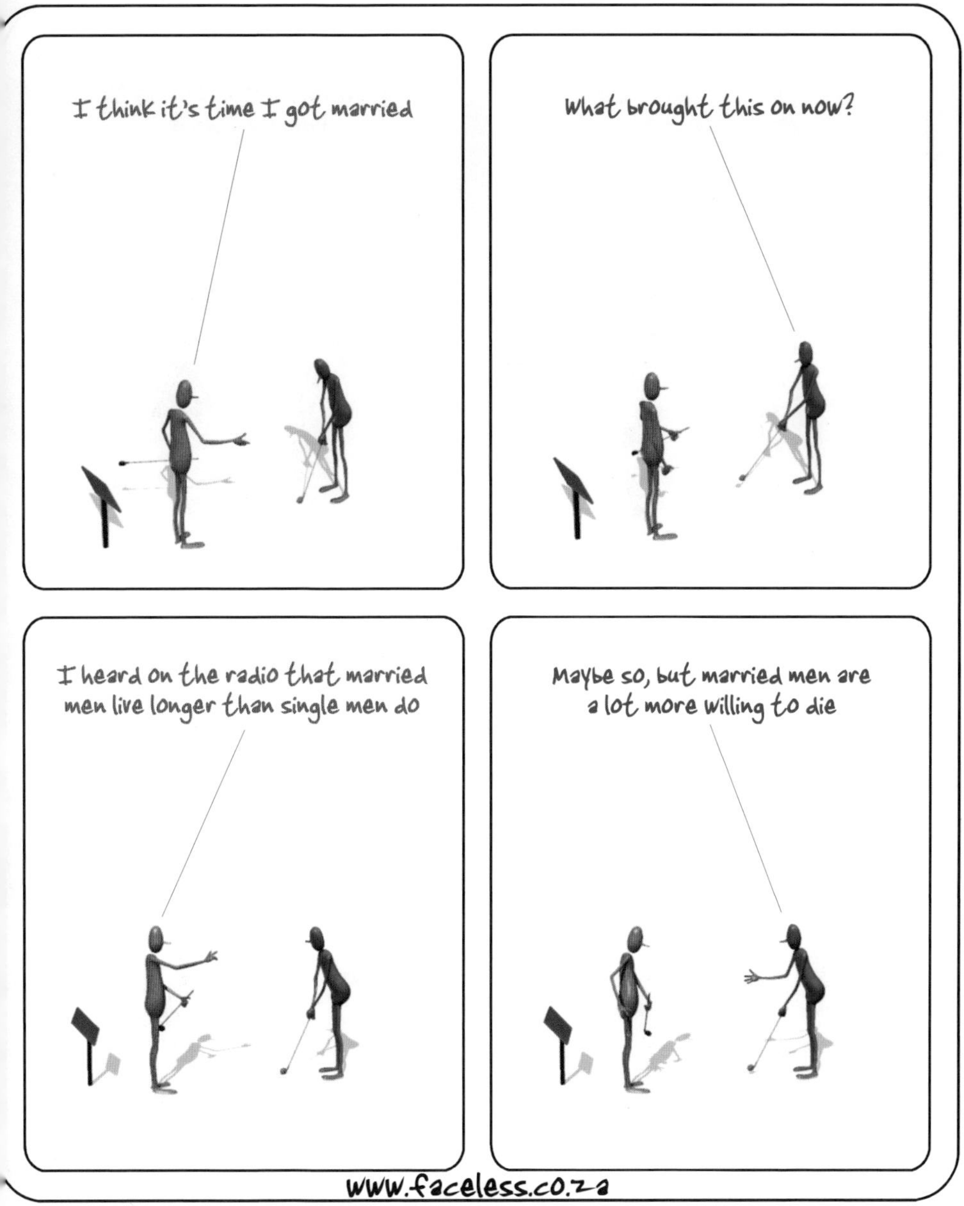
I think it's time I got married
What brought this on now?
I heard on the radio that married men live longer than single men do
Maybe so, but married men are a lot more willing to die
www.faceless.co.za

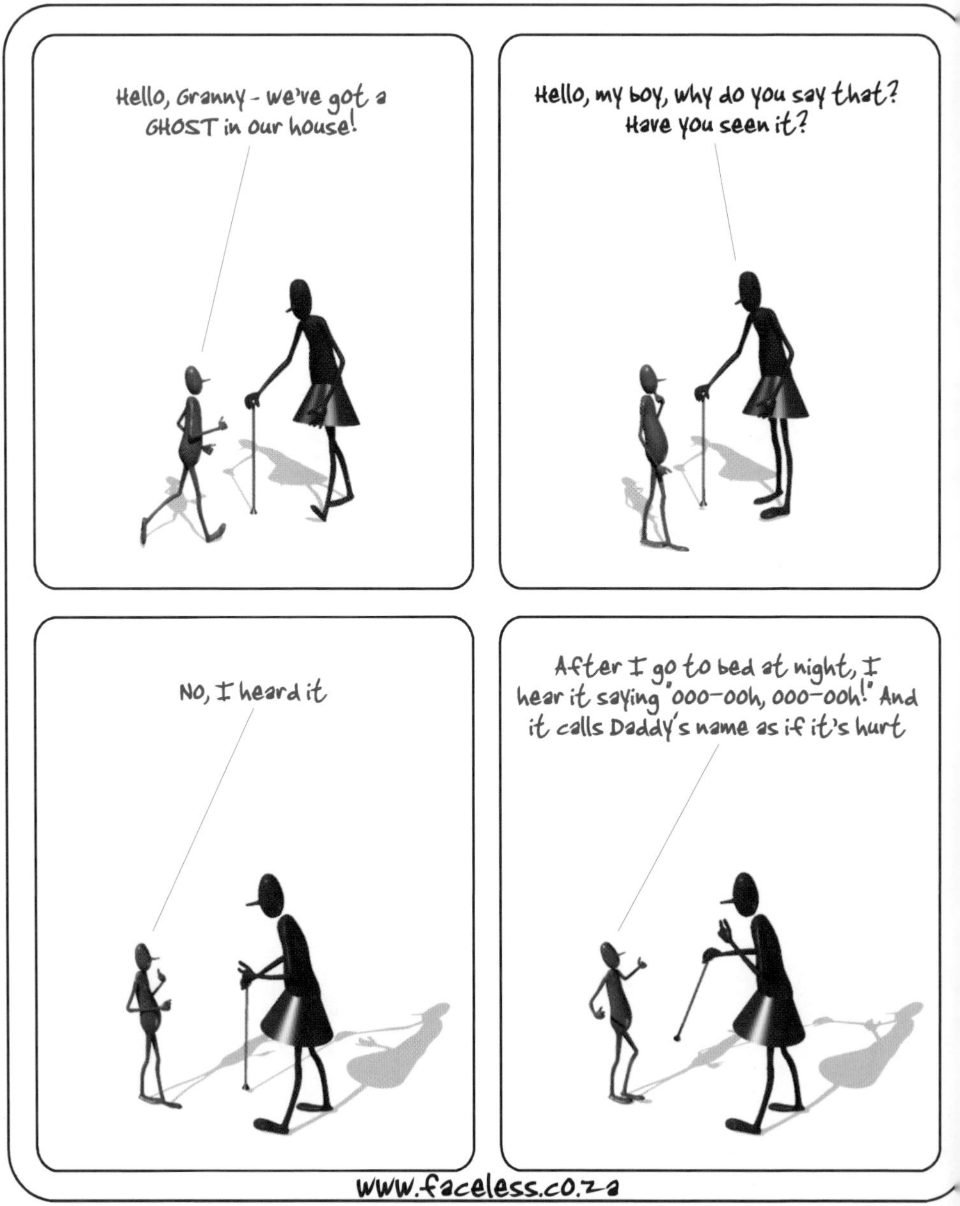
Hello, Granny - we've got a GHOST in our house!
Hello, my boy, why do you say that? Have you seen it?
No, I heard it
After I go to bed at night, I hear it saying "ooo-ooh, ooo-ooh!" And it calls Daddy's name as if it's hurt
www.faceless.co.za

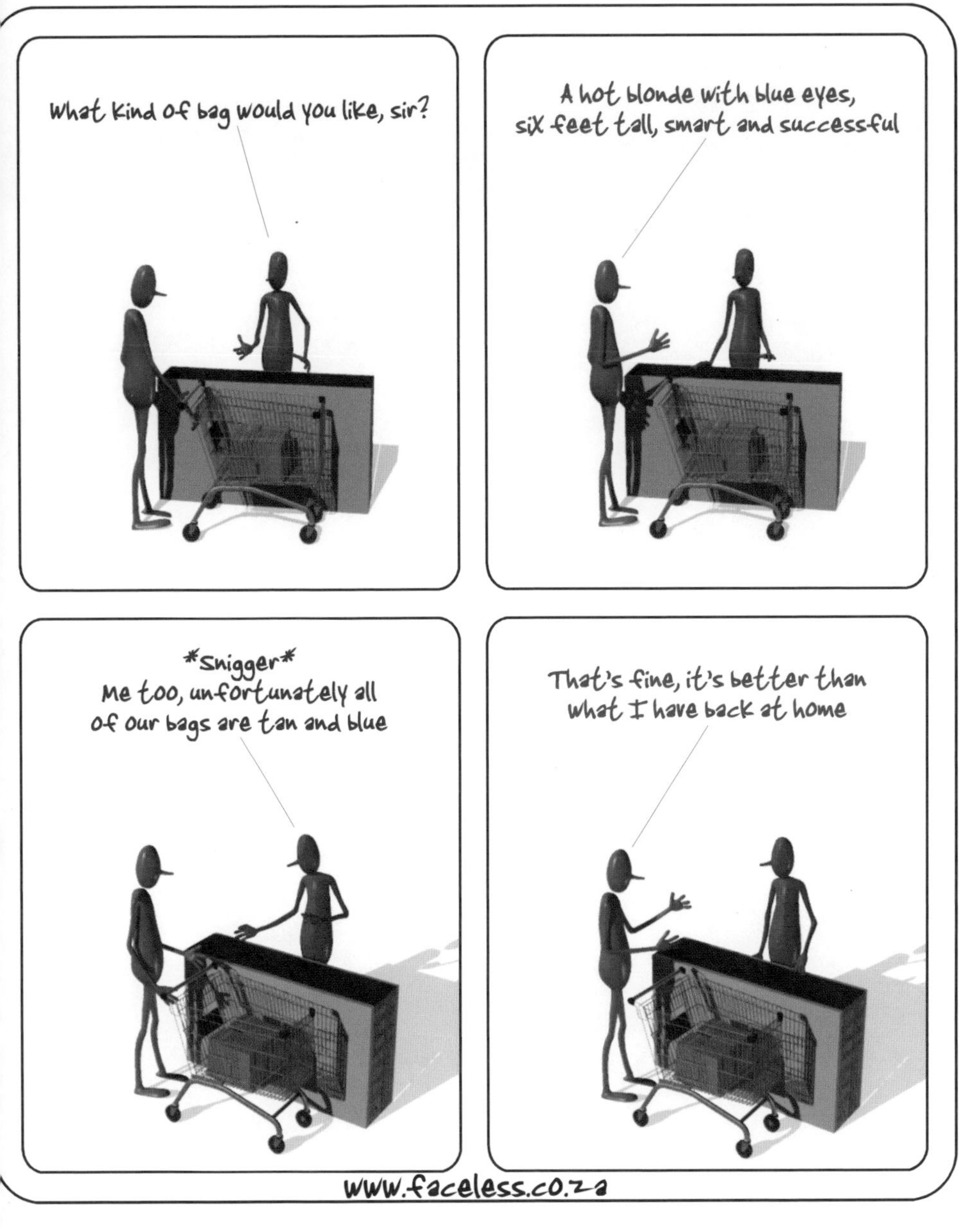
What kind of bag would you like, sir?
A hot blonde with blue eyes, six feet tall, smart and successful
Snigger Me too, unfortunately all of our bags are tan and blue
That's fine, it's better than what I have back at home
www.faceless.co.za

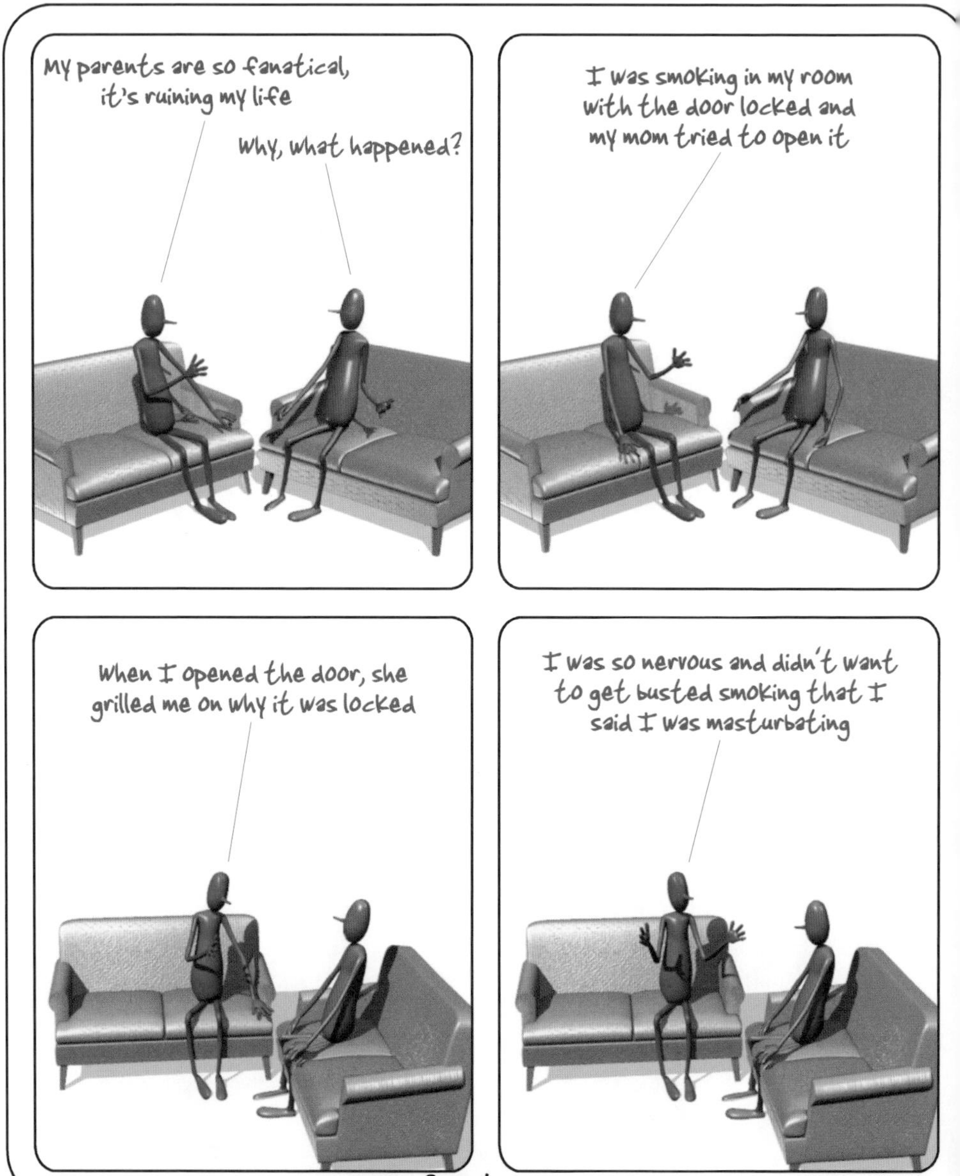
My parents are so fanatical, it's ruining my life
Why, what happened?
I was smoking in my room with the door locked and my mom tried to open it
When I opened the door, she grilled me on why it was locked
I was so nervous and didn't want to get busted smoking that I said I was masturbating
www.faceless.co.za

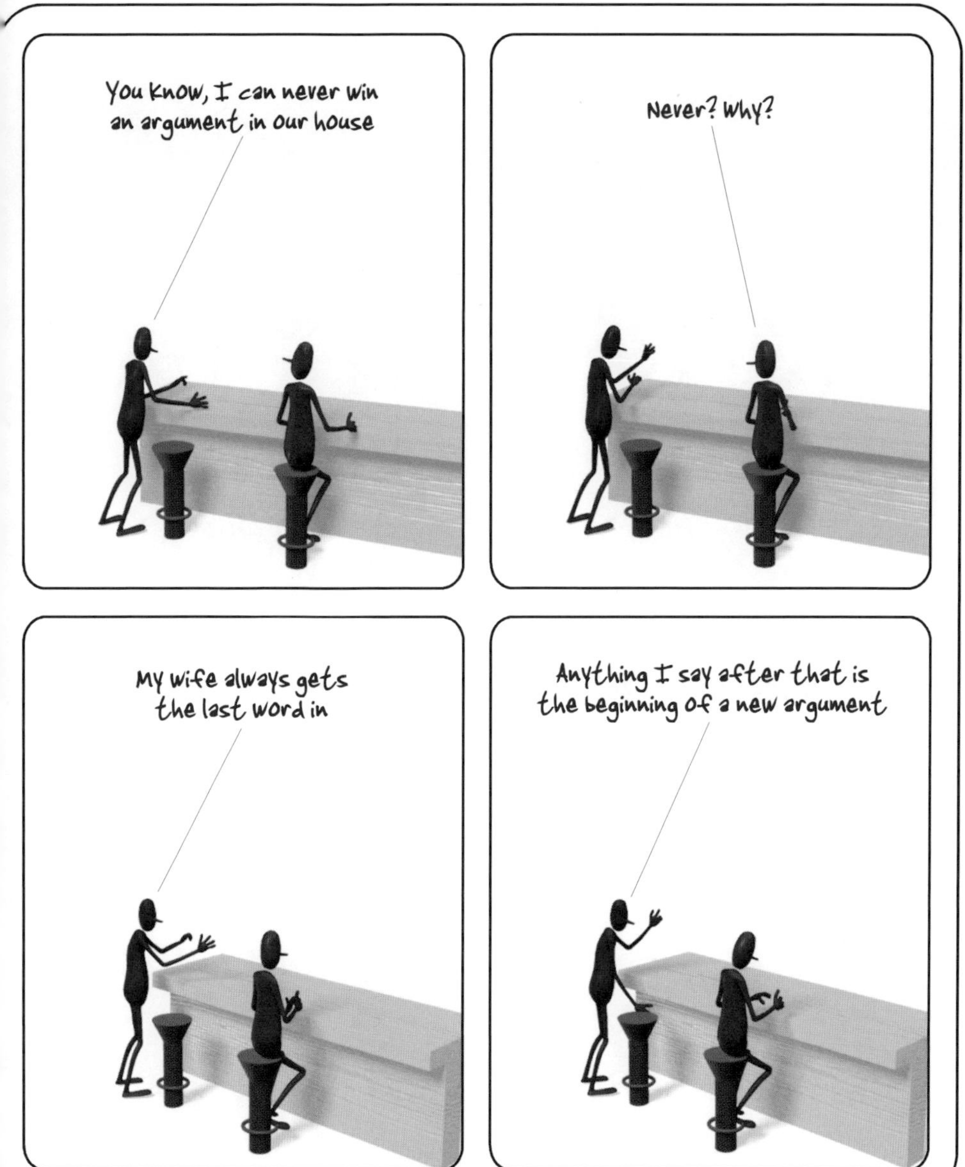
You know, I can never win an argument in our house
Never? Why?
My wife always gets the last word in
Anything I say after that is the beginning of a new argument
www.faceless.co.za

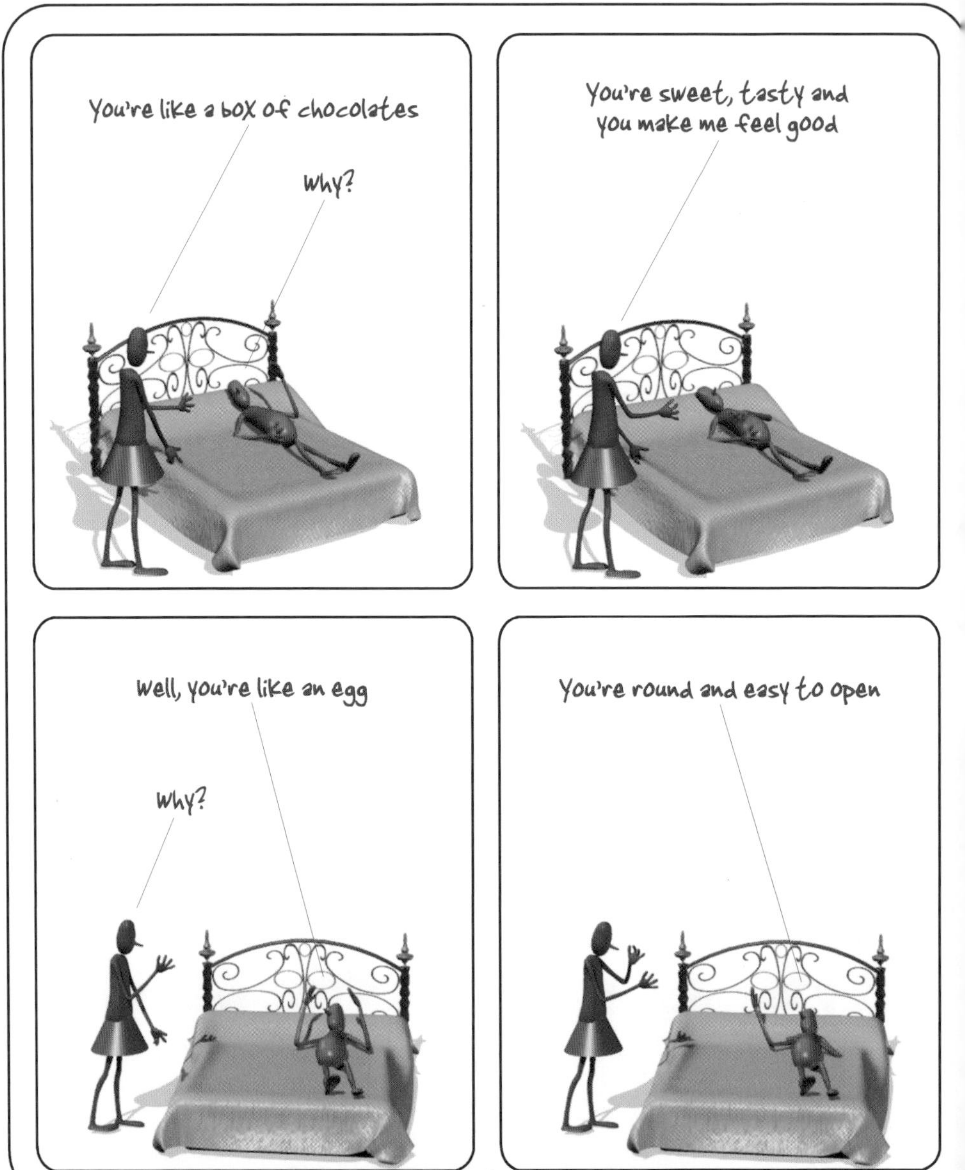
You're like a box of chocolates
Why?
You're sweet, tasty and you make me feel good
Well, you're like an egg
Why?
You're round and easy to open
www.faceless.co.za

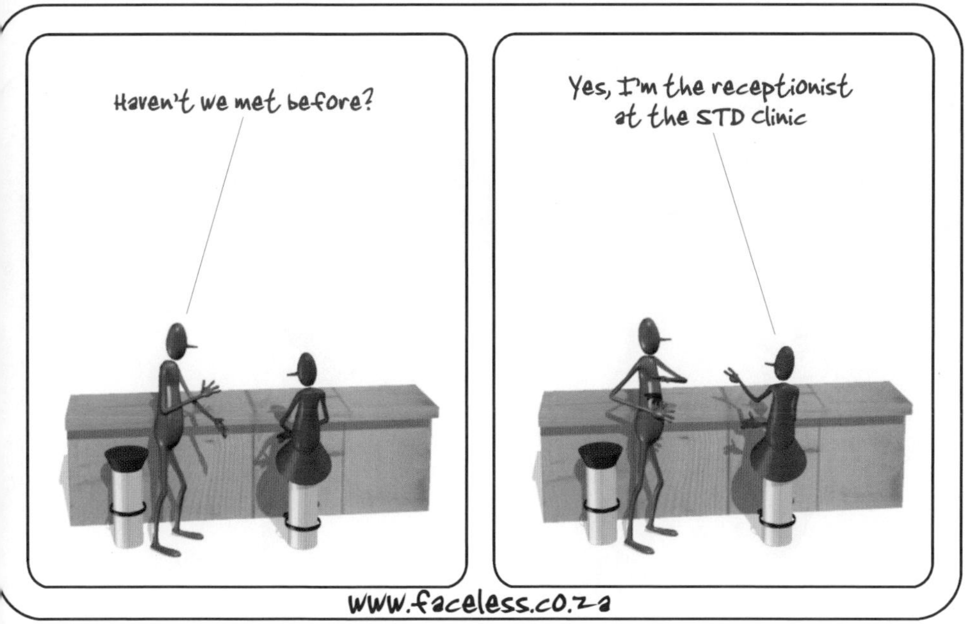
Haven't we met before?
Yes, I'm the receptionist at the STD Clinic
www.faceless.co.za

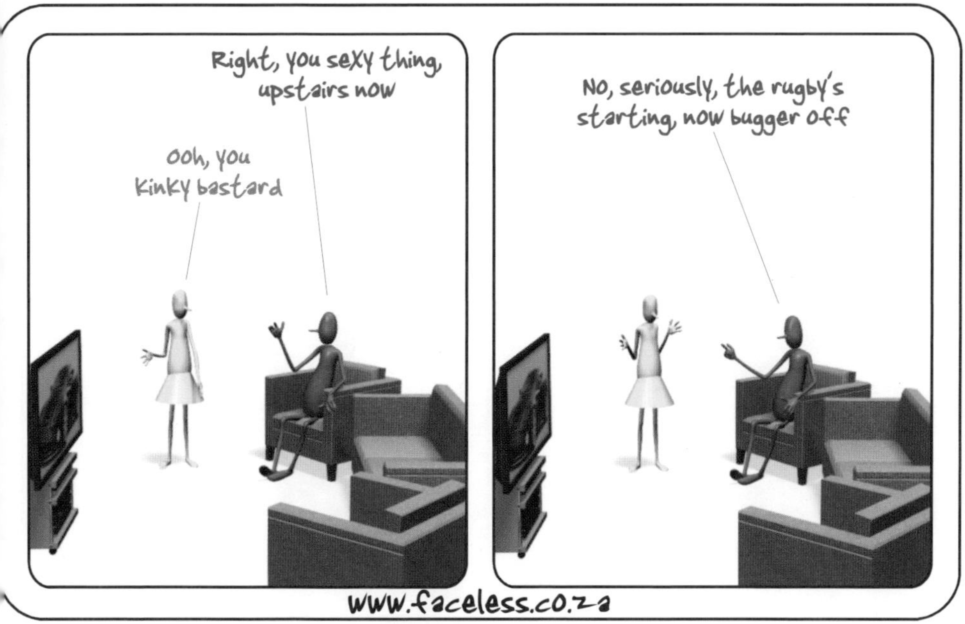
Right, you sexy thing, upstairs now
Ooh, you kinky bastard
No, seriously, the rugby's starting, now bugger off
www.faceless.co.za

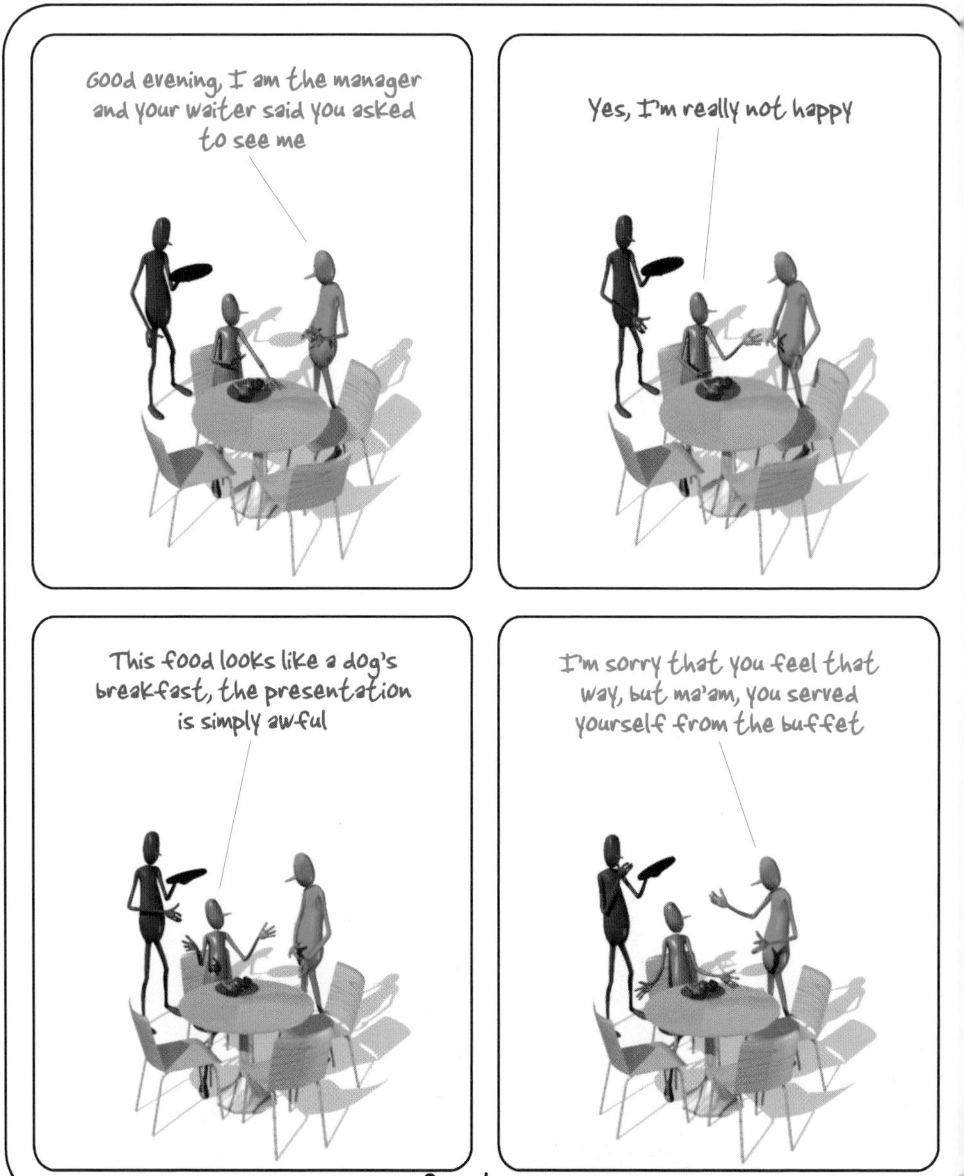
Good evening, I am the manager and your waiter said you asked to see me
Yes, I'm really not happy
This food looks like a dog's breakfast, the presentation is simply awful
I'm sorry that you feel that way, but ma'am, you served yourself from the buffet
www.faceless.co.za

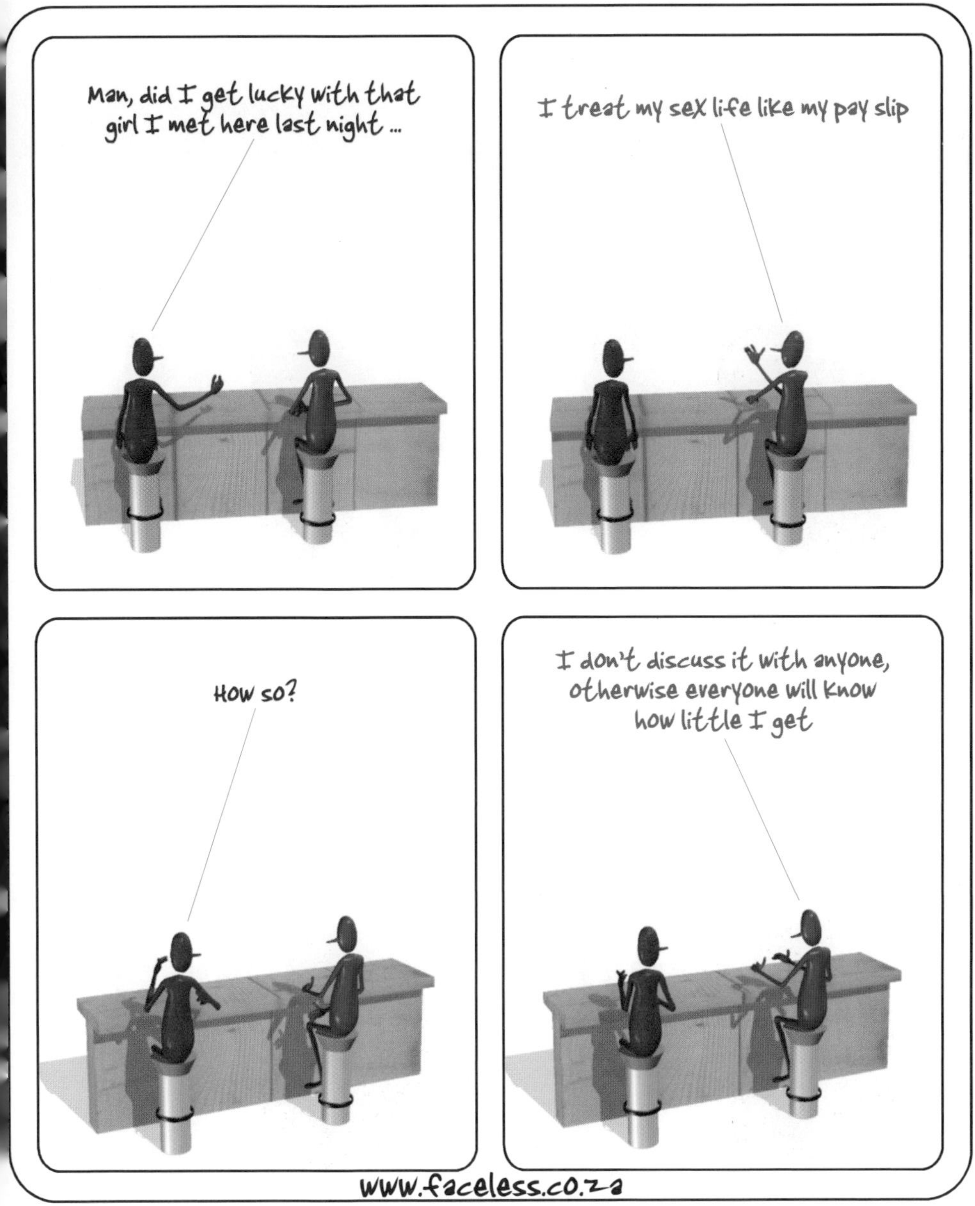
Man, did I get lucky with that girl I met here last night ...
I treat my sex life like my pay slip
How so?
I don't discuss it with anyone, otherwise everyone will know how little I get
www.faceless.co.za

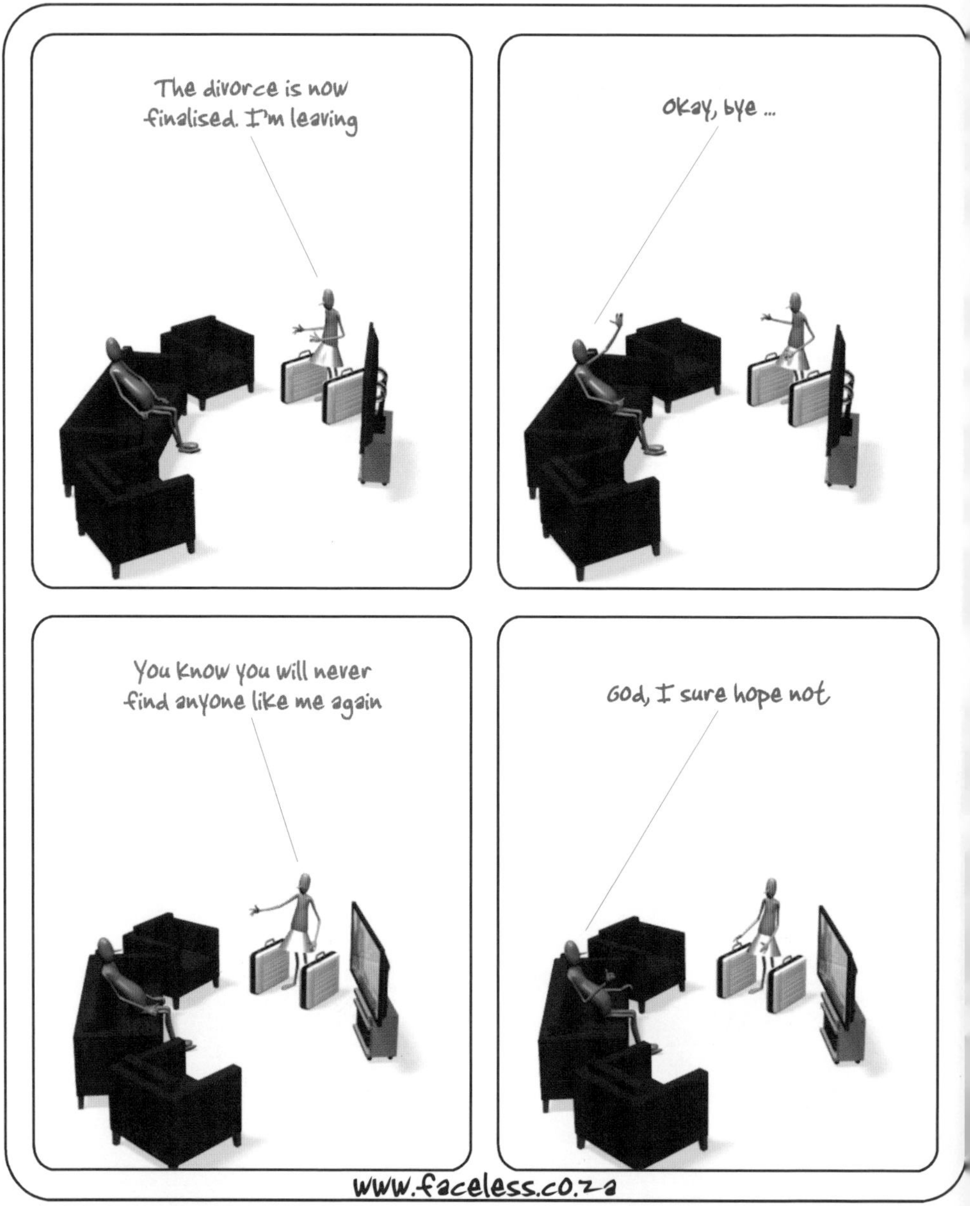
The divorce is now finalised. I'm leaving
Okay, bye ...
You know you will never find anyone like me again
God, I sure hope not
www.faceless.co.za

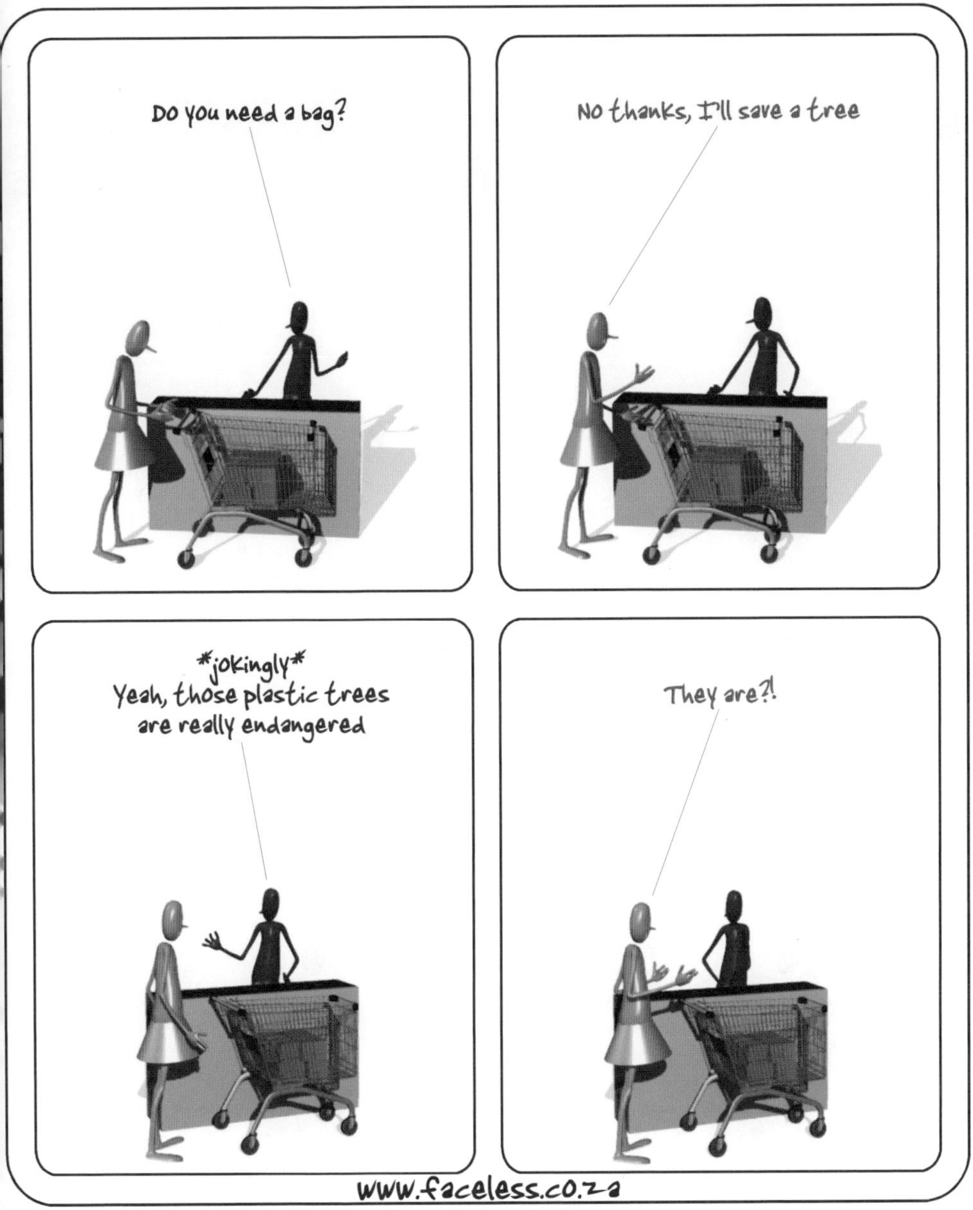
Do you need a bag?
No thanks, I'll save a tree
jokingly
Yeah, those plastic trees
are really endangered
They are?!
www.faceless.co.za

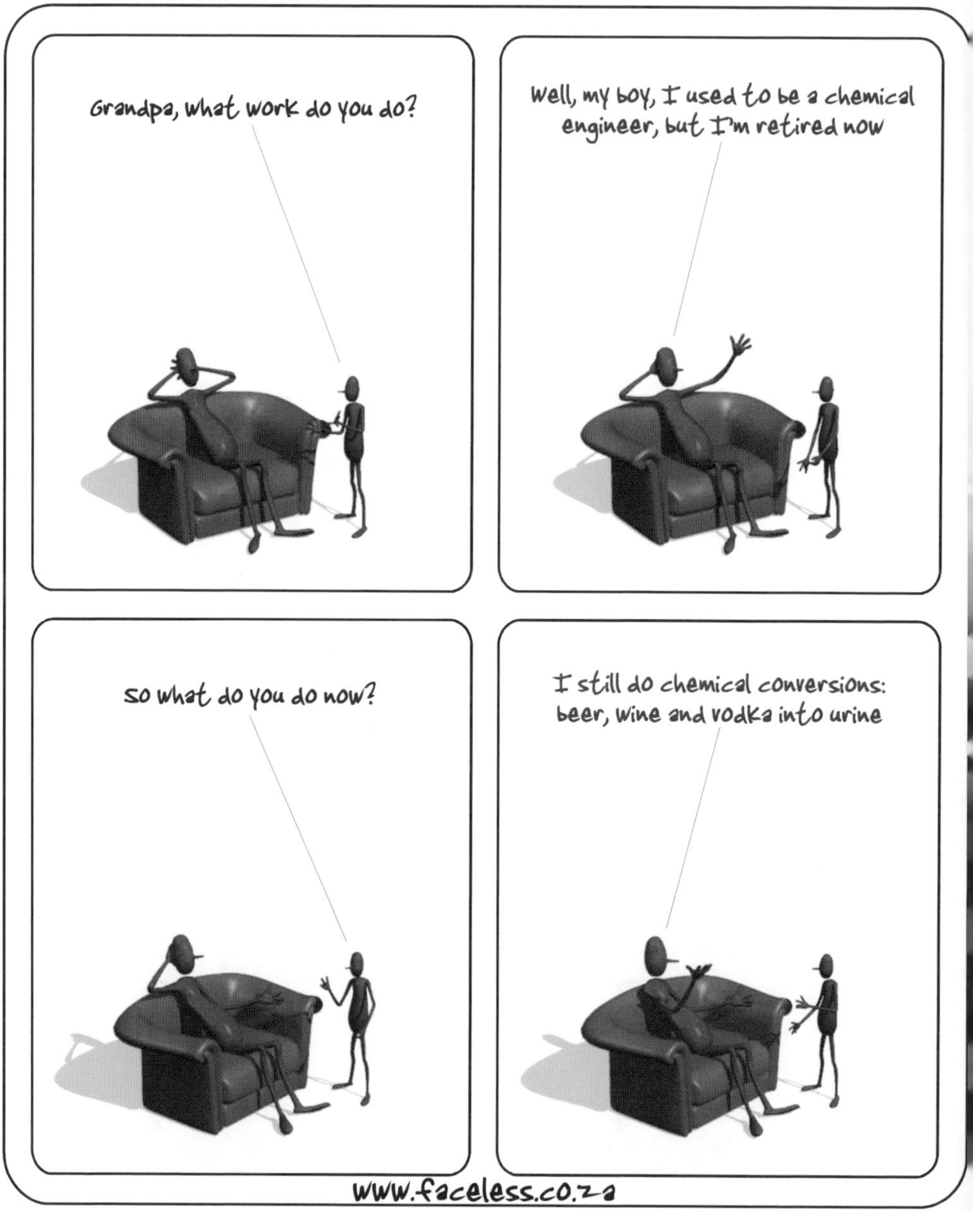
Grandpa, what work do you do?
Well, my boy, I used to be a chemical engineer, but I'm retired now
so what do you do now?
I still do chemical conversions: beer, wine and vodka into urine
www.faceless.co.za

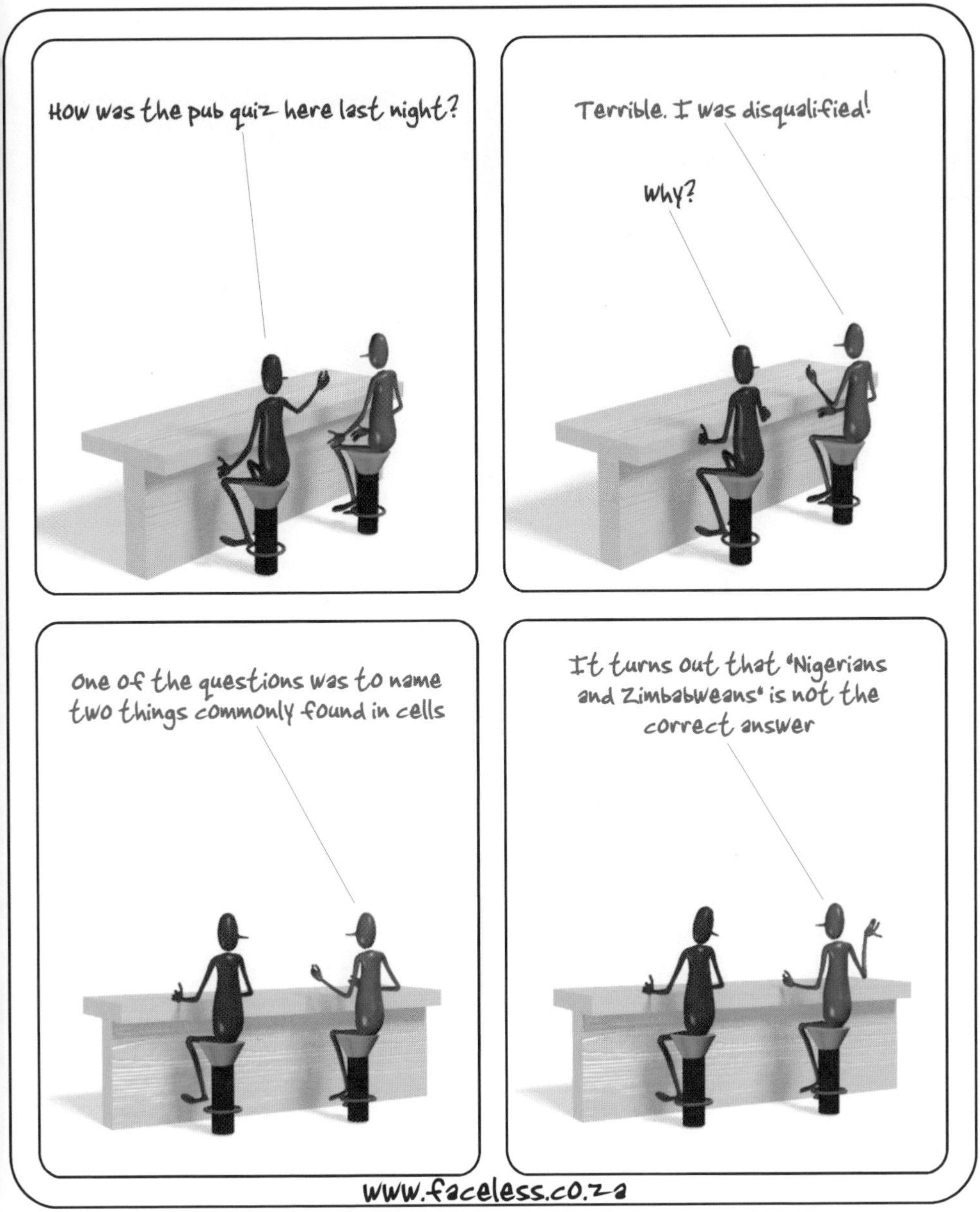
How was the pub quiz here last night?
Terrible. I was disqualified!
Why?
One of the questions was to name two things commonly found in cells
It turns out that "Nigerians and Zimbabweans" is not the correct answer
www.faceless.co.za

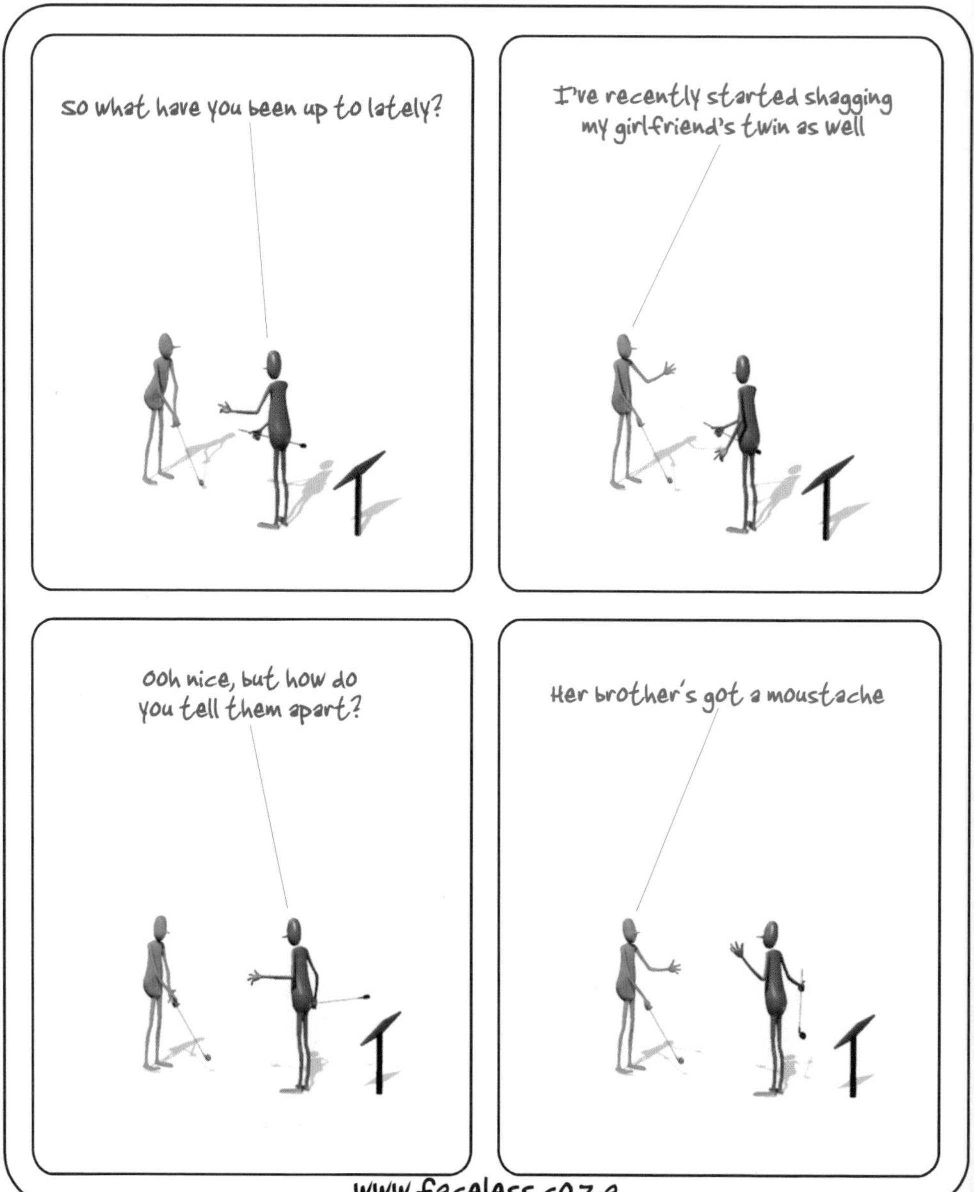
so what have you been up to lately?
I've recently started shagging my girl-friend's twin as well
ooh nice, but how do you tell them apart?
Her brother's got a moustache
www.faceless.co.za

It's that part of your annual check-up. Turn your head and cough, please
cough
Don't worry, it's normal to get an erection during this kind of examination
But I haven't got an erection!
No, but I have
www.faceless.co.za

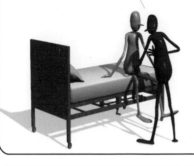

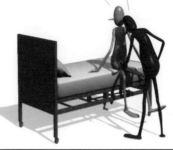

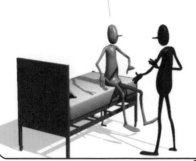

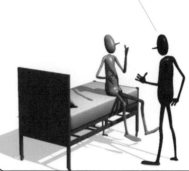

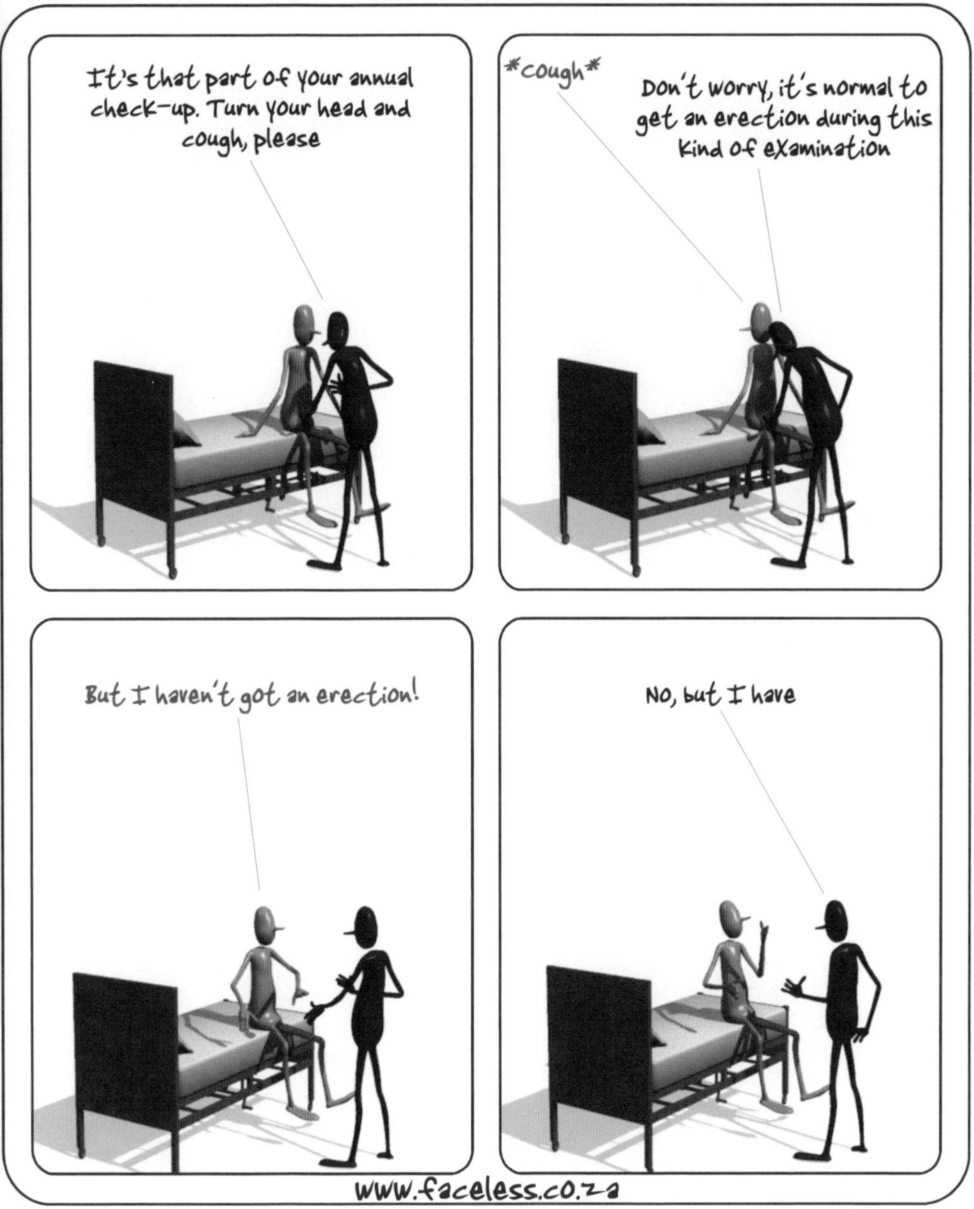

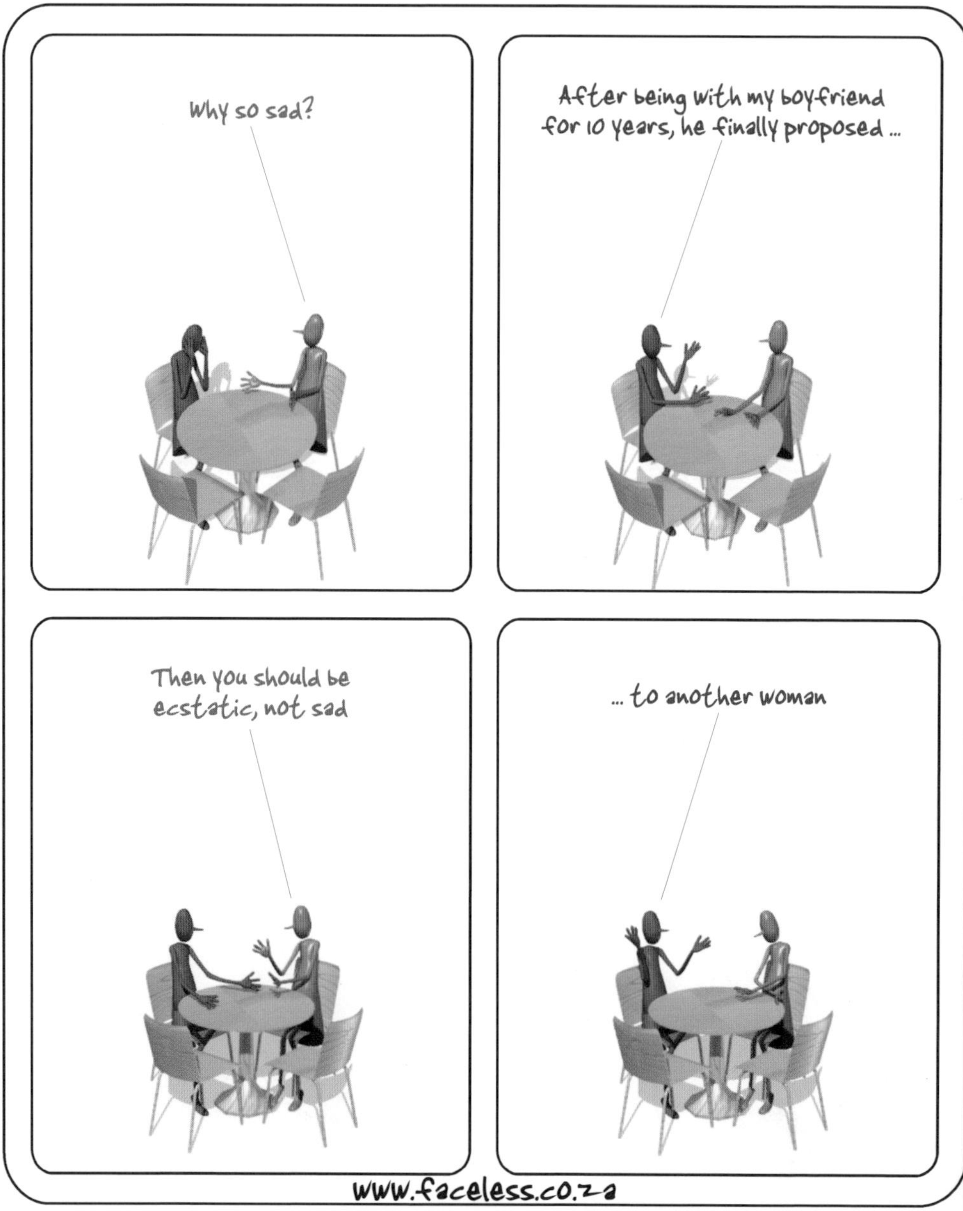
Why so sad?
After being with my boyfriend for 10 years, he finally proposed ...
Then you should be ecstatic, not sad
... to another woman
www.faceless.co.za

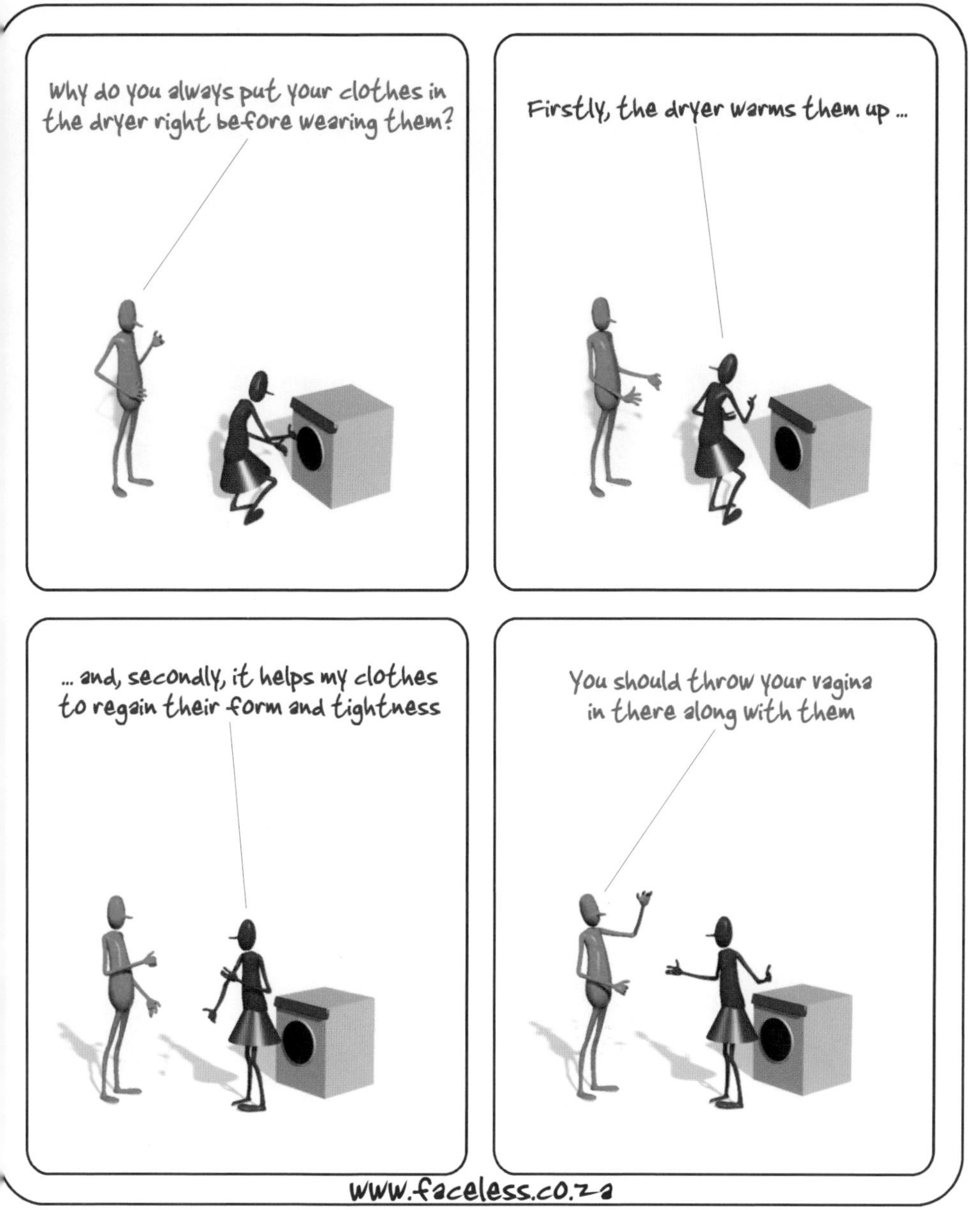
Why do you always put your clothes in the dryer right before wearing them?
Firstly, the dryer warms them up ...
... and, secondly, it helps my clothes to regain their form and tightness
You should throw your vagina in there along with them
www.faceless.co.za

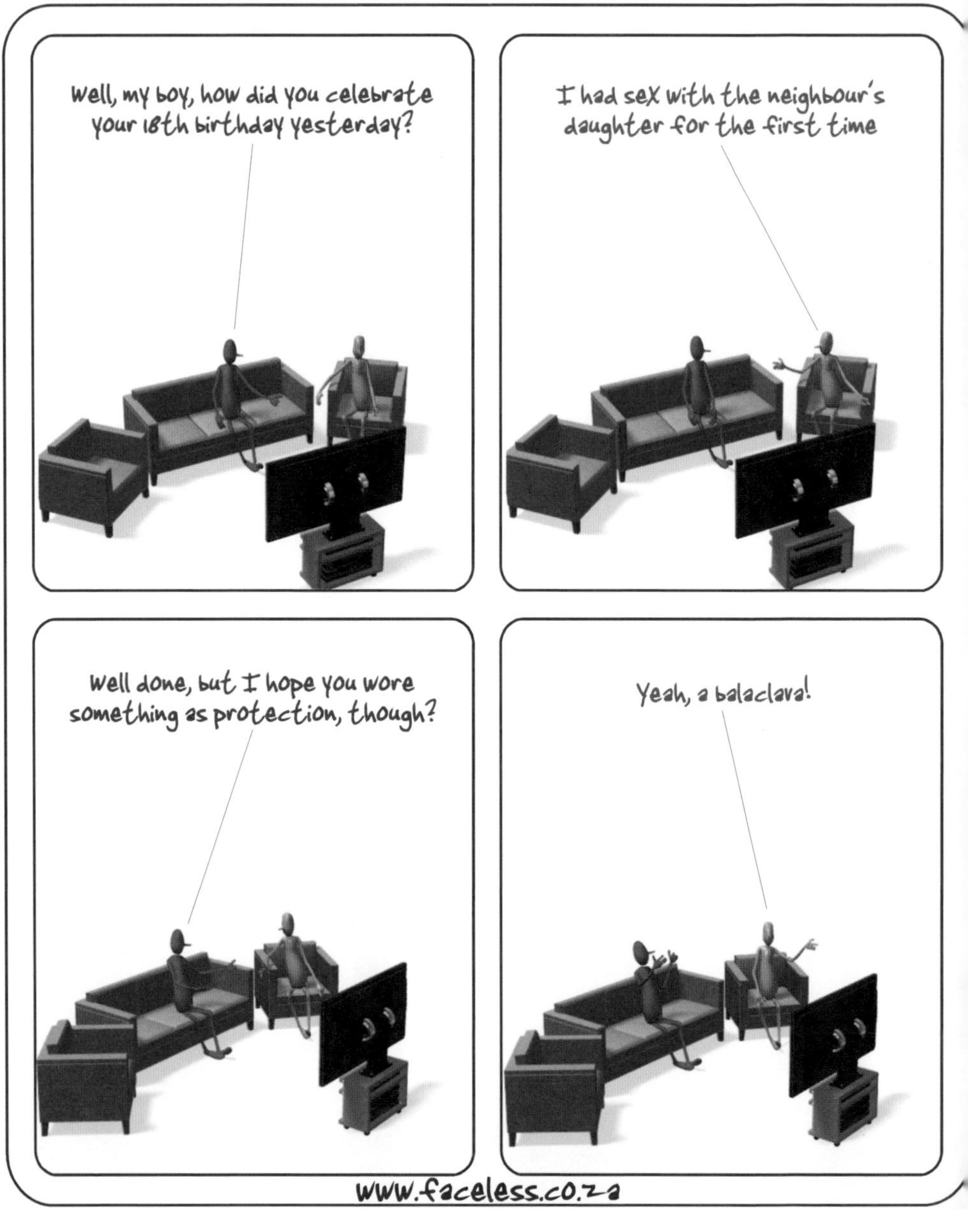
Well, my boy, how did you celebrate your 18th birthday yesterday?
I had sex with the neighbour's daughter for the first time
Well done, but I hope you wore something as protection, though?
Yeah, a balaclava!
www.faceless.co.za

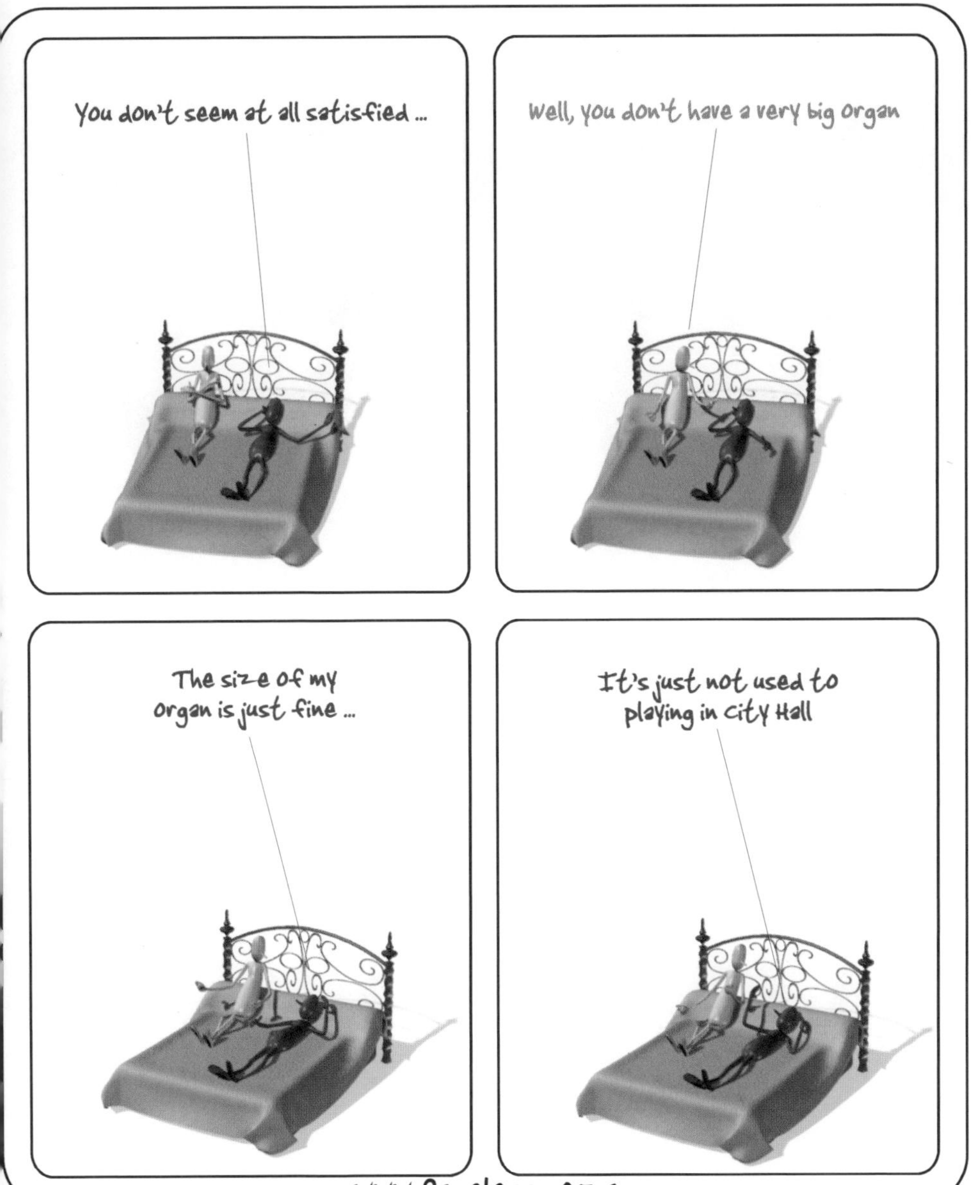
You don't seem at all satisfied ...
Well, you don't have a very big organ
The size of my organ is just fine ...
It's just not used to playing in City Hall
www.faceless.co.za

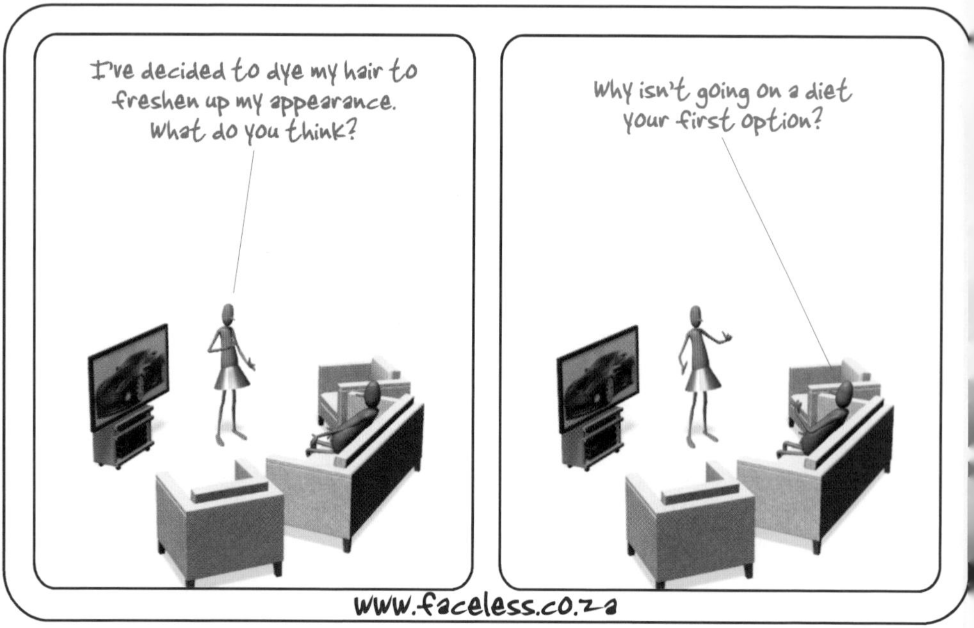
I've decided to dye my hair to freshen up my appearance. What do you think?
Why isn't going on a diet your first option?
www.faceless.co.za

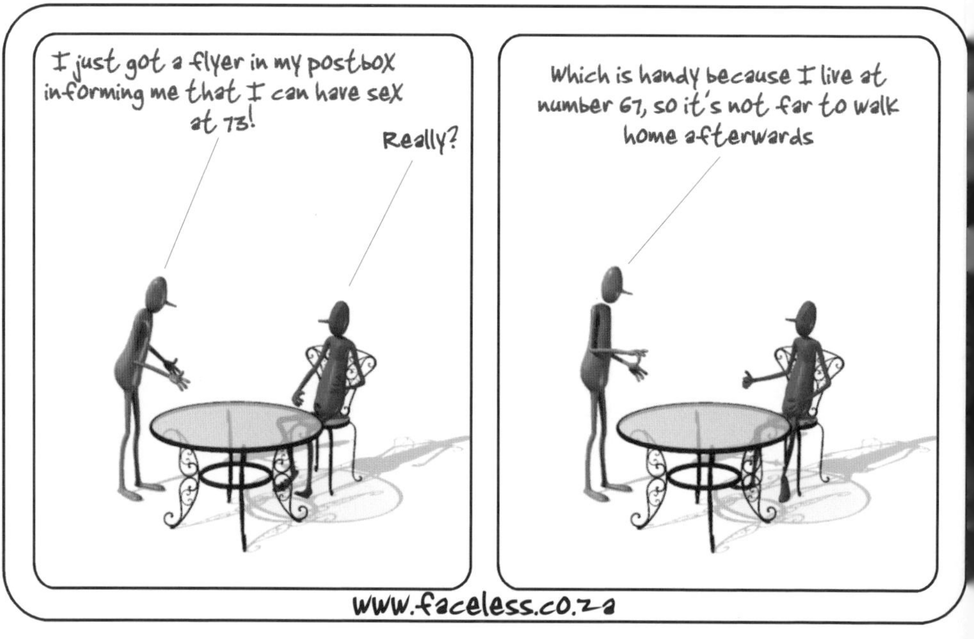
I just got a flyer in my postbox informing me that I can have sex at 73!
Really?
Which is handy because I live at number 67, so it's not far to walk home afterwards
www.faceless.co.za

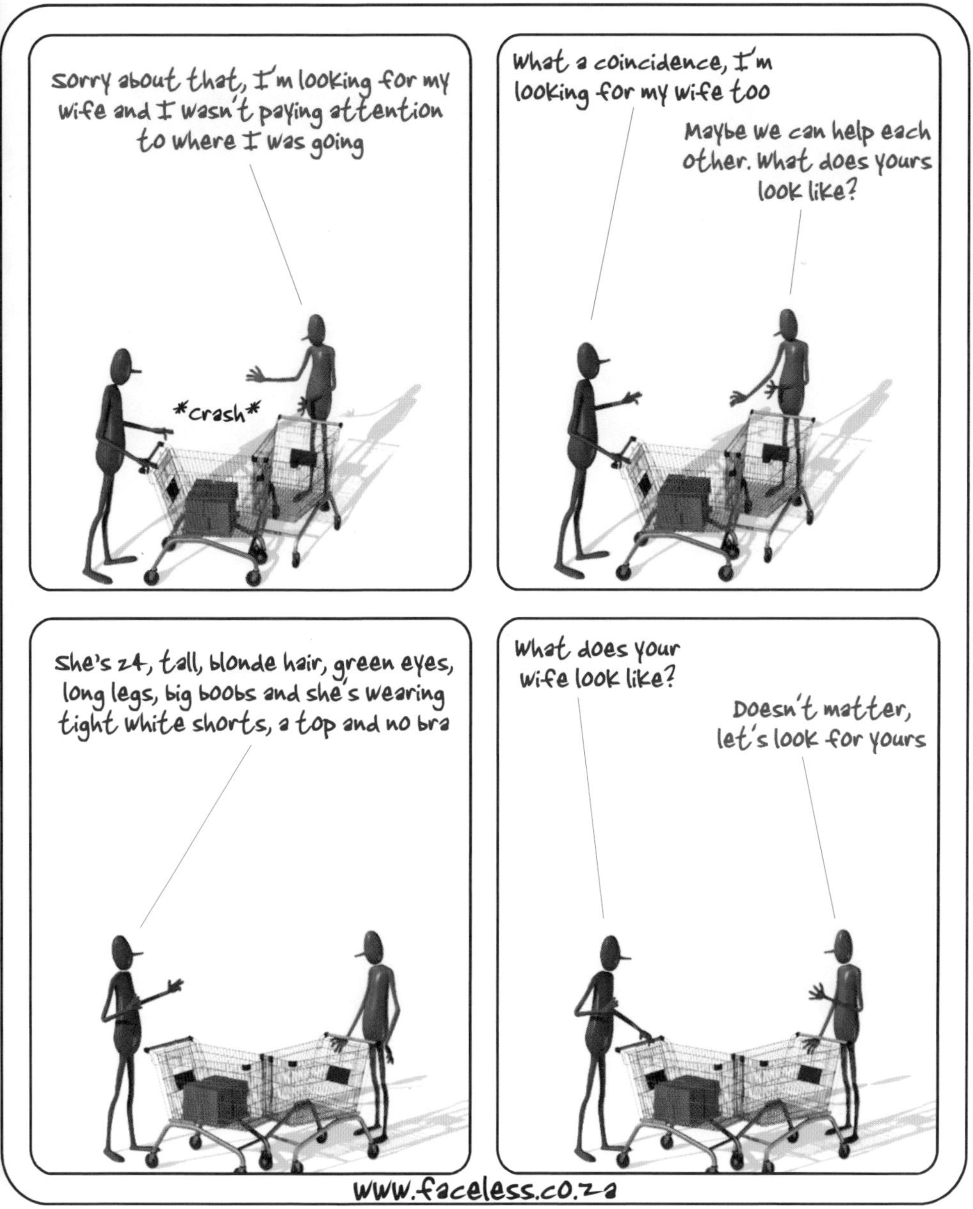
sorry about that, I'm looking for my wife and I wasn't paying attention to where I was going
crash
What a coincidence, I'm looking for my wife too
Maybe we can help each other. What does yours look like?
she's 24, tall, blonde hair, green eyes, long legs, big boobs and she's wearing tight white shorts, a top and no bra
What does your wife look like?
Doesn't matter, let's look for yours
www.faceless.co.za

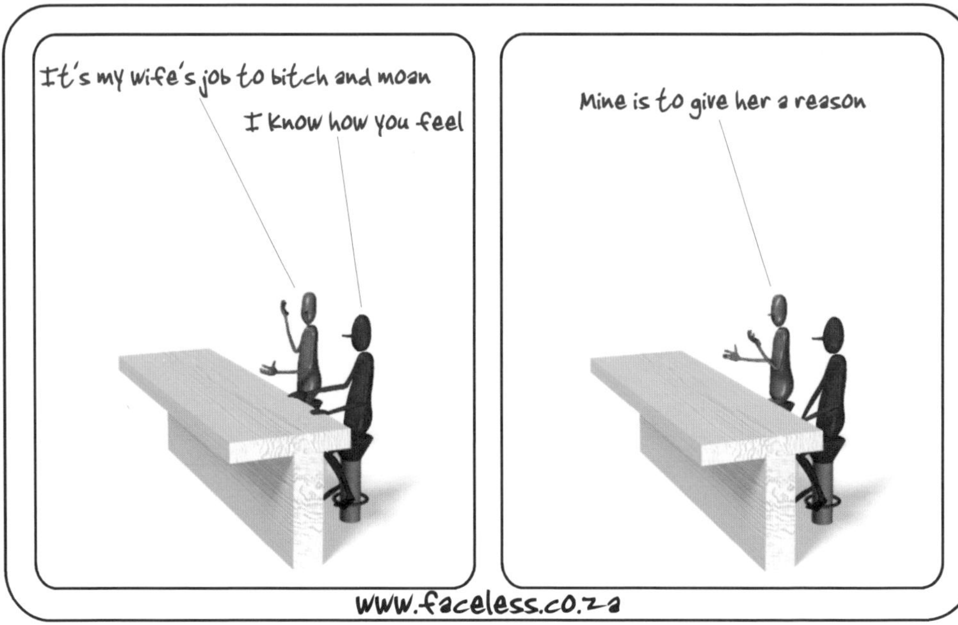
It's my wife's job to bitch and moan
I know how you feel
Mine is to give her a reason
www.faceless.co.za

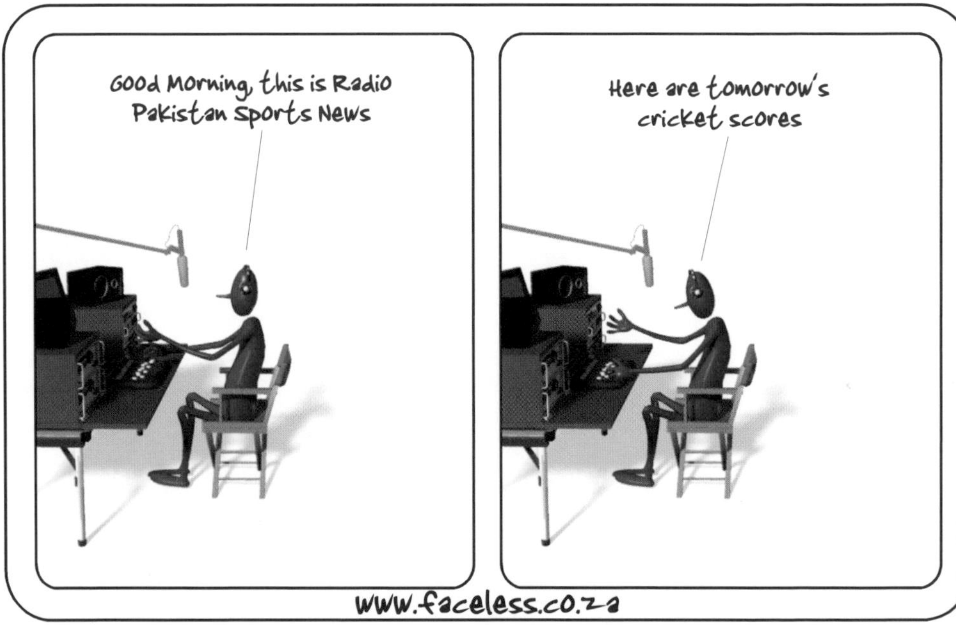
Good Morning, this is Radio Pakistan Sports News
Here are tomorrow's cricket scores
www.faceless.co.za

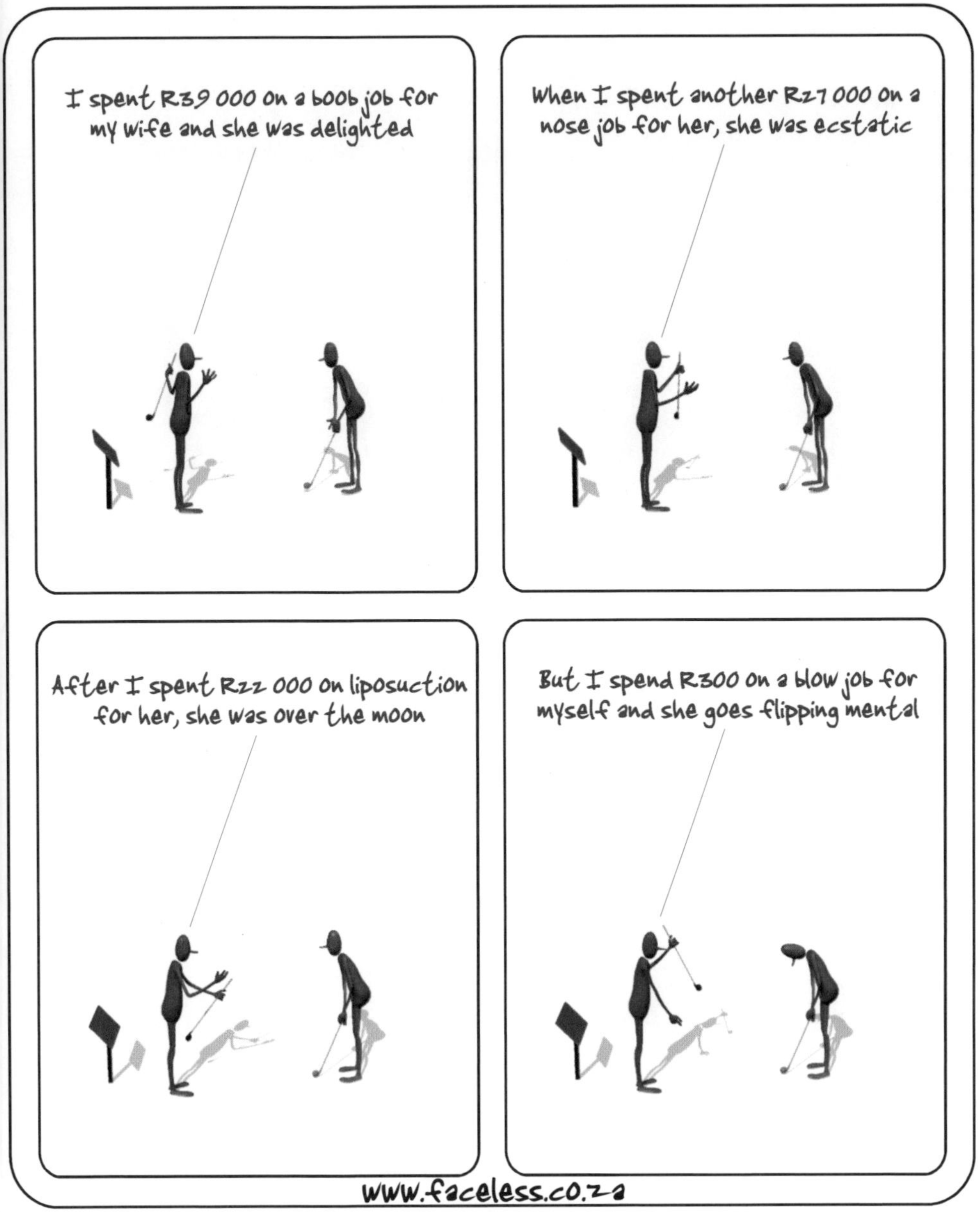
I spent R39 000 on a boob job for my wife and she was delighted
When I spent another R27 000 on a nose job for her, she was ecstatic
After I spent R22 000 on liposuction for her, she was over the moon
But I spend R300 on a blow job for myself and she goes flipping mental
www.faceless.co.za

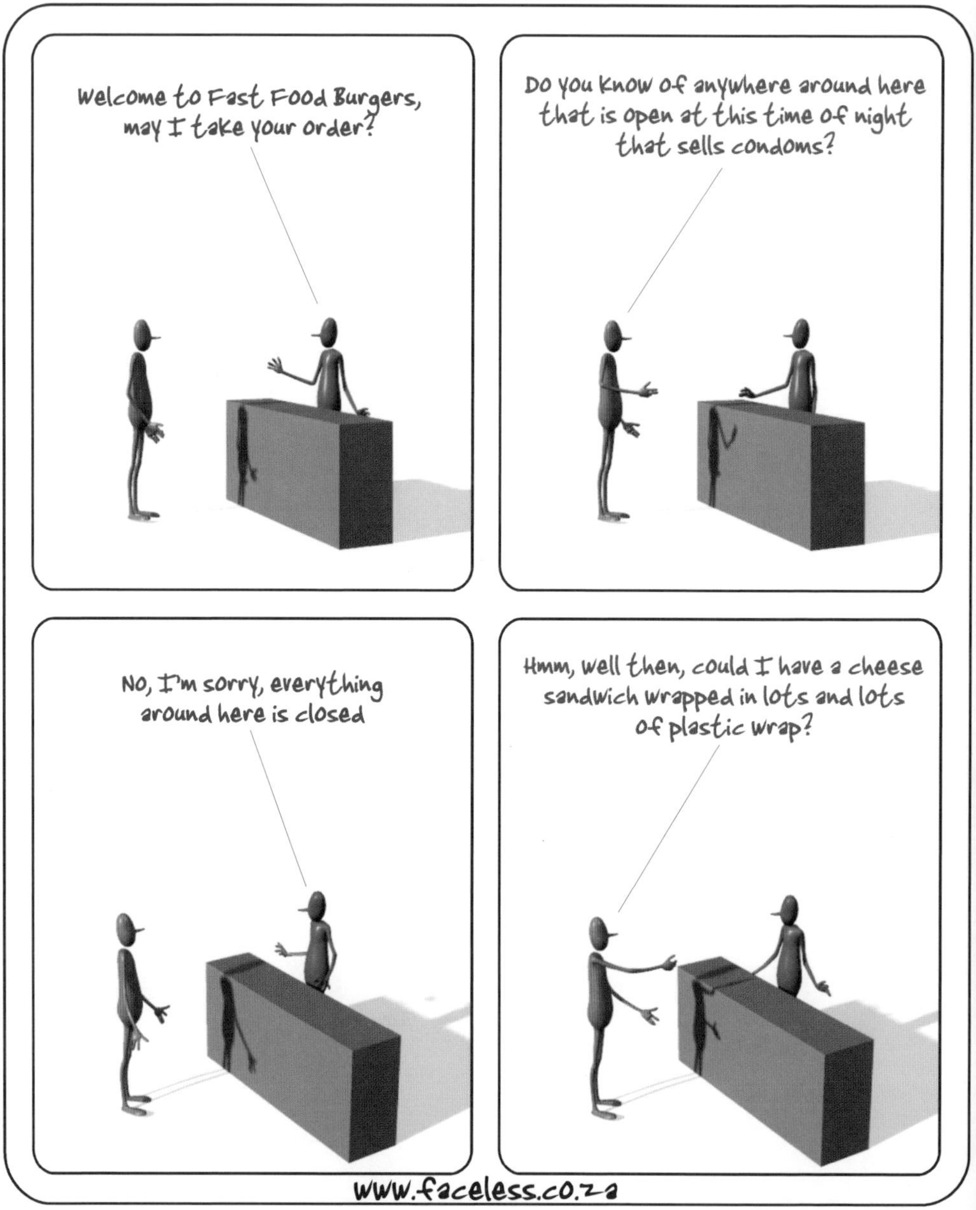
Welcome to Fast Food Burgers, may I take your order?
Do you know of anywhere around here that is open at this time of night that sells condoms?
No, I'm sorry, everything around here is closed
Hmm, well then, could I have a cheese sandwich wrapped in lots and lots of plastic wrap?
www.faceless.co.za

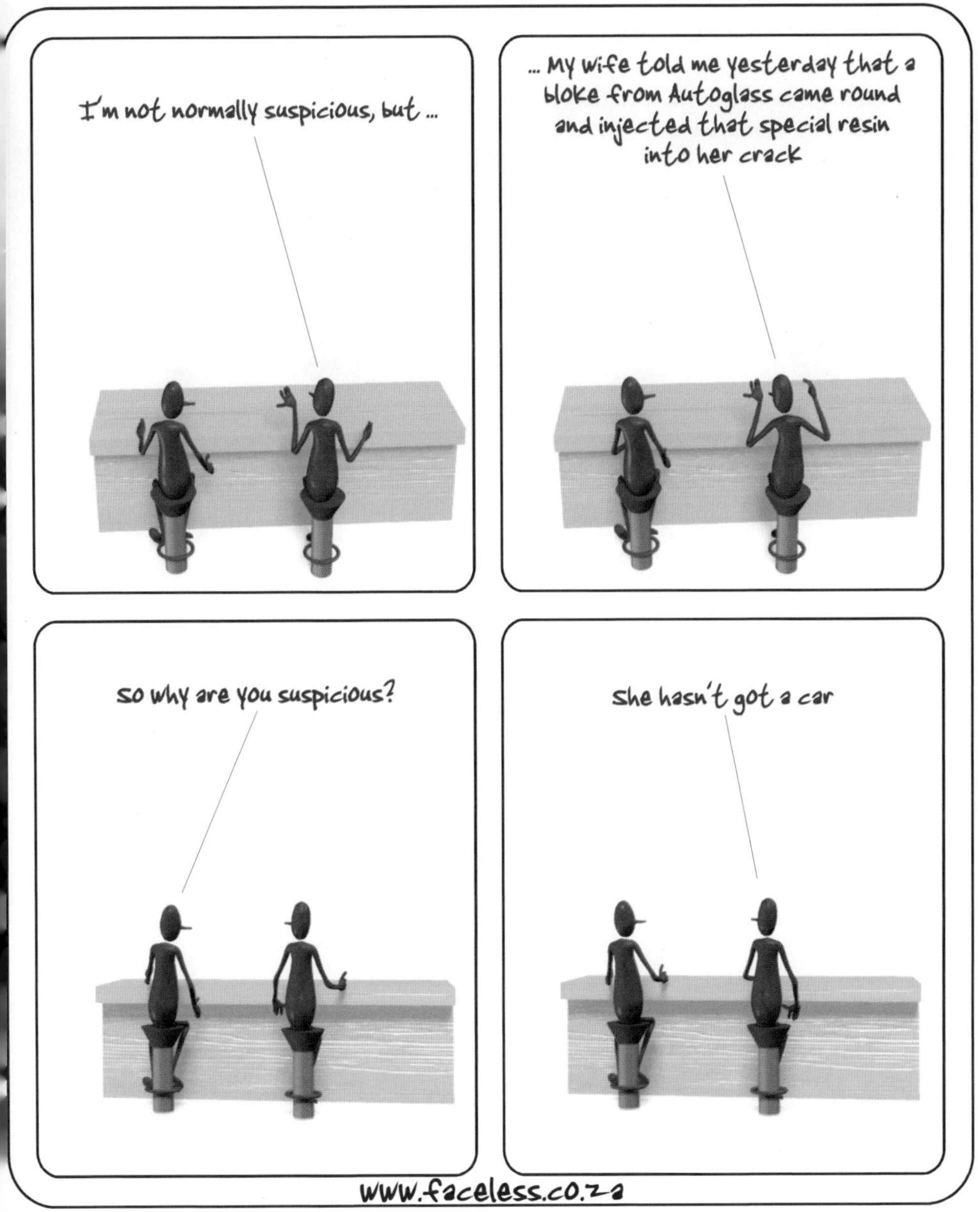
I'm not normally suspicious, but ...
... My wife told me yesterday that a bloke from Autoglass came round and injected that special resin into her crack
so why are you suspicious?
she hasn't got a car
www.faceless.co.za

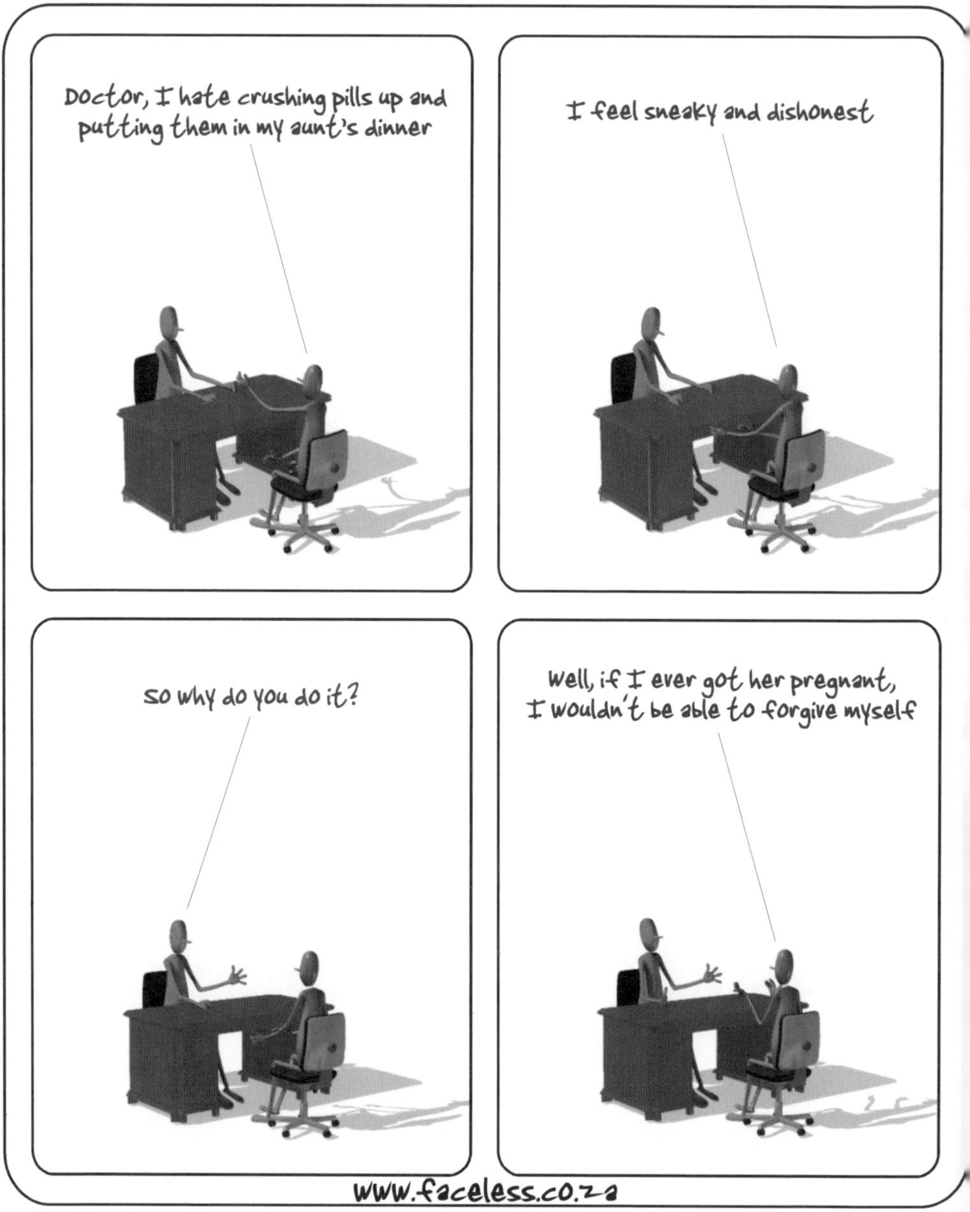
Doctor, I hate crushing pills up and putting them in my aunt's dinner
I feel sneaky and dishonest
so why do you do it?
Well, if I ever got her pregnant, I wouldn't be able to forgive myself
www.faceless.co.za

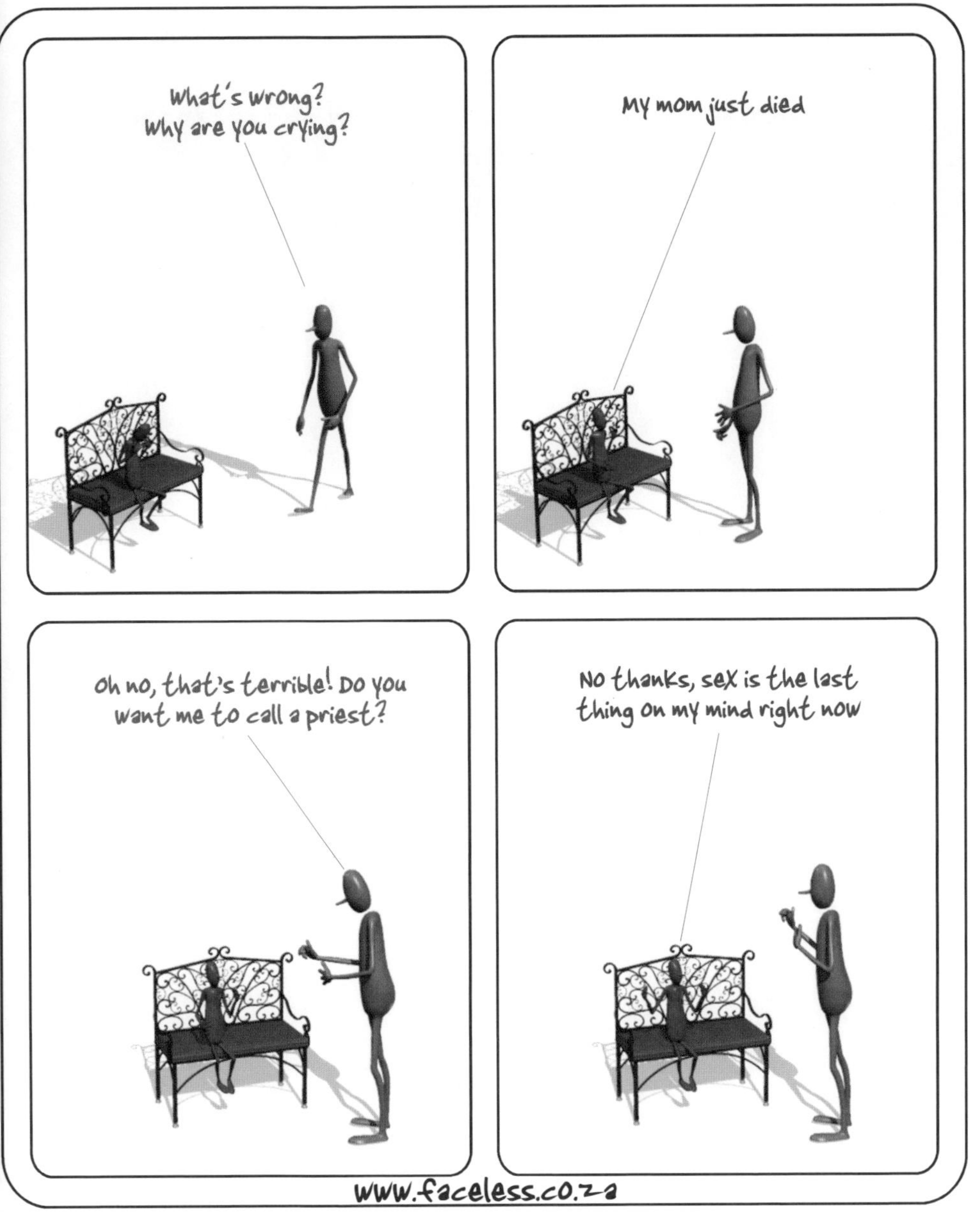
What's wrong?
Why are you crying?
My mom just died
Oh no, that's terrible! Do you want me to call a priest?
No thanks, sex is the last thing on my mind right now
www.faceless.co.za

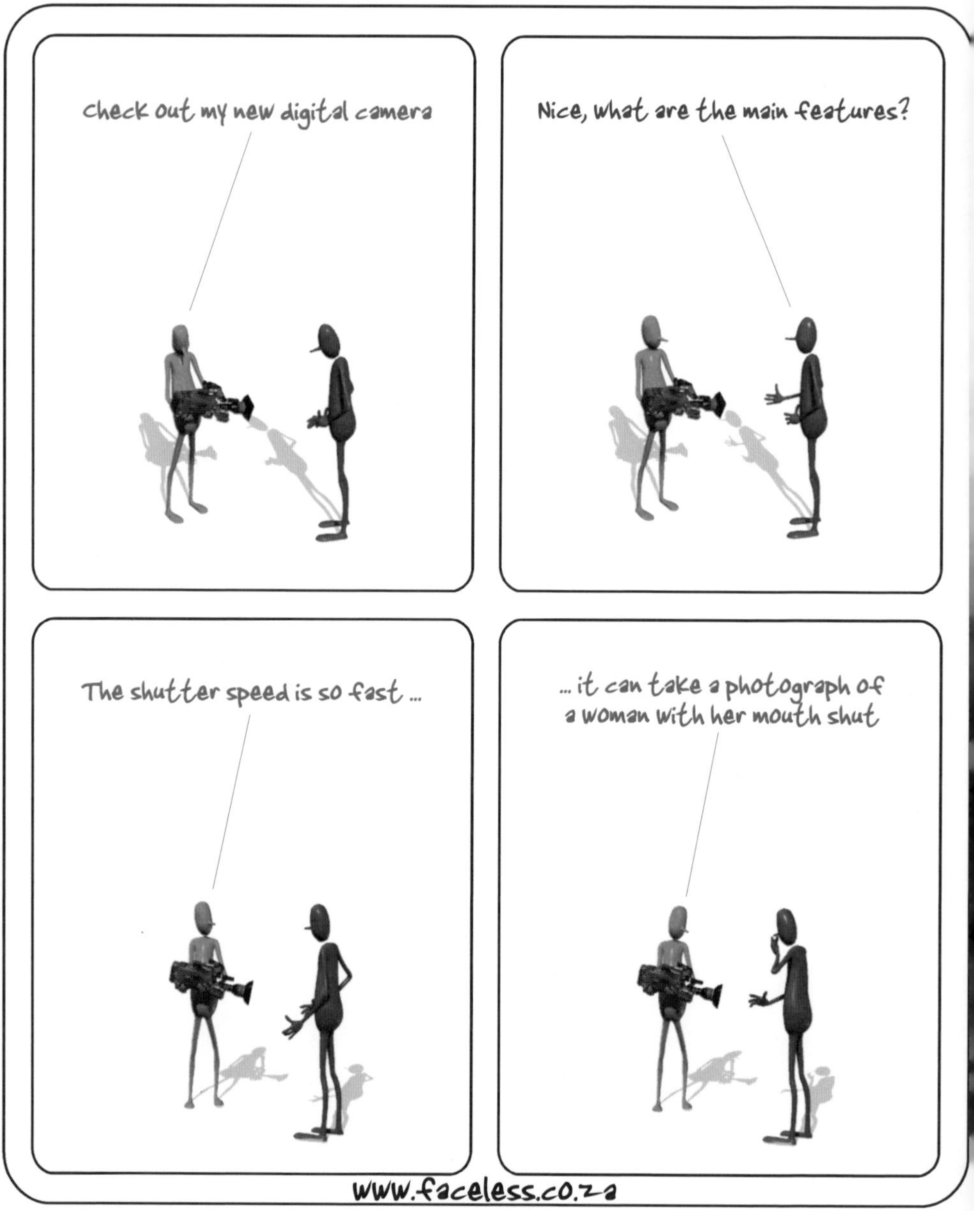
check out my new digital camera
Nice, what are the main features?
The shutter speed is so fast ...
... it can take a photograph of a woman with her mouth shut
www.faceless.co.za

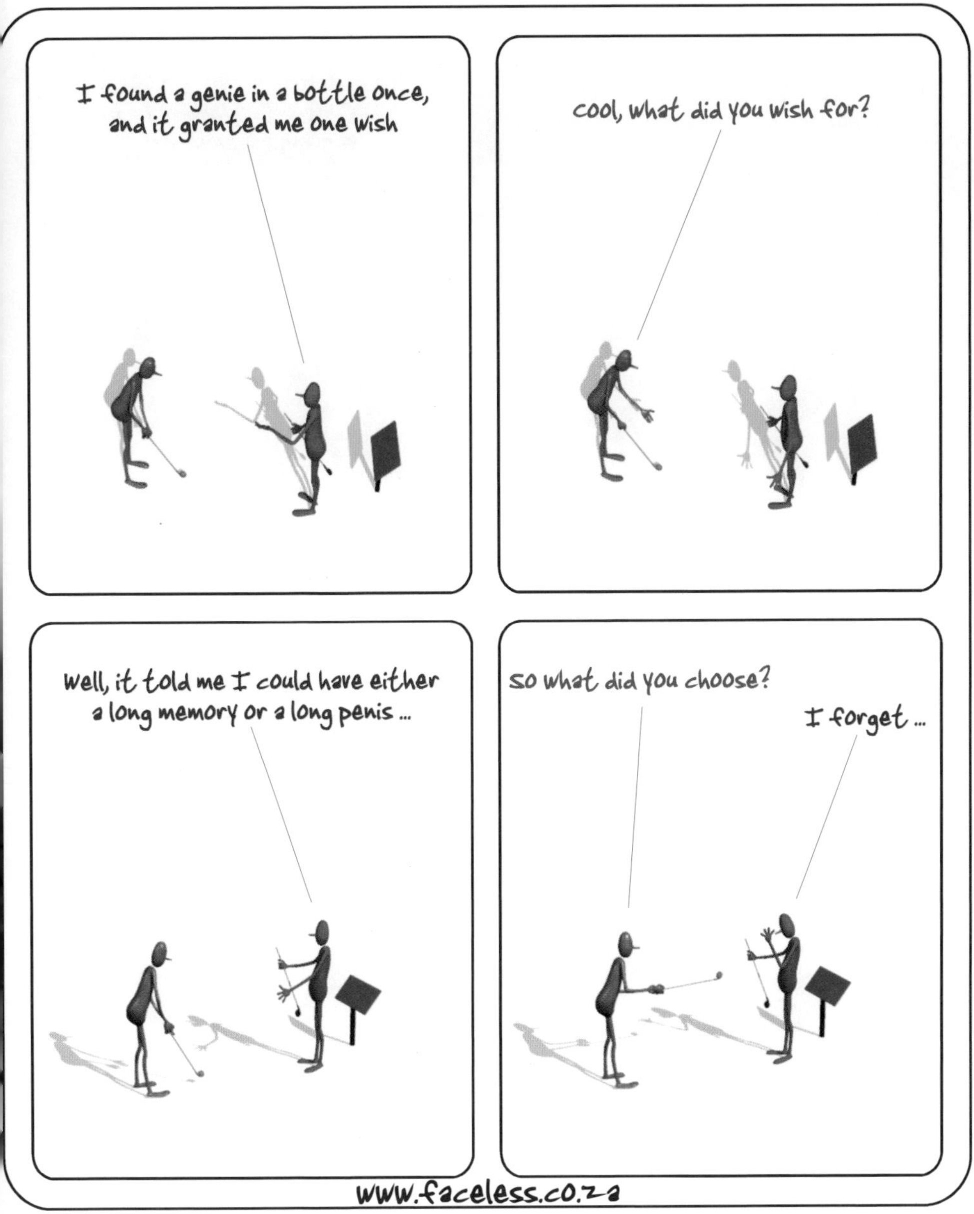
I found a genie in a bottle once, and it granted me one wish
cool, what did you wish for?
Well, it told me I could have either a long memory or a long penis ...
so what did you choose?
I forget ...
www.faceless.co.za

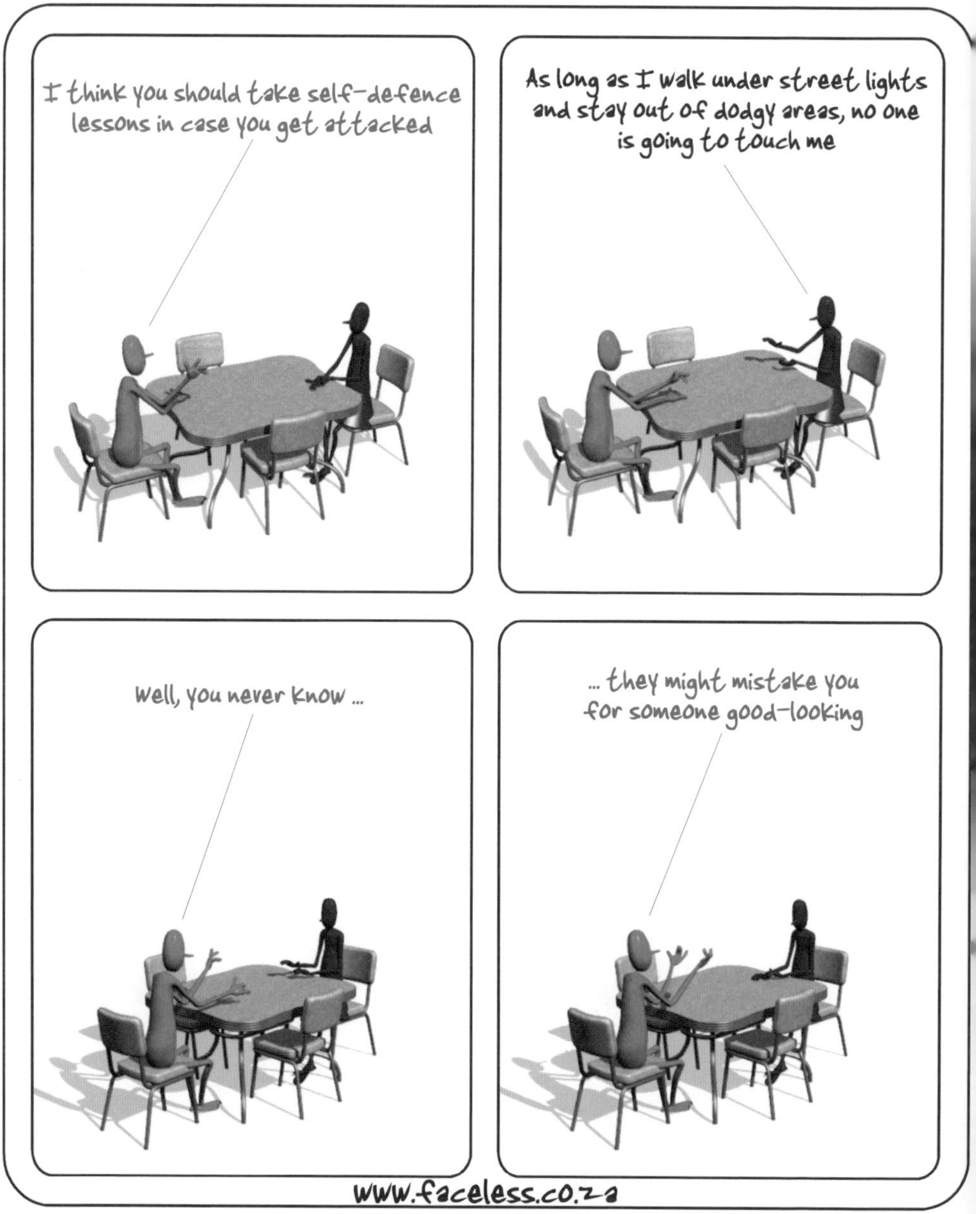
I think you should take self-defence lessons in case you get attacked
As long as I walk under street lights and stay out of dodgy areas, no one is going to touch me
Well, you never know ...
... they might mistake you for someone good-looking
www.faceless.co.za

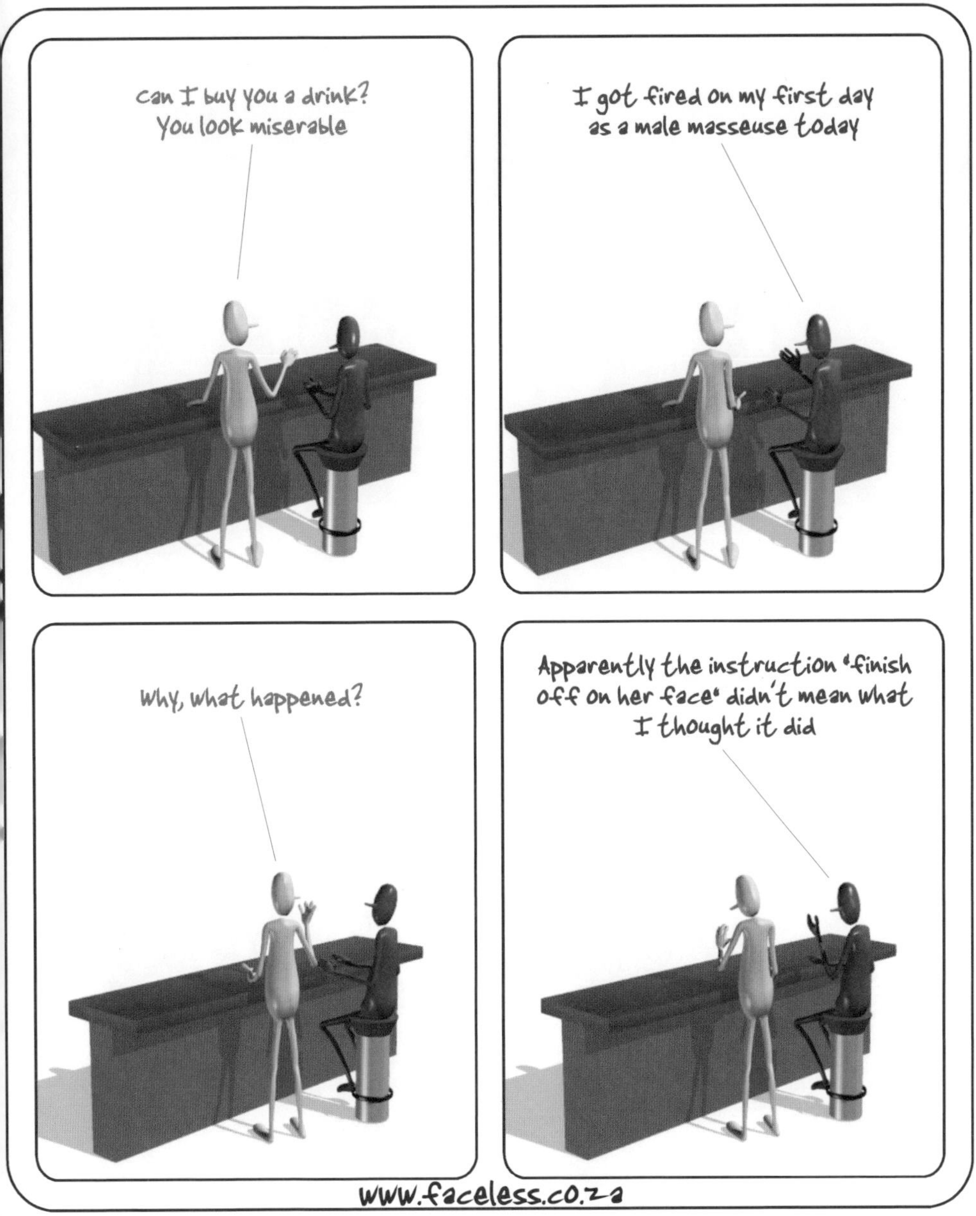
can I buy you a drink? You look miserable
I got fired on my first day as a male masseuse today
Why, what happened?
Apparently the instruction "finish off on her face" didn't mean what I thought it did
www.faceless.co.za

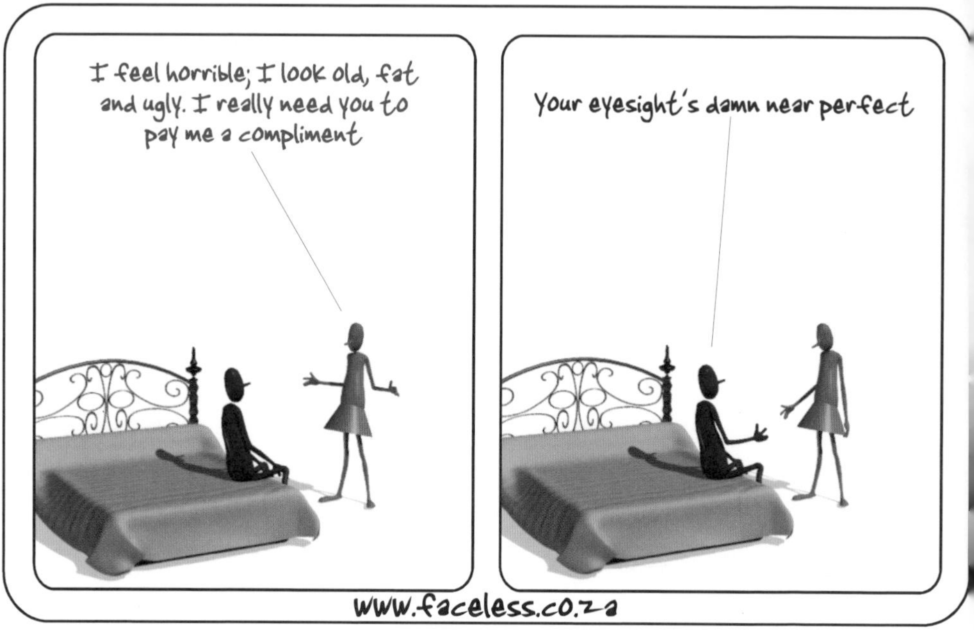
I feel horrible; I look old, fat and ugly. I really need you to pay me a compliment
Your eyesight's damn near perfect
www.faceless.co.za

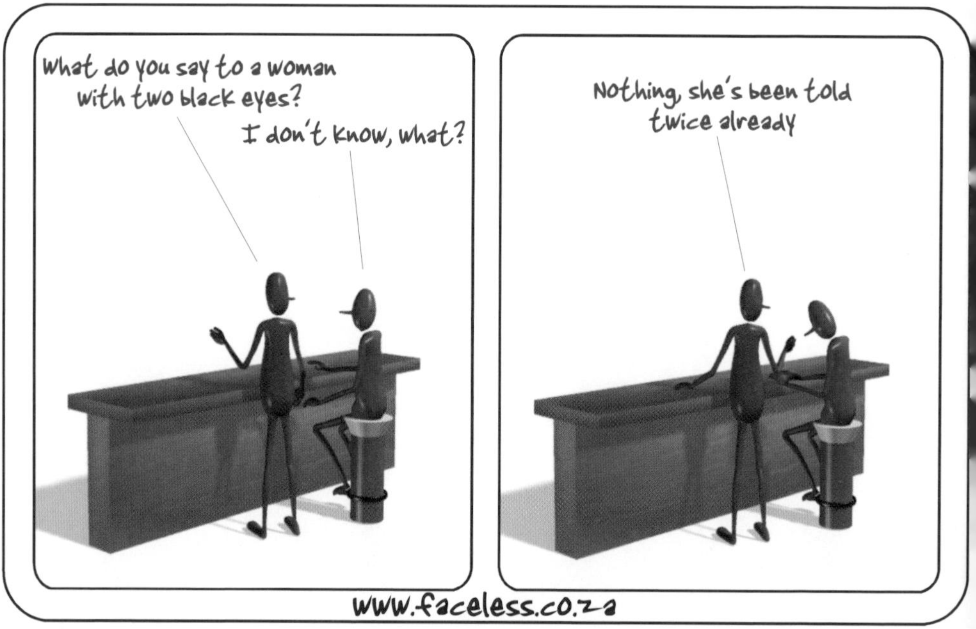
What do you say to a woman with two black eyes?
I don't know, what?
Nothing, she's been told twice already
www.faceless.co.za

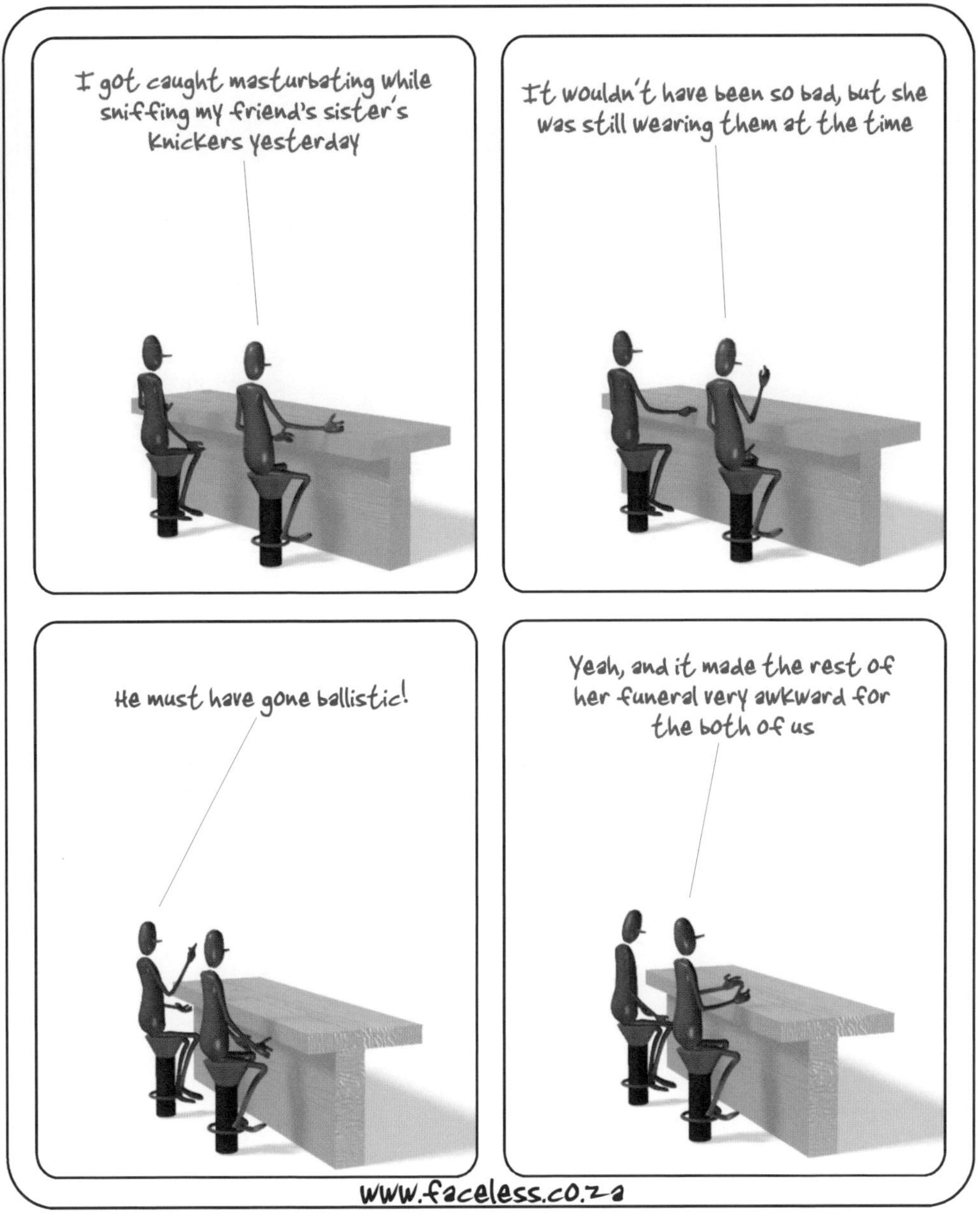
I got caught masturbating while sniffing my friend's sister's knickers yesterday
It wouldn't have been so bad, but she was still wearing them at the time
He must have gone ballistic!
Yeah, and it made the rest of her funeral very awkward for the both of us
www.faceless.co.za

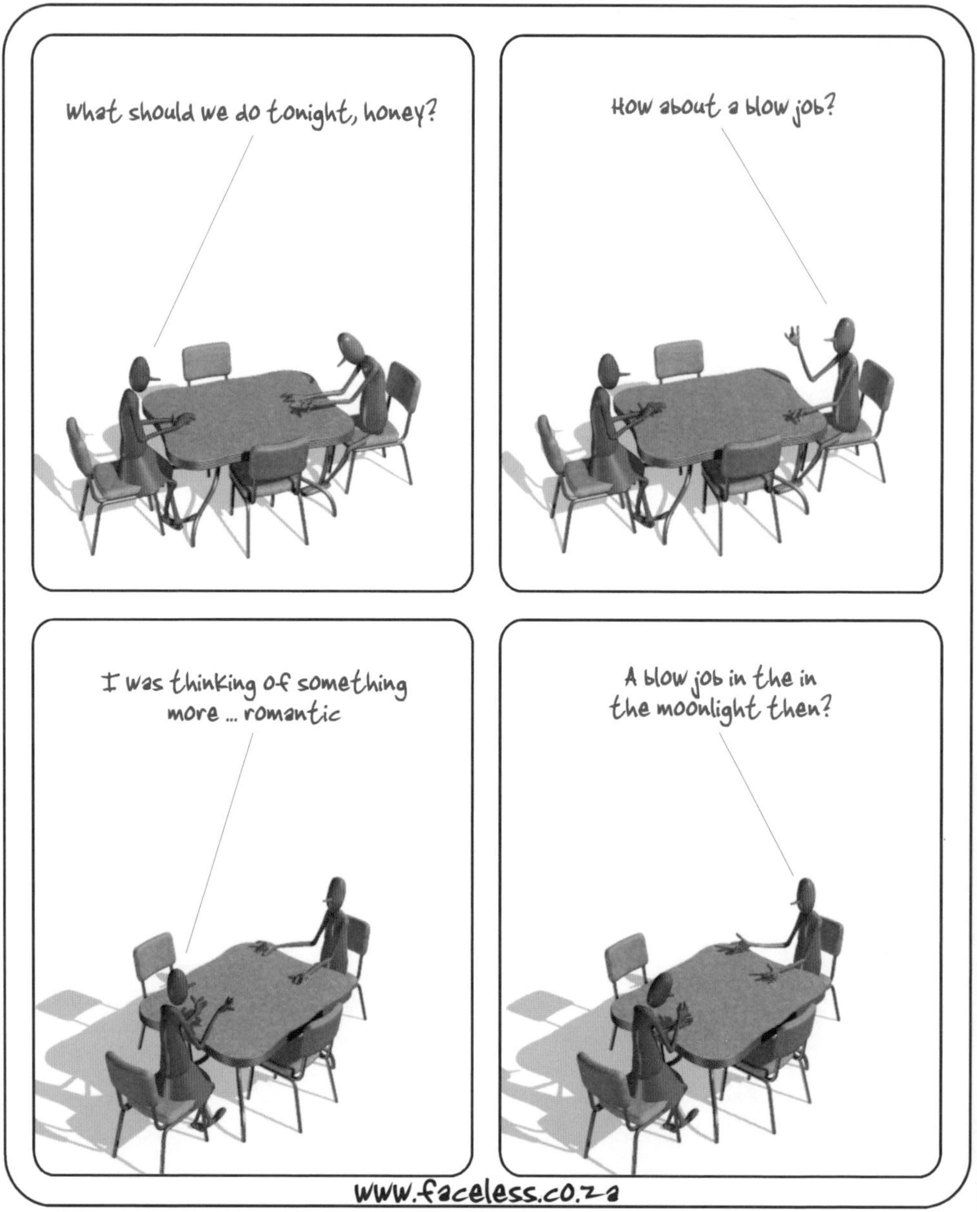
What should we do tonight, honey?
How about a blow job?
I was thinking of something more ... romantic
A blow job in the in the moonlight then?
www.faceless.co.za

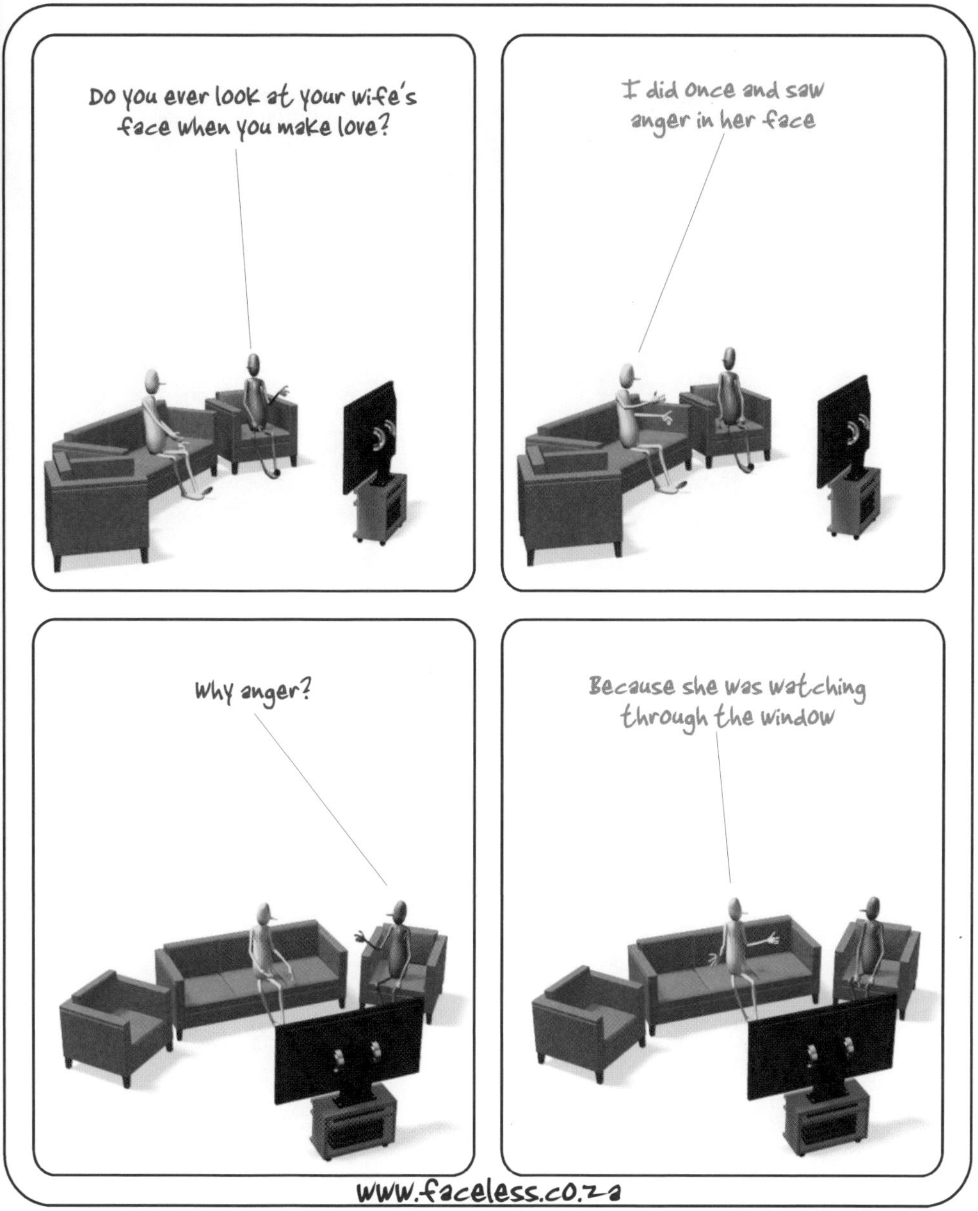
Do you ever look at your wife's face when you make love?
I did once and saw anger in her face
Why anger?
Because she was watching through the window
www.faceless.co.za

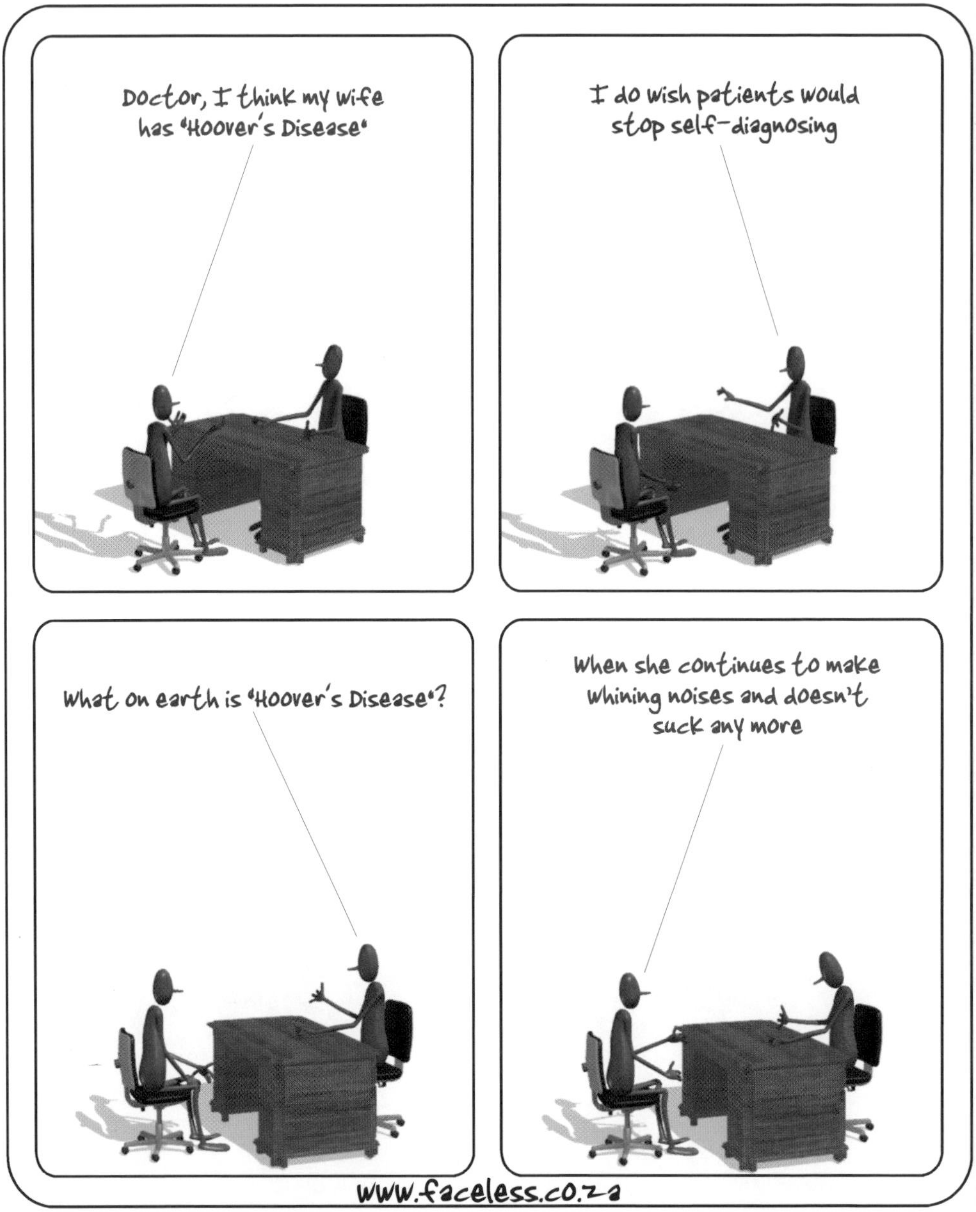
Doctor, I think my wife has "Hoover's Disease"
I do wish patients would stop self-diagnosing
What on earth is "Hoover's Disease"?
When she continues to make whining noises and doesn't suck any more
www.faceless.co.za

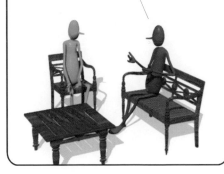

Do your eyes ever burn, your nose runs and you get teary-eyed after having sex?

Yes, all the time

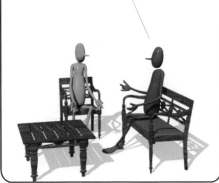

Why is that?

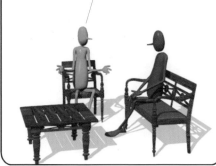

I think it's the pepper spray

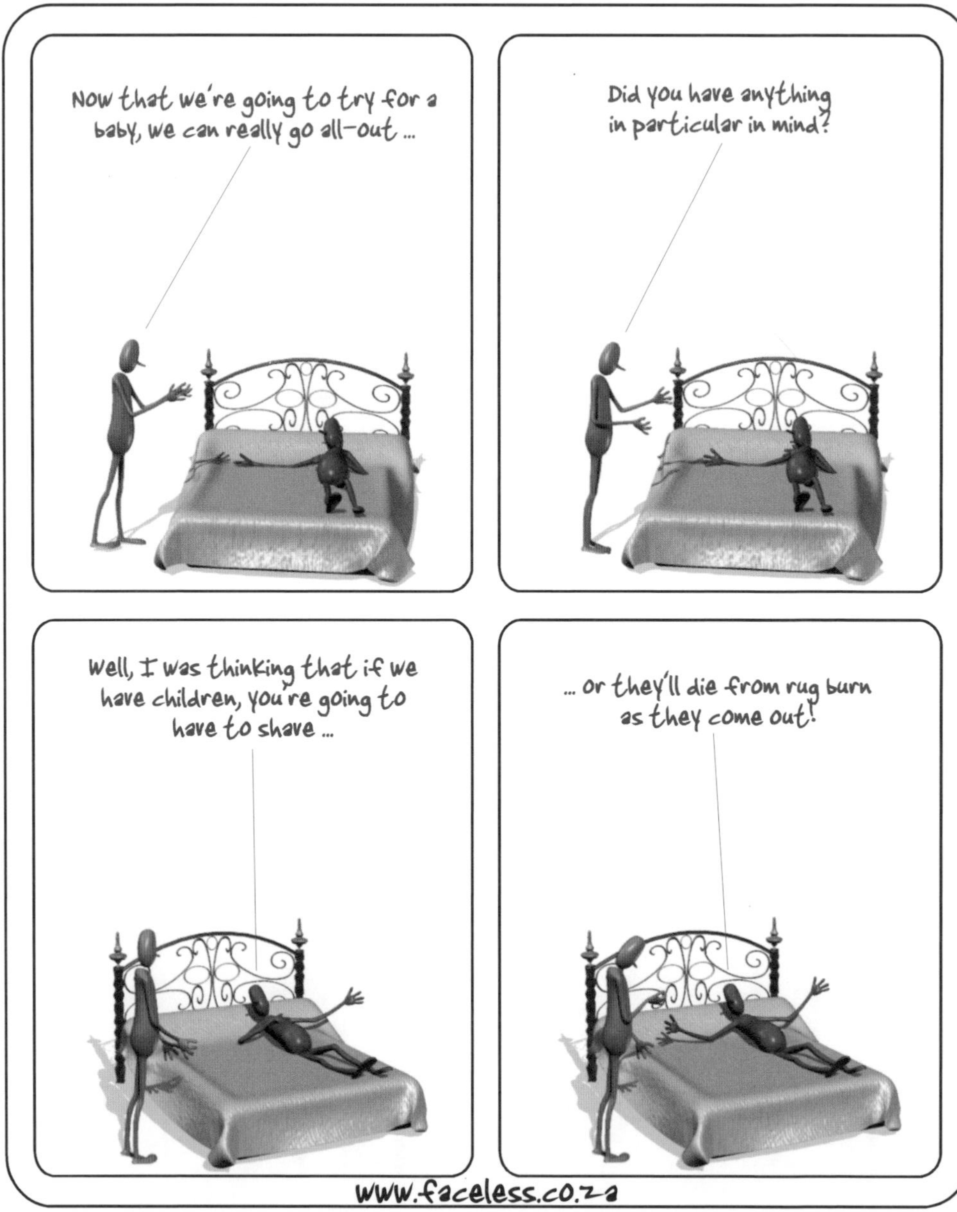
Now that we're going to try for a baby, we can really go all-out ...
Did you have anything in particular in mind?
Well, I was thinking that if we have children, you're going to have to shave ...
... or they'll die from rug burn as they come out!
www.faceless.co.za

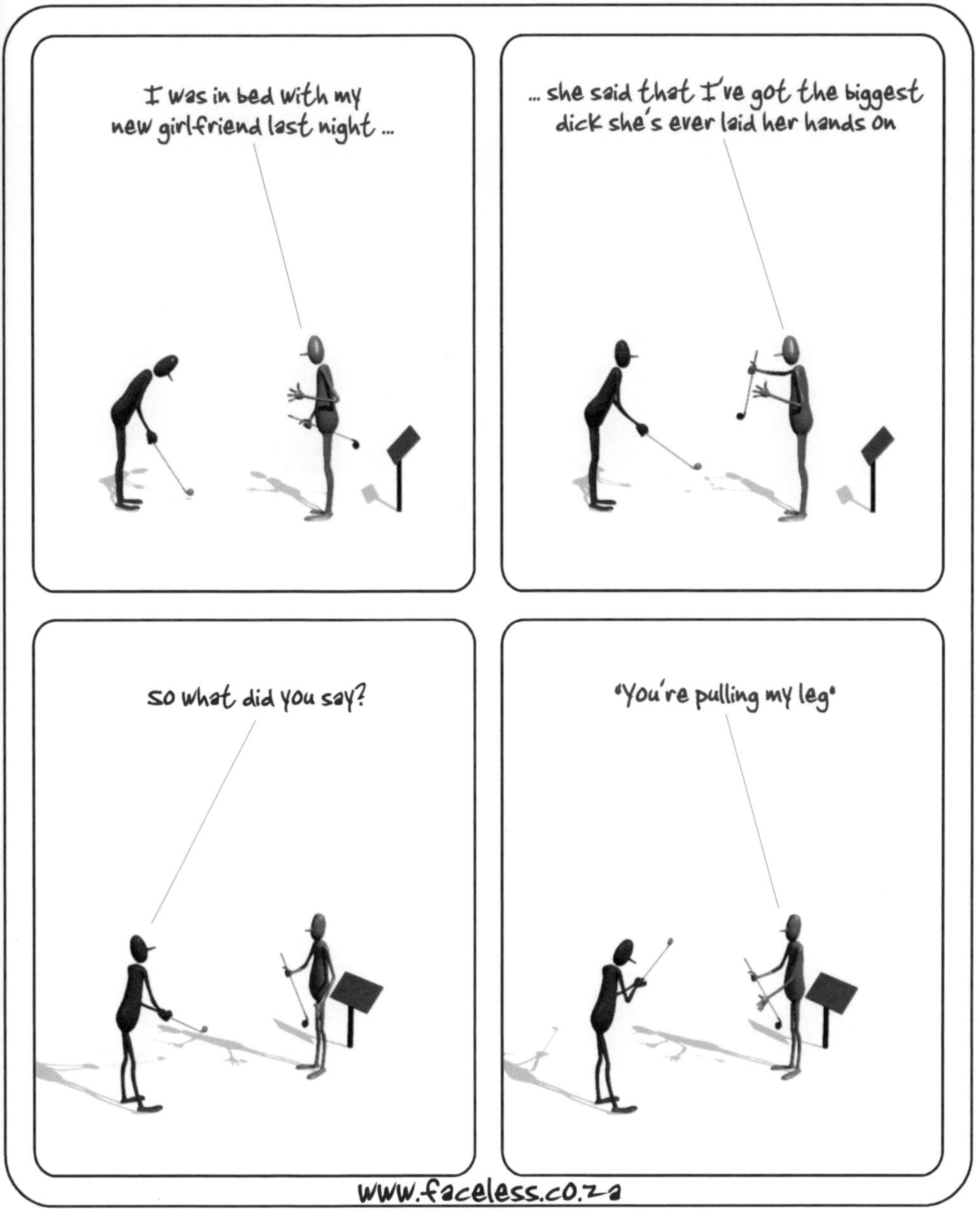
I was in bed with my new girlfriend last night ...
... she said that I've got the biggest dick she's ever laid her hands on
so what did you say?
"You're pulling my leg"
www.faceless.co.za

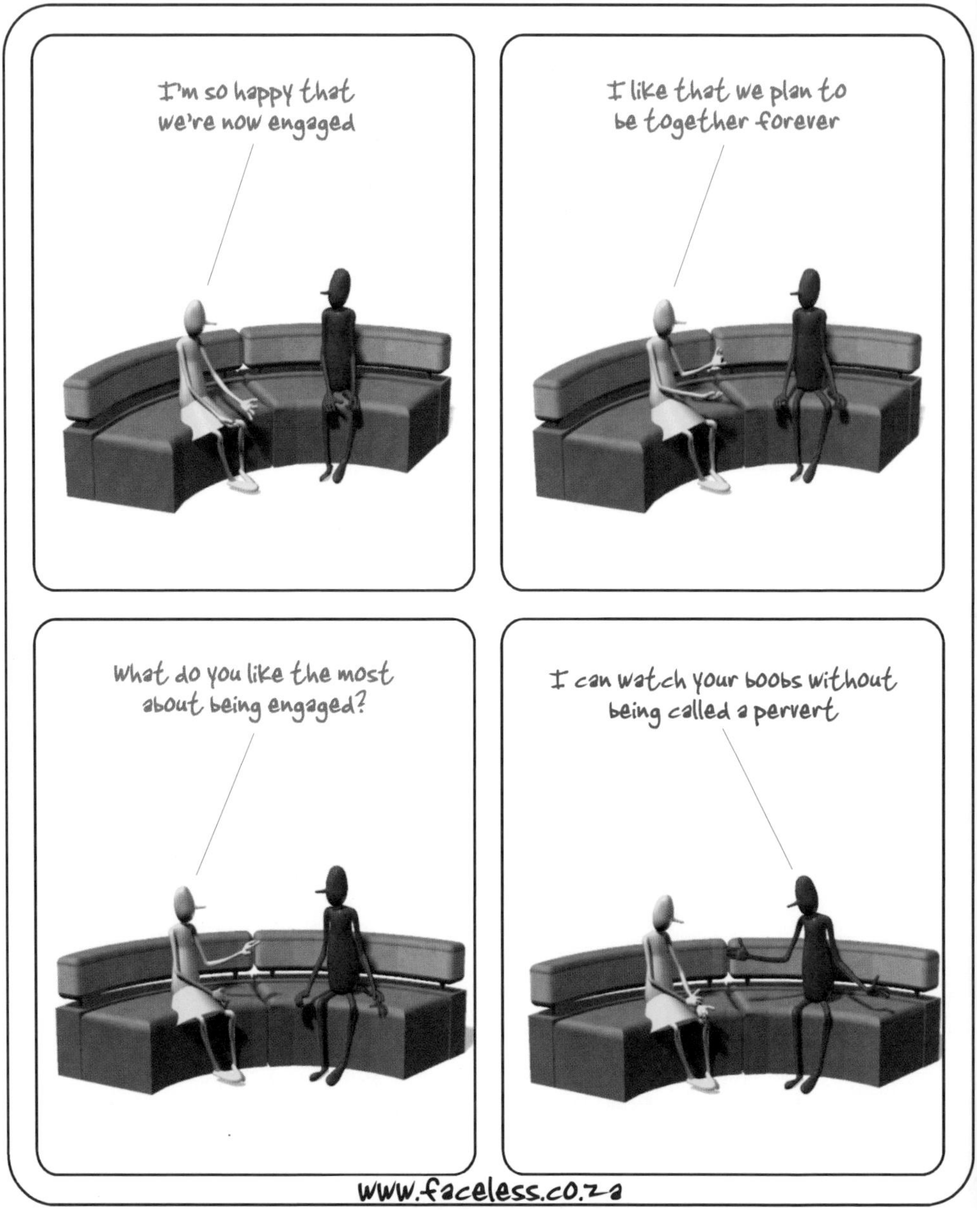
I'm so happy that we're now engaged
I like that we plan to be together forever
What do you like the most about being engaged?
I can watch your boobs without being called a pervert
www.faceless.co.za

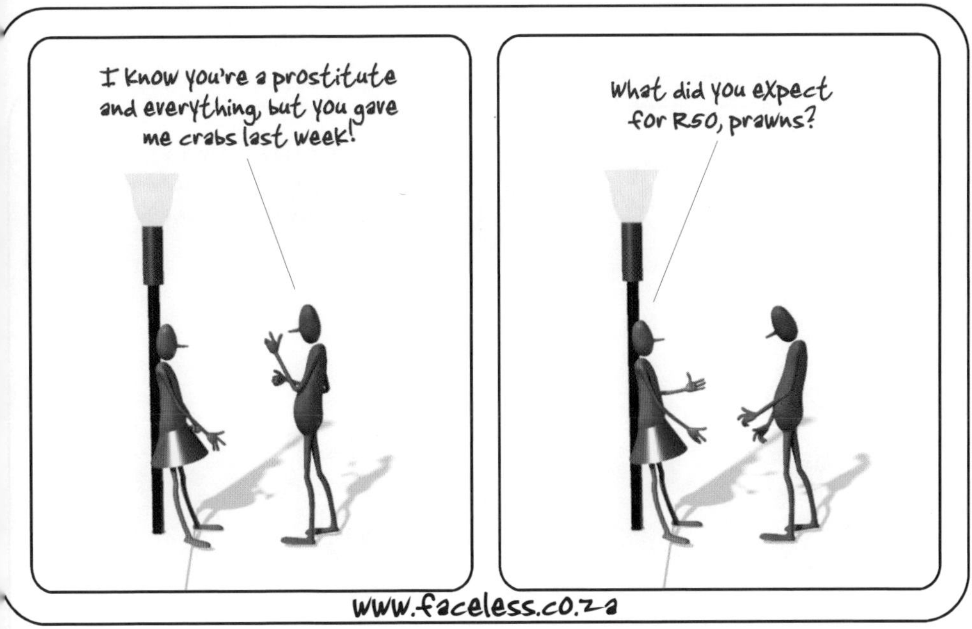
I know you're a prostitute and everything, but you gave me crabs last week!
What did you expect for R50, prawns?
www.faceless.co.za

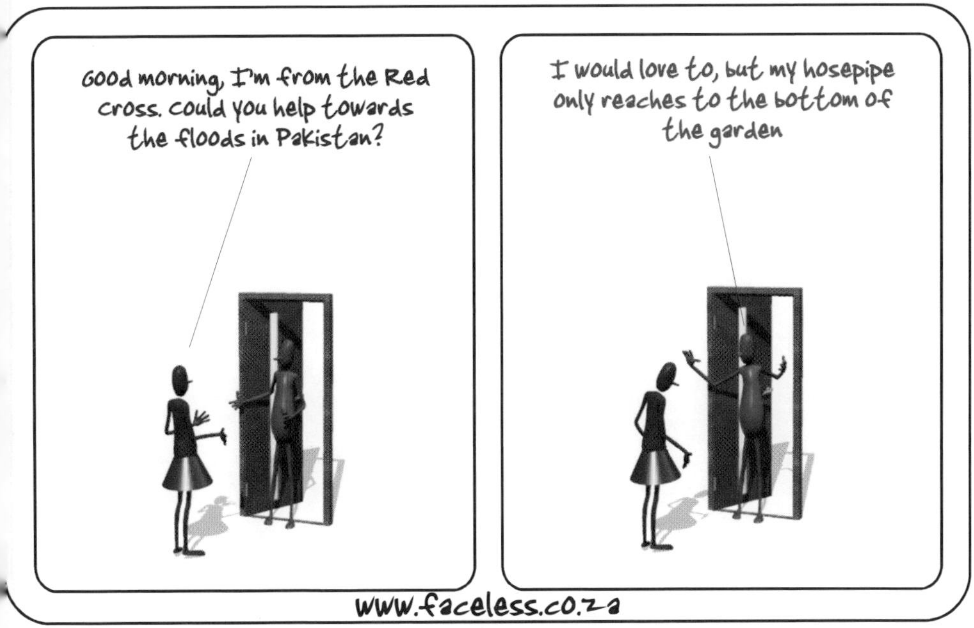
Good morning, I'm from the Red cross. could you help towards the floods in Pakistan?
I would love to, but my hosepipe only reaches to the bottom of the garden
www.faceless.co.za

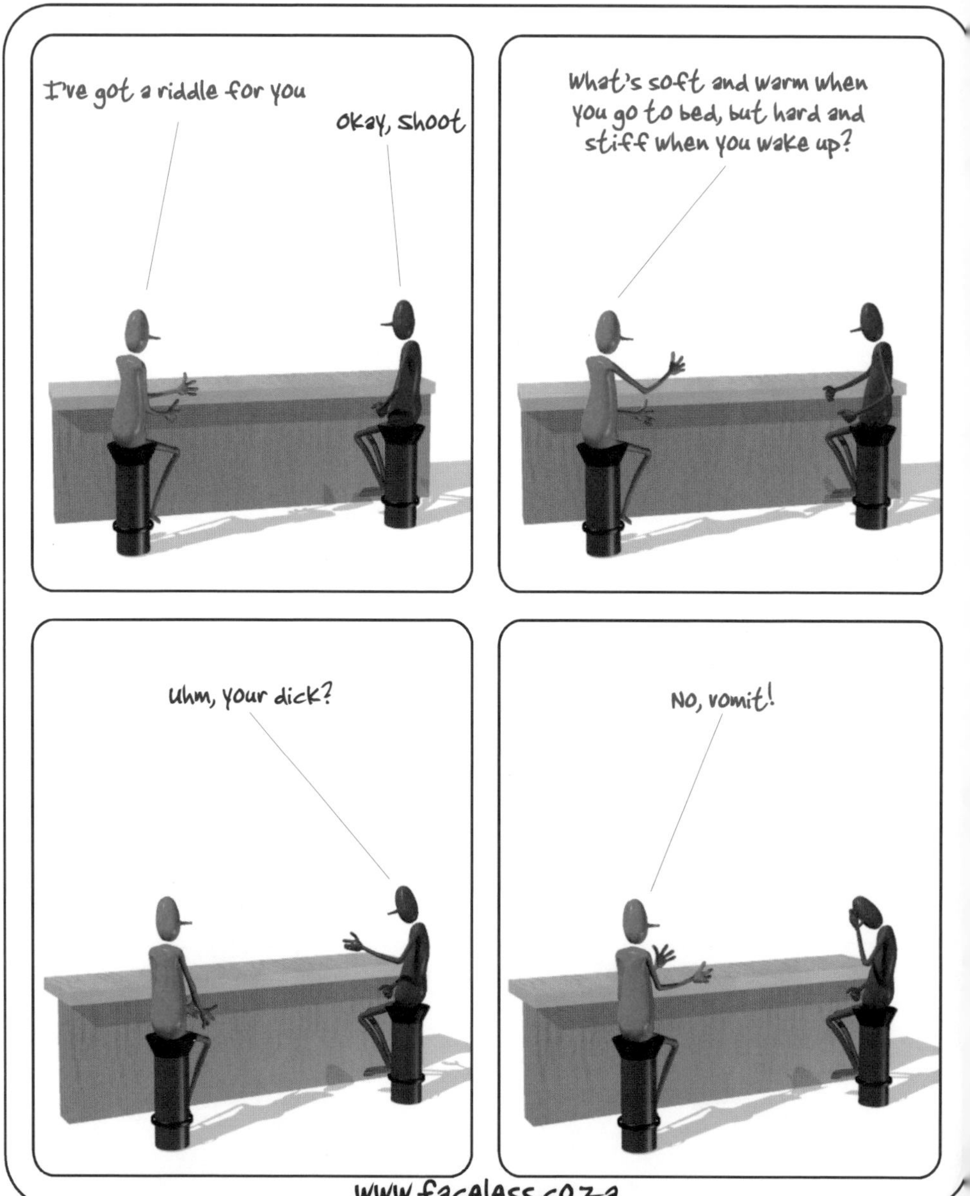
I've got a riddle for you
Okay, shoot
What's soft and warm when you go to bed, but hard and stiff when you wake up?
Uhm, your dick?
No, vomit!
www.faceless.co.za

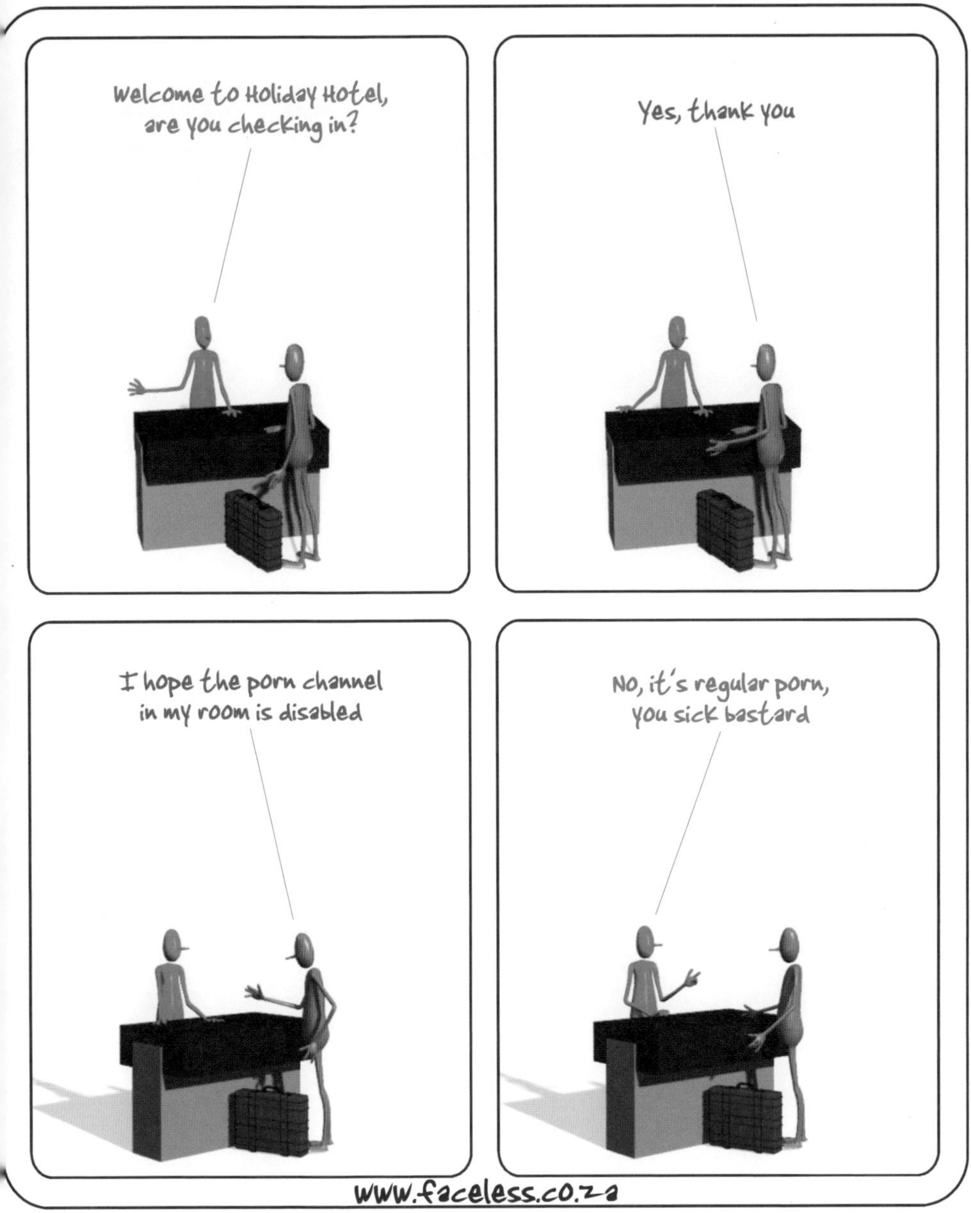
Welcome to Holiday Hotel, are you checking in?
Yes, thank you
I hope the porn channel in my room is disabled
No, it's regular porn, you sick bastard
www.faceless.co.za

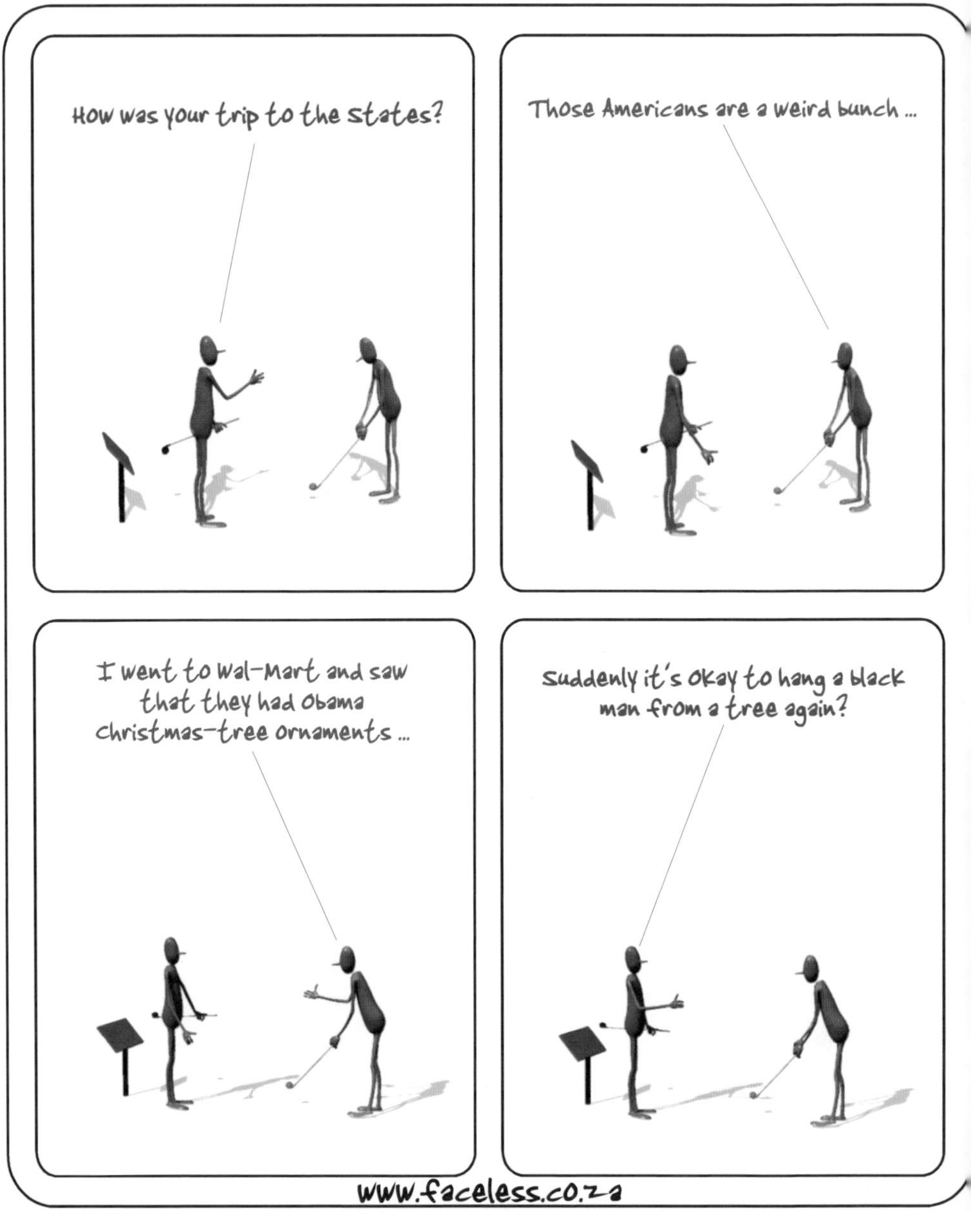
How was your trip to the states?
Those Americans are a weird bunch ...
I went to Wal-Mart and saw that they had Obama Christmas-tree ornaments ...
Suddenly it's okay to hang a black man from a tree again?
www.faceless.co.za

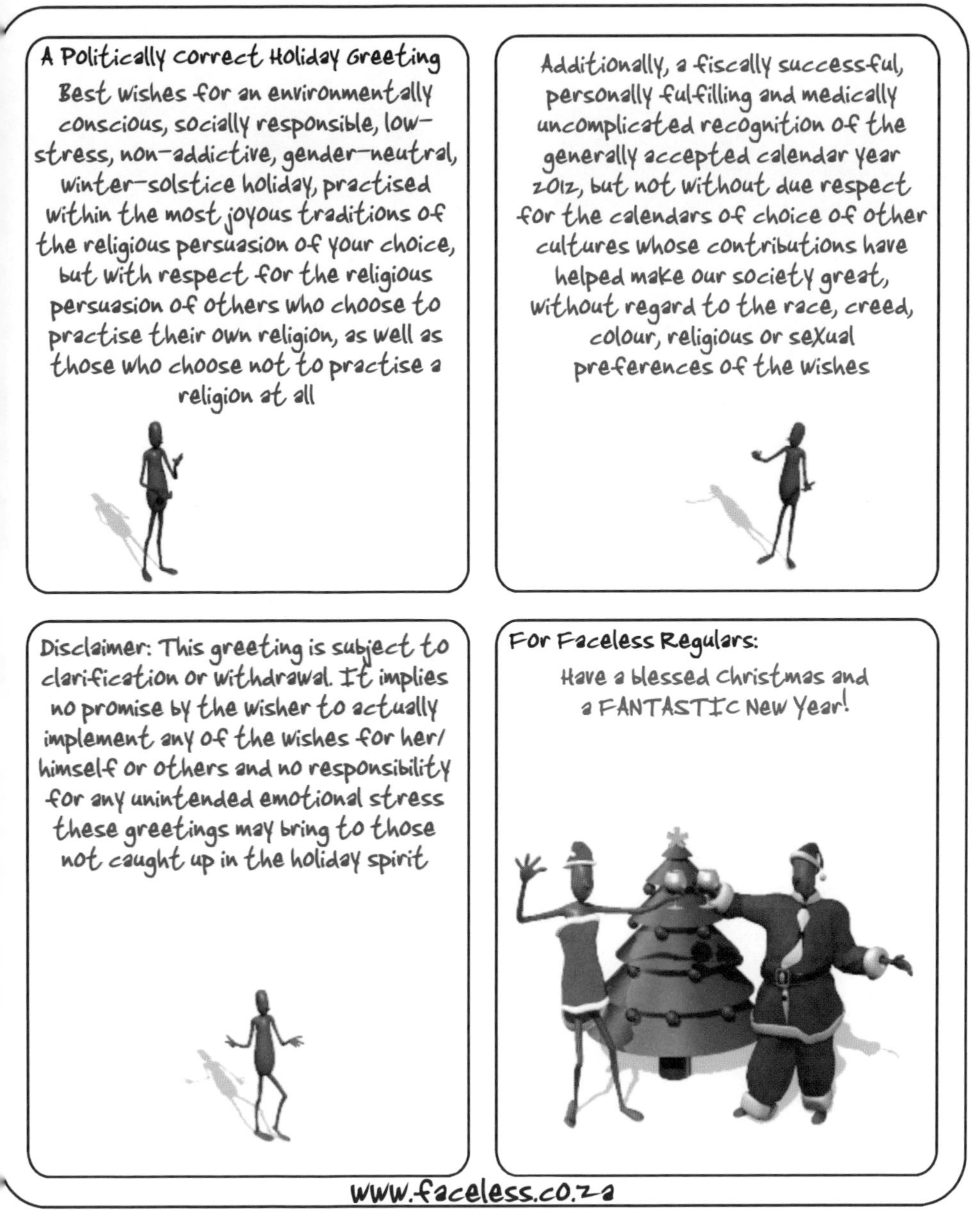
A Politically correct Holiday Greeting
Best wishes for an environmentally conscious, socially responsible, low-stress, non-addictive, gender-neutral, winter-solstice holiday, practised within the most joyous traditions of the religious persuasion of your choice, but with respect for the religious persuasion of others who choose to practise their own religion, as well as those who choose not to practise a religion at all
Additionally, a fiscally successful, personally fulfilling and medically uncomplicated recognition of the generally accepted calendar year 2012, but not without due respect for the calendars of choice of other cultures whose contributions have helped make our society great, without regard to the race, creed, colour, religious or sexual preferences of the wishes
Disclaimer: This greeting is subject to clarification or withdrawal. It implies no promise by the wisher to actually implement any of the wishes for her/himself or others and no responsibility for any unintended emotional stress these greetings may bring to those not caught up in the holiday spirit
For Faceless Regulars:
Have a blessed Christmas and a FANTASTIC New Year!
www.faceless.co.za